Enter
O-ZONE
The acclaimed new novel by
PAUL THEROUX

"This remarkable novel is so powerful that you can feel your perceptions changing as you turn the pages. *O-Zone* is a book about ourselves, present and future, which is as mesmerizing as first-class science fiction, as illuminating as the best literature, and as lyrical and open-hearted as a child's fairy tale."

Susan Cheever

"Theroux possesses a high-tech imagination as inventive as Arthur C. Clarke's.... And nobody creates more vivid characters."

Chicago Sun-Times

"The sheer mass and density of the invention, illuminated by Theroux's crisp style, are ultimately moving and convincing...."

San Francisco Chronicle

(more)

O-ZONE

PAUL THEROUX

O-ZONE

"*O-Zone* is a dark book that deals with dark subjects.... its intelligence is fierce and unremitting."

The Washington Post Book World

"It is Theroux's gloomy vision of tomorrow's human landscape that lingers—a vision that catapults the worst of the late 1980s to its ultimate."

Detroit Free Press

PAUL THEROUX

Also by Paul Theroux:

FICTION

Waldo
Fong and the Indians
Girls at Play
Jungle Lovers
Sinning with Annie
Saint Jack
The Black House
The Family Arsenal
The Consul's File
A Christmas Card
Picture Palace
London Snow
World's End
The Mosquito Coast
The London Embassy
Half Moon Street

CRITICISM

V. S. Naipaul

NONFICTION

The Great Railway Bazaar
The Old Patagonian Express
The Kingdom by the Sea
Sailing Through China
Sunrise with Seamonsters
The Imperial Way

O-ZONE

PAUL THEROUX

IVY BOOKS • NEW YORK

Library of Congress Catalog Card Number: 86-8190

ISBN-0-8041-0151-5

This edition published by arrangement with G. P. Putnam's Sons,
a division of The Putnam Publishing Group, Inc.

Manufactured in the United States of America

First Ballantine Books Edition: October 1987

Contents

PART ONE

O-ZONE

1

THE FIRST THING THESE PEOPLE ALWAYS ASKED, WHEN-
ever they went out, was where were "they"?

But there was no one here in O-Zone—no aliens, and no
Owners except themselves.

It had taken the travelers just under two hours to fly the
fifteen hundred clicks from Coldharbor Tower in New York
City to the large sealed-off territory in the midwest designated Outer Zone. They had decided to fly in a highballing
style and to keep together; it was their party mood—New
Year's. The four jet-rotors were bunched in the flight enve-
lope like a swarm of insects. The eight travelers looked insectile themselves in the last low-altitude phase, with their
masks on. These days it was seldom safe to travel in such a
dense formation, making an easy buzzing target. Even aliens
who had little else had weapons—Starkies had rockets, one
of the travelers said. Yet they knew there was no one down
below now, and no one else alive for the next three hundred
clicks.

"No Starkies, no Skells, no Trolls," Hooper Allbright said
over his radio to the rest of them. "No Shitters, no Diggers,
no Roaches. Not even any Federals!"

He was photographing it all through the sting in his nose
cone.

"And I don't see any Owners either."

The precise pattern of old highways, like wheel tracks,
passed beneath.

Traveling high in rotors gave them a point of view. They
watched the earth through ground-screens in the cockpit.

3

The land was small and scarred, and inhabited by people who looked like flightless ants. They could see the tops of their heads.

"We're the only taxpayers here, so let's enjoy ourselves," Hooper said. "It's better than home!"

There was a squawk on the mike, a shrill *heep-heep*, which he silenced by continuing.

"I like to think places like this are beyond criticism."

In another aircraft, his nephew Fisher said, "Keep flying, shit-wit."

Hardy Allbright glanced back at Fisher and frowned: the radio was open, the mike was live. *Heep.*

"Who said that?"

"This is the unthinkable," Hardy piped up. "But officially this place is not on the map. That's why it's not illegal."

"I thought you had an Access Pass," came a nagging voice from another rotor. It was Willis Murdick in his new Welly.

"The Access Pass is for the Red Zone," Hardy said. "O-Zone doesn't exist. Hasn't for fifteen years."

"You could grow old here!" Hooper was saying. "All you have to do is keep your clothes on."

"Ground temperature's twenty-two cents," Hardy said, from his cockpit. "Forty or fifty years ago you'd have worn winter clothes here at this time of year. Bare trees. Frost in the morning. It was cold all over. You'd have needed mittens."

"But you wouldn't have needed weapons fifty years ago," Moura said.

Murdick's voice exploded on the line: "Peace-keeping weapons! Hey, listen, they work! We're living in the longest period of peace known to the world!"

They were looking down from their rotors at the odd worn and grown patches that might have been city-stains and a discernible pattern of trees in some valleys that made them look like wild gardens. The roads were decayed, but their straight lines were still visible in the wilderness. Tipped-over light poles lay across them, and junked cars that might once have served as roadblocks during the emergency; and bridges—broken-backed.

War had not done that: people had, and weather, and time. This small abandoned part of America had come to resemble the rest of the world. One third of the state had been contaminated and closed off by an excursion of nuclear waste.

Hooper's mike was still going *heep-heep* whenever he opened it, but he fought the *heeping* to protest.

"You think just because there hasn't been a world war or a nuclear explosion the world's okay. But the planet's hotter and a whole lot messier, and that leak was worse than a bomb. And look at crime. Look at the alien problem. Look at money. Forget war—war's a dinosaur. The world is much worse off."

"I'm not worse off," Murdick said, from his rotor. "Neither are you."

"Willis, what kind of a world is it when there are some simple things you can't buy with money?" Hooper added, "I hate that."

Yet he knew that Murdick was right. As travelers they were exceptional. Who else had such freedom to range so far and see so much? It had all been a gradual slide into ruin, though they only noticed it when they left home—flew out of New York City and looked down.

It was a meaner, more desperate and worn-out world. It had been scavenged by crowds. Their hunger was apparent in the teethmarks they had left, in the slashes of their claws. There was some beauty in the world's new wildernesses, of which O-Zone was just one; but its cities were either madhouses or sepulchres. *Fifty years ago* was simply a loose expression that meant before any of them had been born. It meant another age. And yet sometimes they suspected that it had closely resembled this age—indeed, that it *was* this one, with dust on it, and cracks, and hiding aliens, and every window broken: smoke hung over it like poisoned clouds.

But whatever desperation and ruin these travelers saw in the United States they knew it was much worse elsewhere. They had seen that the chaos and despair of other places—the hideous inconvenience of poverty—had made America, even in this condition, seem majestic.

Hooper was leading them in his Flea, a double-seater, but he flew alone. He had worn his mask the whole way: bat ears, a snout, a chrome throatpiece, and a wide tinted faceplate. He had taken charge, keeping radio contact with everyone and chattering throughout the entire trip. The party in O-Zone was his idea.

"Who knows—this whole place will probably be reactivated in a few years."

"It's a relief to talk about the future for a change!"

"That's all anyone talks about!"

"Because the past is a mystery. At least the future's familiar."

"Stop wobbling, Hardy," Hooper said. "You'll make yourself sick."

The spiraling motion was for the camera's sake. In his rotor, Hardy was also shooting—making a tape of the trip through this prohibited area. It was for his own reasons and also because he did not really trust Hooper to complete his tape. Hooper might decide tonight that he hated the whole place, or that he was bored and was leaving immediately. "Nuke it!" he might say, and go back and take his tape with him. Or he might wipe it and say he had never really wanted it and why had Hardy given him this stupid job to do? It would be just like Hooper to say without warning, "I've seen enough of this desolation—I'm reversing engines."

Once, on a long flight to a cluster of his warehouses in California—this was somewhere near Landslip, at a time when he still made inspection visits—Hooper had simply vanished off the screen. He radioed to Hardy in California, "Don't expect me."

Later, Hardy asked why and said, "Were you on a shoot?"

Hooper said he had been fascinated by a particular valley and had seen a good place to land.

That grin of his! He had a space between his two front teeth that was as wide as a ten-dollar coin.

"I just wanted a piss and a scratch," he said.

Now Hooper was saying, "You're endangering the rest of us, banging your ship around like that."

"Sorry, Hoop." Hardy straightened his rotor and made an adjustment to his camera.

"Goddamned rotation—all elbows."

"I won't do it again."

The apologies came easy. There could be none of the misunderstandings of friendship. And it wasn't love or a lack of pride. They had had almost forty years of this, but that was not the point either. The two men were brothers: Hardy and Hooper Allbright were imperfect versions of each other.

"You put the camera on the wrong setting," Fisher said. Fisher—Hardy's boy—did not look like either of them.

But this boy was never judged, never measured, never assessed, and if he was compared it was with himself at an earlier age.

"I'm the human being in the decision-loop," he said.

Today he was navigator, and he knew he was blazing a trail. But programming the new flight path was not a privilege for him, it was a necessity, he said. "Who else has the math or the memory?"

Hardy put Fisher's fussing down to nervousness, but it was not the responsibility for all the navigation—that was a problem with an exact solution, and exactitude made him arrogant, not nervous. No, the reason for the boy's odd squawking was that he was fifteen years old, and this was the first time he had been outside New York City. He seldom left the Coldharbor Tower, and never alone.

He had come today because, Hardy had said—truthfully, as far as he knew—that Fisher was the only person who could get them to O-Zone.

"We're in your hands, Fizzy. We'll be lost without you."

And so the boy had agreed.

"It's a landmark trip," Hardy said. He was speaking to Moura, his wife, who shared the controls. "This isn't just a New Year's party. This is exploration and discovery. This is a new land. We're the first people here."

Fisher said, "How is that different from any other longitudinal field study?"

"There's a lot of romance associated with this place," Hardy said. "The wilderness, the secret transferral of the nuclear waste, the fact that it was all in caves—big strange toothy limestone caves, boy. And then the leaks and the contamination, and half the state evacuated and closed off. Amazing! And it was kept closed, like a secret garden, and given a perimeter and a new name. So the most dangerous, empty, and primitive part of the world was right here in the United States. It was unknown—that's where the romance came from."

"Know what I think about that?" Fisher said.

Hardy wondered whether he had gone too far—the boy hated listening to him.

"That you're a tool," Fisher said.

"I was talking about the past."

"A complete tool."

"Stop quacking, Fizzy," Moura said, because the boy had begun to laugh. He laughed without smiling.

"What a dimbo," Fisher said. "Didn't you believe your satellite imaging?"

"Watch the video readout," Hardy said. "I want good pictures!"

The boy ignored this. He could be relentlessly rude, and one aspect of his rudeness was that he was deaf to friendly cautions. He hung on his safety harness just behind Hardy and Moura—navigating, squawking the coordinates, reading the video. He dangled, like a bundle of badly fitted software, setting them straight. Some of his rudeness Moura found almost charming, because he was innocent throughout and still so young, even if he was not small anymore. But he could be strange. He often said something or did something and then it was clear you did not know him at all.

"Romance! Adventure!" he said. His eyes became wicked with mockery. He was a good-looking boy but too fidgety and nervous to be called handsome. He was never still, and his questions were incessant.

"When I was your age I couldn't just key into my own satellite like that, and even if I had, it would have given me a big monochrome aerial shot, like a cheap road map."

"Why didn't you enhance it on your computer?"

"My computer was so old it had moving parts," Hardy said.

But Fisher hadn't heard. He was looking at the ground-screen. "'Like a secret garden'! You dong!"

"I used to think it was a kind of wasteland," Moura said. "I never imagined this."

Fisher had opened his mouth to mock; but she spoke first and silenced him.

"Something that's been lost—that you can't see or touch or ever have again—can grow in your mind and acquire wonderful associations. It can become almost magical."

But this, the Outer Zone—O-Zone—was an emptiness. They had left the Red Zone Perimeter and identified themselves with their Access Pass and had been allowed to proceed. For over fifteen years it had been forbidden for anyone to enter O-Zone or even to overfly it. It had been a deadly place. The earth, the air, the water—everything here had been dangerous with radiation. The nuclear waste that had been stored in the caves had got loose, the cylinders had

cracked and hemorrhaged—perhaps an accident, perhaps
sabotage; everyone had a theory—and this great tract on the
Ozark Plateau had been soaked in contamination. But that
danger and the rumors of devastation had been its protection. Its peril had kept it lovely. Its name was a fright. O-
Zone became a new word for a special wilderness—a place
that had once been wooded and parklike and settled, and was
now a prohibited area, dangerous and empty, with burst-
open roads and fallen bridges and a reputation for poison.

"The average radiation level here has been measured at
two-twenty rems," Fisher said. "In New York the daily dose
is point one! If we didn't have survival suits we'd die here!"

"It's O-Zone National Park, Fizzy," Hooper said over the
radio.

All the lines were open. The conversation carried from
rotor to rotor.

One of the Eubanks said, "It looks all right to us!"

"This place was so radioactive it used to be luminous,"
Fisher said. "It gave off a greenish glow!"

"—before you were born," Willis Murdick was saying.

It was an immense and overgrown ruin, without people.
And now that it was bright on their ground-screens they
began talking of how the irradiated plants and flowers had
had a freakish beauty, and one of the other women—either
Rinka or Holly—was describing what it had done to the
columbines and bloodroot and wild asters, the walnut trees
and the dogwoods.

Fisher said, "I won't believe that until I get some specimens."

"Those trees scare me," Moura said. "I never see a tree
without thinking there's someone behind it."

"The trouble with you," Fizzy said, "is you only get one
idea at a time." And then he put his glove on the screen and
said, "What's that scab down there on the ground?"

Hooper's voice rang in their earphones. "It's a city-stain.
They're brighter out here, because they've been left for so
long."

"Someday New York might look like this."

"Never!" Fisher shrieked. "Who said that!"

What had been a city was now a low wrinkled wheel of
luminous dust, softened and tumbled apart and lying in the
sea of green treetops. It was in places struck with color, the
footprints of collapsed houses; and some spikes and stools of

buildings—and a few half-towers—were visible at its center. Throughout the stain was the faint tracing of the geometry of parks and squares and roads. The river still ran and had an innocent tinfoil gleam, but Hooper said that the river had carried tons of irradiated slush out of the caves and floated it forth.

"I'm reducing speed and going in to shoot," Hooper said.

"You porker," Fisher said. "You're freaking up my program."

The others hovered just behind Hooper's rotor. They approached the city-stain, going slower and hanging together in the same companionable flight pattern—the Eubanks in their Hornet, the Murdicks in their Wellington, Hardy and his wife and boy in their Thruster Three, and Hooper in his two-seater Flea.

The city-stain revolved under them as they crossed four clicks of ruined houses which had lost their paint, and many of them their roofs. Most had been engulfed by their gardens and looked like old tombs or burial mounds. The roads had been narrowed into tracks by overgrown bushes, and many low buildings had been engorged by thickets of trees, giving the impression of hillocks and humps. The taller buildings were staring things with gaping doors and empty window holes; and yet they seemed to have an elderly dignity and a stillness that amounted almost to loveliness. They were stark and grave in the emptiness and clear air, and among the finely printed shadows they were neither dead nor alive, but appeared monumental. It was a stricken city that had been abandoned, but it had not yet fallen into total ruin. Its abandonment—it was clear from the images on their ground-screens—its desertion, had been a form of preservation. It was at last people that brought cities down.

The travelers continued to track across it, bemused by its gloomy beauty.

Straining forward on the straploops of his harness, Fisher said, "Do we have to go so slow here?"

"What do you want to do?"

"Finish the trip at top speed and then watch the raw tape of it in a unit somewhere."

"Kids," someone said.

"This is more fun, Fizzy."

"Fun," Fisher said, making the word sound stupid. "The

camera's more efficient. We'll have more data—we'll see more. If it's on tape we can stop."

"Willis and I can see plenty!"

It was mostly intact, but it was hollow—a ghost city. Some of its structures had fallen and soaked into the ground; the land looked saturated with those ruins. The rest had not been destroyed, only deserted and blurred. It was one of many in O-Zone. What was its name?

"That information's classified," Hardy said to Moura, who had asked.

"Isn't it on the map?"

"The map of O-Zone is blank," Hardy said.

"Because of the military installations on the perimeter," Hooper called out.

"Bullshuck," Fisher said. "It's because of Roaches and Trolls and the risk of looters when it's reactivated. Anyway, officially it doesn't exist, so how can you have a map of something that doesn't exist?"

The buildings close-up had a softly bulging and bearded look. Dust that had been whirled against their walls had sprouted grass and weeds, and there were plants and bushes on knobby stalks poking out of odd corners of the brickwork.

"We'll come back sometime and look around."

"What's the point of doing this twice, you dimbo!" Fisher said.

Moura turned and looked at him. She wondered whether he was frightened. He had never been out of New York, and here he was in O-Zone!

There was no energy here, the still city-stain had no light source of its own, and so it was full of natural shadows—they seemed to be in all the wrong places. Moura knew that Fizzy was not used to this; she was hardly used to it, the hiding stripy darkness. There was ferocity in it—it seemed tigerish and threatening, and it tempted her with the pleasure of risk. The thickened foliage looked full of secrets—the black oak and slippery elm—as if a lumpy green blanket had been drawn across half the flattened city.

Hooper had been narrating in bursts over the radio in his friendly bullying way as they had descended. Now he was saying, "Check those roads, check those parks—hey, can you believe those compounds?"

He meant that it was a marvel that the roads were so

narrow and unprotected. Even before they had fallen into ruin they could not have been safe—that surprised everyone. No fences, no walls, no barriers, no sign of checkpoints. The parks were densely wooded in a sinister and concealing way, and the yards and gardens of houses were open to the road. It had apparently been a city without walls. It was not tragic, merely a pathetic phenomenon—no lights and too many shadows.

It represented the naive trust of another age, a kind of fatal innocence and incompetence. Surely this would have finished it even if the radiation had never reached it from those caves. The travelers were amazed by sights like these. They had flown today from a secure city of open spaces and high walls and guarded entry points. They were used to wide, walled expressways, fortified against intrusions and ambushes; they were accustomed to busy skies crisscrossed by their own patrols of aerial gunships. It was not that Coldharbor was a garrison area, but that New York was a sealed city—and this nameless stain beneath them was like a city on its back.

The Eubanks could be heard quarreling in their Hornet.

"Not so close, Barry!" Rinka said. "You don't know what's down there!"

"Hooper's down there! I'm following him on autopilot, so will you please let go!"

And Willis Murdick, who had gone off the air, suddenly broke into their frequency, saying, "Listen, I've got irons."

"You pretend like you know what's down there," Holly Murdick said.

"Whoever's down there don't matter to me. The closer we go, the easier it is to burn them," Willis said.

"You porker, Murdick."

"And I hope they're listening," Willis said.

It excited them to see the empty sprawling place, its tumbled buildings, the stain of its stone and metal spread beneath their rotors. This was the dangerous past! Narrow roads and hedges and embankments—and what was that glimmer? Was it the poisonous twinkle of radiation's foxfire?

"There's nothing down below," Hooper said.

"Even if there is, I've got irons."

"But there's no one there!"

He spoke with eagerness and hope, and hearing him, Hardy could almost see his brother grinning and flexing his fingers, as if he'd seen a woman he wanted.

"If there's no one there, it's not dangerous, so why don't you—?" And with that shriek the Eubanks broke radio contact.

Patches of the city were intact and the rest had become part of the enormous oak-hickory woods that surrounded it. To Hardy's eyes, the city was not dead but asleep, wrapped up, protected and snug, and waiting for adventurous travelers to awaken and untangle it.

"It's lovely in a wild way," Moura said. "It's like a town in an old story—it just went to sleep."

"It's full of infection." Fizzy was sulking, not even looking at the ground-screen. "It's carcinogenic from one end to the other."

"Shall we land?" Hardy said in a teasing way to the transmitter, hoping for a listener.

Hooper rose to the challenge and said, "All we have to do is find a hard surface for these rotors."

But this was bravado. He could say anything he liked. He knew it was forbidden to land here.

Hardy winked at Moura. He did not speak—Hooper would hear. Hardy didn't want his brother's submission once again to the strict terms of the Access Pass: protective clothing, sealed conditions, no landings in a city-stain or within thirty clicks, no skin contact, all activities and sightings to be logged, all food and water to be brought in. It was forbidden to leave anything behind, and nothing could be removed.

The two-day trip—the New Year's party—had been Hooper's idea; but it was Hardy who had been granted the pass, to carry out what Fisher insisted was a longitudinal field study. An air corridor through O-Zone had not yet been approved, and yet Hardy—to everyone's surprise—received permission to land. These days, access to O-Zone was rarer than a moon landing, and it was the fact that they would be the first—even if they were only party-goers—that roused Fisher and persuaded him to agree to be navigator. No one asked why Hardy, of all people, secured the pass in the first place.

"—probably bursting with fabulous old treasures," Hooper was saying. "Want to follow me down?"

Hardy smiled at the way Hooper's rotor kept unwaveringly on a safe course as he threatened this rashness. And then he was startled by a squawk from the rear seat, where Fisher had stiffened in his harness.

"This is officially a degraded area!" the boy said. "It's a bone-valley, there's been an excursion, it's marbled with plutonium! You can't land here—they'll revoke Hardy's pass, and the Federal—"

"You sound just like your father," Hooper said.

"He's not my father, you fuck-wit!"

"Murdick here," came the gummy voice. "I don't see why my wife and I have to listen to this."

"It's dangerous!" Fisher was still hollering, his big square teeth showing in the faceplate of his mask. "I've studied these places! You could contaminate us—taint the rotors—and they wouldn't have to let us back into New York. We'd be quarantined!"

"See, that's what he's really worried about. He really wants to go home. Why did we bring this little shit?"

"Who said that? I'm navigator! You wouldn't have got here without me!"

"Oh, shut up, Fizzy," Moura said. "Everyone can hear you."

"If you don't know the risks, you're stupid," the boy yelled into the microphone. It was another squawk, and it made someone in another rotor laugh out loud. Fisher could not modulate his voice, and his mask only distorted it further. He clucked and growled and quacked in his adolescent way, and then there was more *heep* from the mike. And more people laughed, making him madder.

"The risks are infinitesimal," Hooper said. "This is a very old disaster."

Fisher started to say something, but Hardy signaled for him to be quiet. Hooper was still talking.

"I guess we'll have to move on and find a safe strip. And, Hardy. If there's any way of sedating your youthful passenger, I'd be mighty grateful. He sounds like a Fed."

"What's the point of sightseeing if we're making a video loop?" Fisher said. "It's a waste of time. It's for dimbos."

"Are we holding you up?" Hooper said. "Have you got a speaking engagement out here? You going to lecture the folks locally on the subject of antimatter? Or particles?"

"A lot you know about particles, you herbert."

"Or inert gases?" Hooper said, and shot his rotor up, and laughed, and added, "We're the only folks in O-Zone!"

"I hate words like 'infinitesimal,'" Fisher said. "I think Skells and Roaches probably use those words."

"I'm listening," Hooper said crisply, and he was still laughing.

"Everything can be measured," Fisher said. "Especially particles—particles have an inside and outside. They have interior dimensions, and weight and density. They have surfaces, they have topography, they have personalities. Don't tell me about particles! And never mind quarks—"

"Doesn't this kid ever stop?" It was one of the Eubanks, back on the air.

"—I've tracked exodes! I described Antigons! I know all the numbers." He gasped and began again. "We've been flying in circles, slowing down, speeding up. If we had flown straight and let the camera move in circles, we could have calculated exact distances and speeds and fuel to a ten-digit milliliter. All this bullshucking is just creating useless variables. 'Infinitesimal' is crap! Everything has a number!"

"What's your number, then, Fizzy?"

Fisher laughed. It came suddenly, with the quack of his usual voice, but there was a choking behind it. His laughter was a horrible snorting noise. He showed his large disapproving teeth. He said, "You know my number, fuck-wit!"

Moura turned toward her son again. Throughout the flight he had seemed to be suspended by his straploops as he nagged and navigated, appearing to gnaw the mike in his mask. He held his face forward, against the curved window of his faceplate.

He was associated in her mind with masks: she saw his face behind most masks. They had been part of that clinic's ritual. She had worn one, the donor had worn one, and the masked face had hung just above her as he entered her. She had not known the donor's name, but she had approved his pedigree, and she had come to enjoy the sessions—one a month, over the period of two years. When they stopped, with her pregnancy, she had felt abandoned.

The donor's mask had been a soft, beaked thing, with live flicking eyes; and hers had been a human face—a lovely actress who had been popular at the time. After one session Moura had stopped wearing the short smock, after two she dispensed with the stirrups; before a year had passed she went to the clinic as if keeping an appointment with her lover.

It had been a medical fad that had passed through New York—contact with the donor, probably a reaction against the injections and the test tubes and the slivers of frozen sperm. In some contact clinics they wore body masks, like breastplates, and in others they were naked in total darkness. She often wondered whether she had done the right thing. She could have received a sliver or an implant. Now she never spoke about it—people would misunderstand. These days, contact clinics were regarded as little better than brothels.

She had not known the man, of course—that was forbidden. But sometimes—and very often these days—looking at Fisher, she felt that stranger become more familiar and saw not Fisher's face but the face of the man behind the mask. She saw him most clearly in her son as a hovering shadow, and shadows—for the features she gave them—were the most powerful presences of all.

Fisher was fifteen-plus, tall for his age, with a pretty face and some gray hairs. Even though he did not get regular exercise he was hard-fleshed and tight-muscled—probably from tension alone, the nervous way he sat at his console. He was angular; his arms were too long, his feet and hands too big. His palms were always damp. He used body powder but never combed his hair. He had Moura's good looks and like her he was tremulous and attractive, always glancing. The difference was he talked. Mother and son had the sort of pale faces that are brightened and made more beautiful by nervousness. They shared another characteristic: they never smiled.

Fisher yawned constantly, and she could not get him to cover his mouth. He had a phenomenal ability to sleep, yet his mind was tireless and his intelligence easily engaged. He fastened on a problem and would not let go until he had shaken a solution from it, and then he was bored and blank for moments—and deaf—until he snatched at something else to solve. Moura had expected most of these traits in him: she had seen his profile before he was born—before he was conceived.

He was an extraordinary boy. His memory was perfect. He could find his way in pitch dark, steering himself with his memory, or the memory of a picture. But it had been years since he had done so. He was now afraid of the dark. He said, "There's stuff in my nose," when it was only snot—and sometimes it dropped out and he shrieked. He howled at insects, sometimes saying loud simple words to them in his squawking voice.

All this, Moura told herself, was predictable. What she had not expected was his rudeness—his snarls, his corrections, his boasts, his bad manners. He had become worse as he had grown older, and he was harder now to control—impossible, really. He had no humor, no grace, only the rattle of incessant information. He did not converse, he argued and made noisy connections. Most of his questions were belittling or hostile: he seldom listened for answers. And now there was a wobbly quality to his fifteen-year-old's voice that was a bleat or a growl interrupted by a high metallic quack, and he lost his temper with a sound like tin trays dropping. At times four or five strange notes were struck in the same sentence, or in a single word—he knew some very long words. He was completely unselfconscious, and could become angry very quickly—new chords were struck and things snapped in his throat. Moura had not wanted perfection, but she did not want this either. He could be infuriating. He had the asceticism and willful self-indulgence of genius. He was a cold creature and when he was being obnoxious his good looks made him seem far crueler than if he had been homely. People called him "wonder boy."

He was still arguing with Hooper over the radio!

"I love these folds," Hooper was saying. "These little ridges and corrugations of the land—"

"Synclines," Fisher said. "Anticlines."

"Lay off," Hardy said.

"Look at that filthy crawling river."

That was another thing: his horror of dirt.

"It's stupid to put down here!"

He had gone rigid again, because Hooper was leading them in a great circle, around a collection of buildings—two sets of buildings in stone and metal, identical in every way, like gigantic furniture, resembling a pair of narrow matching chests, with balconies like pulled-out drawers.

"It's probably contaminated!"

Moura said nothing. She was afraid of giving away her real feelings—that she was pleased to see him challenged and defeated by Hooper's decision—obviously they were going to land. Now Fizzy would have to accept things. Who cared if he got angry and yelled? He deserved this: she liked the rare sight of uncertainty on his face.

At his age she had traveled across the world, to some of the wildest places. Today these places were off limits and served merely as names and metaphors for hopelessness or terror. "Africa," people said to scare each other; but she had been there, and not in a colony like Earthworks in Kenya, and not in a rotor either. She had seen Starkies and Skells—they had been more approachable then, less aggressive, rather glorying in their own strangeness, like clowns at a party. That was before IDs, before Owners were classified; and yet there had been risks. She had lived awhile in Europe—not always in a sealed city—and she had traveled to the various landing places in Asia. There were fewer Prohibited Areas then. But she had stayed in Red Zones, she had gone with Hardy on field trips, she had traveled in surface vehicles. And now O-Zone!

Yet this was fifteen-year-old Fizzy's first time out of New York City. She saw that it had made him edgy, and at times unbearable. She was glad. A little suffering might do him good. Everything had always been too easy for him. The really annoying part was that he was navigator—that reassured her, but it also infuriated her.

"It's a hell of a long way to go," he said.

Hardy said, "Too far from home?"

"New York is the center of everything! The rest of the world is Roaches!" He was swinging angrily again on his harness. "We're only going to sleep here. That's all you care about. 'Hook me up. Let's buzz out. Let's go into a coma.' You're worse than Skells!"

Moura smiled, because he was known to be so intelligent, and here he had just made this stupid remark. He slept a great deal, but he was too young and too impatient to appreciate the deep sleep known these days as a coma. It had been one of her first thoughts when Hardy had told her of the possible trip to O-Zone: A coma—sleeping in the wilderness—what dreams we'll have in the safety of that empty place!

They were still circling the buildings. The tallest were only twenty stories high, and their stone was soft and slightly pockmarked, terra-cotta-colored, with gilded seams from the afternoon sunlight, and russet-colored where there was shadow. They stood isolated on a low islandlike hill that was banked and terraced with stone oblongs and low walls. The land rose to a shallow flat-topped knob of wide pinky-gray steps that had resisted the bushes and prevented the spread of trees—dwarf hackberries and maples here. The pair of landings at the top of the steps were each as long and broad as a football field, two flanking plazas providing a platform for the buildings. Now that they had made a complete circuit they saw that the buildings were like bookends on a broad shelf—no books—and the shelf surrounded by greenery.

Below the terraces and the plazas, and all around, were dense pine woods, with some black oaks towering, and little half-glimpses of abandoned structures, small and fragmented enough to seem like memories of what they had been. From this height—the travelers were circling just above the tops of the buildings—the old overgrown roads crisscrossed the woods like green seams.

"They look solid—no distress marks in the structures, no cracks visible, no subsidence, no evidence of fire or vandalism. The roofs are intact."

Hooper was speaking to all the other rotors.

"That's one good thing about radiation," he said. "Sure keeps the riffraff out."

"He thinks he can detect high-level mutagens by just look-ing," Fisher said. "What a porker."

"It's beautiful," Moura said. She saw in it everything that was lacking in New York and their own tower—silence, emp-tiness, natural light, wild trees.

"Looks like a great place for a party," Holly Murdick said. "We can have an old-fashioned New Year's!"

They were low enough now to look directly at the buildings without using the ground-screen. They had probably been regarded as towers when they were built, but they were not very old—not much older than O-Zone itself. They might have been finished just before O-Zone was declared a Pro-hibited Area. It was possible they had never been occupied. There were no signs of use, only of weather and neglect, and the effects of boisterous foliage. The brickwork was spotted with white lichens, and the empty blue-tiled swimming pool was cracked. The ornamental garden on the south terrace was overgrown in a strangely symmetrical way—the azaleas and junipers bursting from the edges, and lengths of red-leafed vines spilling into the pool. The thick untended trees had the contours of broccoli.

Sumacs and stinkweed had erupted through the main driveway, but Hooper followed it down to the main road—there was a structure he wanted to shoot, he said. It was a gatehouse, and beside it a large flat slab of stone with letters cut into it.

"It's got a name," he said.

The sign said "FIREHILLS", and beneath that, "Residents Only."

"Guess that means us," someone said.

2

THEY WERE NOT ORDINARY TRAVELERS; THEY WERE wealthy, they were city people, they were Owners. They had a passion for protection. There was no one here, there had been no one here for years, there could be no intruders, because O-Zone was prohibited and empty: it was on that basis that they had planned this New Year's trip. But their habit of security was so strong that they began laying out soft wires and alarms as soon as they hit the ground.

Hooper had spun his rotor down beside the stacked buildings on the hill—he saw that the plaza shelf would both hide them and give them a view of the surrounding countryside. Then the rest of them rifled in, and on the ground the rotors had the appearance of spiders— black bulgy bodies and pop-eyes and fangy jaws and slender bow legs.

"—lick this into shape," Hooper was saying as he paced on the terrace in full sunshine. "We'll be okay here"—but he went on fussing.

Even before the last rotor was unpacked Hooper had hoisted the power supply and set up the first eye. The seven remaining eyes were installed immediately after, and it was only then that the travelers felt safe.

Each eye was a multifaceted ball on a stalk, and any movement it detected caused a blink that tripped a signal and activated a beam. It set a tape going and made a sound-bite of everything it stunned. The soft wire was a separate system with its own lethal beam. These systems were powered by the energy cube on the roof—and it was put there not for the stronger rays of the sun or the absence of shadows, but because it was out of reach of any intruder. When the beams were fixed and the cameras positioned and all the circuits in working order, the travelers began to claim various rooms in Firehills for themselves.

They did not question the effort and expense involved in wiring the place. It did not matter that it took them longer to secure the area than it had for them to fly from New York. It was a ponderous instinct. They carried out the job efficiently, following a diagram provided by Fisher's computer—not only because Fizzy was the most intelligent of the travelers or because he had redesigned the security unit on their tower at Coldharbor, but because he was the most fearful of them and the one most likely to provide a complete profile of the weak spots in Firehills.

"Aren't you overdoing it a little, Fizz?" Hardy said as Fisher printed the design for a new circuit and prepared to bring it to Hooper.

"The system's specified on the pass," Fisher said in his quacking voice. "All overnight landings have to be secured!"

"But this is O-Zone."

"All the more reason!"

The rest of them worked in their masks, saying very little, taking orders from Hooper, who had not stopped talking.

"Let's give ourselves a big area," he said. "It'll take longer but it'll be worth it. We'll have some space to scratch in. And we can go for a hike afterward—on foot. You like hikes and outings, don't you, Fizzy?"

"Less than four hours of sunlight left," Fisher said. He was still agitated from the flight; the computer work had not soothed him. "Sunset is at seventeen-twenty-nine."

"Afraid of the dark?" Hooper said.

"Porker!" Fisher cried. "Herbert!"

The Murdicks and the Eubanks carried equipment, looking up from time to time to marvel at the place—at their good luck in having been granted permission to come here.

"Did you see the birds? Woodpeckers and mourning doves. And Willis says there's wild turkeys around. Isn't this something special?"

"Rinka saw some butterflies. We haven't seen butterflies in ages."

"Wouldn't you just love to pick some of those flowers? Only it's forbidden." This was Holly Murdick speaking. She made a face. "They could make you real sick. They could cripple you. You could grow a hump."

"Listen. Everything's got a different noise here—even the trees."

The whispers continued—the travelers were both nervous and grateful. One of the traits they shared was an alertness for the slightest sound, because a noise so often meant danger. It did not matter that they had been told that no other human beings existed here. Their suspicion and fear had given them an unsleeping habit of stealth. They were like certain timid animals in the watchful way they pricked up their ears and prepared their site; and even after it was wired and the whole of the exterior secured, they did not relax. Beneath their most easygoing expression was a twitch of attention. They listened as if with cats' whiskers, and in their soundest sleep was a monitoring throb that kept them awake to danger. They felt stupid rather than vulnerable, for they knew how dependent they were on their electronic equipment—their systems and devices were capable of spotting things they could never see.

This was proved only minutes after the circuit was complete. They heard a bleep and at the same time the snap of the light switch and a brief camera whine just beyond the area where the rotors were parked.

"Get down!" Hardy said.

They dropped to their knees, then forward onto their hands and elbows, turning their masks sideways to see.

"I knew this whole trip was a mistake," Barry Eubank said. "We didn't have to come all this way to get hurt."

"Be quiet, Dad," his wife whispered, embarrassed by the man's whimpering. "It's probably nothing."

"I've got irons," Willis Murdick said. "I'll burn down the first thing that moves."

"Don't burn me, Murdick—I'm moving," Hooper said, and hurried toward the activated eye. He kept his head down and his weapon forward.

Fisher lay against the stone surface of the plaza shelf. He was squinting and speechless with fear.

Hooper then trotted heavily back, grinning through his faceplate. He tonged a dead thing out of a bag and spread it on the stone surface. It lay like soft gray fruit with bad flesh and dark bruises.

Moura's hands were over her faceplate and she had gone off the air.

"You know she hates rats," Hardy said. "Why are you such a fool, Hoop?"

"Squirrel," Hooper said. "And not any old squirrel."

Fisher raised his mask and angled it so that he could see. It was not large—"Eighteen centimeters," he said—and it had been burned on the beam: the singe mark was printed on its spine. It was still whole. It was skinny and strangely deformed. It had a stumpy tail, and its brain lay outside its skull, encased in a sac of membrane.

"It's a mutant," Fisher said.

"Ain't that good news?" Hooper said, and squeezed the thing with his tongs, making its eyes bulge.

"He means," Fisher said, "we won't find any people here. Not even Roaches or Trolls. They wouldn't have lived through the heavy doses of rads."

"Or their brains might have burst out of their heads," Holly Murdick said.

"They couldn't survive with undeveloped crania," Fisher said. "So that's a stupid thing to say."

"It's a joke, sweetie," Holly said quietly, and kissed her faceplate at him.

"I don't think jokes are funny." Fisher stared at her with cold eyes, then pushed the squirrel into Hooper's bag and sealed it. He said, "I'm keeping this specimen, to study."

There was only one job remaining before they could move in: the sealing of their rooms. Hooper had chosen the units from the lower floors of the second Firehills tower, and each group was responsible for sealing and decontaminating its own unit. It was not a matter of radioactivity—they had measured that before even cracking the canopies of their rotors and they had made sure that the level was safe. "Low-level mutagens," Fisher said, and traipsed up and down with a scanner, poking the others in the leg.

But there was dust everywhere and there was always the possibility of danger from whatever new viruses or strains of bacteria had emerged here. This was the reason they kept their masks and suits on, and wore gloves and boots. The units had to be made safe before they could be used as living quarters; before the cushions could be brought in and inflated or any of the provisions unpacked; or any of the hardware set up—the monitors, the phones, the lights, the insulated pods they called sleep capsules.

Hardy was filling the cracks in one of his rooms. His apparatus was bulky—a sort of plump fire extinguisher which he carried in a backpack. He was working the nozzle over a deep crack when he looked up and saw Hooper enter.

"I was just thinking," Hooper said dreamily, showing the gap in his teeth.

Hardy switched off his machine and shifted its weight so that he could stand straight and face his brother. "You look like you're enjoying yourself," he said.

"Why does that surprise you?"

"You have a rather frightening habit of saying, 'I've tried everything.' You're hard to impress."

"This is different," Hooper said, and began pacing. "Wouldn't Dad have loved this condo? It's not that old, but this is the old world."

Hardy said, "There are probably thousands of them in O-Zone, all empty."

"It's real brick, you know. This stone wasn't poured. There's even wood in some of the rooms. I mean, actual lumber—not this superior sawdust we get in New York. The Murdicks don't like it! They're putting up a bubble outside. Nice and new. You know Willis. And he claims he's got some special food for us."

Hooper was walking around the room—stepping over Fisher as he did so—and rapping on the walls and windows, testing their strength in an admiring way.

"When I dream about buildings, I dream about things like this—old empty towers in a green wilderness. A big sky and no wires."

But Hardy was puzzled by his brother's sour tone of voice. "Why do you sound so resentful?"

"Because of the trouble it took us to get here, and it isn't even far," Hooper said. "And we've only got a forty-eight-hour pass, and then it's back to Coldharbor. That's not fair."

"I'll never get another permit if we break the rules."

Hooper glanced at Fisher, who was injecting the squirrel through the transparent bag, and then showing his teeth at the dead thing as if he had been contradicted.

"Besides," Hardy said, "it's probably not even safe here."

"That's good news. Mutagens, right, Fizz? That'll keep this place in shape."

He started to leave, then paused and returned.

"It's amazing what happens to a place if you leave it alone," Hooper said. "It just goes its own way. It stays alive. It grows. It gets better!" He smiled and looked wildly around and said, "There must be people like that. Do you suppose there are? That were left alone? Innocent friendly little forest people? I'd like to see one with her face pressed against the window. I'd be grateful for her, she'd be grateful for me—that's love, Fizzy."

"This is a cancer factory," the boy said. "Take off your helmet and your gums will bleed."

"There are mutants here!" Hardy said.

"There are mutants all over. I've seen them in New York," Hooper said. "Hairless rats. Blind squirrels. They don't live long. It doesn't mean anything." He went close to Fisher, who was still kneeling over the deformed squirrel in the bag. "How's our friend doing?"

"I'm performing a biopsy. This is raw tissue."

"I thought it was bubble gum. Good thing I didn't chew it."

"I don't think you meant that," Fisher said, glowering at his uncle. "I'm working on the theory that the squirrel's not a genetic mutation, but a chromosomal aberrant—"

"That'll make me sleep a whole lot better," Hooper said.

"—and that it might have been dead before it hit the beam."

"That doesn't make any sense at all," Hooper said. "Listen, Fizzy, do you know where you are?"

"You dong!" Fisher howled as Hooper left, but his mask turned the howl into a honk.

Hardy thought: I've spent the whole day losing arguments; and then: You're all mutants.

Fisher said that simply filling the cracks in the walls was not enough protection. He told Hardy to get out of the unit, and he released a cloud of plastic sealer into the rooms and slammed the main door.

"It sets in seconds," Fisher said, and then showed Hardy how it had given the whole unit a hard glaze on every surface. "It's not just dust—we're dealing with carcinogens. You want a party? Or would you rather have terminal cancer?"

"We could probably take our masks off," Hardy said as they moved in cushions and sleep capsules and personal bags.

"Probably," Fisher said. "Only I'm not going to." He made a face at Hardy. "Because I'm not a fuck-wit."

Hardy said nothing. If he did, he might scream at the boy. Did Fizzy know how near he sometimes came to being hit? Yes, he was intelligent, but Hardy often saw him as a rather pathetic creature—a big dumb animal with an overdeveloped brain and backward in every other way. But he was a brilliant navigator. And he was only fifteen. And this was his first time away from home.

Yet Hardy often wanted to scream at the boy and hit him—not hard, but hard enough to make him think before he delivered an insult. The boy had never been hit!

Outside—he could not stand another second in the unit with Fizzy saying, "I'm taking this side of the room for my mainframe"—Hardy watched the Murdicks setting up their bubble shelter. It was not enough that they had the largest and most expensive rotor—a big black levitating Welly that doubled as a gunship—or that Willis had brought an array of new weapons; he had also insisted on taking charge of the provisions. And he had refused to move into a unit in Fire-hills. He had brought his own unit.

Holly Murdick said, "I think it's super when a person really knows what he wants and then knows how to get it."

"Your best work is always done in complete comfort," Willis said. "But comfort isn't a question of money alone. It also takes great imagination."

His bubble shelter was an inflated dome that was kept tight by a pump that fed it pure air from tanks that he had brought to O-Zone—many tanks, for he believed that the air in O-Zone was unbreathable. He had set up the bubble on the terrace near the empty swimming pool that was now a great sink of vines and flowers.

"And we saw some snakes in there," Holly said. "Willis is going to lay down some poison, before they poison us."

"They're harmless," Hardy said. "Just glass snakes, legless lizards, and salamanders."

"We're not taking any chances."

What was there to fear here? Hardy looked west of Fire-hills, where the sun was sliding through a buttery cloud. The landscape was open, with forested knobs and steeply mounded hills. But you could not look anywhere on this empty-seeming land without thinking of the world of caverns that lay beneath it like a vast dripping and deserted subway. The wilderness had reestablished itself and taken hold of O-Zone and buried it in leaves and branches. But what im-

pressed Hardy most were the clusters of abandoned buildings—so well made, so firmly forgotten in the eerie stillness
of the dust-smothered towns. And it seemed so absurd that
Murdick had brought a bubble shelter to a place where every
dwelling was empty.

Willis dragged himself out of the bubble's front valve.

"I should be making a tape of this," he said.

When Moura, Hooper, and the Eubanks gathered to admire the bubble, Holly and Willis obliged them by scrambling
in and out of the valve, showing off the bubble's accessories.
Its chief feature was its transparency—and the illusion that it
was entirely empty. It shimmered like a window: nothing
behind it. And when Willis entered, he vanished, and yet the
interior of the bubble appeared to be visible. Holly entered,
and vanished—the sun shone through the bubble—and then
she emerged, and Willis poked his head out of the valve.

"And that's not all," he said. "We've got some real surprises for you people."

"Willis picked it up in New York," Holly was saying to
Rinka. "He knows an outfitter. Isn't it neat?"

Willis pulled his head into the valve.

Hooper said, "You just sort of evaporate when you get
inside."

"But I can see you!" It was Willis' muffled voice.

"It's expandable, too," Holly said.

"You all right in there, Willis?" Barry Eubank said.

"It's a downstroke strobe effect, you herberts," Fisher
said, and he walked toward them. In his swollen helmet, his
gloves, his padded suit and big boots he looked like a deep-
sea diver—and the greenish afternoon light helped, too, as
Fisher plodded toward them as if through fathoms of water,
and in a watery echoey voice he continued, "It's done by
negative projection in the double layer—the seams are
wired. If you put an infrared light on it you'd see everything!"

"Except aliens don't have infrared lights," Barry said.

"Or if they do, they don't have juice to run them with,"
Rinka said.

"What planet are you on, porky?" Fisher said, turning on
Rinka and gurgling through his faceplate. "There are Skells
that have jump jets, pilotless aircraft, heat-seeking rockets,
nerve gas, and satellite links!"

"They don't have clothes!" Willis said. He was just out of

the valve, on his hands and knees, and turned his face up awkwardly like a spaniel.

"If you've got nerve gas you don't need clothes!"

In Fisher's voice, Hooper said, "If you've got nerve gas you don't need clothes."

He was a perfect mimic. He did not use exaggeration—if anything, it was understated. It was expert playback, and because it was such an accurate echo, and not overt mockery, it seemed especially cruel.

"Relax," Hooper said in a silencing voice when Fisher faced him—the boy was grunting with anger. "I always have the impression you're being hostile when you give us information. I mean, don't *shoot* it at us, okay?"

"This is your soft-dome model," Willis was saying to the others. "You can actually double its size by just increasing your air pressure and paying out more bubble. Plus, you've got air and temperature control, but with thermal skin there's hardly any heat loss."

"We're thrilled with it," Holly said.

"You should get one," Willis said, and grinned at his gleaming igloo. "You'd be doing yourself a favor. It's solid comfort from top to bottom, and they're developing one with a toilet feature."

"It's no more than a glorified tent," Fisher said. "It's a gimmick. It needs a huge power supply or else it won't stay inflated, and without sufficient power it loses its transparency. I don't think it's comfortable, and I know it's not safe."

Hardy said, "What are you worried about, Fizz?"

"Anyone could slash it."

"You'd need a torch. It's armored fiber."

"Skells have torches. Most aliens have torches!"

"There's no aliens here," Hardy said. "There's no one here but us."

The others had begun to listen, and after Hardy spoke, a silence fell. They were unused to such silences: this one was riotous with insects and birds and the papery swish of leaves.

"So who's for a hike?" Hooper said.

And the silence continued. It was a vigilant pause, as the travelers looked outward from what they had begun to call their camp—beyond the security apparatus, the cameras, the soft wires and beams and the eyes on stalks and the masses of positioned lights. They looked out at the shaggy yellow-green woods that surrounded them. The road was overgrown, there was no path, a building just below the terrace was split; there were insect mutters and the chirps of birds—and mewing doves, and the soft chattering rap of a woodpecker. Overhead, a turkey vulture circled slowly like a severed kite. They were all thinking: Where are we?

"We'll just walk a few clicks," Hooper said, taunting gently. "Who's for some fresh air?"

They murmured at the absurdity of it: they were all wearing masks and breathing Assisted Air.

Hardy said, "We should make the most of the daylight. Establish some kind of satellite link. Keep in touch. Get Fizzy's mainframe working. It gets dark here."

"Really dark," Barry said.

"Imagine that," Rinka said, and still in her flat anxious voice, "That's going to be different."

The thought of darkness brought to them a foretaste of blindness, an intimation of terror. It was never dark in their tower at Coldharbor, and they were used to the skylights of New York and some streets lit from below. It was the simplest fact of life: light was safety and darkness danger.

"We won't be able to see a thing," Holly said, anticipating the night. "I'm not going."

Willis Murdick said, "I've got some lights in my bubble we could bring. You don't even have to carry them—they fit over your helmet."

Moura said, "We don't have any kind of map."

"This is a hike," Hooper said. "It's not an expedition. Just a stroll down the street."

"I don't stroll down the street in New York," Holly said. "Why should I do it here?"

"Anyway," Fisher said, "there's no street here."

"Through the trees," Hooper said.

"There's no path," Barry said.

"We'll make one," Hooper said, but it sounded like a hollow promise. He saw there was no enthusiasm for the walk—indeed, he sensed a degree of fear among them. They were new here, and not yet accustomed to the light and sound of the empty place; he knew the dusk and the darkness would be much worse for them.

"I've got just the thing," Willis said, and brought out a long flat object from a tube. "Ever seen one? A chain-sword? For bushwhacking?"

He also had a thick helmet and mask, he said, and thigh boots, and a new suit of armored fiber. "What's the point of coming to a place like this if you haven't got the hardware?" He salivated and swallowed noisily as he described each new thing. They were the best, he said—based on the most advanced research, made with new substances, developed in outer space, and tested on the moon and in orbital stations. He kept swallowing, as if he were tasting something unusual and splendid. He said his chain-sword had an extension that gave it a meter-long blade.

"There's your blade," he said, shooting it to its full length. "And there's your cutting edge. Oh, sure, your whole edge is heated and high-speed."

He was chomping with satisfaction inside his mask.

"What's that fixture?" Hooper said, tapping a ring and collar at the front of Murdick's faceplate. "Is that going to be useful on our hike?"

"It's a suckhole," Murdick said.

"Your husband is such a total tool!" Fisher said to Holly.

"It's for the food I brought," Murdick said. "You're all going to need suckholes. But don't worry. I've got suckholes and adapters for everyone. You just snap 'em on your faceplate."

"What about our hike?" Hooper said.

The eight travelers in their suits and masks tried to look important and preoccupied, but they were silent, they had no answer: they shifted uneasily on the terrace, avoiding each other's gazes, and glancing out at the woods. The light seemed to be draining out of the trees, leaving a blackening glow in the thickness of ragged boughs.

"What if we trip and fall down?" Barry Eubank said. "I know we're alone here, but that's not it. You could rip a suit, you could crack a mask. You could get hurt pretty bad out there."

The others had turned to see what Hooper's reaction would be. Hooper said nothing. The sun dazzled against his faceplate. So the travelers looked out again, past the security apparatus; and again their odd movements and glances seemed dominated by the thought of danger.

Slowly Holly said, "That could be awful in the dark."

"We can't pick the flowers, we can't drink the water, we can't eat the fruit or cut any branches," Moura said. "And you want to hike it, Hooper?"

"It seems to be getting dark already," Rinka said.

It was only a lumpy pillow of cloud passing across the sun, but it left a chill on them with its brief shadow of darkness.

"Let's have this damned party and then get out of here," Barry said.

They were timid, Hooper saw, and even he had become unsure. They still stood together in their expensive masks and suits, facing the ragged trees and looking for openings or the malevolent eyes of animals. They saw nothing but the irregular wall of woods, so dense there could only be more of the same behind it. They split up again, pretending to be busy, but after a while most of them had returned to the edge of the terrace and paced along the perimeter wire—using their security beam as the margin of their promenade.

They looked outward at O-Zone as if looking offshore. They studied the indecipherable shakings of the trees. Moura spoke suddenly, as if saying out loud what everyone had been thinking. It really was like looking at the sea, she said—the rough waves and changing colors. "We've got no idea at all about what's underneath it!"

"Don't be stupid," Fisher said. "Murdick's got sensors and pods with thermal imaging!"

"What does that mean, Fizzy?"

"It means you can see anything in those bushes," the boy said. "The porker doesn't even know what thermal imaging is!"

But Moura was staring at him.

"Are you going, then?"

Fisher said nothing. There was only the swish and scrape of his trouser legs rubbing as he walked across the terrace. And then from inside Firehills came a reply—a loud quack of anger.

Night came down and everyone said wasn't it a good thing they hadn't gone with Hooper on his hike?

Moura Allbright and Rinka Eubank stayed outside at the edge of their lighted island and stared into the dark. The night had a blackness of unusual depth. It seemed bottomless and mocking, and they were alarmed by the rising tide of night noise—the scratch of insects, the smash of leafy boughs, and was that the wind? And above all this murk and babble was the starlight—a whole sky of sandgrains. It had been so long since either of the women had seen this—they lived under a starless sky in New York.

"Aren't they pretty?" Rinka said.

Moura agreed. But there was no comfort in stars. Their cold light was deadened by distance. She thought how stars only made her feel more isolated and made this darkness thicker.

Rinka said, "Do you remember the accident?"

"The incident?" Moura said. "Not really."

"All that reassuring talk scared the hell out of me," Rinka said. "And then the rumors of sabotage? The evacuation that went wrong? The casualties that were supposedly smuggled out and buried in mass graves? The panic, the blame—"

"My marriage was awful then," Moura said. "All I remember was that."

"They were putting nuclear waste in caves! Just stuffing it in and hoping for the best! No one knew!"

"Lots of people knew," Moura said. "I thought the whole country was destroyed. And then I realized it was just a corner of Missouri, and they were putting a fence around it and giving it a new name. I had other things on my mind."

She turned to face the darkness, to ease her memory, to say more. But the past was a darkened forest like this; she remembered and was discouraged. What did the world matter if you were lonely and sad? Cylinders of nuclear waste coming apart and bursting through the mouths of caves and seeping into creeks and rivers—that did not seem such a catastrophe. It was a local matter. You decided not to go there—as if anyone wanted to! They chose those caves because no one really cared. But even if it had been different and much worse—the world splitting into fragments—you didn't think of the world, you thought of yourself and your own life and grew lonelier and sadder, because there was no one else.

Rinka saw that she had stumbled into a private area of Moura's life. It was so odd to find someone who didn't have an opinion about O-Zone and how it had got that way!

"You always think a place like this is going to be exciting until you get here, and then it's usually either boring or dangerous. This is both! How is that possible?"

Moura was listening to her with a fixed expression—these

were the times when she was glad to be wearing a mask: you just made encouraging noises into your mike and let people go on talking. But Rinka was asking another question.

"Did you?" she was saying. "Did you really want to come here?"

"No," Moura said.

She was thinking of the nightfall. She had watched it and worried. It was as if they had been swallowed by an animal and were inside, in the darkness of the beast.

"Who's that?" Moura said, seeing a big shadow move away from the building.

"It's Fizzy."

He looked so strange—she wanted to say so. But how could she say anything about Fizzy without making it a comment on herself? She went inside with Rinka, to avoid having to talk to her son.

Fisher too felt lost in the darkness. This night made him feel weak and naked. He complained, saying he was hungry—the complaint easing his fear somewhat; but still he was afraid, and he limped, dragging one boot—it was timidity, he was not hurt. He shouted, much too loudly, "I whacked my heel!" He stayed under the lights, and meant to attach himself to anyone who came near.

He saw Hooper and struggled over to him, and then he saw the others, just around the corner of the building, at the perimeter beam, standing like people in a foundering ship, searching the dark ocean for a light or a glimpse of a narrow beach.

Fisher wanted a friend now—Hooper or anyone, even Murdick, whom he disliked: even Murdick would do. He was drowning here in this darkness. He wanted reassurance, he attempted conversation. But he was clumsy. He did not know how to begin.

He gasped at Hooper and began in the worst way, saying, "Why don't you have a woman?"

Hooper thought of Fisher as a supermoron, for his brains and his bad manners. But he knew the reason for the boy's awkwardness now, in this place: he was afraid, he needed human company, he had intended a friendly question.

Hooper said, "You can help me find one."

The boy blinked. He had not expected that. He tried

again, bumping against Hooper and kicking his uncle in the shins.

"What's your problem?"

He was still trying to be friendly!

"I lack inexperience," Hooper said, and laughed at the boy's bafflement. "I don't want anything!"

There was a sudden screech of fabric as Fisher turned, working his arms against his noisy suit, and pulled his too-heavy boot aside.

"Fizzy, that's a big problem!"

And Hooper was thinking that there was something so pathetic in the boy's being overdressed—all those clothes were so sad. Just then there was a flash—another creature caught and killed on the beam.

"It's a mutant," Fisher said. "Yellow stripes . . . and what a smell! It's actually getting into my air!"

"It's a skunk," Hooper said. Fizzy had never seen one. Never smelled one. And he called out, "Another party guest!"

Hooper looked around the terrace, hoping that someone else had heard and would find it funny. But the rest of the travelers were inside it had gone dark. The heavy black sky had slipped down against the orange bar of sunset and narrowed it to a red line and squeezed it into the far-off hills. Then he was alone with the boy, each of them pretending he was not frightened.

3

Even with the lights on it seemed dark to them in the second-floor unit that Hooper had sealed for the party. Perhaps it was too big for their lamp fixtures—it was a pair of long rooms with a balcony (one of those galleries shaped like pulled-out drawers). A hundred bright bristly insects sucked and fluttered at the windows.

Hooper was attracted to the large windows. He glided over like a fish in a glass tank and put his mask against it.

"Look," he said, because his brother had followed him. "People rave about visiting orbital stations and leasing time in space vehicles. This is much better."

"The weather's hurt this place."

"You can do something about that," Hooper said. "You're the landscaper."

Hardy hated Hooper joking about his job at Asfalt, especially as he had made it rain in a dozen countries. And it was a potential contract at Asfalt that allowed him this Access Pass to O-Zone. But this was a party; he didn't want to spoil the mood by contradicting his brother—anyway, Hooper would accuse him of being oversensitive.

"I don't think I see the same things as you, Hoop."

The dark helped, Hooper thought. He saw great soft hills and hidden places, and he imagined being among them, possessing them and burying himself there. It was not the hard lighted place that New York had become. This was a murmuring darkness. It gave him hope until he remembered he would be alone here.

"I could be happy here," Hooper said somewhat defiantly.

"You used to say that you could be happy in space."

"You have to return from space."

Hardy said nothing more. His brother was so impulsive—saying something one day with utter conviction, and regretting it the next, feeling condemned by it, and hating all his moods as soon as they left him. He yelled in fury when he remembered his contradictions, and he was bitterly hurt when he was reminded of them. It was in the end so embarrassing to be that fickle. What did he really want?

It was as if at these black windows they were flying blind through space. They were falling but could not tell how fast. It excited and frightened them—it was total eclipse. And the paradox was the noise. They had naively expected the darkness to be silent. The insects and the surfy noise of trees woke old memories in them—longings and fears and the hopes of early childhood. Hooper thought of the happiness he had always wanted, and Hardy the happiness he had never believed in—he knew that Hooper had not really grown up, or at least had not stopped hoping, which meant the same thing. How was it that Hooper, so much more battered, could still be so hopeful?

"I'd like to buy this place," Hooper said at last.

"This condo—Firehills?"

"No"—and Hooper's teeth flashed at the suckhole Murdick had fitted to his mask. He seemed to be addressing the black territory that lay behind the balcony. "I want to buy O-Zone."

"You're one of the few people I know who could probably raise the cash," Hardy said. "But it's not for sale. It's all Federal property now, and I think the Feds have other plans."

"I'll buy the Feds," Hooper said.

Was he laughing? He was certainly happier and more animated than Hardy had seen him for a long time. He had been whistling ever since they had landed here.

"I already own some Feds!" Hooper said. "Threw some money at them."

While they had been talking the guests had arrived and taken seats with their backs to the glaring lights. The travelers were used to brighter, safer-seeming rooms—this was a temporary shelter, a camping trip!—and so they glanced sharply whenever a shadow jumped on the wall.

This play of broken silhouettes and crow patterns distracted them and made them nervous and talkative. It reminded the Eubanks of a landing they had once made in Africa, when the lights had failed in the Earthworks colony on the coast. And the Murdicks said they had passed a night like this in a town in California, years ago—they'd never forget it. "I thought we were goners."

"It reminds me of being small," Moura said. "This is how I felt when I was about five. I was always looking at the walls of my room and thinking: What's going to happen next?"

"I wish you hadn't said that," Rinka said.

"It doesn't remind me of anything," Hooper said. "That's what I like about it."

Holly said the lights were awful but at least the sputter of the quartz core drowned some of the nighttime cackle—"All them birds," she said, meaning the insects.

Each person had brought a cushion, and most of them had changed into a different suit—they were one-piece flight suits, which were so closely fitted the air-conditioning tubes stuck out like veins along the legs and arms. No part of the body was exposed: they wore gloves and soft boots and masks—each mask had been adapted for eating with one of Murdick's suckholes.

"I'm running the whole commissary," he had explained. The Murdicks had matching helmet-masks, and Holly's large faceplate showed that she was wearing makeup—stripes on her cheeks and around her eyes and the fashionable stripes that continued over her ears and hair. Moura wore a custom-made mask that had been modeled on her pretty face—she thought the suckhole (why had Murdick been so insistent on them?) rather spoiled the effect. Hardy's mask had been issued to him by Asfalt; it had a company bleeper and was equipped with signaling and dust-sensitive devices. Fisher wore a video mask, and he was engaged in watching something on it, which was why he had not said a word. Most of the radio apparatus was in the dome of Hooper's helmet; but all the masks had radios—the party guests communicated by radio on an open circuit that allowed them to hear what everyone was saying, much as if they were sitting in a room and not wearing masks.

They kept their masks on. It was not because of the radiation level—the counter in this sealed unit was registering less than fifty rems—but rather so that they could see and hear better. Their breathing was improved, their Assisted Air was better than whatever stuff was trapped in this room; and if the roof fell in—Murdick said that it had happened before in places like this—they stood a good chance of surviving it.

"I'd love to get these clothes off," Holly said. She squirmed in her suit and wagged her helmet. "Next time let's choose somewhere safe. Then we could walk around naked."

"Barry saw a naked woman shopping in New York the other day," Rinka said. "It's supposed to be very fashionable."

"She was obviously an Owner," Barry said.

"Sure," Hooper said. "You could tell by her tail."

"By her mask," Barry said. "And she wasn't really naked. She was sort of painted. Body makeup, that kind of thing. The idea is to look like a Starkie."

"That could be dangerous—that's what I tell Holly," Willis Murdick said. "Someone might take her for a Starkie. She could get burned."

Holly was insulted, but kept her temper and said sourly, "As if anyone would take me for a Starkie."

"Some of them are pretty nice-looking," Hooper said.

"I know Willis hunts them," Holly said. "And I can understand why people burn them. But if you find them 'pretty nice-looking' I think you're sick and perverted."

Hooper's big mocking face came up against his faceplate—his white stumpy teeth with the wide space between the two front ones, and the bat ears trembling on his helmet.

"Sex with a different person is different sex," he said. "It stimulates a different part of your brain and gives you slightly different desires. You make discoveries. When I say 'you' I mean me."

"But an alien?" Willis Murdick said. "You're risking diseases!"

"Don't believe that propaganda. They blame everything on aliens. Hey, some of them are pretty nice-looking! Better than flesh-pups. I've had flesh-pups!"

Holly had started to smile. "What do you do with a flesh-pup?"

"You butter her and fuck her. Or him. With a flesh-pup you can hardly tell the difference." He turned from Holly and looked around the room. "You're all shocked, because I just reminded you that you're like me. It's like the song—I'm saying what you're thinking! You women are thinking: Let's get disgusting . . . let's have a splash party. And—"

Barry Eubank and Willis were whinnying inside their masks, as Hooper caught them with the flash of his faceplate.

"—and you men are thinking: I like the way your tits jiggle—let me stuff them into my mouth. If only I could tip you onto your back and receive the gift of your young body!"

"When the conversation takes this sort of turn," Moura said, "I always figure it must be time to eat."

The travelers had arranged their cushions in a circle; in the center was a low wooden table that the Eubanks had found in their unit. Murdick said that a table—especially this one—was not required for the dinner; but it was a solid old-fashioned oak table, and everyone else said that it added to the old-time atmosphere of the New Year's party. They were alone, in a place that was prohibited and remote, and the thick lovely tabletop with its dents and dark scratches seemed somehow appropriate.

Willis Murdick had broken the seal on a crate stenciled "Provisions," and unzipped the inner bag, where there were tubes lying in small bundles. The tubes were narrow, the size of soft air bottles. He had passed them around and urged the others to eat.

"Your wife doesn't like my food," he was saying now to Hardy.

Before Hardy could reply, Moura said, "I like it. I just wish I didn't have to squirt it into my mask in order to eat it."

"You don't squirt it, you squeeze it—pressure means everything with space food. And use your suckhole—didn't I give you one?"

"This food was designed for the space program," Hooper said. "Years of research went into this meal. That tube of protein cream you're holding probably cost a million bucks to develop—and you just strangle it and sneer at it."

Moura could not tell whether Hooper was joking—often, at his most obsessed, when he harangued them, the effect was comic. But she said nothing. He was dangerous when he was angry—not physically dangerous, but abusive and growly. Just a moment ago Holly, who had obviously been thrilled by his talk of sex, whispered, "Hooper, sometimes I like your insane notions," and his face had darkened and he had made a dog noise at her.

And he could sound self-mocking when he was being serious.

"I'd like to take something of this away with me," he had said.

"This toothpasty food?"

"No," he roared. "O-Zone!"

Murdick was sorting out more tubes—of pulverized fruit, of nonalcoholic wine, of noodle gluten. "This one's called 'Celebration Seafood,'" and he read the contents on the label and showed how to fit the nozzle over the suckhole.

"Hollandaise whitefish! Shrimp paste! Crab strings!" Hooper said, passing the tubes around. "Here's some oyster pellets and textured lobster—just squeeze this little bottle and pretend you've got your face in a lobster claw. Here's some rice fiber, here's some meat fabric."

"Baby food," Hardy said. "I'd rather be fed intravenously than eat this goop."

"Fizzy hasn't eaten anything," Moura said.

"Fizzy's watching a video in his mask."

"If I can't have a jelly sandwich I'm not eating!" Fisher said—but he had not moved, he was still watching something on his video mask, his voice had come out of his ears.

"Wonder boy needs a swift kick," Barry Eubank said, and looked straight at Moura, as if defying her to respond.

Moura was not ashamed of herself for keeping silent. She felt a certain exhilaration when she heard the boy criticized; it was so much worse when he was praised. Praise angered him, in any case, and criticism merely made him laugh—that terrible braying that upset her more than tears.

"This is a memorable meal," Murdick said. He compressed his lips in gratitude and peered through his faceplate, looking delighted in a pious way. "We've got our vitamins, we've got our bulk, our fiber, and our taste. The product is easy to digest and no problem with contamination. This product is not going to repeat on us. And no impurities."

More out of loyalty than conviction, Holly said, "I agree. We ought to eat like this back in New York—we'd be a whole lot happier and we'd live longer."

"I think I could be happy without forcing this parrot shit down my gullet," Hooper said.

"It's a great product—I know the wholesaler," Murdick was saying. "A friend of mine"—and he brought a tube of crab strings to his mask, screwed the nozzle into his suckhole with a half-turn, then squeezed and swallowed—"good friend of mine, would be mighty pleased to be eating this. That man has been in space for years, rehydrating his food."

Murdick saw that he was being stared at.

"When I heard we were getting permission to come to O-Zone I said, 'We're not having any rehydration! This is going to be deep-space conditions! Forget New Year's—this is a real mission!'"

"Try the meat butter, Barry," Holly said, passing a tube to him.

"'Fortified,'" Hooper said, reading a label, and feeling the words themselves were satire enough. "'Spinach sauce in a matrix of emulsified yeast portions.'" When no one responded, he said softly, "Mother of Christ. This food is a nightmare."

"And it's all got weaving in it," Murdick was saying. "It's great for the guts. Aren't you having a good time?"

They said they were—even Hooper said so, and Moura agreed. It seemed petty to spoil Murdick's surprise treat. This party was very unusual, they knew. They were the first travelers to come here since the sealing and naming of O-Zone—and so they felt like explorers and pretended to be roughing it in the harshly lighted room of this empty building. The food was silly, but it did not alter their mood, which was one of celebration and discovery. They felt brave, being here. It was as if they had come to a distant and inhospitable planet—they would not have felt stranger or more exuberant in space. Talking about it was one thing, and the food . . . well, the food was cranky; but the meal was the important thing, all of them seated and eating it together in this place, all the travelers enacting this old ritual.

Moura tried to put this into words. But she could see that it was unnecessary to say it—they shared the feeling, they were moved.

"Say something, Fizzy."

Hooper tried to get the boy's attention.

Fisher did not reply. He had been sitting cross-legged, but he had tipped himself onto his back, and he lay there with his knees up and nodding inside his mask and muttering barely audible sounds—the murmurs that crept out of the ears of his mask.

"He's still watching his loop," Moura said. She tapped on his mask, but he did not respond.

Barry said, "I used to watch porno with those things. I just locked myself in my helmet and drooled. Drove my parents crazy!"

"It's probably theoretical physics," Hardy said. "With Fizzy it usually is."

"Bremstrahlung!" Fisher's sudden quack—that odd word—startled them.

"I think he's telling us something."

"Give him air, brother," Hooper said. "I think your son's fading on us."

The quack came again. "Electromagnetic radiation!" the boy said. "Decelerating subatomic particles in an electrical field of an atomic nucleus. Lining up the equation!" He un-clamped his video mask, but left his faceplate in place.

They stared at his pink puzzled face—he was still damp from concentration.

"Go shit in your suit," he said to no one in particular.

They ignored this. He was freaky. He was only fifteen! Why should they let him worry them? He was so strange he screamed at insects, and he had mistaken a very ordinary skunk for a mutant—so Hooper had wheezily whispered to them.

Fizzy's abuse was no more than a childish nuisance. Mur-dick told him to grow up. "Wonder boy," Barry said. Hooper smiled and said, "Supermoron." And they went on congrat-ulating themselves at their success in having made camp in this prohibited place. We're actually in O-Zone, they kept saying.

"Who got you here?" Fisher said. "Who's navigator?"

Now they were submerged in darkness—they could see it packed against the windows, like fathoms of dangerous water, a wild ocean in which they lay buried. The night out-side was still noisy, and their lights seemed crude to them. But they felt bold—they were pioneers.

"This is paradise," Hooper said.

That was just about right, Moura thought, because para-dise was difficult—not a settled area, but something wild and empty. Beautiful, yes, but paradise was also a place where you had to figure things out for yourself, and where you might also fail.

"This friend of yours," Barry said to Willis. "You say he's been in space for years?"

"Right. But I agree with Hooper. I wouldn't trade this for anything."

"There are more risks here," Fisher said. He had not put his video mask back on. He sat holding it and regarding them contemptuously through his faceplate. "Those space stations are controlled environments, and there's no Roaches on the moon. But a place like O-Zone hasn't been properly studied—or if it has, that data's all classified. There's no documentation that I could find—only a few weather reports and some soil samples. I think it's full of freaks and mutations. Listen, we found one! And there's probably seepage. Half of O-Zone is underground anyway—caves and burrows, and those Federal caverns where they stored that nuclear garbage. How do we know there isn't more of that slush leaking into these collapsed roads that look like riverbeds? There's no maps! You'd get nowhere in a ground vehicle! This is more dangerous than space!"

"Tell the Pilgrims that," Barry said.

"If you set one of those amateur astronauts down here, he'd think he'd made it into the program," Fisher said. "He'd think he was on a hot planet."

"I am so sick of those people and their rocket talk," Holly said.

Moura said, "The security guard in our tower is a Pilgrim. Only he calls himself a Starling. Captain Jennix. He's very secretive."

"He's a complete porker," Fisher said. "He reads those stupid science-fiction books that all of them read. He believes them! You can see him throbbing!"

"Have you actually talked to him?" Rinka asked.

"Yes," Moura said. "I think he confided in me because he wanted to get some information from Hardy. I wanted to laugh! How can they actually believe they'll be able to settle on the moon—or is it Mars?"

"It's platforms in geostationary orbit," Fisher said. "The porkers."

"They're welcome to all of them," Hooper said. "And the Roaches can have New York, and the Trolls have my permission to infest California, and the Starkies can squat wherever they want. O-Zone is for me."

Barry said, "I know what you mean. I've felt less secure in New York. That night we had that power failure on the bridges. That was worse than this."

"Is this bad?" Holly said.

"I mean, it was dark," Barry said.

Hardy said, "I remember when I used to like the dark."

"Hearing you say that gives me the creeps," Rinka said.

"Relax! Willis has a chain-sword!" Hooper said. "He can slash his way to freedom!"

Sensing that he was being mocked, Murdick said, "I've got some irons, too. And I know how to use them."

His defiant tone brought a silence to the room, and the others sat there, among the jumbled tubes of food, with a buzzing in their earpieces. That was the terrible thing about the talking masks, Moura thought: everyone could hear you swallowing and gulping and pretending not to be frightened.

"For example, that power failure on the bridges," Murdick said. "I didn't care. I was in a rotor—I'm not saying who it belonged to. We burned over a hundred Roaches that night. They were hanging on the bridges. I could show you a tape of it, if you don't believe me."

Fisher said, "Moura wouldn't let me go out that night."

Murdick grinned at him and said, "I wasn't scared. I had irons. And the whole bottom of my rotor was plated with titanium. I might as well tell you—it was a gunship."

"These horror stories are making me hungry," Hooper said. "I wish we had some real food. Next time let's bring pizzas."

No one was listening to him; no one responded. The attention was on Murdick, who seemed both aggressive and anxious, all his talk of aliens and killing. Why were such stories always told by isolated people huddled in a shadowy room?

"If for some reason we couldn't get our rotors off the ground . . ." Barry was saying. Then he stopped and looked at the window. He could not see anything beyond the black glass. "I suppose we'd be in pretty rough shape here."

Hardy said, "There's Red Zone Rescue at the perimeter."

"They'd have to find us first."

Murdick said, "What's to prevent us from getting our rotors off the ground?"

"Holes in them," Rinka said. "Some friends of ours took a trip in that bad zone in California outside L.A.—Landslip, where they had the quake. They didn't know there were aliens around, some kind of Troll territory, and the aliens were all having a war or something. They had three rotors—real expensive ones—and every single machine was damaged. Holes punched in them. Seems the Trolls had got hold of some shit-guns. Luckily, these friends of ours were very well-armed, but if they hadn't been, and if they hadn't burned about twenty of those Trolls, they would have been in serious trouble."

Murdick said, "When people stop coming to places like this it'll be the end. This isn't far—it's a mental distance. You're just worrying about the dangers. And there was that stupid campaign a few years ago to completely deactivate O-Zone. Declare it a wilderness area, the cowards said. But what's the point in staying home in a sealed city and turning the rest of the planet over to the animals? Eventually you'll have animals scratching on your front door."

"So you want to activate O-Zone?" Rinka said.

Before Murdick could speak, Hooper said, "No, leave it alone. It's probably the only empty place on earth. The last chance!"

"You're just saying that because you can't buy it," Hardy said.

"Tell us your plans for O-Zone," Hooper said, and smiled as Hardy fell silent.

Holly was objecting at the other side of the table. "I wouldn't live in a place like this," she said. "A woman in my tower said she knew someone who got deformed after living on a margin of a waste dump. It was in Europe somewhere. She grew a hump."

When she finished speaking, Fisher began jeering. His noisy pleasureless laugh was a nagging noise in everyone's earpiece.

"What is wrong with this kid?" Holly said.

Fisher's ear-scraping mockery stopped as abruptly as it had begun. The boy turned his big mask on Holly and said, "What you just said isn't true. And if a thing isn't true, it's stupid."

Holly tried to dispute this, but Hooper interrupted her, saying, "As usual there is a sort of crude integrity in what our supermoron says. There are too many superstitions about places like O-Zone."

"There's too many laws," Murdick said. "We had to wait years for permission to fly here, even though we've got the right protective gear and all the food. I think we're hampered by regulations."

"I think we should be grateful for what we have," Hardy said. "We're lucky to have safe cities and secure corridors. Who has the money to activate zones like this? They're pretty, but they're uneconomic and probably unsafe. There's contamination—everything would have to be sealed, and food and water would have to be flown in. Water!"

"They shoot water to the moon," Hooper said. "And your company got us under the wire, so they must have some interest in an uneconomic wasteland like this."

Hardy did not reply to Hooper, and yet he kept talking. "Think of the security problems," he said. "It's impossible to travel on the ground, and there are no maps. The high-risk areas haven't been pinpointed. Look at us—we hardly dare leave the building!"

"We don't know what's out there," Holly said.

"There's nothing out there!" Hooper said.

Hardy said, "They've tried to activate places like this before. They've had an easier time on the moon than in some contaminated zones on earth."

"Because imaginary dangers are much worse than real ones," Moura said.

"And there's no Skells on the moon."

Hooper said, "There's no Skells here! We're alone—"

There was a little whimper from Rinka—she was laughing. She said, "This has got to be the strangest New Year's Eve party ever held."

They felt this was true, and that it made them singular, but it left them feeling self-conscious, too. They went silent, still sitting among the blazing lights and the shadows, with their backs to the windows. Yes, it was an accomplishment being here—something they had dreamed of. And yet they knew how timid they were in this huddle, and that they were afraid of the dark windows.

"I remember when this was Missouri."

"Who said that? This bullshuck is boring," Fisher said. "How about showing the tape?"

"We're having a conversation," Murdick said.

"We've got two hours of raw tape!"

Murdick said, "I'll bet you don't remember when this was Missouri."

Fisher crept over to Murdick and put his mask against Murdick's so that the faceplates touched. He said, "Who is that man in there?"

Unzipping a side pocket on his trouser leg, Hooper took out a cylindrical cartridge. "Here it is," he said. "The trip from Coldharbor. I'll play it at three hundred clicks an hour and you tell me when to speed and when to zoom."

Hardy handed over his own video cartridge and then hung the screen on the wall and held it steady while Hooper inserted both video cartridges into the base of the frame. It was a simple self-contained viewing apparatus that was operated by the control pistol that Hooper was fumbling out of a bag.

"Who wants to work the controls?"

"Let me do it," Fisher said.

"The kid'll jam it," Murdick said. "Give it to Hardy."

"Yah, I'll jam it—I'll jam it down your throat so far you'll be showing movies out of your bum," Fisher said, and again he pushed his faceplate against Murdick's.

"You'd better be careful, kid," Murdick said. "Don't make me crazy. I'll hand you your head. I've got irons."

"If I was as stupid as you I'd have irons too."

"You might be smart, but you've got the manners of a Roach."

"You look like a Roach."

"Beautiful irons," Murdick said, trembling as he spoke, and cracking his faceplate against Fizzy's.

"You fuck-wit."

"I've got stunners, I've got beams, I've got fléchettes, I've got burp guns and shit-guns." Murdick's faceplate was clouded with steam and spittle.

"Look," Fisher said, "he's flobbing on his faceplate."

"I don't have to kill," Murdick said in a choked voice. "I can blind, I can deafen, I can sicken, I can burn—I can make you stupid!"

But Fisher had turned away from him, and facing the others, he cried, "Why isn't anyone sticking up for me!"

4

They were silenced by the tape. It began behind them, with Hardy pointing the control pistol at the screen. The light isolated and seemed to quieten Willis Murdick—he appeared ashamed of what he had said: he looked limp and regretful in his expensive suit and mask. And Fisher seemed a little solitary and pathetic; after his squawk, no one had said a word. Then everyone was watching the screen, and video reflections streaked their faceplates and throatpieces.

"There's Coldharbor," Holly said. "There's our block."

New York—its deep walls, its battlements and shining towers—filled the screen and rolled past, like a cluster of castles; and the island's edge followed, the silver shimmer of the river full of daylight, and then New Jersey, and the sweep of empty streets—a Black town, a Troll town, a lightless city of aliens of some kind sinking into its own stain. Occasionally there was a flash—a dull orange smudged by smoky air. So many fires, of all kinds—random fires in the open, burning buildings, black ruins sending up trails of soot, cooking fires in settlements. For those poor people, someone said, fire was their only flamboyance.

The video was shown at a speed slower than their rapid trip, so they saw now what they had missed on their rotor's ground-screens. They saw simple features—the accumulation of snow and the icy lakes in the north; the pretty configuration of hills; the high fences and sentry posts around most farmers' fields. The pleasure of watching this videotape lay in their ability to slow it, or—using the faint grid on the screen—enlarge any part of it, any square, and bring it sharply into focus.

They asked Hardy to crank it up so they could examine the houses, and crank it again to see the people inside the windows, and their faces, their eyes, whatever they were holding in their hands. There were more plated or armored vehicles out here—and more jalopies, too. Hardy cranked them forward, and enlarged the pedestrians and the little dramas being played out beneath them as the trip progressed. They saw a human corpse on a roadside, and many dead dogs, and a house that had just caught fire, and wrecked vehicles.

They saw several mobs rippling down side streets, looking like marbles in a chute. The faces were expanded so that their expressions were readable, and their clothes, and their weapons.

"They're enjoying themselves," Hooper said.

Most of the people below were unfamiliar to them—they never saw them in New York: workers and low-grade Federals, and all the other tribal types who were known collectively as aliens. It was doubtful whether anyone down there had a valid ID, and there were certainly no Owners on the ground.

"There's a mob—that shadow in the corner."

"A Swarm—"

Murdick said that Swarm-crime was common out here: the mob surrounding and surging into a store or a house, or overwhelming a person, and then hurrying on, quarreling over its loot.

"Zoom them, Hardy. Look, they're Roaches."

"What's that in their—"

"Guns, bones—they're looters," Barry said.

"It's firewood," Hardy said, and moved even closer.

Moura said, "They're just poor people. Leave them alone, Hardy."

But he paused and gave them all a glimpse of the gaunt dusty faces and the torn clothes.

Fisher watched with his fingers on his faceplate and in his eyes a clear black light of pure horror.

There were few patches of dense population after that. Mottled woods crowded below, and then there was no one and nothing except hiding trees.

"I've hunted here," Murdick said. "It's good country."

"Good roads?" Hooper asked.

"Never went on the ground. We hunted from rotors."

In some towns there was no smoke, no lights. Perhaps they had been shut down? Or were they pretending, as some towns did, that there was no life in them, no valuables, no property at all—playing possum because of all the roaming thieves. But plowed fields showed farther on, private gardens, and towns with perimeter fences and fortress walls, and towns with main streets and white churches and ice rinks that looked as though they had never changed.

"That must be Pittsburgh," Hooper said. "See the rivers? See the walls?"

Murdick asked for the tape to be slowed in order for the others to see how there were no trees around the city. It was stark on its cliffs, as smooth and simple as a blister, with a margin of grassland around it.

"No hiding places," Murdick said. "They've got a terrific safety record here."

The tape quickened and the view tipped, the horizon rolling down below speeding clouds. They were like laundry that has twitched and blown in the sky since the beginning of time; the clouds were enormous—stretched thin and threadbare with all the beating, and now no more than gauze turning into vapor. Then it was all blue and the ground no longer visible.

"Turning south," Hardy said. "So we avoided all that traffic in the northeast corridor."

"I think it was smart going this roundabout way."

Fisher said, "It completely bent my calculations."

Holly was saying, "I know people who won't fly to Washington anymore, there's so much traffic."

They were quieted by the sight of grassland and fields and smudges of woods, and for the next fifteen minutes they watched the land pass by in an unbroken ribbon. Few vehicles were visible on the roads, and the tape was rolling too fast for them easily to identify the people. When a surface vehicle was spotted, someone shouted "Zoom!" and Hardy aimed his pistol and fired at that part of the grid; and then the vehicle rushed hugely into focus.

"There he goes, old Willy Shucker, in his four-wheel-drive toilet," Hooper said as the elderly driver of the plated car swelled on the screen. "Oh, he's been living out here for years—just him and his carcinoma."

Hearing the rotors droning, the old man looked back, in the wrong direction, not realizing they were overhead.

"No—over here!" Rinka said. "Look!"

The old man struggled with his steering wheel and his vehicle slewed left and then right.

"He's a Rocketman—a real Pilgrim. Look at those wild eyes. His ass is on the ground but his mind's in Mars. He's got his money in space vehicles, paying dues at the local space-cadet clubhouse. He definitely has room on some future launch—look at him, he's dying to leave. He's practically in orbit already. No low-level stuff, but the real whatsit—"

"Geosynchronous," Fisher said.

"You heard the boy."

"Leave him alone," Murdick said, and when Fisher looked up rattling his mask at him Murdick added, "Not you—that old guy, that Astronaut. Lay off him. Those people aren't hurting anybody. I think they're good for the program. It's the other bums I can't stand."

"What bums?"

"Aliens, blacks, prostitutes, polygamists, professional beggars, stowaways, lepers, and psychopaths." Murdick had not taken a breath. He gasped through his suckhole, then said, "Burn them down."

Moura said, "It all looks pretty normal to me," and everyone turned back to the screen.

"Foodplots," Fisher said.

Was that what they were, all these patchy right angles? Moura thought: Then I'm right. And the ground vehicles—the little beads and blobs—seemed to slip along the roadways unimpeded. A portion of the town was clearly shriveled or cut off, but other districts had a look of health—roofs and movement and the occasional flash of glass or metal. Heavy smoke was always a bad sign from below, but there was not much smoke here. Moura asked for a few close-ups and was rewarded by the sight of a dusty convoy trucking vegetables. But when she asked what could be more reassuring than a great hopper of cabbages—or were they beets?—Murdick stood up and began gabbling.

"Don't you believe it," he said. "There's danger there—it all looks different on the ground!"

"Except Willis never goes on the ground," Holly said.

"That's the reason why!" Murdick said.

It was greener as they traveled farther south, and the lakes, like metal dishes and brimming potholes, were more numerous and blacker by contrast. The grassland ended, the farms became more rumpled and hummocky, and were bordered by snaky riverbanks and the dark shag of pine woods. The towns were tufted in these distances—more good roofs and buildings high enough to cast shadows.

"Sometimes, out here, you get thirty or forty aliens going up to a house and just walking in. What use are dogs or alarms against forty reeking aliens? They just chew their way in and devour the place, and then move on. And on some of these roads—"

Murdick went closer to the screen and found a long straight road.

"—you get your major hijackings. Oh, it's no more than a roadblock—it might be a tree or a tipped-over car or a stack of burning tires. But as soon as that vehicle stops, they're all over it, sinking in their claws and wetting their teeth."

He was pointing to a particular truck, a long double-bodied model.

"Your alien," he said. "Your career criminal."

Hooper said, "I've lost shipments that way. But these days we air-freight most merchandise."

The camera drew back again and gave them a wide angle; but Moura was still looking at the truck, a tiny pair of hyphens in all that browny-green wrinkled land. This truck was heading down an unbroken road, about six lanes, and other vehicles strung out on it too. What Murdick said, and Hooper appeared to confirm, made no sense: Moura could not see where the road started or where it ended, and the only indication that things might be strange down there was the fact that each vehicle, and the truck especially, was followed by a trail of dust. So it was unnaturally dry on the ground, but that wasn't crime, that was just bad weather. She thought: He's trying to frighten us.

But reminding them of the dangers was also a way of reminding them that they had overcome them. At a slower speed and in ground-focus—looking at farmers' faces and at barnyards and at washing hanging on the line—their journey seemed to them remarkable. For long stretches they looked with unselfconscious admiration at what they felt they had accomplished. It was as if by flying over in their speeding rotors and photographing every detail of the terrain, they had taken possession of it, and understood it; and more—that now it had no surprises for them.

"Couldn't this be turned into graphics and color-coded and used for navigation on the ground?"

"Of course," Fisher said, to Hooper, who had asked, "but why would anyone want to take this trip twice?"

Now, emptier, the land seemed enormous. Minutes passed, and only a handful of settlements appeared, and they lay on the landscape like scabs. Murdick said that they were lawless places—most of them, anyway—and that no one was to be fooled by the look of the roads or the condition of the buildings. They were inhabited by the worst aliens—Trolls and Skells that had been dumped or driven there. Many of them had been thrown out of planes and somehow survived, all bashed up, and found others and started breeding a very nasty kind of alien.

"And we've seen Starkies here."

Where he waved his gloved hand was a river of oxbows, and a sloping valley that was hemmed and tightly folded and gathered, like an old-fashioned skirt—all these odd features were watercourses. Murdick's glove hesitated over a great patch of woods the shape of a bird's shadow and splashed with blue. It was beautiful.

"Probably bandit country," someone said.

The towns here seemed lifeless. Hooper wondered if they were bust, for in the same vicinity were compounds of fenced-in families and their fields, or so it seemed to him. He said out loud they were probably fugitives, and the others said, Oh, sure, and were glad to see the land below streaking past.

Some hills had been cleared and on their summits were the domes of observatories and some goggling telescopes and big white dishes—look at all that crockery, Fisher said; and Murdick said: Skelly—that was the proof that aliens had technology.

"There—that sort of irregular star-shaped stain—that's a fortified town."

"Where are we?"

"That sort of cleft-chin shape in the river is the bottom of Illinois."

"And there's the murky Mississippi," Hooper said, and asked for the tape to be speeded up.

In the blur and monotony of trees another color swept

fleetingly past, but was less a stripe than a moment of shadow, a sort of beat like an eye-blink, a visual blip, much like the river a few seconds before.

"The margin of the Red Zone," Fisher said.

There was silence—no one had seen it, and there was a certain hesitation in their earpieces, the pressure that builds just before something is loudly denied. But no one denied it. The pressure continued as anxiety and mumbling silence.

More woods followed, with torn patches where there were lakes. They were shrunken lakes, ringed with deep shores: O-Zone was famous for having become dry, and this was one of its driest months. There were stains of settlements, some buildings precariously standing, but no other signs of habitation. Although some of these towns were spattered with colored bungalows, you looked closer and saw they were abandoned and scorched. The power lines hung from discolored pylons; the roads were empty; the bridges were down. The woods piled up and became denser and thickly ribbed with overgrown ranges of low hills, the assertion of a rough plateau, with ridges and hollows dividing rugged bluffs.

"O-Zone," Fisher said.

The boy's eyes twitched at the hurrying tape.

"This is the part I like," Hooper said. "Those narrow canyons, the gorges, the velvety folds of land. Please don't call them anticlines."

"Shut-ins is what they call them here," Fisher said.

"How do you stand him?" someone said.

But the tape was still speeding them on through O-Zone. Among the forested knobs were shadows where nothing else could be seen, and these spaces were pressed deeply into the land, as if old blood had soaked into the ground and still showed. These shadows looked solid and were blindly black, like a depthless lacquer that was a shape without features or details. Where the curves were gentler and had soft bulges and human curves and contours, the crescent shadows lay alongside them, fitting perfectly. In the muscular cushions of green there were scars, but there were no openings among the trees—only the steep lips of old clearings and the tracings of forgotten roads, with the new woods folded over them.

"Caves," Hardy said. "It's all caverns underneath those ridges. This is where it all started."

He slowed the tape and pointed out the creeks and rivers,

which flowed from underground rivers in the caves, and what everyone had taken to be springs actually bubbled from caves, and after the incident—"the excursion," Fisher called it—the water had come up hot. The area was dammed and closed and renamed—Outer Zone seemed appropriate for something that was no longer Missouri. Satellite pictures showed it glowing green.

With the tape crawling on, they saw more city-stains and the eruption of trees in what had been plowed fields, and fat green pads where there had been lawns and parks. And among the fallen settlements the slashmarks of ruined highways.

"Wasn't it a great trip?"

"I've got to have a copy of this tape," Barry said. He turned to Rinka. "Show it to the Etnoyers. They'll scream!"

"I want a print of this too," Murdick said.

Hardy aimed the control pistol at the screen and brought the ground even closer, separating the colors and showing the bristling treetops and the areas of water—with the sun slanting on them they were like bottomless holes. The greater the enlargement, and the more detail they saw, the wilder it looked.

"Those shadows are sinkholes," Fisher said. "Collapsed caverns. Some people think they could have squashed the containers of waste."

"I think it was the Russians."

"It was aliens," Murdick said. "There's documentary proof."

"Anyway, we're here."

"It's not desolate," Hooper said hopefully, and finished the thought in his head: it was only empty.

In this long slow panning shot the land gleamed with radiant darkness, the lines of forest making long troughs of shadow. A moment later the land was flat and fragmented, with patterns of deserted settlements and dead towns like the sprawling symmetry of lifeless flowers and sun-faded colors on the surface design of an old trampled carpet.

An hour had passed. Now their New Year's party seemed more like a mission into the unknown, the sort of expedition that people made into deep space. They were glad to have this unusual tape to show their friends, so they could boast about having been to this wilderness. After letting the people marvel at it they could spring the surprise: This is American O-Zone!

"It's scary," Moura said. "We're so far away."

Barry said, "I can't believe we took that trip."

"It's lovely," Hooper said. He was smiling sadly, deaf to the other comments. He liked the way it went on rising and deepening; he liked the shadowy belts of foliage and the creases at the edges of the fine furrows below, and on the surface the suggestion of caves below.

The camera's eye swept into it and onward, probing it without disturbing it.

"Heads up . . . Look!"

It was Fisher, sitting forward—but the tape was still rolling.

"Rewind!" he said, and set their heads ringing.

His young untuned voice had no note of authority in it. Moura always thought of it as the sort of carping voice she wanted to disobey—the sort of voice that made you want to do the opposite of what it demanded.

"Didn't you see them?"

He was excited and sounded insolent. Now he was standing. He snatched the control pistol from Hardy, and while the others complained, he shattered the picture on the screen into splinters. All this had taken seconds, yet the panic had begun.

"Fizzy, what are you doing? You'll break that thing!"

He ran the film clumsily back and forth, using his thumbs, then said, "That cluster of pale specks. See them?"

Weren't they tiny withered blossoms, or perhaps dead patches on the ground?

He screwed them closer, holding the pistol at the screen. He was squawking with pleasure, and then complaining. "Fuck-wits! We didn't get a sound bite!"

They had heard the aircraft—they were running, half-hidden, he said.

"I don't see anything."

"Neither do I," Hooper said. "Where are these people?"

"I don't even think of them as people," Holly said.

Fisher was crying, "Aliens!"

Someone—was it Barry?—whispered, "But you said we were alone."

They froze. The lights sputtered. Time did not matter, because they felt trapped. They looked up at their black windows in fear, expecting to see half-human creatures come shouldering their way out of the woods.

5

W HAT MADE IT WORSE FOR THEM WAS THAT ONLY THE BOY
had seen them—and they were dependent on him; they
needed him and they disliked him.

"What did we just see?" Rinka asked.

"Aliens," he said, with a clam in his mouth.

No one asked whether those people were dangerous. Everyone was dangerous.

It was as if they had just confronted the symptoms of a fatal
cancer—not goblins or demons, but the plain bony face of
certain death: pickety teeth, a splintered nose hole, and the
unwavering gaze of empty eye sockets.

Just as the travelers had begun to take hold of a shaky
sense of well-being, the fragile feeling vanished. They felt
unsafe and were desperate to do something. It was now late,
almost midnight. They had planned to watch another tape
and then pop enough pellets to give them a long sleep—there
wasn't time for a coma. They had felt more than safe—they
had felt privileged and powerful. Now this.

"I couldn't see anything," Hardy said, and looked around.
He was watched by masks but there seemed to be no faces
behind them.

Why had they all gone so quiet? Why was Fizzy the only
one moving in the room, fussing with the cartridge?

Throughout a long fearful stammer of silence Fisher re-
played that particular strip of the tape three more times, and
they studied it in order to find reasons to calm themselves. It
upset them that nothing was clear and that this boy was

58

squawking and hitting the screen with his glove and saying, "Right there!"

Everything they heard from Fisher frightened them, because it seemed they were in his hands. Afterward there was nervous talk and more hesitation. They did not at first ask the obvious. They did not want to terrify themselves with questions to which they had no answers.

They were tentative but kept talking, in the belief that their fear wouldn't show. Yet it made their fear apparent.

"There probably weren't enough for a swarm," Barry said. "But they sure must have been doing something criminal."

Fisher said, "You can't prove that."

"I think I saw them," Holly said. "They looked real ugly. Did you see their dirty rags? They're like germs, these people."

Fisher said, "They weren't wearing rags."

All these remarks were addressed to Hardy. Hardy was somehow responsible for this. Hardy had got the Access Pass from his company, and he had hinted that he had plans for this place. Also, Hardy was sitting among them, looking ineffectual. And everyone remembered Hardy's remark. Some of the others were whispering it. Hardy had said there was no one here.

His weakness showed in his wet eyes.

"I couldn't see anyone," he said.

Moura said, "I wonder what they were doing?"

"I don't care," Hooper said. "But why were they doing it here in O-Zone?"

He was the only truly angry one and because of the force of his feeling he seemed the least afraid. His anger preoccupied him. He was nervous—not frightened, but agitated and spiritless. He looked undermined.

"They have no right to be here," he said. "This is ours!"

Fisher was staring, his mask twitching at the absurdity of that. Hooper glanced up and nodded and swallowed the rest of his protest.

"They were running," Fisher said. "They heard our rotors. They were trying to hide."

"Could have been poachers," Murdick said. "Like those Skells that poach dogs and cats in New York. I know a lady lost her collie dog that way. I didn't tell her they torture them to death and eat them—but it's true. Torture softens up their flesh, sort of tenderizes it, see."

"Apparently they're always on the move," Hardy said. "That's why they're always looking for food."

He was receiving the glances again, for saying that. Did that mean he accepted what Fizzy had said? He seemed to be acknowledging that fact.

Hooper began saying something more about the aliens' habits, and the rest looked up at the screen. Although it was empty and not even lighted, it seemed now like a window—the creatures had been seen there. That was part of the unreality of it all: they had flown over them, making plans and congratulating themselves on their boldness, and they had not seen them until now—and even so, they had had to be told by wonder boy that the aliens were there. The travelers felt foolish and exposed. The aliens had been there the whole time!

"Maybe the kid's wrong!" Hooper said.

Barry Eubank replied to this by saying, "Rinka and I are going home first thing in the morning."

He was holding his breath, as if he expected to be challenged and was going to say much more. But no one asked him to justify himself.

Hooper said in a disgusted voice, "Who else is bolting?"

No one spoke up. Moura suspected that it was not their determination to stay that kept them quiet but rather that they were ashamed to say out loud that they wanted to go. In their small timid hush was their anger at being asked the question that way.

"We should get some data on them," Hardy said. "What's wrong, Willis?"

There was steam on Murdick's faceplate.

"Nothing's wrong," Murdick said, and his tone said everything—it was a perfect lie-detector phrase. Murdick spoke quickly and tried to shrug. He looked lost in his bright suit and oversized mask. He was panting as he added, "But don't you think we should have gotten some data on them before we came all this way?"

"This is O-Zone—it's empty," Barry said. His shrill sarcasm betrayed all his terror. He was perspiring inside his mask; and he was pacing—keeping away from the windows. "There's no one here!"

"And those are just the ones we happened to see," Rinka

said, speaking for everyone, accepting everything that Fisher had said. She was whispering and staying near Barry—their common fear had made them a married couple once again; their terror was a kind of agreement and bond. "There could be lots more," she said, "right out there in the dark."

Hooper said, "Hardy's right—we should get some data on them."

"Who wants data? I don't care who they are," Rinka said. "If I had irons I'd kill every one of them."

Murdick said, "I've got the irons."

But no one asked him more. He was pathetic about his new equipment and when he mentioned his weapons he seemed frightened rather than strong.

Hardy's hands lay in his lap, his palms turned up, his thumbs out—they were more telling than a facial expression, and they signified futility. He said, "The only thing is . . ."

He did not finish the sentence—did not have to. The same worry was in everyone else's mind: Where were these aliens?

"We'll never find where they are," Hooper said. "We weren't flying straight. And if they were running when Fizzy saw them, they're probably still running. The calculation is impossible."

"That's just"—Fisher was squawking and stuttering—"just exactly the kind of stupid thing those aliens would say. 'Impossible' is another idiot word! If you start talking like them you'll never find them. Look at all the data we have—"

They hated his voice. It was bad enough having to overhear his talk, but it was so much worse being lectured by him. Yet they listened, because there was nothing else they could do, and because he was explaining what he planned to do with his computer. But his voice was so harshly unpleasant it made his plans sound desperate and unpromising.

"I'm pretty sure I can locate their position to within three clicks," Fisher was saying.

"I don't want to know their position," Moura said.

"I do," Murdick said, but without conviction. "Then I could show them my irons."

They all felt foolish in their masks and with all this clumsy equipment. And the litter of tubes from that ridiculous meal! And the complicated alarm and the sealed units in this Fire-hills condo, and the talk: "Our bubble-dome is a totally dust-free environment." But nothing they had brought with them on this trip could prevent them from being afraid now.

They decided not to move—not to go to their units or to sleep or stray outside—until Fisher did what he said he could and established the approximate position of the aliens. But they doubted that the boy could really help. What if the creatures were just outside in the darkness—squatting there and gurgling and waiting with the rockets everyone said they had? There was no more terrifying image than a hairy filthy alien—an Arab, an African, an illegal Hispanic—poised in the darkness clutching a heat-seeking missile; it was an ape with a deadly weapon.

Even if the aliens were not outside the condo—if they were east of that last large city-stain that had no name—how many clicks was that, and was it possible for these marauders to get here on foot before dawn? The travelers did not think their fears were unreasonable: most aliens moved on foot, and they often traveled at night, since none of them had passes.

"I'm standing watch," Murdick said. "We should post someone on the roof to guard the aircraft. I'm not saying go on the ground, but someone's got to watch it." He rocked on the heavy treads of his boots and said, "They're not getting near my bubble! I've wired it! They'll blow themselves up! Raw meat!"

But it was a haphazard vigil—it was a glancing at windows and a peeping over balconies. They were too apprehensive to be efficient. They felt naked and isolated on this lighted hill—it was too late to douse the lights—and they felt peculiarly threatened by the darkness. They prowled inside Firehills, discovering cracks and old furniture and tattered curtains. Using remote control, they set the alarms on their rotors. But who would rescue them when the rotors were snatched and flown away? They imagined the alarms screeching and the lights flashing as the thieves took off into the night.

They climbed to the roof of Firehills and looked blindly down upon the great blackness that surrounded them. The humiliation was that in this darkness they were both blind and naked. They wanted to save themselves. It maddened them to think they had no remedy except this squawking boy.

Murdick startled everyone with his weapons and his threats. Just the sound of him was a worry. He clanked his irons and muttered his confused plans. He was a small man, and because of his obsession with complex equipment and uniforms he always looked overdressed and somewhat top-heavy. He said he had the best irons, and they asked him what kind exactly. He told them rockets and gas-guns.

"We might be shooting into the dark. With these you don't have to aim. And we're wearing masks, so there's no problem."

"I thought gas-guns were against the law," Hardy said.

"They're against the law where there's a law," Murdick said. "But this is O-Zone."

"You frighten me," Hardy said.

"There's a shoot-on-sight rule that applies in places like this," Murdick said. "They might be right down there, steaming and stinking under those bushes."

"Why are you so eager?" Hardy said.

The man did not reply. But it was not the eagerness in Murdick's attitude that worried Hardy. It was the man's stupid fear and wild talk—all those horrible promises. It committed him to action and made him capable of anything. When Hardy left him, Murdick went looking for Hooper.

In the glaring light of the party unit, Fisher wired his computer terminal to the video screen where they had reviewed their trip. The aliens' malevolence still seemed printed there in small smudges, and the travelers had only to glance at the screen for their fears to intensify.

All except Fisher, who was calmed by his data-search. He set his keyboard on the big oak table and began to issue orders in his quacking voice. He had no authority, and he was very clumsy—his arms too long, his feet and hands much too big—yet everyone obeyed him. He had the Eubanks dragging cables for him. They believed that any activity, even this menial work for Fizzy, would soothe their nerves. At the very least it would help them kill time until dawn, when they planned to flee this dangerous place.

Hooper ran up and down stairs, first trying to avoid Murdick, who was raving and stamping, and then trying to keep away from the others, who were watching Fisher seated at his terminal, tapping *tock-tock* with infuriating pauses, and snorting at the screen.

Hooper was gabbling. Finally he said, "What are you doing, sonny?"

Someone mumbled *wonder boy:* the name had never fitted

him better. He was in his element. His youth and intelligence, and most of all his conceit—his importance! he alone could dispel the confusion!—plus the weight of his own drowsy fear, made him tyrannical.

He was now in sole charge. He had demanded that each pilot hand over his audio-log and flight program. Both the Murdicks and the Eubanks had recorded domestic squabbling on the tape, and they hated giving this unpleasant boy access to their privacy. What would he do with them? Yet their recorded outbursts only annoyed Fisher. He wasn't curious about the shouts and accusations; they were an interruption of his work. He frowned and muttered when something abusive was aired.

"What did you say?"

Fisher did not look up at the questioner. "I said I find foul language very relaxing."

He screened the incomplete charts of O-Zone and ran the tape of the flight back and forth, timing it and scanning it for speed and direction.

"How long do you think it will take?" Murdick asked.

"What are you doing now?"

"Do you really think there's aliens here?"

Fisher let the questions accumulate. He was absorbed in building a system; it was too early for answers. Fisher's relationship with computers and machines was physical—you could see it in the way he moved his lips. And there was an intimacy in the delicate touch of his hands stroking the keys. He used his fingertips on them, and when he was lost in concentration he had a way of salivating. He spoke in a slow satisfied drawl, with juice in his mouth.

"I'm feeding it raw data."

And he lightly scratched the keys, as if tricking his fingers into an arpeggio, and consoling the machine that way. Then he gave the whole mainframe a benevolent smile, as if this thing were animate and regarding him with hunger and gratitude.

Hardy found his brother at the window shortly after that. They did not speak immediately. Each glanced at the other's reflection in the glass and saw a distortion of his own face. There was a family resemblance—the faceplate showed enough of the broad nose and heavy jaw, the bright close-set eyes. Each man was just over six feet tall, and physically strong. They believed themselves to be the healthiest in the party.

As brothers they were not made uneasy by long silences. Each knew that the other was only pretending to be looking out of the window, but was in fact comparing the reflected faces. They were fascinated by the possibility that as brothers they might be interchangeable.

At last Hooper said, "I never expected the Eubanks to let us down. They're supposed to be so sophisticated and well-traveled. What a pair of shitters."

"I don't blame them for wanting to leave," Hardy said. "We should all leave."

"You mean run away before our pass expires?"

"If there are aliens here we can get data on them without hunting them down. What's wrong?"

"Nothing." But Hooper winced as he said it, because there was so much to explain, and Hardy's mind seemed made up.

"Murdick wants to burn them," Hardy said.

Hooper merely stared in acknowledgment. Only minutes ago, Murdick had come to him with a plan for mounting guns and beacons on the upper floors of these buildings, Firchills, and luring the aliens out of the woods with food or loud music (he believed the creatures were nearby and breathing hard), and gassing them.

"You know me," Hooper said. "I've never burned anyone in my life. I don't use my iron in New York. As for my warehouses and depots—when they're looted I just file an insurance claim and fix the hole in the fence."

"You sound so passive."

"That's the sound of money," Hooper said. "Money makes some people helpless. No one listens when I complain, because I'm Hooper Allbright of Allbright Cable Sales. A man of my net worth has no excuses."

Hardy was embarrassed hearing Hooper talk about his wealth—especially wealth making him feel weak. He resented it, and felt Hooper was merely indulging himself and overplaying the role of victim. But Hardy felt victimized himself and he decided that it was the time and place that had produced the feeling—it was O-Zone, it was this empty building standing in the darkness; it was the conclusion that everyone had reached: they were trapped here.

Hooper took a shallow breath—it was as if he were sipping at a thought.

He said, "I don't want to burn down those aliens, whoever they are."

"Why are you so gloomy all of a sudden?"

Because we might have to burn them down, Hooper thought.

The beauty of a mask was that it gave you whatever expression you wanted, and you could hide behind that face. As long as Hooper didn't talk, his brother would never know what was on his mind.

The thought of killing those people deadened him and made him feel half-human. He tried to rationalize it. When they're burned they're gone. It was merciful, in a way—better burning someone than injuring him and leaving him struggling for the rest of his life against that damage, and suffering yourself with his lasting reproach. No, that was just hunters' logic.

Hardy filled him with buoyant light by saying, "Maybe there's no one here."

Hooper was still concealing himself in his mask, wondering what to say.

Then he did not have to reply.

"I found them!" It was Fizzy, yelling from what he had begun to call "the Operations Unit."

There were eleven of them, he said, big and small, in a large circular depression near wooded hills they had taped, eighty-two clicks east-northeast of Firehills.

"It's a valley?"

"It's a down-thrown massif," Fisher said.

The aliens had no vehicles, he said. Even if they were in perfect health it would take them three days to walk to Firehills. Amazingly they had no village; there were no huts on the tape, no active dwellings.

"These bastards just keep moving," Murdick said.

"They have no discernible pastoral features," Fisher said in his slow juicy way. He had the maddening habit of making intelligent comments in moronic, slurring speech.

"This kid belongs in a rubber room."

"Who said that?" Fisher cried. And trembling at the computer terminal he went on, "If you say those things about me I'll leave you here. I'll unplug this system! You'll be stuck! You'll die! Those aliens will get you!"

When his honking stopped, the room went very quiet.

"I want a drink," Fisher said into the submissive silence.

"Get him some water," Hardy said.

"I want a bottle of Guppy-Cola."

The bottle was quickly brought, and as Fisher refused to leave his terminal Murdick was obliged to kneel and fit the nozzle of the Guppy-Cola bottle to Fisher's suckhole.

And then, a great deal calmer, Fisher described how he had made projections of travel time, and located obstacles, and roughed out a strip map of the land that lay between Firehills and the aliens. He had plotted the irregular flight path of the afternoon. He calculated the exact quantities of fuel consumed, and all the other critical measurements— elevations, altitudes, temperatures, wind speeds. From his scan of the tape he sketched a profile of the aliens: they were clothed, most wore shoes of some kind. Three profiles were still pending, and of the rest five were men and three women. They had dogs. Several of the men were capable of running very fast.

"They're blacks?" Holly said, and frowned in disgust.

"No," Fisher said.

"That could be worse," Murdick said. "That could mean they have technology."

Two might be black, Fisher said, but that didn't mean anything. They were all carrying what seemed to be simple weapons, and as none had food packs or other bundles he had assumed they either lived nearby or else camped there.

"What were they doing?"

"Chasing some big birds," Fisher said. "Wild turkeys, I think."

"Them turkeys must be sick," Willis said.

"Not as sick as them aliens," his wife replied.

Hooper said to Fisher, "You actually saw the birds?"

"Yes, and that's not all. I saw some deer, and a small bear and a bobcat, and some other stuff—rabbits and raccoons, I guess."

"Mutants," Barry said.

"I couldn't tell."

"Let's get out of here," Rinka said. "It's all animals."

"I wish we knew something about those aliens," Hardy said. "They must be illegals of some kind."

"You didn't even know they were here!" Barry said, and bore down on him, and backed Hardy to the window.

Seeing his hesitation—he was trying to think of a way of

reassuring them—the Eubanks and the Murdicks turned on him. It was very late, their eyes looked boiled in their faceplates, they began shouting. Was this some kind of joke? A whole day had been spent in traveling here and making camp, and just as they begin to relax they find out they're surrounded by Skells! Hey, they could have had all the Skells they wanted in New Jersey!

They went on yelling, competing with each other, their voices gonging in everyone's earphones. It wasn't bad enough that they had come without maps, it wasn't risky enough to be here on their own—no, they had to be here in a flimsy haunted condo with aliens in the bushes. And it was dark! These animals had technology—they could rush Fire-hills at any moment and slip through the alarm beam and kill them all!

"Leave him alone, you porkers!" Fisher said.

But Barry ignored the boy, and went for Hardy again. "You work for one of the biggest research agencies in the country," he said, squaring his faceplate against Hardy's, "and they send you here with false information."

"Not false information," Fisher said. "*No* information! That's different. We're generating data—"

"Those aliens might have penetrated O-Zone just this morning," Hardy said.

"They live here," Holly said. "And we paid money to come here, and we're not even safe!"

"If they live here, then we've made a very big discovery," Hardy said, forcing himself to whisper to these shrieking people. "This is officially a degraded area and it apparently supports a small human population."

"It might not be small," Fisher said.

"It's definitely not human," Rinka said.

It was all going to be so different, Moura thought: a pleasant flight, and then a foray over the new territory—towns and city-stains that hadn't been seen from the ground for fifteen years; and then camp, a meal, and the tape of the trip in this undisturbed place. And hadn't someone mentioned the possibility of a long recreational slumber in the sleep capsules? Afterward, when the party was over, a triumphal return to New York, and a celebration in Coldharbor Towers.

But no—instead, it had become uncertain and possibly dangerous. Two of the couples were panicky. The Eubanks were furious and the Murdicks vengeful. Willis was talking about gassing and burning the aliens. Hooper looked defeated—he wore an expression of helplessness and woe, which he could not conceal behind his mask; he looked as if he had been jilted. Hardy was still trying to fend off the others and deal with their loud cheated-sounding accusations.

Moura's face was set in a frown of resignation. She had never believed in the trip, she had not wanted to take it in the first place. What she had begged for was to be away from Fisher—perhaps Africa, just for a few days. She suspected that Hardy had arranged this O-Zone party for business reasons—perhaps he needed cover. All her fears were confirmed; in fact, this was all much worse than she had feared. But she did not say what she felt. Hearing the others complaining loudly helped her a little and eased her frustration.

Only Fizzy was happy, and pleasure made his mouth grim. Because only he had seen the aliens, he had become essential to them. He knew where the aliens were, he had analyzed them, he had all the information. He alone was calm. He had called out a few abusive names and then gone back to his computer, where he now sat, his head slightly inclined, his fingers stroking the keys. He was playing something, and swallowing in an affectionate way, and still speaking fondly and juicily of feeding it raw data.

"I'm getting a little more color," he said. "Quit the noise."

Murdick was stamping, he was impatient. He wore a glittery silver suit of armored fiber. He was a small skinny man and in his oversize helmet-mask he looked absurd and overprepared. His anger was unconvincing, and, like his antenna spikes and his two-inch bootsoles, seemed like just another aspect of his absurdity. He was overdoing it, because he was afraid.

He had stopped talking about burning the aliens. He said that he and Holly certainly weren't going to bolt, but they wanted to do something before the aliens were on top of them. Rinka was probably right in thinking that there might be many more of them out there: it was a frightening thought. All those eyes!

"Someone should take a little trip," Hooper said. "Before we do anything rash we need another sighting. Something more tangible. A shoot—some more tape."

Fisher kicked the table leg and squawked with a suddenness that silenced the room. Everything they needed to know was on the tube! There was no point in leaving this room! There was nothing more they could find out from the air. Everything that was possible to shoot on a flying trip tomorrow, Fisher could tell them right now.

Hooper was shaking his head. Fizzy, when he was pedantic, was unbearable, and he could not be stopped. But the boy saw pain on Hooper's face and spoke quietly to him.

"I found you a woman," he said, and tapped a line on the screen: *Subject G. Female.* "She's about fifteen, and boy can she run."

"This all sounds imaginary," Moura said.

"I'd like to see them," Hooper said.

"If they exist," Rinka said. She turned her faceplate at Hooper. She was very attractive and so there was something particularly ugly and repellent in her face when she showed disgust. "And you want to go near them?"

Hardy said, "It could be risky to go on a shoot. You'd be taping them on the ground. And it's a violation of the Access Pass."

Barry let his cold eyes rest on Hardy. He said, "You swore there was no one in O-Zone but us."

"That's what he said." Willis Murdick peered into Hardy's faceplate. "There's no one else here."

"And he keeps talking about 'them.'"

"Officially there are no aliens in O-Zone," Hardy said.

Murdick said, "Then officially we wouldn't be taping anyone. I say we go on a shoot."

So the party ended. The Eubanks said they were too frightened to sleep. The Murdicks hid themselves in their bubble. Hooper said he would stand first watch, and he took up a position on the roof of Firehills with a gas-gun that Willis had forced upon him. Hardy and Moura locked themselves into their unit, and Fisher moved his sleep capsule into "The Operations Unit"—he had taped the new name to the door and given himself the title Director. He would sleep there, he said, in case of something additional to add to the data base—another projection or detail.

It was two o'clock in the morning, and in their fear and anger and confusion the travelers had not noticed that the new year had begun.

6

Hooper was impatient on the roof of Firehills, standing watch under the dim flakes of starlight—their shining seemed to keep him in darkness. He was murmuring, trying to remember. When Murdick had given him the gasgun and another lethal-looking black pipe, the little man had said, "Burn all prostitutes, beggars, lepers, wackos . . ." But wasn't there a lot more?

Being alone here made Hooper jumpy. This was serious—this was urgent. He considered whether they should leave as soon as it was light, then decided that it was a necessity to look for the aliens; considered whether it should be a large shoot, then decided on a small scouting party—and decided that he should be leader; considered the time and decided soon, then today—at dawn, or when they could get ready; and finally decided to go after the little bastards right now.

That decision gave him patience. He stopped kicking. He waited another hour and woke Murdick. He knew that Murdick was an irritable man, but he was necessary: he had the best equipment and the most versatile rotor.

Murdick was ready. He too had decided a scouting party would be a good idea. He only needed encouragement, someone to share his nervous anger, someone to take charge.

He said, "Who else?"

Hooper told him.

"I don't want that brat along!"

"He knows the way," Hooper said. "We won't find the aliens without him. He's already got them programmed."

71

Murdick said, "Let's just take the program. I've got a mainframe on board. We don't need him."

But Hooper knew how to convince Murdick.

He said, "We won't have a chance without him."

Murdick sulked—not by saying anything but by stumbling obstinately and bumping the walls as they proceeded to the Operations Room. Then he spoke. "That kid better behave himself."

Fisher refused to accompany them. His pleasure lay in solving problems at his computer, and he sat with one knee jumping—flinging his leg up and down. He was still working at the terminal with long stabbing fingers and making faces at the screen—he said he had decided not to sleep after all. He was surrounded by empty Guppy-Cola bottles. He had discovered more about the group; he had coded the individuals according to speed and size; analyzed their old-fashioned weapons—nets and noise-makers and snares. But where were their shelters?

Hooper said, "I know how you can find out."

"Not if it means going there and landing," Fisher said. He had not looked at Hooper. He was still twisting his face at the screen, where the calculations glowed. "I don't want to be on the ground with them."

"Don't you want more data?"

Fisher said, "I can find out what they have for breakfast using algebra."

"But you don't know where they live."

"Hooper, some of them look crazy. There's four big ones."

Even Fisher's science and precise data were sometimes overwhelmed by his instinctive fear. He hated this in himself, but he could not rid his mind of these visions of beasts —their smells, their wet hair and wild eyes. Mathematics didn't help.

Hooper said, "But you know all about their weapons."

Fisher could not speak. There was something so stupid about admitting you were afraid.

Hooper said, "We need you, Fizz. We can't find them without you."

"Murdick, you porker, turn your radio off," Fisher said, and he waited while the furious little man moved a switch at the side of his helmet. "I don't want him listening."

"He can't hear anything now."

Fisher said, "Did you tell him that you can't find those aliens without me?"

"I sure did—and he screamed his head off."

Fisher turned back to the screen. He said, "If I go, I'm in command of the whole flight. I give all orders. I can abort the mission at any time. Otherwise, forget it."

"Yes, sir," Hooper said—glad of his mask, glad the boy was turned away from him. "This mission is all yours. You're captain."

"And what are you?"

"You can just call me uncle."

"Aliens, blacks, prostitutes, polygamists, professional beggars, stowaways, lepers, and psychopaths," Murdick said as the huge rotor jumped and hovered.

Hooper said, "I was trying to remember."

"Accelerate," Fisher said.

As he moved the throttle, Murdick said, "All of them All aliens. All illegals. Burn them all down."

Murdick's violent talk fascinated Hooper. It was a complex belief in hostility that made his aggression seem as systematic as a religion. But the same talk only bored Fisher with its lack of logic. Its arguments were dangerous and messy, and it was based purely on power-seeking. And it was arbitrary, too. He had asked, "What does 'black' mean?" and Murdick had raged at him.

Now Fisher said, "Are you watching the direction? Correct it one-half degree east."

Fisher sat in the rear seat of Murdick's Wellington, as captain—he had insisted on that. His forearms rested on the computer terminal and he watched the tube and the ground-screen. He had demanded to be navigator as well, but the program was written and there were as yet only trivial decisions to make. Those he dealt with in his nervous pedantic way and always in a voice of complaint.

Without telling anyone of their departure time, they had hurried away from Firehills, making their vertical takeoff in the dark, the Welly rising before anyone could react. The idea was to locate the aliens, to hover and land in darkness, and at dawn go on a shoot—observe and tape them.

"Just like we did in Africa," Murdick said. "Holly and me, at that Earthworks place on the coast."

"Watching aliens?"

"Buffaloes."

Hooper snorted.

"We had to catch them in the early morning," Murdick said. "Antelopes, zebras—everything. Sometimes you'd see a croc making a kill. But it can be dangerous."

"The crocs?"

"Blacks," Murdick said. "Jigs." He became thoughtful. "Some of the worst aliens on the planet. People hunt them. I could tell you stories, except this kid is here, which is kind of frustrating."

Fisher said, "The point about these O-Zone aliens is that they probably live here. And we're visiting. So 'alien' is a funny word for them."

"I don't call them aliens. They're Skells, they're Shitters, they're Roaches," Murdick said. "And that's not funny. These savages might have hit the coast last Monday from the islands—Jamaica, Cuba, Haiti. Or in an unmarked plane from Canada. A lot of them come in by plane—it's the new racket. From India! From Brazil! They're smuggled in like dope. They land in fields and then scatter. Hey, wouldn't you try to come here if you were a jig? This is America! They burned some just outside New York last month that came from the middle of Africa—by plane. They were barefoot!"

"These aliens are wearing boots."

"They could very easily have sneaked into the U.S. a few days ago."

"If that's the kind of shit-data you need, there's no point in going."

"I want to smell them," Murdick said.

"Then stay on course and do what I say. Deck of clouds ahead."

Fisher maddened Murdick by staring at the screen when he spoke to him.

"Because I've smelled lots of others," Murdick said. "Know why?"

He had begun to shout against the wail of the slipstream and the clicking of the rotor, and he didn't wait for a reply.

"Because I'm in Godseye," he said. "I can say that now we're on this mission. Yeah, Godseye."

"I figured that," Hooper said. But he wondered whether Murdick was just boasting, as he had about his bubble shelter and his tubes of food and his chain-sword for bushwhacking. Those boasts had meant nothing.

Fisher said, "What does that mean, Godseye?"

"I guess it means you don't know everything, wonder boy."

"If you want to get on the ground with your ass intact, don't talk to me like that."

Hooper had been expecting this friction. Two of the biggest fatheads in the party! In order to divert them he said lightly, "How are we going to land in the dark, Fizzy?"

It didn't work. Fisher began to complain. "It won't be easy, because this well-equipped Welly doesn't have infrared sensors on its landing gear."

"I've got high-definition thermal imaging!" Murdick said, almost choking. "I've got beams! I've got—"

"Never mind," Fisher said. "I know a place."

He guided them over the sinkhole he had found on the chart he had made. He spoke sharply, then grunted. His manner was severe and, from a boy of fifteen, nearly unbearable to the two men on board. He could navigate, but he could not pilot the rotor, nor could he operate any of the controls. He knew the commands, and that was an even greater irritant, because he always gave them with his head down, in a cross, contemptuous slur, speaking through his lips like an imbecile.

"When I give the signal, hover," he said. He was holding his watch dial against his faceplate in order to see it.

Murdick said, "If anything happens to this ship—"

"Shut up and hover!" The command rattled their earpieces.

"We're steady," Hooper said.

"Start the descent and don't deviate!"

There was always a nag of insolence in his orders.

"Drop it!" he said, just as Murdick recovered and began to complain. "There's an old sinkhole here. And cut the engine as soon as we're down."

They plunged slowly, spinning and tipping slightly, landing like a helicopter, but using jet-thrusters. Then they touched, the thrusters beating against the ground, and Fisher was squawking for them to cut down the noise and kill the lights so that they would be hidden. They had dropped into this hole in the woods. Darkness lay against the portholes and seemed heavy on the hatches.

Hooper screwed open the hatch and switched on his external sound. A gusty breeze barged through the high leafy boughs they could not see.

"They're going to find us," Murdick said.

"Not if we find them first," Hooper said. "Grab that energy cube, Fizz."

"The captain doesn't carry gear." -

"You're not captain on the ground—I am. Now pick it up."

They dropped lightly to the ground and set off in the dark. They were afraid to go very far from their aircraft, and yet the hickory woods rose all around them—they needed high ground to see the aliens. Fisher had plotted the route: the landing in the sinkhole in order to hide the rotor; the circular way out; the climb to a vantage point just above the meadow and field where he had seen the aliens on the tape.

Murdick kept stumbling and grunting. He heaved himself at bushes and caught his toes against small boulders and tripped. He blamed it on bad directions, he muttered about the darkness, he damned his new boots. Earlier he had boasted about the boots, their thermostat feature, their built-in pedometers. "They're state-of-the-art," he had said. "Godseye got a special consignment." But they made him clumsy on the narrow track. His grunts and squelchy curses made him sound in the others' earphones as though he were slowly falling down a long flight of stairs, and bumping on each step.

He said, "It's the wrong terrain!"

"You mean the wrong boots," Fisher said, behind him.

Hooper listened to them squabbling. Fizzy was just as boastful and equipment-conscious as Murdick, but his confidence exasperated the older man, who, aiming to compete, deceived himself and became lost in exaggeration. It was not the boy's wild-sounding talk that disturbed Murdick but rather the fact that he was always right.

"At least they're safe," Murdick was saying. "My feet are completely sealed."

"You're so worried about radiation you can't even walk straight!"

Fisher talked back without letup; he had never outgrown the childish habit of reacting to everything, and he often teased until it became torture. He made no allowances for a person's simplicity or weakness. When he heard a yelp of pain he went on squeezing, and so he could seem cruel in an apelike way.

Murdick was having difficulty concentrating. He gulped as he stumbled, and swallowed his replies.

Up ahead, Hooper told them to take care. Monitoring each other, in their masks and helmets, they were almost deaf to outside noises unless they deliberately amplified them. Hooper listened to the commotion of their footsteps crashing through the thickness of leaves and dead sticks and briars. They had no light, there was not much moon. The risks excited in Hooper a sense of nakedness and a wilder sense of freedom. This was like launching himself off a cliff and trying to fly. He was very sorry his only witnesses were the boaster and the brat.

Murdick was saying in worried tones, "We'll have to find our way back on this awful path to get to my Welly."

"You might not make it back," Fisher said. He got courage from Murdick's fear, and taunted him. "If you don't reach the ship in time, we'll have to leave you behind. That's the rule."

"This isn't space travel," Murdick said in a pleading voice.

"It's much greasier, it's more dangerous. You'll reach chokepoint and jeopardize the whole mission if you make us wait."

Breathless from kicking his big boots through the low dense bushes, Murdick gasped, "You can't leave me! It's my ship!"

"Shut up, both of you," Hooper said. He turned and they saw his towering body outlined against the star-grains in the fuzzy night sky. "I'll switch you off and lose you."

He then hurried forward and shortly after said, "Here we are."

It was lighter on the thinly wooded knob, but they could not risk the open—not even the dusty glow of pale moon-beams. They found a grove of bushes like a large leafy basket on the upper side of the knob and crouched there, inside, kneeling and balancing themselves with their elbows. It was just before five, in the predawn dampness.

"Your yawning drives me crazy," Murdick said.

Fisher had been growling and gargling into his mask. He did not stop. He had discovered one more way of enraging Murdick.

"I hate the dark," Murdick said. He was genuinely afraid, and his bad nerves made him pathetically truthful, even shameless.

Hooper said nothing. He was sighting out of the grove with the double-barreled object Murdick had called his burp gun when he had given it to him.

"You've got irons," Fisher said to Murdick. His own fear was returning and making him shiver in this stillness. "What are you so nervous about?"

"We could be sitting in poison." Murdick sensed that he had torn his suit on briars on the way up. He imagined the thorns like rusty spikes tipped with radiation and that the slightest scratch meant death.

"This isn't an iron," Hooper said. "It's a camera. Right, Willis?"

"That piece is regulation Godseye," Murdick said. "It's got thermal imaging."

"You didn't answer the question," Fisher said. "Didn't you hear me when I told you I'm a theoretical physicist? That looks like a particle beam to me, shit-wit."

In the darkness, Murdick breathed hard and blinked at the dial of his watch, and still in the darkness, crouching and grunting, he said, "I don't have a college education, because I don't need one. Listen, at least I'm not a freak. I didn't come out of a test tube."

"He thinks people come out of test tubes! Murdick, you are such a tool."

"Listen, I'm doing all right for myself. I've been around. I don't have to read about things in books. I've seen them, I've shot them, I've brought them back. I've stuffed them."

"Stuff this, porky."

Each time they spoke, Hooper had to readjust the sight and take a new reading.

"A lot of people," Murdick said—his voice had gone hoarse and threatening now—"people with a technical and scientific background, aren't worth anything in a crisis. In fact, most of them are wacko. But me—I've got money. I've always had money. That's all a sensible person needs."

"Hooper's net worth is ten digits! Why are you such a tool?"

By saying nothing, Hooper made them self-conscious and shamed them into silence.

Before they were fully aware of it the air around them was

fogged and then washed with dawn. The sky lifted, and from a low roof turned into something light and limitless, and it intimidated them with its clarity.

Below them was the meadow they had seen on the tape, but it was messier, with muddy hoofed-over patches and protruding clumps of grass. The woods beyond looked pathless and showed fallen oaks, with redbuds and dogwoods growing beneath. Though it had an appearance of danger and disorder, scaring Murdick and Fisher like an ugly mask, Hooper still felt thrilled by its wildness, the way it seemed young and untouched.

But as it grew light they all felt punier, and soon as spooked as they had felt at Firehills. Their equipment was no good to them here, the woods made them feel like savages, the landscape reduced them, and anxiety made them simpleminded. Then they were in full light of day, three lost souls sighting across the grass.

"The aliens I saw were over there," Fisher said, pointing beyond the meadow. "There's a narrow hollow—"

"I'm not getting caught in those woods," Murdick said. "I'd never have a clear shot."

"What kind of film did you load?"

Murdick didn't turn. "Very fast," he said.

They debated moving closer to the hollow—if there was a hollow. Hooper said they should try to get a sound bite—their wires were sensitive enough to pick up even distant voices.

Fisher said, "What's the range of your mike?" and reached. "That doesn't look like a mike."

"Keep your hands off," Murdick said, and snatched the thing away.

Holding a small trumpet-shaped object, Hooper crept out of the basket of trees and aimed the bell-mouth at the far end of the meadow. He moved it again, then shook his head.

"It picks up every breeze and every bird," he said. "All I can hear clearly are bobwhites. We'll have to shift."

Murdick said, "Never"—he would not move on any account, and he sat surrounded by the telescopes and cameras and the two energy cubes they had brought from the rotor. His small face was pinched in his mask, and he made himself even smaller, putting his knees together and holding his gloves against his earphones like a frightened child. The fact that his gloves were broad and pawlike made him seem even more childish.

"So what good is all your hardware now?"

Fisher's voice was mocking. It made him almost serene to see the terrified little man.

"It's the wrong terrain," Murdick said, and he moaned because the young boy was standing over him.

"He means the wrong planet."

Hooper said, "I wish I knew what we were looking for."

"It's stupid to look for aliens right away—they're too dumb and slow," Fisher said. "We should look for animals. I mean, real ones. I saw deer and foxes on the tape. Animals would give off better signals—we'd pick them up more easily—and animals would distract the aliens. Then, instead of us trailing the aliens, they would be trailing the animals—chasing food, see—and we could hang back and tape the whole show."

Hooper turned completely around, so that his faceplate was level with Fisher's, and he was smiling through it at the frowning boy. It was a good plan, he said. But Murdick looked rueful and stubborn; it was such a good plan it gave him no excuses.

Hooper said, "Yeah. Let's pinpoint some animals. You coming, Willis?"

"He wants to sit on his hardware."

But hearing that, Murdick struggled to his feet.

They broke cover, laden with hardware, sloping forward and keeping their heads down. Hooper whispered for them to watch for smoke or any movement. They crept to the top edge of the meadow and walked just inside the woods, in the crackle of dead curled leaves.

"That's deadly soup," Murdick said as they passed a bowl-shaped mudhole. "It's all cancer here. We shouldn't have come."

They moved irregularly in single file, Murdick and Fisher jostling for second place behind Hooper. For Fisher it was dreamlike, and his feet hardly seemed to strike the ground; Murdick's gabbling fear made him giddy and gave him an illusion of courage.

"Their brains might be growing out of their heads," Murdick said.

They reached a corner of the field. Hooper said, "If you

see anyone, freeze. If he sees you, hold your ground. Don't run, whatever you do, or you'll get eaten."

When they moved off again, Hooper thought of the injustice of having to sneak around here. This was O-Zone! Empty, poisoned, prohibited O-Zone! They deserved to have the freedom of the place—it belonged to them! Its perimeter and commando guards and all its security were paid for with Federal taxes. Aliens didn't pay taxes—they had no legal existence. Hooper felt a mingled annoyance and respect; he was a hunter whose quarry had so far eluded him, and still moving blindly, he sensed in a sort of prickling psychic way that the creatures he hunted were watching him the whole time.

Murdick was studying Hooper's eyes. Hooper looked back, his reverie broken, and saw that Murdick too seemed to be watched by aliens.

"I don't like this," Murdick said.

"And you're in Godseye, Willis?"

"We hunt in packs, we don't take crazy risks, we have air cover." Murdick was being candid—he had been terrified into telling the truth. "We've got bigger irons, we've got real firepower, we stay off the ground."

Fisher was listening to both men and staring at the sleeved pipes they held across their knees.

"Hey, are those irons or cameras?"

Murdick's eyes were red and squinting. Hooper looked away and said, "I see something."

Putting his pipe to his eye, Murdick said, "It's a dog."

"It's a deer," Hooper said, also spying with his pipe. "A white-tailed doe. Look how skinny she is. There she goes."

The animal had a muddy belly and muddy shins and it kicked its hind legs as it ducked into the woods.

At that moment the men emerged—no helmets, no masks. Their bare faces gave them a look of power. They were carrying something coiled. They made no sound at all. When they paused they were like dogwoods, and when they moved they turned back into men.

"Are they mutants?"

The deer was slightly lame and favoring one leg. It was moving and listening, very alert, but it had not sensed anything yet. It was shambling and browsing, leading the aliens on—two of them but it seemed like three, the way they moved, appearing and disappearing. They were gone. Had they ever been there?

Pausing near some wrecked trees, the deer lowered its head to the grass and in the same movement raised it—swung its body round, twitched its ears and tail.

"It saw us," Fisher said.

Hooper said, "Not us," and lifted his black pipe.

The deer was looking away from them, its ears alert and stiff, its hooves planted firmly in the turf. It held its rump high, in anticipation. Then a shudder in its haunches ran a shiver through its stringy leg muscles, and it rocked backward and bounded lopsidedly through the trees, the way it had come.

A man had sprung up behind it, and then the other reappeared, and both gave chase. They were small and ordinary, and their plainness was the most astonishing thing about them. They were real, they were more frightening than monsters. They wore thick vests and heavily patched trousers, and their hair was braided and tied back. They looked like woodsmen—bearded and green—and they were very fast. Aliens. They were gone now.

"It's two of the males—B and D," Fisher said.

"You recognize them!" Hooper stopped shooting with the thick black pipe.

Murdick said, "They were carrying ropes."

"Nets," Fisher said. "They keep them coiled. They can't throw them in there—they'd snag on the trees. They're probably driving that deer into a hole."

It was a hurried conversation. They started after them and saw more aliens gathering ahead and joining the running men—another man, a youth—girl or boy, they could not tell. They went after the slowly dancing deer.

Shadowing them were the three unearthly figures in suits and masks and domed helmets.

"Let's stay together," Murdick said in a terror-struck groan.

The aliens were yelling. It was not fierce—it was a wild kind of laughter interspersed with chatter. More aliens had appeared and vanished: they were uncountable, and were the more alarming for that. They were nimble and fast, and when they spoke they did not seem out of breath.

There was a power in the aliens' confidence, Hooper thought, and it was clear from the way they moved in the woods that they lived here. They neither stumbled nor hesitated as Hooper loped after them, trying to steady his camera. Fisher kept up with him, but it was not bravery; he was afraid to be left behind.

The deer was running back to the meadow, now trying to elude the two men who had confused it by separating themselves from a pair of hackberry trees. As they ran they loosened their lines and shook out the folds in their nets.

It was all magnified in Hooper's viewfinder. He was outraged that these aliens were chasing and poaching this animal—they had probably crippled the doe in a trap. They had no right to be here! His anger gave him speed, but he did not burst out of the woods. He stayed hidden at the edge of the meadow, still filming, as the aliens expertly netted and caught the deer, and then tripped it and pinned it to the grass.

That was the answer. Not burning them, as Murdick kept threatening, but chasing them and catching them in a bag, then emptying that bag somewhere far away. Killing was wrong, and killing was also very stupid—there were too many, it would never succeed, and just the attempt would turn you into a monster. But rounding them up might work—it was what they did themselves. Trap them in their own nets and then take them away.

"They don't look like mutants to me," Fisher said.

"They don't look like taxpayers either."

Hooper was still filming them—the scene, rather than the people. He longed to take this tape back and study it; to let Fizzy analyze it.

The aliens had turned their hunt into a lark. They yelped as the grunting deer was subdued, and when its legs were tied its grunts became rattling cries and snorts. It went on thrashing.

Fisher was breathing hard. "That individual is female. She's coded G."

She was muttering and pointing to the edge of the meadow.

"Murdick," Hooper said.

He had tripped and rolled over, and then climbed upright and was now balancing on his wobbly boots. He was examining his suit for punctures. He picked at the fabric, and when he was satisfied that there were no holes, he looked up and saw that he was being watched by four aliens. He smiled at them in terror.

"Don't bolt," Hooper said into his helmet mike.

There was no signal from Murdick.

"Can you hear me, Willis? Don't raise your hand, don't turn. Just copy. Do you read me?"

Fisher said, "He must have pinched a wire when he fell. The great equipment freak! He's going to choke!"

In his suit and helmet and mask and buskinlike boots, Murdick looked like an astronaut prepared for free-flight—just swimming in space—which was why he looked so strange standing still in those dry slanting woods, up to his knees in ferns, and with yellow jackets buzzing around his helmet.

He was clearly terrified—his arm froze as he motioned to raise it. He held his double-barreled pipe in his gloves, but he did nothing with it. Hooper's was still whirring softly, as he taped this confrontation.

The aliens had become smaller, had silently shrunk into concealment in the brush until their heads and shoulders were indistinguishable from the smooth stones. But Murdick turned away with wooden movements ("Don't!" Hooper shouted, hurting his own ears with his loudness), and tried to drag his legs through the undergrowth. Then the stones became human heads, the aliens materialized again, and rose up. Glancing back, Murdick ran, and one of the net-men started after him, swinging his coil.

Murdick was slow; he pitched against the trees, stamping and sort of free-wheeling, and his helmet swiveled heavily left and right—he had no peripheral vision. He moved into the meadow like a prehistoric animal, lowering his head to look around, and stumbling on his big flapping feet. He had dropped that double barrel and was fleeing in a slow staggering way across the grass. His panic gave him a crazy uncoordinated gait and his boots lurched as if struggling against magnetism.

"They're going to get him!" Fisher said. In his voice was neither pleasure nor fear; it was pure animal excitement—a kind of sudden ignorance. "Chokepoint!"

Hooper did not lower his video camera. He braced himself and slipped his fingers into the grooves Murdick had shown him. He snapped off the safety catch. The net-man was in his eyepiece, poised and steadying himself to fling the net over Murdick—he was arched as dramatically as a spider. Hooper moved him to the center of the cross hairs and squeezed.

The sound of a soft thump reached Hooper as the man

exploded into meat and in the same instant flew apart like liquid.

The camera still ticked in the first barrel. There was no one: what had just happened?

Before the other aliens could check their running toward Murdick—the man they had followed had simply vanished—Hooper fired again. There was no bang. The loudest sound was the plop of the plunger, as the second man exploded—swelling, becoming huge, just before he vanished. This one bloodied the other two with the mist of his red pulp.

Murdick turned to face those remaining aliens—the man, the wide-eyed girl. They were screaming, their shirts were blackened, their faces were streaked with blood. They were appalled, and yet they looked like demons, and when they ran they were still howling. Murdick had hesitated, and then he blundered in the opposite direction, toward the hill where they had left the rotor.

Fisher said, "Did you tape that too?" but he was frightened by the wild look on Hooper's face and he did not wait for a reply.

They stopped by the basketlike grove of trees and bushes to pick up their remaining equipment and then hurried down the slope to the sinkhole. Murdick was already in the cockpit and heaving the hatch cover.

"Move over," Fisher said. "I'm captain."

Hooper said, "Were you trying to run out on us, Willis?"

Murdick's eyes popped in his faceplate. He was speaking, but he couldn't be heard—his mike was broken, he was off the air.

Just before they took off, Fisher peered into the faceplate and saw that Murdick was weeping with pink eyes. He pointed to himself and mouthed "captain," and to Murdick and mouthed "fuck-wit."

In the air, Fisher said, "I knew you'd bring irons!" He was more frightened now that it was over. "You used a particle beam on them!"

Hooper said, "Is that what that thing is?"

"You're turning out a dozen kilojoules per square centimeter and you don't even know it!"

"It's a good thing I did," Hooper said. "They were going to eat Willis."

Murdick sulked and fought for breath and let the others fly

his plane. He was humiliated and broken, and he looked especially absurd in his expensive flying suit and helmet—his small face in the wide faceplate, his gloves making his hands look like fat mitts. He looked like a child wearing a party costume.

"No one believed me," Fisher said. "They were there! You saw them!"

Murdick winced at this. Every mention of the aliens made him glance sideways wearily. His mouth was slack with self-disgust and his eyes were bleak with pain. Disgrace showed on him like a skin disease.

"And now they're all dead," Hooper said.

"There's nine more of them!" Fisher said.

Murdick's face showed pain once more.

"Do you want the world to know that?" Hooper said. "Wouldn't you like to know something that no one else knows, captain?"

Fisher said, "I know a lot of things that no one else knows!"

He was glorying in the speed of the rotor, the way it plowed clouds apart, the slow tumbling of the earth beneath them—all this in brilliant sunlight.

He said, "I once thought I was heliophobic—no crap!"

"Please, Fizzy, pay attention," Hooper said, and braced himself against Murdick in order to look closely at the boy. Murdick was slumped in his bucket seat; Hooper used him as a cushion. Hooper said very carefully, "If we keep them secret, they'll belong to us."

The boy's eyes were cold and almost colorless, but his lids softened them as he became thoughtful; and his lips moved, not in speech, but tightening against his teeth. He was thinking about the aliens. *If we keep them secret, they'll belong to us.*

Hooper saw that the face in the mask was as strange as the mask itself. He knew the reason: it was the closest the boy had ever come to smiling.

But at Firehills it was Murdick who was first out of the rotor—Murdick, because Hooper was at the controls and Fisher was navigating: Murdick had had nothing to do.

His cry was triumphant but he wore a mad grin of humiliation.

"We burned them all down!"

PART TWO

COLDHARBOR

7

IT HAD BEEN LIKE A VOYAGE TO A DISTANT ISLAND. O-Zone *was* an island. And he was now safely back in the world, but shaken.

After all that—two surprising days that had exhausted him by soaking him in fear and excitement—the world looked different to Hooper Allbright. Had the world changed, or had he? The O-Zone trip gave him a way of dating his life. He now had a sense of time, a feeling of before and after. It was scratched on his memory in a long raw stroke that would heal but always remain as a narrow scar. In that sealed wound were the discoveries he had made—the forbidden place, the friends he had seen in a new way, the shock of having seen those aliens in an area believed to be empty. And he had to accept the strange simplicity that O-Zone was America, and aliens were human.

The worst of it was that he had killed two men and nothing at all had happened. Because there was no justice, he had to carry all of the guilt alone. Far away from the shouting lights of New York, among chittering birds, he had become a man and a murderer. *I'd like to take something of this away with me,* he had said. Now he realized that he had left something of himself behind. It gave him a lasting desire for solitude, but an aching sense of loneliness—he who had never been lonely. He wondered who was missing in his life, for surely it is only other people who make us lonely?

He stopped thinking of Fizzy as a supermoron. He felt instead a little insecure—dependent on the boy, because they now shared a secret. He needed him in other ways, too: he saw Fizzy's strength, and he suspected that all this time people had mocked the boy—even Moura and Hardy had mocked—in order to give themselves the courage to face him. It was not that the boy had the answers to hard questions, but rather that his navigation had been crucial to their O-Zone trip. The boy had made maps of this unmapped region. They had all found it awkward to admit how much they owed to Fizzy, which was another reason they jeered. And the boy didn't make things easier. He seemed to have the power of a wizard, but he also had all of the wizard's eccentricity. And his life indoors had made him cranky and demanding. Yet I need him, Hooper thought. Something had happened.

As for Murdick—his fears and obsessions had never seemed worse. The man was stupid and mean, and his stupidity Hooper regarded as very dangerous. He was a member of Godseye!

Yet the memory of the weapon, the double-barreled particle beam, which took pictures, continued to fascinate Hooper. Murdick had called it a burp gun. "I'm going to put it into my catalog," Hooper had said when he'd first seen it. It still seemed a profitable idea. Sell it by mail order; there was a fortune in something as simple and deadly as that, especially as the camera apparatus was said to be as efficient as the firearm. You pointed it in the general direction of the target, and the heat-seeking particle beam found its mark and destroyed it. Hooper was eager to develop the film. He was very surprised it wasn't instant self-developing film, like the stuff they had used to tape the trip out.

It had all been discovery! O-Zone was beautiful, the Eubanks were cowards, Hardy was mysterious (but tactfully didn't ask questions), the Murdicks were frantic, and Moura watchful. Fizzy had put himself in charge and then said, "I like math because there's no people in it!" They had streaked back to New York—and Hooper saw it afresh: another discovery. The city seemed silly and tame after those days in O-Zone.

From his tower in the garrison block of Coldharbor on the upper east side, he looked out at the glittering city and saw a long narrow island of more towers in garrisons, arranged like upright tombstone slabs. Some were glass, some granite or coated steel, others scalloped and black-gray like chipped flint. A knot of small choppers whistled past. Flights of rotors sharked through the sky, and circled, and sank, as they dropped onto the flat tops of the towers or on the barge pads moored on the river.

The choppers' monotonous chugging was in odd contrast to the shriek of jet-rotors, and all of it echoed in the deep canyons between the garrisons, a whole sky of aircraft noise, rising and falling. It went on ringing; it was the loudest city in the world. Hooper was sure that there were more than the permitted number of aircraft at this time of day. But the gunships of the police patrols did nothing but make their incessant figure eights over the city. The aircraft—choppers and rotors especially—had multiplied a thousandfold since the bridges had been secured against unlicensed ground vehicles. Sealing the city had meant a longer trip in and out—more security checks, more barriers, more bottlenecks. It had made the city safer but a great deal slower.

Until that trip to O-Zone Hooper had believed—with most of his friends—that aliens did not have aircraft. Now he was not so sure. The aliens he had seen were not freaks; they looked alert and human. He would have been happier with freaks or subhuman creatures—it was the popular view, anyway. It shook him to be reminded that they were human, and that it was not they but the language that had changed. Similarly, his view of O-Zone had altered his view of New York.

The skylights could not mask the gritty January color of the clouds, or the rolling smoke-laden air from New Jersey, or the purple rotor fumes. The only trees he could see were inside, at the high windows of nearby towers. At ground level he saw great empty spaces—the stone plazas, the wide streets, the fenced-in parks. And everywhere—even on this Tuesday morning—the security lights, so powerful, and shining from so many angles, that New York had a superficial magic, an illusion of castle towers suspended on a watery cloud. The profusion of lights made it a city without shadows.

He had not noticed that New York was bad, because it had become bad so slowly. It was a terrible place. All you could say was that it was safe. But the water was foul and the air was woolly and dusty from factory acid that made the light sulfurous. And all the buglike aircraft with their noisy *wup-wup-wup*. Fizzy was right again! The only solution to living in New York was to stay indoors, in a tower complex like Coldharbor, because indoors there were trees and flowers, there was fresh-cut grass; you could swim, it was warm. And outdoors, however safe, it was a full-time hell. You might be bored in here, but out there you would be suffocated or deafened or blinded by the light; and out of the city—in any direction—eaten alive.

One of Hooper's pleasures was standing on the balcony of his unit and looking through his own windows at his rooms, liking the play of light on his pictures and the arrangement of his furniture and the look of all that warmth and solitude. He became a spectator to his own achievement, and as his scrutiny increased and his interest widened, he became almost disembodied and indulged in the intense vanity of envying himself. It was a kind of pride that he could not suppress, because looking through the windows of his unit he saw that everything was in place: I have what I want. He had only to reenter the unit for the vision to be complete.

But now he knew, without looking in, that something was missing. Over his breakfast of green tea, tangerine juice, and fresh bread, he glanced at the smudged horizon and remembered the two men he had murdered. Not even shreds were left of them. They had been atomized into a fine mist of blood and sprayed apart, and at last blown gently away on the breeze.

He rid his mind of that image by thinking: I want that weapon for my catalog.

Even that seemed tame—his company, his catalog. He laughed to think that he had once been excited by it and had woken up in the morning with new ideas to try. He was the owner of a mail-order business. He had inherited the family chain of department stores, while Hardy—older and more serious—had gone into weather management. There had been almost five hundred stores—most of the old shopping malls had had an Allbright's. But with progressive deterioration, as one city became too dangerous, and another too poor, and another lost its power supply, and yet another lost its population, Hooper rid himself of the retail outlets and changed over to mail order. He was warned—by Hardy among others—that he would probably fail. The warnings liberated him and made him bold; Hardy's tentative cautions meant that if he succeeded he would owe his brother nothing. The only way to get free of the paralyzing grip of family was to break out and risk everything—to frighten the family into disowning him, and then to succeed. By risking everything, Hooper knew he would have everything to gain, and what had seemed a humdrum and predictable business became risky and made him imaginative.

His best idea had been to close the stores and start a catalog. But instead of printing it he put it on tape and film and relayed it to subscribers on cable television. He used still pictures as well as the data in the margin. He also used videos of some products: he knew that some men subscribed merely to watch women's underwear being modeled. Indeed, there was something for everyone: Allbright's Discount Cable Sales was famous for the liveliness of its visual catalog—its drama, its humor, its erotic content. The catalog claimed to sell everything: *Allbright's for All Bright Things.* The sales operations were performed on a computer line, the subscriber ordering his merchandise and paying for it using his own tube and cable link. Allbright's depots and warehouses were scattered throughout the country in secure industrial estates, but as the catalog was available throughout the world, it was a global business—Allbright's sold worldwide to anyone who had dollar credit.

It was a vast but simple business. There was no head office—no office at all. Hooper worked from a computer terminal in one room of his Coldharbor unit. The rest of his staff also worked from home, using mainframes; but the daily operation was little more than updating the catalog, reviewing new videos, ordering merchandise from subcontractors, adding and deleting items, and auditing the cash flow. Hooper seldom saw his employees—it was not necessary, since their performance showed clearly on the computer record. He never saw his customers and he had ceased to take much interest in his merchandise. Because of the credit arrangements he demanded of customers, he was guaranteed payment before an item was shipped. All sales were firm. The problems were usually associated with deliveries. Many delivery points were unsafe for ground vehicles or were far from airports. Yet Hooper prided himself on being able to ship anywhere.

Converting the family business to mail order, and building it up, had been a physical act. He had followed his instincts, and he had been encouraged by all the warnings that he would fail. He could see no point in action unless that action involved risk.

It had all paid off. When asked what his net worth was,

Hooper showed the gap in his front teeth and stuck out both hands and cried, "Ten digits!"

He had become a billionaire by including in his catalog just the sort of innovation that Murdick's weapon was. It was a foolproof, all-purpose item. It was a camera, it was a rifle, it worked in the dark, it had thermal imaging; it was more accurate than the person firing it, and its effect was devastating. It contained no bullets: a light particle pulverized the victim, and there was nothing left. No wonder the camera was so important: the trophy existed only on film, which was housed in a cartridge that was small enough to hide in your fist.

I won't put it in my catalog, he thought, and was suddenly very angry that such a diabolical weapon existed. It had no business in any catalog! What if weapons like this were common? It was bad enough, as Fizzy had said, that some Skells had rockets—and it was well-known that though Starkies were always naked, they were also very well-armed.

Hooper felt that by keeping the weapon out of his cable catalog he was helping to keep it a secret. Putting it into the catalog was like giving it to the world.

He went through the mechanical motions of approving some catalog changes, authorized an inventory in one warehouse and a stock shift in another depot. He answered some staff queries, and he reviewed the Christmas sales and the year-end figures. And then he stood up, hating the mouse in his hand that controlled his terminal; hating his room, hating his tower, hating the prison of this garrison, Coldharbor. It struck him that they had broken the rules—they had committed murder; and they had not simply gone home from the New Year's party—no, they had been expelled from O-Zone. It was a dismal thought, because it left Hooper feeling powerless and poor. What was all the money in the world if you couldn't have the one thing you wanted?

He hated being alone in this city. All everyone said—its only praise—was that it was safe. But not even that was completely true. The limited degree to which it was true was the result of a dreary succession of security checks, one valve after another, at every garrison block and on every bridge: the ID examination, the showing of the pass, the scan, the sniffers.

He had fled Coldharbor, he was walking fast downtown. "You've got something in your pocket, sir."

Was there always a security check at Eightieth and Madison?

"A film cartridge."

"You'll have to show it to us, so we can scan it," the guard said. "And I'll require an ID."

"I'm walking down the street," Hooper said, and sensed he was about to lose his temper. "And you—"

"Without an ID you have no legal existence."

"Don't lecture me," Hooper said, and his temper was gone. He was shouting now, and his anger seemed to have a life and logic of its own that had broken loose from him and was flapping in the face of this uniformed man. It was not even his own voice. "You private security people have no legal standing," the voice was saying. "Half of you guys are crooked. I know all about those body searches you carry out. I know—"

"Most people tell us it makes them feel better," the guard said. He had inserted Hooper's ID in a scanner, he had turned the film cartridge over to another man to be sniffed.

He was still talking; he had interrupted Hooper. Was there anything more infuriating than being interrupted only to be contradicted?

"—That's what most people tell us."

"I am not most people," the voice said, issuing from Hooper's mouth. "I am some people. I'm a few people—very few people!"

He snatched his ID and the cartridge and continued on his way. He was photographed at a checkpoint on Sixty-first, and there was another very strict check at the Midtown Mall when he entered the Greenhouse. He was scanned, he was sniffed, he was made to wait until his ID was flashed; and he realized, waiting in a narrow cubicle, that he was being photographed again.

"Are you jokers looking for someone?" the voice said. "Listen, I'm an Owner!"

He walked a few steps and called back, "You porkers!"

Then he recognized the voice, and realized his affinity with Fizzy. That was what had changed. He was uneasy, he was lonely, like the boy.

Inside the Greenhouse he saw a naked woman—naked-naked.

She was walking toward him, her flesh riding gently upon her as she walked, shaking with each footfall, the up-and-

down of her thighs, her trembling belly and nodding
breasts—all skin and motion. They usually wore jewels, but
she was young; she wore only a gold chain around her waist,
and sandals and a mask—a snout—but nothing else. He saw
that the mask was gilded, and possibly gold, but it was her
nakedness, not the mask, that suggested that she was probably very wealthy. And if you covered your face you didn't
have to cover the rest of your body.

Someone said, "It must be spring."

"Starkie," was murmured several times.

The alien styles had inspired new schools of fashion, and it
was true that this young woman was frankly imitating a Starkie. Other women had smears and stripes on their faces,
mock tattoos and markings, and ribbons in their hair. They
wore poor-folk styles and outlaw styles, and torn-open metal
fiber shirts, and heavy leather belts, and dusty boots. But
there was no mistaking these people had lots of money.

Some of the other shoppers and pedestrians in the Greenhouse were more conventionally dressed in one-piece suits,
but many girls and young women wore aprons—and nothing
else—or skirts that were slit up the back, so that their bare
buttocks showed. These were the defiant winter styles this
new year.

Hooper followed the naked woman from store to store—
she was buying jewelry. There was not much interest in her.
Some people muttered, older men stared. She bought another gold chain and fastened it around her waist with the
first one. Hooper stayed behind her as far as the main exit.
He would have left then, but he wanted to avoid another
security check. The woman breezed through, though she too
was scanned and sniffed.

A car with black windows was waiting for her at the sidewalk, but before she walked the forty feet from the exit to the
car, the woman enlarged her mask, drawing the snout aside
and the mouthpiece over the lower part of her face, making it
a breathing mask. The city was perfectly represented in the
image: the security check, the gold chains, the ornamented
mask, the naked woman.

The Greenhouse in the Midtown Mall was pleasantly warm,
and fragrant with the odor of its own hot blossoms. It had
once been eight blocks of streets and buildings; and then it
was sealed and rebuilt, the streets surfaced with tiles and the

whole mall roofed over in glass, a crystal cover twelve stories high. Trees and flowers had been planted inside the Greenhouse, and in the rest of the mall there were balconies and walkways erected against the buildings. It was on ten levels, a sealed shopping and business precinct which preserved something of the look of the old city and yet had a perfect climate—no noise, no fumes, no crime. But the rents were high, and although there were enclosed shopping malls in most cities, they were not good places for discount department stores. That was why Hooper had chosen to turn Allbright's into a mail-order business.

Fizzy had once said that someday domes like this on the Midtown Mall would cover the whole city.

Why discourage the boy by telling him that it would never happen? The cities would fail and die long before then. There were too many threats to their security. And look at these fools mimicking aliens—bare-assed, tattooed, wearing ragged ribbons, and some in bare feet. It was because of the protection they felt in the Greenhouse—its warmth, its security guards. But these people had no idea that some aliens were tough and intelligent and very fast; that they wore plain clothes, and had long hair, and dirty knuckles, and were simply out there, waiting. He had seen them! And seeing these parody aliens in their silly costumes made him remember clearly the aliens in O-Zone.

Or had he been wrong? But he had the cartridge of film to verify it all. It was the reason he was here. He did not want to release it until he was certain he could get it developed. Normally he would have sent it with a runner, and the runner would make his way around New York looking for a lab. But Hooper wanted to hang on to the film. And at last he was glad he had come in person on this menial errand. The dreariest jobs were the most revealing: he had forgotten how much he hated New York.

He had already been held up at two security checkpoints because of the film cartridge—its seal, its size, its metal strip.

"I'm sorry, sir, but we've never seen one of those before."

His Owner's ID made them polite, but still they ran the cartridge through a scanner.

Anything unusual worried the guards. Hooper loathed and pitied their stupidity—they were carrying out orders, they never used their own judgment or took anything for granted. They told him solemnly that they had to be thorough, but

Hooper saw them as only very slow, and he growled word-lessly at them in impatience and fury.

The irony was that there had been no security check on their arrival back in New York yesterday. Their rotors had been logged but not searched—they could have imported a blob of radioactive sludge, or a flask of poison dust, or a jar of contaminated water (people said O-Zone was full of such dangerous trash), and no one would have known. Fizzy had a maggot-heaving squirrel in a bag: its brain was bulging out of its skull, probably a mutant. Hooper thought: I could have sneaked in a whole live alien!

No one had seemed to care that they had come from O-Zone. It was off the map. No wonder O-Zone was full of aliens.

"I've read about film like that," the man at the lab told him, and Hooper was almost grateful to the man for treating him like a flunky runner. He hardly looked at Hooper, but he was fascinated by the film. "This is the first time I've seen it." Handing it back, he said, "Sorry. Can't help you."

"It's ordinary film," Hooper said. "What are you telling me?"

"The problem is getting it out of the cartridge. The case is designed to obliterate the film if it's not opened with the right key."

Hooper was examining the seamless case. "What's the point of—?"

"Security. So it won't fall into the wrong hands. You know that, fella."

"It's pictures of my kid's birthday party."

The man pinched the cartridge while it lay in Hooper's hand, and he said in a husky threatening way, "That's no birthday party. Stop wasting my time."

Hooper tried at another lab. Two men puzzled over it, and then one of them said, "I wouldn't want to be responsible for fouling this up."

He kept walking in the Greenhouse. He saw another naked woman. This one wore a mask, and attached somehow to the right place was a rubber penis, which swung as she walked. He saw some naked teenage girls painted with mock tattoos and wearing helmets and face masks. And he saw a naked man wearing what looked like a hangman's hood, leather, with a pointed beak and eye slits—a mask probably. And other people dressed expensively as aliens: men as

Trolls, women as Skells. It disgusted Hooper. These people may never have seen an alien in the flesh, and so their mimicry seemed strangely naive and alarming.

The trees planted here in the Greenhouse were taller and greener and far healthier than many he had seen in O-Zone. But there was also something barren and antiseptic about them. They were like overgrown houseplants, with clean leaves, the trunks wrapped in tape, and the limbs neatly pruned. Beneath them were long troughs of flowers, and low fountains; and some streets had been banked into swales, with grass and ferns. It was like a bottle garden or a vast terrarium—greenery under glass—tidy and clean and beautifully lit.

But that orderly place had the effect of making the rest of New York look especially dirty and dangerous, for as soon as Hooper left the Greenhouse—another security check, another argument—he smelled the sour air and was deafened by low-flying one-seaters moving recklessly between the buildings. Cruising above were some booming police gunships. Many people wore mouth-masks and some wore full masks with earphones and receivers: he watched them gabbling as they walked along.

Still looking for someone to deal with the cartridge of film, Hooper headed for a photographic lab where in the past he had sent his own confidential film and tapes for copying. He had never gone to the place in person—had always sent a runner—and it was not until he set off that he realized that the lab was deep down on the west side. He had not expected any problem with the cartridge, so he had not taken his car. Now it was becoming a full day's work on the ground, but it was an instructive day, and moving through the security checks, he was like a man in disguise. There was a humiliation in that scrutiny, but he felt a thrill, too, at the thought that he could be mistaken for an illegal or someone packing a weapon.

But at a hastily set-up checkpoint in the West Thirties his patience failed him. It was perhaps the arbitrariness of it, the temporary-looking barrier and booth, that made him feel victimized. He was subjected to a thorough body search and made to wait.

"I'm just looking for clearance," the young guard said, seeing that Hooper was exasperated.

Was anything happening on the screen? Hooper's number had been keyed in. The guard was blinking at it.

"Won't be a minute."

"I'm going," Hooper said, and started forward in a brawling gesture. He knew he would not be able to open the door, but he wanted to make a scene. He needed to be angry.

"My boss won't like this."

"Don't you know who I am?" Hooper shouted. "I *am* your boss! I pay your salary. I'm an Owner, I'm a taxpayer. You work for me! Now get out of the way and let me through!"

"We're not Federal, sir. We're private."

The city was full of private armies of security guards!

"This street's private, sir. This checkpoint's going to be permanent." Before Hooper could react, the guard said, "You're clear."

And they were all robots!

Hooper did not feel sorry for himself, and he knew better than to waste his sympathy on New Yorkers; but this rare experience of walking left him wondering how these millions of people endured this policing day after day. For Hooper it seemed a milder form of the crime it claimed to have eliminated.

Upstairs, in the lab, the technician said, "I couldn't touch this. It's probably classified. Anyway, the case is sealed—I can't get into those."

"What's so special about these cartridges?"

"They're safe. They're used for highly sensitive visual data." The technician was turning the small thing in his fingers. "Whose is it?"

The question inspired Hooper. He said, "It belongs to my boss."

"He sent you here?"

Hooper nodded. "His name's Allbright."

"It would be," the technician said, and smiled as he weighed the cartridge in his hand.

"You know him?"

"No," the man said, and his beaming expression was the pressure of his memory building behind his face. "But I've seen some stuff he's sent here for copying. They were choice items. Very special, very wild."

The man did not seem to notice that Hooper had fallen silent and had recovered his cartridge.

"I used to do some of the copying. I'd say, 'Now I've seen

everything.' But I was wrong, because a week or two later he'd send us something else—something fantastic!"

Hooper had put the cartridge into his pocket. He said, "I don't think Mr. Allbright would like it if he knew you were saying irresponsible things about his private tapes."

The man was unmoved. He had become possessed by the memory of what he had seen, and that remembrance was so powerful it overwhelmed the present. All he saw in Hooper was a mildly complaining runner with an impenetrable film cartridge.

Hooper was indignant, but the man was still smiling.

"I wish I could help you," he said, "because I'd love to see what's on that film."

Hooper left feeling that he had only one choice left. Of course the weapon had been special, and it was understandable that the cartridge was sealed. This film was the only record, for whatever the weapon destroyed was gone forever. What was it that Willis had said? *Regulation Godseye*. Murdick was a trooper!

Light was safety and darkness danger even here, and especially at night. But New York was famous for its skylights, the long high cones of sharply bent-back light that were particularly dazzling at the margins of the island—at the bridges and wharves and designated entry points. Tonight, diffused and smoky from the cloud cover, five cones shone down on Murdick's garrison in the peripheral district of Midwest.

The garrison was called Wedgemere and comprised four tall towers nicknamed the Bolts. That name had stuck. They were threaded throughout half their height, like bolt shafts, and their tops seemed modeled on the heads of machine bolts, six-sided and thick, for rotors.

"The Murdicks are on thirty-seven North Tower," the guard said. "They're expecting you."

"Don't tell me things I know," Hooper said. "Just open the door."

"I'm getting a shadow." The guard looked up from his screen. Hooper saw the man's blank face as insolent. "We'll have to run it through the scanner."

It could only have been the cartridge. "It's film," Hooper said, and he resented having to reply to the guard. "It's harmless."

"Everything goes through the scanner, sir."

"That sounds like an order. I don't take orders—I give them. So get out of my way, soldier."

As he spoke, the main door opened, but it was not to let Hooper through. It was Holly Murdick, leaving the building. She said, "Willis is waiting for you."

"This robot won't let me through! He wants to look through my pockets."

"Open that door," Holly said, "or else this is your last day on the job."

The guard's face remained impassive—nothing in the mouth, nothing in the eyes; and his body hardly moved as he flashed the door open.

Hooper said, "This is a sealed city. We've got skylights. We've got aerial patrols, gunships, and barriers. I've been going through security checks all day! It's all obstructions! And what is it with these security guards? Why do we let them run our lives?"

"Willis always says, 'Don't blame the guards—blame the aliens for making the guards necessary.'"

Now that the door was open, Hooper deliberately delayed entering. Who exactly was in charge here?

"I'm an Owner," he said. He turned to the guard. "And you're not."

"Relax," Holly said, and took Hooper's arm. Leading him to the door, she spoke to him gently, as if trying to calm him; but when Hooper realized that this was probably her purpose, he became only more agitated. "I'm real sorry you didn't come to see me," she was saying. "'Different people mean different sex.' I liked that a lot."

How annoying it was to be quoted: it was such a tiny mirror. Hooper stared into Holly's little witchy face, and then mentally he tipped her onto her back. But it didn't work, he wasn't interested, she looked too eager. That eagerness meant she wanted everything, and that he did not matter much to her indiscriminate lust.

He said, "I've got a little problem."

"Sometimes people with problems are the most fun," Holly said. "Hey, I know all about your moviemaking!"

Her saying this so lightly, in an excusing tone, made him feel worse than if she had screeched at him for being perverted. She was treating him as blamelessly crazy.

"Too bad I've got a date," she said hurriedly, seeing the anger she had provoked—Hooper's eyes blazed at her. And calling back at him, "I'm seeing Moura. Wasn't that a great time? I got a good feeling in O-Zone. I'm meeting Moura to prolong it a little."

But upstairs her husband seemed to take a different view. "I didn't think I'd be seeing you for another year," he said, and stared at Hooper. "I mean, we saw so much of each other in O-Zone."

Hooper said, "And yet, I had a feeling I was seeing everyone for the first time."

At this, Murdick winced, wrinkling his face as if he had heard a loud noise. He looked away from Hooper, pretending that he had just seen something out of the window. It was seven o'clock, a winter evening, but nearly daylight. The skylights dazzled—the river was on fire with them, and speckled with the insect shadows of rotors landing on barges and the patrolling gunships lumbering back and forth. No stars over the city—only the smoky glaze of skylights deflected through cloud.

"Especially you," Hooper said.

Murdick was trying to hide his face by looking away. But Hooper could see his reflection in the window: wounded eyes, hurt and trembling lips. Hooper was fascinated by the skinny face, the bareness of it, and Murdick's little head and fragile-looking ears. The man was so ugly without his mask!

"Holly's out," Murdick said. It was a meaningless remark: he was changing the subject. He kept talking.

O-Zone, he said, had made her feel claustrophobic: now she had the nutty idea of roaming New York. There had been more restrictions in O-Zone, and they had stayed indoors most of the time! But Holly was restless, he said helplessly, like a man running out of euphemisms. He swung around and faced Hooper in a pleading way, as if imploring him to understand.

Hooper said, "I was a little worried about you in O-Zone."

Murdick pushed his face back against the window and leaned and looked across at some low-flying gunships.

"It all seems so strange," Murdick said. Was he speaking about those gunships rocking in the long columns of light? "Seeing those abandoned condos. The mutation—that squirrel. The creepy noises. The darkness. The poison dust. All the rules and regulations—rules can scare the hell out of me, and the simplest ones are sometimes the worst. 'Wear protective clothing at all times' did it for me."

He moved his lips, showing his teeth—the shape of a smile, but only the shape: it was the memory of fear.

"Those savages, that mission, that so-called shoot," he said. "O-Zone was a kind of nightmare."

He tucked his hands into his metal belt and flapped his elbows in a time-killing way. His fear was fading but his voice was still hesitant.

"Who knows what really happened?" he said.

Hooper smiled at him in a wild disbelieving way, his big eyebrows rising, and with frost in his voice he said, "I know."

"All the confusion," Murdick said. He didn't want to hear Hooper. "It's better forgotten."

Hooper said, "I'll never forget."

Murdick went perfectly still—so still he seemed to twist time around—and after what seemed to Hooper twenty minutes or more, the little man said, "What are you saying to people?"

"I don't have to say anything. I've got a videotape. I can just put my feet up and watch it—or show it, as the case may be." He waited until Murdick's eyes were on his, then added, "It all depends on you."

Murdick made a tentative sound, saying *maybe* by using the air in his nose. He then said, "I'm glad you came. I only discovered after we got back that you took the cartridge out of that weapon."

Murdick was facing him, but Hooper had not blinked.

"I want to buy it from you, Hoop."

He said "buy" with emphasis. He was worried, he wanted it; this was like ransom.

"Do I look like I need money?"

But Murdick was still talking. "I didn't behave very well out there. I'm not used to that—being alone, facing aliens on the ground. I was unarmed. I've never been so scared. That's why I ran."

"You thought they were going to eat you."

Murdick began protesting in an excited stutter. "They do eat people, some of them. Not for nourishment, but as a ritual. It's a proven fact. We have full documentation. Teeth-marks. Bite patterns. Denture templates. We matched aliens' teeth to victims' wounds. We've done autopsies—stomach contents." Then he faltered, working his mouth. He said greedily, "I've got to have that cartridge."

"How do you know I haven't developed it?"

Murdick's smile was genuine and relaxed. He trusted the strength of technology—it was another trait he shared with Fizzy. But human weakness worried him. He was uneasy with Hooper, but certain about the film.

"Impossible," he said.

"Still, I've got it," Hooper said. "You want it because you're afraid Godseye will find out that you ran."

Hooper said it in order to hear Murdick's insincere denial—a *No* like a groan. Murdick's face bore the faintness of the real smile that was fading into worry once again.

"They'd string you up, I guess."

Hooper went on mocking him about Godseye. Each time Hooper spoke, Murdick clenched and unclenched his jaw, grinding his teeth as he listened. It gave his face a peculiar look of concentration, as though he was unable to swallow a stubborn mouthful. The biting made his eye twitch.

He said, when Hooper finished, "They'd understand. They're much more compassionate than you think."

"Oh, sure. I've heard some of these death squads are greatly misunderstood."

Murdick screwed his lips together and said, "Don't use that expression."

"What did you tell them about O-Zone?"

"Not much," he said. But he was using his teeth again, and his biting gave him away.

"That means you told them something."

"I didn't tell them our route, or any landmarks. I deleted the flight plan. They wanted to access it, too—they wanted to know. I didn't mention the mutant, the condos, or anything."

"You blabbed about the aliens."

Murdick started to deny it, and then he said abjectly, "I told them there were only two of them."

"Did you say who burned them?"

Murdick became watchful. He said nothing. He was biting again.

Hooper said, "I see."

"I want the cartridge," Murdick said.

"Armed men never say 'please.'"

"I need it," Murdick said, and the "please" was a whimper in those words.

Hooper said, "You don't need it. All you need is for me to keep it quiet. You need to trust me with it."

Murdick's face was small, but he was thin and had two

distinct sides to his flat head. He turned his skinny face on Hooper and said, "Can I trust you?"

"Sure," Hooper said—so promptly that Murdick smiled unexpectedly again. "And just to prove you trust me, I want you to take me to one of your meetings."

"We don't have meetings," Murdick said, staring hard. He was almost certain that Hooper was trying to slip something past him. Wasn't there a loose connection in what Hooper had just said?

Hooper had taken the cartridge from his pocket.

"It's coded," Murdick said. "It's regulation."

"You'll have to explain that to a simple mail-order man."

"It's secure. Chemical code." He was biting between each thought. "It has an obliterating mechanism. Can't be developed commercially. Used in intelligence work. Can't be copied either."

Hooper was smiling at Murdick in a lazy challenging way.

"It's no use to you now," Murdick said. "And we're the only people who can develop it."

"We'll see about that," Hooper said. "I just want you to know that I have it."

Murdick began to protest, making fishmouths.

"Let's not threaten each other," Hooper said. "We faced danger together. I saved your life. That should make us friends." And he smiled as he pocketed the cartridge. "I want to see this movie, Willis!"

Murdick said, "You swear you won't say anything about that mess?"

"I'll go you one better," Hooper said. He was cheerful. Perhaps it didn't matter what was on the film, as long as he kept it in his possession. "I'll go to one of those Godseye meetings and tell them what a hero you were. That it was your idea. That you planned it all. That you burned them."

Murdick said, "I would have, too." He was nibbling with anger. "You want me to develop the film for you?"

"Not yet," Hooper said. "Let me stick up for you first. Godseye will be proud of you."

"We don't have meetings," Murdick said. He was biting again. "We have hunts."

8

For Moura, the aftermath had all been secrets and sudden silences. She had stood aside at the Firehills tower in Ω-Zone when Murdick's Welly had returned and buzzed straight down, spinning grit and green leaves at the watchers. She had seen Murdick stagger out, still bowlegged from the flight, and he leaned into his faceplate and crowed, "We burned them all down!"

She had watched Hardy stride forward and say rather stiffly and formally to Hooper, "I'm not going to ask you how it happened, so don't tell me."

"You don't want to know?" Hooper seemed relieved.

Hardy was still standing to attention in front of his brother, a little ceremony to make him remember. "It could be terrible for you if I knew."

Afterward Moura said, "What the hell was that all about?"

Hardy said, "Nothing."

But she knew—she only wanted Hardy to deny it so that they would both remember the moment.

She said, "'Nothing' always means 'something.'"

Hardy shrugged, refusing her the courtesy of an explanation, and as always keeping his work secret and separate. Yet she wanted him to realize that she was no ignorant bystander and that she knew that something serious had happened on the shoot; that she knew that it was more convenient for everyone if it remained a secret.

He could be a cold and humorless man, but she admired his fairness. He would not have lied, even about his brother. He would have filed a report, and Hooper might have faced an investigation. They would have wired him and plugged him in to see whether he lit up. His money would not have been much help to him.

And he probably would have lit up, hot with guilt, she guessed. It was undoubtedly serious, because Fizzy's behavior was more unusual than ever. What had the boy swallowed to make him so strange? He had said nothing on the return to Coldharbor—he who had done nothing but talk and criticize all the way to O-Zone! And Hardy, normally very silent, became talkative, as if to avoid thinking about what terrible things had happened on the mission that Hooper, Murdick, and Fizzy had mounted. How could three such thorough misfits have failed to bungle badly?

She saw each one of them as disturbed and divided. So they might have taken a risk. But disturbed people were also accident-prone. So something unexpected had probably happened, which "burned them all down" only hinted at. She was surprised and relieved—everyone was—that they had returned safely.

But would she now have to live with Fizzy's silences as she had once lived with his know-it-all nagging? She tried to talk to him, merely to hear his voice and perhaps detect in it whether he was angry or upset. He looked shocked, he was a bit pale, his eyes drifted in and out of focus. But he was thoughtful: she could almost hear the buzz and whir of his mind, the odd flutter of his calculations.

His silence made her talkative. She remarked to Hardy on the clear sky here and the cap of haze that lay over the cities outside O-Zone; the squarish, furred prints of houses and blocks, the miles of creeping green, the pleasure of having spent New Year's in that place. The secrets, too, were an oblique pleasure—another surprise, for she had so many secrets. How could the wife of such an unresponsive man not have secrets?

During the flight back, Moura glanced at the specimen Fizzy was bringing back—the monstrous misshapen squirrel. How had it got that way? Was it plutonium, as everyone had said—and if so, had they been in any danger?

"It's a low-level mutagen," Fisher said in a dull voice.

"Want to talk about it?"

"I can't talk to you," he said. "You don't have enough math."

Wasn't there something simpler to discuss—something she

knew about? What about food, music, the latest movies, radio programs, money, the rest of the world, or next year's presidential election? What about his acne? Pimples had broken through on his nose and his cheeks. He usually ate badly—he sat at Pap during long study sessions, eating junk, Guppy-Cola, and jelly sandwiches.

"Your acne's improving," she said, being tactful.

"Antibiotics," he said, and yawned at her. "I'm doing two capsules a day."

Back in Coldharbor he kept to his room, muttering to his machines and yawning without covering his mouth: she watched him on the monitor.

The day after, he appeared at his door.

"Just tested the squirrel," he said. He was afraid; he needed to talk to someone; but he was so bad at the simplest things. "I did a brain scan and an autopsy. It's not a mutant."

"That's good news," Moura said.

"No, it's not," he said. "Because it was dead before it hit the beam."

He was talking in his growly uncertain voice.

"Someone threw it," he said, and put on his helmet and clicked his mask into place, and slipped on his gloves. He was dressed as he had been in O-Zone—the same boots, the same armored-fiber suit, the same radio helmet. He was prepared for a zone of deep contagion: it was a high-risk outfit.

He said no more about the specimen. Instead, he did an extraordinary thing. He went out alone. He gave no explanation; he simply left the unit, dressed as if for a danger zone: clump, clump, clump.

The phone was ringing—not Fizzy; it was Holly Murdick's face on the screen. It was an eager face: she photographed well, because she was so used to mirrors.

"Can I come up?"

Then Moura was glad that Fizzy was gone, because Holly had things on her mind.

Holly said she was desperately bored, and she laughed in a convincingly desperate way as she said so, sounding reckless, as if she was ready to try anything. She was a pretty woman in her mid-thirties, and as obsessive about style in a garish way as Willis was about the latest equipment. They were both faddists—he was gadget-conscious, she was mirror-mad. Moura saw something childish in this, something touching and monotonous at the same time. Holly's face and hair were striped, she wore trucker's boots and carried a Skell bag; her short skirt was slashed into a fringe of ribbons, and underneath she wore skintight trousers. Moura was glad that Holly was not wearing one of her embarrassing aprons—the apron and nothing else that showed her big pale bottom and her knuckly spine and made her seem so silly and defiant.

Today Holly was intense, trying a little too hard—her trying showed.

"I haven't been able to pull myself together since I came back"—she was still talking about being bored. "Willis just mopes." She paused and looked sharply into Moura's eyes and said, "You're so lucky to have a child."

"Fizzy's not a child anymore."

"You know what I mean."

"And he's been moping too."

"Their big so-called mission. 'Let's go on a shoot!' Willis is so secretive." She seemed to be poking fun at him because he could not possibly have anything to withhold—he was too dull to have any secrets. She found Moura's eyes again and said, "I never knew how to go about it—having a child. I mean, doing it right, having one worth raising."

Moura could see that it was not necessary to reply to this. Holly had just begun to unburden herself. But Moura dreaded such conversations and she felt sure that Holly was leading up to something painful—probably going to divulge an awkward secret. Maybe she had tried to buy a child on one of her trips—so many people did, and the kids turned out so badly sometimes: feebleminded, diseased, crazy, the wrong color, with faked IDs and misleading medical histories. Years later the awful truth came out; and then they were taken away to be injected and burned.

"So many theories, so many methods," Holly was saying. "Every year it seemed there was something new—implanting, freezing, womb-leasing. I couldn't decide."

"Or just buying one in some other country," Moura said, to test Holly's reaction.

"Willis would never have stood for that. He hates people who buy kids."

Seeing that Holly had become reflective, Moura softened toward her and said, "Having children is pretty straightforward nowadays. The labs start a dozen for you and then implant the best one."

"Wasn't it straightforward when you had Fizzy?"

There was a sudden blankness, a whitening in Holly's face, between the stripes of makeup. The expectancy in her demeanor put Moura on guard.

"You didn't try anything fancy," Holly said. "Or did you?"

She knew something. She was not very intelligent, but that made her all the more tenacious. She was asking all the right questions, because she knew all the answers. Moura smiled to mask her look of caution.

"There were a lot of methods," Moura said. "All those theories —" She stopped abruptly and said no more.

"I'm sure you made the right decision." Holly was still watchful beneath the mask of her makeup.

Moura said, "Do you really want to have a child?"

Holly looked eager. She had not heard that question, only her own provocative remark. She said, "Fizzy wasn't frozen, was he?"

Moura shook her head: No. Why didn't Holly take the hint that she didn't want to discuss this?

"I hope you don't mind my asking about this. It's just that you're so sensible and practical—and everyone else goes chasing after the fads."

"I chased after the fads," Moura said.

Holly's mouth was open, but there was the suggestion of a smile in the way it gaped. This was what she wanted to hear.

"I think it was a mistake," Moura said. "Hardy wanted the best. He's so scientific—so careful. He insisted I have a matched donor."

"It must have been a great match. There's a striking resemblance between Fizzy and Hardy."

"I'm afraid I don't see it anymore," Moura said.

"So you went to a clinic."

"I didn't mention a clinic."

"Sorry," Holly said. "You mentioned a donor. I just assumed."

And then Moura knew there had been whispering. Holly had got the information from Rinka about Fizzy—the pedigree, the donor, the clinic. Moura had told Rinka, and she had not sworn her to secrecy. Most of Moura's friends knew that Fizzy was a clinic child, but until O-Zone no one had known the method. It was that trip that had made Moura remember—Fizzy's face, his nagging, the masks. And the excitement; her nervousness. O-Zone had seemed an innocent wilderness, and their isolation at Firehills had given her a glimpse of the past and made her truthful.

She said very precisely, "What is it you want to know?"

"I was just curious, just wondering—"

"It was a contact clinic," Moura said.

Hearing that, Holly relaxed. Moura could hear the breath. It was not modern to be shocked, but Moura saw an old-fashioned thrill register in Holly's shoulders, a little shiver of pleasure, as if something small and lively were moving within her.

"They probably don't even call them contact clinics these days."

Holly said, "They do, they do! But—"

Her excitement, and the wish to conceal it, distracted her. She was so full of questions she had trouble phrasing them. The most banal were obviously the easiest.

"Weren't you frightened?"

"I wanted to be frightened. That made it more human."

"Yes," Holly said—but it was hardly a word; it was a little gasp of pleasure.

Moura understood now, and she was glad that Holly did not want to talk about having a baby, even gladder that she did not want to talk about Fizzy. She wanted information, that was all. Discussing the contact clinic was simple: it involved only Moura herself. Hardy had been very scientific, so Moura had been the opposite—taking the risk of a donor, of twenty-four sessions, and at each session prolonged contact.

"It seems such a long time ago."

"Only—what?—Fizzy's fifteen, isn't he?"

"It was over a year before it took. That's almost seventeen years ago. I forget how many sessions. Two years' worth, I guess."

How thrilled Holly would be if she told her how she had counted the eighteen sessions, and knew exactly when and for how long. But it was impossible to be truthful about that without being truthful about the other thing—how she had been devastated when they had come to an end.

"Two years," Holly was saying, and now she did not bother to conceal her excitement. "You must have actually gotten to know the guy—the donor."

"He was wearing a mask."

"Oh, God, really, a mask? What kind—was it scary?"

"It had a sort of beak. It looked like an owl or an eagle,

one of those blunt hooked beaks. A bird of prey, I remember thinking. But he was probably a Harvard student."

"He was young?" Holly asked. "How could you tell?"

"Masks make you look at other parts of the body," Moura said. "Everyone's feet are different and easy to remember. Their knees, their hands, their knuckles. And everyone's got a different odor, even someone who's very clean. These donors were scrubbed and sanitized, but still I knew. He was young. He had light bones. He was tall. He—"

"He must have known you, too!"

"I never thought about that."

It was her second lie—and she was angry. She had vowed not to lie, because she had always been misled by her own lies and had trouble with the truth afterward. Anyway, she hated liars—their stupidity—they were usually half-convinced by their lies. Yes, of course she had thought about the man recognizing her! She reminded herself of this forcefully now. Seeing Fizzy, she had seen the donor. Had that donor ever thought of her again?

"Did he say anything to you?"

You love it. You—

"No," Moura said, and she knew she was safe with this lie. There was no danger of her ever forgetting or distorting the words the young man had whispered. But she could see that Holly wanted to know everything and, in her frustration, did not know what to ask next.

Moura said, "I had very definite ideas about it. I thought: If Hardy's going to be so scientific, then I should be as unscientific as possible. I wanted to take risks. But I didn't really think they would be serious risks, because I had it all worked out in my mind—what it would be like, what my reactions would be. I had it all under control."

Holly was nodding, her face lit with approval and admiration. You knew what you wanted, she was thinking, and you went out and got it.

"The thing is," Moura said—and paused to make sure that Holly was listening—"I was totally wrong. It wasn't anything like that, and my reactions were strange. I was shocked—I lost all control."

Yet Holly was still smiling.

She said, "I like that even better, honey."

"It was frightening," Moura said. "You don't think I'm serious. You're still smiling."

"Because I like it frightening."

"Risks change you. You take them and you're different afterward," Moura said.

"Yeah," Holly said, and darkened slightly in her seriousness, "but you weren't hurt."

"Not hurt, but changed," Moura said. "The physical part was actually rather tender and innocent at first, but . . . I'm not going to tell you any more. I just think it might have been a mistake."

"To have contact with a donor?"

"To have a child," Moura said.

"Why did you bother!"

If it had been a question, it would have been the hardest question of all, and Moura's answer would have incriminated her. In the end the child had been a necessity, for it was all that remained, the only thing she could hold on to. And that was why Fizzy's heartless brilliance was so discouraging. But thankfully, Holly wasn't asking a question.

"I don't care about children, really," Holly said.

Already her self-deceiving and meddling friend had forgotten her earlier lie: *You're so lucky to have a child.*

Moura saw in Holly's face a wild willingness. She looked very happy and very hungry, as if she were about to laugh out loud. She had carefully put on these savage clothes, and at last her savagery suited them.

Moura said primly, "I thought you were asking about Fizzy."

Holly brought her knees together and pinched her face and said, "Don't tell me *he* goes to clinics!"

She really had forgotten her pretext for bringing up the subject of the contact clinic! She had no memory. Such people were often liars. But it was their salvation: they would never be seriously hurt by their actions.

Holly said, "Let's get up a party and go."

"I'm sure they've changed," Moura said. "No one goes to contact clinics for implants or fertilization anymore. They've got a bad reputation."

"They're still licensed. They're very strictly controlled. They're supposed to be clean."

Moura could not help smiling at Holly, who looked so eager and happy now, nervously smoothing her hair—so bright-eyed.

"You actually want to go to one."

"Yes." It was another half-formed word, another gasp of pleasure.

Moura said, "I wouldn't dream of going through that again."

"You don't have to do anything—just prop me up a little. It'll be fun, like the party in O-Zone. We'll get Rinka." She was chattering eagerly. "Do you think they still wear masks?"

Before Moura could answer, the door alarm sounded— Captain Jennix from Coldharbor Security, announcing Hooper Allbright. Moura was glad for an interruption to deflect all this talk of clinics. Hooper was just the person to change any subject.

And yet this evening he seemed unusually reserved, almost suspicious. The women were at once too quiet and too interested in his arrival. He detected something conspiratorial in their politeness. What had they been talking about?

He saw Holly as fickle and out of touch, but he liked Moura, and he always thought it a deficiency in himself, not her, that she was the sort of woman he would never be able to make happy. His studious and rather chilly brother had not succeeded with her, he knew, but they were still together. Happy marriages were inexplicable to him, and probably meaningless anyway; but long marriages were another matter—they had a mystery ingredient, something subtler than love, like sympathy or patience or even comedy. However, it was not comedy in Hardy and Moura's case, and he knew they regarded his humor as aggressive and his instincts as impulsive and unpredictable. This knowledge made him self-conscious and more impulsive, and because he hated being watched, made him wilder, too.

He smiled at the women, not knowing what to say. He had become weakened by the apparent futility of his other purpose—the cartridge of film that no one but Godseye could crack open.

Holly said, "It's all right, Moura. Hooper's here to see me. He's been following me around all day."

"Where's Fizzy?" Hooper said suddenly. "I couldn't get him on the radio."

"Hooper's pretending he doesn't see me. Men always do that," Holly said. "He's just waiting for me to make the first move. Woof-woof. Like I'm some animal."

Hooper turned to her and said, "I don't mind your saying

that, because you're not really talking to me. You don't know me. So what you say doesn't matter."

He felt that she usually seemed to be talking to herself, and something in him was always on the point of signaling to her: *Yoo-hoo! I'm over here!*

"You girls look as if you're planning something," he said. It was a kind of nervous smugness with an air of concealment: their exaggerated interest in him was an awkward lack of interest.

"I'd love to hear your plans," Holly said.

"Fizzy's out," Moura said. "Sit down, Hoop. Talk to us."

"I can't sit down. I've been trying all day to get one chore done."

Holly said, "Don't you wish you were back in O-Zone, where there are no chores to do? Just the wilderness and abandoned buildings. Those towers looked so exposed—so naked—with no one in them, and there's something sexual in all that solitude. I mean, being alone in a place like that gives me ideas! I thought: One other person and this would be perfect!"

Hooper objected to the woman saying this, because the sentiments were his but her way of putting them sounded crude and stupid. There were better ways of expressing the simple wish that had woken in him in O-Zone.

"That's very silly," he said, angry that she was making him deny it.

Then he sat down. They had noticed that he was irritable, and so they were trying to please him by being playful and giving him information.

Moura said, "We were all wearing masks in O-Zone. We come back to New York and suddenly everyone is wearing masks."

"It's like we started a fashion," Holly said. "I like that. I love masks. You can get away with anything in a mask."

This made Hooper even more uncomfortable. He had detected something sexual rising in the room. He saw it was Holly, a sort of glow on her: she seemed to shimmer from where she lay on the sofa, propped on one elbow, with her hand cupping her striped face.

She was saying: Look at me.

Hooper was not attracted to women who bore the marks of other men on them. Holly was like that, like those women whose manhandled bodies had slight discolorations, bruises like thumbprints, little reddened patches of pressure. Old lovers and brutes and strangers, and most husbands—they all left their damage on them. The most desirable women looked to him as though they had never been touched—not virginal or innocent, just unscathed and solitary.

Moura and Holly he saw as bright New Yorkers. They had all the money and all the savvy and they had always lived among powerful men. Holly was reckless, and Moura practically unknowable, which puzzled him, because she was almost his own age, and very attractive—those long legs, that smooth serious face—yet there was no evidence that she had ever been manhandled.

He said, "Someday New York could look like O-Zone. It wouldn't take much nuclear trash to take the stuffings out of this city."

"I can't imagine New York without people—like O-Zone."

Hooper almost replied, *Don't be silly!,* but he remembered how they had sworn to the others that O-Zone was empty, that all the aliens had been burned. It was probably full of aliens!

Holly said, "Don't be depressed. This is a great place."

The glow was on her, and there was something else in her expression that seemed brainless and sexy—perhaps the way she worked her mouth and kept it open.

"It could happen. New York could turn into a city-stain," Hooper said. "It might be a good thing. The trouble is that it wouldn't end up as pretty as O-Zone."

"You've been saying that a lot lately," Holly said. "Catastrophes," she said. "Burnouts." She spoke each word with a dreamy smile. "The future."

"Sometimes I think your wishing for a sorry future is your way of taking revenge," Moura said. "It's a kind of threat, because you've had a bad day. But really it's just cursing."

Where am I? Hooper thought, and surfaced again from another conversation. There were so many playing in his head.

He said, "What do you mean Fizzy's out? He never goes out!"

9

NORMALLY, FISHER WOULD HAVE HAD A LONG STUDY SESsion at the mainframe in his room today. He had never gone to school; he had always had high-level classification—Remote Student, Type A, the category that had given him the nickname "wonder boy." He was not alone in the category, but the mention of anyone else made him overprecise and competitive. He had all the strengths of his classification, and the weaknesses, too—hypertension, impatience, humorlessness. He disliked human company. His pleasures were the symmetry of math and the solitude of his room, and a session like today's, where he was rapping back to a study team and propounding his own new description of particle behavior, Fisher's Theory of Subsequence. He went through his proofs and thought: You porkers.

But he canceled the session, and after that muttering to Moura, he headed over to Hooper's unit, which was in an adjoining tower in Coldharbor. He needed to see his uncle. Much more than verification, he wanted reassurance. He could not be calm about the squirrel autopsy—it had not been a mutant, it had not been contaminated, it had not even been alive! But who had thrown it? It shocked him to think that aliens had crept so close to Firehills. And he had been shocked by the mission—the rapidity of the deaths—the burning of those two trotting men in O-Zone. He had thought that the difference between particle theory and particle practice was a pool of blood. But there had been nothing left of those men. He was a supremely confident boy, and had a flexible if narrow imagination, but he was shaken when challenged with the idea of nothing.

He mindlessly, uselessly signaled Hooper with his phones, and when there was no reply from Hooper's unit, he set off to look for his uncle outside Coldharbor. He had never been alone in the city—there was always Moura, or Hardy, or a driver, or a pilot. He was walking, and he knew there was something momentous in this move, as there had been in their trip to O-Zone, and the mission. He had never thought of himself as living in New York. He was a resident of Coldharbor. So this was no stroll—this was like flinging himself off the roof.

He had no real hope of finding his uncle in this huge city, and what good was his tracer signal among all the radio waves here? Hooper might be anywhere! But Fisher knew that he was only half-looking. The important thing was that he was outside, skimming—he had liberated himself. It was the effect of O-Zone. He felt braver now. He had seen aliens face to face—and not simple trampy Skells, grubbing in garbage cans, but wild people, net-men, living like settled beasts in a prohibited area.

And the extraordinary revelation was that he had seen that these aliens were not very strange at all. He despised himself for the intrusive superstitions that had made him imagine them as snarling doglike creatures with broken fingernails and dirty feet. The truth was so different from this irrational goblin species. They were clean and fast, they had beards and bright teeth, they seemed self-sufficient. He was overwhelmed by the obvious: they were not beasts. He was surprised and ashamed to discover what logic had told him all along, that they were fully human. They were not like him, but they were very similar to everyone else he knew.

All his terror had come later, on the trip home, when he was safe. Then he went rigid, considering how he might have died. The memory of Murdick had made it worse, because he easily imagined himself being just as defenseless and clumsy, with a pinched wire or a blocked air supply, shuffling in front of the aliens in mute terror, maybe gabbling and pleading just before he was netted and his head twisted off or his bones broken. The forest aliens killed their victims by hand, to save bullets—that was what everyone said about forest aliens. Two of them had been killed—"beasts," he would have called them, yet no one could have looked more human than they had at the moment of impact, when the particle hit, just before they were turned into smoke.

But Fisher had survived. He had steered them out of that place. After that, what terrors could this walled-in city hold for him?

He walked from Coldharbor to the Midtown Mall, but did not enter. He told himself that he was looking for Hooper. He still felt safe, in his mask and headphones, his suit, his big boots. He paused at Madison, somewhere in the East Forties, and clicked his mask out of position and switched off his headset. He was holding his breath, but not voluntarily: there was a catch in his throat, he could not speak or cry out, he was being slowly throttled by a paralyzing yawn. All contact was broken; he felt very weak.

A tear gathered at the corner of one eye, then spilled and ran quickly to the tip of his nose. Air hummed in his head, and his breath and strength returned. He became buoyant— first his face and head, and finally his whole body. He was momentarily weightless—outside, still alive!

The city stank, it screeched, its rough stone was cold. He noticed, as Hooper had, the large numbers of policemen and guards, city cops, private security men, and even some gray-suited Federals. Above him were cruising gunships that did nothing but buck and slide low in the sky. It was a towering city of soldiers and policemen.

He heard the donkey-bray of an alarm and saw nearby lights raking the street and mounted cameras swiveling. He was on the point of running away when he saw that no one near the alarm seemed to notice the pounding noise or the flashing light. Often in the past, when the sound of alarms carried to his tower room in Coldharbor, and he saw confusion on his external screen (he had no outside windows), he put on his headphones and turned up the volume—music or the voice of a teaching panel—merely to calm himself. As an indoor creature, he had always been made anxious by the racket of distant alarm bells or sirens. Now he was outside, up close, and he saw that it was nothing but noise—a false alarm.

"They're too sensitive," a watching man said. "They can be triggered by vibrations—by dust particles."

"That means they're not sensitive enough," Fisher said. "They're calibrated wrong."

He wanted to explain what he meant, when the man

frowned and said "Bullshit" and walked away. The abruptness of it scared him a little.

The other streets were full of people, and the air pulsated with the regular beat of rotor noise and rising choppers. Like Hooper, Fisher was reminded of the emptiness of O-Zone, the great spidery wilderness of hickories and oaks, the sinkholes and swellings of the plateau, and the distant glimpse of prairie. Empty buildings, standing like tombs, with the peculiar nakedness of abandonment. The whine of insects, and birds fluttering like blown paper. The reassurance of wilderness; and then the sudden violence of that shoot.

The O-Zone trip had given him a taste for flying, for navigation. He was restless here in New York, and he was proud of his boldness in wandering the streets. But the wandering also proved that there was nothing to be afraid of here. It seemed to him a somewhat ordinary city, and certainly on the ground it was a great deal less special than it looked from fifty floors up. New Yorkers talked about dangers, but where were these dangers?

"You'll have to pass through this checkpoint, sir."

Sir, because the guard could see from the expensive mask and headset that he might be wealthy. He had slipped his mask on again. The fumes and the noise in this part of New York—surely this was one of the dingier parts?—were too much for him. Another alarm had started, and just the sound of it had shaken him. It might not be dangerous, but it was bad-looking. You needed nerves, not brains, here. The tramping crowds and the traffic had driven him east, where he had hoped to get a look at a sealed bridge. He had not expected a checkpoint.

"Your ID, sir."

He handed over his plate and watched the guard push it tape-side-down into the machine. It was returned to him with a salute by the armed guard on the other side of the metal detector.

"What do I do now?"

"You may proceed, sir."

When had he ever been called sir? Afterward he relished the idea that he had been under suspicion. He might have been armed; he might have been illegal. He might have been dangerous!

Feeling powerful, he stared at his reflection in a store window. The mask and headset gave him an insectile head and beetle jaws, his pimples made his nose look lopsided, the corner of one ear was folded forward under an earpiece. He saw that he was skinny, and he suspected that one arm was slightly longer than the other. He was overdressed in his padded jacket and boots. He was wired. He peered into the reflection of his faceplate and thought: Goofball. He felt ridiculous, and so he squinted until he went out of focus and his image was bearable.

At times like this he remembered that he was fifteen years old. In his defense, he wanted to tell people that he had traveled to O-Zone. I've seen it, he wanted to say. I've seen aliens in the wild—we killed a couple of dangerous ones. I navigated a Welly and hid it in a sinkhole. I collected a specimen—not a mutant, but it was dead before it hit the beam!

Who was there to tell who would understand him?

He found a weapons dealer on East Thirty-fifth. It was six flights up in a rattly elevator, and then through a security check and a very thorough frisking by an armed woman guard smelling sweetly of flowers—a gimmick, Fisher thought, this pretty woman carrying out body searches on potential customers. From the side window he could see the East River—the drive, the wall, the cones of skylights.

Nothing was displayed on the counter except catalogs, which he pushed aside.

"I want to see a particle beam. It's got a camera with thermal imaging and a weapon built in that can work independently or in conjunction, reviewing data. There's probably a pure laser model."

The clerk was grinning, but it was not amusement—he was only resting his mouth as he listened to Fisher, who was still talking.

"It's got a heat-sensitive director for self-centering on the target—if it's a soft target. And if it's—"

"Weapons like that are regulated," the clerk said, interrupting him. "They're not for civilian use, anyway. They're Federal army, special forces."

"I know someone who's got a nice one," Fisher said in a needling way. He had gone into the store in order to tell the man this—to boast. "He's not army."

The clerk was a young mustached man with the slightly sulky mouth and skeptical eyes of a weapons dealer.

Fisher said, "Whatever they blast, they just atomize."

The man looked unconvinced, but Fisher did not mind. Boasting was his way of talking to himself.

"It's probably the best antipersonnel weapon you can get," Fisher said. "It's not perfect. I'd like to see it modified for high-density targets."

"Beat it, kid. I'm busy."

Fisher laughed at the man's ignorance. The laughter came honking out of his helmet, and he left saying, "You're a complete tool."

He spent the remainder of the day testing his nerve on the streets in Lower East, clumping in his boots and keeping his helmet on. He saw a large number of blacks—no masks, no suits, only bubble caps and hippy-dip jackets like jigs in stories. He could not understand why they were allowed to roam the city. Were they legal? He wondered why they weren't arrested, or stopped and searched. They were probably Pass Workers, he thought, over for the day to do things like shift trash and sweep.

Two came toward him, and Fisher began radioing the emergency number.

"Hey, Bubba!"

"Rocketman!"

They were staring at his helmet, his boots, his contagion suit, as he steered clear of them.

They were gone!

"This is Mobile Task Force. Please identify yourself—"

He tuned out, feeling brave, and yet still mystified by the blacks simply swaggering and shouting along the parkway. But he told himself that he would be able to identify them if he were called on later, summoned by security, and with that in mind he noted the time, fifteen-thirty-seven.

He did not eat lunch—no money; nor take a bus, nor a tram—no pass; nor enter any other buildings. He stayed on foot, keeping by the river, thrilled by his nearness to Brooklyn—right across the water—which had a reputation for danger and squalor. It was filled with illegals. He heard sirens and thunder flashes from that greasy shore and he knew they were not false alarms.

In the late afternoon, he was walking back to Coldharbor worrying about illegals they had started calling "worms," for their ability to burrow beneath the city, and he saw a chopper shining a strong light on the river just below the rail. A support boat also shone a light, and he could see from its markings that the boat was part of the task force nicknamed "Moat Patrol." He was encouraged by the large number of armed police, and crossed over to the rail to see a Skell being fished out of the river.

It did not matter that a chopper was hovering, and a support boat waiting, and four men of a foot patrol had their weapons leveled at the creature—Fisher was frightened. He was frightened by the appearance of the Skell and he was frightened by what the Skell represented, the millions more. Whether this one had fallen in accidentally or was trying to enter the city illegally, Fisher could not tell. But it was certainly an alien, and here at the edge of New York, the slangy name was apt. He had a lumpy face, and a miserable, wicked expression, and his skin was gray-blue, bristly and bloodless like a cut fish or a fragment of old plastic. He was shaking with cold, and his shoes had been removed to prevent his escape—his ugly feet were blue and white, and he had terrible toenails. He was whimpering to a policeman, trying to explain something.

The Skell was dripping on the cold stones of the terrace, bedraggled like a sea monster—Fisher had the impression of air escaping from the Skell's body. When the creature was strapped and restrained, Fisher went a bit closer. The policemen guarding him seemed to be joking among themselves. Another policeman, punching buttons on a handset, looked up as Fisher approached.

"Good going," Fisher said, feeling he should congratulate the patrol on a successful capture. "Was he carrying a weapon?"

"Just a lot of old rope."

But the policeman stared at Fisher as the blacks had done. What was so odd about being addressed by a Type A in a fiber suit and boots with the latest gear on his head? Fisher guessed that it was his bravery in being here at all, alone in New York—the cop probably guessed that he was only fifteen and was surprised by his courage.

Fisher's voice came quacking out of his mask: "He might have been making a net. Some illegals in outlying places use nets as weapons."

"Is that a fact?" the policeman said, and went on punching buttons in his hand receiver.

"Oh, sure," Fisher said, and then he glanced at the Skell

and became frightened again—it was the blue face, the filthy skin, the white feet, the wet shaggy clothes. He lost his voice in fear, and tried to talk it into existence. It came creaking and whistling. "I've seen some—as near as I am to you. I was on a search mission. It was supposed to be a shoot, just taking a sound-bite, but they ended up burning two of them. Now, those guys were carrying nets."

The policeman did not reply. He had looked up as Fisher was talking, and he seemed to be mumbling to himself: Search mission? Sound-bite? Burned two of them? Nets?

Fisher made a face, shifting his mask, and said, "The only thing is, they're the wrong kind of ropes. Density, see. Too stiff, too heavy."

But the policeman was still staring at Fisher's expensive mask and headphones.

"You sure you should be here, kid?"

"I thought I might be able to help. I've got some data—"

"Wait a minute," the policeman said, and adjusted his receiver. "I'm getting a sighting."

But still his fascinated gaze strayed back to Fisher.

"I've been in much worse places than this. I'm talking about contamination, I'm talking about city-stains—"

Squawk, quack: the policeman was staring at Fisher's faceplate. Contamination? City-stains?

"—You probably wouldn't even believe me," Fisher was saying.

That made the policeman smile. He said that having worked this particular stretch of the river wall for almost ten years, he would believe anything.

Fisher wanted to tell him the rest—about the dead squirrel, the broken roads, the forests, the sun flooding the empty towers at Firehills, the sound of insects and birds. He wanted to say, *I've been to O-Zone,* because he was sure the policeman had never heard anyone say that.

But in his talking he had ignored the policeman's word "sighting"—another creature had been seen—and now he remembered it, and the fear took hold of him again.

The fear had something to do with being very hungry, and it was aggravated by the light sliding like yellow crockery on the river's surface; by the echoing alarms and the jangling of cars; and the idea that this was all routine and happened every day.

So he simply turned and walked away from the policeman and the scene at the river wall (the Skell was being hauled into the chopper). On the way to Coldharbor his nerve failed him—it was the panic that he might have to spend the night out alone on these streets. And hurrying home, he got lost, though he was only three blocks from the towers. He used his phones—the emergency number—and had to ask directions. After that courageous day, this humiliation!

"It's him," Hooper said as Fisher entered the unit. Hooper was delighted to see the boy. When had this kid ever gone out alone?

"I've been trying to call you all day," Moura said.

"I was off the air," Fisher said. "I decided to tune out and do some exploring on the ground."

He said it carelessly but he believed he had just survived another hazardous mission—one not very different from the shoot in O-Zone. He waited for their reaction, and was annoyed that no one expressed surprise or asked him where he had been. He wanted to describe the blacks—how they had threatened him; he wanted to tell them about the Skell and the task force and how he had explained ropes and aliens to the cop. He felt he had been very reckless in switching off phone contact and staying off the air.

"Don't worry," he said, to encourage them—why weren't they saying anything? "I'm all right!"

Moura said, "You missed your study session."

"Theory of Subsequence," he said.

"You never know—it might come in handy someday," Holly said.

"I wasn't learning it, shit-wit. I was teaching it and going over proofs." He looked at Hooper. "What do you want?"

"Private," Hooper said. "Let's go into your room."

What was oddest about Fisher's odd feety-smelling room—a wilderness of screens and tubes and consoles—was that although it had a skylight, it had no windows. Hooper had never noticed this before; but he had never before taken Fisher seriously, nor had he ever needed him as he did now. Imagine, needing Fizzy!

"Blacks," the boy was saying. "It's all blacks out there."

"How do you know that? You don't have any windows."

"I was actually out there. I mean, on the ground. I saw them. Incredible number of blacks." Fisher was pleased with himself and snorting with satisfaction. "A few of them thought they could give me a hard time. They didn't get anywhere!"

What was he talking about? Hooper said, "What do you do for windows?"

Without speaking, Fisher went to a console panel and threw a switch. A window image appeared on a large square television screen on the wall where the outside window ought to have been. The boy manipulated a remote camera and panned the other towers, the skylights, rooftops, gunships, and a wall of blackness at the perimeter of the city. Fisher had not been looking at the image; he was looking at Hooper, and when Hooper nodded—his question had been answered—Fisher stabbed the switch and the image shook and vanished.

The boy was still snorting in a confident way. "You think from up here that there's all kinds of trouble down there. But most of that is just false alarms. Oh, sure—they pull Skells out of the river, but some of them don't even have weapons."

"They're tramps," Hooper said. "Where would they get weapons?"

"I'm just giving you an example. Like the blacks. You wouldn't think there are any blacks in the city from up here."

"New York is full of blacks," Hooper said. "Just because you're black it doesn't mean you don't get a residence permit or a work pass. Or an ID. Lots of Owners are blacks."

Fisher looked at Hooper with suspicion, as if he had not known this simple thing.

"I know," the boy said defiantly. "What's that?"

Hooper had taken the cartridge out of his pocket. He handed it to Fisher.

"Ever seen one of these before?"

"No," Fisher said, and held it under a desk lamp. "But I've studied those seals. They're used in intelligence work."

"There's film inside."

"I know," the boy said.

"The problem is opening it without destroying the film."

"I know," the boy said.

He made an ugly mocking face at Hooper, twisting his mouth, as if to say: You must be a fool if you think I can't open this!

"It's apparently a very sensitive mechanism."

"I know," the boy said. "What's on the film—those boonies?"

"Unlock it and we'll watch it," Hooper said. "But listen, this is secret."

Just the word, whispered in that way, was like an affirmation of friendship, because they were alone, and each suspected the other of being weak and needing a friend.

10

Hardy had filed his preliminary report on his longitudinal field study in O-Zone and submitted it with his tape of the trip two days after arriving back. Now, almost a week later, he had his reward: a coded message on his computer screen in his inner office. He unscrambled it and read: *Budget approved for further topographical field study Project O-Zone. Please update and verify. Scramble this immediately. Do not print. Do not use data base. Treat as classified.*

If it was this secret, then they were serious.

He scrambled the message and then phoned Operations.

"Allbright here."

"This is Operations," the woman said. Why didn't she give her name? But he knew why—Asfalt bureaucracy made employees that way, and it was the reason he had no friends there.

"I want to discuss Project O-Zone."

The voice said, "Seems it was a good party."

"Excellent."

"No problems?"

"None." Hardy was glad that he was ignorant enough to be able to say that.

"Then there is nothing to discuss."

"I wanted to ask about Access Passes," Hardy said, persisting.

"These will be granted to authorized personnel, or anyone you nominate."

He wanted to say more. He was happy about the approval. He just wanted to talk about the project.

128

He said, "I was wondering who's supervising—"
The voice said, "Weathermaker—"
His company name came like a warning.
"—this subject is highly classified."

Nothing to be written, or spoken, or recorded: they were very serious. And it was a measure of O-Zone's reputation in the United States: the place was believed to be wild and inaccessible and poisoned and dangerous, and so the project had taken on these same attributes. It was the first time that had happened, though Hardy had carried out many similar projects.

Hardy Allbright made mountains. He had designed and built mountains in West Africa, Mexico, and Saudi Arabia. So scientific, Moura always said about her husband. It was true, and it was the chief reason that Hardy had not inherited the family chain of department stores. "You're smart enough to stay out of business and look after yourself," the old man had said. "Perfesser!" he had always yelled in an admiring way at Hardy, and he had left him a large sum of money. "Perfesser!"

The family thinking was that Hardy had the brains, and Hooper the personality. In retail trade, personality mattered more than intelligence, especially as the business was long-established. And if it was a question of expansion or alteration, brains did not help much; then it was series of chess moves, which had more to do with being able to borrow money. And yet no one had ever expected that of Hooper. It surprised everyone when he restructured Allbright's and turned it into a mail-order business.

It also surprised everyone when Hardy, who was indeed a professor—a meteorological scientist specializing in weather modification—left his lab at Columbia and went to work in the downtown offices of Asfalt, which was part of the Petroland Oil Conglomerate. Hardy in business! But his work was classified—always Federal contracts or else contracts with foreign governments. Construction, people thought. What else could it possibly be? And because it was Asfalt, they suspected defense work, probably airstrips. Not even Moura knew. Few secrets were safe from Fizzy's restless intrusions and yet Hardy felt that even wonder boy did not know the exact nature of Asfalt's work. Rainmaking was always rumored, but no one knew how.

Hardy was mistaken. The boy had long ago hacked into Hardy's computer, and he copied everything that entered it. He knew all of it, but scorned it as obvious drudgery, and he could not understand why anyone would treat it as secret. It was no more complicated than roadbuilding. It was simpler than runways.

It was mountains—flat mountains, hot mountains, thermal mountains: vast black patches in places that were dying of thirst or simply in need of additional rainfall. The mountains were great unbroken areas of black asphalt. In the Ivory Coast they had paved 3,400 square kilometers, and the Sulayyil Stripe in Saudi Arabia was almost a third larger. Moura had gone on both trips without knowing, without guessing; though she too had suspected airstrips and runways. Asfalt had a projected mountain in central Australia and another was being studied in the middle east—but fighting in the region, and finance, cast doubt on that middle-east mountain ever being made.

They looked like enormous parking lots. They were flat and featureless and black. They created rain. Hardy's job was finding their dimensions and their placement. Shaping them and siting them properly were crucial, because it was not merely that they were placed in areas of low rainfall, they also needed the right prevailing winds and the correct angles. The wide black mass became a hot spot and created a convection current, boosting the air passing over it. This heated air rose rapidly, as if against a mountainside and, rising, it cooled and the moisture in it condensed. And then there were clouds and, quite often, rainfall on the far side of this thermal mountain.

It was, most of all, a way of using millions of barrels of excess oil. It meant that oil production could be maintained, and it kept the price up.

The oil side had nothing to do with Hardy. He had invented ground patterns—black crescents—that modified wind direction, shifting the air to his mountain. It meant a greater use of asphalt. Thermal mountains had intensified Petroland's drilling and refining, and it was the making of the company, now one of the five big oil producers in the world. And in every country where the Asfalt Division had built a thermal mountain, the weather had been significantly modified. There was now rain—and trees and crops—where there had been desert.

But Asfalt dealt in disruptions. Secrecy was a necessity because of the scale of the projects—the large oil shipments, the land areas, the finance; all the things that could go wrong, the downside, the shortfall. When Hardy was asked how he made his living, he never mentioned that Asfalt was mainly concerned with weather modification on a grand scale. He said engineering, the oil industry, and sometimes he used Hooper's private joke: landscaping.

He had told Hooper, because Hooper had asked. He had never been able to withhold anything from his brother, and so he was particularly resentful that Hooper seemed to have so many secrets.

Asfalt was an American company, and yet all its work so far had been carried out abroad. Apart from one stripe in Mexico of relatively small proportions (though the precipitation yields were good), no plan had ever been put forward for an American mountain. All the good land was spoken for—it was owned and managed—and so no tract available was large enough for a thermal mountain that would make a difference. One was needed in the midwest, but no one could agree on where it should be sited. Federal agencies had obstructed all development plans so far.

Several enormous tracts of land had been put on the market, but as soon as the sellers discovered that Asfalt was interested, the price had gone up, the sellers thinking: Oil money! Defense contracts! Airstrips! Bases! And so the prices were prohibitive. Hardy had never believed that Asfalt would build a thermal mountain in America.

And then, by chance, the exclusion order was removed from O-Zone. Asfalt provided Hardy with Access Passes and instructions to camouflage the visit. Hooper said, "Let's spend New Year's there—have a party!" Murdick said, "I'll find the food!" The Eubanks had promised backup, and after pleading with them Fizzy agreed to navigate. But it was Hooper's enthusiasm that kept Hardy's intention secret: after Hooper took charge of the trip, no one asked why it was that Hardy's company had secured eight Access Passes. Asfalt had warned Hardy of the dangers in traveling in a Prohibited Area. But there were advantages, too. It was Federal, so it was protected, and it might be possible to lease it from the government. It was contaminated, so it was empty—who would dare go there, who would want it, or fight for it? It was large. It was a wilderness. It was one of the largest tracts of empty usable land that might ever be available to a private company. And some of it, Hardy now knew, had been cleared.

But Project O-Zone was classified: the very idea of it was secret. And Hardy knew that if the land was still radioactive it was useless. But what a coup if he could reactivate O-Zone! The first trip was meant as a way of getting a general impression and trying to decide the safety factors. That was the beginning of the longitudinal study. Later, if the budget were approved, he would do some preliminary plans, establishing its elevations, making maps. There would have to be many more trips, more studies, and especially needed was a grid of film and some satellite photography. Yet he knew now that O-Zone could easily contain a thermal mountain, and with this—perhaps the largest in the world, perhaps a chain of thermal mountains—it might establish a modified weather pattern for this part of the United States. That was for the future. The main thing at the moment was to get onto the ground again and make it look like another picnic.

He had come to see that it was a wonderful place, O-Zone—low hills and broad fields and sunken cities: perfect, really, and all ready to be poured full of asphalt.

In his office at the division, just before he set off for Coldharbor, Hardy Allbright shut his eyes and saw it very clearly—the immense space, the emptiness, the ruin. Fifteen years ago its appeal was not merely that it was centrally located and unlikely to arouse suspicion—it was already underpopulated and somewhat wild; and most of all it was full of caves. They were deep limestone caverns, with the dimensions of the gorges aboveground: they were in some cases believed to be bottomless pits. Put nuclear trash in sealed containers in these holes and it would never be heard of again. Who could possibly tamper with them? That was the theory.

The contamination was so bad, so catastrophic when it came, that it was hardly publicized, for fear of its being so demoralizing. And even after it became known that half the state had been uprooted and moved, it was regarded as a precaution rather than a necessity; and it was never known how large an area in the heartland of the United States had become uninhabitable. It was one of those events which occur on such a scale and are so tragic and empty of hope that they are kept secret—any publicity only adds to the misfortune, and simply knowing about them seems like a curse.

But time had passed. There had been changes. The place had gone from wilderness to civilization and back to wilderness; it had been returned to America again. Now it was ready for anything. The woods could remain as protection, the roads and some of the towns might be reactivated, and part of that new state would be determined as an area of high rainfall. It did not matter whether the prairie in the western quarter would be affected, or whether the rest of the plateau would return to intensive agriculture—it was not a question of food. It was all experimental, and an American first. The point was that O-Zone could be controlled, so what did it matter whether the input of rain resulted in a hydroelectric scheme or altered topography? It was a sealed zone, and when it was unsealed and its weather modified, it could be penetrated according to a scientific plan, and colonized like a new planet. In a world of dead ends, it would be a fresh start. And there would never again be any accidents there.

He saw the land rising up before his eyes, the long swards and knobs and rough escarpments and tumbling woods, and the vast empty spaces that filled his dreams as a weathermaker.

Now the trees were clumped and denser, and in between the clumps were chutes of grass; up ahead, protrusions of original forest showed as great smudges. This new view was from the ground, in a semidarkness highlighted with heat impressions. The land was iron-blue and dusty on the film, with smear marks of leafy boughs and above them naked branches lying across the sky like cracks. It softened to pale blue, but still there was no movement, only the black branches in the foreground, the frothy wall of trees at the far side of the watery-looking meadow, and the long slashes of new light—dawn rising.

"I was just thinking about that," Hardy said, holding the door open. "That's O-Zone."

"What are you doing in here, you dong!" Fisher said. "This is a private room. You didn't buzz."

"That was not O-Zone," Hooper said, and killed the picture.

"I recognized it!" Hardy said. He was still looking at the

blank screen, where the meadow had been. Now he turned to face the two seated people. "Hooper! In Fizzy's room!"

"The kid and I were just kicking a problem around," Hooper said, hating himself for sounding adulterous and apologetic.

"Why did you switch off the screen?"

"Out of politeness."

"Go away," Fisher said. "Why are you bothering us?"

"You're wearing a mask!"

Fisher looked like a louse, or a sucking insect. He said, "Hay fever!" and stood up.

Hardy was surprised by the boy's bad posture—the way he hunched his shoulders made his long arms seem even longer. And what huge feet! His hands were red and very damp, and his wrists newly hairy. He had grown up in this room, and so he had the strange shape and habits, and even the same lowered head and bumping motion, of an animal in a cage. His appearance and the way he moved—the noises he made, the yawns, the squawks—always caused Hardy to forget the boy's intelligence.

"You didn't buzz! You didn't signal! You just burst in— and now you're not going away!"

"I was looking for Moura."

But the boy was right. Hardy knew he was lingering here because he had just had a new glimpse of what he was sure was O-Zone. Was it the tape they had made on the shoot they had mounted with Murdick?

"Moura's not here. Obviously."

Hardy pointed to the blank screen. "Those trees and fields—that's O-Zone."

Hooper said, "That was the tape of the trip out. We got it on macro. That was the Ohio valley. You interested in the Ohio valley? Got plans for it?"

Hardy shook his head—he didn't want to encourage any of Hooper's talk about Asfalt's plans, especially in front of Fizzy.

"Do you want to discuss something?"

Hardy said nothing: he was annoyed that they were now asking the questions. It was an unlikely pair, Hooper and Fizzy, but he saw them as formidable and possibly a threat. They had all the right combinations, and they had apparently made peace. Hardy felt especially uncomfortable, and almost envious, seeing Hooper succeeding with Fizzy where he had failed.

"Why don't you go away?" Fisher said. He was not being aggressive, only showing incomprehension that he wasn't being obeyed. He poked toward Hardy with the snout of his mask and let his long arms dangle.

Hardy said, "I have no interest at all in O-Zone. And I don't want to watch your tape. Don't forget, I've got one of my own." But as he shrugged and turned away, he glanced at the video screen: the quality of their tape had been noticeably better than his—it was ground-focus, close-up, high-definition. He wondered, was it Murdick's? "I'm just surprised to see you two in here, looking so guilty."

"Don't be such a dong," Fisher said. He seemed suddenly bored, and began sniffing in impatience, sucking air noisily through his snout. "Now get out!"

Hardy went, but hated being sent away like this.

Fisher locked the door and said to Hooper, "My parents are insecure. They don't know what to do with me. They're not as intelligent as I am, so they can't tell me anything. See, the trouble is, they don't have any authority. All they could really do is bully me or report me to my session team leader. But they're afraid to. They know I could double up and really wreck things for them—I could file against them. I could be taken away from them and sent to a guardian."

He plucked his mask off and yawned. It was one of his loud slow yawns. He didn't cover his mouth. Hooper had to turn away—his immediate reaction was an urge to slap the boy for yawning like that.

"I know all about Hardy's work—everything he does!"

"It's supposed to be classified," Hooper said.

"I hacked it."

"And you know all about your mother?"

"No," the boy said—so logical he could never be untruthful. "Moura only thinks things. She never stores them. It's all in her head."

He yawned again, another gravelly roar, and showed Hooper his scummy tongue.

"They really have problems!" Fisher said.

Hooper was staring—too fascinated to smile.

"That's why I have to be careful not to criticize them,"

Fisher said, growling through another yawn. "They'd freak if I did."

Hooper said, "Let's roll this thing," and pointed the mouse in his hand and squeezed.

The screen deepened with an image: daybreak over that meadow in O-Zone, as the two troopers peered through the basketwork of branches. Murdick's helmet was visible, and the upper bulge of Fizzy's, as the camera panned slowly back and forth. Human murmurs drowned the birdsong on the soundtrack. There was a dragging racket of what seemed like scraping.

—*Your yawning drives me crazy.*

In the blurred imaging the meadow had a frozen look.

—*I hate the dark.*

—*You've got irons. What are you so nervous about?*

—*We could be sitting in poison.*

—*This isn't an iron. It's a camera. Right, Willis?*

—*That piece is regulation Godseye. It's got thermal imaging.*

The mike was bumped, and then: —*looks like a particle beam to me, shit-wit.*

The dusty blue of the set of woods behind the field turned to a pinker, grayer powder, and was stirred and liquefied into paler light. Yellow seeped in at one edge and soaked the foreground, making it a tufty green. It was dawn on the meadow.

—*I don't have a college education, because I don't need one. Listen, I'm not a freak. I didn't come out of a test tube.*

"Fucking Murdick," Fisher said, and whirred the tape forward. "He is such a fucking truncheon."

When the tape resumed, the images rose and fell, and the nodding motion continued in the long tracking shot through the yellow woods. Hooper was photographing the running figures of the aliens, who were chasing the lame deer. The accompanying sounds were of tramping feet—the troopers' big boots—and of branches being punched, and *They don't look like mutants to me*—and the aliens' laughter.

Hooper had remembered the slant of morning light striking through the leaves, and the surprising speed of the aliens as they high-stepped through the ferns and low hollies that grew beneath the hickories. But he had forgotten all those unusual sounds—the muttering birds, the screeching insects, the aliens' delighted yells.

The men had raced ahead and were circling in order to maneuver the deer into the clearing, where they could use their nets. As they changed direction, the young woman crossed over, and there was a clear shot of her turning just in front of a curtain of sunlight.

Hooper pointed the mouse at her and froze her.

He caught her in a hurdler's posture, her legs fully extended front and back—she was leaping a fallen tree. Her face was bright with effort and strength, and she was barefoot. She wore a loose shirt and thin green trousers. Her shirtfront had jumped and he could see her smooth stomach and the curved undersides of her bare breasts. Her hair, sunburnt in patches, whitened and blond, was cut short, except for a single braid at the back of her neck. Her hair was shorter than that of the men who ran ahead, and for a moment she had seemed like a beautiful boy among dark witches and hags. She was well off the ground—a good healthy bounce—and she was young. Sixteen, Hooper thought, because he did not dare tell himself less.

"Subject G," Fisher said. "One of the survivors. She's about fifteen."

She was smiling. Hooper envied her her happiness, and for that instant he wanted everything she had. But she had nothing. Hooper thought: Yes, I want that—I've never had nothing. He saw an unassailable safety in that simplicity, and he was aroused. But it was more than wanting to possess her. He wanted to *be* her. He wanted to live her life. She was welcome to his. She would think this was crazy, because he was wealthy and considered powerful—an Owner, after all—and had an apparently pleasant life. She could have it! It no longer interested him.

And Hooper, who had never loved—did not believe love existed apart from sexual desire, and that desire itself burned it away—Hooper began to speculate. Perhaps that is what it is, he thought: sharing someone else's life, living it, serving it, believing in its value—challenging yourself with this new person by offering everything that person wants. And the lack of love was the empty prison of your own life lived alone.

He did not think he was such a fool. That alien—that savage—must have felt the same. He felt powerful again and saw the use of his strength: I can give her everything she wants. But although in that instant he had started to live her life and be with her, he could not imagine what she might want. And she was far away, not in space but time. She might be infectious—many of them were diseased. She might not speak English. She might be a psychopath.

She's lost, he thought, and pitied her. And then he began to worry: Or am I?

All this took a few seconds, and some of it he remembered later and put in its proper place, the blaze of those seconds.

"It's jammed!" Fisher said.

The girl completed her leap, and bounded over the fallen tree trunk, and ran out of sight.

"I was thinking," Hooper said. He had remembered his unspecific wish in O-Zone to take something of it back to New York. Now desire had made that wish specific.

"Move it forward to the burn."

"No. I want to watch it slowly."

He glimpsed her through the trees. She was lingering in the woods, watching the men in the meadow. He was aroused by her peculiar health and by her carelessness. He loved her old clothes. And she was dangerous!

"Quit pausing it!"

"I'm trying to get a fix on these people."

"They're not people—they're aliens. They're really dimbos and they're probably sick. No masks, no gloves, and look at that footgear. They're running around practically stark! They're almost pure monkey!"

Hooper said nothing. The tape still whirred.

"They sleep under trees! They don't even make camps! No technology!"

Hooper sat forward. He had just seen her again, her hand on her face—she was thinking. What was she hoping?

Whatever she wanted . . . But Fizzy was still talking, and Hooper could not finish the thought.

"They're really dirty," Fisher was saying. "Hey, dong-face!"

Hooper had killed the picture. He fumbled with the electronic mouse in his hand and moved the tape up to the moments just before the shooting.

"If it weren't for me you wouldn't even be watching this. I cracked the seal, I decoded it, I developed—"

"If you say one more word, I'll kill this thing," Hooper said. "I'm showing you the burns, and that's all."

Fisher started to reply, but a male alien filled the screen and commanded his attention. Murdick's hands became visible, then the helmet, and the terrified face in the mask. No wonder Murdick wanted this tape—it showed more clearly than Hooper had seen at the time what a coward Murdick was. Murdick was trying to smile at the alien. The trooper in Godseye was about to grovel.

And then the alien was in focus—his beard, his sinewy shoulder, his net. The blast came—a hiss preceded it on the tape—and the alien was changed from a solid substance to a jelly, and trembled deep red and contracted, withering and fusing to a tiny doll image of its bigger self. It flew apart, disintegrating, a mist becoming a gas. The fine spray of the destroyed man slightly darkened Murdick's suit.

And the second alien, just the same, losing his look of surprise and vanishing in a mist. He was enclosed, then gone.

"What a weapon . . . what amazing burns!" Fisher said. "How about the rest—the early part you skipped?"

Hooper could not answer immediately. He was nauseated by the deaths. Seeing them like this, in slow motion, frightened him, too. No wonder a camera was part of the weapon: there was no other way of knowing who the victim was.

He removed the cartridge from the video unit. He was still trying to think.

"The chase," Fisher said. "How about the chase?"

"You're too young for that stuff."

Fisher laughed, because he was not really interested in those animals, he said, and he told Hooper that he had spent a whole day out on the streets alone.

"You've done it once," Hooper said.

"I'd go out again anytime," the boy said. But trying too hard to sound brave, he sounded terrified.

Hooper went back to his own tower and watched the tape four more times. It maddened him that he could not copy it or print from it. He did not watch the burns—they had badly upset him. But the girl: he watched her closely, concentrating hard. She did not know him, she had never heard of him. And she was a stranger. He wanted her. It had been years since he had really wanted anything, and until that moment he had never wanted any person.

He tried saying it a number of ways, but nothing worked until he whispered, "She needs me," and then he saw her face again.

11

Going out, Moura approached the Coldharbor main gate and saw the security guard inside reading a book. Captain Jennix was not a captain in the Coldharbor Security Force but rather in his local "ship." The man's title irritated Hardy, who had once told Moura, "'Captain' means something, which is why I will not call that man 'captain.' He's not an Owner, he's never been in the service, and he's done nothing to earn that rank. Frankly, I think all these Pilgrims and Rocketmen are crazy in an uninteresting way." Moura still didn't know what "captain" meant.

Captain Jennix was a youngish man, thirty or so, who called himself a Starling. He had a very small head, and unfunny blue believer's eyes, and wore an immaculate uniform. He had a way of glancing skyward and talking about "the program" and "weightless motion" and "emigration"—he meant into space.

He looked up from his book and spoke to Moura in his flat plodding way. "Preparing my mind for the mission."

You didn't ask about the mission—not because it was awkward and imaginary, but because they would keep you there all day describing it with facts and figures, and they could be fanatical recruiters if they felt they could use you. Moura was aware of Captain Jennix's interest in Hardy, and so she was always very circumspect.

He was smiling at her, showing her the title of his book, *The Time Lords of Titan.* She wanted to laugh, but his passion frightened her, too. The books were always science fiction, and they always seemed years out-of-date.

"Read it?" Captain Jennix said.

"No thanks," she said, to be ambiguous and polite.

"I've got lots of others you might like," and stooped and brought out a stack of paperbacks with lurid covers showing troopers and Pilgrims and lunar settlements. Captain Jennix showed them to her title by title: *The Settlers of Planck, Beneath the Ocean of Storms, The Synodic Month, The Lunar Pole, The Gardens of Tranquillity, Crossing Mare Frigoris, Mission to Fertility*—

"Please," she said. They were like a peculiar form of devotional literature, and she found them singleminded and upsetting.

"It's unusual to see you out on a Sunday morning," Captain Jennix said. He had the Pilgrims' belief in strict routines.

She hated being noticed that way, especially as she knew that something had changed within her. Until the O-Zone trip, she had spent most Sundays at Coldharbor off the air and sealed in her room, sometimes with Hardy, in a deep deliberate sleep. A coma, most people called it; and not beds or sleep capsules, but "coma couches."

It had started as a fad and turned into a pastime. When it became very popular it was associated with good health—not physical strength, but a sense of sanity and well-being. But it is the fate of some pastimes to become obsessions.

I've done fifteen hours, people said; I've done twenty; I've done a day. When Barry Eubank said, "I've done two dozen," the Murdicks replied, "We're working on thirty." It had attracted them to O-Zone—it was so empty it must be very safe. That was what everyone had thought. What a place to sleep! But in the end no one had slept at all in O-Zone.

"You were away about a week ago," Captain Jennix said, stating it as a fact.

How surprised he would have been if she had told him where they had gone. He might not have believed her. He expected her to believe that at some point in the future he was going to take his place in a lunar mission, make a moon landing or else live for a time in a space station with other Pilgrims, or Starlings—Rocketmen, anyway—and yet he would find it inconceivable that she had spent two days in the Prohibited Area of O-Zone.

"New Year's party," she said, enjoying the preposterous sound of the truth.

"You can pass, Mrs. Allbright," Captain Jennix said.

He sat at a bank of monitors on which various parts of Coldharbor and even districts in New York were visible. On one a space vehicle was shown. Was this why Captain Jennix was in such a thoughtful mood? Perhaps he was anticipating a space launch—always an emotional moment for a Pilgrim. Their hope lay in being transported into space by just such a rocket. Captain Jennix wore two stripes on his sleeve, which meant that he had paid a certain amount toward a place on one of the vehicles. He had not said so; it was talk—but it was probably true. All the Pilgrims paid, and all hoped, but very few of them actually went up. Still, they were great supporters of the Federal Space Program, and there were so many of them it was sometimes said—Hardy often said it— that highly placed Pilgrims boosted the budget for space travel, and the Federal government encouraged this zeal.

Now Captain Jennix pushed his chair away from the monitors and said, "I don't blame you for hesitating, Mrs. All-bright. New York—"

But it was not New York. It was that Moura did not want to spend another Sunday in a coma. That wasn't rest—it was active sleep: not forgetting but remembering. She and Hardy used gas. It could have been the gas as much as the motion of the couch that tired her. Other people used injections or capsules. The longest period she had managed was eighteen hours, and she had regretted it. She had thought that the silence and the emptiness in O-Zone might change her manner of sleeping, somehow alter the experience. She had always woken exhausted.

Captain Jennix was saying, "Take this book, for example"—she saw it was *The Settlers of Planck*. "It shows you the importance of pushing on. There's no sense going unless you *keep* going. Out of the house, past the wall, off the earth, until you're weightless. Learn to fly and you solve the problem of time. You never just go out and come back. Know why?"

She must have glanced at him, because he spoke as if in reply.

"Because once you've gone out you can never come all the way back."

What was he talking about? She was thinking of O-Zone, how it had stirred her, shown her the land and the sky. Because she thought they had been alone, the place had frightened her with its emptiness; but it had frightened her more when Fizzy's suspicion had passed through Firehills that there were aliens nearby.

"There is no recorded crime. There is no disorder. No instances of madness. The training program is foolproof, so its success is due to the caliber of the troopers who go—good caliber, the best people."

Moura listened to him, but behind his small head she saw the old world of O-Zone. It seemed remote, and as separate, as isolated and hard-to-find as an island. Never mind that it was in Missouri, because America had become an ocean.

"The great complaint is that not enough people go on these missions," Captain Jennix said. "But all the *good* people go. Isn't that everyone?"

She had been exposed to danger—reminded of it, even if it had not existed. Fear was fear, whatever the cause. And fear had made her feel solitary. She had begun to think intensely about her life—more intensely than any coma had made her remember. Fully awake and afraid, in the clear light of the O-Zone trip, she had seen Fizzy changing into whoever his father was—the masked man at the contact clinic. He had spoken to her!

"I'll give you an example," Captain Jennix said.

An example of what? What was Jennix trying to prove? She stared past his head and on the bank of monitors she saw street grids and various corners of New York—the river, the perimeter, the bridges—and she wondered . . .

But Captain Jennix said, "We have a unit in the Starlings' divisional ship code-named 'White Girls.' This is basically an intelligence unit, but it won't move until the day comes for transporting personnel. In other words, they're basically on standby alert until just before countdown."

"I'm sorry," Moura said, but it didn't seem to matter that she had not been listening. Captain Jennix had stood up and become rigid when he had said *standby alert.*

"White Girls," he said. "Basically they could be on standby alert their whole lives. They move when they get the signal"—now he moved, but it was only to slap another book for emphasis. It was *Mission to Fertility*. "Mrs. Allbright, you could qualify for White Girls. The point is, you don't go out until the last day, and then you go out and you don't stop until you're locked into space."

He sat down and frowned at the video screens on the bank of monitors. He was clutching *Mission to Fertility*.

"It's all in here," he said, flexing the book.

What a bore he was, waiting his turn for the rocket. And it probably would never come. Moura knew she wanted something else. Since returning to New York she had felt dissatisfied. She had a vague feeling of imprisonment. Holly's visit had stirred her, too, and given her a direction. Holly could be foolish, but she was funny and uncritical and a good prop. Moura had known her too long to be able to find fault with her. After that length of time you accepted everything in a person or else ended the friendship. And Holly was useful because she dared to say things out loud to Moura that Moura only whispered to herself. Moura sometimes wished that Holly were more subtle, but she also thought: Maybe I need her to be unsubtle in order to flatter myself.

"This is an awful city," Captain Jennix was saying.

In her mind, Moura had gone into New York and found the clinic. She had entered and registered and made her request. Was it still such a hive of rooms and cubicles? And all the scanners and sound equipment; and the air knifed with disinfectant. In her mind she waited there, crouched at the cliff edge of her willpower, listening hard but hearing nothing but the white noise which hissed in her ears during those sessions; and his beaked mask hard against hers. *You love it. You—*

He could not have been an ordinary person, because Fizzy wasn't.

She had rehearsed the trip, tried out her questions, and imagined what the answers might be. But she did not want to go out alone.

"It's a much worse place than anyone admits."

Was Captain Jennix reading her mind? Pilgrims—Starlings, Rocketmen, Astronauts—often claimed to be telepathic.

"The things I've seen!" he said. "And not just on those screens. I'm not talking about over the river, which is pretty terrible. Or beyond that, where it's hell. I'm talking about right here. The power failures, the inefficiency, the new so-called styles of clothes, some of which means no clothes whatsoever—supposedly decent people, Owners, pretending to be Starkies. And self-delusion. And old technology. And junk people."

Moura brought him into focus.

"New York," she said.

"The world, really."

And he frowned again at the monitors, this time importantly, as if to say *I'm leaving*.

"This planet is very backward," Captain Jennix said.

But Moura didn't believe in the salvation of space, and she certainly was not going to pay for a time-share in a rocket. You weren't supposed to call them "rockets"! The Pilgrims were so fervent and deluded, always glued to the launch channel, and pathetically thrilled when another vehicle was boosted into space with a colonist on board. What happened to them? Perhaps they were killed or else stranded; perhaps the few that went were opportunists—merely joyriding. They never advertised their disappointment, or their eager despair.

"When the last good person leaves," Captain Jennix said, scrutinizing her with shrewd pleasure, "we'll burn this planet."

"Don't burn me, captain."

"Join us and we won't have to."

It was wrong to argue with fanatics, or even simple believers—they always ended up by insulting you. Moura had wanted to go into New York, but had only made it to the park beneath Coldharbor, which was no distance at all. She was not consoled by that stupid man who kept telling her it was dangerous out there. If he was so brave, why was he double-locked in a checkpoint and dreaming of a trip to the moon?

Hardy was saying, "Aren't you ever going out again?"

This was at Coldharbor, in their unit high in the tower. He was talking to Fisher and waiting for Moura, who had said she might not be long.

Fisher yawned without covering his mouth, as if replying to Hardy—but a harsh reply of scouring breath.

"Why not go?"

What a change it would be to have Fizzy somewhere else on a Sunday, especially if Moura was coming back soon. He was hoping to persuade Moura to help him sleep. It was no fun sleeping alone, and it was terrible to be observed. He was grateful for her interest. It was what remained of their marriage, their willingness to sleep together—sleep in the recreational sense: the coma. For Hardy it was an important activity; but he always made a point of waking first—he wasn't a distance sleeper.

"There's nowhere to go," Fisher said, because the idea still frightened him. He became slightly nauseous and unsteady on his feet when he remembered that he had spent one whole day prowling New York. That was how his timid and tentative sniffing had seemed—like bold prowling, a kind of confident balancing act, the awkward boy imagining himself like an indestructible cat. But something else within him, a dull inarticulate instinct, held him, and this dumb memory of the danger had kept him indoors ever since. "And there's nothing to do out there."

Against his will, and in silence, like a shadow on the window, he saw the old Skell again—the blue bristly face, the risen veins, the white feet, the black rags. It dripped against the river wall and it whimpered. The creature possessed a dangerous hunger. Fisher hated his own irrationality—these were small cockroachy pests! And then he hated Hardy for rousing the feeling in him. Why was Hardy harping on that lately—about going out?

He had another favorite subject these days, and just then, to Fisher's annoyance, he reverted to it.

"Those pictures," he said, and as the boy began to yawn at him again he went on, "I wish I'd gotten pictures like that in O-Zone."

"They weren't taken in O-Zone."

"Even so"—but he didn't believe Fizzy at all—"they were extremely good. High definition, thermal imaging, overprinted with that data on elevations and distances. What sort of camera was it? It must have been Murdick's, right? I'd like to know where Willis gets his equipment."

Fisher wanted to say, "He's in Godseye." But that reminded him of Murdick's gibe: "If you don't know what Godseye is, you're not as smart as you think you are."

"That was the Ohio valley."

"It doesn't matter," Hardy said. He knew that Fizzy was telling Hooper's lies. He only wanted him to listen: he needed the boy's help.

Pictures of that quality were what he needed for his Project O-Zone report. But it was not only necessary to have good pictures on the ground; he also needed willing scouts.

Asfalt had not confirmed that the project was secret, because it was more than secret: it was what the company called a ghost—it did not officially exist. Its sensitive nature meant that any research had to be Hardy's voluntary idea. All the responsibility was his, all the risk, all the blame. O-Zone was still classified as highly dangerous, a Prohibited Area. No project could be officially contemplated for such a place.

Yet Hardy had already decided what his next step must be. He was influenced by Fizzy's sudden decision to go out alone in New York—a whole day in the city, off the air! He had been such a coward before. And there was Hooper's new relationship with the boy. Perhaps Hooper had given him the encouragement to spend a day outside the garrison.

This was the answer. Those two could shoot the preliminary survey, the elevations, the aerial grid. They could distribute sensors for relaying wind data and carry out some fieldwork to complete the longitudinal survey.

If Hardy himself took the return trip he would have to keep a secret. With Hooper and Fizzy acting for him, shooting O-Zone for the hell of it—for the pleasure of having a unique Access Pass—no one would suspect him of having a secret. The ghost would be safely invisible. There was another bonus—they apparently had the right equipment and knew how to use it.

Hardy said, "And when I say out, I don't just mean New York. I mean wild places."

He was changing the subject again, and again Fisher saw Brooklyn, the view from the river, the bridges that had been secured against alien gangs, and the lights that could never reassure him, because all they illuminated were the scribbles and the greasy river water and the blackness on Brooklyn's walls.

When he looked up at Hardy, *wild places* was printed on Fisher's face. It showed in his eyes and on his mouth—doubt, uncertainty, shadows, strangeness.

Hardy said, "I was really impressed with you in O-Zone. The way you took charge and drove the mainframe. Keeping everyone calm. Locating those aliens. Gathering that data—"

Fisher seldom listened to Hardy. He looked at him but his mind was elsewhere, solving problems, usually a kind of baggy geometry of particle physics, like socks he slowly turned inside-out and tucked into matched pairs. In the streams of particles he tried to seize each speck and enlarge it and give it a name. Exodes. Squarks. Antigons. And lately he had become interested in the concept of "wabble," which he saw as the sideways movement of particles, something that had never been described, but crucial to his Theory of Subsequence. His mind was working that way now, but then something urgent in Hardy's voice made him begin to listen.

"Hard information and reliable maps," Hardy was saying. "The graphics could be very useful. In fact, the whole program—"

"It's not a program," Fisher said. He never allowed his work to be praised. He was a perfectionist, and he believed his mind was perfect, but a thing was blunted and coarsened as soon as it was made: pure thought could not be transformed into matter, and nothing could be brought to perfection. "It's just sketches."

"They're great sketches."

The boy shrugged. "There's a lot we don't know." He stared at Hardy and said, "Microscopic data. Subterranean temperatures. Soil analysis. Take those birds you were raving about."

"The quail—beautiful bobwhites." And Hardy saw their round tufted shapes, pecking and making for a thicket at Firehills.

"We haven't got anything on their bone marrow."

Saying these things awakened Fisher's interest, and he became curious about the answers.

"I never expected you to go with Hooper and Murdick. You were in unknown territory!"

The boy was encouraged. He said, "A Prohibited Area. Evidence of high-level mutagens," and licked his lips.

"Exactly," Hardy said.

"No one's been on the ground there for fifteen years," Fisher said. A wordless anxiety trembled in his mind—something small darkening within him like an infection. "We were the first."

"There were aliens there. You could have been in serious danger."

"We *were* in serious danger," Fisher said.

"You burned them."

"Yeah, we burned them all down." And he thought: Murdick, that total dong!

The boy was frightened again. He saw clawing aliens, the other man, the running girl. The burning of the two men had bewildered him, and viewing the tape with Hooper had only given him nightmares. He still had horrible dreams of being trapped there, of ragged aliens wrenching him through the smashed window of the stranded Welly.

"And then you went out in New York!"

This new reminder weakened Fisher further. That small dark thing trembling within him was terror curling like a dead leaf. He wanted Hardy to stop talking about what he had done.

"Wait," Hardy said as Fisher turned away. "That's pretty impressive for a kid of fifteen."

The boy had already crossed the room.

"I'm a theoretical physicist, not a trooper."

"You proved that you can be both. It's the most valuable human on earth—the field scientist."

The boy did not react except to say blandly, "I'm not a spaceman."

Hardy walked across the room toward him, and waited until the boy acknowledged him before saying, "You can help me."

It didn't work. Fisher was unmoved. Of course he could help him!

"Are you interested in going back to O-Zone?"

The boy thought Yes and became afraid once more. He could only calm himself by thinking No.

He said, "I have work to do here."

"I could get you a couple of Access Passes."

Fisher stared. Hardy was always so evasive, but Fisher was never surprised where Hardy's work was concerned. Since he had hacked into Hardy's computer, he knew this longitudinal field study concerned weather modification in O-Zone, probably a thermal mountain. It was old-fashioned stuff, just a way of using surplus oil and inflating its value. He saw something savage in Hardy's naive trust in the benefit of rain.

"Imagine being the only human in O-Zone!"

If that were possible, Fisher thought, I would go. But that thought was crowded with the sight of jumping aliens—monsters! beasts! net-men! He saw their hungry faces, their teeth, their big filthy hands.

He said, "No one really knows what's there. Hooper calls it a desert island."

"You can find out what's on it."

"Why not you?"

"I don't have your skills, your insights, your resources. I don't have your pedigree. I'm not a Type A." Hardy had found it difficult to begin, but then he spoke with conviction, fascinated to know what Fizzy's response would be. Again he mentioned how Fizzy had taken them there, and led the shoot, and brought them back to New York.

"That's obvious," the boy said.

Hardy was staring—feeling doglike.

The boy went on, "I've been listening to that for years, people saying, 'We could work with you,' 'We could use your talents,' 'We could find room for someone like you.' Of course! It doesn't flatter me. I know what I can do. I know myself better than any of these dongs. I'm even better than they think I am! They never say how badly they need me. No, they put it in a patronizing way, how much *I* need *them*." He had started to clench and unclench his hands, reddening them and leaving bright white marks from the pressure of his fingers, and he was blinking with fury when he said, "I don't need them at all!"

"I'm saying I do need you, Fizz."

"And they tell me what they want, but they never"—the boy's voice had become a squawk—"they never ask the really crucial question."

Hardy was about to speak when Fisher interrupted.

"I'm going to be burned out at twenty!" the boy cried.

"Fizzy—"

"And they never ask what *I* want!"

"I'm asking," Hardy said.

Fisher said nothing. His fear had come back. But he did not think: I want more courage. He believed his intellectual strength made him unusually powerful. But in a small awful way his irrational fear of darkness and of imaginary terrors crippled him badly. He knew that. It was not a large handicap—that was the worst of it. It did not really limit him, and yet it would not go away. It was absurd and maddening, like having a stone in your shoe.

"I'll let you know," the boy said.

"What are you doing?"

He was pulling his helmet on, the one with the faceplate and phones; and the suit, and gloves, and the big boots. Survival gear.

"Going out," the boy said, and shoved his nose and mouth against the faceplate, and squashed them, making himself ugly. "Going out!"

Moura had come back sometime after that, and now they lay side by side in the darkened unit, she and Hardy. They were relieved that Fizzy had at last gone out. Into New York wearing survival gear! They imagined the boy roaming the city, being watchful, seeing blacks and Japanese and weirdly dressed Owners, and believing he was in great danger.

But it was a start, like his friendship with Hooper. The two had nothing in common, so it had to be true friendship, perhaps the beginning of maturity.

"We're losing him," Hardy had said as he administered the gas to Moura.

"When was he ever ours?"

To Moura, Fisher seemed completely out of reach. She had left the building intending to visit the clinic. But her nerve had failed her: she had not even gotten past the gate. I'm as bad as Captain Jennix, she thought, dreaming of empty planets and the serenity of space stations.

"He thinks I should be in something called White Girls."

Hardy did not hear her. She was murmuring, going under. And she wondered what had become of the clinic after all these years.

The same thought continued in her coma—the clinic, the cubicle, the underwater noise. She was received, she was examined; smears and scans were carried out. She was injected. Then she realized that she was not alone. In the soft semidarkness a beaked man rose up beside her. She recognized him, in spite of his mask; and what was more, he knew her. He held her and she was struggling, thrashing, and worrying that it was going to stop too soon.

In his own capsule, watching across an expanse of black, Hardy saw full piles of thunderheads rising and gathering.

Fisher had clumped past Captain Jennix. He thought the man was an idiot. The credulous Rocketman had a question for him, something simple about vertical shear. Fisher refused to answer—he called him a tool. Jennix squinted; he was taken by the boy's helmet and boots. He said that he had just seen Moura. Fisher said, "You are such a total herbert!"

It was another bright night; but the rush of rotors and ground traffic, the rattle of trams, and the yowl of punctured alarms kept him back. The sounds weakened him physically, the noise making his muscles go loose. When he tuned out, the unnatural silence spooked him.

In front of Coldharbor was a lighted park—a plaza of dense yew hedges and bare trees. Beyond it, the street led downtown. There was a station of the Tram Rail and the coaches flying along it. He could get in and go. He could take the subway. There were taxis. But he did not move: that stone in his shoe was making him afraid.

He buzzed Hooper. "I'm out—prowling around," he was going to say.

Hooper did not respond.

Fisher sensed that the city noise was hammering him small. He wondered now where he had ever got the courage to go out before, and he felt a retrospective fear—anxiety at what he had done a week ago, alone.

He tried Hooper's number again. "How about prowling together?" he practiced saying.

But Hooper was off the air.

12

"WE'RE GOING HOT AT OH-FOUR-HUNDRED. WANT TO watch a video while we wait for Murdick and the others? Hey, mister, I'm talking to you."

The big man with the cartridge belt over his shoulder was talking to Hooper by helmet phone, though the two men were only a meter apart in the new-model assault rotor. Hooper thought of it as a gunship; the man called it a "Whoopee." The man's helmet and mask had the Godseye insignia of a sunburst, and the local unit's name—"Snake-Eaters."

His name was Meesle. He was tall, with a full gut and narrow shoulders. Hooper could see that he was proud of his big belly—the way he clapped his hands on it and measured it with satisfaction and seemed to steer himself forward with it. He was not fat overall but he was an assertive shape. He had met Hooper just after midnight and led him blindfolded to this spot. All the while Hooper was thinking: I'm a wealthy man and I let them blindfold me!

Now the blindfold was off, but the rotor's windows were dark. This gunship, Hooper guessed from its size, was probably parked on a tower top way uptown. He could hear the air traffic clearly here.

"This video," Hooper said, "is it something special?"

He suspected that it was a porno disc, for passing the time—or possibly a violent murder. It had always been whispered that some of these squads made tapes of their executions; and now Hooper knew how. He's going to show me a burn, Hooper thought. That's how they get into the mood, all these trigger-happy executives and Owners, these millionaire

153

vigilantes. Yet there was something rather vulgar and scruffy about Mr. Meesle, who probably had a title like Colonel or Commander.

Hooper had come here out of curiosity, but already he regretted it. He was afraid it would all be too much for him, and what was the point? Why had he browbeaten and blackmailed Murdick into getting him a candidate's pass? Because Godseye was only a name, because he knew so little about them. But now that he was here he suspected why he had so far always stayed away from this bunch.

"We had this flick made for us," Meesle said. There was a wink in his voice that Hooper hated. "Special."

That made it sound as if it might be worse than murder.

"What do you think's keeping Murdick?" Hooper said.

He was stalling. He did not want to watch a videotape with this man Meesle. It was too cozy, the pair of them side by side in the parked gunship. Hooper did not want to be near enough to be nudged by this eager man. His distrust of the man had become resentment, and he was angry with Murdick. After that invitation, now he had the nerve to be late! Perhaps that was the little creep's way of getting even.

"That might be him," Meesle said.

Careful, rung-creaking feet rose up the metal ladder that led to the belly of the gunship.

"Murdick."

But the door opened and it was Sluter—so his name badge said—the pilot. He was a slow, suspicious man with sniper's eyes, who in a deliberate way said nothing to Hooper, and when Hooper smiled Sluter stared at his mouth—at the space between his front teeth.

To Meesle, Sluter said, "There's some artillery shells on the pier. Who left them there?"

"That would be Cleary, from Ammo."

"It's no place to leave them."

"Not much we can do about it."

Sluter said, "There's a lot we can do to Cleary."

He was speaking to Meesle but staring crookedly at Hooper. "We can burn his car and kill his dog."

It came out quickly in a monotone. Hooper thought: He's crazy, he's dangerous.

Sluter's jaws had bony hinges protruding from the back of his cheeks, and his teeth were clamped together. Hooper wondered whether this sense of danger was merely an expression of his own resentment and unfamiliarity here—a first-time feeling, and something cruel in the man's face.

Meesle said, "I'll get him to winch them aboard."

"Artillery shells?" Hooper asked Sluter, and at once he knew the man was antagonized by questions.

Sluter turned his back to them and stuck his elbows out. He was nodding—probably angry; he seemed to be counting.

"Simulated artillery shells," Meesle said. "Noisemakers." He spoke in a friendly way, using his big hands for emphasis. "They startle and disable. We've got real ones, too, but we don't normally use them inside the city limits."

It was after three o'clock in the morning, and even Meesle's friendly voice seemed harsh; time was slow-moving, and the lights too bright. Hooper felt inattentive and fragile because of the hour. He hated missing sleep, not because it made him tired but because he became stupidly wakeful—extreme fatigue gave him insomnia. He was risking that just to have a look at Godseye!

Abruptly, breaking the silence, Sluter said, "We might have a surprise inspection tonight. They'd want to see everyone's pass."

Hooper understood what he was driving at. Who is this stranger? Sluter was thinking. Doesn't he know this is a secret organization? What right does an outsider have to be here on a hunt? And is he really an Owner? Hooper had always believed the typical Godseye trooper to be someone like Sluter—a man whose feverish suspicions misled him and kept him from knowing anyone well.

"You're responsible, Meesle."

"I've got a pass," Hooper said. "It's signed by Murdick."

"Murdick says he's a snake-eater."

"I've seen some of Murdick's snake-eaters," Sluter said.

"Listen, this is the guy who was with him in O-Zone when Murdick wasted those aliens."

It seemed to Hooper just as well that Murdick had told them the lie, because he did not trust himself at this moment to sound convincing on Murdick's behalf.

"He saw Murdick burn them all down!"

Sluter did not hear any of this—chose not to hear it. He had walked over to a porthole and cranked it open.

"Those artillery shells are still sitting out there," he said.

Meesle didn't react. Hooper now admired the way Meesle could be both friendly and stubborn.

"Well, it so happens that we're planning to watch a video. You're welcome to join us, Skipper. We'd love to have you. And after that we can worry about the artillery shells."

He placed his hands on his belly and spread his fingers to contain it in a good grip. He seemed very contented that way, holding himself like a man dangling in deep water with a flotation device.

But Sluter was gone. He had the sulky person's way of suddenly disappearing—eclipsed by his own shadow and muttering as it happened, the mutters becoming part of the incoherent background, like another eclipse, the sound equivalent of shadow. There was something about his bad temper that made him seem insubstantial: he easily vanished.

Meesle did not mind. He looked happy in the fishbowl front of his black helmet. He pressed a switch on the video machine and lit the screen. He said, "Are we nice and comfortable?"

"Let's get this over with," Hooper said, rotating his chair toward the screen.

The word "INTRUDER" solidified on the screen, and then melted into the shape of an actual man entering a darkened house through a window. Finding his way with a flashlight, he opened a desk and removed a small tray of rings, and then rifled some drawers for papers, and moved quickly through a room, snatching small pretty figures of glass and silver from shelves and pocketing them.

Then the lights went on: the burglar looked up and saw that he had been surprised by the home-owner, who was smiling and holding a gun on him. He threw the burglar a pair of handcuffs and ordered him to put them on, and then brought him into the cellar of this luxurious house. The burglar had a tough, vicious face which, in close-up, had the fixed expression and mute darting eyes of an animal. But then the face reacted, fear slid across it, and the camera drew back to show that the interrupted burglar had been brought to a torture chamber—whips, straps, chains, prods, a bondage chair, and more.

"That's enough," Hooper said, and turned away.

"It just started!"

"I'm not interested in pornography."

"He doesn't kill him. He just tortures him."

"That's what I mean."

"The burglar asked for it! He was robbing the guy's house." Meesle looked hurt. "Afterward, the guy goes to the burglar's house and burns it down. This isn't porno. This is about justice."

"Forget it."

"Hold it," Meesle said. "I've got another one."

This one, called *Alienation,* could not have been simpler, and yet Hooper's bafflement kept him from protesting.

A young man appeared on the screen. His handsome face and strong upper body were shown—he was barechested. Behind his head the sun was breaking through a cloud. The young man was not smiling, but neither did he look solemn. He was serious and self-possessed. He said, "I am an American," and stared.

"I am an American," said the next person, a woman— head and shoulders, her fresh face shining. She had white even teeth, full lips, soft hair, and if it were not for her eyes she might have been taken for the sister of the young man just shown—there was certainly a family resemblance. But this woman's eyes were the hard gray-blue of knife metal and had the same warning glint.

An older man, just as healthy and dignified, followed the woman. His hair was pure white, and his face lined, but his voice was steady, with a hint of defiance in it.

"I am an American."

Hooper wanted to laugh, it was so naive. And Meesle perhaps sensed his restlessness, because he said, "Wait, you're going to love this."

Another face appeared. It was an abrupt shift, the face bumping into view. This man was swarthy and had rumpled hair—a piece of string in the hair—and a torn shirt. When he opened his lips to speak there was a great square gap, and his whitened tongue twitching in this toothless hole.

"I ain Nerican," he said, moving his furtive eyes sideways, like a thief.

"I in Mokin," the next one said. His face was black and swollen, pustules on his forehead, his hair a mop of little medallions of filth. He was almost certainly a city Skell.

"I aim Mocking!" an old woman shrieked. She had a ruined face and was balding. White scars showed like chalkmarks on her scalp.

"Arm Marrycan," muttered a grizzled man with wild eyes. He had the dirty outdoor look of a Troll, and greasy cheeks, and plugs of snot in his nostrils.

Hooper was startled by the ugly faces, and there was something objectionable—harsh and mocking—in their voices, each creature saying in broken English that he was an American.

"Argh Maakin!" This man's pulpy nose was split open, and his eyes were bloodshot.

"Me!" cried another sweaty head. "Me Marican!"

"Meiguoren!" a Chinese man howled, showing tooth stumps, and then his head was displaced by another howler, a gleaming monkey-face with slobbery lips and pendulous ear-lobes. "Mollikan!"

The faces were hideous, animal, lunatic, foreign—alien. They grunted. They were scarcely human, and they were not speaking English; but that did not matter, because Hooper knew they were illegals and that in their shouts and barks they were claiming to be Americans. There were more. Hooper was fascinated by their ugliness. They had wild eyes and broken teeth. They were furious. They looked extremely dangerous.

The faces became fiercer. They were stupid with rage—defiant and demented. One mouth had long canines, the dog-teeth of a baboon. And then they became wholly unintelligible and simply gibbered—but Hooper knew they were saying, "I am an American."

There were gunshots, and these loud blasts made the faces disappear. There was no blood. This happened twenty times, beginning with the last faces: the gibbering ones—*bang!* Dog-teeth—*bang!* "Mollikan"—*bang!*

And, in spite of himself, Hooper felt lighter and breathed better as each figure was blasted away. He relaxed, settling into his chair, waiting for all this to end. He was relieved that it was not porn, not torture, not murder, really; he was not sure what it was. It seemed to him a kind of comedy—the grotesque faces, the absurd ways of saying "I am an American," and the bangs were no worse than custard pies.

In the last sequences, the three healthy people from the beginning reappeared—first their faces, and then "I am an American," and finally a wide shot showing that they were wearing uniforms with the Godseye insignia and carrying blunt black weapons. That was the end.

"Didn't I tell you it was kind of cute?" Meesle seemed pleased in a wistful way. "How about another one?"

Hooper said no, but softly and suppressing a half-smile, because in a small way that video *Alienation* had worked on him. He had found those faces horrible. Insisting they were Americans! What made him somewhat objective was that all the faces annoyed him, even the three Godseye troopers that he was supposed to admire.

And he also said no because it was like pornography—he was disgusted and aroused at the same time. He could not honestly say that he hated the video. But he hated himself for feeling ashamed and fascinated.

He guessed that Meesle saw him weakening. The peak of Meesle's helmet was wagging at him.

Meesle said, "I know you want to watch another one. You're just not sure whether it's good for you."

Hooper did not want to incriminate himself by denying a thing he saw some truth in.

"You like it," Meesle said, leering at Hooper through his mask. "Or else you wouldn't be here."

Exaggeration was better—that was easier to deny. But Hooper had forgotten why he had come—something to do with the other tape, the particle beam, his surprise when the skinny-faced little man in the shiny helmet and new boots had become very nervous and confidential and said, "I'm in Godseye." Murdick, of all people!

"Just curious," Hooper said, and thought: No wonder I'm disgusted.

Meesle was still good-natured, still trying to entertain him.

"Some of you first-time guys are great," he said. "Sluter thinks you're all security risks and you're all going to give us clams. But I'm for opening up more and getting fresh blood. A lot of what we do is just routine. Even the Snake-Eaters sometimes forget about the real objectives. We need new people." He peered at Hooper from the gleaming faceplate. "Really angry people."

Yet Hooper was surprised by Meesle's cheery tone. It had always been Hooper's impression that men in squads like Godseye were very angry. In other respects they were totally anonymous and secretive. Upside-down, over forbidden O-Zone, the terrified Murdick had revealed his secret.

"We had a guy on board a couple of months ago. He was a first-timer."

Meesle smiled and savored the moment. He was full of the story he was about to tell.

"Sluter wanted to kick him off the ship. 'He's a clam. He's a dick.' That kind of thing. But I insisted we give him a chance. He didn't say a word the whole time. He was an older man—mid-sixties or so."

Spreading his fingers on the ground-screen, Meesle said, "Pretty soon we had a Skell cornered down at the Battery. He'd run behind a building and had sort of squeezed himself into a doorway. Some of those monkeys can get into cracks. We couldn't use gas on him because of the location. I was for popping his eardrums—blasting his head open with some noise. Hum some stunners at him. But before I could load them, this old guy—who we've never seen before, meek as a lamb—he says, 'Put me on the ground.'

"'Put him on the ground,' Sluter says, only too happy for him to draw the Skell out, so we can burn him down.

"But no. This first-timer rushes forward and tears the Skell out of the doorway with his hands. It's not a Skell—it's a Roach. He doesn't know the difference! He begins bashing him on the head with an iron pipe. There's blood everywhere—the Roach's head is smashed into a bag. Hey, this was getting strange! We had to pull him off. It wasn't that he killed the guy, which he did, by the way—no, it's all that anger coming out. I hadn't seen blood for years. With these new weapons you never get that kind of open wound. I never expected a Roach to have that much blood. The wet mess! The raw meat! I had forgotten that you could kill someone with an old iron pipe. But he had more than an iron pipe."

Meesle had stopped tracing out the murder on the ground-screen with his fingertips.

"That's why we need you guys," he said, raising his eyes to Hooper. "We need your anger."

Hooper said, "I wonder what happened to make that man so angry."

"I asked him. Screaming Skells. Years ago, he was trapped by some in New Jersey—Screamers. They cornered him and just howled at him. Then they took his car. You never forget a thing like that. The thing about aliens—"

But Meesle stopped in the middle of the sentence: the outside hatchway had opened, the rubber seal making a plump satisfying punch as it shut a moment later.

It was Murdick, feetfirst, his new boots and short legs and fat knees descending the ladder into the body of the aircraft. Then his bubble-head showed—another helmet! This one was blue-black, with antenna plugs, a chin mike, and a faceplate that looked to be an inch thick—perhaps a combat model. It made Murdick's white face seem trapped in a fish-eye monitor.

"The thing about aliens," Murdick said, finishing Meesle's sentence and pinching his face at Hooper, "is that they're responsible for everything in this city that's inconvenient. Forget their crimes, forget that they're illegal. I was just stopped three times on my way here—that's why I'm late. Two checkpoints and one Federal patrol. What am I doing out at three o'clock in the morning? Where am I going? I'm an Owner! Sure, they were apologetic after they saw my ID, but do you think we'd have to put up with this if there were no aliens?"

In addition to the helmet, which Hooper now saw was onion-shaped, Murdick was wearing a green padded jacket and gauntletlike gloves and yellow knee boots. He was obviously bullet-proof and completely wired, and though he was only two meters away from Hooper he had spoken over his phones, probably unaware that the phones made him sound like a cricket.

"The fact that there are aliens around means that we're under suspicion," Murdick said. "Owners!"

When he said "Owners" he lifted his arms and Hooper saw that in his right hand he held a weapon. It was riflelike, but obviously very light—Murdick easily swung it in one hand. It had a short barrel but was not bored, and its shape was that of a slender lamp rather than a gun. Yet more of Murdick's paraphernalia, another fancy weapon.

"It's not fair," Meesle said. "We're not fanatics. We've got a right to be out anytime of the day—anywhere we like. We shouldn't have to carry IDs. This would be a freer society without them."

Hooper had heard the issue of aliens discussed many times before—there were few other issues that roused such passion. But he was struck by Meesle's tone: it was reasonable and just a touch annoyed. There was nothing obviously brutish about it; and even Murdick's argument seemed to have merit. It was true that the aliens and illegals were the reason for the endless barriers and security checks.

"In a way, it's not their fault," Meesle went on, smiling softly and adjusting his helmet. He shook the helmet and something inside rattled; it was such a beautifully made helmet Hooper imagined that the odd rattling sound came from inside Meesle's own head. "They're foreign. They don't understand our society. They don't know American rules. A lot of people will tell you, 'They're animals.' But they're not animals. Unfortunately. Their big problem is that they're human. Their curse is that they somewhat resemble us. And because they can never fit in, they'll always be predatory. They can only do harm, to us and themselves.''

There was patience in Meesle's voice, and a mildness that Hooper found maddening.

Then Murdick said in a quietly amused way, "Some of them don't even wear clothes."

And seeing nothing on Hooper's face—no anger, no agreement, no objection, because he was suppressing everything— he turned to Meesle and said, "He doesn't believe me!"

Hooper said, much too loudly—it all came out at once—"I saw a naked woman two weeks ago at the Midtown Mall!"

"An Owner," Murdick said.

"She was naked!"

"A naked Owner has clothes at home," Meesle said. "A naked alien doesn't have any at all—not a stitch. That's why they get burned."

"Right," Hooper said, still fuming. "And that's just the way they talk about you. Godseye is a secret organization that burns people for throwing paper in the street."

Murdick said, "He called them people."

But Meesle didn't quibble.

"We sometimes do," Meesle said. "We have to. Your paper-thrower is your rapist."

"And vice versa," Murdick said, his voice chirping out of his helmet. "The same ones commit all the crime."

Meesle sighed and seemed to relax, and he gazed at Hooper in a comfortable upturned way through the faceplate of his mask.

"That's a very important point to remember, Mr. Allbright," he said. "At the simplest level it is throwing paper in the street. At the highest level it is killing or raping, or stealing something valuable. But you see we are dealing with the same offender. Your alien is not a person with clean habits. Your rapist or your thief is also someone who will throw paper, just as your murderer or your mugger is also someone who will commit petty crimes—spitting, shouting, defacing property."

"So if you arrest people for spitting, and maybe kill them, you've solved the problem?"

"You don't have to take my word for it, Mr. Allbright,"

Meesle said, seeming to agree with him. "There have been scientific studies, carried out by teams of experts. We have documentation. In some places, your spitters were actually apprehended and burned—and your crime rate went down. Or your noisemakers were apprehended and burned—and your crime rate went down."

"The crime rate should have gone up," Hooper said, "because isn't burning people a crime?"

Meesle looked pained at Hooper's ignorance. "But we don't always burn them," he said. "And we never call them people."

Murdick went *cheep-cheep* on his phones, trying to protest and put Hooper straight. "Polygamists, professional beggars, stowaways, lepers," he was saying. But Meesle interrupted softly.

"We pick Skelly up and we put Skelly down."

Hooper said, "Aren't you curious to know why aliens commit these crimes?"

"Skelly doesn't actually have a choice in the matter," Meesle said, raising a debating finger at Hooper. "A cat that kills a bird is merely following his nature. You either accept a cat's nature as a bird killer, or else you eliminate all cats. That's why we're against putting Skelly on trial. He won't have any defense—it's not fair to him. Skelly is acting instinctively. He can't help himself. It's his nature. See, Skelly is not really committing a crime— Skelly *is* a crime. A walking, breathing, living crime. And of course we're also talking about your career criminal, who sees himself as doing a job. We want to put him out of work."

After saying this—still in his friendly reasonable tone—Meesle went to the microphone at the console and tapped it and said, "Load the shells, Cleary." Then he returned to where Hooper still stood, trying to find logic in the cat analogy.

Hooper said, "You didn't answer my question."

"Mr. Allbright," Meesle said, "an alien, or a cat, or anyone, commits a crime for one reason only—because he thinks he can get away with it."

Meesle and Murdick smiled in pity at Hooper, the simple soul who had to be told that.

"And most of them are feebs," Murdick said. He then chirped at Meesle, "Who's on board?"

"Sluter's forward," Meesle said. "Flatty ought to be here any minute. We're going hot at oh-four-hundred."

Murdick said, "Flatty's the navigator. He's a damned sight

better than your nephew, wonder boy. Flatty knows all the best locations. He's found us some great specimens."

There were four sudden thumps. The gunship pitched each time. Hooper looked around in alarm.

"That's just Cleary, loading shells."

The man named Flatty arrived soon after. He explained that he too had been detained at several checkpoints, and like Murdick he was not angry with the guards, but rather with the aliens who made the checkpoints necessary. He was somewhat undersized even by what Hooper had taken to be Godseye standards, and in his heavy uniform—big helmet, big boots—he had a funny little strut, like a self-important cripple, as he made his way through the gunship. He was fluent and easygoing and good-humored in ways that reminded Hooper of liars he had known.

"Hooper Allbright," Flatty said. "Any relation to Allbright, that billionaire with the cable catalog?"

"I was going to ask him that," Meesle said.

"I used to be him," Hooper said.

"Very funny," Flatty said. "But that's good, because everyone's treated equal here."

"Flatty's pretty famous, too—for some roundups he made in Florida a few years ago."

"When you lose sovereignty over your borders, you're finished," the little man said. "That's why the world's jiggered. We can't let that happen in America."

The trouble with these particular fanatics was that one or two of the things they said made sense, and it was their rare flashes of rational thought rather than their usual craziness that worried Hooper. He was facing little Flatty, thinking of what Murdick had said about roundups.

"I remember those raids," Hooper said. "You loaded transport planes with people—with aliens—and dumped them in Africa."

"Or on the way," Flatty said.

"There's nothing on the way."

"The Atlantic."

"You dropped them in the ocean?"

"Very gently."

"I never thought of that."

But now that he had been told, he saw them spilling out of planes, tumbling through the air into the open sea and sinking.

Flatty said, "It's better than dumping them in Prohibited Areas. That's what some units used to do, years ago."

"You mean, tossing aliens into places like O-Zone?"

"Sure. So they could catch cold," Flatty said. "But you know all about that, don't you? You and Willis burned a couple, didn't you?"

"Murdick did," Hooper said.

And Murdick, who had been irritable from the moment he boarded, smiled and looked very pleased.

"What's O-Zone really like?" Meesle asked in the tones of someone speaking of a fabled land.

"Incredible," Murdick said. "Dangerous. Full of ghost towns and contamination. Oh, sure, we're talking high-level mutagens. You're looking at an animal population that's maybe fifty percent droolies and limpers, and a high proportion of outright deformos. I'm not counting extra toes and cleft palates. I'm talking heavy mutation, I'm talking monsters."

Meesle and Flatty had turned from Murdick to stare at Hooper in scrutiny, because only he could verify what Murdick was saying. O-Zone was well-known as a wilderness, but was this true?

"O-Zone is an island," Hooper said. He was going to say more, but checked himself: that seemed to explain everything.

Sluter's voice came over the intercom. It was sharp, snappy and commanding—all business.

"This mission is code-named 'Streetsweeper.' Strap yourselves in for takeoff. And mask the passenger until we clear the tower. We're going hot in zero minus sixty."

The others began counting, chanting the numbers.

Murdick blindfolded Hooper with what looked like a hangman's hood, and as the gunship surged and tipped, his voice chirped at Hooper's ear.

"We're cooking ass," he said.

13

So far, this Godseye unit had made Hooper feel like an outsider himself—him an alien! The troopers' crass antagonizing opinions made him defensive, and he was fearful of making hostile jokes, afraid they would turn on him and say, "You too!" He hated their seriousness, he was insulted by their bad logic.

Murder is always easy, murder is for bunglers, Hooper murmured in the darkness behind his blindfold. When he put it into words it sounded true. These murderers did not want him to know the location of their rotor pad. As if it mattered. And all the rest of it, the talk about anger and aliens, the videotapes, the whispers, the insignia, the expensive weapons, the jargon, the silences, the silly helmets—it all reminded Hooper that he had no business there. It was not just that Godseye hunted aliens; it was rather that Godseye was suspicious of anyone who was not in Godseye. These so-called troopers were suspicious of him!

"Murdick, where the hell are you?"

"Up front here," Murdick said; and nervously, "We'll take your blindfold off as soon as we clear these buildings."

The man was uneasy now with the secret of his incompetence in O-Zone. It was hard enough for him to conceal his cowardice, but so much harder to pretend to be brave. He badly needed Hooper.

Hooper said, "I'm an Owner!"

This rattled Murdick, who had no idea why Hooper was protesting. If they know so little about me, Hooper thought, what can they possibly know about aliens?

"We're going to work a few areas in Lower East," Flatty said.

The croaky voice helped Hooper remember what the little man had said about dumping aliens into the ocean: *It's better than dumping them in Prohibited Areas. That's what some units used to do, years ago.*

They had populated O-Zone! A self-important unit of Godseye troopers had abducted some pathetic aliens. Instead of killing them quickly, they threw them into O-Zone and wished on them a slow death—cancer and skin diseases and softened bones from the contamination, the whole colony turned into a colony of lepers and zombies. Godseye, with its loathing for litterers, tossed aliens into America's only real wilderness.

This revelation had two effects on Hooper. It made him loathe Godseye—the Snake-Eaters, as this unit was called; he hated their ignorance and their presumption as much as he feared their casual murders and their hypocrisy. But it also intensified his feelings for those others—the victims, the aliens he had seen in O-Zone. Somehow, these people had survived. And they had looked healthy enough, racing through the woods.

Every time the Snake-Eaters had used the word "alien," he had a flash of that running girl he had isolated on the tape. And when Meesle had said, "We don't call them people," he had seen her very clearly—pale eyes and straight sun-drenched hair and brown legs—hopping over a log, her dancer's way of jumping and pausing. Women were to him first physical and animal: she was that, fleeing, and it excited Hooper to see her running away.

Hooper's blindfold was taken off, and two different face-plates gloated at him in the gunship—Meesle and Murdick in new helmets, a skull and a demon face. Murdick was the demon, because he was talking to Hooper breathlessly about his new weapon—a stunner—and his chirping was the giveaway. It was the tiny voice of a violent sparrow.

But skull and demon faces? They were probably intended to scare aliens, yet they were like Halloween masks—over-sized and ridiculous. And their voices were eager and definitely birdlike and boyish.

"You can usually get some real good action there," Meesle said as the gunship nosed slantwise down among the towers on the lower east side. It was at the margin of the city's skylights, where they splashed on the river.

With their gloves on the ground-screen, the masked men twitched and looked alert—the Skull and the Demon, pot-belly and sparrow-chirp; party masks and real weapons. Sometimes Hooper had thought how his Allbright Cable Sales catalog accurately represented America, everything in it, and that in the future this civilization could be understood from that catalog alone. He had believed it to be real and truthful, and to contain everything that mattered. Now he knew he was wrong, for there was no hint in it of these men or their equipment. Their suits did not look like suits, nor their weapons like weapons.

What am I doing here? Hooper wondered. There was darkness in the sky ahead. He thought: She's lost. And then, remembering how far away he was from her: I'm lost.

He simply wanted that girl. He was proud of his desire, but he was also afraid she might vanish. He was impatient now to go back to her. In this gunship of hunter-troopers he felt like a betrayer. It was not only guilt that worried him, but also a prickly sense that this hunting mission was unlucky and maybe risky. He knew that desire made him solitary and singleminded, but he had never been able to explain his impulses to anyone.

The lighted grid on the ground-screen showed them to be hovering just above Lower East.

"We're going to drop down and get some lights on," Flatty said, speaking from the cockpit.

Sluter groaned over the intercom about visibility, while Flatty gave altitudes—meters from the ground.

"We've had reports of some sightings around here," Flatty said.

Hooper had put on a pair of headphones. "I don't get it," he said. "The city's secure. The bridges are safe. The whole perimeter's sealed. And even the perimeter in Brooklyn is patrolled. All the trouble spots are contained, so how—"

"There's plenty of leaks!" Meesle said.

His old sober voice had changed and become gleeful. The patient pompous man had become jaunty at the prospect of catching aliens within the New York perimeter. *Plenty of leaks*—he sounded delighted.

Murdick said, "Oh, sure, there's got to be lots of them down there," and practice-aimed his elaborate stunner.

"There's too many irresponsible people in this city who encourage aliens to enter illegally, just so they can get some cheap labor. I'd shoot half the manual workers for a start, and I'd deport all those goons on temporary permits."

"You could round them up and dump them into O-Zone," Hooper said.

Murdick chirped at this—already he had forgotten his disgrace; and Meesle cried, "Sure thing!" Even with masks on, Meesle and Murdick were visibly happy. The masks made their pleasure look frivolous and silly. The men were bright-eyed, actively impatient, working their fingers on the ground-screen as they busily watched for a victim.

"Is that one?"

"No, it's a city cop on patrol. See his shield? It shows up on ultra-v. And there's his partner. The trouble is, they have to make arrests and do a lot of paperwork."

"What about you?" Hooper said.

"Generally speaking, we stick to the areas where shoot-on-sight rules apply."

"That's why we stay off the ground," Murdick said.

"I'll bet there's a Roach around the corner of that building," Meesle said. "We're on low power. This bird is quiet. A Roach around the corner couldn't hear us. We'll just swoop and take his head off as he's whistling—"

Meesle sounded very pleased as he scrutinized the ground-screen. He spoke hungrily and in a mocking way.

"We can see in the dark, you know."

"We'd probably catch more of them if we could smell in the dark," Flatty said from the cockpit. He was eavesdropping on this conversation.

"Skelly likes alleys and doorways. You never find Skelly on a wide road. Skelly loves tight places. Give him a crack and he's happy."

That other talk, all the theory about crime and career criminals and scientific studies and "We have documentation"—that was just guff. These facts were plainer. Meesle and Murdick were having the time of their lives, and they were very proud of their expensive weapons. The grouch, Sluter, actually adored flying the gunship and declaring, "Burn his car and kill his dog." Little Flatty's fun lay in navigating them into corners and seizing aliens and then flinging them out of cargo planes into the sea. This was a picnic for them.

Hooper imagined that all this was so. And then he had

proof of it. In the narrow streets of Lower East a speck on the ground-screen was enlarged, and proved to be alive. It was warm-blooded, it moved; but it was very small.

"Make sure it's not a dog," Meesle said, and explained why to Hooper. "We made hamburger out of a guard dog the other week. We pinned him down and were ready to fire when we saw it was a mutt. 'Burn him anyway,' Murdick says—he's all excited, see. But it was a patrol dog, beautiful thing, got loose somehow, poor bastard. Murdick didn't care! If Sluter hadn't hoisted us out of there it would have cost us a few bucks. Hey, there was dogmeat everywhere."

"I had a spasm!" Murdick said, thrilled at the reminder of *Burn him anyway*. "I just wanted to wail away with my bazooka."

He moved his demon face near Hooper's.

"Fléchettes," he said. "I hit him with two cluster bursts of exploding fléchettes."

Hooper saw a flight of arrows, Murdick blasting the hound to shreds from the safety of the hovering gunship.

"It breaks my heart to see a good dog burn," Meesle said.

"He didn't have a leash," Murdick protested. "The shoot-on-sight rule applies."

"Watch the screen," Sluter said—there was a sob of enthusiasm in his voice. "See if that Skell has a leash."

Because the speck was not a dog. It was a human male in heavy clothes, and as soon as the gunship's lights were turned on him he began to run.

Then Hooper experienced something he had only seen secondhand on videos or on very big and very teasing projection screens—the wraparounds that could be so vivid.

He held on tightly as the Godseye gunship tumbled sideways toward the street. It pulled up sharply and went after the running man. Hooper had been in many different aircraft, but never in one that could make such sharp turns as it gave chase; never so close to the ground or so near the sides of towers; and never in this part of New York at this hour. Now they were upside-down, and now flying backwards.

Hooper was secured by a body clamp, but still he felt the sharp jolts of the gunship as it changed direction. The others called out—the man on the ground was darting in and out of doorways; then into an alley. Sluter could have waited at the entrance—it was blind, there was no other way out—but instead he raced in and somersaulted against the blind wall, drenching the man in bright light and driving him out.

"Drop something on him!"

"See who it is first—zoom him."

"It's a Troll. He's ugly, he's got scabs. He looks black. Burn him."

"Stun him," Murdick said, holding his new weapon to a valve in the side of the gunship and aiming out. "Stiff him, save him. I can turn him into rubber. We can make an example of him."

Hooper said, "Take it easy, Willis."

"The mere fact that he's running gives us the right to burn him," Murdick said through his chirping amplifier.

They were trying but failing to pin him down; there were too many streets, and too narrow and enclosed.

But Meesle said, "This is the part I like best." He pressed his skull mask to the porthole. "Chasing them." His eyes were fixed on the running man, and there was a gentleness in them—a calm satisfaction and a certainty. "Watching them get tired." He seemed to be smiling within the skull. "Running them down."

"He's shooting at us," Murdick said. "The asshole's got a handgun. Bang-bang. He's going to tip over."

"I've got a profile on him," Flatty said. "We just scanned him. He's using an ordinary automatic, he's wearing a metal detector and a radio. We just monitored him calling his headquarters."

"What headquarters?" Murdick said.

"He's a security guard. He's legal."

"Aw shit," Murdick said, with feeling.

"Leave the bugger alone," Meesle said.

They were still tracking the man, but no longer so recklessly.

Hooper detected in their sympathy a certain kinship with security guards. He felt otherwise. When he realized that the man was a guard and not an alien, he hoped they would go on chasing him—not shoot but disable the man somehow and give him a taste of his own terror. Security guards were never Owners, and they seemed to take acute pleasure in giving Owners a hard time at checkpoints. Owners were absurdly tolerant with them and often even grateful, as if these big slow fools made the whole world safe.

"Don't burn him if he's a guard," Meesle said.

"Why not burn him for being a guard?" Hooper said.

"That would be a clam," Meesle said, and turned his skull face to the ground-screen.

Hooper had heard the word before. "What's a clam?"

"A mistake," Murdick said. "One you can't correct. Like someone you can't bring back from the dead."

But the incident had shown Hooper an important aspect of the hunt: a person chased by a gunship—no matter who—behaved like an alien: panicked, ran, shot back if he had a weapon, and tried to hide. And really, from this height, in a racing gunship, everyone below looked puny and furtive, like an alien.

There was more movement on the ground-screen—another man. Using lights and howlers, the Godseye troopers quickly pinned him down. He crouched against a tower, and though his face was averted and his hands were over his ears, they knew they could hold him there as long as they wished, blinded and deafened, until they scanned him.

"I hate the ones that don't run," Meesle said. "He's got no fight in him. He's a stiff."

"If he makes a break for it, let's stun him," Murdick said, poking his weapon into the valve and aiming down.

"He's not going to make a break for it," Meesle said. "He's just sitting there, forcing us to do all the work."

Meesle sounded disgusted with the cowering man.

"I hope he's an African or a Hindu or something in Category F," Meesle said. "We won't need clearance. We can fry him in his own fat."

Murdick's unwavering weapon was pointed at the man below.

"They all have diseases."

"He's not carrying any metal," Flatty said, and then cutting down the howler and using a microphone, he demanded that the man produce his ID, so that it could be scanned and validated.

"I'm praying the monkey doesn't have one," Meesle said.

But the man fumbled in his jacket, and wincing at the skull and demon pressed against the portholes of the shuddering gunship, he held up his ID.

Sluter shone a beam on the disc and said, "We're getting a readout. He's local. Works here," and then called over the microphone, "Look up!"

The man turned his naked white face toward the gunship. His eyes were slits and his mouth was puckered in terror. It was as if he were facing a firing squad.

Sluter said, "We are looking at Vernon Morrisett, thirty-nine, a file clerk. He lives in a tower on Thirteenth and B. No offenses."

"I wouldn't live down here," Meesle said. "It's all legal Orientals and approved blacks."

Hooper looked at the frightened face of the crouching man. His clothes were blown by the rotor of the chattering engines. He moved on his hands and knees to keep his balance, and his face was full of the bewildered fear of a man having a nightmare.

"He's never going to be the same again," Murdick said. "The very least he's got is burst eardrums."

"So what? He's not an Owner," Meesle said. "Anyway, he shouldn't be out so late."

They kept talking about the man, and they were so frustrated in not having killed him that after very few minutes they were reproaching themselves for their hesitation and were fully convinced that the man was an outlaw—a Roach or a Skell who had stolen an identity disc.

"Next time we won't be so kind."

Hooper in anticipation pitied anything now that moved on the ground-screen.

There came a shadow, no more than a sliver of darkness, and they gave chase— Murdick poised at the firing valve with his new weapon. But they lost the fleeing thing before they had gone one block.

"Just as well we didn't shoot," Murdick said. But it was insincere consolation—his fury at not shooting was still burning in his voice. "It might have been someone's pet—maybe an expensive attack dog. They don't wake up from these."

"What exactly is that thing, Willis?"

"This is a Wardley Sonic Stunner," Murdick said, chucking the weapon up and sighting with it, and then jerking it in his mitts. "It's made under contract in France. It delivers sonic shock."

Hooper hated the man's silly helmet. The demon face-plate, made of bulletproof high-gloss Velmar, had red flames painted on the eyebrows, and red pointed ears—the concealed phones. And Murdick's monotonous chirp the pitch of a busy signal came out of the grillwork behind the blood-spattered fangs. Murdick was thirty-seven years old!

Still chucking the weapon and gloating, Murdick said, "It directs ultrasonics at the target. It's antipersonnel, so you've got absolutely no peripheral damage. But it has a devastating effect on muscle fibers—makes them go all floppy. You know anything about the principle of sound-chains? It's not on the market yet, on account of some negative data."

"I love those Fizzy phrases," Hooper said.

"It dropped a few animals in some labs," Murdick explained. "Heart attacks. I mean, their hearts just arrested—plop. But see, that's the great thing. When it's calibrated right it just melts the target. I'm talking jelly-effect. No more muscles, and your target's hardly ventilating. It wears off in a day or so, with no aftereffects at all. I know what you're thinking—heart attacks. But they were very small lab animals."

Through his skull teeth, Meesle said, "Murdick and his magic irons. Ever see anyone so well-equipped?"

"You've got to have the right tools for the job," Murdick said. "I just wish," he went on, thrusting the sonic stunner once more through the firing valve, "I just wish we had something to use them on."

Hooper believed they were more dangerous in that frame of mind than in the mood of pretend-outrage he had seen earlier—their reasonable tone on the ground. After three chases there were no trophies, no prisoners; not one shot had been fired. Their impatience was worse than anger, because it gave them a false sense of urgency and made them careless. The gunship seemed to swim amid taunting shadows. The more frustrated Murdick became, the more he hugged his weapon, making adjustments.

"It's important to experiment," Murdick said, knocking his mask against the window.

The gunship still hummed and bumbled between the towers, shaking the passengers and yanking them against their clamps when it changed direction.

Then it climbed steeply, seeming to swallow air.

"Going up," Meesle said in the voice of an elevator operator. "Top floor. Skells, Trolls. Roaches. Outlaws. Pimps—"

He is curing me of being a fool, Hooper thought.

No joke was possible by a man wearing a death's-head

mask. Everything he said in that faceplate made him seem either cruel or foolish.

"We've taken a risk-benefit decision," Sluter said over the intercom. "We're crossing into Brooklyn. There's always action in Redhook. Watch the ground-screen and stay on alert."

Murdick clutched his weapon and put his horror-helmet against the porthole of the banking rotor. Meesle stuck his face against the ground-screen.

"Let me know if you see anything," Murdick said. He was already in a firing posture—excited again.

"Don't you worry."

But they were both fearful too, Hooper thought. This could be dangerous, crossing into a no-go area of Brooklyn at four-thirty on a black winter morning, out of the range of skylights. They had dropped south in the course of their several chases. They now passed over two sealed and lighted bridges. Hooper recognized the Navy Yard in a pool of light, and then the gunship banked and brought them southeast over low dark rooftops. They spotted a figure on the ground, and as the gunship descended the figure moved, began to run.

"That one's definitely from out of town," Meesle said.

There was a kind of silly humor—never funny—that always was a part of violence, and Hooper regarded murderers now as terrible clowns.

"Bring us down," Murdick was saying. "Give me a clear shot and watch him melt." He turned his demon face on Hooper and said gloatingly, "Liquid!"

Meesle said, "Why not chase him a little bit?"

And they did, with teasing hesitation, letting the man get away, and then piling over him and turning on the howlers and driving him into a different direction.

"He looks guilty as heck," Meesle said of the stumbling man.

Hooper was touched by the murderous man using the word "heck."

The man on the ground seemed confused—cornered, panicky; and once again Hooper was reminded of how anyone chased by a gunship like this looked and behaved like an alien.

"Easy," Murdick said, taking aim.

"The way I look at it, that clam's dead already," Meesle said, and sounded disgusted. He was addressing Hooper, who had stayed in his safety clamp because of the gunship's jolting. "The ideal thing is to find a hot one. Home in on a crime. A swarm, say, or a mugging, or someone jogging home with loot in his hand. Then we go howling in and scorch him."

Hooper noticed for the first time that certain details on Meesle's skull mask were luminescent. These features glowed at him from above the ground-screen. This childishness made Meesle seem more dangerous.

"Sometimes we drop someone down as bait or a decoy. Some Roach we've had in the jug. Or one of those moldy guys they call worms, that turn up in the subway." Now the man's real eyes looked as hideous as the painted features on the mask, and they widened in the greeny glow of the sockets. "As soon as they wet their teeth on him, we scorch. That can be beautiful. With a woman or a couple of kids as bait it's"—and he paused, savoring the pleasure of it—"hey, you can make movies!"

"Watch," Murdick said.

"But winter in Brooklyn," Meesle said. "Perimeter Redhook. It's too cold. They don't run. It's just scabs like him—"

The man was cornered, averting his eyes from the lights.

"Listen to how quiet this beast is," Murdick said.

He was speaking of his weapon. There was no sound. There was no light. There was only the tock of the start button. The man simply collapsed on the ground and remained there, flopped over his twisted legs.

"Now he's pliable," Murdick said. "Now he's open to suggestions."

"And now you can pick him up and drop him in O-Zone," Hooper said, "so he can get nosebleeds and raise a family of Roaches."

"We don't do things like that," Meesle said. "We just run them out of here."

"Ever think maybe they belong here?" Hooper said, throwing his body clamp off and facing Meesle.

But all Meesle said was, "I never think that," and to Murdick, "Your friend's getting excited."

"It's crime prevention, Hooper."

Flatty's voice came from the wall: "We just did a scan on

him. He's not carrying anything. What shall we do with him?"

"I don't want that garbage on board," Sluter said.

The gunship hovered in the uprush of steadying air.

"Burn him down," Meesle said.

"Don't!" Hooper said.

But Murdick had already fired. The crumpled man moved under a dart of light from another of Murdick's weapons; and then the corpse shimmered and seemed to rise, and went black. It was then only a smear of gray ashes.

"I used a fléchette," Murdick said.

"I took his picture," Meesle said. "He was smiling."

The gunship had risen, they were spinning. Hooper moved away from the two men for relief, and he watched at the porthole, wishing he were elsewhere. Across the river, New York was bright and tall, lovely under its skylights, a narrow island of turrets and towers. There were glistening pinpoints of frost in the winter air, and the flashing blips of other rotors moving among the buildings. Here the streets were dark; only in the distance were there stripes of light—the corridors and access routes through ruined and unsecured areas. They were passing over these ruins now, staying low and keeping silent on reduced power, moving like a heavy insect toward Greenpoint.

At the ground-screen, Meesle said, "I've got a clear image of something upright."

"A woman," Murdick said, studying the image. He was excited. "Don't let her see us. She's just walking."

Hooper sensed the gunship lift and pause, but the figure on the ground-screen kept moving, still tracking slowly—a gray shadow crowded by darkness. What was she doing at this hour on a Brooklyn back street?

"It's like I said—ideal." Meesle was peering at the screen. "She's like bait. She's certain to attract an outlaw. She's probably a scab herself."

Hooper said, "From this altitude, doesn't everyone look like a scab?"

"That sounds hostile," Meesle said, and then he murmured, "Stay high and get a clear image of her."

They did so, and the shadow on the screen was replaced by a red point of light.

"Here comes Skelly. What did I tell you?"

Another pinprick on the screen moved toward the first one.

Murdick said, "Shuffle, shuffle."

Meesle said, "Let it happen."

The two glowing points of light came together and made one red bud.

"We're dropping," Sluter called from the cockpit.

But before he had finished speaking they had dropped the whole distance, an accelerated fall that was checked just above the couple on the street. Murdick was at the firing valve, fussing with the lighted numbers on his sonic stunner, bumping his gloves and saying, "Aw, rats."

"I think it's a rape—she's fighting back."

"Throw something at him!"

Murdick raised his weapon and took aim. This time there was a sound that accompanied that of the start button—of liquid sluiced down a plughole, the suck of rapid water and air—and both figures dropped flat.

"You got the two of them, T-Bone."

"It wasn't me!" Murdick said, and smacked his weapon in disgust. "It's a design fault." He looked again at the victims. "They were too close together."

The bodies lay on the ground, arms and legs all the wrong way, and their hands looking very small and helpless. The gunship's spotlight was so strong it took the color from them.

"Someone's got to go down there," Sluter announced. "They might be carrying IDs."

He was brisk, he was at the controls, he would not have to go down himself.

They feared the ground—especially here, especially at this time of night, in winter-dark Brooklyn. But the ground, anywhere, always held the prospect of danger. Hooper believed that it was partly superstition, because they lived in high towers and usually traveled in rotors. Now no one spoke up. There was no movement in the gunship. Rushing air in the stabilizers was the only sound—that, and the gulp of the rotors. Even the expressions on the horror-helmets seemed peculiarly blank—the dumb things gaping at Hooper. There was silence from the loudspeaker, too, so Sluter and Flatty were holding their breath.

The bodies were wrapped in ragged clothes, and under the bright light of the gunship they lay like a burst bag.

Hooper said, "I'll go."

"On the ground," Murdick said, as if thinking out loud at the audacity of it.

"I've been there before."

They set him down gladly, and encouraged him, saying they would burn anyone who came near him. They sounded violent: they probably meant it. Their dread of being exposed on the ground had made them murderous. "Snake-Eaters" said it all. It made Hooper feel superior to them—braver, smarter, more sensible; and he was pleased because they must have known this, and there was nothing they could do except take the same risk themselves. They didn't dare. Snake-Eaters!

He took his time looking over the figures. In spite of the thickness of the rags they were poorly clothed for the weather. Had this been an attempted rape? It was impossible to say. It was an abduction, there was no doubt of that—the commonest crime these days: stealing people, for any one of a thousand reasons. Hooper dug the woman's face out and uncovered it. She was ruined-looking but young, possibly an addict. She was no Skell. He found proof— an identity disc.

The man was frowning and very pale, with the sudden cutdown look of a dead animal, wearing a surprised expression of useless effort in his frown. His eyes were open and empty.

The young woman had suffered pain, the lower edge of her face was twisted aside, and Hooper saw that it was this agony that made her seem old. From her date of birth on her ID Hooper calculated that she had just turned sixteen.

"They're both dead," Hooper said into his mike.

"Get aboard," Sluter said, "or we'll leave without you."

But Hooper still took his time, mocking them by being slow, reproaching them with their own cowardice. They were afraid of the ground!

"He thinks he's a meat inspector," Meesle said.

Smiling up at the spotlight, Hooper palmed the ID; and then he signaled for them to open the hatch.

"She must have had a bad heart," Murdick said. His voice was screechy and defensive. "I blasted the guy, but some of the shocks must have brushed her as I swept it sideways. It's supposed to have a narrow focus."

"Two more clams," Meesle said. "Which reminds me. What about their IDs, Mr. Allbright?"

"No IDs," Hooper said.

"Then they're not clams," Murdick said. "They're Roaches. See? It didn't matter!"

But he was pacing the belly of the gunship, looking for a place to stow his weapon.

"It's got to be a design fault," he said. He seemed disgusted with the weapon, and held it lightly, as though he wanted to get rid of it. "Or maybe I had it turned too high. You should see the circuitry."

"Give me that thing," Hooper said, and snatched it.

"This mission is complete," Sluter was saying over the intercom—and the gunship was rising again. "We are proceeding back to base, to go cold. Blindfold and secure the passenger."

14

THE SLEEP CHAMBER IN HOOPER'S UNIT IN COLDHARBOR was dark and soundproof. He gave himself a "kind" injection and stayed in his sleep capsule for the next twenty hours, kept all his windows blacked, re-routed his messages—Allbright business. In spite of the injection, an equalizer, he dreamed badly of the Godseye hunt. The drug perhaps worsened the effects, by making his terror into clownishness. He had always been frightened of clowns, and dolls, and most masks. Now he saw terrible masks. He heard wounded notes played on a stringed instrument. The last stage of the dream was all struggle—thick gloves, and slow legs, and clumsy shoes. When the four clowns glared at his guilt—they knew what he was thinking—he tried to laugh. It made an awful sound. Even he hated it, and at last he woke himself with this hideous laughter.

Awake, he could endure that fear, but the experience of it aroused his pity for Fizzy. In his garden, a glassed-in room tall enough for a grove of full-grown bamboos and wide enough for a lily pond and a fountain, Hooper felt stronger. He strolled; he marveled that his fear was gone; but he kept seeing Fizzy's face.

"Poor Fizzy."

The panic Hooper had felt on the mission had given him a taste of what the boy's life was like. Everything was a threat! For example, one day, working at Pap—the name he had given his computer mainframe—a little crust of snot had dropped out of Fizzy's nose. Seeing it fall on a pressure key, Fizzy had squawked at it. He stood up in fright, rising on his tiptoes, shocked and disgusted—and what a sour face! He tried to go on working, but he paused, uttering nauseated groans, and avoided touching that key.

The boy had a well-known horror of dirt, of strangers, of surprises. Anything unexpected was a shock. It was the reason he never went out alone. The memory of Fizzy's fastidiousness made Hooper ashamed of himself—his behavior the other night. Fizzy limped and squawked, yet for all his little-boy rage he was truthful. His superstitions proved that he was innocent. But Hooper himself had no excuse.

Hooper walked through his glassed-in garden, squinting at the hot colors of the flowers, pushing the overhanging palm leaves, feathery shapes that went on swaying after his hand left them. Peeping through the greenery were marble statues—a headless woman, a Chinese lion; and at the far side of the lily pond, a nymph pouring water—his fountain. There were rotors and loud planes motorboating in the gray sky outside, but it was always quiet in the humid heat of this garden. It had always consoled him in the past; but now he saw that his isolation had made him naive.

He had been naive about Godseye, and realizing it shamed him and made him feel lonely. This lonesome feeling also contained a vision of himself as ridiculous and selfish. He had always known that the city was corrupt—and dangerous too, though not in a filthy obvious way like those dark parts of New Jersey and Brooklyn and the no-go zones of America where there were ruins and no skylights and even the police were dangerous. But now he was close to home, on New York's perimeter, and that made his loneliness so much worse. When have I ever been lonely? he wondered. And why now?

He made for his office and his computer terminal. But he did not work. He took out the ID disc of the murdered girl, and held it until it heated his hand. He wanted to rid himself of his sickening and poisonous feeling of criminality, but he could not bear to focus on what he had done and seen.

He wanted to be innocent. He was innocent, in a way. His friends had always assumed that being so wealthy and worldly, he knew all about hunters, all about death squads and vigilantes and weapons, and all the workings of the security net. But he had known nothing. Those troopers were at once so bold and so stupid! Their secrecy irritated him, their arguments were illogical. From one point of view it had seemed boring, pointless, masonic in its foolish rituals and routines. And those horror-masks! But no—it had been a real hunt, committing real murders: he had seen those people fall, and heard the hunters rejoice. "Burn him down!" The masks had been truthful—truer than the men's faces, the skull and the demon. Cowards of their kind made the worst murderers; and Hooper knew that he had been a coward himself.

It was not evil, it could be explained: it was bad and ugly and cruel. What haunted him was the knowledge that they would all get away with it. He deserved that to be turned into a punishing memory, and guiltily wished it upon himself; but he also felt reprieved—a sense of relief in waking up in his own apartment, among familiar things, his unit, his office, his garden. The worst of being with murderers was in afterward noticing his similarity to them.

They were efficient and powerful, they had either money or else connections; they felt they were securing their own city—they were Owners. They had everything they wanted. But power could also represent useless muscle. All this time, ever since he had crawled out of his sleep capsule, he had been opening and closing his hands, grasping air. Then he gave up. His hands were heavy; two thick things lying in his lap as he sat at his terminal.

He ran the video again, scanning it for the girl with bright hair, freezing it when she smiled, freezing it again when energy stiffened her long strides, freezing it and zooming on her face and figure. She was not glamorous; she had the look of a fox; her hair was burned—streaky and short; she had a small head, her feet were large, she had long legs. She was exactly what she seemed: young, pretty, bright-eyed, strong, very fast. She had to be intelligent to have survived there.

"How do you know she's fifteen?" Hooper had asked Fisher.

"I analyzed her bones," the boy had said.

"Her bones!"

"And her teeth."

Her skin was smooth and unmarked. In several shots she was a boy with breasts. She had probably lived her whole life in O-Zone. She had that look. There was a simplicity in her clothes; in her face. Hooper saw this as her strength. She might never have heard of New York, might never have seen another city, apart from the collapsed cities and city-stains of O-Zone.

Still Hooper worked the video, all the time watching for her. He let her expression change in close-up. She was fresh; and was it innocence or bravery that made her seem so fearless? Hooper felt that for her this city would be magic. And he could bear to live here, if she were with him. You could look anywhere in New York and not see a face so fresh—so eager and happy.

She would want everything she saw. Hooper, who had had all he had ever wanted, had forgotten what desire was like until he had seen her face on the video. He had not even noticed her in the flesh.

"DECODE UPDATE" appeared on her face. The urgent message had found him on a classified emergency circuit, from where it had been re-routed. Obviously it was something needing immediate attention.

Hooper tapped in his security code and released the update.

The girl's face still showed on the screen, but just at the level of her eyes and passing over her brushed-back hair there was a message on a ribbon: "HOUSTON ALLBRIGHT SHIPPING FACILITY AND WAREHOUSE RAIDED AND PARTLY DESTROYED BY FIRE EARLY THIS MORNING. SEE DATE AND TIME ABOVE. SUSPECT ORGANIZED GANG ARSON ATTACK. REQUEST OWNER'S PERMISSION TO CARRY OUT SURVEY OF DAMAGE AND LOSS. FURTHER REQUEST URGENT FUNDING FOR POLICE ACTION AS IN SOUTH FLORIDA STRIKE-FORCE MISSION ON BEHALF OF MIAMI ALLBRIGHT."

The message continued, lengthening and reminding him of last year's terror in Florida—the roundup he had financed. He severed the ribbon and keyed in his orders.

"PERMISSION DENIED," he typed on the screen. "FUNDING DENIED. TAKE NO ACTION." He frowned: he was happy.

Once, a worker had written in one of the anonymous criticisms that he encouraged: *The Owner, Hooper Allbright, is conspicuously absent, and in communications he has an abrupt and arrogant manner that does not inspire loyalty.*

He thought of that criticism now. He added to his orders: "THANK YOU ALL FOR YOUR PROMPT ATTENTION," and keyed in his Owner's code. Then entered it and sent it down the wire and concentrated again.

She was running. All exertion was revealing, but hers was

particularly so. It was not only her simple strength he found attractive—he had seen enough athletes; it was her enthusiasm, an energy that hinted at happiness. She was probably fierce, too, and as different from any woman he had known as a wolf from a dog.

She was an alien, always hiding, always hunted, totally temporary, with no education, no rights, no legal existence, no individual identity—no disc. All this made her more attractive still to Hooper. She was like a flower in the forest—so new she had no name yet. And he had found her. She was, finally, wild, and Hooper knew that bringing her out of that Prohibited Area might make her wilder still. The idea excited him. She deserved to live.

All this time, while he watched and froze the video—enlarged the image, looked closely at the girl—he saw lights accumulating on the panel of his console. He had activated his receiver for Allbright messages. What was it? Probably warehouse inventories, weekly reports from the depots, losses and gains. Perhaps another raid. He had come to hate the business.

He left the girl on the screen and, watching her, pressed the print button. Out the stuff came—pages of it from the glowing chattering printer, all of it requiring his attention and comment. He reached into the basket and drew out a report, began sorting through it, then dropped it and switched off the printer. He diverted the remainder of the messages to his committee. But the printer was finishing a report. It was programmed to complete a task before it went cold, and with a mind of its own it chattered and pages kept coming.

Hooper shouted at the thing and clawed the pages out of the basket. He was infuriated by this particular report. The raid in Houston had pleased him, and "TAKE NO ACTION" exactly suited his mood. He had asked for a defeat. But this spat-out report was of year-end profits, Christmas sales, cash input, dividends—ten-digit numbers, like new words, like phrases, figures so large they were like whole sentences.

Infuriated—ripping mad—because an outsider would always say how hard it was to make money like this, how easy to find a friend. The girl still leapt on the video screen. If a man could make that much money in the mail-order business he could certainly persuade that girl to join him.

But, no, it might not be easy at all; he was afraid it might be impossible. He would need the best plane he could get—a gunship like Murdick's that could fly backward and sideways and vertically and scan the ground the whole time. He needed a stock of equipment—not the standard gear from his catalog, but sophisticated weapons, like the stunner he had taken from Murdick (but a stunner that worked properly). He needed navigational devices, like Murdick's; and a bubble-shelter, like Murdick's; he needed help—but he did not need Murdick.

He imagined the tight spot—a strange noise, a shadow, a threat. And Murdick sweating inside his mask and stumbling in new boots. "These are authorized for lunar locomotion!" And perhaps an encounter and unnecessary violence. "I had a spasm!" And perhaps a death. "Aw, rats." Then a hurried flight out and the girl lying wounded or else startled and fleeing. He did not need Murdick at all. It was not that Murdick was wealthy, though that was certainly an important disadvantage—Hooper had begun to see that the rich greatly resembled the aliens, but being more powerful, were a greater threat to everyone. Murdick's special danger was that he was almost certainly impotent, like so many fortyish men whom Hooper knew—like Hardy perhaps; and that limpness, that unwillingness, that lack of response, with his money and his anger, made him a killer.

But Hooper could not navigate, did not have a flight program, and—most crucial of all—did not have an Access Pass. And he knew that even if the miracle happened, giving him solutions to these problems, he was still alone, and if something went wrong in O-Zone he would probably die.

He puzzled and hungered for a week: his desire was a thrilling insufficiency, always leaving him unsatisfied. The New Year's trip to O-Zone had just about wrecked him, and the Godseye mission had done the rest. He had discovered the one thing on earth that he could not have!

Afterward he laughed, because he was thinking just these thoughts—cursing at finding no connections, frustrated that money didn't help, teased and weakened by desire, and sensing that at last he had no control over his life—and he was maddened by his inability to plan a mission to O-Zone. He laughed later and remembered all this pressure, for in the middle of it, perplexed by another imagined difficulty—what if the aliens were armed and attacked his plane?—he heard a call sign.

Heep.

It was like being woken by a disruptive dream: a sudden shock that made him remember the dream—like the killer clowns.

Heep.

Was the printer jammed? Maybe choked on one of those vast reports? Strangled by Allbright input, overheated by the length of the profit sheet?

Heep. Heep.

Machines were either works of art or else dumb animals. They were never human. This was an animal sounding an alarm. But it was not the computer. He had shut it down and diverted the messages in order to concentrate on the girl's face. It was not his telephone: that too was re-routed.

Hee—

Across the room, on the floor, was the helmet-mask he had worn in O-Zone—the one with phones—ridiculous thing with bat ears and a chrome throatpiece. He was being signaled on that frequency. It was a summons, but so unexpected it was like a rapping in a séance.

Hooper put the helmet on, feeling foolish.

"Hooper—"

It was Fizzy, snarling, squawking—would he ever have a normal voice?

"Hardy asked me to go to O-Zone, and you too"—and yawned: it was a long growling in Hooper's ears. "You probably don't want to, right?"

Hardy worked underground, in an enclosed office complex under the Asfalt tower. He had no windows, no glimpse of the sky; the one external monitor showed the security desk at the entrance—people having their passes checked. The secrecy demanded of him in his weather work meant that he seldom knew what the weather was outside, whether it was rainy or sunny or, this month, snowing. He did not mind that. It would only have exasperated him to see unplanned precipitation or unanticipated sun, and he hated weather jokes. People were stupid and complacent about the weather; they behaved like the most primitive aliens and believed themselves to be ridiculous victims, constantly fooled by its changes of mood. They knew practically nothing of the secrets of weather management.

Hardy's own research had always been classified. He had never been tempted to discuss it with anyone. Even if he had

had the intention, where would he begin? Should he start by saying he had once drowned an entire valley of Mexican peasants in a weather effort? But, no, he had gone too far now in his work for it to be easily explainable—its simple beginning was so long ago, and he was past the point of anyone outside Asfalt understanding it. Today was typical. He was preparing a report on the subject "Weather as a Weapon"—proposing a Subdepartment of Storm Creation in the Department of Defense. What did it matter what anyone thought of it? And anyway, Hardy hated discussing anything until he had come to his own conclusions. People gave you ignorant opinions, not informed judgments—they told you how they felt! Fizzy was one of the few people Hardy knew who could take an idea and consider it with intelligence.

Hardy became distracted wondering whether Fizzy had put the plan to Hooper.

Moura had said, "Fizzy's so strange. I hardly know him now. I'm starting to dislike him."

"We should have been more careful," Hardy said. "You should have."

He felt sure he could have managed the birth better. He had seldom had a problem with his work, and that was a similar sort of calculation. He had always been successful himself in managing nature.

He had grown excited about the idea of a thermal mountain in O-Zone. He paced; he reflected; he had done most of the calculations—billions of liters of oil would be used for the black patch. The patch would cover—and seal—the radioactive hot spots in O-Zone, and if it worked, the same process could be used in other Prohibited Areas in the world, making them very valuable. The precipitation in the adjacent space would probably increase tenfold, and rivers and lakes would be created, and the configuration of the landscape changed, like clay molded by a gigantic hand.

He saw the immensity of black asphalt, and the clouds massing over it—chutes of them, darkening and swelling until they became a great Gothic cathedral of vaults and spires made of the storm. And between gaps of silence, the groans of thunder like breaking hammer-beams released shafts of blinding light—fiery cracks in the stirring clouds, and finally a slow hiss growing to a roar of water, as the rain fell hard on the land, slapping it and giving it life.

The vision brought him back to the theory in his report. A

bomb was an isolated convulsion: it was a matter of technique and simple explosives. But to take control of the sky, to manage the insubstantial air—that took genius. To Hardy, there was more beauty in a well-made cloud than in any tower or bridge or city wall; and more use. Those drowned peasants in Mexico: the point was that after that sacrifice there was plenty of water. Those people had not died for nothing. Yet the thought of so many people dying at once in his own flood and mudslide had given Hardy a thrill that shamed him and made him even more secretive, as he dreamed of that black sky over O-Zone or making war with weather.

His report was a sober reasoned thing, but he thought: What a wonderful weapon. What a triumph it would be to drown your enemies, to rain on them and watch them dissolve, to make their country uninhabitable. To parch them and kill them with the slow fire of a drought. To choke them on dust, batter them with hailstones, or bury them in snow. Flood them! Freeze them! Starve them!

And people say to me: What do you really do?—and expect me to give them an answer that will please them.

Storms that could be made to rage day and night for months, beating mountains down in their fury!

That was the substance of his report to Asfalt: Bad Weather. He argued for controlled periods of severe weather as a useful thing. There were disputed areas of Africa and Asia which could be held in check and perhaps settled with storms. He had made videos of the possibilities—mock disasters. The crackle of rain, the whisk of snow; successive spasms of flood, or a prolonged dry spell. No Owner could truly be hurt by bad weather, but for everyone else the lash of weather was splendid and impartial; and the land would always remain.

Here he ended his proposal, but he went on thinking—of storms, and secrecy, and his thermal mountain. His project in O-Zone could prepare the way for other large-scale storm projects. His success would mean a promotion in Asfalt, but that mattered less to him than the fulfillment of his vision of the world: sitting in the windowless concourse under the Asfalt tower and—somewhere in the world—making it rain, making it snow, allowing the sun to shine; making the desert bloom.

He would have promised anything to Fizzy to get him to go

to O-Zone for the raw data. Then he saw that the boy really wanted to go, but was afraid. Hardy knew he had no influence on Fizzy—he was not a father but a foster parent, a silly flunkying figure. He was counting on Hooper's boredom and bullying to carry it off and help the boy make up his mind—Hooper's impulsiveness. And he knew, without knowing why, that Hooper badly wanted to go back to O-Zone.

15

FISHER HAD EXPLAINED WHAT HARDY WANTED, AND Hooper said "Yes" before he asked what it was all about. The boy took this eagerness to be pure stupidity.

He had crossed over from his unit to Hooper's, in an adjoining tower at Coldharbor. "Hard copy," he said, looking at the Allbright profit printout scattered in the room. "I'd suffocate on all that junk. What kind of a fuck-wit is it that doesn't store it?"

It was an accusation, not a question. He was not interested in a reply. He saw the Wardley stunner and snatched it.

"That looks like one of those crazy sound-forgers. It works on animal tissue. You can do anything with it. You can bruise, you can disable, you can maim—you can melt!"

Though he had only crossed from his tower in a tube, staying inside Coldharbor the whole time, Fisher was dressed for the outdoors. He was dressed for contamination conditions. He was dressed for the moon. He wore leaded boots and mechanical hands and a high collar. He wore a radio helmet, and his mask hung loose around his neck on a strap. He wore a survival pack on his belt—Hooper knew there was a body bag and a week's rations in the bag. His suit was thick and air-conditioned, and his radio crackled as he talked.

Hooper was touched by the boy's seriousness, his belief in the expensive equipment. It was another example of his innocence—his thinking that because he wore this stuff he was safe. He did not yet know all the ways he could be harmed.

He had hardly looked up from the weapon. He seemed

191

genuinely interested in its workings, unlike Murdick, for whom it was just another deadly boast.

"I was out a week ago with Murdick."

"That porker."

"It's his. I took it off him."

"That porker," Fisher repeated, but he was still studying the weapon, scrutinizing its options panel.

"It's got something to do with stunning people, using vibrations. It makes their muscles seize up."

"Tell me about it," Fisher said—mocking in his clumsy way. He sighted with it, screwing up one eye. Then he placed it on the floor and knelt over it. "This thing's lethal."

"Murdick says it's safe."

"Murdick's a porker," Fisher said. "It's got a design fault. The controls are housed under the sonic generator and they're not isolated. As soon as you start wailing away, the sound penetrates the panel. Look, it's on the highest setting. Plus, it's got a flare on the muzzle instead of a pipe fitting. There's a unit missing."

Hooper loved him for his jargon, and though Fizzy's tone was his terrible squawk, Hooper wanted him to continue.

"What should I tell Murdick?" he asked to encourage the boy.

"Murdick must know this! With a pipe fitting to squeeze the vibes, you have to aim, but with a flare you can't miss. It sprays a beam about a meter wide. Hey, did you see him use this thing?"

Hooper said yes.

Fizzy's lips were drawn tight. "He didn't miss."

"He stunned some people. I saw it."

"He probably melted them," Fisher said. "He certainly stiffed them. It's highly sophisticated but it's set on overload. It could be very useful. But it's dangerous at the moment. I want to take it apart. I want to fix it. I know how."

He probably did know how—he was usually right. But once again Hooper was on guard, feeling both admiration and uneasiness in the boy's presence. Sometimes Hooper wanted to laugh out loud; then he would pause and become thoughtful. Fizzy was such a strange boy. He noticed everything. He never smiled. His bad manners were his major fault, but it was his bad manners that reminded you that he was human, and that reminder made him bearable.

It was then, while Fizzy was describing how he would go

about fixing the weapon, that Hooper remembered he had said yes to O-Zone.

"What's it all about?" he asked.

"Don't know," Fisher said. He had seen the earlier inquiry, the prospectus, and he was almost certain that Hardy was planning a thermal mountain. All this he had gathered by hacking into Hardy's computer, and he had known before the trip to O-Zone that it was not a New Year's party but an exploratory look for a longitudinal field study, for Asfalt.

"You didn't ask?"

"Don't care," Fisher said. It was just an excuse to sell surplus oil! Hardy imagined himself to be Jove, hurling thunderbolts, but he was just a tool of the oil people, telling them where to squirt it. He was an oil can! "Hardy's a dong. All he does is lie to me."

"That's very uncharacteristic of you, Fizz. I think of you as having an inquiring mind."

"I'm not too sure I want to go." There was a twang of timidity in his voice.

"You're not afraid, are you?"

Fisher said, "I'm not a field scientist," and his eyes went black in anger. His skin was very pale—almost chalky near the red eruptions of his pimples. He looked absurd in his spacesuit.

He's fifteen years old, Hooper thought. He said, "O-Zone just the two of us. It could be a good trip. We could learn things. This time we could do it right."

There was nothing else on earth that he wanted. The young girl was now very clear and within reach. Hooper was on the verge of telling Fizzy exactly what he planned and how Hardy's offer could not have come at a better time.

But Fizzy had begun to bristle. He looked like a stuffed toy, and his inner trouser legs scraped as he stalked to the wall, where there was a full-length mirror.

He said, "They could have done a whole lot better. They didn't have to settle for this. I know I'm smart, but I could have been a lot taller. I could have been stronger. I could have had risk training when I was, say, four or five."

He was challenging himself in the mirror, and still sneering at what he saw, and seeming to glare past his reflection at his parents.

"But they were stupid," he said. "Especially Hardy. He ordered Moura to make her own choice. I'd like to know

where she went. She could have done better. She could have
made me taller."

Hooper stared at him, and smiled, and licked the smile off
his face. He realized that Fizzy was talking about fertilization—the clinic, the pedigree, the achievement and type
number. The boy was facing himself and complaining.

"I could have been a lot bigger," Fisher said sourly. He
opened his mouth and showed his teeth to the mirror. "They
starved me."

"What's wrong?"

"I hate my teeth. And I'm too small."

"Your teeth are fine. You're a big boy. You're big
enough."

"Hardy gave me an anxiety attack!"

Hooper didn't know what to say.

"Some people are really stupid!"

Fizzy seemed on the point of smashing the mirror, for the
image he saw in it.

"Why bother getting a high type-number if you don't get
the highest one?"

His voice had cracked in the middle, and the absurdly high
note combined with the growl of his trying to recover his
voice made him sound particularly pitiful.

Hooper said, "You're fine, Fizzy! You're a remote student.
You've got university exemption. You get great scores. Look
at me. I had to go to college. I wore a beanie! I failed my
exams! I drank beer!"

"I'm not talking about you," Fisher said—merely moving
his eyes to glance at Hooper. What was the connection between this rich foolish man and himself? Hooper had come
out of another age—he was probably thirty-nine. When you
asked him a question he grinned like a goon and showed you
the big space between his two front teeth. But Fisher saw
himself as a new man, and so he was maddened each time he
had to contend with the evidence that he was imperfect. He
knew it made him anxious, it made him overdress.

"They got me a brain, but they screwed up all the basic
factors. I'm not big enough, not strong enough. I hate my
face. I get nosebleeds. I have shallow breathing. I grind my
teeth. I'm fear-oriented. I've got shitty reflexes. It's all her
fault. I could have been a trooper!"

"Take it easy, kid." But with this plea the boy looked
especially sad in his expensive suit and wired helmet and

bulgy boots. And the survival bag flapping against his thigh made him seem pathetic. What was it about equipment that made people look weak and uncertain?

Perhaps Fizzy had seen the same pathos in the mirror. He turned away from it and said, "I wanted to go out the other night. I tried. I was afraid."

There were tears in his eyes.

"I hung around the checkpoint talking to that idiot Jennix about space travel. He's a Rocketman. He's lining up a place on a station, he said. He wants to migrate to a space platform. He's such a fucking wonka. He's afraid, too! He's worse than me!"

Hooper was sorry for the boy, but he was so uncertain about what to say that he felt that if he said anything he would giggle. And something in him made him glad to see Fizzy squirm. He was growing up at last. He saw his weaknesses—so that was an approach to adulthood. When, years from now, he saw he was ineffectual, he would be a man.

In a hopeless voice Fisher said, "I wanted to go to O-Zone."

"We'll go!" Hooper said, glad that he was able to shout it. It meant everything to him now.

"I can't," Fisher said. "And it's their fault. Moura's especially. She went to some stupid clinic and got stuffed with some defective implant. I could kill her for that!"

Hooper said, "There are two of us, Fizzy. We'll get the best gunship, the best gear, the best weapons. You've got all the navigation. We'll bring back some brilliant descriptive data—"

All the time he was speaking he was thinking of the girl's face. It was a good humorous face. And her pale eyes and slender legs. If I don't take her I'll never have her. He had always imagined that she would leave willingly, but there was something in Fizzy's fussing that made Hooper think that he might have to capture her.

"If we're to find anything new we'll have to get onto the ground. Otherwise they can use satellite pictures and spy planes."

"Eye level," Hooper said. "I'll be right beside you."

"It's dangerous. We'll die."

"No—it'll be fabulous. We'll look at those blind big-headed mutants!"

"They weren't blind. They were anophthalmic. Their skulls were normal-sized. But they had exencephaly."

"Whatever you say, Fizz."

"They were dead before they hit the beam. Someone threw them at us—to scare us."

"So what?"

"It worked—I'm scared! Hooper, you don't know me. I'm serious. I'm not strong enough. I haven't got—"

But Hooper had known for years what Fizzy had just discovered. That weakness, which Fizzy thought was a revelation, was all that Hooper had ever known about the boy. And the boy did not know that admitting the weakness was a strength, and knowing what it was would help the boy survive in the wilderness—that kind of anxiety was a greater advantage in O-Zone than a feeling of power.

Fizzy had discovered that he was not perfect! So there was hope for him. He had taken off his heavy gloves. His hands were hot and flushed pink—very soft, almost delicate hands.

He said, still pleading, "There's something missing."

"You might find it in O-Zone," Hooper said.

When the Allbright brothers, Hooper and Hardy, were together they felt much younger, usually like boys, and at times ageless. But they were sensitive to slights and could easily be wounded, so they were very guarded about what they said. They were wise and infantile at the same time.

Hooper had thought: I won't go to O-Zone for his reasons—only for my own reasons. Then he remembered the Access Pass: it was being handed to him on a plate, and it seemed to him as if there was no way he could refuse. It was a brilliant gift, and what was best about it was that the giver had no idea of its great value. Hooper knew in advance that he would accept. His fear was that in seeming to equivocate he would appear too reluctant, and the offer would be withdrawn, and he would never see that girl again.

Make me give in, he thought when he saw Hardy. He found it hard to accept a gift from anyone, least of all from Hardy. This dislike of gifts was a domineering trait in him, he knew. He was always somewhat surprised to see what people would do when they were given some small token, and he distrusted the vanity of anyone who solicited favors. It was another strength of Fizzy's that he mocked all such offers of presents.

They had met in a restaurant in West Harlem, a bulldozed and newly colonized part of the city, and a compromise location for the brothers—Hooper had come from Coldharbor, which was off York Avenue in Upper East, and Hardy had been looking for office space in Washington Heights, where he hoped to locate what he now thought of as his Storm Center.

"I just saw the Eubanks downstairs," Hardy said. "I haven't seen them since our party in O-Zone."

This was his cue—Hooper was sure of it—but he resisted it, and let it pass, and only said, "They smoke, did you know that?"

"They were actually going into the Smoking Room," Hardy said. "They seemed a little sniffy with me. I'm sure they expected something else in O-Zone."

"They didn't smoke in O-Zone—probably scared they'd catch fire," Hooper said. "They drink, too. It makes me gag to think of a cigarette in one hand and a drink in the other—"

It was a false note. Hardy could have said: You inject yourself, you swallow happies, you photograph women. But Hardy was a tactful brother, and he responded in the same way, talking about the sickening habits of the Eubanks. And now both brothers knew they were stalling. They had no secrets from each other. Guile only worked because they allowed it. Hardy wondered why Hooper did not have a woman; and Hooper wondered whether Hardy was really impotent—and what was at the bottom of his weather research? But this was all. It was not very much. As brothers they understood the delicate nature of each other's pride. And they had real admiration for each other's achievements—Hardy's status as a weathermaker, Hooper's as a mail-order tycoon. There were no confrontations, they never talked about the family or the fortune; there were no hard words—that would have been the end.

They studied the menu and then ordered by keying the numbered combinations into the selector at the edge of their table—the steak dinner for Hardy, the fish for Hooper. Any mention of food these days provoked talk about Murdick's meal at Firehills:

"Meat butter."

"Crab strings."

"It was designed for the space program!"

It was another way of stalling, though. The subject, so far

evaded, was Hooper's willingness to take Fisher to O-Zone. It was a conspicuous evasion for a number of reasons, but brotherhood came into it again.

Each brother to be polite had to give the impression that the other was doing him a favor. But each believed the opposite at the same time—that he was doing the other a favor. And secretly, at the faintest level of awareness, each had a dim sense of satisfaction that he could not put into words, that he was doing exactly what he wanted.

Hardy said abruptly, "We're very worried about Fizzy. I think the proposed mission to O-Zone would be good for him, frankly. I sometimes feel he's cracking up. This might pull him together."

Ah, so we can discuss this tricky thing by discussing Fizzy, Hooper thought. That was tactful—so tactful as to be a bit spineless. But in this way they could spare their own feelings. They proceeded very tentatively like two fat acrobats balancing on wobbly chairs.

"He's not cracking up. He's a little awkward, maybe. But he's normal, for his number."

"He never goes out. That's not normal."

"He went out once, a few weeks ago."

"Only once is weirder than never."

"He doesn't have any reason to go out."

"That's crazy too, because he doesn't have any reason to stay in."

"His computer. His mainframe. His studies."

"He calls the thing 'Pap'!" Hardy said. "Listen, this is the safest city in the world!"

Hooper said nothing. That statement gave him a glimpse of the Godseye gunship.

Hardy said, "He's getting strange indoors. In his room. He's developing a wacky eye-blink. He chomps his teeth. He's weak. He sleeps irregularly. And that yawn."

Hooper knew the yawn. "He'll grow out of it," he said. "He's only fifteen!"

Their food was brought by a man with a trolley. He wore a face mask—it was catching on! Hooper wondered whether the thing served a practical purpose. He slid the sealed trays in front of them, and made a little bow and pushed the trolley to another table.

"Fizzy's a slug," Hardy said. "I've seen kids like that just collapse and cry when you talk to them, and spend the whole day watching their fingernails grow. They stop taking baths. Liquid diet. They develop this tremendous interest in germs and fecal odors. They start talking about dirt. They receive strange orders over their headsets. They get very unscientific and monotonous."

"Are you talking about your kid?"

Hardy said, "You should hear him describe the right way to open a can. Gloves, tongs, tweezers, hot water, plastic bags—"

But Hooper thought: We are here to talk about O-Zone.

He said, "The mission might do Fizzy some good. But he's not crucial to it. And if you want elevations and temperatures, you could use satellites or send a plane over."

"I want eye-level stuff," Hardy said. "I want to know what it smells like. I want your feet on the ground."

He wants secrecy, Hooper thought, so he wants me. Who else could he trust? His favor to Hardy, and Hardy knew it, was that he did not ask why he wanted eye-level videos, and the smell of it, and his feet on the ground. Secrecy certainly, and he also suspected that Hardy was a bit of a coward—it seemed to go with the limp dick of impotence, and if Hardy wasn't a coward, why was Fizzy so fearful? The boy had never learned courage. Hardy had neglected him that way, and in so doing had made him think that courage was something special and unattainable. The boy was a brain, but not more than that. It was like being a moron.

"I'm pretty busy," Hooper said.

Hardy nodded slightly, to show he had heard.

Hooper was grateful to him for not challenging this. Hardy knew he was lying—that he had been restless but never busy.

Hardy said, "It would mean a lot to me if you took over. I think the kid likes you. You can set him straight."

"What if we find aliens?"

"Probably none there. And didn't Murdick say you'd burned them all down?"

"But what if?"

"You know how to handle yourself," Hardy said. "Anyway, they're all sick. They're cranks and cancer patients. They don't fight back. I can't see them worrying you."

It was the popular view—aliens are sick and diseased—and it was a measure of its pervasiveness that even someone as scientific and well-informed as Hardy appeared to believe it. Maybe he's just trying to urge me to go, Hooper thought.

But Hooper knew that the aliens he had seen in O-Zone and on the Godseye hunt were not sick at all, and what had struck him most was the way they resembled Owners and passholders and everyone else.

"They could delay our research," Hooper said. "And we might want to study them."

Hardy smiled and shook his head. "People make a mistake in thinking aliens are interesting. They're not. They're empty. They're diseased. They're very easily intimidated. Very few of them have killer instincts. They don't make anything. See, if you don't bother them they won't bother you."

All this talk had made the meal mechanical, and concentrating on what Hardy was saying—especially this bullshit about aliens—had made Hooper incapable of tasting his food. It was there one minute; then it was gone. He could not remember having eaten it—it had something to do with pauses in the conversation, with listening. It was a form of punctuation.

But Hooper had his answer—he was still suppressing his urge to blurt it out. He pretended to worry a bit longer. He dropped his eyes, then took a deep breath and expelled it slowly, so that Hardy could see and hear that he was being judicious. It was such a charade! He had never been so eager to do something, and he felt foolishly grateful to his brother for this favor, and for sparing him other questions.

At last, almost bursting, he said, "I'll go on one condition. That you don't give me instructions—no warnings, no advice. If you want to be in charge you can go yourself. I'll carry out your instructions to the letter—whatever data you want, I'll get. And I'll look after Fizzy. But I'm in charge."

Hardy had already begun to nod in agreement as Hooper was talking. Then he said, "That's fine, as long as you treat it as secret. Not a word to anyone."

Hooper opened his mouth to speak.

"Not even Moura," Hardy said (and his quick interruption made Hooper stammer). "Let her keep her own secrets."

It was perfect for Hardy: nothing official. He had no job, no project, no research, no proposal—nothing existed except the words they had just spoken, which had risen and disappeared like vapor over their food in this anonymous restaurant. It was perfect for Hooper too. No one knew what he planned—he hardly knew himself. So there was no mission, no purpose, no plan. Nothing existed, no routes, no check-points, no aliens—

"You're smiling," Hardy said. "That's good."

Only the girl existed, waiting to be rescued.

The brothers had managed to please each other again. It was not a gift, but an agreement—a mutual favor that went back and forth. Hardy was glad, for whatever reason. And Hooper was delighted. It was all he wanted and yet he had never revealed more than a mild willingness. Give someone something and they go on dogging you, if not traipsing after to thank you, then trying to return the favor, which was worse, like giving the same thing back.

16

Moura had always stayed clear of her son, as from a biting animal or one of those toothy household trash extractors, the garbage-chewers that ate everything and were so hungry and vicious you needed a license for them. Fizzy hated to be touched. If it happened, he quacked—or worse, he laughed. His laugh was both a bark and a squawk, and always abusive, with the stink of his bad breath in it. He laughed, always without smiling, and it had the rhythm of a rotor blade.

The distance and the hands-off might have helped them succeed as mother and son. Moura had never liked to touch him, or be touched by him either. Once it had been like politeness, but now it was closer to revulsion, and Moura was so amazed by her behavior that she told Holly Murdick.

They were at their exercise class on the roof garden of Coldharbor—Holly had come over from Wedgemere. Each woman was on a muscle machine, looking as though she were being snatched and swallowed. Holly was glowing, damp and pink with exertion, groaning in her body sock. And yet, even twisted in the machine—but perhaps it was the way the machine held her in its grip—she looked fleshy and eager. Lust gave her a silly face and a doggy friendliness—heated eyes and a wide stare and a slow half-smile, all lust.

"It might mean you're repressing your sexual feeling for him," Holly said.

Moura wanted to laugh—and it was not just the idiotic idea that she might have a sexual feeling for the supermoron ("I've got an on-line program waiting for me on Pap, quack-

202

quack!"), but the way Holly said it, hanging there with her arms out, like a bondage queen, sweating as her legs were being worked. There was a panting lunacy in Holly's lust that made the woman impossible to take seriously and aroused a protectiveness in Moura, something almost motherly, because in that mood Holly had no defenses. But she was still theorizing about Fizzy!

"—and sort of masking it in self-disgust," she was saying. "It's fairly common among a lot of mothers."

And the other thing about Holly's ignorant defenselessness was that you had to listen to her nonsense or she would be dreadfully hurt.

"I've never been his mother in that way," Moura said, trying to be tactful. She was on the next machine, being stretched. "Holly, I don't even like him very much."

"That's what I mean by disgust," Holly said. "Or maybe he's attracted to you and you somehow understand this." She was full of theories, many of them contradictory, and perhaps it was because she had so many that she was seldom dogmatic. "Maybe it's your way of thwarting him. You're discouraging him. You suspect that he wants to jump you."

The trouble with Holly's seldom being dogmatic was that she seldom sounded serious.

Moura said, "Now I wish I hadn't told you."

"Willis says that kid is nothing but trouble."

"Fizzy's fifteen. He's got huge teeth, long arms, and his hair is already partly gray. He insults Hardy to his face and he calls his mainframe 'Pap.' He does nothing but yawn in my face. And to him I'm an old hag, because I'm thirty-six."

"I was reading about this witch instinct they've discovered in aliens that might be some indicator—"

"I'm not a witch, not a whore, not a mother, not a little girl, and I despise the word 'wife.' I'm a woman!"

The outburst did not startle Holly. She was now dancing slowly and still fastened to the arms of the machine.

"You should act like a woman, then, and be practical about this obnoxious kid of yours."

Sex was the last thing, but it was just like Holly to think of it first. Moura was baffled by her own reaction to Fizzy. As an infant he had been a frail inert creature, and she had loved him—his milky breath, his tiny fingers, the way he slept in a little bundle. He was a part of her, a live thing that had become detached, that still belonged to her. But then he opened his eyes and began to move and make noise, and nothing she did pleased him. She had no power to quiet him. He was the same infant, but a beast, and from the moment she recognized that it had been a battle.

Moura coped by handing him over. It was easy to find school sessions for him—all the agencies wanted to take credit for his genius. But these days when she heard that meaningless word she thought: Who is he?

The schools found him volatile, quick to master anything, but with intelligence to spare—it brimmed in him, and he used it to mock the teachers, and he mocked the work they gave him, too. The work he found easy, it was thin he said, there was not enough of it. He said, "Everybody knows this!" He laughed his unsmiling laugh. The school authorities said that he was like a certain kind of computer that could perform well only when a wise operator was driving it. They could not master his operations.

But Moura did not see him as a special machine: he lacked the stillness, the repose of a mechanical object. He was active. He was like a hungry monster that could eat anything you fed it. He gobbled up the problems that were set before him—demolished them and then laughed because no more were provided. Finally, he was classified as a remote student. He worked at home, and his lessons were transmitted to him on a cable—his own channel, his own program. He was granted high school exemption, and this year, aged fifteen, university exemption. He was now doing advanced research in particle physics. He was not boasting—he was too truthful ever to boast, and yet everything he said about himself sounded boastful. Moura was not impressed: she knew the schools had not been able to handle him.

"University exemption!" Hardy said. He was the one who boasted—and he had no cause, and knew it. He was not Fizzy's father.

"They're procrastinating," she said. She was just as wary of his boisterous intelligence; and still she asked: *Who is he?*

These days she watched him cautiously—for example, unscrewing the lid of a jam jar. He wore gloves, his hands like big broad paddles; he did it under a disinfecting light; he wore a mask. He grunted miserably—these noises meant he was thinking—and he seemed to be sniffing, smelling what he was doing. He moved his lips and wrinkled his nose behind his faceplate. Opening a jam jar! He folded his gloves on the lid and let the light play on it, and jerking one leg back for balance, he struggled until the lid was off. He shrieked when he saw that he had smeared jam on the fingers of one glove, and kept quacking until he had flapped the glove into the trash extractor.

Beside this, what was particle physics? As he had grown older, changing from day to day, he had become less familiar to her. On occasions she regarded him as, if not a threat, then a potential source of danger.

Moura had finished her exercises with a swim in the Cold-harbor pool and had come back to her unit feeling refreshed—relaxed and strengthened and, as always after swimming, a few pounds lighter. She looked out and saw the dusty lavender sky of midafternoon, which meant the winter day was ending—the tame skylights would soon be switched on, a whole dome of curved light, making it a city without shadows.

But she preferred it the way it was just now, before the skylights came on—the wide empty streets of winter, few pedestrians, the grinding of the trams, the swarms of tipping rotors with their flicking lights—like fireflies. She loved this shadowy daylight, on the narrow seam between day and night. And it soothed her to know that Hardy would be late. She was planning ahead, allotting the hours to herself. She wanted to call up the figures on some investments she had made, and analyze them as she ate—she enjoyed eating at the console; Hardy never did so himself and hated seeing her do it. She wanted to compute her exercises at the same time—the hours on the machine, and under the lamp, and swimming; and the breakdown of her food figures. It made her feel even better when she saw her effort turned into statistics, because numbers were unalterable and they always seemed in a solid authoritative way like investments. A first-night was being televised at eight, and after that tennis, and she promised herself a long phone call later to Rinka, to fix a day for their outing. By the time Hardy came home looking for sympathy and a listener, she would be ready for him; but she felt free only when she was alone.

She had just seated herself at her console when Security rang—Captain Jennix at his most military, imitating a space-man. Before she could respond, Fizzy burst out of his room.

"That's for me!"—his elbows raised like a penguin.

It annoyed her that it *was* for him, a large parcel in the tamperproof wrapper that meant it was classified—about a meter long and rather narrow. She wondered whether it was a weapon—it was rifle-sized, and Fizzy carried it in a certain tough-nervous way, one end of it sticking ahead of him as he pushed toward his room.

His sudden appearance spoiled the rest of the evening for her. She succeeded in ignoring him because she tried hard, and she always returned to what she had convinced herself was an empty unit—not thinking of Fizzy at all, because he never left his room. And then there he was, flapping like a penguin and with the same shuffle-shuffle, full of corrections, big teeth, spiky hair, and holding his head to one side, yanking his door open as the phone went. He had snatched the parcel from Jennix's runner and limped back into his study, which was his whole world, where he sat and squinted at Pap. If that thing was an iron it was the end. It was bad enough that he had become a stranger—but a weapon-freak!

Moura had not been in his room lately, not since the return from O-Zone, just after New Year's. That was a month ago. She resented the thought that Hooper had been admitted: all that whispering that day over the video cartridge.

No, "resented" wasn't right; and not "irritated" or "offended." She wanted, consciously, to have no feelings at all; she wanted to see the boy as clearly as possible. But he was such a little shit and know-it-all, her anger always got in the way.

"Let me in," she said on the phone. "I'd like to talk to you."

"Don't come in here!" This was four quacks.

Maybe he's attracted to you. Some things Holly said were so wrong they could never be offensive. This was actually funny! Holly's obvious lack of perception made her a safe and easy friend. Moura could not bear being observed by an intelligent and critical woman—it was so exhausting, and what was the point? Were you supposed to listen to all their wise questions and give them humble answers? At least Holly let you laugh at her occasionally.

There was a noise. Had Fizzy dropped something? He was probably trying to unwrap the weapon, or whatever it was. He could be very clumsy, dangerously so, as his slow hands sought to keep pace with his racing mind.

"Don't be a nit," she said. "I'll be right in."

But the next moment he was at the door, breathless, swallowing with apprehension, his eyes wide. He had rushed out and confronted Moura, to protect his room. How could you be angry with someone who looked like a penguin?

His panting was like a demand that she leave. His breath was humid. He was trying to speak.

That was another thing—she could never tell these days when he was afraid. His fear seemed like just another kind of rudeness. And hunger always gave him bad breath.

"I thought you might want some food," she said.

"Too busy!"

"And I wanted to talk to you about going away. The Murdicks are getting up a party to go to Africa in March."

Holly had said, *I'm going to be a naked savage for a month.*

"I hate those places," Fisher said.

"It's completely zoned and secure. The beaches are beautiful, all of them are fortified. I haven't been there for years. When I was your age I went with my parents. I met a boy and had a really good time."

She wanted to say more. He looked so bored she wanted to shock him.

He said, "Those places look safe because of all the soldiers and police. But really they're full of diseases. The food's buggy, the water's contaminated. All those jigs, all those monkey-men."

"It's a lot safer than O-Zone."

"Wrong!" Fisher said, and his repeating the word turned it into a honk. He was protesting with his hands—batting the air. Upset at that little thing!

"What is it, Fizz?"

He fussed, started to speak, then gagged and gave up. Later she heard him banging in his room; and talking. But he often talked to himself. In a sense he talked only to himself.

But tonight she heard him shouting in a ducklike way.

"Negative," he said. "Negative." And more: words so unfamiliar to her they might have been another language. And then a familiar cry of his, "Nuke it!"

I don't know him, she thought, and it frightened her more to think that she once did.

He was more and more a mystery, but she pitied him. That was the first week of this new seclusion. Then crates began arriving for him. He had always been interested in new equipment, yet this interest had apparently developed into an obsession. She could see him trying the stuff out—she had a glimpse into the skylight of his room from a corner window upstairs. She saw him in a bewildering variety of masks, staring out. He had weapons. He pointed these ugly objects at the tall, safe city and its emptiness. He was living out some bizarre fantasy of siege, she supposed.

That was when she bugged the room and listened.

"Mission Westwind Command speaking."

He was full of code names. She had always found men's code names madder than their masks, and insane, as well as simply childish. Women never went in for this ridiculous naming and playing. Hardy was a tremendous user of codes. Perhaps Fizzy was imitating this secretive man, who refused to be a father.

Fizzy was still quacking: "When a risk arises and is canceled out by a solution, there is no risk. I have run a computer check of every possible downside event, from suspected cannibals and a verified biting-death, to foot-rot from boot condensation. I have a matching tally of remedies. I will not consider any move until the mission has been declared risk-free. I have drawn my list from all the recorded and projected incidents in all other missions by self-contained vehicles in comparable zones, and nothing will be taken for granted in the decision-loop, not even any loss of—"

Who was he talking to in this severe voice?

Moura went on monitoring the bug: he was not talking to anyone. He was recording this on his memory machine and storing it in what he called "Mission Westwind's Archives." Was he sick?

"Mission Westwind Command, speaking from Headquarters—location confidential. This is the Commander with an update of the details of risk-elimination intelligence—"

Sometimes, clinic kids went hoopy. They blazed with insights until they were in their mid-teens and then burned out and spent the rest of their lives watching cartoons on television, doing jigsaw puzzles, and working on coloring books. They became very pliant and told you what they wanted for Christmas. So she had been warned.

Poor kid, she thought.

Books arrived. He snatched them from her. She heard him stumbling with them in his room. When he was done with them he fed them into the trash extractor, grinding his teeth as he worked the switches.

"What are you doing, Fizzy?"

"Shredding these classified documents."

She pondered whether he was wacko by trying to remember a time when she had believed him to be normal. She was left, still wondering, as video cartridges arrived. He watched them in his helmet and then wiped them.

A two-day silence—and nothing from the bug—impelled Moura to try his door. She knocked.

"Fizzy, can I come in?"

"Negative!"

But his voice sounded so strange and choked she got her own key and unlocked the door.

Fisher was hanging upside-down, his legs crooked over a chair back, his head in a helmet.

"Classified!" he howled, and in his fury he fogged his whole mask.

He was growing odder. Any day she expected to see him grinning from above a jigsaw puzzle and quacking in joy as he pounded a whittled piece into place.

Physically he had changed a great deal. Not long ago he had her lovely solemn face—Moura thought of it as her mother's face—but this past year, the onset of his late adolescence, had coarsened it. He was taller and skinnier, and his face was paler and blotched and bony; his neck was thin; his feet were very large. Those feet! Expedition boots arrived. He limped in them and made snorting noises and ordered more, not bothering to send back the rejected ones. Moura could see some of the equipment from her upper window. She imagined Fizzy's room to be piled high with it.

One day a warning light flashed on the unit's signal board, indicating a fault in Fizzy's room. At first he denied there had been anything wrong, and then he admitted—because Moura threatened to call Jennix—that Pap had overheated.

"Commander," she heard from his dead-ended messages. "Mission Westwind."

It was not that he was mad, but that he was growing madder.

Hardy was no help at all. He was seldom at home these days, and when he was at home and Moura told him of her bafflement, of Fizzy's strangeness, he agreed. But his agreement was useless, and his sympathy was as bad as ridicule. She wanted Hardy to shake the boy, or else plug him in until he lit up.

But all Hardy said was, "He's a fruit all right. No question about it."

Hardy had never taken any responsibility for the boy, and after the novelty of Fizzy's intelligence had worn off he had taken no interest. *He's not mine!* he seemed to say. It was true, but so what? And it made Moura wonder further: *Yes, whose is he?*

Hardy's ambition and singlemindedness were no bad thing, but the trouble with ambitious people was that they were invariably secretive and even sneaky, and that made their ambition intolerable.

"I think we should send him for observation," she said. There were whole hospitals filled with kids his age—all problem kids who had become cartoon freaks and jigsaw addicts, who did other odd things like pulling down their pants in public; kids who had been reared as remote students, doing theoretical physics. Though personally Moura did not think it was such a long way from discussing Black Holes to coloring in Donald Duck. Yet she was sure now that Fizzy had to be plugged in or else fed through a wringer. He needed a year of it—a real pasting.

"It won't do any good," Hardy said.

It was just like Hardy to be so self-absorbed. He agreed there was a problem but refused to discuss a solution.

"If only he were calmer," she said, realizing that she was the one who was fretting.

Sometimes at night she heard him grunting over Pap, voice-printing, and once doing a random check on the bug she heard Hooper's voice. Hooper, of all people! She thought of confiding her fears to Fizzy, but how could she without revealing that her gravest anxieties were provoked from what she heard on the bug?

The "Mission Westwind," the "orders," the "Commander" business, worried her most, because they seemed the most fantastic and unlikely. And all those weapons—they *had* to be weapons. And the boots—boots for a penguin of fifteen who had been in New York City alone only once in his life, and that for a mere afternoon! That one time was only about six weeks ago: perhaps it meant something? Maybe he was gearing up for another expedition to Battery Park or Tribeca!

"I think it's war games," she said to Hardy. "I hope it's war games."

Hardy smiled. What did he know? Nothing: where Fizzy

was concerned, Hardy was a total stranger. He was not the father. He knew that. She hated his detachment. He was so ambitious—such a sneak.

What was Hardy's sympathy worth? It was worse than his humoring her. When she became agitated he made it seem as if the problem were hers. She was the worrier, she was stranger, and she was probably causing it all—that's what his sympathetic tone said. He was still smiling in that horrible unhelpful way.

"The kid's fifteen years old. He's a Type A. He's a clinic-genius. What do you expect? What do you want?"

From the upstairs window she saw Fizzy dressed as for a moon landing or a space flight, holding his arms out like a deep-sea diver, and walking stiff-legged among all his packages and parcels, all those weapons, that equipment, the rejected boots.

"This is Commander, Mission Westwind. Risk-elimination weapons check commencing at oh-nine-hundred—"

Moura thought: *I want to find him.*

The three women usually took turns dividing the day. Lunch in Connecticut was Rinka's idea. She provided the rotor and the pilot.

"We could have taken the train," Holly was saying over the *whup-whup-whup* of the blade. "You meet people on the train," and she winked. "Real-lifers!"

"This is quicker," Rinka said.

"This old thing!"

It was old. It was noisy. It was a low-altitude model. They were still not in Connecticut—at least nowhere near the restaurant—and already Moura was sick of *Can't hear you, darling!* and everyone shouting everything three times.

"I said, you could have taken your rotor," Rinka yelled.

"Willis loaned it to someone who's doing a long haul," Holly said. "Hooper Allbright, I think."

Moura said, "Did you say Hooper?"

"Can't hear you, darling!" Holly smiled back at her, and then turned to Rinka, who was sitting next to her. "It's so dull here I want to puke."

"Give me a chance. You'll get your turn later," Rinka said. "Anyway, we're not in New York anymore. That's something."

"Connecticut's worse. All those fortresses. All those shantytowns. All those trees. It's riddled with roadblocks, you know. Checkpoints. Scanners. You can hardly move!"

"That's why I didn't want to take a car."

"Who said anything about a car?" Holly winked again at Moura, who could scarcely follow the conversation. "I was on the train once. It was when that germ scare went around and everyone wore masks. I had a really devastating one, with huge eyes and little jaws, like a hornet. The man next to me had a shiny leather one. He had a sort of muffled voice, but I knew what he wanted. 'How about a little privacy?' he says. He had a room on the train—he was an Owner, from upstate, going home. We went to his room. He took his clothes off—everything but his mask. I found that incredibly sexy. I did the same. He said, 'Want to dance?' Did we dance!"

All this while Moura had been leaning closer in order to hear, and then she smiled and said softly, "I know what you want, Holly."

"Can't hear you, darling!"

Soon the rotor was setting them down on a circular pad in front of an old brick building with a white wooden porch and freshly painted trim. The three women paused to admire the chimney, and wondered whether the smoke coming out of it was real—and decided it was not.

"The food's supposed to be very good," Rinka said. "They grow most of it themselves in those hothouses."

The bright bubble-domes gleamed on the next low hill.

"Fresh asparagus in February. They even do their own mangoes and guavas."

Moura said, "I'm in the mood for textured lobster."

"Meat fabric," Rinka said.

"I'm sick of that joke," Holly said. But she seemed angrier than was justified by her friends' mockery of Willis' provisions. Perhaps it was her forced smile which made her seem so cross. She said, "Look at us. Three attractive women spend one day a week together because we're frustrated and restless. What is our brilliant solution?" She turned to face them and said sharply, "We eat lunch."

They were met by a boy in a pale blue one-piece suit. He was not much older than Fizzy, Moura noticed, but in his slow attentive way he seemed both wiser and saner, and quite a bit more intelligent.

"I'd like to make your lunch here as comfortable as possible," he said. The name badge on his suit was lettered *Royce*. "Just let me know if there's anything I can do for you."

Holly said, "Do you mean anything?"

"I hate it when people are rude to workers," Moura said when the boy left them. "You embarrassed him. You're always doing it. Hardy's always doing it. Hooper's the only one who gives them a break."

"They're used to Owners here," Holly said. "Don't worry, I'll pay him."

And her mention of Hooper made Moura remember something else: "Were you talking about Hooper when we were in the rotor?"

"No," Holly said, but she was not listening—she was glancing around the restaurant. "Look at the people here. Where did they get their permits! They're all duds. Sometimes even Owners look awful. Look at him— I'd rather get jumped by an alien!"

They ordered their meal, and because they were not hungry and were so eager to leave, they only glanced at the menu, and they ordered too much. When all the food came—bowls of vegetables, a salver of beef, a half-meter of salmon—they wanted to go.

"There's nothing special about this stuff," Holly said after they had picked at it a little. Then she spoke into the microphone: "Royce, darling. Take this garbage away." She looked at her friends. "When I'm not hungry," she said, "I don't even think of it as food."

"Sorry," Royce said, gathering the plates.

Holly fixed him with a smile and said, "I'd much rather eat you."

Back in the rotor, Rinka said in a challenging way to Holly, "Your turn, darling."

"Coffee at the Greenhouse," Holly said. "Hooper told Willis that he saw people walking around naked—it's apparently a new Starkie fashion."

"These fashions that copy aliens give me the creeps," Rinka said.

"There's no one else to copy," Holly said. "Anyway, I want to see if it's true. I haven't been there since before Christmas."

That was the routine, each woman taking a turn. On the way back to New York, Rinka said, "Is something wrong, Moura? You're so quiet. Is it our bitching?"

"No. It's Fizzy. I think he's breaking down."

"Clinic kids have a wicked record for breakdowns," Holly said in her cheerful rattling way. "But you didn't go to any old clinic, did you? Why are you looking at me like that?"

"Because I just thought of my turn," Moura said.

"First give my turn a chance," Holly said.

Just before they landed on the rotor pad on the roof of the Midtown Mall, Holly changed into a short apron, and but for this she was naked.

They strolled with everyone else in the warm scented air of the Greenhouse, on the lookout for a naked woman. Soon they saw one. She was leaving a bank. She was not more than thirty and rather tall and slender, but her jewelry was the most striking thing about her. She wore a heavy gold chain around her waist, which was fastened by a gold padlock; a heavy knotted necklace; and bracelets and ankle loops. Holly said it seemed a little tacky to wear that much jewelry without any clothes.

"And that's just plain fussy," she said when another woman approached them. This one was also naked and wore gold chains, and her pubic hair was dyed green and cut in a leaf shape.

"There's one with a mask," Rinka said. "That's attractive."

It was a breathing mask, but an expensive ornamented one.

Moura said, "When I see New Yorkers wearing breathing masks in this clean air, and these rich women going naked—"

"Aren't there any men?" Holly asked, and quickly answered her own question. "Of course not. Men are so pathetic. Owners are the worst." And she continued in a wondering way, "You don't know anyone until you know what their sex life is like. Then it's all horribly clear. And if you think very hard about your own sex life you know yourself pretty well. Oh, God, your turn, Moura."

Then they were in the rotor, Moura giving the pilot precise directions, and Holly was still talking.

"You could have a friend for twenty years, but if you don't go to bed with them they're a mystery. Don't laugh, darling. Sex makes you rational. What are we doing?"

"Making our descent," the pilot said.

The rotor was straining and tipping against a vibrant muscle of wind.

"So we don't really know each other that well. But I know some strange men very well. Where are we?"

Moura explained: Upper West, in a district called River-west, just north of Columbia. And then they landed in an open space.

"Where all the hospitals are," Rinka said.

They were private hospitals and small clinics, street after street of them in the new towers and in old dignified brownstones. In the glare of the ground-level lights, the brass plaques shone. Most of the windows were false or else heavily curtained. The whole area gave the impression of thick walls and secrecy. All the buildings had broad diameter dishes on the roofs and tall antennas. The heavy doors were severe and anonymous.

"They look like banks," Holly said.

"It's all clinics," Moura said.

"Sorry I can't take you nearer," the pilot called from the cockpit. "There's a noise restriction here."

The three women walked from the landing pad to one of the smaller buildings. It was ten stories high and unadorned, in the old style: pale brick, granite, and square windows, and only a number on the door—no plate.

"This used to be the Sanford Clinic," Moura said.

Holly said, "I hope it still is, darling."

Even approaching from the street, Moura had the feeling they were being watched. She had always had that feeling here, because there was never anyone visible from the windows. They buzzed and were admitted to the lobby, where they were quickly scanned by a stony-faced security man, who sent them into a reception area.

There a nurse met them. She was Oriental, probably Chinese. "Do any of you have an appointment?" She wore a crisp white suit and gloves and a cap that hid her hair. Only her face showed, in an oval in this uniform, and the face was smooth, like a doll's, and perfectly painted.

Moura said, "If this is the Sanford Clinic, we're here to make appointments."

"The consultant will be right with you," the nurse said, and stepped softly away.

"Does she think we want babies?" Holly said.

"It's a licensed contact clinic," Moura said.

"That usually means whorehouse," Rinka said. "I would never have come here alone."

Just as the door opened, Moura felt herself tremble and she knew she was afraid of seeing the consultant. She remembered him as very nervous and so eager to please he seemed unsure of himself. She had wanted him to take charge and release her from the embarrassment of making decisions herself; but no, he had said, "It's up to you, Mrs. Allbright," and she had had to explain what she wanted.

That was, she knew now, the old days. The consultant was a woman, heavy, about fifty, very businesslike, and there was a briskness in her voice and an assurance in her manner that indicated to Moura that it was routine for her. And Moura was glad of this, because it meant that she had seen such women many times before, and she would not look closely at them. They would be anonymous, really; just clients.

Even as she was thinking this, the consultant was saying, "Protecting your anonymity is one of our main concerns. And of course your health—"

Moura realized now that the woman was not interested in any of them personally; she only wanted their business. She probably did not mean much of what she said—these clinics were not in the fertility business anymore—and so Moura was grateful for the woman's insincerity. How she would have hated her concern or her scrutiny.

"We'd like to work with you on your program," she was saying now. "We'll be meeting with you to discuss your requirements and your options. I'll explain the insurance scheme and the short-term contract. I take it you've never been here to Sanford?"

Holly said no—"First time!"—answering for them all in her enthusiasm. And Moura was so touched by Holly's eagerness she did not correct her. Holly was saying, "Tell us what to do."

"Before we can begin any sessions we'll need some details. These are strictly confidential. And I also suggest a complete physical—a blood test and a smear. This is as much for your protection as it is for ours. And I do urge you to take advantage of our insurance scheme. We can get most of this over with today, and then you might be interested to watch some training discs. I'm sure you'll want to be examined separately. Excuse me—I'll just see who's free."

All this was said by the woman in a confident voice, without much emotion, and it took Moura this amount of time to realize that the lights were so low that they could see the consultant's face very clearly, but she could not see theirs. Moura was glad it was a woman, and she liked her rapping voice and lecturer's manner.

"A blood test! An insurance scheme! A physical!" Holly said when the woman had gone. "Hey, don't laugh—it's sensible!"—but she was laughing.

"Is a training disc what I think it is?" Rinka asked.

"I imagine it's porn, with a woman's slant," Moura said. "They didn't have training discs in my day."

Holly said, "I like this place. Our 'program'—that's nice. When can we come back?"

"What about next week?" Rinka said. "Our next outing."

"I don't want to wait a week."

The Oriental nurse returned and directed them to the examining rooms.

"I'll need a blood sample," Moura's doctor said. He was a man and wore a gauze mask. He used his hypodermic syringe to motion her to a chair.

"Don't touch me," she said. "I don't want a physical. I'll pay you, but skip the charade."

"No one gets in here without a physical," the doctor said. "So if you want some action—"

Moura was startled by his directness, but because she didn't want a man she kept her composure.

"I'm looking for someone," she said.

When she had explained it to the doctor, he said, "That's rather an unusual request. I'll have to refer you to the director. You can make an appointment at the front desk."

All of this, Moura knew, was for Fizzy's sake. He had made it necessary, and he had been on her mind the whole time: that was where he had come from; that was what he was.

And because of her concentration she called him as soon as she returned to Coldharbor. There was no reply. She used the bug, she peered through the skylight from the upper window, and—unable to find any sign of him—she unlocked his room with her emergency key. She had prepared herself for a loud complaining quack and flailing arms. She had prepared herself for worse—for his swollen face, a blue tongue, a brassiere around his neck. But there was nothing. He was gone, with all his boxes.

17

"ARE WE STILL ON COURSE?" HOOPER ASKED.

Fisher did not reply. The land below was scratched with old roads. It was empty and sunlit and wide-awake green. It seemed safe—Hooper felt he could put this jet-rotor down anywhere. But he was not navigator. The navigator was silent inside his helmet.

"Is there something wrong, Fizz?"

"Call me captain," the boy pleaded in his quacky voice.

"All yours, captain," Hooper said, and thought of Jennix at Coldharbor and his space-station dreams and the fantasy of his funeral on the moon. Was that normal?

None of Hooper's talk could rouse the boy. Fizzy had not blinked since they'd crossed the Red Zone. When they had received a sharp command at the perimeter to give details of their Access Pass, Fizzy had opened his mouth. But no sound came out. He breathed hard, like someone trying to steam up a window, and had a glum, laborious look on his face. Hooper had transmitted the details and they had been allowed to pass over that great shaved strip of land, with its upturned dishes and low-level gunship patrols.

Hooper was almost sure they were on course. They were using the flight program from the New Year's trip. But Hooper wanted Fizzy to relax, or at least to say something—anything to lessen the boy's apparent terror.

"We are filming, captain," Hooper said. It was still early in the O-Zone part of the trip, but they were speeding, and he did not want to miss the aliens' camp.

218

The horizon and the white sky were a shining reflection on the curve of Fisher's faceplate.

"I wish I knew where Murdick got this stuff," Hooper said. "Jet-rotor. Burp gun. Sonic stunner. Sealed video equipment. And that food of his was like slop, but you've got to admit it was unique." He glanced again at the boy. "It must be true about Godseye having government connections."

How could Fizzy sit there so long and say nothing? Hooper had never imagined that fear would make a person deaf, but rather the reverse—make him hear every crackle and whisper. Or was it something muscular? The boy was rigid in the bouncing rotor.

"I get mad when I realize I can't buy what I want with my money. Hah! Tell me what I'm supposed to use if I can't use money."

Now Hooper knew he was talking to himself, so he was brisker and friendlier.

"But it's humiliating—you bet it is. That a guy with my net worth and my credit can't buy Special Forces gear. That I have to blackmail Willis Murdick, so I can use it. That I have to take orders. No, sir, scrub that last objection."

He glanced again at Fizzy and hated the boy's helmet and found the padded suit unnecessary and the shoulder patch ridiculous: *Mission Westwind Commander*, it said. The boy was dressed for a moon landing. "Lunar suits"—that's what people called the temperature-controlled suit that Fizzy had chosen for this trip. And the boots made his feet look elephantine.

"We are still filming," Hooper said, and then remembered: "Captain."

There was a murmur on his earphones. He waited for more babble, but no clear words were uttered. It was grunting—Fizzy. The fact that the boy was grunting meant that he was thinking hard and might say something. Hardy had once said that Fizzy's farting was also an indication that the boy was deep in thought. Still, bursts of air were forced down the wire—no words. The boy's thought showed like the rumbling surface of a cooking stew.

"Viruses," he said at last.

Hooper looked hard at Fizzy's faceplate and tried to penetrate it to see his expression. Surely the craziness would show on his face. But all Hooper saw was the tilting land and empty sky of O-Zone mirrored on the plate.

"Psycho-killers," Fisher said.

Then there was a long silence—fifty clicks or more.

"You can't really do anything about either one." And he turned, the reflection slipped away from his faceplate. Fear had given him one mad eye and dry lips. "There's no remedy for bugs or wackos."

So that was it: he was still afraid of the risks. He had boasted about eliminating risks, but Hooper had noticed that he had come on the trip reluctantly. He had waited until Moura had left with her friends in the rotor, and had met Hooper on the rotor pad of Coldharbor looking like a moonman—padded "lunar suit," stratospheric helmet, high boots, finger-assisted gloves, and a container of weapons and equipment so heavy the rotor had to kneel to receive it. Fizzy had struggled through the main hatch, looking sick.

"You all right, Fizz?"

"Call me captain." That was the first time. The boy's face was yellow.

Now they were in O-Zone airspace. They flew low over the green tufty fields and the hills of blue rock and the hardwood forests. The thin brown rivers were all loops and oxbows. The city-stains were like the ashes of vast fires. They were circular and gray, littered with scrub and untended trees, and there were scorched saucer patches where there had been explosions. These craters brimmed with stunted trees. The land was lumpier where there were caves, but from this height nearly everything else looked flat.

"I had forgotten it was so dry," Hooper said. "But spring breaks through nonetheless."

The bright hot dust showed through the mottled woods. They knew that the green on the rocks that gave them a soft appearance was a crust of lichens. They had started their long descent.

"Still filming."

Fisher had not looked once at the ground-screen. He was holding on, bracing himself on his safety clamp, his head bowed.

"There's Firehills," Hooper said, and saw that Fizzy's eyes were shut tightly.

The towers, the terrace, the whips of foliage, the empty swimming pool and its snaking vines, the oaks and hickories surrounding the complex, which was set securely on the stoollike hill—it all looked lovely to Hooper and he felt, hovering there, as if it belonged to him.

"I see a fire," Fisher said, glancing out.

"Wild azaleas," Hooper said.

The boy winced and withdrew to his helmet.

"We'll make a sweep around it to get it on film. Okay, captain?"

After a slow circuit of the buildings they dropped into the very spot they had vacated almost two months before and saw that the alarms were still in place.

"How long do we have to stay?" Fisher asked.

Hooper threw open the hatch and lifted his faceplate and breathed the clean air. It was a beautiful day in O-Zone. Then he turned toward the boy and deliberately did not smile.

He said, "You tell me, captain."

In silence, they verified that the alarms still worked and the power packs were still charging. They used scanners and sound equipment to search the interior of Firehills for intruders. Fisher followed Hooper, doing nothing but grunting and growling—thinking hard; he stayed very close to his uncle, and from time to time Hooper bumped him, or stepped on his toes, and several times Hooper himself was tripped by the boy. Hooper calmed himself and moved on.

He was reassured by Fizzy's anxiety and he knew that for his purposes the boy was the perfect companion here. He was so spooked by aliens he would be a genius at spotting them on the tape they had made. Fizzy had devised a complicated program for scanning the videotape.

They were outside the condo now, at the edge of the clearing. The wall of dense trees prevented them from going farther, but for the moment Hooper was satisfied. He loved the partially broken brickwork, the grass growing through the terrace cracks, the oxidized metal foxed by tiny lichens, the desolation of the place. It was like an ancient ruin of hot solitary stones, but one he understood, because it was not really ancient—it was only abandoned and entirely empty.

It was not until he heard the small flute notes of a bird that he said, "There aren't many birds here."

All this time Fisher had been silent, bumping and tripping Hooper as they walked the perimeter of Firehills.

"What a shame we can't live here forever," Hooper said.

Something careless and lighthearted in Hooper's tone made Fisher stiffen.

"I'm afraid," the boy said, and sucked air.

Hooper put his hand on Fizzy's shoulder and felt the boy recoil slightly and then draw nearer to him and relax slightly, comforted by the simple touch of Hooper's glove. Hooper wanted to hug him for responding that way, but he didn't want to frighten him. Usually the kid hated to be touched! But he saw into Fizzy's loneliness, his isolation in his study at Coldharbor. He had a clear memory of seeing Fizzy bent over Pap, and he found the posture pathetic—not like someone driving the computer but rather like a fearful little Skell praying at an altar.

"We'll be all right here," Hooper said. "You're captain. I'm chief of ground operations. I'm responsible for your safety."

He had never been closer to the boy. He felt powerful as his protector and in an intense imagining he saw Fizzy as his own son, and wanted to hold on to him. It gave him heart to continue searching for that girl, because in seeing Fizzy as his son he took possession of the girl, too, and saw her as his wife. In that moment at Firehills—the green woods blazing around them and the sharp smell of dry dust in the air and the solitary rattle of a woodpecker—Hooper understood what it was that he lacked on earth: simply, a family that needed him.

It put him in a generous mood, and that generosity helped him see the boy clearly. Fizzy was a calculated product—the result of a plan. He had a type number; he had been designed; he had specifications and predictability. He had done everything that had been required of him. But he had not lived. His mind was a vivid island of intelligence in an innocent body. Now inexperience made him dumb, though it had never done so in New York. Faced with the real world of dust and insects and empty valleys, and the prospect of aliens, he felt terror.

That was proof of his worth. His fear was his humanity. His fear would save him. When Fizzy said, "I'm afraid," Hooper loved him.

And later, after sunset, when Hooper said, "I need you, captain," he meant it. Only Fizzy could read the videotape for aliens, only Fizzy could operate the scanner program. Without Fizzy's wonderful brain, Hooper knew that he would be blind and stumbling in this wilderness. He would never find that pretty girl. Fizzy was inarticulate and strange, gulping and farting in the echoey corridors of Firehills; but he could speak to these machines and get answers.

In the operations room—it was Fizzy's idea—they hung a row of monitors and installed a computer console. Fizzy looked at home here. His breathing was better. He didn't quack, he didn't grunt. He ran the videotape of their inbound trip and watched the main screen.

"Explain how these bleeps work."

"I can't, because you don't know the first thing about stealth or radar avoidance."

"I know about sneaky people."

Fisher said, "Alien clandestine exfiltration, you mean."

Hooper had to bite his lips to keep from smiling. "How do I find an alien on this thing?"

"You'd never understand."

The selfish little snarl in Fizzy's voice gave Hooper a lift. Fight, he thought—fight and live.

But he spent the second day dragging Fizzy up to the roof, and he took sightings on every side, while Fizzy knelt behind the parapet. The third day they were airborne, flying through the markers on a grid they had traced over this part of O-Zone.

Fizzy said, "Do we have to do this?"

"Hardy said so."

"That porker."

"He wants us on the ground, too."

"I'm not going on the ground until I'm sure we're alone."

At night, behind blacked-out windows in the sealed operations room at Firehills, Fisher scanned the videotape for aliens. He grunted, he gasped, he found no one.

Before they set off in the morning, and every night using starlight scopes and infrared sensors, Hooper wandered through the corridors of Firehills, looking for treasures. Everything he found was a treasure. He was like a beachcomber searching the tidemark for something familiar. He enjoyed being in these low buildings, among collapsed and dusty furniture, and old pictures, and faded paint, and brittle magazines. Firehills was a museum of recent artifacts—not very old, but how dated and useless! And their frivolity condemned him—the left-behind shoes, the cracked mirrors, the thick broken televisions and sunburned curtains. Nothing was so harsh as time in dimming brightness, or in shrinking objects into triviality, or in grinding great things very small. Time was an impartial leveler of everything. And what reproached Hooper here was that much of this junk was Allbright's merchandise, bought before he had introduced his cable catalog, and unpacked here to molder in the ruin and radiation. He saw his name on the lining of a lampshade, on the label of a towel, and printed on the dome of a dead bulb.

He thought how you had to look hard for ruins in America, and you were lucky if you found them, because they didn't last. When they were gone, they were gone for good—not like the ruins in Europe, but more like the mud huts in Africa, which simply crumbled and became earthworks again, with trees growing out of them. And when the ruins were gone you were lost, the past was a mystery, and not even the future was familiar. He thought: I need a family.

He had found his way to a sun-faded room at the top of the second tower and was looking off the balcony at the distances of trees.

"Hooper!"

Fisher's voice rang on the helmet phones.

"I've got a bunch of aliens here!"

Hooper found the boy rigid at his mainframe, his goggles misted, his mask and faceplate fogged—he was breathing hard, grunting, as if trying to speak.

The aliens were not in the old place, near the flat valley, that enormous depression surrounded by bluffs, where they had looked for huts. They had moved out of the valley and were in a heavily wooded part of O-Zone. They had built flimsy shelters—that was the meaning of those freckles on the screen; the hot pinpricks were humans. They were nearer to Firehills—not more than fifty clicks away.

"A bunch?" Hooper said. "A whole *bunch*?"

He smiled at the back of the boy's helmet, and still murmured the ridiculous word. The boy had never been so imprecise before. There was hope!

"Three," Fisher said, and grunted again. "I'm pretty sure the rest of them are hiding. There are lots of caves in those rocky hills nearby."

"Nothing to worry about." Hooper was relieved that Fizzy had spotted them. He would not have been surprised, after those killings, to find that the aliens had fled O-Zone. But it seemed they had only shifted away from the valley—if they were the same ones.

"Aliens!" Fisher said, fogging his faceplate again. "We didn't come here for them. We're shooting a video for Hardy. We're on a shoot!"

"We'll still have to go on the ground."

"I'm not going on no fucking ground if those dongs are there!"

"Take it easy, Fizz. They're probably a different bunch."

"They're the same ones from the meadow!" In his threatened mood, Fisher had begun to quack again. "I identified them. Two net-men and that skinny girl—"

Hooper lowered his face to the pinpricks that Fisher had enhanced on the monitor, and he warned himself against reacting.

"Hooper! You're responsible for my safety!"

"Stop worrying."

"I'm worried, so how can I stop?"

"I need you, Fizz. I'm not going to let anything happen to you. You're my navigator. I can't go anywhere without you."

"I'm the captain!"

"Leave them to me," Hooper said, still nodding. "I can deal with them."

But he was nodding at the tiny image, that bright star on the ground which matched perfectly the pretty girl in his imagination.

They blacked out more windows that night on Fisher's orders. They ate in silence—Hooper, with his mask off, grinned at the meat he was about to tear apart in his teeth; Fisher screwed a tube of protein fiber onto the suckhole of his faceplate and slurped it. At Fisher's insistence they checked all the alarms and all the infrared sensors.

Fisher said nothing: he was listening for aliens. Hooper thought of Hardy, of Moura, of Murdick, and Holly and the Eubanks, of everyone he knew in Coldharbor—in New York. He looked at his world from a distance, and from here it seemed very clear to him. He seemed to be looking down from space. Was this the sensation that Jennix craved? Everyone he knew was small and exposed, like those aliens. They were isolated. They vibrated in empty space.

He pulled out his sleep capsule—the long pod that lay under the blacked-out window. He switched it on.

"I was just thinking how we're always alone. Each of us is alone."

He knew he was rambling. Now he was thinking of the girl and feeling sorry for himself and pitying her.

"Ever notice?"

Fisher said, "No."

He had already crawled into his sleep capsule and was flexed in it on the floor like a white worm. His face showed. His eyes were dark—closed off like the windows just behind him.

"I never noticed."

No! Of course he hadn't! The boy had never known anything but solitude.

"But I was home then," Fisher said. "I had Pap."

The room hummed with silence.

"How do you feel now?"

"I've got you," Fisher said.

"Right, captain."

They were back at the clinic, the three of them. Two days after that first visit, Holly called Moura and said, "I want to go back to the clinic—now." Moura said, "Fine, I'll join you," and Holly was slightly shocked at how quickly Moura had agreed, just like that. But it was only a moment's pause, no more than a blink of Holly's long eyelashes—the shock excited her and made the visit even more urgent.

Moura noticed that Holly was dressed differently this time—not the teasing little apron and bib and bare bum, but a jacket and skirt and warm boots and goggles. Holly had realized that she could have what she wanted. It had probably just dawned on her that she didn't have to make an effort to attract a man at a contact clinic.

"I've never seen you looking so sensible," Rinka said—she had come reluctantly, she said. "For laughs," she said, using a phrase that Moura never believed, no matter who uttered it, no matter how.

Holly's smile was her lively one of lust and eagerness, and there was an edge of hilarity that lent a giggle to her voice.

"I told Brad he could land on the roof," Holly said. "I wish he had. It's so much better going through the roof. I think going through front doors in New York is really vulgar."

Moura hated this evasive chatter, but she was also grateful

that she was not required to talk. What could she say that would not condemn her?

"We've got four-o'clock sessions," Holly said. "I opted for soft sessions—they're open-ended for my client area, and they're more expensive, but I told them I didn't want a time sleeve."

Moura thought: Hunger, greed, unlimited fucking—poor Holly. The jargon did not disguise Holly's mood. She was twitching, blinking behind her goggles, smoothing her skirt. But it moved Moura to see her friend nervous.

Rinka was sheepish. She seemed hesitant and embarrassed. Moura would have been touched by that embarrassment, except that Rinka persisted in her insincerity.

"I'm doing this for laughs more than anything else."

"There aren't many laughs here," Moura said.

The others fell silent, and she realized that she had been too sharp. What a stern remark to make to her uneasy friends.

To help the moment pass, she said, "But it's safe. It's got a reputation. It's not in the baby business anymore, but so what? It's got all kinds of men, and a good health record."

"I know a gal who caught that chronic clap from her husband," Holly said piously. "You get these red dripping blebs all over your pelvic area. You begin to smell. She started to drip—this gal I know. It was her husband! She would have been a lot better off here."

She sounded disgusted and self-righteous, but Moura knew it was poor Holly's confusion—virtuous one moment, devilish the next. Moura wanted to say, *You'll get used to it here,* but didn't—not because it wouldn't calm Holly but rather because it was such an ominous thought and probably true in a dreary way.

And Moura, too, was uncomfortable. She had the suspicion that they had wanted her as a chaperon, but now that she had eased them into the clinic they wanted to be rid of her. No one liked to have witnesses here.

I enjoy being with them but I don't like myself when I'm with them: she went on confessing to herself, because being here meant that she had to scrutinize herself and look for motives. All this was the past.

She thought: *I have to be with them to understand who I am and where I have been.*

"We're real-lifers," Holly whispered. "This is action."

It wasn't boasting—she was merely trying to raise her morale. Moura knew that first-time fear. It was mostly imaginary—there were few risks—so that when you overcame the fear you quickly felt brave, and that was the sudden beginning of a greedy stuffing habit.

"Where are the other women?" Rinka asked.

Her nervousness had made her prissy. As she sat in the reception area she kept pinching different parts of her suit in a modest tidying way.

"The idea is that you don't see anyone else," Moura said. "Except the donor. They apparently still call them donors."

"I love anonymity," Holly said. "It really switches me on." She touched the shine on her eager cheeks. "Most people will do anything in a mask!"

For Moura there was something painful about waiting here. It was torture, a well-informed fantasy, that reproached her. She had returned to an old love and seen that it had not existed. She had always been alone. She felt remorse, the humiliation of broken hopes. She thought: It is heartbreaking to be reminded of your old dreams.

The three women were instructed by another kindly nurse to pass to an inner room. They blinked and tried to widen their eyes: it was darker here, lighted only by lamps above bright not-very-good paintings and bronzes. The statues were of naked dancers—perhaps dancers—men and women. And the lights and the way the sculptures were positioned made you look closely—too closely: the things were really poor and plainly sexual. But the low music was clever. It didn't come from those rooms but rather seemed to be playing in your own ears.

"It must have been so different before," Holly said.

"Yes," Moura said, for her friend's sake.

"I guess this is it," Holly whispered, seeing another nurse, and she leaned toward Moura. "When we get to the room, what do we—?"

But the question was lost. The nurse gave Holly and Rinka their room numbers and then she waited with Moura until the other two had left.

"I'm here to see the director," Moura said, and thought: No, it was just the same, and wanted it to be over.

* * *

The fragrant odors in this place—perfumes and flowers—reminded Moura of their opposites: sweats and stinks; and a whiff of strong disinfectant from one doorway made her think of venereal poisons. The bronze statues and bad paintings were truly vulgar, and she hated the potted palms and soft music. None of that had changed. Years ago it had been slightly more shadowy, more pretentious and unsure of itself, although its business had been strictly regulated and the clients came to be fertilized, not fucked.

If there was a difference it was that now the place had more airs of being a medical facility: the white uniforms and gauze masks, the many reception areas, the solicitous instructions and needless clipboards; and all the staff so kindly and courtly, as if they were dealing with problem people. It was that atmosphere that depressed Moura and made her feel like a problem person.

"The director will see you now, Mrs. Allbright."

His name was Varley Sanford. He had founded the original clinic, but Moura had never met him before. He could have been a man of sixty, but he was probably much more than that. He was healthy, old-handsome in the way men sometimes were, rather slim, with a lined, sun-browned face and soft white hair. He had perfect teeth—capped and probably sealed, but a good job. All his gestures suggested a man used to calming women and gaining their confidence, and he had an unhesitating vanity.

His eyes were the giveaway—they were cold and colorless and bulged slightly. He hardly blinked. And his hands were those of a very old man—twisted and a bit shrunken in the slack skin. But it was not the age or that look that frightened her. There was also something reptilian about them—the thin digits with sharp narrow nails, the yellowing cuticle, the slippery skin that had a dry sheen on it. He had a lizard's unwavering gaze, and a limp reptile's handshake—he merely presented his hand and let Moura weigh it in her own. And her attention was drawn to the hands again, because just as Moura sat down Sanford clawed a piece of paper from his desk and held it rattling near his face—those fingers, those eyes.

"You don't have to introduce yourself," he said. It disconcerted Moura that Sanford still clutched the paper printout. "We know you. How is your son?"

"He is the reason I'm here," Moura said.

How could the man stare like that without blinking?

"I want to ask you about his father," Moura said, and she decided to be careful. Sanford had the sort of stare that made you talkative.

"We don't use that word. I'm sure you mean the donor. What do you want to ask?"

"His name."

Sanford's hands became very still. There was a pause on his face, and his features tensed and swelled slightly, as if the man were resisting an expression trying to surface. Moura was impressed by his control, but she was also impatient for him to speak.

"I'm willing to pay you for the information."

His hands were hairless and slender, with knobby joints, and the skin was covered with crescent wrinkles, as if cut with scales. The paper was pressed between his fingertips.

"Please say something."

He slowly drew his lips apart and said, "I've had stranger requests than that."

"I am only interested in my request," Moura said.

"Of course." Now he seemed to be smiling, and this was worse than his other frozen face. "Strange requests are always considered, and if they are granted there is always a surcharge of some kind. But we have strict regulations. As a contact clinic, we are working in a very sensitive area."

Moura said, "Don't make needless explanations. I know what business you are in now."

"Our business has always been family planning."

"How many of your clients want babies?"

"Not wanting them is also family planning."

Moura said, "Nowadays, women come here to be fucked."

He had put the printout down, but now, using only his nails, he scratched it from the desktop and took it into his hand, and he rattled it as he spoke.

"You sound indignant," he said. "But you were a steady client of ours for almost two years. We have no record of any complaint from you."

"That was sixteen years ago."

Sanford stood up. He did not speak. He locked the printout into his desk and beckoned Moura into the next room.

It was the sort of security room she had seen at Captain

Jennix's checkpoint at Coldharbor—monitors, a bank of them, covered one wall. There were fifty or more, and their square screens made a chessboard pattern on the wall. Jennix's were always lighted, showing parts of Coldharbor—corridors and sidewalks—and parts of the city. But these screens in Sanford's room were cold and like his eyes had a surface gleam that was colorless and impenetrable. That's what it was about his eyes—he could see out but you couldn't see in.

Still he had not said anything. She hated his silences most of all. He reached and activated a dozen pressure pads, cutting the light and glare, and then he shook his control pistol at the monitors and in a drizzle of light blobs eight or ten of the screens came on.

The images were green-tinted orange at first, and then the flesh tones of naked bodies—so frail-looking and plain on these small screens. A hooded man lay with his head between the scissors of a woman's legs on one. On another a woman knelt over a man's face. They seemed feeble and a little frantic—that woman on all fours impaled by the man behind her—their close embrace like that of a pair of copulating frogs. In two others the woman sat on men, in another a woman was tied to the bedposts. The sound was turned off, but in one a woman was obviously shrieking with pleasure. Holly—

"Don't turn away," Sanford said. "Look."

But she had looked—she had seen everything. She tried to complete a thought: Sex is always solitary and selfish, and—

"We had those screens sixteen years ago," Sanford said, switching them off. "We were years ahead of our time." He had moved to the door. His voice was almost without emphasis. He seemed very sure of himself. "Go home, Mrs. Allbright, and think about those screens." He might have been giving directions to a small child. "They are the answer to everything. Think carefully, and come back if you like. But please be warned. They are also the answer to questions that you haven't yet asked."

18

It was dark enough now, Hooper thought—late on their fifth day at Firehills. He played a small light on Fisher's closed eyes.

The expression on the boy's face when he was asleep made Hooper love him more. He was so young! And he was innocent, his face unmarked, no scars—only a scatter of pimples—and so pale. With his eyes shut he seemed very fragile. He had a temporary, suspended look in sleep, his lips just parted, as if he were about to fall and break. The awful word "genius" was perfect, because there was something useless and unearthly about a genius.

The boy stirred in the light, then blinked—compressed his cheeks and squinted, giving himself a mole's squeezed face.

"You fucking herbert!" he said. Now he was awake.

He tried to say more but he choked on his fear, and he had stiffened in his sleep capsule. He did not move—he was deader than he had seemed asleep.

"It's me, Fizz—don't yell," Hooper said. "We're shooting."

Fisher just managed to groan, "I'm staying here."

"You're safer with me."

"Negative!"

There was no alternative: tonight, Fizzy could not refuse. It was to be Hooper's final push. But he had not said so.

Each night he had slipped out alone and muffled the rotor and flown to the forward base he had established. He had then trekked ten clicks, to where the aliens had moved. He waited; he watched; he filmed, returning at dawn to Firehills. There, Fisher scanned and interpreted the videotape.

These shoots were possible and productive because the aliens were also hunting at night, and they had put themselves at a disadvantage. They had moved their camp—obviously because of the New Year's Day ambush and those killings. So this was for them new territory: they were truly aliens here. They had no gardens, no huts, no defenses. Their dogs were gone—had they eaten them? They seemed to have little food. They went in search of small animals, which they trapped. They gathered wood. They grazed their animals—a skinny cow, a pair of goats. All this in the darkness of the woods, when the moon was down. They had survived so far, but they were having a difficult time, Hooper could tell. They were divided and desperate; they were blind.

And because they were blind, Hooper's shooting was easy. He used the starlight scope to find them, and he shot them with Murdick's heat-sensitive camera. Fisher had identified all of them. There were nine aliens. Monkeys, Fisher called them—herberts, dongs, tools, wackos, jigs. He hated and feared them. But he described them minutely for the data base; he knew all their movements, which ones were scavengers and berry-pickers and diggers, which were hunters and sentries. Without realizing it—he still thought they were shooting for Hardy—he had helped Hooper isolate the girl. There were hours of her on the tape. Hooper had her hunting, he had her standing guard and burying food. That food business was interesting—the other aliens did not seem to know anything about it. Hooper watched the tapes after Fisher sealed himself into his sleep capsule for the night. This secret food-burying fascinated him, but there was another in which she washed in a shallow pool that was fed by a spring. Hooper had shot that one at some risk, because dawn was just breaking and until then he had always traveled in the darkness. But seeing her stripping off her clothes, he was not about to sneak away in his rotor simply because the sun was coming up. In fact, the light dazzling between the saplings gave the moment a powerful poignancy as she tossed her clothes aside and stood, as slender as a taper. The girl's nakedness and the rapid, splashing way she washed made her seem like a creature of the forest.

Her name was Bligh—that was the spelling Hooper gave

it. He learned it by shooting her in whispered conversation with two men, one she called Gumbie, and another she called Rooks. Rooks was black. Fizzy analyzed their lip movements.

"They probably saw you. They probably want to kill you. Especially that jig."

As he muttered—this was back at Firehills—he inserted the lip-reading program into the computer.

"They're hungry," he said. The data was coming through now. "They're talking about food."

"Hunger makes people irritable," Hooper said.

"You know all about it, don't you, herb? You and Hardy are such big talkers when you've got me to do all the work!"

The boy's fear made him quarrelsome, and quarrels upset him further.

"I appreciate your help," Hooper said.

"I'm the captain—you're the helper!"

"What are they saying?" Hooper asked, not daring even to try to calm the boy anymore.

"I'll tell you, but just stop giving speeches. 'Hunger makes people irritable.' I can't bear listening to shit like that."

"Right, captain."

Hooper was always surprised that Fizzy did not take offense when he spoke to him in this ludicrous way—the boy even seemed to like it.

"They're arguing," Fisher said. "'Listen, Bligh, if I find out you've been hiding food I'll kill you'—correction, 'kick you.' She says, 'Don't you threaten me.' The jig says, 'Don't make problems.' He should talk!"

That was last night, a typical night. Hooper had stayed near her and she had taken the same path to the shallow pool. He wondered whether she would remove her clothes again and wash; but she didn't—perhaps it was too cold. She waited, and when she seemed satisfied that no one was watching her, she foraged in the trees.

Hooper had been on the point of stunning her when he saw she was not foraging—she was hiding food. He was so fascinated by her deception that he allowed her to get away. So he had not isolated her: she had isolated herself. Perhaps she was planning her escape; perhaps she did not trust the others; perhaps she was merely hungry. He shot her going.

Usually, just before dawn the aliens hid themselves, to sleep. They had been frightened into new habits. And when they vanished, Hooper returned to Firehills. He watched the video he had made; but it was more than watching—it was like a form of prayer. It was sometimes worship. His desire for the girl, Bligh, dominated him totally. He told himself that he needed her, and that it was urgent. He believed it might make him strong. Instead, he felt sick. If he did not have her he would die. He reflected that he could have just about everything else on earth and it became a greater urgency that he should have her, because none of those other things mattered.

But it was not simply a reaching out and clutching her: he wanted her to possess him too. He wanted her to feel the same desire. She did not even know he existed! It was all like old magic, and he thought he sounded like a savage when he mumbled to himself that he loved her.

"We didn't come here for this," Fisher said.

He meant watching the tapes and drowsing all day and kicking around this old condo, Firehills. He also meant that they were too close to the aliens. He meant everything, because he was so frightened.

"It's what Hardy wants us to do," Hooper said.

"Hardy's got a secret weather scheme here," Fisher said. "I know all about it. I hacked his computer wide open."

"What's the scheme?"

"I don't know—the fucking tool stopped using his computer! But I'm sure it's one of those thermal mountains. He wants to get a contract, so that he's the only one in O-Zone."

"Except there's some people who got here ahead of him."

"I mean, he wants to be the only human being."

Hooper marveled at how all of Fizzy's reading and intelligence had failed to persuade him that aliens were human. His fear had made them into wolves and monkeys.

Hooper said, "We agreed to Hardy's terms, captain."

"That porker."

"And we can't shoot these ground elevations until we've isolated the aliens."

He meant Bligh—without her there would only be misery in his mouth.

All this time, Fisher had stayed at Firehills, behind the blacked-out windows and the wires and alarms and infrared sensors. Hooper had allowed it. But tonight, their fifth night at Firehills, Hooper needed the boy with him.

"Negative," Fisher was saying as he rolled his head in refusal.

Hooper said, "I think a couple of them could have just slipped under our wires."

He regretted the lie when he saw the effect it had on the boy's face: Fizzy was drowning.

"So we're moving camp, Fizz. Leave the hardware and follow me. I've already loaded the food."

But in the end Fisher said he was too weak to follow. Hooper helped him up and half-carried him into the rotor. And then they were on their way, heading for the forward base.

"Did you say something?"

There had been a murmur in Hooper's phones.

Fisher was whimpering. "You fucking herbert."

The landing spot for the jet-rotor was a sinkhole, ten clicks from the aliens' camp. It was a wide hole and deep enough to hold and hide the rotor. These sinkholes, Fisher said, were caused by the collapse of the limestone caverns that were so numerous in O-Zone. The roof fell in and a bowl was formed. Everyone talked about the sabotage that might have caused the radiation leak, or was it a ransom attempt, or blackmail that had contaminated O-Zone for so long? Fisher's own theory was that it was none of these. It was an earth tremor, like the one that had created Landslip in California, and simultaneous collapse of these caverns all over the Ozark Plateau. The weight of this rock had ruptured the drums of nuclear waste that had been hidden in the caverns; and so the place was poisoned.

Hooper was doubtful. "Then why did the Feds make a mystery of it and imply that a dark foreign power had made a mess of O-Zone?"

"Because the Feds didn't want to admit that they had been hiding nuclear waste in Missouri for twenty years. It was a blunder, so they invented a conspiracy."

"And it never occurred to anyone that it was the roof falling in?"

"How could it? No one was allowed to enter O-Zone. It was evacuated and sealed."

"Smart kid," Hooper said.

"And now we're sitting in one," Fisher said, looking out of

the rotor at the steeply sloping sides of the hole. "It's probably hot!"

"It's safe. I've checked it for radiation levels."

"I hope it's hot. I hope your knob drops off!"

The hole was perfectly situated for Hooper's purposes. He had flown from Firehills with the rotor's muffler engaged—it was almost noiseless, its sound was something like the thin whine of a nighttime mosquito, and didn't carry: it was the pelting of the rotor blades. In the hole, it was hidden. This was Hooper's forward base.

Fisher said, "I hate it here."

The base of the hole was soft and silty, probably from soil that had washed down, and on its upper edge were trees, many of them withered and bent down.

"You think it's pretty on the ground-screen," the boy said. "But it's just smelly green rock."

The false barren green of O-Zone covered the exposed limestone here. It was a crumbly, scaly green, the fungus crust of lichens. From a distance it was velvety and ravishing; up close it was hard and ugly and very dry, and every surface was thick with it. Beneath this layer of scrubby lichen was solid rock. At night, in the darkness, it seemed to have a sweetish stink.

They had traveled in the dark. The landscape had showed crimson and gray on the ground-screen, the woods mottled, the hills had been blotches and black holes.

"Lights are dangerous," Hooper said. "They make you overconfident."

"You dong," Fisher said. "You're supposed to be responsible for my safety. How did those Skells get under the wire?"

"There are no Skells out here," Hooper said, amazed at the boy's ignorance of this simple fact. "You only find Skells in cities. You saw them yourself on the tape. They're not tramps and bagmen and cannibals."

"You tool."

"They're sort of ordinary people," Hooper said, persisting.

"Grubbing in caves. Climbing trees. Chewing branches. Oh, sure, ordinary people!"

"We drove them out of their camp. We killed two of them! They're scared—wouldn't you be? They're hungry. They're desperate."

"You feel sorry for those monkeys!" Fisher said. "What a

fucking porker. It's a good thing I'm captain. If you were captain you'd probably be making contact with them. Chewing branches with them! 'Okay, jigaboo, pass me a branch'"—Fisher was honking, because it was all so preposterous—"And there's Hooper and his monkeymen, all having a feeding frenzy! Boy, am I glad I'm captain."

He stopped talking as the rotor shut itself off—something in its whine had kept him talking. But now he sat in the darkness, simply breathing. Hooper said nothing. The boy bitched and breathed hard when he was afraid.

"What about me?" Fisher cried finally. "I'm hungry. I'm desperate. And I'm not a monkey!"

But it was so hard to reassure this ranting kid. Hooper was calm because he was certain of success—certain of its necessity, too. He saw the three of them in the rotor—Fizzy navigating, Bligh in the rumbleseat, and flying east with a tailwind in a clear sky. It was a lovely vision but it was so complete he could not describe it—he had gone too far in imagining it, given it too many specific details. He had let it accumulate around him so that he was already living within it. And he knew that it was his own vision, not Fizzy's; so the boy might find no consolation in it at all.

"Let's stick to the plan," Hooper said. He meant his own plan. "And then we can go home."

"I'm not leaving this rotor."

"It's only ten clicks to the camp," Hooper said.

"I'm completely hidden in this sinkhole. I ain't leaving, porky."

"I'm telling you, you're safer with me."

"Walking in the dark up a hill in monkeyland!"

"Suit yourself, sonny." Hooper was too angry to risk saying anything more.

"Herbert!" Fisher called out. "Don't go! Don't leave me!"

But Hooper had already pushed away his safety clamp and lifted himself free of the hatch. The darkness poured past him. He did not think of the risks but only of the urgency of this mission. He was not worried about these blind aliens. He only thought how much easier this whole business would be with Fizzy's cooperation. And now the stubborn boy had wedged himself in the rotor and wouldn't leave.

Hooper dropped to the ground. Outlined against overlapping masses of stars, the rotor—parked on its long crooked-out legs—looked like a monster insect.

There was a breath of wind tonight. No, it was a suffocated voice in the rotor crying, *I'm captain*. A little gnat shriek. *I'm captain*.

Over these past days it had become Hooper's practice to climb the hill quickly and descend the other side more slowly, scanning for aliens. He had safe stopping-places where he crouched and listened for voices or footsteps. He had discovered that people who hunt at night establish regular routes and never deviate from them. Night hunters were the most predictable creatures, and they all behaved like raccoons, blindly treading paths that were clearly visible by day as worn-away grooves on the floor of the woods.

Darkness was the cover for their routine; but Hooper also had a night routine, and he could see their paths in his starlight-scope. He always knew at which point in the trek he would hear Bligh stealthily toeing the leaves, and where he would see her foraging, and where bathing or waiting. He had become accustomed to watching her when she was alone, like a bird on a branch. He felt he had come to know her well. He loved her face. When she was alone her face was real.

But he was surprised tonight at not finding her in any of the usual places. For an hour he trekked and stopped, and for another hour he scanned—nothing in the imager, nothing on the scope or the phones. He went to the spring. Because of the water, it was the only dense greenery around, the only seclusion. Hooper did not want to be trapped by daylight. Bligh was not there. Hooper waited, listening to his own breath in his ears, and the rattle of the dry leaves.

What he first took to be voices were running feet, closing in on him quickly. He had heard Bligh running before—she was fast; but these were swifter echoey steps. He decided that it was two people, one just ahead of the other.

He set his scanner at those sounds and waited for an image. He was always excited by the rising image—a pinprick became a seed-shape, and swelled to a wavering blob, grew legs and arms, and was whole and human. It was a kind of birth in seconds.

So he saw Bligh, like this, growing out of a point of light; and then saw an unformed thing behind her. In the imager it became a bearded man in a heavy coat. Bligh outran her pursuer and then the man stumbled among so many trees. "I can see you!" the man yelled. But it was Bligh's own territory. She knew it in the dark, and it was the man—this stranger—who was lost. Yet he was not that far away. Bligh might not be able to hear him, but Hooper monitored his gasps at thirty meters.

Crouched, and with just the imager and the mike raised in the dark, Hooper could see them both, Bligh and her pursuer.

"It will be light soon," the man called out. Who was it? Fizzy would know. He had identified them all. The kid even had nicknames for them, like the Jig, and Dimbo, and Beaver-Face. "I'll get you then, when it's light!"

With this the man was silent and still, waiting for the night to lift. Bligh lay against a fallen tree, her hands on her face, her knees drawn up.

The man remained a melted shape, a swatch of pink, pulsing on Hooper's small screen. Hooper wanted to do something, but what could he do without alarming Bligh? He might lose her in that attempt. It was past four-thirty and the sky was changing from a starry blackness to a murky blue, like deep ocean overhead. In one quarter, the sky was lighter but the wooded land here was still dark, and the hillsides like black walls with cold shadows.

In this silence and ripening light the man stood up and everything happened.

He ran forward and picked out Bligh. He flung himself at her. But as he did so, Hooper fired the stunner and the man dropped. He fell with a flop, like a heavy sack, and his grunt was the air thumped out of his mouth.

It took several seconds for Bligh to realize she was safe from the man.

"Don't run," Hooper said. "I'm over here."

The light was enough.

She seemed curious rather than afraid. Hooper could see the wonderment on her face, the thought: *Who . . . ?* She was thin now. She wore an old coat, and her hair was bright and chopped.

"Bligh," he said.

She looked closer and almost smiled at hearing her name—she seemed touched, as if she had just heard someone praying.

In his mind, Hooper had always pursued her and taken aim with Murdick's sonic stunner, which Fizzy had repaired—Fizzy had the new model with him in the rotor. (It was the boy's peculiar selfishness that he kept all the expensive and elaborate equipment with him, and never used it.) Hooper had imagined stunning her with one shot, and on waking she was his—he had never questioned how.

He was amazed by how very different all this was. He was improvising—it was new to him, and clumsy. He observed himself taking off his mask and dropping it, and throwing his stunner aside, and taking off his gloves. His hands were bare—he could see he was trembling.

She watched him very closely with alert eyes—they were big and pale; they missed nothing. Her head was erect on her long neck, and steady like a deer's in a breeze.

"I love you," he said, and felt liberated by saying the word.

It was only then that her face clouded and she backed away.

That morning Moura had said, "He's never been gone this long before." But Hardy was just as evasive as he had been at the beginning. He was evasive in an active hectoring way. He first went deaf and demanded that Moura repeat what she said—the worry; then he ridiculed her for worrying; then accused her of being suspicious, and finally of wasting time— it was too late, he said; didn't she know that simple thing?

It was probably the only thing that he had in common with Fizzy, that he was overbearing and abusive when he was nervous; at his most truculent when he was fearful. Then you poked him and he collapsed.

Now he was saying, "Hooper got him out of his room somehow—for almost a week so far! That's more than we ever managed to do!"

It was all blame. He meant: You failed him, you neglected him, you turned him into a robot, a tool, a supermoron—and you're his mother!

"I don't know whether you understand," Hardy said, "but Fizzy's childishness humiliates me. I feel as though I have to carry him—and I don't like it. I'm not his father. I'm not responsible. I don't know him—I used to, but I don't anymore. It's sometimes that way with children, isn't it?" But he did not wait for a reply. "You don't understand."

And then Hardy went about his business. He might be late, he said. He was working in the Asfalt Annex—more evasions: there was no Asfalt Annex, Hardy must have just invented it.

But he was not stupid. It had occurred to Moura many times that in creating these evasions Hardy had made himself a free man.

She wished she had some of that freedom. But she felt burdened by her past and had only lately realized how much of it was Fizzy—how this horrible-handsome boy disturbed her. Her conversation with Hardy had upset her. She had been worried, and it was related to Fizzy. But how could she tell Hardy that she was making another visit, this time alone, to the contact clinic? He would have said, "What are you trying to prove?" and she didn't have an answer to that.

It was her third visit to the clinic in less than a week—but "clinic" was the wrong word. It was a meat market, it was a doghouse, it was a stud farm. She hated its hidden exits and entrances, all its face-saving secrets, the rotor park on the rooftop, the blacked-out windows. Its pretense of being involved in medical research and technology was a shallow mockery, and all that talk about fertility and babies and programs! She hated the bad expensive decor and the subdued and cheating lights, and the oversized plants, and the tests and examinations. Most of all she hated the solemn medical manner of the staff, who were all pimps and whores.

"You can go up now, Moura"—she hated the way these so-called nurses had quickly gotten onto a first-name basis— "Dr. Sanford is expecting you."

And she hated the nurse's knowing face and her brisk bullying manner—standing watch over her until she started upstairs.

"To be perfectly honest, I didn't expect to see you again," Sanford said. "But here you are, so let's get down to business."

They were in the room with the checkerboard wall of video screens, and Sanford had begun switching monitors on and activating machines, tapping pressure pads and pushing chairs forward as soon as they had entered.

Moura was intimidated by the monitors—by her memory of the glimpse Sanford had given her: that awful combination of high technology and poor frantic flesh. It went against her upbringing for her to feel ashamed—and she wasn't ashamed. Yet she wondered whether her anger and indignation were a mask for shame. The clinic was perniciously spic-and-span, and she was disgusted with herself for being there. But she held on to her doubts, because always in her life it was her doubts that saved her. She thought: This is what I was, but is this what I am now?

She knew the sad greedy women who came here and stuffed themselves full with sex. They acted out their fantasies. No one was shocked here, because everything had a price: some fantasies were merely more expensive than others. None were priceless. That was the logic of the meat market—every cut was for sale. She had never believed that she was one of those women, and that was why she was able to return here.

Sanford's fussing distracted her in these thoughts and brought her back to her immediate purpose.

"Shouldn't we be discussing terms?" she said, because she saw him slipping a video cartridge into a slot.

"We're very old-fashioned here—"

Why was it that crooks and liars always used that phrase?

"—we're in business to make money. And I've found that for people in certain moods, money is no object."

He had not turned to look at her as he spoke. It was a gauge of his contempt, not to turn. It was also a medical man's arrogance; and it was the arrogance of a pimp.

Now the largest screen was lighted. Sanford said, "All this was a long time ago, of course."

She guessed that his elaborate manner was a way of wrongfooting her, and she felt that he was behaving this way because he suspected that she was in a weak position—she had come with a request: she needed him—so he must have thought. Perhaps he also suspected that she despised him. Beneath his fluttering phrases and gestures there was mockery. She was convinced of his sadism, because he was so much worse when he smiled.

He was smiling at the screen. It was an old video; she could tell from its scratchy surface and occasional jumps, its rattled lines, its poor color quality—parched in some shots and garish in others.

But there was no mistaking the young man. She looked upon his beaked mask thinking: A mask is also a face.

"Is that him?"

She only watched; she said nothing. But she felt as if she were at the edge of a cliff that was breaking beneath her and bearing her down. The man had entered a room. He was naked except for the mask—and that looked a little fierce. There was no sound, but she knew the man was speaking.

"Tell me his name," Moura said at last.

"Just watch," Sanford said.

She said, "I'm almost sure it's him."

But Sanford kept facing the screen. What did he see with those empty eyes? Moura realized that she had deliberately not looked at his hands, so as to keep her composure.

The masked man walked forward, his penis like a tassel making an odd short arc as it wagged. She had always thought of sex in a disconnected way because penises seemed like something added on, with a separate existence—rather comic and bulgy tassels one minute, and the next minute terrible truncheons.

He was very young—tightly muscled and tall, with a flat stomach and slender legs. It was Fizzy's body—Fizzy's hands and feet; the same penguin's walk that made her feel safe.

"That's enough," she said. "His name and whatever other details you can give me—that's all I want."

Sanford smiled with only his mouth—his cold eyes were no help—and his effort made him seem particularly sinister to Moura.

"I'll pay you whatever you want," she said. "And no one will ever know. I realize you value your confidentiality, so I give you my word that it will remain my secret. I'll sign anything you ask, I'll swear—"

"Not necessary," Sanford said. He was confident, and yet not relaxed as an assured man might be. He held himself stiffly in his chair, and began to turn. "I know you will never sue us."

He was facing her, twisting his hands—one hand throttling the other.

"This is why."

As he turned back to the screen the angle of the camera changed—a new camera, a different corner of the room.

And now Moura saw the young woman on the bed: she was propped on a stack of pillows, one hand lying just between her legs in what was not modesty but a kind of teasing. As the man approached, she opened the fingers of that hand, making a wicket of them, and the mock-modest covering gesture became gross and explicit. Spreading her fingers, she spread her legs, and showed the lips of her vulva reddening, and its moistened throat.

She too wore a mask that perfectly fitted her: it was the face of a lovely woman.

"Shall I turn the sound up?"

"No"—and she surprised herself by sobbing. "I don't think I could bear—"

She did not finish, for now the man had embraced the young woman, and she received him, taking his face in her hands and kissing it. It was a clumsy coming together of puppet heads—staring and expressionless, the most meaningless caress: mask kissing mask. But it did not matter that their faces had the fixed expressions on the masks; it was their bodies that thrilled her. She saw pleasure, drama, and a subtle change—even an expressive sadness—in the bodies of the young man and young woman. And there was something that moved her in the way their feet responded—their lovely feet.

Tears were streaming down Moura's face. She watched willingly, punishing herself with the sadness of it. She wept for herself and the young man. She wept for Fizzy. She wept at the sight of the solitary act. The young woman did not know that she was lost.

Finally she could not bear to look anymore, and could not see through her tears. Alone, she saw the woman alone. There was no loneliness in love. But sex was narrow, sex was private. It was like throttling a small animal—choking it until it was dead. It was sometimes like twisting your own arm off. It was not shared—not really—and when the desire was gone there was nothing. Love involved someone else; but all sex was always sex with yourself.

"Now you know almost everything."

"He's gone," Hooper said when they got back to the sinkhole where the rotor was parked.

The sun was just breaking over the brow of the hill, and the whole sky was visible—liquid with light.

"The food's gone. The weapons too."

As soon as he saw the hatch lying open he had let go of Bligh's hand. She watched without surprise as Hooper blustered. He was saying: *How? Why?*

"They've snatched him—we'll never find him," Hooper said. He hated saying these things, because his words made it all real. But he couldn't help it; he was babbling, and now he spoke directly to the woman, who had not said anything so far. "Where are they taking him?"

She had pale eyes, a child's face, and her skin was damp

and dusty from the tumult of the night. Her clothes were torn and so threadbare, and she was facing a man in a gleaming rotor-suit, standing tall in expedition boots, and wired for survival.

In a small surrendering voice she said, "Where are you taking me?"

Just then dawn dissolved the simple darkness of night and the clear air showed the beautifully lit disorder of the day in this wilderness—the green-caked rocks and gaunt trees, the blue dust, the pathless woods, the emptier distances.

PART THREE

HAPPY VALLEY

19

Two men who in the darkness were no more than hard hands and grunts smelling of glue had plucked Fisher out of the rotor and swung him to the ground in a net. The boy screamed once sharply and punched and pulled at the ropes. He had howled all the way to the camp, and was still howling. But no one heard him. He was still wearing his helmet and mask.

It was dawn at the mouth of the cave, in the dampness and dust and the sting of smoke.

The man called Mr. Blue watched him twisting in the net of ropes and said, "Let him out the bag, Rooky."

Once he was out of the net and disentangled, Fisher stopped howling—stopped everything. He had just lost his helmet and mask struggling in the bag. He cowered and tried to make himself small. He went absolutely rigid.

"Spiderman," someone said.

"He turned into a stick."

He heard them talking about him, but it was like a dream in which you know all the dangers, and know you are probably going to die, but are helpless to save yourself.

"You got a name?"

He stammered saying "Fisher."

"Fish," Mr. Blue said, and looked satisfied.

"Mighty goddamn far from the water, I'd say."

"Throw him back."

He was flat on the ground. Each time he opened his eyes he saw feet. Their sandals, the ragged straps, their toes, frightened him; and so did the stains on their faded pants. He saw ax heads and black dented pots and some of his own provisions from the rotor. Seeing these stolen things in their protective wrappings stacked in the dust reminded him that he had been stolen himself, and was captive and couldn't move. Now and then they touched him—pinched his suit to examine the metal-fiber material. He screamed, or tried to scream: it was a miserable whimper, so insignificant no one noticed it.

"It's strong lightweight stuff, but it's for cities and space. It can't take much abrasion. Even those boots won't last here. The gloves might be useful."

"The helmet's a beauty, but I can't get a buzz out of it."

"He's real pale. If he's sick with something I say dump him. He might make us all sick."

They were still talking.

But he was more terrified by their smell. To Fisher they were more like plants and animals than human beings. They had the ragged stinking look of wild things, they had wounds and bruises and chafed faces. They did not talk to him. They wore very little equipment, only old tools—a knife, a coil of rope, a sharpened screwdriver, a hatchet or ax. He could tell they seldom washed. He imagined them to be sick with dirt, probably wormy, or with fleas clinging to them, with nits in their hair. He thought of them as a type of poisonous weed, and he did not want them near him. He was afraid of their touch—their filthy hands and hairy arms, their damp rotten breath. Some were women, some were black.

"Wrap up this fish, somebody."

"No, don't bother. He's not going anywhere," Mr. Blue said. "And I hate his yelling. He'll just yell in the bag."

"We don't need him, Mr. B."

"Who knows? He's a fair specimen. We might be able to do something with him. Maybe use him for a swap."

Fisher was pleading, "Find Hooper. He'll give you anything you want. He's responsible for my safety—"

But they did not reply. They said nothing to him. It unnerved him, and he began to doubt that he was making any sound at all. Was he only imagining the words and his voice just an unintelligible mutter?

Their ignoring him was worse than if they had threatened him with their full attention. It made him motionless, it kept him rigid. It's driving me crazy, he thought. They'll let me die. He whimpered—it came out of his nose as a hum. He tried to speak—*Who are you?*—but his lips would not move. They were talking about food—the boxes they had lifted from the rotor; they wondered whether to eat them. They examined the thick wrappers and the seals on the bags: they could store them, they said, for a time when they might be even hungrier.

"Who are you?" Fisher whimpered, but now he was convinced that the question had not left his head. "Let me go!" It didn't matter what he said—they couldn't hear. "I hate you!"

They went on talking.

"You're aliens," he said.

This word roused one man. "You're the only alien here, piggy."

Fisher screamed to himself: *Herbert!*

"And take him back to that rotor and swap him for Bligh," Mr. Blue was saying.

Yes, hurry, Fisher pleaded to himself, too fearful to speak again. The man had terrified him by calling him "piggy."

The woman Valda said, "Bligh and some equipment. Make a bargain. Maybe some money too. We'll never get another chance like this. He dropped in our lap!"

"He belongs to someone—probably an Owner, from the way he's dressed up. He's worth something."

"I say leave him and walk away. He's going to give us trouble. I can tell from his freaky face."

Freaky face! They were skinny and bug-eyed with hunger, and Fisher had the idea—in spite of what they said—that they were planning to kill him. This fear persisted in his mind with another related one: that they intended to eat him. It was the worst of his thoughts and he couldn't rid himself of it. He had heard stories about cannibals and had usually laughed at them—and he had mocked people who believed such things. But this was his punishment, for he had laughed at the stories of people living in places like O-Zone, too, and that was precisely what these aliens were doing. Their presence defied available data: why weren't they dead?

But Fisher was not impressed with their ratlike ability to survive here, against the odds. If they had a secret, it was a savage secret. They were rats, they would eat anything, they floated, they gnawed, they slept in lizard cracks in this rocky hill. There were no children here, and yet there were men and women: that meant something. Fisher also thought that they were sick and dying from the effect of living among low-level mutagens that had slowly soaked into their bones. They probably knew it, and in this desperate condition had turned into beasts—the sort of vermin that would do anything to survive.

They lived like beasts, he could see that. It was a temporary camp, but that was no excuse. They could have done better than these flimsy shelters propped against tree trunks, and that hole in the hill, and that firepit and foodbox. There were nests of grass and leaves where some of them were sleeping now, because they had been up all night, like rats and monkeys.

It seemed horrible to him that he knew all their names. He had lip-read Hooper's tapes and stored the conversations. He had classified each of these people according to age, sex, and body type; he knew their coloring and how fast they moved and what weapons they carried. Hooper had said that Hardy wanted all this data. Where was Hooper now? *I'm responsible for your safety*—that's what the porker had said!

"Eat this," Mr. Martlet was saying, showing him a handful of dry turds.

I don't eat stools, Fisher wanted to say.

Martlet (thirty, male, black, stocky) said, "It's meat. Go on."

How could crumbling black strips of stool be meat?

Covering his face, Fisher turned away. He refused a drink, he saw filth in it. He slapped a plate of wild plums from Valda's hands.

"Give him something from those tubes we took out of the rotor," Rooks said.

"No—save them. Their seals will keep them forever. It's better than money. Give him some of those pole greens," Mr. Blue said. "Or some of that cottontail stew."

"He won't eat anything," the woman Tinia said.

From his grass nest Echols said, wagging his beard, "He doesn't recognize any of it as food. We might have to analyze some of that sealed food to see what his diet's like. We don't know what he'll accept and eat."

"Choke him on this," Martlet said with a growl—what was he holding down there?—"Or else let's get rid of him."

Knowing their names made it a greater shock for Fisher to discover that these aliens with identities and ages and body classifications were such animals and stank so fiercely. It was a humiliation for him to consider that all the time he had spent with the computer, sorting and storing data, and scanning and enhancing the images, was for these savages. He had enjoyed the data, and he liked inventing ways of classifying these creatures, but up close he found them unbearable.

So his study was no help to him; it only showed how superficial his data was. All his hours of classifying and scanning had not revealed what he had learned minutes after being abducted: that these aliens were dirty, haggard, foulmouthed, and ill-equipped. They lived like rats. They scratched. They stank. They were desperate, they were dangerous!

"Are you interested in getting out of here alive?" Mr. Blue said.

Fisher's pale pleading face was fixed on the man kneeling over him at the mouth of the shallow cave.

"Then write what I tell you."

Mr. Blue's words were harsh, but his tone was reasonable. It disconcerted Fisher, because the man's danger was like an echo. They were peaceable-looking creatures, but on reflection not so peaceable: the aftershock was their ferocity. They were killers—he knew that now. It had not shown in the data, but as their captive Fisher could feel it and smell it.

Mr. Blue was holding a pen and a square of lined paper that had been torn from a pilot's logbook—both items snatched from the rotor.

Sitting up in silence, Fisher took the pen and smoothed the paper against his thigh. It was Hooper's pen—he called it his stylus. The porker was always scribbling with it when he should have been doing something useful, like making sure that no intruders could get into the rotor when it was parked. And why hadn't he found these aliens and blown them away?

"Write exactly what I say," Mr. Blue said. Then in a halting, dictating voice, "'I am being held by a large number of people'—correction—'well-armed people. If you follow instructions they will release me unharmed. There are certain conditions and demands'—you're not writing, Fish."

Fisher had been doodling nervously. This pen and paper were useless; anyway, he could scarcely write, and did not consider it anything but a pointless labor, since he had a voice-printer in the rotor, and even a pocket voice-printer. But the pocket printer had smashed as he had struggled in the net.

All these filthy-faced aliens were staring at him now.

He wrote, *Bng hld bi lg no amd ppl,* and then the message appeared to become incoherent. Still stabbing at the paper, Fisher glanced up.

He thought at that moment the man was going to hit him— Mr. Blue had raised his hand.

The bearded man, Echols, snatched the paper.

"This is just a stupid scribble!"

Fisher had not been shouted at by any of these people until then, and when it happened he almost fainted. The sharp sound pierced him and gave him a pain in his heart. It rapped against his head, and when he saw the man's open mouth and his huge teeth and tongue his fear of being eaten came back. It was not a fear of death, but rather of teeth sinking into his flesh—of being eaten alive.

He could not speak, though an imploring voice within him was saying: *Get me a printer or a frame and I'll key in anything you say and transmit it to my uncle! I'll do what you tell me!* He knew he could not write well, nor use a pen with any skill. But he wanted to send the message and he was paralyzed by the fear that if he didn't they would tear off his arms and eat them—or simply start chewing his shoulders and biting his cheeks.

"He's saying something—"

Fisher himself did not know what he was saying. It was all a moaning in his ears.

"He wants a printer," Rooks said, as if translating.

Mr. Blue said, "He means some kind of cable rig. He thinks we have computers, frames, screens, phones, satellite links. He can't write."

Someone else was crumpling the paper. "This bullshit is no use to us."

"He's retarded—handicapped or something," Echols said. "Maybe he's got a motor problem. He seems a little dystrophic, the way he moves, the way he was holding that pen—could hardly get his fingers around it."

"He acts like a cripple," Martlet said. "He'll cripple us."

There was a sudden chatter of opinion, everyone talking at once, but Mr. Blue made himself heard.

"Who wants him?" he said.

The question silenced them.

"Then we hand him back now, and no big negotiation. Come on, we're just wasting time."

"He's a drooly."

They pulled him up roughly and tried to trot him through the woods. But he resisted. He moved slowly. He was stiff and frightened. He had never run before in his life. His head felt small and fragile without the helmet. He could barely breathe.

"Can't run either!" Gumbie said. He was laughing at the way the boy stumbled.

Fisher knew why they were so rough and careless—because they would be rid of him soon and they had no regard for human life. He thought: Good, they don't want me. But he was also ashamed. He had tried to talk to them, he had tried to write a message to Hooper, he had tried to run. He had failed, and he had had to listen to someone say *He's a drooly*.

They carried him, four of them swinging him in a net, the way they had snatched him out of the rotor an hour ago.

The sun was higher—not above the trees yet but still striking brightly through the boughs—and the huge sky was one simple color that seemed to drown the eye. Fisher was watching it through the branches as he swung, his face upturned, hating these dusty woods and the men trotting beside him and gasping *ump-ump-ump*. He thought: Get me out of here.

Hooper would save him. Hooper was chief of ground operations, and Fisher was captain. He would demand that Hooper agree to the bargain, give them anything they wanted. And then when they saw Fisher ordering Hooper around, and Hooper saying *Yes, sir*, they would understand that Fisher was actually a very powerful person—not a drooly, not handicapped, not a cripple, but the captain and commander of a delicate mission to O-Zone.

And when he was safely aboard the rotor he would take the particle beam and destroy these monkeys.

Already, in his mind, he was burning them to dust. During this run to the sinkhole where they had put the rotor, this thought kept Fisher breathing. He would climb into the rotor and rise in it, and then just hover and pour fire on them and blow them all away. He saw them dancing in pain and then dying among the dead trees.

The swinging bag made him nauseous. There was something about nausea that always intensified his fear by weakening him still more.

"The hole's other side of that hollow."

"Just hand this pig back," someone was saying.

He did not recognize anything here. Hooper had landed in darkness, and it had been dark when they had manhandled him out of the rotor.

"It's gone."

"What did he do with Bligh?"

Fisher began yelling, "Where is he! Where's Hooper! Put out a Mayday call and raise him! Use my helmet phone!"

But no one responded, no one spoke to him. Perhaps they had not heard his voice? He knew he was hysterical. He was gagging on mucus. But was his voice merely a shrill noise in his head?

The men were discouraged that the hole was empty, and probably because they were so hungry they went suddenly limp from the effort of this run. They were saying, "He got Bligh" and "We're stuck with this fish," and cursing.

Fisher had begun to struggle again in the rope bag, trying to get free of it so that he could actually see into the sinkhole. They let him struggle and loosen the drawstring, they let him kick the bag until he realized that he could simply step out of it. It was as though they had just given him an intelligence test, but a simple one, to prove he was not a complete basket case.

Fisher pushed the ropes apart and ran to the edge of the wide hole. He saw four faint dents in the dust from the pads on the rotor's feet. The hole had an odd scoured look from the whirling rotor blades.

"You dong, you wang, you fucking tool!" he screamed. "You're responsible for my safety!"

He was on his knees.

The others did nothing but watch him in a vaguely irritated way. But he would stop his squawking soon—he would never be able to keep that up.

When the men came for him he said, "I'm still captain," and began to cry.

He could not walk. He had lost his voice. He could hardly see. The pains in his arms and stomach were a kind of gnawing, and a torment, telling him how it would feel when they held him—tearing his flesh, biting his toes—and ate him alive.

Back at the hidden camp he covered his face and became very still. His fear had distorted all his senses. His eyesight was poor and yet he heard everything as twice as loud. He had no sense of taste at all, but what he smelled was rotten, filling his nostrils with the furry stink of decay. His hands and fingers and all his hinges were numb, and yet the gnawing pains persisted in his body. He had never had such an awareness of his body, the frailty of it—its stupidity; of such a devastating sense that his intellect was useless. He could not seem to help himself from growing stupider.

The odor of food made him sick. They called it food! He could not eat. He could not distinguish between their feeding him and their torturing him. Wasn't it the same thing? They insisted that he eat, showing him a burned bone, and they kept up their punishing demand. But he refused. It was the odor, the sight of hanging meat—some dead animal that they wanted him to take into his twisted stomach.

"I saved that meat for him," Martlet said. "And he didn't eat it."

A black man offering him food! Probably flobbed on it!

"He's got to eat sooner or later."

Fisher was nauseous, but he was also very hungry. His hunger gave him a severe headache, and tired him; yet he could not sleep. He spent the rest of that long day and the first night shivering at the back of the cave in a mouse nest of dead grass, thinking: I am dead.

In the morning he saw a gray patch on the cave wall that was the size of the screen on Pap. He tried to calm himself by staring at it. He fastened his dim eyes to it and got some strength from this concentration. The sky, the sun, all the empty space—the smells, the noise—deranged him. He felt he could go mad in all this bad air. He had no helmet! His suit was torn! These people had no protection, but they were aliens, they were hardly human. They were probably mutants, or else sick, or crazy.

Fisher held his head lopsided and continued to stare with a crooked intensity at the lozenge of granite on the rock wall. It gave him strength, but still he whimpered as though he were grieving.

"He's more than wacko," Gumbie said.

He heard it and said nothing.

Mr. Blue said, "They're probably glad to get rid of him. They might have taken him out here to dump him, like they dumped all those others. Only he had connections, so instead of blasting him out of the rotor they set him down gently."

"And then that rotor just highballed out of here."

Hooper hadn't come back. He had abandoned the captain and aborted the mission. He had disobeyed orders!

The young woman called Kylie asked in a small voice, "Why did they take Bligh?"

"She might have gone willingly," Mr. Blue said. "She hasn't been right since those phantoms burned Murray and Blayne. And she freaked when we couldn't find the bodies."

Valda said, "What do we do if they come back for Fish?"

"No one's going to come back for him," Rooks said. "Would you go anywhere for him?" And he started to laugh.

That was the second day. In the evening they tried to feed Fisher again. He would not open his mouth. He ground his teeth. He would not drink. His gaze was fixed to the wall. He was solving problems. He was reporting Hooper for disobedience and making sure he never flew another mission ever again. Fisher's face was very dirty.

"Flatten him. I don't want him squatting there all night."

But when they dragged Fisher down he struggled—not against them, but their touching him triggered a fit, and he thrashed on the ground. Finally they got him into the bag. He squawked and tried to stretch. They stepped on him, jamming him down with their cheesy feet.

"As if we don't have enough worries!"

No food, no sleep—Fisher was dreadfully cold. And now his whole body hurt from their kicks. Strangely, the pain had driven out some of his fear. They dragged him near the fire but it only heated one side of his body: burned it—while the other side ached with cold.

"What do you say, Mr. B?"

He had been silent for a while, thinking. Then he said in a decisive way, "Okay, let's sell him."

20

THEY STARTED THEIR MARCH AT DAWN. FISHER HAD hardly slept—the darkness made him think he was going to die. He had watched the moon swing and dissolve. *Let's sell him*, Mr. Blue had said. Fisher had the idea that if he was sold he was saved. That hope kept him marching.

They walked slowly through thin woods of cedar and short-leaf pine toward one of the round hills in a low range of them. Their circling and climbing took them the whole day. Fisher refused to eat anything except two wild plums which he peeled himself by picking flaps of skin away. He did not speak. Carefully, in fastidious steps, balancing himself in his torn boots and choosing his way, he walked in the middle of the file. He calmed himself by considering various methods of killing these people after he was safely rescued. He favored stunning them and then atomizing them, one by one, leaving the trees intact.

They camped under a limestone hill in the late afternoon. All that walking and they still weren't there? They did not build a fire. They muttered about hunters and searchers. They had carried all the stolen provisions but they did not open them. They ate meat strips and potato beans, and when the whole sky was black they lay in the leaves they had heaped.

For most of the night Fisher was awake, listening to their snores and gasps. He was now too weak to escape—they did not even trouble themselves to cram him into the rope bag or to tie him up. They left him squatting in his own pile of leaves. He imagined them thinking: How can this cripple get

away? It demoralized him to know that they had not bothered to secure him while they slept. It was another sign of
their contempt. He was too simple and stupid to save himself,
they figured. He hated them, and pitied himself, and despised Hardy and Moura for the shortsighted fertility arrangement they had made. If they had been shrewder he
would have been different—powerful, never afraid, taller,
nothing missing.

He was impatient for the sun to come up. He wanted to
move on. The prospect of change gave him confidence. At
least the new people would not eat him. You didn't buy
someone and eat him! He knew he would be handed back to
Hardy and Moura for a ransom and then he would start
proceedings against Hooper for dereliction of duty—a huge
lawsuit—and bring him down. Sometime he would return
here and burn them all.

His anger gave him life and restored his thirst.

"Who's that moving?"

It was the mutter of the little man Gumbie standing watch.

"That you, Fish?"

Fisher grunted "Yum," and Gumbie turned his back on
him. That was how much they cared. And Gumbie was cracking something in his teeth. There was no greater show of
indifference than a guard eating in front of a prisoner. Eating
demonstrated a brainless absence of fear. Gumbie was eating
like an ape. He was hunkered down, with his elbows out. He
seemed to be crunching bones and blowing the broken pieces
off his big lips.

"What are you eating?"

"Pine nut," Gumbie said, turned to the boy.

They were both pale blue in the moonlight.

"Crack one for you?"

Frog-eyes, they called this man—Froggy—because of the
protruding hoods of his eyelids, and there was always a
froggy frown on his big mouth. Fisher suspected from his
unresponsive alertness—staring and never seeing anything—
that he was dimwitted. He felt safe in the presence of this
small man's inaction.

Fisher said, "I want a drink."

"There's a jug in the cooler."

"Not from the jug," Fisher said. "Get a sealed can."

"Mr. B said don't touch the provisions."

"I'm captain," Fisher said, steeling himself.

Gumbie went *pah* spitting nutshells.

"And if I die," Fisher said, "you won't be able to sell me."

Without a word, Gumbie rummaged in a bag and brought out a can. He handed it to Fisher, who sat down and fumbled with it. He had never opened a can without tongs or clean gloves. Finally he unsealed it, splashing some of it on his sleeves. He drank it so fast it went down his throat like liquid flapping through a pipe—the sound of a drain.

It was his first drink for two days. It cleared his head and strengthened him. He saw this as a victory, something to be enjoyed. He was alone in O-Zone with eight aliens! He was sorry there was no one he could tell—not to boast but simply to have on the record: an Owner, Type A, on his first mission actually living with hostile aliens. He thought: I'm not dead yet!

More than ever he wanted to be rescued, so that he could return and thunder down and kill all these people, especially this half-wit, Gumbie.

He said, "Where are we going?"

"Like Mr. B said, we're selling you, fella."

"Tomorrow?"

"Yump."

"Who's going to buy me?"

Gumbie was crunching a pine nut. He blew and swallowed, then paused, picking nutshells from his lips. He was thinking.

"Some Diggers in the town over there."

"Which Diggers, which town?" Fisher sensed that Gumbie was weakening. "I'll give you a swig if you tell me. It's glucose. It's real sweet."

A snort rattled out of Gumbie's hairy nostrils.

Gumbie then uttered an extraordinary sentence.

"The Bagoon family at the Mooseworks Pit in Varnado, near Summerville."

Fisher repeated the words to himself. They seemed to say everything, and yet they told him nothing.

"Now give me that swig," Gumbie said.

Gumbie's suckings and swallowings on the nozzle were too much for Fisher. They were monkey noises, they made the boy think of germs, and of viruses for which there were no known cures. He went and lay down on his leaves.

From the darkness there came a low accusing voice—the growl of Mr. Blue. "So you're not so stupid after all."

Fisher did not move, did not breathe. He kept very still, wondering who Mr. Blue was speaking to.

"I'm talking to you, captain."

The next day they talked about him as if he were not there. Mr. Blue said the kid was tricky: it was best to ignore him.

"Don't touch him, don't talk to him, don't listen, don't give him anything. I don't want any relationships to develop."

They were sorting their equipment, distributing it in equal loads prior to moving on. They made a great effort to remove every trace of their having spent the night in this grove— scattered the leaves they had slept on, swept away their tracks, filled in the garbage pit. There had been no fire. It was especially important to make the place look innocent, Mr. Blue said, because they were leaving the stock of sealed provisions behind, buried in a hole.

"I want this to be a simple transaction," Mr. Blue said. "If they suspect the kid's a dip, they won't buy him."

"What are we going to tell them?" Martlet said.

"That they can have him. They can negotiate with the search parties and collect the ransom. They've got radios."

Valda said, "But he probably is a dip. He won't eat, and there's no one looking for him."

"That's his problem," Martlet said.

"His people just left without him."

"Don't tell the Bagoons," Mr. Blue said. "They'll see a good hostage. A little dippy and obstinate, but otherwise a normal eighteen-year-old, I guess."

"I'm fifteen and a half," Fisher said.

"I don't hear anything," Mr. Blue said.

"Fuck-wit."

Someone laughed.

"I'm a clinic-classified Type A, upper number. I've been a remote student since I was seven—"

"Nothing," Mr. Blue said evenly, and shouldered his pack.

"Fiber optics, particle physics, theoretical densities, the Bremstrahlung effect, wah-wah-wah—"

He had started a stammering quack in the confusion of his protest, because no one seemed to be listening; and the more he quacked, the more incoherent were his words. It was as if he had lapsed into another language.

"Mutagens! Thermal receivers. Fictile circuitry!"

"Let's move," Mr. Blue said. "We can be in Varnado by noon."

Their camp had hidden them at the foot of this range of hills, but when they climbed a low ridge and began descending again Fisher saw that it was the last range of hills. To the southeast was Firehills—Fisher knew the patterns of scarps and knobs and shut-ins; to the northwest, clearly visible on the edge of what looked like prairie, was the place they had been calling Varnado, and the surrounding township of Summerville.

"I know where we are," Fisher said, and blinked at the tumbled town.

"Not a thing," Mr. Blue said, with his hand to his ear.

"That city-stain."

They did not seem to know the term. Someone mumbled, "Varnado."

"I've been over there in a jet-rotor. I've even hovered there and shot close-ups. It's totally uninhabited. They've stopped putting it on maps, because it's still pretty hot. It doesn't have a name."

"Dip," someone said.

This sight, the land ahead, was Fisher's earliest memory of O-Zone. He had seen it first on the ground-screen when they had come for the New Year's party: the wheel-shaped city-stain of ruined and roofless houses, and tipped-over stacks, and the standing towers with bearded brickwork; the terraces and painted pools. From the rotor it had seemed a large figure flattened on the ground, like a pressed flower or a footprint. They had shot it and gotten a sound-bite, and then they had buzzed it and made for Firehills.

That New Year's party Fisher now saw as their undoing— all of them had been wrecked by it, and he had come out the worst.

Today this city in the distance scared him. It was vast and irregular. There was no way out. Its farthest edge was rucked up like a rug into folds on the horizon. A light dust cloud swelled over it like a puffball. Beyond the broken suburbs in the foreground—streets bursting with grass and bushes, collapsed houses, faded cars resting on their axles—there were empty apartment buildings, and the stone towers and condos of the old town.

It all looked so different and dangerous: from the ground it was an aching sight of abandonment. They had just left the steep hill paths that gave Fisher vertigo, and now he was faced with this city-stain, where he felt he might sink and disappear—because "city-stain" was the wrong term. It was only a stain above an altitude of three clicks. He could see now that it was deep and shadowy, and was dusty with desertion. There was not a live thing anywhere in it. But his captors did not hesitate at the edge. They were still tramping. But where were they taking him?

It did not even occur to him to run. And the dark and the disorder of O-Zone frightened him so much they overwhelmed his other fear—of being eaten alive. What had remained of his willpower had almost stopped twitching in him. The thought that he was going to be sold to some new people no longer gave him heart. He could not find anything in the look of this ruined town to give him hope.

He saw a good walled-in house, but it was only a place in which to die. He thought of worse things. In one particular horror-vision he saw a gang of savages enacting a ritual sacrifice and roasting him over an altar fire. In another he was left to scream himself into suffocation in an airless room. He was tortured with biting insects. Or he was simply abandoned in this deadly place. He did not want to be let loose; he needed to be rescued by that porker who had demanded the title "chief of ground operations."

"I hate this place," Mr. Blue said. "I hate Diggers."

Fisher moaned to think that this savage alien was afraid and hated it here.

They were still scuffing through the outer town. They kept to the middle of the street, away from the dead or else grotesquely overgrown trees and hedges. The cracks in the street made it seem as if it were made entirely of puzzle pieces. The sun sifted through the puffball of dust.

"We'll drop this dip and then take off."

They were going to sell him and then leave him there!

"Maybe we should send Martlet ahead to let them know we're here," Tinia said.

"They already know," Mr. Blue said.

He said it in a kindly way. Tinia and Kylie, the two other women, stuck together and usually let Valda do their talking for them. Fisher now regarded these women with a sense of envy: they were going to be leaving this place today, and he was being sold—to stay.

Echols said, "They have sentries everywhere." He was

wearing Fisher's broken helmet, with the faceplate up, and carrying a weapon he had stolen from the rotor—one of Murdick's particle beams. "They have radios, too. We've probably passed a half-dozen Bagoons in those empty houses. They'll send word ahead. They hate strangers in their quarter."

They talked as if O-Zone were full of people and places, with names and reputations. Not a Prohibited Area, but twenty counties still more or less ticking over. It was supposed to be empty!

"When will we see them?" Valda asked.

Fisher guessed that none of the three women had been here before, from their ignorant questions.

"When they want to become visible they'll stick their heads out."

The women looked up at the windows.

"Out of the ground," Echols said. "They don't live in those buildings. They live underneath them. Hey, they're all Diggers."

Overhearing this talk aggravated Fisher's fears, and after almost an hour of what he guessed were the Summerville suburbs they came to the granite buildings and the headless towers of Varnado. He was alarmed by the shadows and he felt sure he was being watched from these towers. A cone-shaped one had once been made of glass; every window was broken and what remained was a fragile structure of rusted frames. He had been fearful flying over it in a jet-rotor. He was now traipsing through it on foot! He wanted someone to know this! His fear was tinged with amazed pride at having achieved it.

"There's someone in that doorway," Martlet said, deliberately not looking.

The scrap of pride left Fisher then, and his terror returned. Terror was a sense of his being big and soft and very easy to kill.

Mr. Blue had started to say something, but the person in the doorway interrupted him.

"Stay where you are." It was a young grunting voice using an old loudspeaker that seemed to shred the words.

They saw it was a small ugly child with a thumblike nose and long dark nostrils and tiny eyes. It wore a long shirt and stood on bare feet, but whether it was a boy or girl they could not tell.

Echols said, "See, they put kids in all the dangerous jobs aboveground. They're expendable."

Valda said, "What bastards!"

The force of her outrage distracted Fisher and made him see this woman as almost human. Until that moment he had not imagined any of them to have normal emotions. She cared about the child!

The child had given Fisher a fright. This little creature intimidated him more than a full-sized adult would have done. He found most small children subhuman, apelike, and dangerously unpredictable. Even ones in Coldharbor upset him. "Children" was a horror-word.

The child's grunting came again. "Use the phone!"

Mr. Blue slung down his pack and left the group. He went through the doorway, where the child still stood watching, but he was not gone more than a minute.

"It's just me and the Fish," he said when he returned. "The rest of you wait here."

Fisher said, "I changed my mind."

They looked at him.

Fisher said, "I've decided I don't want to be sold."

"Dippy," someone said.

"Don't say that!" Fisher cried out. "Don't leave me here."

But the others had stopped listening to him. More faces emerged from behind pillars and window frames—they were children of remarkable similarity, with round, sunburned faces, rather doglike and snub-nosed, and squinting and frowning at the strangers like bad-tempered old men.

Fisher had become very afraid. The aliens hadn't answered him. He had told them his decision. They didn't care! And now, at the moment of being separated from the group that had abducted him, he stopped seeing them as savages and stopped believing they would eat him. Valda had convinced him by saying disgustedly *What bastards!* He began to fear the unknown Diggers who lived like moles in this ghost town of Varnado.

They entered the building, just the two of them, Mr. Blue leading, and descended the fire stairs—three flights to an old concourse, with lamplit tunnels leading from it. It had once been an underground shopping center—the troughs still stood, holding dead ornamental trees. The store signs were intact above shop fronts: shoes, salads, sandwiches, jewelry, books, bedding, drugs, flowers, chocolates, ice cream, auto accessories, clothes. It was so odd in this buried mausoleum to see the empty shops and the dirty signs: Casey's, Hi-Rite, Soop's, Van Allen, Heather, Speed-King, Grover's Drugs, Hax, Mackie's—there was even a cavernous Allbright's, one of the old retail outlets.

This large underground area had the smell of humans. The light was poor—there was no electricity. That was very scary. There were oil lamps and reflectors and ceiling wells where shafts of dusty sunlight came from street level. And there was a stink of burning fat or grease—probably the lamp fuel—and a smell like dead cats.

Mr. Blue said, "Let me do the talking."

Fear had silenced Fisher. They were following another ugly child.

Mr. Blue turned. Was he smiling? He said, "I was just getting used to you."

The quack that came out of Fisher's nose was pitiful—even he was startled by it. Mr. Blue's features softened when he heard the harsh despairing sound.

"They call this the Mooseworks," Mr. Blue said, in a chatty way.

It pained Fisher to hear this man be friendly now, as he was about to sell him. Perhaps that was why he was being friendly, because Fisher no longer mattered, and the man was relieved at the thought of getting rid of him and making some money. What good was money here?

"To distinguish it from the Buffaloworks. That's another network of Diggers."

They were met at the far end of the concourse by a man with a flashlight. He held it and twirled it in a self-important way, as if it were his badge of authority. And because he kept it shining on Fisher for most of the time, Fisher had only the dimmest sense of the man's appearance—merely an impression of clumsy fatness, and whiskers, and greasy overalls. The man breathed loudly through his nose. This was an alien! He made Mr. Blue seem rather tame and gentle.

"What have you brought me, Mr. B?"

From behind the light Fisher heard the disgusting scrape of the man's fingers scratching his scalp.

"I've got a valuable hostage."

"He doesn't look very healthy." The fingers reached beyond the light and pinched Fisher's arm. "Where did you get him?"

"Out of a rotor, in a gully in our quarter. Hunters, probably. New Yorkers—the rotor was registered. They're looking for him, but we've avoided them. We can't deal with ransom. We don't have any resources. We had to leave our camp two months ago because of a raid. We lost two people. We're on the move. This kid's just in the way."

"What makes you think we can handle him?"

"You can make radio contact," Mr. Blue said. "There's some big bucks to be made out of this kid. See his suit?"

"You only took this creep? You didn't take food or weapons?"

"Nope."

"That's got to be a lie," the man said, flashing his light into Mr. Blue's face and giving Fisher a glimpse of the man's own head: he had the flat broad frowning face of those children, and was dirtier, and had hair to his shoulders, and tiny eyes—hardly a face with so much hair.

"I wouldn't trust their food," Mr. Blue said. "They put poison in it. And they never leave weapons behind."

"Yet they left this kid," the man said, and made Fisher wince with the flashlight. "I don't blame them! He's a bone, he looks sick, he's probably carrying something infectious. Unless he's hoopy. What's his name?"

As the man asked, he reached out, and thinking he was going to be pinched again, Fisher recoiled with a squawk, crying *Wah!* He had also gotten another glimpse in the shifting light of the man's face, his bad skin, his cracked lips and matted hair. He received a strong gust of the man's stink.

"His name's Fish," Mr. Blue said. "We haven't got a machine to read his ID. It's coded. I'm telling you, if he's not an Owner he belongs to Owners. They pay big bucks."

"He's a dip," the man said, and scratched his head. It was like a rake dragged through sand.

Fisher had reacted to the man in a monkey movement, and he was still whimpering. But he had already processed what he had seen so far. This large filthy family of Diggers had been undetected because they lived underground, at the lowest level of this abandoned town. There was no way a scanner could reach them, and any shooting missed them too: Fisher's own shooting had missed them. Wrong again!

"I've got enough dips," the man said. "We'll take him off your hands, but we're not buying him unless we get some food and weapons."

"We need food too," Mr. Blue said. "That's why I'm here. We're hungry. We can't feed hostages."

"You mean this dip is all you've got?"

"He's worth money. When they come looking for him—"

The two men argued. Fisher had long ceased to feel that he would be saved here. He doubted that he would even survive in this awful place. His eyes had grown accustomed to the darkness: he could see enough of these littered shops and tunnels to fear them. It was bad enough on the ground—but belowground it was ratholes, with suffocating smells.

Mr. Blue was saying, "These hunters and prospectors have money. They're going to want this kid back."

"There are no hunters here," the man said. "They call it O-Zone. I think they dumped this kid. I think you found him in a bush. I think you're lying."

"I'm not."

"You're lying about the weapons, too. One of your men up there has a helmet and some kind of laser gun—new stuff. My kids saw it. Don't bullshit me!"

"Broken," Mr. Blue said. "Try them if you like. You can have them with the kid if you pay. But I swear they're cracked."

"This kid's cracked—he's a dip." Again the light was on Fisher, dazzling his eyes. "Look at those teeth, look at those big lips. Why are his hands red? He's got pimples and sores. Don't lie to me—someone dumped him. They'll never be back. Look, he's crying!"

Tears were brimming in Fisher's eyes. He had started to crouch in despair. His breathing was sudden with sobs, and he looked stricken. He had no hope at all now.

"I like that—look!" the man said. He was peering closer at Fisher, he seemed amused by the child's weeping.

Mr. Blue said, "Leave him alone."

"I'll take him," the man said. "I want him!"

Mr. Blue had knelt near Fisher, and so had the man. Fisher snatched at Mr. Blue's hand and held it tightly, pressing it to his face. Long labored groans came out of Fisher's mouth. Fisher glanced up and he was shocked by the look of pity on Mr. Blue's face. Or was it pity? It was an expression of sympathy and disgust, and perhaps anger, too.

Fisher was unable to make one word. His fear had reduced his speech to animal sounds. He was drizzling and honking snot. The sounds frightened him and his fear made those same sounds worse.

Mr. Blue stood in front of Fisher as the big man reached out with his dark hand.

"Hoo! Let me have him!"

"Leave it," Mr. Blue said. "I changed my mind."

"I think you're a dip."

"I think so too," Mr. Blue said. "I guess we're going."

"Stick around. We can have some fun with this creeper!"

"I'll have to discuss it with my people," Mr. Blue said, hoisting Fisher, jerking his arm.

And they left—Mr. Blue hurrying the stumbling boy along the concourse. In his panic, Fisher had become wordless. He grunted, he shambled, he tripped on the stairs.

On the second landing, Mr. Blue fussed and hesitated, changing again, reproaching himself. He said, "Why didn't I leave you there!"

But he stopped when he saw Fisher stammering, trying to speak, and his eyes became kindlier watching the boy's struggle.

"It's . . . it's not a laser gun," Fisher said at last. "It's a particle beam. I can fix it for you. I can fix the signal in the helmet. I can get the radio working. I can get anything you want. Please don't leave me here!"

Mr. Blue had become very calm, and Fisher saw in his calmness the kindest face. He did not see a savage anymore: he saw a rescuer.

Mr. Blue said, "I occasionally have the feeling you might be human."

Outside, he did not reply to any of the questions from the group—and they were heckling him. He did not slow his pace. He pulled on his pack and, still walking, he said, "Let's get out of here while it's still light. Diggers are dangerous in the dark, and I don't like Varnado."

"Why didn't you sell him?" Martlet said. He had been nagging the whole time. "Why didn't you swap him?"

"They didn't want him," Mr. Blue said, and kept his face forward.

The lie gladdened Fisher and made him march harder. People had always told lies against him, but when had anyone ever lied on his behalf? And it was an alien!

21

Mr. Blue was a young balding man whom most of them called Mr. B. Though he was strong and had the upright and stiff-backed posture of a man in Federal Security—and that in itself amazed Fisher, because Mr. B was an alien—and always carried his own pack, and was always at the front of the file, and a wonderful walker, he was mostly made of bones. He was so skinny his knees showed as big bulges; he had sharp elbows and shoulders; and Fisher could see the clear angles of his skull beneath his thin flesh—even the way his jawbone was hinged just under his ear.

At times his thinness gave him a kindly aspect, and at other times it made him seem suspicious and dangerous. His thin face and long fingers always made him appear cautious, as if he was willing to take his time, and didn't mind being slow. Fisher looked at him and expected him to say "No" or else nothing at all. He often said nothing. He had a habit of suddenly falling silent—breaking off in the middle of a sentence, tilting his head slightly, and listening. When he listened like that everyone else went quiet. His silences gave him authority.

It happened that very afternoon, as they marched away from Varnado on the track they had followed in. Fisher was talking—he was so relieved to be alive and with these people that his fears were suspended, and he was gabbling.

"I'll tell you why the satellites have missed those Diggers so far"—though no one had asked the question—"and why they still figure O-Zone is empty. If the Diggers aren't using any energy except a little oil and a little solar, and they're

271

staying belowground or undercover in watchtowers, there's no way they can be detected. You could get a satellite fix on them if you knew how to program it. I could program a satellite to find something five millimeters long. I've got enough information now to get a wire on those Diggers, and burn them out, too, if you want to—"

"Shut up, fish-face," Martlet said.

"Mr. B's listening," Gumbie said.

Fisher was flustered. He did not know the words for any apology, and had never placated anyone before, and so he became very nervous. He could not remember what he had been saying, or even that he had been monologuing.

They all held their breath for a full minute.

Then Mr. Blue signaled that it was all right—just a plopping noise made by a branch.

"He hears things that we don't," Echols said. "That's why he's in charge and you're not."

"I heard it," Fisher said brightly.

They glanced at him: all those cold faces.

"It was random," Fisher said. "Percussive. Organic. No threat quotient. Yeah, it could have been a branch."

"Dip," someone said, but Fisher was still talking.

"If we had the right box I could print those sounds and analyze them. We could store sounds, make a memory bank for every gleep, program a listener alarm. We could have bands with pitches represented, so that every sound was categorized, and then—"

He sensed a rising antagonism toward him, a growing intensity of rejection. It was like a certain quality in the air—like a smell vibrating against him. And it seemed to awaken a receptive sense in him that he had never used.

"Then we could go on talking," Fisher said.

"We don't have a box, we don't have a frame," Mr. Blue said. "We've got nets and jackknives, that's all."

"I can fix the particle beam or the helmet if—"

But Mr. Blue was still talking. That was another habit of the man, the way he would go on in the same even voice, overriding any interruption—which was why his anger seemed so terrible. His shouting was rare, so it was like madness.

"We were raided last January," he said quietly.

"New Year's day," said Rooks.

They kept track of the months and days? January? New

Year's? Fisher was on the verge of saying, *It wasn't me—it was Hooper!*

"We lost two good men," Mr. Blue went on. "We had to leave our camp—we've been on the move ever since. That's why, when we hear a noise, we listen."

"The particle beam has a heat sensor. That's better than a human eye. And the radio scanner in the helmet can pick up anyone shadowing us, on any frequency. I mean, you don't have to stop walking and stick your ears out just because a branch falls down somewhere, or a bird poops in its nest!"

They had started to walk again. Fisher sensed that no one was listening to him, and stopped talking.

"I'm hungry," he said after a while.

Martlet said, "Now he wants to eat!"

There was not enough daylight left for them to get back to their previous night's camp, where they had buried their provisions. But they were eager to be as far away from Varnado as they could. They climbed to the ridge on the first range of hills and stayed there. It was too dangerous to make the descent on the narrow track in the dark. They ate pine nuts and hawthorn buds they had gathered on the way up, and they promised themselves a better meal tomorrow. It was a cool night, and there was drifting dust, but Fisher was comfortable enough in his insulated suit, in a nest of pine needles and leaves. The others slept together, huddled in a heap under some woven blankets.

In a groggy voice Fisher spoke to the darkness: "People in New York think O-Zone is peaceful."

He still marveled that he was alive—after his abduction, after the dirt, the bad food and no sleep, and the marching, after the frightening encounter in Varnado: those children, that Bagoon man, the Diggers. I am alive, he thought.

He had begun to relax, and as his panic left he discovered that he was very tired. He had loosened his grip on wakefulness and was already plunging fast into streaming fathoms of sleep. He was wakened from this slumber by a reply—one of the men.

"Ozark, not O-Zone."

"The Outer Zone," Fisher said, slipping under again.

He woke, shivering, and heard the crackle of a fire. It was daylight. He had noticed that they only made fires during the day, and often no fires at all. They lived lightly in a skimming way on the land, with no signs of their having passed through.

This morning they were all on their feet, standing in a circle, warming themselves. They were laughing—talking about thick soup and hot tea and fresh bread—what they would do to get some.

They were handsome in their headcloths, their scarves wound around their faces against the dust and the chill. And their shawls and their cloaks gave them the look of Arabs or Gypsies. They had the right clothes for this hot-cool place and its dryness. Fisher no longer noticed that they were wearing faded rags; they seemed camouflaged and well-equipped.

"We could strain some water through Gumbie's socks."

"Would that give us soup or tea?"

"Oh, man," Gumbie said, and looked at his feet.

Fisher stood up and staggered. He pushed at his hair and yawned and limped over to them. He chucked a large stick on their fire, scattering sparks and killing the flames for a moment. Warming his hands, he bumped the others and stumbled, stepping on someone's toes. Then, to be companionable—though no one had said anything—he laughed abruptly. He opened his mouth very wide and honked *Ha! Ha! Ha!*

The others looked at him slowly, with polite horror. They were startled and suspicious, and their silence silenced the boy's honks.

"Where do you brush your teeth around here?"

Fisher did not see their apprehension or their mockery.

"Where do you squirt?"

They laughed at this, and he was glad. He was so happy to have woken up among them. One of his nightmares last night concerned torture in Varnado. It was a stone or a stick pressing into his back, but his nightmare made it into a knife blade. And the odd burr of insects in the night had given him a glimpse of the filthy Bagoon, that Digger scratching his scalp.

But now he was drinking air in the clear morning light by the fire—you needed permission for fires in New York, and this kind was forbidden! Anyway, you'd never find the wood! This wasn't civilized but it wasn't too bad. He now saw Diggers as dangerous cannibals, and decided that he was safe. Mr. Blue was decent, for an alien. Fisher liked the way these people had risen early and made their fire. He had somehow thought that they would be snuffling under their blankets all day, and biting each other, or else waiting for it to rain. He couldn't imagine what you did if you didn't have a room.

They were outdoors all the time! But he was reassured by their human laughter, even if he didn't understand their jokes.

He wanted to please them. He had never tried to please anyone before in his life. He believed that his laughing very hard and very loud was one way; that asking dumb questions was another; and that being useful—repairing the signal and the beam—would make them grateful to him. It would surely please them to know that he was very powerful; but he regretted that they were not intelligent enough to understand his particle theory—Of Subsequence. He longed to impress them, but they did not have any math, so it was perhaps impossible—unless he was able to turn his learning into a trick. He kept laughing in odd stuttering shouts—he honked, he hee-hawed like a jackass.

He said, "Do you aliens notice the cold? You probably think I'm a herbert but if it's a couple of degrees down I can't move!"

They stared at him, scarcely believing.

He said, "I was just joking about brushing your teeth, by the way. Mine are sealed. But you've got to do something or else you'd get wicked bad breath."

They said nothing to him, and yet still stared.

He said, "I used to think you people were cannibals. Hey, you must have heard the stories!"

He spoke to Rooks.

"That you kept Owners for their meat!"

Rooks was a wheezy-faced black with blown-out cheeks and a flat head and a deeply pitted nose. He had made himself a thick collar with his scarf. His color frightened Fisher, even though Hooper had said there were legal blacks all over New York. Fisher had never spoken to one, and he could not imagine that this man understood English. He had not seemed to hear; he had not blinked.

But now he took his mouth out of his scarf and spoke back to Fisher.

"If I was a cannibal," Rooks said, "I certainly wouldn't eat you. I'd only eat you if I was a vegetarian."

Broop-broop, someone was laughing.

And so Fisher laughed—gave his sudden honk—and it was such a surprise to everyone that they laughed with him.

"Those Diggers!" he cried between honks. "I was scared! I thought I was going to brick myself!"

Mr. Blue interrupted him and said they had a long day ahead of them. He said, "And we could take those provisions home. We should go back to the valley."

"Which one?" Fisher asked. "This zone is full of down-thrown massifs and cave tectonics!"

"Happy Valley," Gumbie said.

"Sounds like a funny kind of depression," Fisher said. "Hey, get it?" He became very grave and added, "I don't blame you. I hate jokes myself. You always get them from porkers. 'What's four feet high and has three ears?' That kind of wonk. I don't even listen to it."

They boiled water and drank it.

"White tea," Valda said.

Fisher had some and complimented them. "It's pretty sensible to boil it, you know. You guys aren't doing too bad."

Then they kicked the fire into a hole and scattered the piles of leaves and dragged branches over their tracks. They walked along the ridge and down the hill to the place where they had buried their provisions.

"This isn't the place," Fisher said. "It was farther down the slope!"

No one said he was wrong. Mr. Blue moved a rock and dug out some soil and lifted a box of provisions.

"We could bury a bug or a sensor, and then afterward we'd know just where to dig," Fisher said.

"We could bury you, sonny," Martlet said. "And then you'd know."

Mr. Blue had knifed open the box. He said, "We'll split open one of these protein packs and rehydrate some of those vegetables. But that's just to get us started. We're going to spend the next few days finding our own food—as much as we can."

"Like animals," Fisher said, showing his teeth and grinning, trying to please them. It was not a smile; it was merely a way of twisting his mouth.

They were watching him.

"Just food-gathering! Using the whole day to grab food, and storing it up, and just thinking about eating! That's what wild animals do! Ha!"

Their silence overtook him and smothered the echo of his laugh.

In a challenging voice Martlet said, "What are you planning to do, Fish?"

"Fix the hardware!" Fisher said. "When you come back from your nut-gathering you're going to hear a radio going zip-de-zip. You might even have a particle beam. You've never had one of those before. You're going to like that!"

"Dippy-dip," Rooks said.

Mr. Blue broke open a tube of textured protein.

"It's made for the space program," Fisher said. "They've got all different flavors. The nozzle's for fitting on a suckhole, but you can eat it without a suckhole. I'm the only one here with a helmet, right!"

"It looks like shit," Tinia said; and the other woman, Kylie, said, "Sure does."

"It tastes like shit, too," Martlet said.

Fisher said, "You guys eat dead animals!"

Their stare was like a disapproving noise.

"Hey, I eat meat now and then," Fisher said. "Really!"

They were all chewing fragments of the protein mixture now, and this chewing was more intimidating to Fisher than their stares.

"Fart-food," Echols said.

Fisher said, "It goes good with glucose."

"No glucose, no scaled drinks," Mr. Blue said. "We can dig for water. Then we set off and collect some grub."

They filled a soup pot with some freeze-dried vegetable flakes from the sealed provisions, and boiled them in water, and let the flakes swell—the contents were thick and sludgy, they soaked up so much water. And the people ate them using wooden implements out of their packs. Mr. Blue ate sitting on the ground. His back was perfectly straight, like a classical musician in a chair—a man with a violin, except he had a wooden spoon and wet vegetable flakes. He ate without a sound, listening hard, as he scooped each flake neatly and raised it to his mouth.

When they were done, Mr. Blue gave them tasks. Most were to gather food, or else process it; one was to keep watch on the ridge. Fisher, Echols, and Valda were to stay in the camp.

"I don't need help from them," Fisher said. "They're ignorant about this stuff. It's very sophisticated circuitry—just slugs and chips. It doesn't have moving parts, you know!"

"How old are you, Fish—fifteen, right?"

"Sixteen in a couple of months. Hey, listen, a theoretical physicist is washed up at twenty-five or so, and a mathematician even earlier. Your brain turns to mush. Einstein did all his serious thinking in his twenties. So did Ravensdale, the particle man—he did this big thing on densities and speeds. I was working on the interrupted mode—beam-bending. You don't understand any of this stuff, do you? What I mean is, I'm old!"

"Sure," Mr. Blue said. "And that's why I want you to keep an eye on these people, Fish."

"I'll be captain," the boy said.

He fretted about finding the right place to work, but when he found a flat rock, he worried about dust getting into the works of the helmet. He whimpered about the light being bad and about not having the right tools. He had only the emergency kit from the lining of his suit. He seemed very young and very nervous, and he snapped at Echols and Valda, "These are caveman conditions! This is year zero! And you don't know the first thing about this category of helmet. You probably think it's some kind of hat!"

But when at last he opened the helmet and set to work on it he became calmer and conversational.

"This helmet's a Velmar Victor. It's got about a hundred functions, and that's just in the communication mode," he said. "You don't have the slightest idea." He removed the dome with his bony fingers. "This is where your energy cells are housed. This is how we test them—"

In a patient but doubtful way, Valda and Echols sat watching the boy. They were each knitting, moving two short spikes through some coarse yarn. It was one of the habits of these people, Fisher had noticed, their routine of knitting whenever they were at rest. They made narrow lengths of woven ribbon that matched the patterns in their clothes. Every scarf they wore was sewn together from such woven strips. Their spikes clicked as they watched Fisher.

"I hate my head," Fisher said suddenly, looking up and making a face. "The shape of it, the way it bulges in the back." His gaze met Valda's. "I know what you're thinking. Too bad about his ears. They're way too big."

Valda said, "I hadn't noticed."

"Then there is something really wrong with your eyesight," the boy said. "Plus, my left ear is smaller and a fraction lower than the right. God, I hate being asymmetrical." Now his head was down, his nose against the helmet. "The cells are fully charged, from your wearing it, Mr. Echols. Though you had it on wrong. Probably thought it was a hat, right?"

Echols said, "How long are those cells good for?"

"Stymax—no upper limit!" Fisher said, poking inside the mask. "And my sinuses, too—they fill up. I get wicked sneezing fits and my nose drips. And I've got flat feet, practically no arches at all. If I took these boots off and walked through this dust—which I would never do, because there's probably hookworm here, but let's say I did—you'd see duck prints. I'm not kidding. Webbed feet."

He was still tinkering.

"This is such a beautiful thing. Look at the circuitry, all those chips. This was developed for high-risk areas. It's shockproof and sensitive. Look at the technology, the bands, the slugs, the sniffer. This baby doesn't sneeze!" He handed Echols the dome. "Hold that—don't drop it."

"I'll try not to," Echols said.

"If you do," Fisher said, "you're wasting about two million bucks' worth of research technology."

"We'll try to remember that, won't we, Valda?"

"If my parents weren't such porkers I'd have a head like this"—he was gripping the temples of the helmet. "I wouldn't have these stupid ears. These duck feet. These spastic reflexes. My sinuses wouldn't be fouled up. It's their fault."

He glanced over and saw them staring, and for a moment their stares held him.

"My mother decides to go to a clinic. She gets a printout. The clinic's a meat market, staffed by wonks and weirdos. She doesn't run a check on the printout, so obviously there are negative factors. She just looks at a few items instead of the whole data profile. Then she goes for about two years. This is a contact clinic, I'm not kidding. She's up there playing Mrs. Sandwich and Hide-the-Sausage, and all the rest of it. She figures there's a problem. Two years—she's still wondering! She could have gone on to frozen angels, but no, she's got Mr. Sausage and his magic knob doing the job. Finally, she's positive, barf-barf, and she gets scanned and plunged, and here I am. And you're wondering why I'm so pissed off?"

He had returned to the helmet.

"That red bulge is the signal," he said. "See if we can get it talking to us."

His tongue was clamped between his teeth, and he looked like a small boy struggling with a toy. He twisted a cartridge and pressed his thumb on a bulb. A sound came out of its perforations like fingers snapping.

"This is what I'm good at. What are you porkers good at?"

"We know how to evaporate," Echols said.

"What does that mean?"

"We can evaporate. That's how we've survived. That's what we're good at."

"Half the time I don't even know what you're talking about," Fisher said. "Hey, hear that clicking? That's the synapse heating the inducer. These things are beautiful."

Valda leaned over to see.

"And I could mention my knob. It probably doesn't even work."

"What's a knob?" Valda asked.

"Hear that? She wants to know what a knob is!" Fisher said to Echols.

"Why don't you tell her?" Echols said.

"A knob is something you don't have," Fisher said. And when Valda looked up he honked at her. "Know what I mean?" And he nudged Echols and honked again. "A dingle-dangle. A winkle. A sausage. A worm. Know what I mean?"

"Yes," she said, "but are you sure it doesn't work?"

"You're getting a buzz," Echols said, for a *heep-heep*, like an alarm, was sounding from the helmet.

"I know," Fisher said. "Don't touch it. Give me the dome, but don't drop it, dong-face!"

"Is that buzz the radio?"

"Can't you tell the difference between the radio and the scan signal? It's two totally separate functions and sounds!"

Valda said, "You can tell us all about it."

"Sure," Fisher said. "But would you understand it, is the question. You don't have enough math. Hey, do you have any math? You certainly don't have enough high-tech. Have you done sequences?"

Valda said, "I didn't even know what a knob was."

"Ha!" Fisher was honking again. "I've been a remote student since I was eight!" And he put on the mask. "Listen, this dong is humming!" And he jammed the faceplate down. "I'm getting signals! Want a news update? Want some weather?"

"How about a commuter-traffic report?" Echols said.

* * *

When the others returned with their bags of food, Fisher gave them all a demonstration of the helmet, fastening on satellite signals and relaying radio news.

He said, "It's got lots of functions, but it doesn't have much range."

"We want the weapon," Martlet said. "We don't need a radio."

"Weapons!" Fisher said. "I know all about your weapons. You go around scaring people. You fling mutants at them!"

"Diggers do that," Gumbie said.

Fisher experienced a retrospective fear, for that meant back at Firehills that Diggers had been lurking near the wire, those Bagoons, and had chucked a dead squirrel at them, so that they would think *Cancer!* and *Mutants!* and go home.

Echols startled Fisher out of his reverie by saying, "The helmet's probably got a scan that will help trace the fault in the particle beam." And he smiled at Fisher. "It's got to be a break in the transducer."

Fisher said, "Know what? You're pretty smart for an alien."

It was later that day that Fisher realized there were conflicts within the group. It made him uneasy to hear them arguing, and Mr. Blue did nothing to stop them. The leader simply sat on the ground, hardly listening, while three people pulled one way and four people pulled the other. Then night fell, and they were speaking in the dark, the woman called Kylie leading one side, and Martlet leading the other. Kylie, Gumbie, and Tinia were for heading west, to the next range of hills; and Martlet, Echols, Valda, and Rooks wanted to cross the nearer ridge and make for the valley, to see whether the camp they had abandoned was still intact. This camp was news to Fisher: he had not seen signs of any camp on the tape they had shot, either at New Year's or more recently. If he had seen a camp none of this would have happened. He would have said, "Nuke it," and that would have been that.

Why didn't Mr. Blue intervene? The skinny man was silent, which disturbed Fisher, because the boy did not have enough data to take sides—and he wanted more data—and furthermore, the fact that there were sides to take made him feel insecure.

It was this way for part of the night. And then at dawn,

around the fire, they started again—this way, that way. They probably didn't even consider data, they probably were just hungry and hostile—some kind of psychotic depression before they started biting each other!

He put on the helmet and locked the faceplate in order to isolate himself from the yakking. But what was that noise?

"I'm getting a buzz," he said.

No one heard. He pushed up the faceplate.

"Someone's using a radio around here," he said.

It was then that Mr. Blue spoke. It was one word, which he hissed: "Diggers."

22

"I LOST THEM," FISHER KEPT SAYING—TALKING TO HIM-self inside his helmet. He had been left alone in the temporary camp, but even if someone had remained the boy would not have been audible, because his mask was on and his faceplate was down. The others had gone out for more food. Fisher fretted over the beam but did not fix it. He was still saying "I lost them" inside his helmet when the group returned with stashes of food.

And then twilight: the first darkness drifted down like dust and thickened on the ground and deepened until it was over their heads. With it came a rising vibration that was both sound and movement on the cliffs above their camp.

Mr. B said, "There's someone stirring around us. It could be Owners looking for Fish, or it could be Diggers. Let's move higher up the ridge."

"I'm getting that buzz again," Fisher said, and wondered whether it was Hooper. But how could Hooper mount even the simplest search-and-rescue mission without his help? Fisher's gloating was checked by a feeling of abandonment.

The helmet was an acorn shape on his head, and the mask's distortion squeezed his face small in the faceplate. His suit was already frayed, and the padding torn and tufted. His bulgy boots were scuffed.

"They're using a bleep," he said. "There are two packs of them bleeping each other."

His voice had not left his helmet.

"It's a routine signal, but they're not far off. I could esti-mate it."

He saw the others muttering. He could not hear them. He did not know they were not listening to him. In fact, he felt they were following his words closely.

"There it goes again. Seems to be a five-second interval."

Mr. Blue was saying, "The Diggers won't buy him if they can steal him."

"They never came into our quarter before," Martlet said.

"If they're Diggers," Echols said in a doubting way.

"They're Diggers," Martlet insisted. "Owners would wait for daylight—and they don't have to sneak with their equipment. They could throw gas over us. They could zap us like they did Murray and Blayne. No, what Mr. B hears is night people. Let's give them what they want."

Martlet had not looked at Fisher as he had spoken, but now he looked directly at the boy.

Gumbie said, "He'll run off."

"Not if we tie him up," Martlet said.

"He'll undo the knots."

"Possibly three packs, two overlapping," Fisher said.

He was giving information. No one heard him. His head, miniaturized by the faceplate, was like a furious walnut.

"Splice his ankles. Hang him by his feet."

"They'll find him and leave us alone."

"Hook him on a branch," Rooks said, and the lisp of his tongue bunching against his front teeth made it sound slushy and sadistic, and gave him a fishmouth.

Still concentrating hard, Fisher said, "I'll try to give you an update in a couple of minutes."

"They can have him," someone said.

Mr. Blue trampled the small fire that Valda had started, and said, "Shut up," very softly in the darkness he had just produced.

The silence and stillness that followed made Fisher conspicuous.

"I can confirm three packs," he said, and stood up and pushed his faceplate into a visor position. "I'm still getting bleeps."

"He's getting bleeps," Martlet said.

It was the first time Fisher's voice had been heard, and they were all listening now. Eight faces had turned upon the boy and by the light of a yellow blade of moon they looked pale and expressionless. The moon was still low in the night sky, tangled in the branches of the hillside trees.

Fisher plucked off his helmet. He was threatened less by the white faces than by the darkness behind them.

"Whaup?" he asked, in a nagging nasal way.

The darkness returned his yap to him.

He began to speak again, but the silence overwhelmed him with the sense of savages and savagery, and he was reminded again of how different he was. He sensed—really, it was like a strong smell from them—that they wanted to leave him behind. Their faces said: Ditch him. The darkness had suffocating depths.

"I fixed the helmet!" he cried. And then, promising and pleading, as if bargaining for his life, "I can patch the particle beam!"

"You'll need that beam, sonny," Martlet said, with his lips drawn tight and his eyes like ice. "You'll need some muscle."

He started to say more, but Mr. Blue glanced at him and he swallowed it all.

Echols said, "Switch off, Fish."

"I was getting their bleeps," Fisher said, and moved his thumb over the pressure switch on the helmet.

"And they're getting yours."

An alien telling him that! Fisher felt Echols was challenging him. For the third or fourth time since his abduction, Fisher suspected that this man might be intelligent. And yet when he looked hard at the man's lank tied-back hair and cut-off sleeves and bruised hands and big sniffing nose, he could not believe it. Echols' words were like the muttery and ambiguous woof and growl of a so-called talking dog: it wasn't intelligence, it was just a certain kind of noise, and it meant nothing. You were a fool for trying to translate it into something sensible.

"Their scanners can pick up any frequency," Echols said.

He had very yellow teeth—they all had—and so their smiles were never a reassurance.

"I wasn't emitting a signal."

"They have energy-sensitive scanners. You were switched on. They could have heard."

Fisher again looked at Echols with interest. How could this yellow-fanged savage have figured that out? His toes stuck way out of his broken sandals! And the insane thing was that the dong was right: if the Diggers had that sort of scanning equipment—but how was he to know that?—you couldn't listen without being detected, at least not with this wonky helmet. It was like making noise or giving off a smell: if you were switched on they'd find you. Hooper had left him with nothing!

"But that gives me an idea," Echols said. "Leave a bleep behind—leave something here to throw them off. Diggers are pretty cautious, and they only hunt at night. They'll stalk it slowly, and that will give us time to get away." Echols turned to Mr. Blue and added, "We can hide somewhere and work on the beam. Martlet's right—this weapon has muscle."

"We've got nets and axes. We've got knives," Rooks said. "We can beef those Diggers."

Mr. Blue said nothing, but as always his silence made him authoritative. He had a lordly way of listening.

Fisher said, "If we leave this helmet behind, I won't have a scanner to find the fault in the weapon. I need my tools."

Echols was smiling, and Fisher thought: Why is this savage making that ugly face at me?

"Not the whole helmet, Fish. Leave an energy cube behind—just one cell on a wire. Then we move out."

The science of this and its obvious truth from such a ragged man made Fisher resentful. He said nothing more, but instead broke open his helmet hatch and took out a cell and gave it to Echols.

"That's it," Echols said.

Fisher hated the way this man had taken charge, and Echols only spoke to Mr. Blue, no one else, and Mr. B was nodding as if to say: It's all yours, Echols, you get us out of this. But whose helmet was it? Whose cells? And who had fixed it, using nothing but his calculator and his thumbs?

Fisher said, "You know that stuff because I told you, right? Because, listen, none of that is news to me. Theory of Subsequence—ever hear of it? It's mine. I developed it. I'll bet you've never heard of it."

"Instead of leaving an energy cube behind, why not leave that mangy little brat?" Martlet said. "With his ankles spliced."

The boy was startled and weakened hearing the crude words he had dreaded. They did want to dump him!

But Echols was suspending a cell from a wire on a low tree branch. "They'll smell this and chase it."

"I can hear them," Fisher said. He had put on the helmet again and was yakking through the open hatch at the front—

the faceplate was up. "They're circling, they're bleeping, they're setting up a kind of search pattern."

They're looking for me, he thought, and saw them—red-eyed Diggers moving hunched over in ragged packs, dirty salivating kids and old men stepping on their beards and scratching.

He was still talking, but no one was listening to him. Mr. Blue was giving orders to carry the food they had gathered: hickory nuts, plums, pole greens, potato beans, and a pile of skinned animals—all the trouble they took with these poisonous parcels of garbage! Fisher had noticed that they stuck it into their mouths without commenting on it—obviously because you'd be sick if you paid any attention to it.

"Leave the sealed provisions buried," Mr. Blue said.

All the good stuff! The pure water and glucose, the meal bags, the tubes of textured food, the chocolate. Fisher wanted to say: That food belongs to me! You have no right—

But Mr. B was still whispering his orders in a hurried way: move to higher ground, he said, on the ridge that lay well inside their quarter, and even if the Diggers were not fooled by the pulses from the energy cube, and they went on searching, this high exposed ridge would be the last place they'd look.

They picked up and left with no ceremony, climbing fast in the dark. The rocks and trees were speckled with moony highlights, but the path was hidden.

"No lights," Mr. Blue said when Fisher switched on his helmet light. Fisher didn't hear those words, but he heard Mr. B's knuckles rapping on his dome.

"I can't walk without this!" Fisher's voice was shrill with terror. He had been wound up again by the fear that he would be caught by Diggers. "I can't even see!"

"If we wait till the moon is high they'll catch us."

"You want me to walk in the dark!" Up went his faceplate.

In the soft voice he used for his most serious statements Mr. Blue said, "They're very hungry people, so consider the alternative."

The weak light from the fragment of moon—it looked to Fisher like a nail-paring—and the scattered droplets of dew glowing on the ground gave the boulders and bushes a dim watery look. They were lost: the landscape made no sense here. People with sophisticated tracking equipment and sat-

ellite photos got lost here—Hooper, for example. And
Hardy didn't even dare!

The horrific thought was that he was in O-Zone—a prisoner of aliens. Only one fact made that thought bearable:
that somewhere out there were hungrier and more violent
aliens, sniffing toward them.

He watched his aliens moving quickly and without a sound
up the hillside. He wondered why they didn't stand their
ground and burn all intruders, and then he remembered their
weapons—axes and knives and hairy homemade ropes. They
had no choice but to run into the darkness!

"I'm blind," he said, kicking his feet and stumbling on the
path. But there was no path, that was the problem. "I'm
blind!"

They did not pause and pity him, as he had hoped. They
kept him moving, jerked him along, and hissed at him to be
quiet, and when he slowed down they pushed him.

For Fisher this was like climbing through the black baffles
of a stairwell in a dark tower. It was worse when they stopped
to rest and he could not make out their faces in the murk.
Then someone snatched his mask—Echols, who pretended
to be so smart.

"They're converging," Echols said, holding an earpiece to
his head. "They sound like a swarm of bees."

Fisher said, "Hey, porky, whose helmet is that?"

Echols said, "I can hear them buzzing."

"Huh, dong-face? Did you ask permission to use that helmet?"

He was not angry, but rather panicky and talkative because
he felt so naked without the thing on his head.

"We should have helmets," Valda said. "We should have
masks like Owners."

"We have a weapon—that particle beam," Echols said.

"I might decide not to fix it," Fisher said.

"Then we'll have to hand you over," Mr. Blue said.

"And they'll eat you alive," Martlet said.

Fisher said, "It shouldn't be too hard to fix."

"You can fix it," Gumbie said. "You've got the creative
juices."

"I hate that expression, 'creative juices.'"

"Get them flowing."

"Flowing!" Fisher said. "That's worse. That's disgusting."

Toward dawn they plodded more slowly, picking their

steps, until, just at sunup, when the red edge of the horizon blazed at them and bulged from behind the blue plain, they seemed to grow tired, as if the light was making them stagger. They lay down in pairs, except for Fisher, who covered his head and muttered until he was asleep. They were woken hours later by the sizzling insects and bright heat of midday.

Echols handed Fisher the long tube of the particle beam.

"Better be careful with that thing," Fisher said. "It's not a spear, you know. It's not an ax. It's not some kind of net."

Echols was smiling. Their yellow smiles were worse than anything, Fisher thought. It was an animal sneer—a hairy alien face showing its bony fangs.

And Fisher squawked when the savage said, "It's probably a fault in the transducer."

"I hate know-it-alls," Fisher said. "Especially ignorant alien know-it-alls," and snatched the beam from him. "Anyway, the fault might not be there, because the transducer in this unit is a coil, not a clip, and it's self-regulating. This delivers a dozen kilojoules per square centimeter. Get it, dong-face?"

Echols had not lost his smile. He said, "What are those marks on your hands?"

They were circles drawn in green ink on Fisher's skin, and there was a small red swelling in the center of each one. Fisher pushed up his sleeve—more circled swellings covered his arm.

"That's what happens when you get rips in your gloves," Fisher said. "They're bites, of course. Haven't you ever seen bug bites?"

"I mean those green loops."

"I circled the bites with a marker."

Echols nodded, saying nothing more, and so Fisher chattered to fill the silence.

"That way I know just where to scratch when they itch. That way I get the right spot. Otherwise—"

Was Echols, that fuck-wit, smiling again? Fisher suspected that he was, but the alien said in a horribly solemn voice, "That's a very sensible measure. Oh, yes. Circle your bites so you know just where to scratch. Oh, yes."

"I think they're under us," Mr. Blue said. He spoke suddenly, as if revealing an inspiration. "I think they know we're here. They're waiting for nightfall."

"We'll blast them with the beam," Fisher said. "As soon as I've fixed it."

"He still hasn't fixed it!"

"If you're so smart, you fix it!" Fisher said. "Anyway, I thought you said that Diggers don't go out in the daytime."

"They don't have to. They have special scopes. They can detect warm bodies—"

"Thermal imaging," Fisher said impatiently.

"Right. And I think they're sitting under us."

"How do you know that?" Fisher asked.

"I can feel it."

Fisher laughed his jeering hee-hawing laugh.

"When you don't have high tech you tend to listen a little more sharply," Mr. B said.

Although it was only midafternoon, Fisher imagined that it was growing dark. He too sensed the Diggers stirring now. He was still testing the circuits in the beam's transducer. As he worked he mumbled, "Dingle-dangle, peeny-winkle," speaking to the weapon. "Open up. Where's your clasp? Wonky-works!"

Echols saw him and said, "You're using a high-energy scan. They have ways of detecting that emission and tracing it."

"Your nose has a magnetic field, porky, so don't tell me I'm doing anything risky, because they can hear you blowing it."

"I think they're monitoring you heating those circuits."

"Let them listen. Let them find us. At least we'll have something to burn them with."

"You look a little worried, kid," Echols said. "Are you afraid it doesn't work?"

"How do I know if it works?" Fisher said. "If I test it the Diggers will certainly hear."

"That's interesting," Echols said. "We can't test it until we see them." He spoke to the others, who had taken up positions on the ridge. From this vantage point they could see the hollows on both sides, and there was no movement.

Fisher had dug himself in between two boulders and was listening to the others murmuring, "Nothing . . . nothing." Except for this, they remained silent. Fisher knew that they feared the onset of nightfall, when the Diggers might emerge from their hiding places.

Martlet put his head between Fisher's boulders and breathed and stared.

"Why don't we run?" Fisher said.

"We live here," Martlet said. "This is our quarter."

"Then why is everyone so scared?"

"It's you," the man whispered. "Why don't you creep down there and hand yourself over?" Martlet moved, and the purple firelight of sunset flashed across him and lit his lumpy face. "You're just trouble for us."

Then it was dark and Fisher was fully awake, thinking: What if it's not Diggers—what if it's Hooper, or a search party? He still did not believe that Hooper or anyone else was capable of tracking through O-Zone—not without Fizzy himself as navigator. They would be flying blind. And yet what disturbed him in the aliens gave him a little hope for his rescue. The aliens showed flashes of intelligence, and if they were capable of understanding the basic structure of particle beam—certainly Echols seemed to—then might not some Owner be capable of making sense of O-Zone and perhaps finding him? It was possible that searchers might have located his signal, and that within a very short time they would be springing him—and flinging shit and misery down on the aliens. But it was also possible that the Diggers were lurking in the darkness, and that was why he did not budge. Who was out there?

Every sound upset him, the dry crackle of leaves, the purr of grass blades sieving the wind, and the way this same freshening wind wrapped itself round the rocks with a sigh. Among the rat-tat of insects he felt a peculiar nakedness. It was not irrational fear—these aliens, these savages, were afraid, and they were wild men, and strong, too.

He had rebuilt the weapon and in doing so had practically reinvented it. But having heated every circuit in the beam, he had risked being detected by the Diggers, or whoever was out there. It had been a necessary risk. And so he had done everything except fire the thing. The aliens thought he was a fool. He wanted to tell them that the last test might be a matter of life or death.

He longed for the time to pass. He searched the black sky for signs of dawn; he put his eye against his watch. Time seemed to stand still. He had always been afraid of the dark.

Sleep had helped him through it before, but now sleep seemed a different kind of death.

The indignity of his fear shamed him and made him feel like an animal. It was not self-contempt—it was not his fault that he had been stolen by these savages! But it made him feel stupid. He was like a turtle torn out of his shell to bleed here. It brought a raw ferocity to his feelings. He wanted to destroy first the Diggers, then these people, for his humiliation.

He thought: I'm dying because I don't belong here!

Had he gone to sleep just then? He must have, briefly, because he heard Mr. Blue's voice in his dreams and when he woke up the dream was still draining away like daylight leaking from a room and then the cracks themselves vanishing as the last door closed for the night—something about New York without electricity, the whole place turned into dark hills and valleys, for wasn't O-Zone New York without lights? The dream was gone but there was still the voice, and black night gave it the crispness of command.

"Put on your helmet, Fish."

It was Mr. Blue, one of his quiet orders. The boy obeyed. "I don't hear anything," he said. "They're not signaling."

Mr. Blue sighed and said, "I can sense them there . . . and there"—perhaps he was motioning. Fisher could not see the man's hands in the dark.

Fisher said, "Who?" and regretted it as soon as he spoke. "Night crawlers."

The words gave him a sight of fat-faced beasts sliding toward him on smears of body slime. He knew exactly what he wanted: a hook to reach him and get him out of here and swing him to safety, and a jet-rotor with blasters and howlers, to strafe and plummet and hover.

He was looking up, searching the sky for the rescue party, when the attack came. Nothing happened, and then everything happened.

His first feeling was that they had come to save him. He wanted to see Hooper, but instead it was a pack of Diggers. It was such a nightmare of assault that he could not grasp the whole of it. He was pushed back into his dream again, and struggling to wake up from the fright of those hairy faces and the tumult and the thudding of their feet and their yells. It was so much worse in the dark, that motion and sound, and only the smallest glimpse of the attackers.

They had sneaked up behind the northern side of the ridge and overwhelmed the sleepers while the sentries' backs were turned—looking down as the Diggers dropped onto them from a higher ledge. Who would have expected them to scale the far side of that sheer cliff? Fisher watched from between his pair of boulders as Mr. Blue and Echols threw themselves at the Diggers and flung their nets high, trying to snare them. It was confusion: they were hardly visible, a jumble of bodies and ropes. And then there were gasping cries.

"Where is he?"

"Grab him!"

But who was shouting and who did they want? Soon no answer was necessary, because there were no more cries. There were grunts. There were terrible noises—the sickening chop of bone hit by a rock or a club, the odd pulping noise of ax blades on flesh, and startled gasps of either the attackers or their victims. That was the pity of it—there were no demons in the darkness, they were all blundering animals, fighting an animal fight, using their claws and fists to bruise each other's flesh.

"Lift the nets!"

But apparently the nets were no good—it was too dark, the attackers too agile.

"Don't shoot—take him alive," a grunting man said—surely a Digger?

"Push them back," Mr. Blue said. "Get them at the edge."

This had all taken moments—ten seconds, no more. It was all fury. The fighting in the darkness was still strangely dreamlike and primitive, like people struggling against drowning in a dark sea. Fisher stuck his weapon out of the boulders, and then was shoved to the ground.

"Stay down," someone hissed at him, and swung him aside. That was Echols—that whisper, that smell.

Fisher thought he was lost, then realized he was safely back between his boulders.

"Take the beam," he said, and held it out until it was snatched from his hand.

It was a simple weapon, the thickness of a baton, the length of a cane, a funnel on its muzzle, its works in a small box. But as soon as he had surrendered it Fisher became hysterical and began screaming.

"Nuke them! Nuke them! Nuke them!"

There was a flash—not the beam itself but the man it hit as

he died in a flare of light. It struck and spread, and in that fire
he saw a man melt so fast he could not tell whether it was a
Digger or not. The particle beam itself was noiseless, inno-
cent-seeming even; yet its victim hissed and crackled in a
lumpy corpse of blackening fat.

In the light of the burning man were upraised arms, and
twenty startled faces. The beam had frightened everyone,
because no one knew for sure who had fired it and who had
died. That puzzlement produced an odd chastened pause,
and a greater darkness, and then an explosion of leaping
light, the meteorite of a Digger's tracer misfiring in a sound-
less streak over their heads.

Fisher had put on his helmet and gloves and buried himself
in the boulders' crack. Looking out, he could see in the bright
silence of another tracer Echols holding the particle beam,
and the Diggers backing up, and several bodies twisted on
the ground.

He did not recognize any of the Diggers. He guessed from
their irons that they were troopers or warriors of some kind,
but their clumsy irons were no match for the particle beam.
One Digger was burned in the act of raising his flare to aim,
and another went up like a torch exploding into flame. Both
burning Diggers became simpler silhouettes of themselves,
smoldering black and falling. And soon the attack collapsed.
The next moment Fisher heard the fading sounds of the Diggers scrambling away and jumping from the ridge. They leapt
into the darkness and disappeared.

"They got Martlet," someone said.

"Give me a light," someone else said. "I think they got
Tinia, too."

"Broke open her head."

In the ensuing silence, Fisher realized that he had not been
harmed, and hyperventilating, he began gasping, "We nuked
them with my beam!"

"If it hadn't been for you we wouldn't have needed the
beam."

He could have killed Gumbie for saying that, and yet he
knew he had been responsible. The Diggers had come for
him, and three had been burned and the rest driven away.
But was he really to blame?

"It's your fault," he said, and then screamed, "You stole
me!"

Seeing their faces near him, angry, and with the gleam of the fighting still on them, he became alarmed.

"You saved me," he said.

That night gave Fisher the soundest sleep he had had since being abducted. It was more than the satisfaction that he had an efficient weapon. It was the sense that, faced with the chance of getting rid of him, they had fought for him and protected him. Martlet had hated him, but Martlet was dead. That was another cause for relief. He had been afraid of the black man, his mockery, his cruelty. He thought: That alien wanted me to die.

He woke up and wanted to thank them. He did not know the words for his feelings of gratitude. He felt the desire to speak this foreign language, but he was tongue-tied—simply making mewing noises.

Hearing him, someone struck open a light, and the glare obliterated every face. But the blaze remained like an unanswered question.

Fisher said, "I'm glad you saved me."

He spoke into the blinding light. He tried again.

"I'm glad I'm alive."

It was the nearest he had ever come to saying thank you.

Mr. Blue's voice became audible behind the light.

"We don't care about you. We fought for our own sake. This is our own land."

In Fisher's mind this statement was proof that, no matter how they seemed in their actions, underneath it all they were savages.

They buried Martlet and Tinia the following day. Most of the others had spent half the night digging—the savages used axes for that, too. There were no coffins, no shrouds, no coverings. The corpses were stripped and the clothes and weapons—and the few possessions—of the dead people were distributed equally by Mr. B among the remaining members of the group. Fisher watched without sharing.

In New York he had seen cremations and funerals on television—the death of old grandfather Allbright had been a spectacular ritual of pompous mourning, one of Fisher's earliest memories. He still laughed when he remembered Hardy's and Hooper's superstitious stage-managing of the occasion. They had hired buglers and black rotors and they had spent millions to ensure that the ashes could not be stolen from the vault.

This burial at dawn on the hillside in the alien quarter of O-Zone was almost perfunctory. But this was more like it: naked corpses, no worshiping, no tears. All life was gone from the bodies, all hope: no promises, no blessings, nothing false was said. It was not a celebration of any kind but rather a ceremony of concealment, but a plain one, like a form of planting.

"This isn't bad," Fisher said, watching with cold eyes. "No prayers anyway." He suspected that prayers would have frightened him—especially the sight of aliens praying.

"We don't believe in second chances," Echols said.

The graves were like postholes—deep and narrow. That was why they had taken so long to dig. Fisher watched with interest as the bodies were slung in headfirst and lowered by their feet, until their foot soles showed about thirty centimeters below ground level.

"A few months ago there were eleven of us," Mr. Blue said.

"Where are the others?" Fisher asked. But he knew: Hooper had burned two and snatched one, and the Diggers had done the rest.

"Dead," Gumbie said. "Gone."

Fisher was staring at the yellow-gray feet in the holes.

"These bodies are empty," Mr. Blue said. "There is nothing left inside. Our friends are gone."

He chucked some dirt in with a mattock.

"They're nowhere," he said.

Then the rest of them piled in dirt and rocks, and they filled the holes and sealed them. They hurriedly shoveled until the holes were indistinguishable from the surrounding land. There was nothing to mark the graves, nothing left behind. Mr. Blue led the small group away as soon as it was done, and only Fisher looked back. He believed that this burial made more sense than a tombstone ceremony and was much better than the voodoo ritual that accompanied old Grampy Allbright to his ridiculous mausoleum.

Fisher liked this, the way the dead went back to the earth and broke down. Clean degradation; no sentiment. And he liked the way these people had fought. These feelings gave him his first stirring of hope and made him proud of surviving among these animals.

"Except," he said, continuing his thought aloud, "as a result of your probable contamination from exposure to radiation in O-Zone, and the gene mutation in your somatic cells—"

The six remaining aliens had turned from the rubble on the graves to stare at Fisher, who was quacking at them.

"—as a result of that, you've got a very short life span." They all looked black with the rising sun right behind them.

"What makes you think you've got a long one, Fish?"

23

NOTHING MORE WAS SAID ABOUT THOSE DEAD ALIENS. Fisher wondered why, and asked, but there was no reply. He was stared at and the stares said: *Who are you?* They did not talk about the past: what was dead was gone forever. They had few memories. They had no ancestors, nor any ghosts.

They had decided to dig up the sealed provisions and take them back to their original camp at the center of their quarter in O-Zone. Fisher did not tell them that he had been near it at New Year's with Hooper and Murdick. He pretended to be interested in the place—they called it variously "The Valley" and "The Frying Pan," because it was an enormous circular depression. But the area was not noted for its caves, and he had not been able to find any huts there; so where did they live?

He asked.

"You'll see, Fish."

"What are we going to do there?"

"We'll decide when we get there," Mr. Blue said.

A squawk shot out of Fisher's helmet.

"Until you came along, we never thought much about the future," Echols said. "Never had to."

"Now it's the only fucking thing," Rooks said.

Someone grunted, "Shut up."

Fisher knew he was different from the rest of them. It was more than a suspicion or a feeling; it was a visible fact. His intelligence, he knew, made him a member of a superior race—but he had long felt that he was superior to Hardy and Hooper and Moura, and they knew it too. He had proven himself to these aliens by repairing the helmet and the particle beam. Now they had a radio and a weapon, though they hardly seemed to care. Their uncaring attitude to his technological genius was further evidence that they were savages, Fisher felt.

He still wore his padded suit with the baggy pants and boots. His long red hands and bitten fingers protruded from his sleeves—his skin was still circled where he had insect bites. He usually wore the helmet, and often with the faceplate down, so that he seemed bizarre and doll-like in that wilderness.

They asked him to take the helmet off, and when he refused, they wanted to know why.

"The faceplate's optical—I lost my contacts. Hey, I need it to see. You want me to be blind! You're afraid of me!"

It was a lie, all that squawking—the first deliberate lie he had told them. But he did not blame himself. He was still very frightened and often when he reviewed his situation he was in fear of his life.

Savages were unreasonable and unpredictable. Aliens had no legal existence, no legitimacy. He felt that they were parodies of his own life, for they gambled and halved their chances every time they mated; and though Moura could have made a better match at the clinic, she had taken no chances.

But living in O-Zone had improved them, for although they were certainly aliens and savages, they were also tough sunburned people—strong and very silent and watchful. They could move very fast through the trees and hills of this place. They wore knitted hats and knitted clothes—they were always knitting, even the men, when they were at rest. They also wore surprising clothes, like bomber jackets and bush hats and old-style slacks and sneakers, and Mr. Blue wore a brilliant silk scarf.

But he did not have to ask where they had gotten them. O-Zone had been a Prohibited Area for over fifteen years: its inhabitants had been evacuated but they had left a great deal behind—in their houses and shops and hotel rooms. Even Firehills had been full of abandoned belongings, and though it had disgusted Fisher, Hooper had taken pleasure in looking this stuff over, and opening drawers looking for treasures. It was all secondhand junk, Fisher felt, and probably contaminated; but for an alien the whole of O-Zone was a treasure house.

He knew that being aliens, they were predatory. How else could they have survived here so long? His suit and helmet protected him from them. He hated hearing them and being reminded that he was their prisoner, and that they were somehow stuck with him. *Until you came along we never thought much about the future*—that crap.

He wanted to tell them that he had always thought about the future—how it was contained in the present, and was familiar and visitable; how it was always a version of the remote past; and how it could be discovered and accurately projected a thousand years hence. But he spoke a different language. This mode of life in O-Zone was worse even than the prison of the present or the usable past. This was the chaos of prehistory, the aliens like the first beings sniffing the world.

But he also thought: I am farther away from people like Moura and Hooper, than people like Moura and Hooper are from aliens like these. And there were times when these aliens were just as exasperating and stupid, in just the same way, as many New Yorkers he knew.

Yet in New York he had seldom been self-conscious. But here in O-Zone, the way they isolated him forced him to think about himself and his effect on other people. It had an unexpected result.

He said, "When I was a baby, my parents bored me."

And Valda laughed. She had been walking behind him. She laughed out loud.

Fisher was not used to laughter. He was startled and in an obscure way thrilled by it.

He said, "I hate to hear people laugh. Or talk. Or eat. Especially eat."

Valda laughed again. In spite of himself, he was flattered: he felt it gave him strength. He turned and saw that she had thrown her head back. She was a young woman with heavy breasts, and the gesture lifted them and gave them life. He watched them, liking the weight of them, the way they moved as she laughed. There was something careless and wild—and perhaps brave—in the way she leaned back and laughed. He could see the root of her tongue, and her small discolored teeth. Now they excited him, and her body smell teased his nose like new paint. The sound of her laughter seemed to say that she was not afraid of anything at all. He wanted more of it.

"And sometimes," he said, "people have underbite, or a wacky jaw, or teeth missing, and then it's horrible to see them eat—the wobbling way they masticate their food. By 'masticate' I mean 'chew.'"

"We speak English," Rooks said.

But Valda said, "Your teeth are so white, Fish."

Of course he was different, but it was a novelty to him that it was noticed and remarked upon. People in New York took him for granted—all the "supermoron" business that they thought he never heard. Valda was properly paying him a compliment.

"They're sealed," he said, chomping and showing her his bite. For a moment it looked like a smile, but when he stopped you knew it could never have been. He said, "Epoxy. I get them recoated every couple of years."

"That's pretty interesting," Valda said.

But it seemed wrong to him to be producing envy or awe in this alien, and he pitied her for her simplicity and the way she was carrying a heavy pack of provisions.

"But I've got bruxism," he said.

Valda was silent. Rooks turned and stared at him.

"I know you speak English," Fisher said.

"—the fuck's that?" Rooks was saying.

"I grind my teeth," Fisher said. "Especially when I'm asleep."

This was the second day of their march to the camp they called home, carrying the crates and packs of the sealed provisions they had stolen from the jet-rotor. Going to the Frying Pan, they said; wait till you see the Frying Pan. But Fisher had seen it. It was where they had burned the two netmen to save Murdick that misty New Year's, when it had all begun.

There was no path, they stayed away from paths, but they kept in a file. They were climbing again, rising to the low hills at the distant edge of the depression.

"I hope you know where you're going."

"This is our quarter, Fish."

It was true: they seemed to know it—they had names for every city and town. At the top of one hill Mr. Blue pointed and said that over there was Sutton Bluff, and down there

Alton and Shannon and Saint Clair, and farther along was Dexter.

For the moments he was saying these names O-Zone did not seem a wilderness or a Prohibited Area, but rather just another state in the Fifty-two, with prettily named counties and picturesque towns. But Fisher looked across the treetops and saw nothing to justify those names. And a town was not a town if all that was left of it was a contaminated stain.

"I suppose it's all right for you here, but I'd rather live in a room in New York with a secure seal on it."

Valda laughed just behind him again, and she laughed harder when he tried to explain the work he had been doing on particles—describing the Squark, the Wabble Effect, the Antigons, his own Theory of Subsequence.

"I've coded a whole suite of variables for that theory, and by the time I'm twenty and my brain turns to mush it'll be a new law of physics."

Valda was still laughing.

He said, "That's not supposed to be funny. I've been looking at the sideways movement of particles. And Antigons are destructive particles that emit—"

He was unexpectedly encouraged by the fact that she was laughing harder than ever. He liked the sound of it; he wanted more.

He said, "When I was small I used to say 'pisghetti.'"

Valda fell silent.

"I named my computer Pap. Everyone wondered why!"

She began to stare at him.

"And 'jellyshiff,'" he said. "For 'jellyfish.'"

Valda had begun to frown at him uneasily.

"And 'dobba' for 'poops.' It's a corruption of 'job.' You know, like sitting on the hopper and doing a job." Now he was frowning back at her. "I see. You don't have hoppers, do you?"

She did not reply.

"I was a horrible baby," he said. "Actually, I was a Type A, but they thought I was a spazz."

He waited for Rooks to turn, and then he explained.

"A wonk. A dimbo. A wimble."

Valda made a new noise—it was a soft sudden croak, like a baby's burp.

"And then when I was about three I started problems," he said, and quickly added, "Solving them."

Was she listening?

"I managed Pap with two fingers. Bash-bash—boop-boop-boop. When I was five I was hacking. They sent me to school, but what was the point?"

He expected Valda to be impressed. She did not say anything.

"We were living in another garrison then. They didn't call them garrisons, though. Just condos and co-ops. This one was Wedgemere. Very English."

"Wedgemere!" She was laughing again. "Very English!"

"It gobbled," Fisher said. He did not smile, yet he was pleased. "Full of fossils—really old people and foreigners. I mean, I know they had IDs, but they probably bought them. Half the people who worked there were illegals, though— I'm sure of it. That was one of the reasons we moved. We started getting thefts. Then they had a strike force. It was ridiculous. That's one thing I like about you guys—you might be illegal but at least no one's old."

Echols was listening. He said, "This is no place for them."

"And no children—that's great. I can't stand kids." Then he asked, "But how come there aren't any here?"

They did not answer. What did the silence mean? Perhaps that the old folks had died—and the children too, if they had managed to be born somehow. And there was that fifteen-year-old that Hooper apparently snatched, the porker. Aliens were abducted, or else they died here, and it was as if they had never lived. They were plowed under and returned to the earth and forgotten, like the clothes and weapons that were shared among the others.

Fisher said, "How could you live here so long and not invent anything useful? All this walking. All this shitty food. You don't have protective clothing. It's just foraging—hand-to-mouth. What's the point of it, or does it have a point?"

"It keeps us moving," Mr. Blue said. "And it helps us evaporate when we have to."

What was that supposed to mean?

"And no cash."

"What do we need that for?"

"You need weapons. That takes cash."

"So it's your fault we need money. And you don't have any."

"Hey, listen, you stole me!" Fisher said. "You took me away from my uncle!"

They said nothing more. It was noon on this new hill, and they prepared to make camp.

"Other people's lives fill me with depression," Fisher said. "Especially yours."

Another night.

He had thought he did not belong: he did not sleep well, he was still afraid of the dark, he hated their food and their fires. And then he remembered how well he had managed at Fire-hills with Hooper only—what?—ten days ago? They had established a command post, a terminal, a data base, and a communication center. They had enough food for two months. They had been completely secure, with a soft-wire network of alarms. They hadn't cowered behind a rock listening for the hoarse gasps of Diggers! And none of these wonky séances with skinny Mr. B whispering *I can feel them . . . I can sense them.* What porkers!

I was commander of Mission Westwind, Fisher thought. This is my food, my radio, my weapon. These people have not stolen me—I have rescued them.

They were still trekking to the place they called the Frying Pan. Fisher wore his helmet and carried the beam.

"That is one hell of a lethal beam," Echols said.

Marching along, people said whatever came into their heads, and often someone would take up a point made two days before. Echols mentioned the beam as if they had been talking about it; but in fact this was the first time he had raised the subject.

Fisher did not reply. He told himself that he was very suspicious of this man's math. He had done some of the work, but not all of it.

"You got it working beautifully, Fish."

"It might still have phases of bust and spinout," Fisher said, brushing aside the praise. He would not let himself be complimented by these people. What did they know about fiber optics? But he was proud of the weapon—he knew it was a deadly beam, and it was better than they deserved. It had saved their lives.

That was when it struck him that they had no business here. They didn't belong in O-Zone. They really were aliens. They were bewildered, they had not adapted. They had no reliable water supply, their food was disgusting, they slept on the ground, they had a doggy smell, they wore clothes they pilfered out of the musty rooms in the ghost towns of O-Zone, they had secret ceremonies—like that burial.

They screamed at planes.

That was the oddest thing of all, though Fisher had not noticed it at first. How could he? There had only been a few planes—low-flying, radar-avoiders, very loud, possibly search planes looking for him. These aircraft made so much noise streaking past that Fisher had not heard the screaming. The second time they had kept it up until a moment after the plane passed by—the plane was gone, but in the time lapse just after the roar of jets there was a cut-off scream. It was like hearing an echo but missing the original sound that caused it.

But he had seen the aliens, the whites of their rolled-up eyes, their fingers tensed, their mouths wide open—howling at the sky. Even Echols, even Mr. B. The next second it was over and because the jet engines had drowned it all he could not ask why: it was gone, nothing had happened. It was like the dead aliens. When something was gone, so was the memory of it. And, strangely, they did not raise their voices, apart from that.

It pleased him to have proof that they did not belong here. They were truly aliens. Of course he was their prisoner—they were like members of another species. He was one of a small number of special people—now he knew just how special; and he could rely on Valda's laughter—he had always felt that laughter was a kind of submission. But this was not enough, and it hardly calmed him, because he also knew that they could kill him—just punch him down in the most brutish way. Or they could do it with more style, since he was now sharing his weapon with them. Behind all of this was a question to which he did not want to know the answer: What plans did they have for him?

They were not cannibals, but he was still afraid. He suspected that they had diseases and that they were outlaws. He learned a little of them; but they could be so vague.

"How long have you been here?" he asked Rooks.

"Since that explosives thing they tried to hang on me," Rooks said. "Making explosives. That was years ago, but they don't forget."

"Is Rooks your ID name?"

"No. My ID name—before I lost it—was Kenway."

Fisher said, "It's funny. I can't imagine someone named Kenway wanted by the police."

Then Rooks gave him that *Who are you?* look.

Gumbie said, "They claimed I was raping women. It wasn't rape. They wanted to and I was willing. There was absolutely no use of force. Is sex a crime? Hey, they were thanking me! But afterward they changed their minds and I was the one who suffered. That's what happens if you're willing."

"What about Gumbie—is that the name on your ID?"

Kylie said, "Don't ask me any of these questions."

Gumbie was still replying. "Truth is, I never had an ID. Where I came from, they never checked, and we just lost interest in them. I always figured I was a pretty good American until that rape thing came up. But that made me want to leave the country. I lost all respect for the Feds then."

"What you're saying is that you were wanted by the police," Fisher said. "And you're saying that O-Zone isn't America."

Mr. Blue said, "Give it a rest, Fish."

"I was just asking him about his name."

"Gumbie's my family name."

"What's your first name?"

"DeWayne."

Echols said, "Me, I abused my position."

It was a new day but he still did not know them much better, and the raw data he had only confused him more. But it was clear from what they said that the country was in a greater mess than he had ever imagined sitting in his room in Coldharbor.

It also struck him that they were telling him these things, and would probably tell him anything, because he didn't matter: he would be dead soon. That gloomy hunch made him less inquisitive.

One more day.

"Tonight you can sleep with me," Valda said.

She had dropped behind to speak to him—just a whisper. They had started their march, they would eat something farther on. They didn't have mealtimes, they only had hunger, and they did not always obey it.

Valda was smiling at him, still whispering, "If you want."

"Do you mean sleep?" he said.

She murmured something and glanced ahead of her, where the others were tramping. Some carried crates on slings, and others used two-man litters—poles that had been hanked together and lashed like stretchers for the big boxes.

"Because I might not be tired," Fisher said.

Valda laughed again and walked on, and the next time she saw him—it was a rest stop—she said, "That's good!"

Fisher was pleased. He liked her face and her heavy breasts and her smooth hips. He wondered what she looked like naked, but he also worried that she might be strange— diseased and hairy. He was faintly repelled by the thought that she was an alien. And there was her age: Valda he had calculated to be at least twenty!

He liked to watch her body move when she was marching or preparing food, but he reminded himself to be careful: these people were notoriously unhealthy. Aliens carried viruses for which there were no known cures. Some of these viruses had actually been developed by the Feds as weapons, and had been dumped in Prohibited Areas. There might have been some truth in the rumors that these viruses had been tried out on aliens. He wished that he had hacked into more Federal data, but he had never believed it to be of any practical use; he had never imagined leaving Coldharbor, much less being on the ground in O-Zone.

Fisher grew sad at the thought that Valda was perhaps his only friend. The rest of them were skinny and silent. They ate without any pleasure and they had little interest in him. He sat apart from them, trying to eat. He managed to swallow some, but he had plenty left—what they called pole greens and the dried-out muscles of a dead animal.

Gumbie knelt next to him. "If you're not going to eat that, Fish—"

"I was planning to throw it away."

"We don't throw anything away." Gumbie gathered the scraps into his outstretched fingers. "This is for me. Yep. Yump."

Fisher said, "You eat anything."

"It's not hunger," Echols said, because Gumbie's mouth was full. "Whatever you leave behind is evidence that you passed through. We don't leave traces—no food, no footprints. That's why Rooks marches at the rear, dragging a bough to sweep away our tracks."

Fisher had seen the man doing so, but he had imagined it had something to do with the porker pretending to have a tail. Maybe they weren't completely stupid. But in the time they had been in O-Zone the technology outside had developed and left them behind with fifteen-year-old fantasies. For example, everything that Echols knew was out-of-date.

"I hate your food," Fisher said.

"When you're hungry enough you'll eat it," Mr. Blue said.

"That's a sick idea," Fisher said.

Gumbie, still chewing on the scraps he had cadged, said, "What kind of stuff do you want, Fish?"

"Jelly sandwiches," the boy said. "Guppy-Cola. Burgers. Chili. Fries. Ice cream. All kinds of tuna fish. I like that fortified one-meal drink they call 'Marvel Milk'—though it's not milk." He became lonely thinking about it. He said, "Fudge. Chocolate. Spaghetti. Grapefruit segments. Those white things known as 'fish cheeks.' Glasses of juice with condensation on the sides. I'm not supposed to eat dairy products, but I do. Honey, bananas, Sammy Syrup, and those fiber crackers they call Poker Chips." He looked up and groaned. "Chocolate-chip cookies."

They were staring at him and he suspected they hated him, but in telling them what he privately craved he had made himself too sorrowful to care what they thought.

"At least drink your tea," Kylie said.

"Boiled bark!"

"It's good to have a bellyful of warm water inside you," Kylie said, and Fisher thought: She has never tasted Marvel Milk, or Sammy Syrup, or Guppy-Cola.

Later that day they found a shelter in a rockslide. Mr. Blue put down his pack and told them where to make a fire and prepare the sleeping places.

"We don't see the same things," Fisher said.

They ignored him. He had sensed that his listing the food he wanted had created a greater gulf between himself and them. It was as if he had blurted out a belief in a strange god. He wished he had not told them—not because it made them suspicious but because it had made him homesick; and it had also reminded him again that he was a prisoner. The sense that he had been victimized made him antagonistic.

"You point to a pile of rocks and say, 'This is camp.'"

He had slid his faceplate up. His face was squeezed between the cheekpieces of his helmet.

"You rake some leaves into a pile and say, 'This is a bed.'"

He didn't care whether they were listening or not.

"You grab a bunch of weeds and say, 'This is our salad for tonight.' "

Valda was smiling at him, but for the moment he saw her too as an enemy.

"Hey, dimbos, I know the difference!"

That night—Fisher suspected they were taking revenge—Gumbie showed him a thick brush of green weeds. Gumbie was eager to talk, and he had the bright eyes and the wide grin of an explainer.

"There's eighty-seven million kinds of weeds," he said, shaking the bouquet. "If they have milky juice you don't touch them. If they have regular juice you rub some on your skin and wait eight hours. If there's no rash after that, you chew a little piece and spit it out. Wait eight hours more. If there's no stomach problem you chew another little piece, and swallow the juice and spit out the piece. Wait eight hours—"

"That's twenty-four hours," Fisher said. "No food, just flobbing."

"If your stomach's still okay, you chew the weed good, and eat it. If it don't make you sick after that, you can eat a whole handful of it. Yump."

"That's how we discovered stinkweed salad," Rooks said.

Savages, Fisher thought, with fear and pity, and he sealed himself into his helmet so as not to hear them tearing the leaves in their teeth. But he also thought of what Gumbie had said: Why didn't I know that?

He clicked his faceplate up.

"You've got no right to steal my provisions," he said. But the thought of that pilfered food was displaced by a woeful thought, and he sobbed, "You've got no right to steal me!"

"One of your people stole Bligh," Mr. B said.

"I don't know why he bothered," Fisher said, and felt himself trembling. "Because you're savages."

"No more than you," Echols said. "Probably a lot less."

They were still sitting on the ground.

Fisher said, "You scream at planes!"

"You yell at insects," Echols said.

It was true, but so what? He howled at ants and flies when they came near him, and when he saw an insect on his suit he yelled "Cootie!"

"They're vectors in disease," he said. "Especially flies and lice. They're just like you aliens!"

But he was upset; he wanted them to plead with him and to promise to take him home. He was surprised that his screeching had not cowed them. He wandered away to where he planned to sleep and switched on his helmet light and saw Valda lying down and smiling at him. She raised her leg at him, offering him her boot.

"Get this thing off my dog," she said.

It was certainly safe to do that, away from her body cavities. Fisher worked it loose, liking the warmth of her bare leg and the heat of her foot.

"Have you changed your mind?" she said.

He was sniffing in mild alarm: he had forgotten to put on his gloves when he removed her boot.

"About sleeping with me?"

"I'm all right," he said, and his helmet rattled when he shook it. "My suit has coils in it, and I've still got a power pack. I'll be warm enough."

She made that noise again that was like a baby's burp. He could not determine whether it was another laugh. She seemed strange but at least she was on his side.

Never mind sleep with you, I'd like to squeeze your oinkers! That was what he wanted to say. He was afraid of disease— he looked at her and he imagined fungus in her crevices. And if she was twenty she must have plenty of both—funguses and crevices. But still his eyes ached with desire when he saw the pressure of her breasts against her shirt, and her delicious nipples like toggles.

He inflated his suit and warmed its coils, and he slept on his back like a toy bear on the ground, sighing slightly and fogging his faceplate, his arms clasped over his belly and his legs apart.

The next morning he remembered the raw tape clearly as they marched through the rising meadows and tree clumps to the last hill. He could have led them from here: he had studied the profile enough just before his mission with Hooper and Murdick. The repetition of that trip annoyed him. Why come back? He saw all repetition as useless and ignorant routine. Being back here was like failure.

But where was their camp? He had never found one. He had never located any huts, and if it was a cave, where was it?

He only saw the valley—the great flat depression between two ranges of hills.

"The Frying Pan," Echols said.

"That's the center of our quarter," Valda said.

Mr. Blue did not descend the slope to the camp, but instead walked in a halting way—glancing, peering, moving on—like a man shuffling in a museum, possessed by concentration. He did not bend his knees. He nodded at the wide circular valley.

"It's a pan," Mr. Blue said. "It's all ours. No one else has been here for over fifteen years."

"Except me," Fisher said.

Mr. Blue turned to him, stiff-legged, and lifted his face in a question.

"I mean now," Fisher said.

But he had meant before, with Hooper and Murdick—another lie. He had this place in twenty-color overlay, all the elevations, even an infrared version. He had found the paths they had thought were hidden; the sinkhole where they had landed and secured the rotor. The Frying Pan, Rooks said.

"It's got a bottom and sides," the man said. "It's got a handle."

"Incredible geological qualities," Echols said.

"You mean geomorphic features," Fisher said.

They were still at the edge, Mr. Blue still gesturing at it.

"Remember when we used to call it Happy Valley, and mean it?" Mr. Blue said. "Because we thought we were safe here?" He had glanced back at Fisher. "And you wonder why we scream at planes."

"Because, geologically"—Fisher was quacking loudly—"this depression is a down-thrown massif of the eastern O-Zone platform."

"I like them cracks and ridges," Gumbie said. "Yump."

"Delimited on each side by conspicuous fault lines," Fisher said.

"We figure it's been here a long time, looking like this," Mr. Blue said. "That radiation leak certainly didn't affect it."

"At the end of the Tertiary, this platform was composed of an extensive uplifted massif, flanked by down-warping areas on both the north and south sides. During the Quaternary, these down-warping areas were folded and uplifted by neotectonic movements of the limestone plates. That produced caverns elsewhere in O-Zone and the depression here."

"I guess that's why we call it the Frying Pan," Rooks said. "Why are you laughing, Valda?"

She could not answer. She had started while Fisher was speaking, and she was still laughing. It was like frantic hiccuping.

"That was before the radioactive excursion," Fisher said. "Before the human intervention."

"When they fucked it," Rooks said.

No one commented on that. They picked up the boxes and crates and started downward, skidding on loose stones. The sun was up and they were perspiring, on their last push.

Gumbie dropped behind, where Fisher was stepping carefully down the steep sides of the valley.

"Boy, you're real area-dite," Gumbie said in an admiring voice.

24

"No—not over there," Mr. Blue was saying. "It's right here."

But even with the man pointing, Fisher could not see a thing, and it was only after they began climbing again that Fisher saw the slash in the hillside, under a great hanging cliff. It was a stone vault in the mouth of the rockface, this cave they called home.

So he had been completely wrong—he understood that when they had assembled at the cave. He had not expected huts—he had not found any on the raw tape. From the way they had been living and camping on this march he had come to believe that they were tramps: huddling under bushes at night, and then in the morning burying their fire and scattering their leaves, and marching on to find a new bush and scavenge for some food. It was a grubby, prowling animal existence, based on hunger and fatigue. But now he saw that that was not it at all: they had a home, they had possessions, they had beds, they had comforts.

But this place also worried Fisher. It was a high limestone cave, very deep and full of chambers, but from the outside it was hardly a shadow. Even when he had stared directly at it he had not seen it. It was invisible to any search plane: Fisher himself had not seen it with any of the scanners or scopes. He had seen—it was pure luck—aliens scurrying on the video. And no wonder they scurried. In that New Year's party were the first aircraft they had seen for fifteen years. And no wonder, afterward, they had started screaming.

Not even satellites had picked up the presence of these

aliens. That was how ingenious their living arrangement was. And that was why Fisher became very silent when he was led through it and shown its various entrances and its hidden corners.

We're bluff-dwellers, they said. These castaways had solved their problem of how to survive in O-Zone. But what was a solid and secure home for them was a prison for him. He had not detected it, so how could anyone else—like Hooper or Hardy or a search party or a strike force?

He thought: They'll never find me.

"I know they're looking for me!" he said, quacking in a kind of protest. But it was empty defiance: he had no proof. In fact, the reverse seemed much more likely—that he had no chance at all, for more than a week had passed since his abduction and there was no sign of rescue. But still he quacked at them. "They'll find me!"

"That's not necessarily a good thing," Mr. Blue said.

"Why not?"

"Because they'll have to find us first."

They were standing on the open platform at the cave mouth, Mr. Blue and Fisher, while the others had dispersed into the cool shadows of the interior chambers. Water ran in a continuous blabbing somewhere deep in the cavern, and this platform that gave onto the valley smelled of fire and burned corn. It was like living on a shelf in the wilderness.

"Troglodytes," Fisher said.

And yet, in this setting, these people appeared to be almost human. They were not sleeping under bushes anymore; they had food; they had rugs and chairs and tables and lanterns—most likely stolen from the abandoned houses of a nearby town, where they got their clothes. The whole of their quarter of O-Zone was available to them, every house, every hotel, every condominium. Everyone in America spoke of the ghost towns of O-Zone, and these aliens were its ghosts.

"Put him to work," Mr. Blue said.

Fisher said, "You don't mean me."

But Mr. Blue had spoken to Rooks, and Rooks was smiling.

"Get that helmet off so you can hear me better."

With another quack of protest, Fisher yanked the helmet from his head.

"Now get that suit off."

"No," Fisher said. "I won't."

"Do it now," Rooks said, insisting with the kind of whisper Mr. Blue used.

"I was sealed into this suit!"

Rooks had a knife. "I'll cut you out of that suit and you'll never get back in, because there'll be nothing to get back into."

After he unfastened the clasps and the zips, Fisher peeled the suit down and stepped out of it. Standing in the liner, long johns, and a T-shirt, but still wearing his boots, Fisher felt more naked than he ever had among these aliens. Once he had felt distinctly like a turtle torn out of its shell—it seemed to sum up his situation. But that had been fanciful then, a random image to describe his sense of nakedness. Now it precisely described him, for he stood wearing only the thin liner, and there was his shell, folded in a pile with his beaky helmet on top.

He felt weak, but he was bigger than Rooks, with a big boy's thick legs and wide shoulders. And he was tall, roughly the height of Mr. Blue, who was the tallest of the aliens. Yet he had never felt that he was at any physical advantage, and out of his suit and helmet he felt terribly reduced. His great fear now was that he might burst into tears if anyone threatened him, and to calm himself he fantasized again about how he planned to destroy these people, first deafening them with howlers, and then blinding them with lightning bolts, and then burning them down, one by one.

Rooks said, "We've got some boxes down there—food boxes mostly. But other boxes, too, because when we left here we left in a hurry—never got time to hoist those boxes."

"What are we going to do with them?"

"When I said 'we' I meant you," Rooks said. "You're hoisting them, Fish. Get them up here. All of them."

"That'll take me a week!" Fisher said, and he feared that he might not be able to do it at all.

"We've got a week," Rooks said. "We've got time. Now go to it."

Fisher was on the point of asking what the others were doing to help, but before he spoke up he saw them. They seemed very busy, and some of them were engaged in harder tasks than his. Gumbie was carrying huge dirty boulders, and Valda was digging, and even Mr. Blue was hacking away at something.

All that day, Fisher labored with the boxes that lay against the hillside. His job was to raise them fifty meters up to the shelf at the entrance to the cave. The first day he fumbled with them—carrying one, dragging another, pushing a third. He bruised his hands and knees, and quietly—in frustration and rage—he wept to himself in the shadow of the hill. He was too tired to eat that night, but he noticed that they had broken open a crate of sealed provisions, and the next morning he found some packets of cookies and some Guppy-Cola.

He felt weaker the second day, but he had devised a system for raising the boxes. Using a long crank from an old meat grinder, and a ratchet from a truck jack, and a sequence of pulleys, Fisher made a hand-operated lifting machine that he predicted would allow the person lifting the weight to rest, as the ratchet prevented the ropes from slipping.

The question was, where to hang it? There was no tripod, no beam heavy enough or long enough to make into a crane, and the only logical alternative was a hook over the cave entrance.

"Don't you think we tried a block and tackle like that before?" Echols said. "You must think we're pretty stupid to have lived here this long without trying a gizmo like yours."

"Where is it, then, shit-wit?"

"Didn't work, and yours won't either."

"Yes, it will. All I have to do is find a place to hang it."

"Find me a point to put my lever, and I will move the world," Echols said. "There is no point. That's why ours didn't work. My advice to you is start heaving them boxes."

But he was too weak today to lift the boxes, and anyway he had a solution.

He said, "I need a deep hole with a twenty-centimeter radius about two meters above the cave entrance. Stick a beam in and suspend my machine from it."

Mr. Blue and Gumbie and Rooks had wandered over to hear the discussion, because they knew that Echols had a scientific background and was perhaps a match for Fisher.

Echols said, "If you chipped away for two months you wouldn't get a hole that size. That's solid limestone."

"You've tried it, eh?"

Echols nodded and smiled at the boy. He said, "I'd be glad to lend you my tools."

"Keep your wonky tools," Fisher said, and went into his chamber in the cave and returned with the particle beam.

"Stand back," he said. He aimed it over their heads and

made an adjustment on the magazine and fired, blasting a smoking hole with a twenty-centimeter radius two meters above the cave entrance.

"Fuck-wits," he said, and jammed a log into the hole.

He set up his lifting machine, and all that afternoon, and all the following morning, as he hoisted the boxes, he reflected on the drama of what he had done. And he fantasized about doing it differently—saying he was going to blast a hole in the rock, and then turning the particle beam on the aliens and wiping them out. It was a valuable fantasy, because at the end of it he had showed himself that it was impossible. Wiping them out meant only that he would be alone, on the ground, in O-Zone, and that, he knew, was much worse than being their prisoner.

"You ain't working," Rooks said, the day after Fisher had completed the lifting of the boxes.

Fisher was not surprised by Rooks's annoyance. The moment he had finished with his lifting machine, Fisher had picked it to pieces and scattered it, so that they would not be able to use it without his advice. He had left the log in place, not for any practical reason but rather as a reminder of the violence that was contained in his particle beam.

"I've done my work," Fisher said. "I'm finished."

"We're never finished," Rooks said.

And now Fisher realized that he hated Mr. Blue much more than Rooks, for it had been Mr. Blue who had assigned Rooks the job of supervising him.

"You're needed at the forge," Rooks said.

They called it a forge, but it was no more than a sheltered niche in the hillside where a fire was kept burning. "Tin bashing," Gumbie called it. They heated pieces of metal and hammered them flat. Mr. Blue said he planned to use them for armor plate, but Fisher suspected that it was just another way of his keeping the other aliens busy. He hated it for its crudity, its jailbird routine.

The metal was mostly cans and containers, and they heated them by filling them with hot coals and attaching wires to them and swinging them so that the rushing air acted like a bellows and got them white-hot. Then they were easily flattened.

These days there were three or four of the aliens at the forge, swinging cans of coals, stacking pieces of metal or bashing it on the anvil.

"This is what you call centrifugal force," Gumbie said, though the word came out sounding like *centuryfiggle*. He was spinning a can on a whistling wire.

"Bullshuck," Fisher said.

"He never heard of it," Gumbie said.

"It doesn't exist."

Gumbie said, "You think you know everything, but you don't. Everybody knows this is centrifugal force!"

"Then everybody's wrong," Fisher said, and he was never colder than when he was correcting someone, because he believed that to need correction the person must be a fool. "There is no such force. It's just a device causing a circular motion, and if the device is removed, Newton's First Law is obeyed and the object moves off at a tangent to the circle at the same speed it's been swinging. It's an apparent force, dong-face, like aliens are apparent human beings."

And that same day, Fisher found a way of using the particle beam to heat the pieces of metal and even to melt them over the anvil, so that there was no need to use hammers on them.

He believed that he had begun to succeed with them. It was now obvious to them, he knew, that he was intelligent, and certainly not the dip they once accused him of being. More than that, he had proven that he was useful. He felt that it was far harder for a Type A to prove his intelligence to an alien than to prove it to an Owner or someone legal. After almost two weeks of living with them in their complicated cave he had become stronger: he was eating regularly from his own provisions. He saw that it was within his capacity to be physically stronger and more agile than any of them. All he lacked was practice, but this exercise had the effect of building his muscles. He had always thought of himself as inadequate. But he had not tried. He was a Type A, and already, feeling fitter, he had visions of overpowering them and making his way out of O-Zone.

He was not fully convinced that they had no plans to harm him, but as the days passed and the weather grew hotter, he wondered what their plans were for him and for themselves.

In his room, he had a rope bed and a wooden chair and stolen rugs. He still wore his suit most of the time and, often, his helmet, in order to listen for broadcasts. But the range of this radio was pathetic—you could scream farther than it could transmit; and if there were planes, they flew at such a high altitude he could not hear them. Now and then he heard a wasp or a fly and believed it was an aircraft come to rescue him.

He had a window, a round eye that was dazzled all day by the bright valley and the blue sky. He had blasted it through the rock with his particle beam, hoping the aliens would be afraid when they saw the limestone spatter.

Sometimes he believed that he was their secret leader—that they were on the point of recognizing his true strength and then serving him, carrying out whatever orders he gave them, as he had commanded Hooper before that hopeless porker left him exposed. As their leader he would use them to escape from O-Zone, and the moment he was safe he would burn them all, for the uncertainty and fear they had subjected him to.

Sometimes he believed that he was their burden, their pest. Although they had stolen him, they made him feel like an intruder. He was their alien.

And it was no good that he simplified the tasks that were set for him. When he had solved one set of problems, they came up with others. He couldn't win, and so he dragged his feet, and used the hammer and the ax, and refused to simplify them. He saw that they were merely killing time. Aliens were deficient in most skills, but that did not matter, for like animals they had so much time they had no notion of time passing. They were dominated by hunger, danger, and fatigue.

Fisher too was losing his sense of time. Once, he had an awareness of the rhythm of a week. A Monday was unmistakable, and so was the length of a Wednesday and the promise of a Friday and the stillness of a Sunday. But these aliens had no days off, and because the routine was the same, the days were the same. He always knew the date but seldom the day of the week, and he was often appalled to see by his watch that it was Saturday and he was plucking the feathers out of a wild turkey that Echols had snared. That was another thing. They gave him the worst jobs to do, and then they stood around talking about him as if he were deaf, just the way they had when they'd first snatched him from the rotor.

"The question is what to do with him."

Him only meant one person here.

"Make him take a hike," Rooks said.

"He's a germ—he's infecting us," someone said, behind the helmet, out of Fisher's line of vision.

"Push him over the edge." Was that Gumbie?

"Why do you want to keep him so much?" Echols said.

Mr. Blue said, "I want Bligh back."

And if it was true that this alien had been taken by Hooper, then it proved that he had sacrificed Fisher for a monkey-woman. He had hurried away with her and left him to the mercy of these aliens. *I'll burn him, too,* Fisher thought, but of course if Hooper had gotten what he wanted, then he might never be back. *He swapped me for that monkey.*

"You'll get her back," Fisher said with his usual bravado, but his quack took all the menace out of it. "My uncle's got a jet-rotor that's so fast it's practically invisible. He'll come whistling in and burn you all down."

"Tip him over," someone said.

"Leave him alone," Valda said—more and more he noticed that Valda defended him, probably more because she disliked them than liked him; but he was grateful nonetheless. "Bligh might not even want to come back. She certainly wasn't very happy when she was here."

"She was a kid," Echols said.

Fisher was reminded that this monkey-woman wasn't a woman—she was a fifteen-year-old, probably diseased little creature with no ID that his rich uncle just whisked off, the disgusting porker.

"This discussion is closed for the moment," Mr. Blue said.

Fisher found himself giving thanks that nothing was going to change. Whenever he felt safe, as he did here and as he had at certain places on the march, he wanted everything to freeze: no change, no alteration, nothing. Let everything continue just as it was. Packing, burying their fire, hoisting their packs, all the activities of setting out filled him with apprehension. And it was only in the course of the day, in the evidence that nothing bad was happening to him, that he became convinced that this move was sensible. But two weeks in this cave on the bluff had calmed him. He wanted things to change, he wanted to be found—rescued—and for the aliens to be burned. But not right now—not while he was feeling safe. He had come to depend on these aliens, and he knew their moods, and so far they hadn't killed him. He did not really believe they would, and he felt that any change implied risk.

The food was a great help. Eating familiar provisions from the stock he had selected and packed gave him a feeling of well-being. Perhaps the aliens were trying to make him complacent by feeding him this way. But he did not think they were that devious. Much of his confidence arose from his suspicion that the aliens were very stupid and gullible. In a sense, Mr. Blue's spiriting him away from the Diggers was proof of that. Mr. B was sentimental. Fisher was glad of it—he knew he would have been eaten alive by those apes—but he also believed that it gave him power over Mr. Blue.

He had none of their superstitions. They had no idea of change, none of time. Their whole effort was toward survival. And so they had not separated themselves from the land—they saw themselves as part of O-Zone, which would have amused any New Yorker: O-Zone was a contaminated wilderness. And they seemed to see themselves as existing in a place that was not attached to America.

Fisher said, "You aliens are out of this world."

They had heard him say "aliens" so often they had stopped objecting to it.

"This is the world," Echols said.

"Bullshuck."

"The rest of it doesn't count, because it doesn't matter to us."

"You pretend this is some kind of island," Fisher said.

Valda said, "I like that. It's true."

"We don't have to pretend," Mr. Blue said. "We live in our quarter. We have everything we want. And all the perimeters are dangerous. It is an island."

Fisher said, "I'd like to leave it, somehow. Not today or tomorrow. But pretty soon."

He meant he wanted to be scooped up by a battling gunship and to wake up in his room in Coldharbor.

Rooks said, "Why are you listening to this dip? He's nothing, he's nobody!"

Still, they fed him—they fed him like a cat. And he congratulated himself that he had lasted with them. He had been out of Coldharbor alone once in his life; had wandered in New York one day. And the rest of the time had either been in his room or else shepherded by Hardy and Moura ("Look at the lights, Fizzy"). But for weeks he had lived in O-Zone, and not simply survived but had brought technology to this wilderness—it really was an island—and had repaired his helmet and his beam. He knew the aliens did not like him, but he felt sure they respected him. He was their prisoner, but he had not broken down. He did not think that any of them except Mr. B had seen him cry, and he drew strength from that, even though he was aware that he had wept several times. Often he had felt stupid here, as if O-Zone was not the world.

Mr. Blue had protected him from the Diggers. Echols had enough math to know he was a brilliant boy. Gumbie had not really regained his confidence after the business about the so-called centrifugal force; though Gumbie was too stupid to be consistent. Rooks hated him, but Rooks was only one alien. Kylie hardly existed, and after the death of Tinia she had seemed greatly diminished—just a small-faced woman who worked without speaking.

And there was Valda. Whenever he had felt particularly stupid she had propped him up. He was grateful to her. He knew that the other aliens thought he was infantile and selfish, but what did they know of the world? O-Zone was the one place on earth where even a Type A would have difficulty, and where an alien had the advantage. What they took to be his brilliance was actually a considerable handicap, but only Valda seemed to understand this paradox.

Valda entered his chamber early one morning in the third week. It was that hour when his fear of the dark subsided into the impatience and uncertainty he felt in daylight, though both paralyzed him with a numbing sense of imprisonment. There was either no light at his window or else too much—he was blinded by darkness or its opposite. This was the brief in-between phase, and he was startled to see Valda standing over him.

She knelt next to his low bed, where he lay in his inflated suit, his helmet and boots on. He felt very small beneath her, like an infant, and very passive—he was intimidated by her eagerness. She quickly unbuttoned her shirt, and then parted it and held her breasts to him, one in each of her hands, offering them to him.

Fisher looked at the soft crushed nipples and despised himself for liking these imperfect things.

"Don't be afraid," she said. She was smiling at him, her face shining with excitement.

He had not known how tender any breasts could be until she touched them and they were plumped in her hands. Their fragility kept him away, and yet he wanted them. The morning light at the window whitened her skin and showed its tiny veins crazing its tissue, and its dusting of pale hairs, its moles scattered like flakes, and the soft contours of breasts lying like full pouches of milk against her fingers and thumbs.

Facing her, Fisher felt as if he were made of wood and wet clay, sort of stuck together. And though something was struggling within him it felt like an ineffectual rattle—less like a sign of life than a reminder that he was dying. He groaned and a patch of steam clouded his faceplate. He lifted off his helmet, not sure what was expected of him.

"Shall I stick my finger into your bum?" he asked.

"Why would you want to do that?"

"To get you hot," he said, and looked for a reaction on her face.

Valda thought a moment, and smiled at him pityingly and then said, "Let me tell you what I like."

Now the eagerness was in his eyes, too, and still her hands gently lifted her breasts.

"Touch them, suck them, lick them," she said. "Take them."

He thought: They're all she has—they are everything.

She said, "Baby," as his hands went to them; and there was a clap and a roar—a jet-rotor, he knew at once. Fisher sat up but it was too late to run out.

In those seconds she had let go of her breasts and begun to scream. There was no sound of her voice above the racket of the rotor, but he was frightened by her convulsive movement, her open mouth, her teeth, the whites of her rolled-up eyes. A split second afterward the echo of her scream rang on the walls of his chamber, and he heard the distant growl of the jet-rotor.

It broke the spell—shattered the magic with noise. Valda stood up awkwardly. She seemed embarrassed. She buttoned her shirt and knotted it and without looking at him—she had already begun to leave—she said, "You look so funny in that suit."

"Aw, jings," Fisher said, and felt flustered, as if he had

stumbled reaching for something he badly wanted—not only had he fallen but he had ended up with nothing. And now he could not remember what he had wanted; and Valda was gone.

"They're searching for him," Mr. Blue said later that day. They were eating again, but the old stuff—pole greens and stringy meat and bean cakes.

Mr. Blue still talked as though Fisher were deaf or stupid, a dim alien who had washed up on the shores of O-Zone.

"They'll kill us if they find him here."

"And how are we going to swap him for Bligh?" Gumbie asked.

"If we find his people before they find us, we might be able to make a deal."

"He's a dip—he isn't worth the trouble," Rooks said. "Sell him to the Diggers. Give him away. Tie him to a tree and just walk off!"

They usually spoke softly, but Fisher heard everything, because even a normal voice made the vault chambers stutter with echoes. These aliens seemed threatened by echoes, but no whisper was too weak not to reach these walls and be flung back. Fisher stayed away from the echoey darkness at the back of the cavern, and he avoided the blinding glare of daylight at the front. He kept to the edge of the shelf, between the darkness and the light, tuning the transmitter in his helmet and playing with his phones, listening for another rotor. He imagined it swooping, and taking him up and away, and blasting them. But more days passed and there was nothing.

A decision came quite suddenly.

Fisher had been staring at Mr. Blue's skinny face. He thought: I don't know this alien at all. He said, "What's your other name?"

"Elroy," the man said softly. "Elroy Blue." And then he responded to the suggestion and said, "What's your other one?"

"Allbright."

It made an echo, three bounces, and someone was listening inside. That person said, "Like the department stores. That rich family from New York."

"That's my family," Fisher said. "But they closed the stores. They've moved into cable sales—it's all mail order.

What are you looking at? They're all herberts. My uncle's a porker. My father's a dong. He's not even my real father!"

He was surprised by their interest and wanted to mock it: these aliens were perhaps even dumber than they looked. They were impressed by the Allbrights! Fisher disliked the Allbrights and every aspect of the business. But the aliens were murmuring and seemed to see possibilities in the name. They kept repeating it, as if trying it out and listening to the sound of the echoes. And now they seemed to know what to do.

"Take him back," Echols said.

"New York," someone said. "That's the States."

"We can walk to the States."

PART FOUR

EARTHWORKS

25

I**T WAS THEIR THIRD SEARCH-AND-SCAN MISSION**—H**OOPER**
laughed to think that that was what Fizzy would have called
this afternoon flight to and from New York—the picnic in
Firehills, the low-altitude photography. Hooper felt he was
flying blind, but he knew that Fizzy would easily have been
able to locate the aliens. Hooper was lost without the boy; it
seemed impossible to find Fizzy without Fizzy's help. Today
was typical. Unless something specific showed up on the
film—the band of aliens, a settlement, a hot spot, a glimpse
of Fizzy, or any sign of life—it would be another failure. But
it had been another lovely day with Bligh.

"We used to scream when we saw planes like this," Bligh
was saying.

"I don't believe you," Hooper said. "Only wild men would
do that. I mean, real burned-out Skells. Anyway, there are
no other planes here. Overflying is forbidden."

"This year there were people," Bligh said.

New Year's: Hooper said nothing.

"They came down like thunder and lightning," the girl
said. "But it's so quiet inside here!"

He loved her for not being afraid—he loved it that her
wonderment and curiosity overcame her apprehension.

"What's this for?"

"It's a program scanner, a sort of analyzer. Fizzy's. I have
no idea how to work it."

"And you said he's stupid!"

"Not stupid," Hooper said. "Just foolish."

The land streaking beneath Hooper's jet-rotor was wild

and misleadingly green. He imagined that it was all contaminated, and felt like an outlaw and an adventurer. He saw
an exciting similarity between Bligh the alien and O-Zone the
Prohibited Area. It was a lovely lawless place with a terrible
reputation; it was solitary and cut off, an island outside time;
and it was her home. She was a child of all these dangers.

He wanted to believe that Bligh belonged to him now. She
was everything that he lacked. He had been desperate to find
her; he was desperate to keep her. "Love" was the word he
gave his desperation.

In spite of his pleasure in her being with him on the flight,
he was uneasy and superstitious traveling with her in O-
Zone. He was superstitious most of all, because having found
her here, he feared that he could also lose her here—something about just being in this place. And O-Zone still seemed
very dangerous.

It was the only part of America that was genuinely
empty—empty by law, feared by everyone, and heavily
guarded. People dreamed about it and used it as a backdrop
for their fantasies. Its very name was a word for wilderness
and waste, and all its associations made it a complicated and
ambiguous metaphor, as if it were not merely a closed-off
area in the state of Missouri, but a remote place, with the
features of another planet. It was not just a foreign land. It
represented misjudgment and disaster—perhaps trickery,
perhaps sabotage. Maybe Fizzy was right about the collapse
of those caverns causing the radioactive leak. Yet no one had
known until after the catastrophe that the Feds had hidden
the waste there! Something unspeakable happened and then
people said: *There was something I meant to tell you* . . . O-
Zone had been like that. One day it was just the Ozarks, and
the next day it was an island revolving in outer space. It was
lost beauty—spoiled, people said, ruined and poisoned. But
now Hooper knew better, and somewhere down there so
probably did Fizzy.

Bligh had been with him for over three weeks, and all that
time he had methodically and conscientiously been kind to
her. It had become almost instinctive to him in a tall fatherly
way—his attention, his tenderness. He gathered that she had
been unhappy with her people—those aliens. She said they
had been driven out of their camp. What camp? He had not
seen one, and neither had Fizzy. She said she had wanted to
leave at about the time he had abducted her.

"You took me away," she said. "You stole me!"

Then she laughed, and he was so glad she had made it into a joke, because for him it was no joke. And he was still not sure of her. He had not touched her—didn't dare. He was amazed to think that after three weeks Hooper Allbright had still not made love to her. He wanted her to ask why. "Because I'm very serious about you," he wanted to reply. But the girl didn't ask.

Lovers are cannibals, he thought, and in his hungry, despairing way he wanted to devour her and have her at the same time. He wanted to inhabit her; he wanted her to live within him. But he hung back. He didn't want to frighten her; and he was also nervous. While he mocked his desire with the sad self-parody of cannibalism, there was in his mind the actual suspicion that aliens were animals. It was an irrational thought, he insisted, yet he did not want to rid himself of the notion, because he also found it very exciting.

Bligh enjoyed these trips—the search-and-scan missions, these outings. She recognized the features of the land—she told Hooper their names. The word O-Zone meant nothing to her; she called the area "our quarter" and explained that there were also people living in the other three quarters of "the Territory." What people? Hooper wondered. O-Zone was officially empty, and it was certainly a Prohibited Area. Bligh claimed it was full of people. They had camps—some had houses! They had water! They farmed and hunted! And what they didn't have they found in all the abandoned houses in the empty towns. Deserted and radioactive O-Zone was a sort of thriving state of industrious aliens!

"The first time I saw it I thought it was paradise," Hooper said. "But that's because I thought there were no people in it."

"That's selfish," Bligh said.

Hooper was surprised by how quickly and easily she said it; and she was right, of course.

She said, "Don't you like people?"

"I like to think there are places in the world where there are no people," Hooper said. "Empty places, that will never change. I thought O-Zone was one. I guess I was wrong."

"We didn't change it," Bligh said. "We lived close to the ground, and I thought it was a pretty easy life, until you took me away." She was now looking out of the side porthole of the rotor. "Now I know how hard it was. And we've been very hungry lately. The hunting was bad. We ate our dogs."

Hooper asked for more, but she had fallen silent. She often fell silent and shook her head when trying to talk about the past. She resisted, pretending there was nothing to say. She was not superstitious; she was doubtful, watchful, wary.

"Was it there?" he asked, because she seemed to be looking at something.

He took her silence to mean no.

He said, "Fizzy would know," and felt helpless.

This third trip was the last reentry allowed on the Access Pass. Remembering that, Hooper radioed Hardy.

"Homeward-bound, brother," he said when he found Hardy's frequency.

"*Leave a message,*" Hardy's line automatically replied. "*We will find you.*"

Hardy had specifically said: No detailed messages on this subject, unless in an agreed code—so Hooper said nothing. He was becoming discouraged, and what was so frustrating was the thought that if he hadn't lost the boy this would all be perfect. He hated the thought that Fizzy was both a swap and a sacrifice, and he knew that it would be very hard to snatch him back. He hoped he was alive. He counted on the boy's indestructible intelligence. And they had all that food—those weapons, the suit and helmet. And yet Hooper went on punishing himself with the thought that Fizzy was living among wolves.

Bligh was still looking away. Hooper said, "See anything?"

She had a way of wincing that made her seem both innocent and incompetent: that wince meant no, too.

She probably thought of him as a wolf. He knew she was not yet sure of him. How could she be sure in such a short time? So he was careful, he didn't want to frighten her: no shocks, no surprises, nothing heavy. Anyway, New York was strange enough for now. After all the trouble he had taken to find her, he did not want to lose her.

He wanted to say: Through you I can understand the world. Everything looks different and better.

"Why are you smiling?" she said.

"Because I've just realized I want to go on living."

She shook her head, indicating that she did not understand. Did a fifteen-year-old ever doubt that you went on living? She said, "I love these straggling ravines. Those are all pines." She was narrating over the ground-screen, fascinated by the images. "The roads are just black stripes. A few roofs. Now I see why you didn't think there were any people here."

She moved her small stubby finger on the screen, and frowned at it—a strand of hair coming loose from her helmet and brushing her cheek as she turned her head. He was especially touched by her slight flaws. Every imperfection in her roused his love.

She saw him watching her that way—his eyes pleading and possessive.

"You could have had anyone," she said. His steady gaze seemed to make her uncomfortable. "Why did you choose me?"

Hooper laughed to think that she meant she was unimportant. She still did not realize how difficult she had been. She had seemed just about unattainable. She was practically a child, she was an alien, she was living in the most forbidden of Prohibited Areas.

"I almost killed myself trying to find you," Hooper said. "And of course that was one of the attractions," he added, anticipating her next question. "The difficulty of it all"—but he was smiling—"the risk." Then, remembering, he said, "I lost my nephew!"

"They'll look after him. They're not killers."

"He's a strange boy. You don't know him."

"You didn't know me," she said. "You still don't."

"When I saw you I wanted you," he said. "That was enough."

She became silent within her helmet and looked out of the side porthole to think.

"And you didn't know me," he said. "That's another reason I love you. I don't trust the word of anyone who knows me."

He wanted to add, *Everyone lies to the rich,* but it sounded like a whimper, and nothing was more disgusting to him than the rich portraying themselves as victims—and it was one of their most common complaints, saying they were weak, and rather burdened and powerless, and often claiming to be poor. Once, he had whimpered. No more.

"It was dark that morning," she was saying.

She believed that was the only time he had seen her. Hooper did not say that he had watched her on tape, or that he had murdered the two net-men who had cornered Murdick. He was thankful that she never mentioned those deaths. Her fearlessness was her best characteristic; and he loved her most at her most animal. Animals never mourned.

"You say you wanted me," she said, her voice breathy and incredulous. She did not know how strong she was. "But I had nothing. Nothing."

He said, "Yes!"

She winced slightly at his enthusiasm.

"I loved that most of all," he said.

"That word," she said.

"What's wrong with saying 'love'?"

She shrugged. "It's such a waste of words."

But her wide-awake way of saying that made him love her. "I thought I had everything," he said. "And then I realized I didn't have you."

She pushed the faceplate of her helmet up, as if to see him better. The clear sky brightened her eyes, and they pierced him.

"And that you didn't have me," he said. "Maybe I shouldn't tell you these things."

"Maybe," she said. "I'd feel a lot sexier if you weren't so serious!"

She laughed. He now knew that laugh. It was not companionable, and it was not intended as encouragement. It was more like a warning that he had gone too far.

She did not say anything more for a while—for minutes, which was many clicks at ground speed. They were nearing the perimeter. She looked at the ground-screen and said—it was the kind of whisper that is like a vagrant thought—"I thought I was going to die there."

Not there below: by the time she got the words out the rotor was far beyond it, homeward-bound at high speed. Bligh had no idea of air distances, but that ignorance was in Hooper's favor. She believed the short flight meant that they were still very close to the camp she called home. She did not know—how could she?—that New York was fifteen hundred clicks from O-Zone.

A Federal attack rotor escorted by two chase planes drew level with Hooper.

"Reduce speed and identify yourself."

It was only then that Hooper realized he had entered the

Red Zone of the perimeter. Fizzy would have given him plenty of warning.

"Hooper Allbright and passenger, en route to New York."

"Identify passenger and give Access Code."

He first radioed the Access Code—their permission to use Red Zone and O-Zone airspace—and then he gave the name on Bligh's ID.

Moments later, the clearance came, and "That was your last reentry, Allbright. Your Access Pass is now invalid. You may proceed."

It was another reminder that he had failed to find Fizzy. How easily he forgot the boy when he was with Bligh, and he thought: What now?

"I wish I knew who this person was," Bligh said, holding the ID disc and glancing up. She had misunderstood Hooper's questioning look. "It's certainly not me."

"It doesn't matter," he said. How could he begin to tell her of the hunt in New York with Godseye and those miserable troopers, and how Murdick had burned that Owner? "But you need an ID."

"We know all about IDs," she said. Her harsh laughter said, Watch out. "If you don't have an ID in this country you're a zombie. That's another reason we didn't live in the States."

"O-Zone is the States."

"Then why do you call it O-Zone?"

He smiled because she had challenged him. It pleased him to see her in a defiant mood.

"Because it's an island," he said.

She was still studying the ground-screen.

"Where are we?" she asked after a while.

"Pennsylvania," he said. "I haven't been down there for years."

Bligh was still looking, but by the time Hooper had finished speaking they were over New York.

Out of her element, Bligh noticed everything. And she was illiterate. It was not a handicap: it made her especially alert and sharpened all her senses.

She was thrilled, as before on their return to New York, by the lights rising in the city—so much brighter than the low cooling sun settling into the depths of gray dust in the slipstream aft of the jet-rotor. The slender glass-and-silver tow-ers and turrets of the city glittered, and the lights on their steep galleries outshone the dying sun. The dark spaces at the margin of the narrow island only served to make the city seem greater, more imperial and unearthly. It was a city of light.

"It's like a beautiful castle—a gigantic one, with a moat around it," she said.

"How do you know about castles and moats?"

She laughed in her warning way, to put him in his place: How dare you accuse me of being ignorant of simple things? the laugh said. But it was only a laugh, a sound with the merest echo. A moment later it was gone for good.

Everyone Hooper had ever known believed that aliens were naive and that they hated and feared technology. And at the beginning—three weeks ago—he had been apprehensive about Bligh in the jet-rotor, Bligh in New York, Bligh in Coldharbor, Bligh carrying a dead girl's ID. He knew his apprehension was childish, but it was understandable. In his whole busy life Hooper had never known an alien—never been alone with one, never spoken to one. Bligh was human, and Hooper was deeply ashamed that he had ever doubted that in her or any other alien.

And the city was well-planned: Bligh was quick to appreci-ate it. Wasn't the technology of the city meant to allay anx-iety? Surely that was the point of the castle and the moat—not the island's incomprehensible size, but its beauty? Tech-nology was either aesthetically pleasing or else it was worth-less and awful. Fizzy's preoccupations had shown him that technology was an art, not a science.

Hooper was glad that Bligh was not intimidated by New York, but after all, it was an easy place to live. Sleeping in the open and hunting in O-Zone took guts; but not this, not flying in a speeding rotor, and not the rich tower-life in the garrison at Coldharbor. If Bligh was silent it was not terror but bewilderment. It had not taken long for her to under-stand that Hooper was wealthy. She clearly knew what an Owner was, but Owner did not quite describe him.

Now as the rotor slowed down and turned, the twanging sound of the rotor blade reached them through the portholes, and the jets subsided. The slower this aircraft went, the noisier it was. But Hooper was circling around the island to impress her. The lights dazzled her and made her sigh.

Watching them—this pleased him—she seemed to become a very small girl. She was overcome by the sight, and did not speak but only uttered soft gasps of amazement. The towering city shone on the curvature of her faceplate.

"I think I love you even more now," Hooper said. "And—"

She had gone very quiet and was holding tight, as her thick helmet vibrated. They were hovering over the rotor pad at Coldharbor; they lowered and settled on the tower roof.

"And I like myself a little better," he said.

He cut the engines. Bligh lifted off her helmet and shook her hair into place—it was streaked light and dark and it jumped in thick hanks around her face.

"That's a strange thing to say." She had a way of staring at him that made him think he could never conceal anything from her.

He wanted to tell her that his desire, his sex instinct, was roused. He felt younger and more powerful. He wanted to say: Sex is magic.

He said, "I was getting very bored with myself. I'm much happier now—thanks to you. What's wrong?"

"I'm happy when you look after me"—but she said this in a solemn voice. "You're very kind. But when you talk about love, I get worried. I don't really know what you mean—it makes you seem unpredictable. And it makes me feel somehow unfair to you."

He was smiling—glad that they were able to talk, glad that they were alone and safely back at Coldharbor.

"Because I don't love you," she said—not apologizing but stating a fact.

"You don't have to," he said. And then he became solemn himself and said, "You're right. Let's not use that word."

"You haven't eaten much today," he said as they went down in the elevator.

She shrugged; she smiled. "I've never been so well-fed!"

"Please eat something."

"All right," she said softly. It was the small surrendering voice of a child.

He saw that she had agreed to eat, not out of hunger, but purely to please him, and that made him happy. Her willingness meant everything to him.

"And then I'll take you out. We'll buy something."

"You keep buying me things!"

"You can have anything you want."

"You'll make me greedy."

"I want you to be greedy," he said, because she had never shown the slightest sign of greed. "Promise me you will be."

She laughed—her cautioning laugh: another warning.

26

IN THE UNIT AT COLDHARBOR, BLIGH WENT DIRECTLY TO the suite Hooper had given her. It was five rooms on the south-facing side of the tower, where she could look downtown, ninety blocks under the skylights. "I'll be right over," she said, using her helmet phones. She had been very quick to master the phones and the signaling devices, and Hooper could not help wondering whether Fizzy had adapted to the rigors of O-Zone. If he hadn't, he was probably already dead. This thought made Hooper feel fatalistic and made the whole matter of rescue somehow less urgent.

"Dinner," he said to himself, and put two sealed meals into the oven. That was another favor to her. She had been fascinated by the sealed meal trays. Hooper had stacks of them in the freezer, but was much prouder of the fact that as an Owner he had chests of fresh vegetables and fruit, milk and eggs, real meat, real fish.

"I don't eat meat fabric or textured protein," he had said at their first meal. "None of these pastes or formulas, except when I'm on a mission of some kind, and that's pretty rare. I mean, I don't run around rehydrating stuff to heat."

She stared at him: What was he shouting about?

"We actually peel potatoes around here," he said. "We chop our own spinach. Sometimes it has dirt on it! I've got asparagus in that refrigerated drawer."

"Good for you," she said.

But he did not want her to miss the point by mocking him. He said, "I've got a stack of firewood in the fuel room. For the fireplace."

339

Was she smiling at this?

He said, "It's probably the only firewood in New York. I've actually got a permit to burn it."

"What else would you do with it?" Bligh said.

"I've got real apples and oranges," Hooper said. "I've got onions! I've got greens!"

"Maybe that's why I feel so at home here," she said.

He thought: That's possible. He had always resisted the banalities and high tech of New York eating, and he was wealthy enough to afford real food, and a fireplace, and a private car.

And then Bligh smiled and said, "I've never heard anyone boast about onions before," and he realized that she had been sarcastic earlier.

"There's not much fresh food around," Hooper said. "There's not much water. We've got our own supply in Cold-harbor—our own generator, too. Most New Yorkers eat meal trays."

And he explained how you rehydrated or thawed the meal tray. He showed her the tray, and the meal program, and the picture disc, and was about to say that city workers and pass-people from New Jersey and Brooklyn ate trays—and so did Federals, and guards, and probably some aliens too—when Bligh spoke up.

"That's what I want!"

Now, waiting for her, he switched on his monitor. She had been smiling when she left him. Was she still smiling? He watched her moving in her suite. He was heartened by the way she still smiled and sang to herself when she was alone. Hooper became very attentive in front of the monitor.

Being with Bligh meant that he had to isolate himself. He did not think it was wise at the moment to introduce her to Hardy or Moura—he believed that his enthusiasm for Bligh might seem as if he were indifferent to the missing Fizzy. Nor did he want to leave Bligh on her own. Yet it was a satisfaction to be with her. It made him feel useful and human, it allowed him a perspective on himself and his world.

And, after all, he was glad that he had not been impressed by his firewood. She had sense. She had not once mentioned drugs or money or weapons—the monotonous topics of all the other people he knew. Her presence in his unit gave the place life and color—the way dull rooms had been trans-formed for him by the presence of a singing bird in a cage, or cats magnificently slumbering on sofas. But he had long ago abandoned house pets.

She was singing now on the monitor screen—singing as she removed her clothes: not audible words, but a slowly lilting melody that was half in her head. She folded each garment as she took it off, and Hooper went on watching as she stood in her underpants. Liberated from her close-fitting flying suit, she stretched her arms and legs. She was fresh-faced and long-legged and smiling—the way he had first seen her.

She passed a mirror and then glanced back at it, perhaps wondering: Is this what he sees? The faces that people made in mirrors were never the faces they made in public. They seldom smiled. Bligh was not smiling now. She was looking enigmatic. They saved their secret expressions for mirrors.

Bligh went into the bathroom and took her pants off, as Hooper switched monitors, following her to the shower. She ran it so that only a dribble came out, and she washed as someone who had experienced a scarcity of water—sponging herself thoroughly but not wasting any.

She called out, "Almost ready!"—speaking to the closed door and unaware that a camera had followed her here.

And then with an urgent expression on her face, Bligh straddled the width of the tub and, still standing, and holding her slim legs apart, she arched her back and smiled. She took her vulva in both hands, parting it where it was reddest, as though she were holding two halves of an exotic mushroom. Where it was ripest its lips were softly squashed like the thin leaves on the underside of a mushroom cap. Lifting herself with her fingers, she let fly, pissing with a scorching splashing sound into the glugging tub.

Hooper turned up the volume until the sound she made was a loud crackling. He had never known another woman to piss like that, shooting it in an arc as she stood with her legs apart. She was a girl of fifteen: did that explain it? Hooper was fascinated, staring, holding his breath, hanging in front of the monitor and suffocating.

He told himself that he needed to know all her secrets. Then he sighed and came alive, and peered at her resuming her shower, and drying herself, and dressing for dinner, first her underwear, and then sheathing her slender body into another tight suit.

In that same moment Hooper felt accused by small squinting eyes and murmuring voices. He was forced to justify himself, almost to say it out loud. *This is not spying,* he thought. *This is my only chance. I could lose her tomorrow and this would be all I'd have.* And he swore to himself: *I won't betray her.*

"It's true," he said as they were eating.

Bligh looked up from her meal tray. Hooper had spoken out of a trance, surprising her after a long silence. He had been thinking again about what he had seen on the monitor.

"I don't know much about you," he said.

She looked uncertain. She had stopped eating. Then she recovered.

"Can I tell you something?" she said. "I've never loved anyone—I don't even like the word. I always thought it was something that would happen to me later, when I was older."

"You're so young," he said.

"I don't feel young," she said. "And I don't think of you as old. But I feel that you've loved other women. That you've used that word lots of times before. Lovers go on finding other people to love."

"I was married," Hooper said, feeling oddly as if this little girl had put him on the spot. "She was like me. I didn't love her. I pitied her. Because she was like me."

"Was she an Owner, too?"

"Everyone's an Owner," he said.

She laughed at him with a suddenness and a sharpness that reproached him. He knew he deserved it, and to cover his embarrassment—what made it worse was that she was not in the least offended—he said, "It was a few years ago. It was a sort of romance." He was trying to explain, but he was also trying to improve the moment and disperse the echo of her laughter. "Haven't you ever had the feeling, after someone has played music or sung a song beautifully, that you're in love with them?"

She still faced him. She said, "In that case, I would be in love with the song." Picking up her fork, she added, "But as I said, I don't know anything about love."

Hooper watched her closely. He felt insecure when she said something very logical or very wise. Then he realized how little power he actually had, because it hinted at strengths in her that he had not anticipated.

He said, "Eat up and we'll go," and she obeyed him.

On the way out, Hooper radioed Hardy, using the helmet phones.

When Hardy came on the line and heard Hooper's voice, he said, "*Don't say anything more, don't explain anything— say nothing.*" Hardy sounded as though he were repeating something he had carefully rehearsed. "*Talk to me tomorrow on my private line, and in the usual way.*"

He meant in code. He hung up as abruptly as he had answered.

Bligh said, "I like these helmets!"

She had already learned the trick of using a line and phones rather than hollering out of the pushed-up faceplate, and only her boots gave her trouble—she was a trifle unsteady in them.

"Masks are very stylish these days," Hooper said.

"But they're tough, too. They're safe. And the phones really work!"

She took nothing for granted. It was this lively appreciative quality that Hooper valued most in her. When she saw a button, she said, "What does it do?" and faced with a machine or a strange object, she said, "How does it work?" Hooper explained, and she liked the explanations as much as he enjoyed detaining her with them. Teaching her made him feel useful, and it renewed his interest in the city. It also reminded him of all the skills it took to live here.

She was at times so impressed with these details of life in New York City that he suspected that she did not understand them. And then he felt safer, knowing she needed him.

She was astonished by the lights at night—the skylights especially, and the blips and flashes of air traffic, small private planes and rotors, in their clockwise progress around the city; the streaks of their high-level landings and vertical take-offs. Hooper knew from the monitor that the light sometimes kept her awake (Bligh slept naked, with the blanket over her head). But the light also reassured her. Whenever she saw darkness she said, "What's in there?"

She was eager to know more: Hooper had not imagined that New York was so interesting. Bligh's curiosity made the city special. Hooper, seeing it with her eyes, realized that it was fantastic—the heights of the residential towers, the indoor parks and glassed-in gardens, the quack of rotors and the hiss of expresses aboveground—trams and rail cars; the complex rules of entry, the roadblocks, the security checks, and the surrounding darkness.

"I live over there, don't I?" she said, tossing her head at

the wall of black beyond the west side. She still believed that
O-Zone, her quarter of it, lay across the river, just beyond
New Jersey.

Leaving Coldharbor that night, Hooper took Bligh past the
checkpoint, so that she could see Jennix and his wall of monitors. He showed her that they did not simply record what was
happening in the towers and grounds, but also monitored
different parts of the city.

"That's Upper West, that's Lower East, there's the
bridges," Captain Jennix said helpfully. "There was an incident at a tunnel entrance earlier on—Lower West. Might
have been Skells. And we were getting reports of an alien
alert right next door, at the Lansdown Tower. I think they
nailed someone. There was an all-clear. Going out?"

"We were thinking about it," Hooper said crossly.

"Taking your car?"

Hooper faced the man and said, "I hate questions!"

But Jennix was not put off. He said, "It's just that with
these incidents tonight, and the way the world's going, I
thought you might be interested in some literature."

"Not today," Hooper said.

"The young lady might be interested," Jennix said, turning
his smile on Bligh. Jennix wore a long-visored cap and earphones, and a high-powered particle beam was strapped to
his waist. He approached Hooper and said, "Time is running
out, you know. A fellow like you, with your net worth, could
have a swell place on a station. You could do yourself
proud—be totally self-sufficient. You could upgrade yourself
at any time. You could be in orbit, Mr. Allbright."

Hooper said, "It's so kind of you to think about my future," and started away, taking Bligh by the arm.

But Jennix left his station with a leaflet in his hand.

"You don't have to accept this planet," he said. "Millions
are rejecting it for a better life in space. The day is coming
when you'll need it."

The leaflet said, *Reserve Your Space*.

"And we're looking for recruits for White Girls," Jennix
said, glancing again at Bligh. But he had strayed too far from
his station. As Hooper walked on, Jennix said, "If you
weren't hurrying away she'd listen to me. I can tell she's
interested. She'd sign up for the program."

On the plaza outside Coldharbor, Bligh asked who Jennix
was, and what had he been saying?

"He's a Rocketman, a Pilgrim. He lives in a workers' development in Queens with his wife and reads science-fiction novels. He's got an entry pass to New York and a work permit. He brings his lunch in a paper bag. All his savings go to the Pilgrims. It's a space cult—Survivors, Starlings, they have different names. The Federal government actually encourages them. They've made a sort of scientific religion out of the space program—they're rocket people."

"They actually ride in rockets?"

"So they claim. Along with the scientists, the Astronauts, the politicians, freeloaders, and millionaires, you'll find a Pilgrim or two on most missions. They're pathetic—it's just a publicity stunt. I think it's a trick to get their money."

They walked for nearly a block before Bligh spoke again, but she did so in a marveling tone. "I'd love to go up in a rocket. I've only heard about them," she said. "I was so cut off in our quarter. The world is such a wonderful place!"

"This isn't the world," Hooper said.

They had reached the rail-car station. A red Circle Line car hissed to a stop, and many of the passengers were wearing helmets and suits—some with masks in the high style that had recently become popular, with faces and phones and breathing options. Above the station were rotors and skylights, and all the towers were lit. A canyon of light led downtown. The city was best at night, Hooper thought. It was certainly safest: the security patrols were at their strongest at night, and the checkpoints and scanners were all in operation. And it was at night, surrounded by darkness, that the city seemed complete—an entire world, castle and moat.

Bligh said, "What else is there?"

She seemed overwhelmed by it and Hooper guessed that she had already begun to trust in it.

"Dark and desperate places," Hooper said.

But she was smiling.

"Not very far from here," he said.

She was still smiling; she believed she knew those places.

"And all over the States."

"I'd like to see!"

She looked so eager because she didn't know.

"And Asia, South America," he said. "Africa—God, Africa."

"I wouldn't be afraid."

Her upturned face was bright in her faceplate. Hooper

held her. She was trembling, and he thought how small she
was, how thin, for someone so strong.

"Take me there," she said.

"First you have to see New York."

She had said, "I want to go as far as I can possibly go in this
city," and Hooper took her by taxi to South Ferry.

He said, "We could have come here in my own car."

"This is probably quicker." Her gaze was intent upon some
men in masks strolling on the promenade.

She had not understood him. He said, "No. I actually have
a car at Coldharbor. I keep it on the ramp. I hardly ever use
it. It's a new one."

Bligh said, "This is fine"—missing the point.

Hooper paid the driver, and they got out and headed down
the steps to the promenade. Hooper said, "I mean I have a
real car—that I drive myself."

"We found cars in our quarter, in those ghost towns,"
Bligh said. "I used to sit behind the wheel when I was small,
going *brm-brm*. Mr. B drove one. But it was no good, and
there was nowhere to go. You should see those roads! We
heard that some people out there lived in them—too lazy to
put up houses."

Hooper said, "Listen, do you know how few private cars
there are in this city?"

But saying it, he realized that it was a pointless boast: it
really didn't matter.

Bligh said, "Why is this called South Ferry?"

"There used to be a boat here that went across to Staten
Island. The ferry was much bigger than those patrol boats. I
don't think you'd want to go there now . . . or there."

His sweeping gesture took in Staten Island, New Jersey,
and the Brooklyn shore. They were like the dark edges of
distant countries, all shadows and tiny lights, as if they were
slowly drifting away. Gunships and rotors patrolled the bay
as if engaged in battle maneuvers in a silent war.

"Are they really dangerous?"

"Not really," Hooper said. "Just bleak and boring. And
unhealthy. They're full of housing blocks and workers' towers—too many people. Only about half the people have entry
passes to come over here."

"Have you been there?" She was pointing at Brooklyn.

"Sure. And not just flown over it—I've driven through it.

The road's pretty well fortified. You don't see much. That's probably a good thing. It stinks. It's full of the worst kind of aliens."

He remembered too late, but the word had not offended her. It was simply that she had not understood it.

"Just slang," he said. "The polite word is 'illegals.'"

They walked a little more, keeping New Jersey in sight— Bligh said she found it reassuring to see it and to know that her quarter was in that direction. Hooper was impressed by her stamina: after a full day, the flight to O-Zone and this ramble around New York, she was still on her feet and eager to know more. It was after midnight!

Hooper radioed for a taxi, but passing through midtown on their way to Coldharbor, Bligh recognized the Greenhouse— it had been the first place Hooper had taken her—and she asked if they could stop for some chocolate.

"There's one," Bligh said, inside the place.

It was a naked woman in a mask. She wore thick chains around her waist and thinner ones around each ankle. She was with a man in a flying suit and a helmet and high boots. They made an odd couple—the nude woman, the over-dressed man.

Bligh was fascinated by them and saw two more—an older woman, rather heavy, looking terribly untidy Hooper thought—even disheveled—although she was stark naked; and a naked man in a helmet and boots. As the man passed them, Hooper noticed that he was wearing a green penis sheath.

"A year ago you wouldn't have seen any naked people in here," Hooper said. "It's recently become the fashion— something to do with wearing masks, I think. You can get away with anything in a mask."

It gave the place a carnival atmosphere—a feeling of anonymous hilarity; and it was not only the masks and the naked-ness but the other fashions that had the look of costumes, the backless dresses, the women who wore nothing but aprons, the security men who wore protective gear and looked like troopers and Martians and Rocketmen of long standing.

Hooper was surprised that Bligh liked the Greenhouse. For Hooper, it was just another frenzied shopping mall in competition with his mail-order business, but for Bligh it was a carnival crowd and tropical warmth, the scent of flowers, the overhanging trees, and stores crammed full of merchandise. She even enjoyed the ritual at checkpoints—the scanners, the sight of armed guards and Federals. She squealed on the moving sidewalks and on escalators, and she seemed fascinated by the electronic equipment—videoscreens and monitors and flashing lights on the towers beyond the glass roof.

He bought her some chocolate, and when she lingered near a store selling masks, he urged her to choose one. She chose a pretty face, and Hooper bought it for her. He told her how much lovelier her own face was, but he was grateful to her for wanting it. He said, "What else?"

"Are those real?" she asked, and walked to the side, among some trees, crushing a leaf in one hand, then a flower in the other. She sniffed her fingers and laughed. "They are!"

But a guard had seen her.

Hooper moved close behind him. "Owner," he said, and showed both their IDs.

"Keep away from the plantings," the guard said through the grille on his mask. His amplified voice was menacing, but Hooper's ID cut him short.

After that they took another taxi back to Coldharbor. It was a sealed taxi with an air system, so Hooper took off his breathing mask. Seeing him, Bligh did the same, and sighed and sat back. Her face was gleaming with pleasure.

"It's like a dream," she said. She looked very secure, very safe, and happy.

Hooper almost kissed her. He touched her once again, and put his face near hers. But he held back. She was smiling, as if daring him and watching him weaken. He considered the flesh of her lips.

His bleeper went. He could have ignored it or killed it, but he welcomed it now. It was Murdick, on his private line.

"Lost anything recently?" Murdick said.

When Hooper began to reply, Murdick went on, "Anything stolen, anything ripped off or broken? Because—"

"Willis, I'm heading home."

"Because we caught Skelly at the Lansdown with his hands full," Murdick said. "We've got exclusive possession. We're not turning him over. We thought you might want to ask him a few questions."

"I don't have any questions."

Murdick said, "We're going to squeeze him."

"Squeeze him without me."

"What's that?" Bligh asked as Hooper switched off.

He shook his head, and thought: I almost kissed her! He was relieved he hadn't—yet he had come so close. He had vowed to be very careful, not only to avoid frightening her but also to avoid infecting himself. He had not rid himself of the notion that as an alien Bligh might be a carrier of disease. It was his intention to have her undergo blood tests, and not to touch her until then.

But it had been a miserable interruption. It must have been the alert that Jennix had mentioned. Murdick and his trooper friends had caught a thief red-handed—a Skell or someone without an ID: a person without a legal existence. There was always a quarrel when a thief was caught—did he belong to the local security unit, or to the city police, or to the Federals? Usually it depended on what he had stolen. But this was obviously a private matter. Godseye had captured a thief. Anyone who had recently been robbed could join in the interrogation. They would kill him eventually, but it was a slow death.

It was too dark in the taxi for Bligh to see the troubled look on Hooper's face—and anyway, she was more intent on looking out of the window.

"I like this," she said, and took an energetic breath through her teeth.

"There's more," Hooper said. His voice had become very solemn. "There's much more."

He was thinking of black places and city-stains and ruined towns and some of his own depots that had been burned to the ground. But then he got a clear image of Fizzy. It was a pathetic picture and, in sympathy, he had made it old-fashioned in his mind. Fizzy, poor boy, was a lamb on a rocky hillside far away, bleating and trying to keep upright on wobbly legs; and he was surrounded by high winds and wolves.

27

IN THE MORNING, HARDY FOUND ANOTHER MESSAGE FROM Hooper gleaming at him from his monitor and he knew he could not put it off any longer. He phoned his brother and felt at once that Hooper was in a businesslike and just-returned state of mind.

"Please don't ask me to go up in the rotor again," Hooper said. It had been for secrecy, Hardy said. They had gone up at midnight about a week before, and hovered, talking of Fizzy. It was then—certain that they were not overheard—that they had worked out the code.

"In that case, be brief," Hardy said.

"Still no luck with the package. Not even a sighting."

"These things take time," Hardy said. "When you've got some hard news, plug me in."

Trying to be circumspect, he sounded calm—even indifferent to the abduction. He was concerned, he knew that Fizzy was valuable—might even be crucial to the project in O-Zone—but he could not risk anyone getting wind of the disappearance. If Fizzy were reported missing, Federal Rescue would make inquiries, and Hardy would be forced to disclose the reason for the mission. Then the whole plan for the thermal mountain would be known, and the other oil companies would start a free-for-all in O-Zone.

The project had to be kept secret, because O-Zone was still a Prohibited Area. No one else knew that it was now safe, that it might be profitable, and that it could be leased and reactivated. Hardy intended to apply for the permits as soon as Fizzy provided the survey data—Fizzy was perfect for that. He had already done a profile and a field study. With a thermal mountain, a new weather pattern—with plenty of water—it would be a tremendous piece of real estate. What had been a disaster area was now the last great chance in America.

"Anything else?" Hardy asked. He hated this inconclusive conversation and wanted to hang up.

"My ticket's expired," Hooper said, sticking to the agreed words.

"I'll try to get you a new one."

"It's been over three weeks without a signal!"

Hardy said, "The package is well-wrapped."

"The package might be coming apart by now," Hooper said. "Its ass might be hanging out. Holes in its boots. A dent in its head."

"I'm getting static," Hardy said. It was the code signal to change the subject. Hardy was nervous about Hooper's obvious language—anyone would know!

"It was a pretty flaky package—"

"Hooper!"

"And it sort of vanished furiously off the screen," Hooper said. "I wish we had some strategy."

"We need more data on the real estate," Hardy said.

"I've got some elevations," Hooper said, ignoring the code. "Some scattered temperatures and wind speeds. But I can't work the program alone. You know who I need."

"I'm getting more static," Hardy said. Why was Hooper going on in this agitated way? "But thanks for news of developments."

"There are no developments," Hooper said, breathing hard.

A message came up on Hardy's monitor. *Weathermaker,* it said. Hardy said to his brother, "I have to go to a meeting."

But Hooper held on. "What does Moura think?"

"Moura doesn't know. She is a little preoccupied at the moment."

"She's bound to ask," Hooper said, and Hardy guessed that what his brother was really asking was to be excused for this and given an alibi, as if he'd guiltily lost the boy.

But Fizzy was not lost, Hardy felt. Fizzy was stronger than any of them—that was one of his problems. Moura was the one who needed help.

"I think she needs a vacation," Hardy said. "The Murdicks are still looking for people to go to Africa with them."

"Africa." Hooper said the word in a wondering and appreciative way. "What would Moura say to that?"

"Who knows? You ask her how she is and she bursts into tears."

"I have an idea," Hooper said with gusto.

But the words alarmed Hardy. "More static," he said, and this time he hung up.

He had told Hooper he had a meeting, but it was more like a summons; and what was even more surprising was that it was with an unnamed member of the Asfalt board. The key name Control said everything, though: it was one of the budget people.

That too was surprising. Hardy was confident that he had unlimited time and money to gather the data he needed for his thermal mountain in O-Zone. Fizzy, unexpectedly, had become essential to the data search. Who would have thought this difficult child would have a practical use? But he had proven himself, and he had opened up new areas of study: he asked the right questions.

Hooper had felt Hardy was being cold toward the boy— Hardy sensed the criticism in his voice, and he knew his brother was impatient. But he missed Fizzy much more than he had suggested. It was not sentiment, or even stepfather's duty. It was a much greater urgency—it was business. Hardy missed Fizzy deeply, because—apparently—only Fizzy was equipped to find the necessary project data in O-Zone.

"It's awful," Hooper had said in the rotor during their conference. "Fizzy is the only person who could find Fizzy."

"Then he's not lost," Hardy said.

"Where is he?" Hooper said.

"He knows where he is," Hardy said. "We're the ones who are lost."

Now they knew that Fizzy had mastered all the moves. They had doubted him, because he had never left his room. But he had proven to be the best navigator—he had guided them to Firehills; he had the most versatile grasp of the equipment; he could locate aliens, he could complete the survey and program it, put it in code, and enable Hardy to present his project to the board. But the boy had been missing for almost three weeks. Until he turned up, Hardy's job was impossible, and O-Zone remained a distant and featureless island. That was Hardy's lament.

But he was sure that Fizzy would show himself, and when he did he would be more useful than ever, having spent time on the ground. He would have examined the surface of O-Zone, and being Fizzy, he would have kept a log of what he saw—not only temperatures and elevations, but the pattern of variation and the whole geomorphology of the area. He didn't need a wire. He would remember everything: his memory was perfect.

In Hardy's view it was not a tragedy that Fizzy had disappeared. In a crucial sense it could be the answer to the project. The boy would undoubtedly return with the data, and the longer he stayed away, the more he would collect about this unknown area. Hooper had said that the boy might have been abducted; but what proof was there of that?

Once more Fizzy was there, driving the computer synthesizer and squawking. Hooper had taken a walk and returned to find the boy gone—so he had said. No message. Some provisions missing. A weapon gone. Fizzy in his survival suit, waddling away, squawk-squawk. The likeliest explanation was that Fizzy had deliberately dropped to the ground, as he had that January day in New York; and for the same reason—to test his nerve. He had lived in his Coldharbor room for fifteen years! Hardy was certain the boy would be brave. He was equipment-conscious. He had food. He had a weapon. And he had a radio.

"No aliens," Hooper had said. "Fizzy's the only alien in O-Zone."

"Then he's all right," Hardy said.

If I had thought he were in any danger, Hardy explained carefully to himself, I definitely would tell Moura.

Hardy could see the boy fleeing the jet-rotor and hurrying away, daring himself as he went; he saw him sniffing and blinking—making camp, peering out of his helmet, collecting data. He was a strange boy, practically unknowable, a sort of human O-Zone; but with his sixteenth birthday coming up, not really a boy any longer. He may have dropped to the ground for any number of motives. The aspects of his character that made him indispensable also made him unfathomable. He was highly intelligent, he was selfish, he was scientific, he was unpredictable, he was a brat, he was immature, he was perhaps even crazy: he had reasons.

And Hardy felt he had stronger proof that the boy would return. He cynically believed that Fizzy would be back, not because he needed him but because he didn't like the boy. Of course he'd be back—squawk-squawk; and that horrible yawn, and that honking laugh. And Hardy did need him—very badly.

Weathermaker—the message had appeared on the monitor of Hardy's office computer in the middle of his phone call with Hooper—*be on the roof prepared to fly at 1430 hours.* It was signed simply *Control.*

He was being summoned to attend a rotor conference. It had been just such a confidential meeting that had given him the idea for his briefings with Hooper, in his own gyrating rotor: their first discussion about Fizzy's disappearance. Hooper had hated this way of conferring. The tight holding pattern and the turbulence upset his stomach, he complained. It was a noisy and distracting way of having a meeting. Hardy said that the beauty of it was that no one at all could monitor them, and the Fizzy problem had to be kept secret.

Looking down into the Hudson River, Hooper had groaned, "I get the feeling that at any moment I'm going to give the wrong answer and be ejected sideways out of the hatch."

"It's not like you to worry about things like that."

Then Hooper had said with real feeling, "I've got a lot to live for, brother."

Now it was Hardy's turn; but he was not discouraged—indeed, he was glad for a chance to discuss his project in confidence. He had not been able to say anything to Hooper, and that was maddening. He was proud of his idea, and he imagined the results being celebrated: Hardy Allbright, weathermaker, reclaiming this portion of America for Asfalt! And not only opening it to settlement and industry but giving it a new weather pattern—giving it more clouds and rain—and creating a garden where there had been luminous radioactivity, and city-stains, and the footprints of roads and broken houses, and caverns glowing with contamination. He would be bringing O-Zone to life.

Not long ago, in a kind of despair, the Feds had spoken of making O-Zone a dumping ground for unclassified pass-abusers, crazies, and petty criminals!

Hardy appeared on the roof early, impatient to talk. Just at two-thirty the rotor settled—it was a four-seater, one window, no markings; and Hardy saw that it was pilotless—command-controlled—someone was working it from below. The rotor blades stuttered but did not stop. Hardy fought the buffeting draft and climbed in.

There was only one person inside. He was strapped to a seat, he wore gloves and a mask (coated faceplate, monkey-mouthed breathing apparatus) and a green Asfalt suit with white piping. What flesh Hardy could see was sallow—perhaps elderly—and Hardy was annoyed that in his small breathing mask and headphones he himself was so easily identifiable.

"I don't know you," Hardy said.

"Good. I don't know you either."

They were now off the roof, the city beneath them—the spires and turrets, the guarded parapets of garrisons and heliports, the black streets, the castellated heights and smoky distances. It was a warm hazy afternoon.

"We are waiting for your numbers," Control shouted.

Yes, there was definitely a little old man inside all that equipment: the voice became breathy when he tried to shout.

"I'm waiting for data," Hardy said, and thought: I am waiting for Fizzy.

"It's been almost three months!"

"I understood there was no time limit in this scheme," Hardy said. "And the budget has been approved for the project. I've got funding."

"We are a commercial enterprise," Control said.

Nothing was more insulting than being forced to listen in silence to the obvious, Hardy thought. There was something so aggressive about a deliberate show of stupidity.

"We have to make long-term plans—"

Hardy wanted to pinch the old man's breathing tube.

"We need to know whether your site is definite and viable."

Hardy began to screech: "It could be the largest thermal—"

But the man's plodding voice had not stopped: "And we need to know how many barrels to commit to this project."

So that was it. They had a glut of oil, they couldn't store it and didn't want to dump it. They needed an early answer.

Hardy had given them a probable figure—an enormous one—and now he could not confirm it.

"This is a weather project," Hardy said. "It's not just an oil-burner."

"We are in the oil business—"

Again, that tone: the obvious—to insult him.

"—and we wonder whether you're taking this seriously enough."

There was another implication here. Hardy, because he was wealthy—the famous Allbright fortune—was sometimes thought to be a dilettante, passing the time at Asfalt and attaching himself to prestigious schemes. He knew what they said about him—he was an Allbright, didn't need a job, playing at being a scientist, and he was also a very large stockholder in Asfalt. But that stock didn't give him a right to waste company time. The family money was always held against him; he was suspected of being unserious. And it was felt, he knew, that he was prepared to take absurd chances— a rich man's risks.

That was why they had sent this faceless man to interrogate him. Hardy was on the verge of losing his temper. But it was no use. If you lost your temper in a rotor, the aircraft simply went on spinning noisily until your anger was wrung out of you.

Hardy said, "I'm dealing with a Prohibited Area. I need time. Don't worry—it'll pay off."

"We need a backup or you'll lose your funding."

They must really be stuck with an ocean of oil, Hardy thought. They weren't interested in the weathermaking prospects; they just wanted a project, any project, that would allow them to dump the oil—and the best way was to turn it into hot-top asphalt for a thermal mountain.

"Your Project O-Zone might fail."

It seemed so odd to hear the man saying these forbidden words, but of course no one could overhear him in a chattering pilotless rotor high over New York.

"If Project O-Zone isn't viable, we'll need another project just as big."

Hardy hated this man—hiding behind rotor noise and a coated mask and his company code name: "Control." He was a budget man, an oil-dumper. Finding wind, pouring a mountain, building clouds and steering them, making rain, reclaiming land, filling reservoirs, growing food—none of this mattered to him. He thought only in terms of disposing of as many barrels of oil as possible.

"I'll be thinking of one," Hardy said coldly.

"Think fast—we're making our descent."

The man adjusted his mask and Hardy saw that his face was without any expression at all, and that seemed to him a merciless form of gloating.

He could not help thinking of Fizzy—what the boy would say to this man. "Porker!" he'd cry. "Dong-face! Dimbo! Fuck-wit!"

"I'd go with China or India," Hardy said, loathing the silly hiding mask.

"Too much bureaucracy. We have to be in charge, for the maximum benefit. That's why we liked O-Zone. It would have been all ours."

"You keep saying 'we,'" Hardy said. "Is there someone in that suit with you?"

"A backup, Weathermaker," the man said. "A big one, and no strings."

"Africa," Hardy said, because he wanted the man to ask why.

Because my wife needs a vacation, he would reply: she cries easily these days. Because our friend Willis Murdick has been trying to organize a party there. Because I need time for my son to make his way out of the wilderness of O-Zone, and for the boy to find me.

But the man didn't ask.

"Okay, Africa. But go soon, and cover yourself. We have competitors, you know."

"Fine," Hardy said. "My wife needs a vacation."

Moura thought: I have nothing else to do but this, and yet I can't do it. She was still looking for the man, Fizzy's father. The problem was in the nature of the search itself. Men would not help a woman look for another man. They just stood in the way and obstructed her and said, "Why look further—what's wrong with me?"

It proved to her that men who foolishly believed that women were all the same, also believed that men were all the same. Hardy would have known what to do, but he was the only person she could not go to. He would be blunt: Do you want to find this man for Fizzy's sake, or your own?

"I want to prove that I'm not alone," would have been her answer.

Then Hardy would probably shout, "That's just sentimental!"

If you know someone well, she thought, you don't hold conversations—you each have your own monologues. She seldom had intimate talks with Hardy—she did not need to. She always knew what his side of the conversation would be.

But searching for the man in a luckless way made her feel weak and silly and exposed. She had now known the donor's name for a month, and his ID number, and his most recent address. She had gone back to the clinic with Holly, who still used it—still called it a clinic, still used the jargon. She was making progress in broad areas, she said, expanding the range of her responses, and developing new and subtle patterns of sensitivity.

It was sex. It was probably nonstop. It was probably movies, too. They were urging Holly to fantasize, giving her an appetite for something bizarre, and charging her more. The roasted look on Holly's face said it all: it was rosier and greedier in an eager way—now she knew everything. Her face was flesh; there was no thought on it, but there was a .epy look of pleasure—her eyes were restless. She usually looked very hot. She is cooking in sex, Moura thought. She is going to catch fire.

Holly said that she had not realized how much she had been missing.

"Now I know why men are so demanding," she said. "I never knew that I could have whatever I wanted."

She was happy now; she never listened anymore. She said she felt braver and bolder; and she made Moura promise to go to Africa with her.

Moura said yes, because Moura was her only friend; and Holly was the best reminder possible of what Moura had been. Once, sixteen years ago, Moura had gone to the clinic with that same ardor.

Dr. Sanford had demanded a high price for the information about the donor, and he had insisted on a number of conditions. The most severe condition was that Moura could do no more than establish the man's whereabouts—what he had become, his position and designation. She was not allowed to tell him who she was, nor even speak to him; and resuming contact was out of the question.

She promised, because she would have promised anything; and she paid, because she would have paid any price.

"You keep in touch with these men," she said.

"Donors," Sanford said. "They're not all men. We update their files regularly for ten years."

Moura hated the way doctors combined coyness and pedantry: the doctor always taking charge, either saying nothing or putting you down. And this doctor was also a pimp.

He said, "There is a one-in-a-million chance that the donor will die of an undetected disease that had been incubating for many years—hiding in the central nervous system, let's say. Or the donor might go mad. In such cases we would warn the recipient."

Moura was not thinking of Sanford's warning about disease or madness. She was pondering the word "recipient."

"After ten years we put the file in limbo," Sanford said, and it was then that he had torn the printout on its perforations and given her the strip showing the name and number.

Again she said, "Don't worry. I promise to follow the rules."

"It is not necessary for you to promise," he said.

But he was not being kind. He reminded Moura of what she had seen in his monitoring room, and that he had in his archives over forty hours of raw tape in which she was shown—as he put it—trying to conceive. He spoke of the excellent quality of the tape, the detailed close-ups, the color and sound quality. She realized that in this boasting way he was threatening blackmail.

He said, "I am very sure you'll do the right thing. You won't misuse this information."

"Boyd," she said, reading the name from the printed strip.

"We always called him 'Boy,'" Sanford said.

Moura had never seen his face, but "Boy" was a name she could easily connect to his slim body. Sanford dismissed her, saying that names were notoriously unreliable but that numbers never changed. She had Boy's fourteen-digit number, and although he was not in the phone book or any of the current reference guides, she found him in an out-of-date ID directory, listed with his parents, who were Owners. Their address was a tower in Upper East, twenty-eight blocks north of Coldharbor.

That was the first day it struck her that Fizzy was perfect for this world. With that ID number and the various scraps of information he would have sat in his room scanning lists for more details of this man. He would have hacked into the data banks and compiled a complete dossier; he would have found what he wanted.

But that was the last resort—sending Fizzy to find his father. Yet, when all she could do was pick up the telephone and try to call the place, she resented Fizzy's skill. She was glad he was not around: just the sight of him would have aggravated her resentment.

There was no answer. She took a taxi to the address—a granite apartment house called Cliffden, one of the older buildings still standing in an area that had been recently redeveloped. The tower was on its own, not in a garrison. The windows on the lower floors were barred and the front door was caged—but beautifully, in silvered steel. It was not heavily guarded—nothing around here was—but Moura was aware of police patrols as soon as the taxi drove off: a checkpoint, a barrier, a roadblock—her ID was examined three times before she found the building, and one of the security men had asked her, "Purpose of journey?"

"I'm seeing an old friend."

She was always startled by her truthful replies to other people's questions.

The doorman at Cliffden was middle-aged and had the torpid and humorless smile of a Pilgrim—so many guards were Rocketmen: you couldn't rattle them. Moura tried to hide her nervousness. Each stage of her search made her think that she had gone too far, that she was pressing her luck.

In a pressuring way, the doorman said, "Maybe there's something I can do for you," and let his sentence hang. He saw her as any woman looking for any man.

He smiled at her shyness; her timidity made him friendly. Yes, he remembered the family, the Boyds. Yup, and the son—big strapping fellow. Nice people, but they'd had setbacks. Moved out of the city. They were in Long Island—Jamaica. He had the forwarding address.

"Must be the Estate," he said. "The rest of it is real jungle."

Moura set out the following day in a taxi. At first the driver had refused to take her, and then he began asking insinuating questions—"for the checkpoints," he said, "for the bridge"—but before they reached the bridge Moura lost her nerve and demanded to be taken home.

"Why won't men ever help you look for another man?" she asked Holly that night.

But Holly liked men these days—the clinic, she said, had made her rational. She only wanted to talk about the trip to Africa, and she reminded Moura that she had agreed to go.

At last she said, "Fizzy would help you."

"But he's not a man," Moura said. "He's nothing, really. And anyway he's not here."

Hardy had kept asking her what was wrong.

She cried because she could not tell him. He might have thought she had a lover who was making her miserable. If so, he would have been right, in a way. A sense of defeat intensified her feelings of loss, and she could not distinguish between despair and passion.

She tried again, driving toward the Jamaica Estate in her own car. It was a mistake, a terrible trip, she was frightened the whole time. She kept thinking: I should have flown, I should have taken Holly, I should never have risked this. The delays at the checkpoints were bad, but then she'd had to leave the sealed boulevard, Jamaicaway, and was subjected to a recorded warning at the barrier. It was not the Estate after all, and not even a garrison. Was it possible he lived in a house? It was still patchy all over Queens—garrisons surrounded by isolated ghettos—Asiatic, Spanish, and black, legals and aliens mingled. The high walls of Jamaicaway hid this dangerous mess, and the bridges protected New York itself—only legal and registered workers in these outlying places had entry passes to the city.

Her fear of the neighborhood was increased when a group of leather-clad boys thumped the doors and kissed the windows of her car as she slowed down. The smears of their lips stayed on the glass. Then she saw someone being screamed at—another gang of leather boys howling at a cornered Asian, probably Korean. Screaming had become a popular method of assault out here; she had never seen it in New York. Some of the gangs claimed they could paralyze their victims with screams—so she had heard.

She found the address, but though it was a listed building and had a number in the directory, Moura was too frightened to get out of her car. Owners' license plates meant very little out here, it seemed. The building was squat and gaunt and gray. She remained parked in front, and waited, trying to call the building on her car phone. Then a man emerged from the front door. He was armed and wore a mask and phones, but whether he was a criminal or a security guard she could not tell. She was glad the car was reinforced—Fizzy had designed it, though he had seldom ridden in it. He had always said: What if we're hijacked?

The man motioned for her to open her window. She refused and instead set her phones on scan and spoke to him with her helmet on.

When Moura told him who she was looking for, the man offered himself. What was wrong with these men? She had ceased to be angry and insulted by this, but was still frightened, still impelled to keep her hand on the panic button beside her seat.

"He's in his mid-thirties," she said, trying to be businesslike. "I have an urgent message for him."

"Too bad it's urgent, because it's going to take time to find him."

He was smiling, seeing the eagerness she could not conceal; and he was pleased, because his bad news gave him power over her.

"He's gone. He's been picked up. This was a year or so ago."

"Picked up by whom—police? Federals?"

"Could have been any of them. They might have been private. I wouldn't like to say."

She said, "Was he registered when he was picked up?"

Still smiling at her weak questions—an Owner here, asking him these things!—the man said, "Only the Feds know that, but they won't tell you."

She saw that he was reaching down to try the door handle.

"Stick around—we can talk about it," he said.

"Keep away from my car or I'll call the police." The car was securely locked, but even so her hand was on the button that would summon a strike-force rotor from New York.

"I'm a policeman!" The man laughed, and threw open his jacket, showing her his badge.

His laughter was still crackling in her headphones as she shot down the street and, two checkpoints later, she was back on the Jamaicaway. She drove on frightened and bewildered, wondering how an intelligent young man, the son of two

Owners, with an excellent pedigree, could have been picked up—and what for?

But she thought: Fizzy will know how to find him. He would be able to break into a data bank and find the name, if he were still registered. He would find the right file. And if "picked up" meant arrested, or if he had become an outlaw, or was wanted, or had lost his pass for some reason, Fizzy would still be able to trace him. Fizzy had once said in his humorless and truthful way that he could open any line anywhere and find anyone. No one could keep a secret from him, he said.

Let him find Boy, she thought. She would not tell him that the man was his father, but if he found out, so what?

Moura always felt stronger when she was away from Hardy. Her conception of marriage was that it always weakened one of the partners and strengthened the other. Hardy was secretive and slow, yet he dominated her. She believed he drew his strength from her.

Tonight he said, "You're looking a little better."

She had felt fine until he made that undermining remark. But if she protested now, he would say she was being hysterical, and she would probably become hysterical because of his saying that, and he would weaken her in that way.

"I need Fizzy's number," she said, vowing not to be sidetracked. "I've got to talk to him."

That silenced Hardy, for a reason she could not understand. He seemed to be thinking hard. But she trusted him to tell her the truth. He was too literal-minded ever to lie convincingly.

"I don't have his number," Hardy said.

"You told me he was in O-Zone with Hooper."

"Yes, that's what I said—a month ago, when you asked."

Hardy, she saw, had been studying a map illuminated on a videoscreen—a very empty map, she thought: perhaps O-Zone.

Turning back to the map, Hardy said, "He's still there, in O-Zone, but he's off the air. However, Hooper's back."

Moura said, "It's Fizzy I need."

"So do I!" Hardy said. "But he'll be in touch."

"He can't be totally unobtainable," Moura said. "You can get him on a satellite relay."

"No, he's using a helmet phone. He's out of range. But if Fizzy wants to be found, he'll be found."

After Hardy said this he realized that it was indisputable: they could not find him; the boy had to find them—and it would be easy for him, when he chose to look.

"Is he all right?"

"Yes," Hardy said, and hearing himself say it convinced him that he believed it. "I know he is."

Moura remained silent. She was trying to imagine Fizzy's face, but the face remained behind one of Fizzy's very complicated masks, one with swollen eyes. In a mask like that he had tramped back and forth in his room saying, "This is Mission Westwind, the commander speaking—"

Hardy said, "Isn't it odd, both of us stuck here, needing Fizzy's help? Fizzy, of all people!"

"Fizzy's my son," Moura said. "I have to talk to him."

"You can't—not just now," Hardy said, and was glad to have a truthful excuse for the delay—time for the boy to show himself. "Have you forgotten? We're going to Africa"—he was gesturing to the map on the screen: so that's what it was. He said, "It was your idea!"

28

"F IZZY USED TO CALL THIS STRETCH THE MOST DAN-
gerous part of any trip," Hooper said, turning to Bligh.

They were one click out of New York, Hooper driving his
own car, and Hardy and Moura in the back seat. They had
just left the tunnel checkpoint and were in the brightly lit
expressway trough, on the way to the security checkpoint in
the barrier that surrounded the airport, forty clicks into Long
Island.

But this was more than a rackety speedway—it was like a
continuation of the tunnel: high walls along the side, and a
canopy of wire mesh overhead. Bligh leaned back to look at
it through the sunroof.

"'Enemy territory,' he used to say." Hooper was speeding,
not because he thought it was dangerous, but because he
hated the look of it—another shabby fortification.

Moura thought: I was here alone, four days ago. But she
felt it was no achievement: she had been very frightened, and
she hadn't found what she wanted. Fizzy was right!

"Full of aliens," Hardy said. "I don't see the point of going
to the airport by car, frankly. If we'd gone with Murdick in
his bug we'd be there by now."

"Bligh's never seen the outskirts," Hooper said, and in his
doting, overattentive way he repeated that she was new to
New York and was seeing this for the first time. He seemed to
be taking pride in offering her this experience.

He was in love—Hardy knew that; and even Moura had
said, "I didn't think people like that existed anymore. It's
probably her age—she can't be more than sixteen." Yet

Bligh was not girlish at all: she was straightforward and strong and very curious about things. For the tenth time, she was saying, "What's that?" And she had an odd effect on Hooper. He seemed different—innocent and kind, unembarrassed and submissive, anxious to please. Hooper Allbright! It was love, certainly—they could see that—but there was more to it: he was that fussing fidgety creature, simpering and stern, the fatherly lover.

A gap in the expressway wall had been mended with a hundred meters of steel mesh. A ruined building flashed past, a black chimney, a stack of flattened cars, and the sight of several orange fires. In the greasy smoke, twenty or more people stood with their arms high and their fingers hooked on the wire and their faces against the mesh. They were motionless, and yet the swirling smoke seemed to give them a sideways movement. Then the expressway wall resumed. It had been like a glimpse through a window to a terrifying interior.

"That was nothing," Hooper said, because it had frightened him and everyone else badly. His smile was not a smile, but rather an expression of the same fear.

At another break in the wall beside the road there was a much larger group, high up on the mesh—hanging and sprawled like smashed insects. Some of them looked both desperate and threatening, as if they were trying to break through, and yet they too were motionless, watching the stream of cars, holding on. Behind them, under a blue and bulky chemical cloud, was a brick township, and it too was smoldering and scribbled on with angry patches of paint. There was writing everywhere, and all of it looked fearsome, all of it like warnings, and fires, and more smoke, and glinting faces in ragged hats and masks, and trash packed against the mesh of the fence.

"Is that Africa?" Bligh asked.

She was alarmed by the laughter—it was sudden and very sharp and full of wordless worry.

"Owners, Owners, Owners!" the porter cried, preceding them with a handcart of their luggage.

The Murdicks were waiting at the departure checkpoint— Holly in goggles and a semitransparent one-piece, Willis in a flying suit and helmet. He was cross, he said: they had made him hand over his weapons and he wouldn't see them until he arrived. "Some stupid new rule," he said. And Willis was the first to say, "If only Fizzy were here—"

The boy was missed at the luggage check: he would have known which bags to bring aboard and which to send to the cargo hold. He was missed on board when the captain made his rounds: Fizzy would have known which questions to ask regarding flight times and traffic and wind speeds. He was missed in the compartment: there was a built-in computer but no one in the party was sure which flight data should be fed into it.

"If Fizzy had come we could have leased a bird and gone in on our own," Murdick said. "I've always wanted to go transatlantic in my own big bird. Fizzy'd be navigator. He'd drive the computer."

They were seated in a private compartment that they had approached through tunnels and gangways and down the narrow corridors of the plane.

Bligh said, "Are we on the plane yet?"

The others laughed, but it was appreciative laughter this time, not the hysteria of the expressway.

"Bligh's used to smaller units," Hooper said. He loved her wonderment and her capacity for surprise. And she was wise enough in her innocence not to be a danger to him.

"Not only are we on board, but we're about to take off," Hardy said.

"I love your hair, sweetie," Holly said, and leaned forward, tightening her suit against her body. She was damp and very white, like meat wrapped in cellophane. "I want to know how you get it that way."

You live fifteen years in O-Zone, Hooper thought, seeing Bligh smile at Holly. Her hair was chopped short and sun-streaked, and her eyes were pale gray in her tanned face. She was young and rangy, she had small breasts and stubby fingers and smooth fleshy lips. She wore one of Hooper's suits—she said she preferred it to buying a new one, and it was attractively loose on her. Today she was looking even lovelier, Hooper thought—her face softened by the weeks in New York, the food and good living.

"Over a thousand people in the belly section alone," Murdick said, praising the plane. "And there's three more levels. It can be pretty crappy in those central areas," he said. He was smiling, because he was relieved that he did not have to endure it. "All those slobs. But you'll be real comfortable in here. We've got all the facilities."

After takeoff, a steward pushed a hot table in and served the dinner. There was an argument over whether the meat was real or woven, whether the potatoes were powdered or just-peeled, was it spinach or processed seaweed, and what flavor were those fiber chips supposed to have?

"It smells right, but it don't chew right," Holly said.

"It tastes right if you cook it right," Murdick said.

"Fizzy would know," Moura said. "He's always so funny about his food. Jelly sandwiches and Guppy-Cola."

She had begun to miss him, and missing him, had begun to pity both him and herself. Now that he was gone she felt she knew him better; he did not seem so much a stranger. She chewed the food without tasting it, in a quiet and forlorn way.

"I feel lost without the little monster!" Hardy said, reading his wife's expression.

Hooper held his breath and waited for more, and dreaded it, because his explanation was so thin. But nothing more was said. There were nods and glances that said, yes, they too felt lost without the little monster. But no one said: Where is the beast?

They were all subdued in the plane. It was late and dark. But also none of them now wore a mask. They had become used to traveling in masks, and wearing helmets, and they were shy without them.

They finished eating to the low roar of the slipstream against the windows of the enormous plane. Bligh flicked a screen up and saw it was black outside. Hardy said, "We're at twenty clicks. That mean anything to you?" Then they wheeled the table with the remains of their meal into the corridor and extended their chairs into recliners. Hooper yawned and said, "We've only got about three hours more."

Bligh was the first to wake. She put her eye against the window screen and through the crack saw the sweep of the bay and the irregular crusty reef. Then she worked the shade up, and the rest of them woke, dazzled by Africa. The sun burned in a cloudless sky, and beneath was water—green and blue—and a mottled seabed of sand and coral was visible. The plane banked and turned: now they crossed a gleaming green strip of savanna. They flew on and got glimpses of a light brown desert crisscrossed with the dry veins of stony riverbeds, and tumbling hills and great dark cracks in the ground; and turned again over pale patches of dying trees, and blue boulders, and wide orange cones of earth—mountains shaped like anthills; and were flying low over the blue-green sea again.

"The coast," Hooper said. "That's where we're staying."

"I'm going hunting up north," Murdick said. "There's an awful lot of action there. Real wicked trouble"—but he was smiling. "You can shoot poachers on sight." He became solemn and certain. "No questions asked."

After the landing, the loud brake-blasts, and the tow to the terminal, they transferred to a waiting bug, an eight-seater that Murdick had chartered and was piloting.

The copilot was African—the first one they had seen. In his lapel was a gold rocket pin.

"He's a Pilgrim," Holly said. "Imagine!"

"They're all Pilgrims," Hardy said. "It figures. There's nothing for them here."

Murdick said, "You got a name, fella?"

"Navigator Jimroy," the African said.

Holly put her mask on and faced the African. She said, pointing, and speaking in a little girl's voice, "Mr. Jimroy, are you going up in a big rocket to a space station or a lunar base?"

The African said nothing. He had a gentle apologetic smile—it was the enameled smile of the Pilgrim—and he kept his eyes on the ground-screen.

"With Fizzy along we could have done without this fucking Astronaut," Murdick said. "Anyway, where is he?"

But the question was lost in the noise of the rotor whirling them to the ground.

They had seen from the air that the green ribbon of coast was thick with hotels. Theirs was Earthworks Lodge, at the edge of the sea and under the rattling coconut palms. It was arranged in a number of connecting villages—a dozen or more. Each village was a cluster of thatched-roof huts. They only seemed primitive from the outside: they were air-conditioned and had four rooms apiece and were set in gardens among fountains and flowers. The grass was a moist carpet of green and the entire lawn was continually watered by a system of sprinklers that cast forth a glassy mist, like a hologram that

contained a number of dim rainbows. In the sky, big slow
birds circled without moving their wings.

The other guests hardly seemed to notice the visitors from
New York. Most of the guests were naked, and many of these
were painted. They slept under the trees; they lay on lounge
chairs, wearing video masks; they walked slowly through the
heat, the sun gleaming on their oiled nakedness.

"You're in here," Hooper said to Bligh, inside their hut,
and he showed her to her bedroom.

He could not make out her expression. Did she want more
than this? Was she disappointed, or was she relieved by the
way they always slept separately?

"Don't worry," he said. "I'll keep an eye on you."

It always stopped him, the thought that she was an alien.
He was afraid, but his fear excited him, too. It made him
hover intensely near her. It kept him from touching her; it
made her fascinating to him. For now, he was content to
watch. But his was not a glance now and then: it was a
burning scrutiny. He wanted to know everything about her—
to see everything—which was why, even here, he had re-
quested a one-way mirror on the wall that divided his room
from hers.

All the rest of that day they rested. The sun was terrific,
beating through the branches, spangling the sea, and covering the land in a powerful silencing light. Holly went naked;
Moura was bare-breasted but wore a sarong; Bligh wrapped
herself in a loose gown which gave glimpses of her naked
body when she walked and which Hooper found more thrilling than the waxen nudity that Holly flaunted. The men wore
sarongs—Murdick had fastened his with an ammunition belt
on which he hung a pistol.

All the guests were burned dark brown by the sun. These
naked wandering people sauntered in the shade, many wearing pistols, and nearly all wore floppy hats and sandals. Some
of them were painted with fantastic designs—flames and
feathers and loops—like garish snakes coiled around their
arms and legs. Their faces were painted with masks—their
hungry bloodshot eyes peering through the greasy designs.
Leaves were painted on them, and shattered circles, and fragments of the alphabet, and tiger stripes, and fire. One woman
was a zebra, another wore giraffe blotches. Some of them
were caked in white, others were totally black.

They wore jeweled belts and nothing else; they wore necklaces of bone and ivory. Some wore plaited hair, some wore plumes, one girl wore a devilish tail, another small girl was tattooed; all of them were naked. Except in the middle of the day, when the sun was unbearable, these people emerged and paraded in the grounds and gardens of the hotel compound, promenaded among the various clusters of huts in the villages, and walked along the white beach. There were guests in canoes and on surfboards and in sailboats. Some of them bravely played gasping games of tennis. But most of them simply prowled, or slumbered in the shade, amid the urgent screeching of birds.

Holly immediately adopted the painted style: she went naked, with red spirals and streaks on her body, and her hair dyed yellow, and a thin mask stretched around her eyes. Willis wore an African mask he had bought at the shop in Earthworks Lodge. It was made of a whole turtle shell, cut beautifully and fringed with feathers; and it was fitted with electronic detectors, a radio, an air-filter snout, and phones.

"I've always wanted one of these," he said in a quavering ducklike voice that came out of his snout. "You can see the workmanship. These aren't available anywhere else."

Murdick practiced shooting with the other guests. They fired at coconuts that were lobbed over the water—blasting them with their beams. The weapons were silent, but the coconuts split apart and exploded with a loud cracking.

The atmosphere at Earthworks was African, and still wild, in spite of the clusters of other nearby hotels. A heavy odor of salt and seaweed saturated the air, and farther in, near the huts, the smell was of flowers and cut grass and the rankness of damp animals. The sunlight was of shattering intensity. The heat came and went. With all of this was the oddly jubilant sound of birds and insects.

In this isolated and drowsy place there was also activity—waiters carrying food and trays of drinks, gardeners on their knees, men raking the beach or, at sundown, musicians in the twilight playing drums and flutes and twanging harps. All of them were black—perspiring heavily. They were obedient, beaten-looking people. They seldom spoke. They were civilized and solemn in the most old-fashioned way, in thick cloth suits and neckties. They did not seem to notice or to care that the guests were naked, and what Hardy had said about Navigator Jimroy seemed to be true: nearly all of them were Pilgrims—they wore the rocket-pin and read the books and had the short haircut and military manners. They used the lingo.

"Are you a member of the program?" one African asked Murdick.

"No, thank you!" Murdick said.

Bligh was fascinated by the Africans—by their silence and good manners. But more than anything else she was fascinated by the food—vast amounts of it appeared every day on the buffet table on the lawn of their village. Even the New Yorkers, and the other Owners from America, and the various Europeans—Germans mostly—were excited by the food. The sight of so much of it got them shouting and reaching—snatching food from the tables and from each other's plates.

These high spirits caused horseplay and the result was usually a food-fight. The guests' nudity contributed to the riotousness of the event. Tureens of soup were emptied and fruit thrown back and forth, and the naked hollering guests kept it up until the table was bare. There was no check on them—no one stopped them. Afterward, the waiters vied with the marabou storks and the crows for the fragments.

There was a food-fight after lunch on their second day—they always seemed to happen after lunch, when the tables were still piled high and the guests no longer hungry. Hooper steered Bligh away when he realized what was about to happen. But he was a moment too late—before he could get her past the hedge she looked back and saw them flinging food and swiping at each other.

Tears welled in Bligh's eyes and she watched sadly as the buffet table was brought down. It had held a roasted pig and a long filleted fish, vegetables steamed in palm leaves, wooden bowls of salad, pots of stew and spitted chickens and cold platters of peeled fruit.

"Real food," Hooper said angrily, wanting Bligh to know that he too was disgusted. Bligh did not hear him. Hooper had seen food-fights before, but seeing them now with Bligh they seemed much worse—and he was grateful to her for inspiring in him a sense of outrage.

"That's murder," she said. "Those people are worse than animals."

Then it was forgotten. They spent these hot days in idleness, strolling on the beach or else sleeping in a hammock. They slept and ate and lay in the sun.

"Why are so many people wearing weapons?" Bligh asked.

That was the other worrying thing about the food-fight—most of those rowdy people had been well-armed.

"There used to be trouble here," Hooper said. "Everyone had weapons—the local people legalized them for visiting Owners. Then they just became fashionable, like the masks."

"Do they shoot them?"

"They kill poachers," he said.

"What's that?"

"Someone who is very hungry," he said, and surprised himself with the truth of it. He was seeing more and more with her eyes. That was what he meant by liking himself better.

Moura was at the pool with the Murdicks, wondering where Hardy had gone. It was supposed to be a vacation, and yet Hardy was rising early and catching planes, and returning exhausted at nightfall as if he'd done a day's work. And where did Hooper hide with that young girl? The Murdicks stuck with Moura, eating and napping and talking about the other guests. They gave the other guests names: Sweaty Betty, the Moonman, the Teapot, Knockers, and the Monkey. There was another breathless man who sat sloppily in a wicker chair watching Holly with his perspiring face.

"I've got him throbbing again," Holly said.

She called him the Haystack, because of his hair.

Moura was occupied by her own thoughts. She lay on a rock by the pool, like a lizard, her eyes half-closed. Occasionally she slid into the water with a narrow splash, to cool herself.

"Apparently Fidge is still in O-Zone," she said just before she dropped into the pool one afternoon.

When she surfaced, Murdick was gaping at her.

Murdick was equipment-conscious, even here. He wore a wide-brimmed safari hat, and a khaki flying jacket, and goggles and a wrist radio. His concession to Earthworks was his sarong, but he had a short-barreled rifle on his lap. Beside him, Holly was naked—she wore nothing but paint. Her breasts and nipples were outlined like popping eyes, and a nose was painted on her belly, and her groin rouged and marked and made into a mouth: her torso turned into a large leering face.

Murdick said, "You mean Fizzy's alone there?"

*   *   *

Hardy stayed away from Earthworks in his chartered rotor, looking for sites for a backup Asfalt project, in case Project O-Zone should fail. Murdick still went hunting; he left early and angry, and returned unusually silent and somewhat shamefaced. Holly looked for men. Out walking on the beach, she surprised the Haystack, who was sunning himself. He spoke to her in German: he had the loud breathing of a lazy animal. Before he could rise, Holly knelt and straddled him, and sat on him until he stopped struggling. "See?" She shook her breasts. "Googly eyes!" She left smears of her paint on every part of him.

Hooper and Bligh hiked beyond the gardens of the compound. Hooper said they must be in the jungle, but at midday they came to a high fence, and they saw faces flickering in the leaves beyond it. They called out, but the faces vanished.

Hardy returned from his traveling and swore to the others that it was safe to visit the interior of the country. He had seen evidence of animals, he said.

"Count us out," Hooper said. Bligh was his excuse. He wanted to be alone with her, to watch her, to film her.

But the rest went to look for wild animals in the area where Hardy had seen the tracks. Spinning above the tall palms and green grass of Earthworks they saw how small an area they were living in. It was tiny, really; a narrow ribbon of green on the coast. Behind it, the land sloped rapidly away and degenerated into scrub—thorn bushes, and low yellow flat-topped acacias, and cactuses. Gravelly basins as large as valleys lay baking where there had once been lakes. There was no water here at all. Hardy had located several sites for possible thermal-mountain projects. But what was the point here, and who would pay for it? The dark world was full of wastelands and deserts like this. He saw it as the inevitable senility of the planet. Let it die, he thought—Africa was half-dead anyway. But America was different: and now that island of O-Zone could be reactivated.

They looked for gazelles—gazelle tracks and some droppings had been seen here in the long smooth hills of this new desert. They saw skeletons, large exciting ones—thick black buffalo horns growing out of wide skulls, and smooth neat hooves, and the tumbled bones of other creatures. Several animals lay twisted and shrunken in the sacks of their own leathery hides.

All the way to the horizon it looked as if it had once been covered with water—an ocean of it; and the tide had gone out, leaving this dry strand and these dead drowned-looking animals and cracked stones. Now it was blazing—the bones most of all.

They found a steep hill and put the rotor down on its shady side so that they could eat their lunch in the cool shadow of the ridge. The food was served by Holly and Moura.

"We should have brought an African to do this," Holly said.

"There's one," Hardy said, looking up at the embankment.

"Are you kidding?" Murdick said.

It was a small solitary creature on spindly legs and it had appeared from behind an orange sandstone slab. While it moved it was an animal, but when it stopped and raised its head toward them they saw it was human—and it was not the child it seemed.

It crept forward on its hands and knees, with its mouth open. Its few teeth were broken and fanglike in its dark gums, and its skinny arm was out: it was a shriveled man.

"It's an alien," Holly said. "Get him away."

Murdick chucked a hunk of bread at him—not to attract him but to make him stop crawling. It worked. The African seized it and began gnawing.

Hardy said, "There are thousands of them in the north, just like that."

"They can't burn them fast enough," Murdick said. "They're like locusts. I'm surprised he's the only one here."

It was then, because he said those words, that the party looked around and saw the others—fifty, sixty, probably more—it was impossible to count them. They were a mass of dusty rags and death's-heads, big and small, moving slowly, close to the ground. Their faces were sunken and hollow, and their frail skeletons showed through their skin.

"It's all aliens!" Holly shouted, and she stood up—naked, the paint gleaming on her body.

The starved people shrieked, but they were so weakened their voices were like the cries of small birds. They held up their hands, clutching the air. They were still moving.

Hardy led the travelers back to the rotor; and their desperation saved them, because in their hurry to get away they left all their food. The poor creatures pounced on it and ignored them. And then the travelers were safely in the air, and underneath them was the mass of scavenging people that had swarmed out of the crack in the hillside.

Murdick said, "For a minute there I thought they were going to hoist a spear into my guts!"

"They didn't have weapons," Hardy said. "It was a feeding frenzy."

At the rotor pad in the Earthworks compound, Holly said, "That shouldn't have happened! All those aliens! I hated that!"

Moura helped her out of the rotor and took her to her hut.

"They weren't supposed to be there," Hardy said. "Why are they leaving the northern sector?"

"Same reason the buffaloes left," Murdick said, and lowered his voice. "To get away from the hunters."

And Hardy guessed from the conspiratorial tone that Murdick was one of the hunters. In such circumstances, what good was a thermal mountain? Hardy imagined bringing wet weather here. There would be millions more Africans then. It would be like rehydration, and then the hunters would be out, chasing scavengers, shooting poachers. Hardy did not want that. He wanted O-Zone and its emptiness.

"Fizzy could have made a terrific tape of them," Murdick was saying in an admiring way. "From the air! With mirrors!"

"Fizzy could have prevented it," Hardy said. "Holly's right. That shouldn't have happened. They might have mobbed us. But Fizzy would have seen them. He's developed a program for spotting humans from very high altitudes, and he can describe them and build data based on their spoor, their shadows, settlement patterns, what-have-you."

"Is that what he's doing in O-Zone?" Murdick asked. "Looking for the aliens?"

"No," Hardy said in an energetic riddling voice, as if he were confounding Murdick with an obvious truth he'd overlooked—Murdick himself had said they'd burned them all down! "Because there are no aliens in O-Zone."

The dinner gong was being rung. It was sundown: torches were being lighted along the paths, and bats were tumbling like swallows in the sky. Murdick waited for the dinner gong to stop, and then he spoke.

"O-Zone's leaping with aliens," he said.

That was the day that Hooper flew inland to the capital in a hired jet-rotor. He took Bligh and watched her closely, photographing her when she was not looking, and filming her face on the rotor's own recording monitor. He wanted Bligh to enjoy herself, and yet he also wanted her to be shocked and fearful in this precarious-seeming place. He felt they were perfectly safe—much safer than it was possible to be in O-Zone. And yet the African landscape looked vast and desperate: it was dust bowls and high plains, it was strewn with stones, a land without topsoil. He wanted Bligh to believe that the danger was real, and still for her to feel secure: he wanted to show her that she could trust him.

"There used to be lions here," Hooper said.

He had been here before, but purely to buy industrial diamonds for an item in his mail-order catalog. But now with Bligh he felt a greater satisfaction: her presence enlarged his interest. Already he had come to depend on her!

"Most of the animals are gone," Hooper said. "Starved, killed, eaten, made into handbags."

"There are plenty of birds," Bligh said. "I've never seen so many."

There were sunbirds, weavers, fisheagles, falcons, and owls; there were vultures and hawks. They flocked to Earthworks, staying near the coast, where food was still available.

For a while longer they flew over an area so bare that it hardly looked like land at all, but rather like the remains of a place that had blown away. And then ahead was the city. It lay beneath a range of hills that rose to a set of knucklelike peaks. The capital had a look of prosperity—white buildings, granite towers, brick chimneys and walls, the city piled up in the dust. But that look was misleading, for closer it was like any of the places they had seen in O-Zone, and for a moment Bligh seemed to think she was back in her quarter. This was a city of broken windows and ruined streets and overturned cars and burned-out parks.

There were Africans on the roads below, many more people than there were vehicles. The Africans possessed the city: they were everywhere, crowding the buildings, filling the roads; but they hardly moved. They were standing and sitting and lying down. They had built their own shelters on the sidewalks, and against fences and trees.

Hooper did not dare land the rotor, but he went close enough for Bligh to see how the city had been turned into an enormous camp, with shacks and cooking fires lining the main road, and shantytowns stacked against the old abandoned towers—the banks and office buildings and ruined hotels.

"That could have happened in the States," Hooper said. "But they got smart and sealed the cities."

Bligh said, "I never lived in a city," and looked down at the mobs in the streets.

"They'd eat you alive," he said.

He went lower and lingered over the upturned faces, the reaching arms, the whirling woodsmoke. The rotor's noise drowned the voices.

"Where are we going?"

From her tone he knew he had succeeded in frightening her. He wanted to say: This is the world, too. But he also wanted her to know that she was safe with him. He wanted her to love him for taking her here, and for being able to fly this machine, and for getting her out of here. He swooped between two narrow buildings and scattered the people on the street, and then he rose in a cyclone of dust that he had created, lifting the rotor free of the city.

She said, "I want to learn how to do that."

It surprised him. He had not counted on her wanting to fly a rotor herself. He almost said: But you're an alien!

He said, "I'll show you how, someday."

Talking about the future made him feel hopeful. He wanted to prolong this pleasure. He began to make more promises, but he saw that his eagerness was silencing her, and so he stopped.

They were over the plains again, flying above the blowing dust. "Imagine lions and elephants and rhinos," he said, looking down. But he could not picture it; he could not imagine animals living in the dust of this empty plain.

They passed over the dry riverbeds and the red crumbling hills. Nearer the coast, Hooper showed her the system of perimeters and roadblocks that prevented anyone from entering the coastal strip; and the way the airport was fortified, and the harbor blocked. They flew on, over the shoreline of settlements and hotels, and beyond the reef, where there were patrol boats.

If Bligh was impressed she did not say so. Hooper was not sure whether she was afraid. He had expected her to feel both thrilled and insecure—it was the reaction of most people to Africa, living like islanders on the small patches of luxury that were reserved for visitors. She had been alarmed

by the sight of all those Africans living wild in the capital—
the sight of them had startled her.

But none of this bothered her half so much as the other
guests at Earthworks—naked, painted, wearing masks; their
laughter; their late-night parties, and their cruising in the
compound, looking for pickups; the food-fights. Their weapons worried her. And the way they fired them—shooting at
the coconuts that were flung out over the surface of the sea.
Africa did not frighten her, nor did the Africans, who seemed
merely pathetic or docile workers—and it seemed everyone
called them aliens. Yet the Earthworks Lodge and its guests
made her silent and watchful.

She kept her wits about her. She saw and heard things that
he missed. She was stronger than any of the others. She did
not swim or sun herself—she couldn't swim; she waded by
the shore; she regarded sunbathing as absurd and unhealthy.
She ate—slowly, gratefully—listening the whole time.

It had been dark when they arrived back at Earthworks,
and they had seen Murdick's rotor being washed by an African.

"Too dark to look for shells," Hooper said.

Bligh had collected a bag of them. He had bought her a
gold bracelet, a mask, a bowl of polished onyx, the swordlike
horns of a now-extinct buck, a set of sharks' teeth—African
treasures. She had not said so, but Hooper knew she preferred the shells she found on the beach.

They sat on the veranda of their hut that evening, listening
to the splash of the sea, the waves breaking softly on the sand
with a gasping sound.

He said, "Are you happy?"

"I never ask myself that," she said. "But I am!"

The path was lighted with the torches that were stuck into
the grass beside it. He had turned off the veranda lights; he
wanted to be with her in the darkness.

After a while she said, "What's the sound—that little
buzz? I always hear it at night."

It was the camera. He used an infrared one here. He had
believed it was inaudible—anyway, it was supposed to be.
But she was so alert, so sensitive to movement and sound.

He said, "Must be a bug."

"Sometimes I think you're afraid of me," she said.

He wondered whether it was true.

"Because you keep giving me things," she said, and before

he could question that, she added, "But you never touch me."

"Would you like me to?"

"I'd like to please you."

He thought ahead to the video: to seeing her and hearing her say that, and playing it back, to hear her repeat it.

"Tell me what you want," she said. "I'll do anything you want."

He tried to see her face in the darkness. He was glad he was shooting this. He liked her seriousness, her confidence in saying this—her believing that she was able to do anything he asked. He liked the stillness of the shadows on her face, her odd straight hair that was so fine it picked up the firelight from the torches down on the path.

"I want you to go on saying that," he said.

Hooper wondered if their long day together had produced that peculiar intimacy. If so, he looked forward to longer days with her.

He wanted to show her he trusted her, by divulging his most secret thought and saying, *I am one of the rarest, luckiest people in the world. I have had everything I have ever wanted.*

It was a vain boast that he had always been too superstitious ever to say aloud, yet he was on the verge of blurting it out now—then she would know everything about his wealth, his luck, his vanity. He wanted to record her reaction to it: he was still shooting. What would she say?

"Look at me," he said.

But before he could begin, he saw Hardy and Moura on the path, making their way between the flickering torches. Hooper could not think straight. In his reverie with Bligh, that intimacy that was a suggestion that they were very similar—not that they belonged to each other or were possessive in that way, but wanted the same things, the same simple happiness—time had faltered. Only when he saw his brother and Moura on the path did he remember that they were in Africa.

Moura was nearly naked, and the way she walked in her nakedness revealed an anxiety that her clothes would have concealed.

Hardy was behind her, but he spoke first—and sharply: "You told me there were no more aliens there!"

Hooper thought: Africa?

"It's Fizzy," Moura said. "I'm so worried about him."

Hooper stood up. He wanted to speak, yet he could not summon any deception. The long day and the heat and Bligh saying *I'll do anything you want* had made Hooper passionate and truthful. It struck him just a moment too late what they were talking about: the kidnapping about which they knew nothing. He forgot the boy easily, and the crime, because it was such a serious matter.

But he was also startled by their abrupt concern. They were talking about Murdick, telling Hooper things he knew. *Leaping with aliens!* Hardy said angrily. And Moura was crying—but when had she ever cared so deeply about her son? They had come striding out of the darkness and the bat-screeches demanding the truth as Hooper stood up and tried to begin.

"They won't hurt him," Bligh said, and sat up straight. "They'll keep him safe."

Then Hooper remembered everything.

Hardy and Moura were silenced. They seemed bewildered by Bligh as by a bright light that had just clicked on—by her sudden intelligence and what seemed like inspiration in this unexpected protest of assurance.

But it was a puzzled silence and full of piercing questions: *How do you know that? Who are you? Where are you from? How old are you? Who the hell are*—

To distract them, Hooper said, "Yeah, it's full of aliens—illegals. We were getting data on them."

"Why didn't you tell me?" Hardy said. It was much more than a question—it was an accusation and a protest. He felt like a fool with his O-Zone project now, imagining that the zone was empty, imagining that he could reactivate it. It was full of aliens—even this little girl knew that!

"They stole him," Hooper said, talking fast. "They wanted him—probably wanted some technology or food. They were stalking us. I blinked my eyes and they took him away."

Hooper kept talking. He was relieved to be telling them the truth. He smiled and he realized how he hated these needless secrets. And as he talked he had a proud giddy fear, a kind of vertigo from the heights of his determined honesty, that he would go on chattering and say too much—that he would be so possessed by the truth that he would tell them everything. But they saved him from that by shouting at him and rushing away.

29

THEY LEFT AFRICA FOR NEW YORK SO ABRUPTLY THEY had to carry their argument onto the plane. Hardy was still thrashing. Hooper listened and tried to calm his brother—but how? Murdick winced, marveling at the fury he had produced in Hardy by telling him there were aliens in O-Zone. Murdick was proud of possessing the news—it was like knowing there was life in outer space. There was no letup in Hardy's anger and he filled the compartment with the repetitious abuse of his questions. *When! Why! Where!*

"Take him out of here!" Holly finally said, snatching the door open. "Delete him!"

But Hardy was still talking as the two men helped him into the gangway.

"Why did you lie to me?" Hardy said. "Why didn't you tell me he'd been kidnapped?"

Hardy then turned on Murdick, saying, "And you swore to me that you'd burned them all down!"

Murdick had not stopped smiling.

"They breed like flies," he said. The drama of the moment made him stupid with self-importance. "Hey, we were lucky we weren't taken hostage. They swap hostages, they enslave them, they sell them. People are snatched in California and end up in Japan. Remember when they found that Jewish kid in Australia? It's a business! Ever since the value went out of money, aliens have been making fortunes from kidnapping. I've seen the studies. Hey, this could cost you plenty."

Hooper said, "I honestly don't think he's been kidnapped."

"Know what I'd like to see?" Murdick said. "I'd like to see some Owners, some troopers, sweep in there and kidnap a few aliens. What do you think, Hoop?"

"We have no proof it's a kidnap," Hooper said.

"'Stolen'—that's what you said!" Hardy had taken hold of Hooper's flying suit, and looked violent.

But Hooper was gentle with his brother, and at least Hardy was not listening to Murdick. How could he tell them that Fizzy had almost certainly been grabbed in revenge for his taking Bligh? If he said that, he would lose her—they'd hand her back. He did not want to be separated from her. It was bad enough standing here in the gangway while Bligh sat in the compartment, frightened into silence by Hardy's outburst.

"I think he might have gone willingly," Hooper said.

"Fizzy wouldn't have done that," Hardy said. "He's afraid of strangers and he's a physical coward. He never left the house alone—and you think he'd walk unprotected into a Prohibited Area!"

"He was armed," Hooper said. He still believed what Bligh had told him, about Fizzy being safe with those people. "He had his suit and helmet. He was wearing boots. He had food and water."

"They would have swiped his irons first thing," Murdick said. "That'll make it tough for anyone who goes after him."

"They kidnapped him and they're holding him," Hardy said. "Why didn't you tell me there were aliens in that fucking cacotopia!"

Hooper said, "Have you gotten a call? Any ransom demand—anything that sounded like contact?"

"No," Hardy said. "That's why I didn't suspect you of lying. It's been a month! Who are these Roaches!"

"I don't want to be gross, but sometimes they eat their prisoners," Murdick said. "I've seen documentation. They shrink them. They stuff them. They sew them up and hammer them into boxes."

"Shut up," Hooper said.

His sudden shout stiffened them, and in silence they reentered the compartment. Holly was wearing a video mask; Moura and Bligh sat side by side, not speaking—but how similar they looked, Hooper thought, like mother and daughter, the alien and the Owner.

The huge multilevel plane flew westward into the unchanging light. The travelers did not eat—you had to be calm to sit and eat. Instead, they paced; they used the phone link to collect the messages from Coldharbor. There was no word of Fizzy—nothing from him or his captors.

Hooper saw that the news was not merely upsetting to them—it was frightening. An unexplained disappearance was much worse than a certain death. They worried about Fizzy, but they also felt insecure themselves now—as if they too might be snatched at any moment.

Near the end of the five-hour flight from Africa, Hooper saw this fearful self-pity on their faces and said, "You used to hate him—all of you. Isn't that right?"

No one replied until Hooper's stare hardened. In his stare the question was repeated, demanding an answer.

"I need him," Hardy said, and thought of his project—how crucial Fizzy was to it. *I need him to make it rain in O-Zone.*

Hooper challenged his brother with a smile. Then he relented and said, "I'll help look for him. I'm sure he can be found."

"You've had your chance, Hoop," Hardy said, dismissing the offer. It was as if he had been waiting for Hooper to extend a helping hand, so that he could slap it away. Hardy had regained his vindictive spirit now that Hooper was being conciliatory: it was the way their old brotherly games always went. "You didn't find him before—you didn't even tell us he'd been snatched. I don't trust you."

"We'll get up a mission," Hooper said. "We'll plot one of Fizzy's own grid programs and search every square."

He seemed hopeful. His explanation made it sound possible, even somewhat simple, as if they were looking for the boy in a section of New York and not in the wilderness and ruined towns in the thousands of square clicks of O-Zone, which was itself a byword for everything unknown and unfathomable and empty and strange.

O-Zone was associated in the American mind with such strange imagery—nothing was more frightening than the land that was never visited; and saying the word was less like mentioning a part of the United States than a distant island or another planet. And because it was never visited, people believed it to be much bigger than it actually was. They thought about it all the time. It was an area of darkness in most people's consciousness, and Fizzy was lost in it.

"Fizzy's the only person who could write that kind of program," Murdick said.

"Sorry, Hoop," Hardy said—and all his bitterness toward his brother was in the word *sorry:* it could be the cruelest word, for nothing was more insulting than an insincere apology. "You'd need an Access Pass to get back into O-Zone. I won't get one for you. But you'll make out all right"—and he glanced at Bligh—"you've got your young flesh-pup."

Hooper checked himself in his reply. He had been on the point of shouting at Hardy. But there was always a problem in arguing with his brother. Because they were brothers, Hooper knew that at some stage they would have to settle the quarrel and make up. They knew each other too well to use words casually—anything spoken in the heat of argument was likely to be intended. Angry words sounded just as truthful as calm ones, and they cut much deeper. They were never forgotten. The brothers had always talked too much; and that was always an error, it always made things worse. Still, *flesh-pup* hurt.

"Fizzy doesn't concern you," Hardy said. It was another cut—as if Hardy was provoking Hooper to hit back, in order to justify himself and put Hooper in the wrong. "Forget it."

Hooper hated that from his brother; and it was more than a rebuff and worse than a rejection—it was a deliberate slap. But even Moura had joined him in it—even she wanted Fizzy back. "He's my son!" she said sadly. Even she was sulking.

"All at once the supermoron's very popular," Murdick said—and kept talking, because he did not understand how insulting his words were. "Still, the kid's got to be rescued."

In New York, they did not say good-bye—it wasn't necessary; it was a bit too polite, it was certainly too late. Anyway, the argument over Fizzy had done that. It seemed to Hooper that arguments were always either a hopeless beckoning or else a terrible kind of farewell.

That left Hooper isolated. At any other time he would have clung to Hardy and swallowed his pride and made an effort to repair the friendship. He believed that a break between his brother and himself explained the hatred in the world: it made the world look wasted and desperate. He did not want to be forced to admit the truth of this—but if a family was divided, what hope was there for any people?

Fizzy was the rallying point: they had to love him in order to love each other.

In the past, Hardy's anger or any friction between the brothers caused Hooper to grieve—and he knew that he had caused Hardy to grieve in the past. But tonight in Coldharbor Hooper did nothing. He thought: *Find him if you can. Go buzzing and yomping through O-Zone in your humping rotor—*

What they would discover was what Hooper had known for much longer: that Fizzy was not the pathetic squawking supermoron they had always made him out to be—tripping over himself and afraid to leave his room. No, Fizzy had begun to grow, and he might find his manhood in that thorny place. He had all the skills it took to live there. Perhaps that was what really frightened them—the suspicion that Fizzy was strong. They needed him.

They said they were worried; but O-Zone was fenced in. The boy was not on the loose—he was trapped. He would not be found until he wanted to be found. Hooper had convinced himself that the boy had already overcome his sense of strangeness and had probably conquered his irrational fear of aliens. The odd experience was liberating him—releasing him from his lonely terror. *Or am I thinking of myself!* he thought. Hooper was isolated, but he was not anxious. For once he was not alone.

"Your brother's so angry," Bligh said. "I shouldn't have said anything. You told me never to—"

"I'm glad you spoke up," Hooper said.

He wasn't glad at all, but he was ashamed of having to hide Bligh on a false ID. And because he was hiding her from his brother she was dearer to him. That phrase *flesh-pup* still rankled: it was another insult he'd have to endure. Now, cut off from his few friends and his family, he needed Bligh more than ever.

This isolation contained a smothering darkness that generated heat and power—the airless-attic intensity that made things explode into flames. It was the first time that Hooper had felt alone with Bligh. The responsibility for Fizzy had been taken away from him. That offered him a greater isolation. This hot solitary feeling, being alone with Bligh, excited him and made him grateful. It also filled him with desire.

He observed her, and his secrecy made him passionate. It

was keyhole adoration: he knelt and watched her with one eye.

It was late in the evening of their return from Africa. The last leg had been a rotor flight to Hooper's car, and then the drive through the layers of night smoke in Long Island to Coldharbor in New York. They were exhausted. Bligh had gone to her suite—to wash, she'd said, but she had lain on her bed and had not moved.

Having lived wild—and also, Hooper suspected, because she could not read or write—Bligh had developed the capacity to be very still for long periods. She was a light sleeper; she woke at the slightest sound; she heard everything—but she could spend the entire day motionless, only her eyelids flicking, like a bird on a branch, just sniffing and blinking. That was her daytime dozing. At night her sleep was a form of sensuality, and she lay and turned slowly, as if falling from a tremendous height and learning to fly.

Hooper watched her until very late, until his eyes burned. Then he too went to sleep. But still he saw her, bright, naked, making solemn truthful faces at him— her mirror.

The next day at breakfast—real food for Hooper, a meal tray for Bligh—Hooper said, "I'm going to be very busy for the next week or so."

"Tell me when you want me."

He loved hearing her say that, but he took just as much pleasure in spending the rest of the day watching her on his monitor. She undressed, she folded her clothes, she stretched, she scratched herself as she gazed downtown—and he focused on her fingertips relieving the itch. How thoughtful she looked when she scratched herself. She washed, taking more care than before, using more water. She wiggled her toes, she picked her teeth, she took her buttocks in both hands and warmed them. She tried on the clothes that Hooper had put in the room—nothing exotic; in fact, the opposite. They were the sort of clothes worn long ago by his first girlfriend, when they were both fifteen; but "girlfriend" had not meant much then. White silk panties, and tight shorts, and a frilly halter that left her midriff bare. Bunny, she was called. She was bad-tempered and a tease. She had an insolent way of walking that excited him—like that: Bligh was prowling the room. She found a soft spot and folded herself compactly like a cat, and dozed and blinked.

If I were in that room, or beside her, Hooper thought, as if replying to an accusing voice, I wouldn't be able to see her. I would hardly know her.

He needed this distance to see her clearly, and yet it had all started so simply—with his determination to know, when she had left him and gone into her suite weeks ago, whether she had kept her happy expression. He had wanted to know whether she was still smiling, hadn't he? Or had this monitoring grown out of his earlier habit of watching her on the first tape they'd shot in O-Zone, the morning of those murders?

During the days that followed, he went on watching her twitch and glide like a fish in a glass tank. He wished it could have been literally so—her swimming alone in the pool; but she couldn't swim. Yet her sleeping was a form of swimming: she rolled over and came up for air, and surfaced and sipped; and then she seemed to sink slowly and doze on the bottom. Often, when she was at rest, Hooper shot her face, the clasp of her nostrils gripping air when she breathed, the flutter of her eyelids and the hiding eyes beneath, the way she dampened her lips with her tongue, or slept with her fingers against her cheek. He shortened the focus so that he could see the veins in her neck, and the way the sun struck through her ears.

When she was active—striding to the windows, or hurrying to the bathroom—he remembered how he had first seen her like this, on the original tape, shining on the screen in Fizzy's room after they had unlocked that film cartridge; how, seeing her running in the dry woods of O-Zone, among the thin trees, he had decided to hunt her and capture her and bring her back.

He could not explain his helpless urge to watch her. Calling it voyeurism merely turned it into a decadent passion. And that was inaccurate, because it was not fulfillment but rather the most intense form of waiting. Watching her prolonged his ecstasy, and gave him the element he valued most in sensuality, which was suspense. Photography was foreplay, and it sometimes seemed to him the gentlest sexuality imaginable. It was also, with Bligh, a longing in him for a simpler world—the one she had inhabited: the past. The activity took hold of him and thrilled him. He was discovering another man inside himself, and this creature, a kind of timid twin, surprised him as he emerged: not a beast, but a patient kindly soul, who was bewitched by a little girl. And he thought: I'm the one who is trapped—not she.

There was also something pathetic in this watching and filming—he knew that, too. You filmed the thing you could not have. You had it this way—just the narrow image of her flashing like a fire on the screen: her body always looked so hot to him. Then it all went black, and he was alone. He had other moments of supreme confidence, when he felt they would never be parted, and when he saw them both much older in New York or elsewhere, still in love. He counted it as a measure of his love that no other person entered that imagining: he and Bligh were alone, needing only each other. Their love was not a way of making other friends, or trying out other lives. He had hope.

But just as often he felt panic—the idea that he was filming Bligh so that he would have something of her to hold on to long after she was gone: this image. He knew that if he had had no doubts he would have taken things as they came and allowed himself the rest of his life to love her. But he watched her, he filmed her, he kept his distance, he burned; and he suspected that he was running out of time.

He had once thought that it would all be simple, because she was an alien. Now he knew that nothing would ever be simple, because she was an alien.

His fortune, his future, all his time, and all his hopes were concentrated on his success with this young girl. For her he had risked a jail sentence, and following her he had trespassed in a Prohibited Area. He had left Fizzy behind in the wilderness for her. Taking her away, he had abandoned the boy.

In the morning he worked at his console, doing Allbright business—messages to his employees around the country, directives and memos to the managers. And still he watched her: rising, bathing, dressing, eating, undressing, squatting, roosting, dozing. He knew all her secrets, and at times she seemed fascinated by her own body, the way she sniffed and peered. It seemed as though she had begun to enjoy the complacencies of captivity.

He said, "I want to feed you," and gave her lunch. Her breasts moved when she chewed. In the afternoon they used the whirlpool bath, or the hothouse, or the sleep chamber.

He made films of this; he watched them after she went to her suite to sleep, and then he watched her sleeping.

A rigid schedule was important, because these days they did not go out. It was easy in the tower to lose track of time and turn day into night. Fizzy had lapsed into that lonely pattern of reversal many times before—it was the hazard of living indoors, a sort of sleepwalking, nighthawk life. But Hooper had always been careful, and he was careful now. A week after their return from Africa they were still keeping to regular hours, rising at dawn and dividing the day into four parts.

And still he went on monitoring her. He made copies and often watched them again the same day, and he stored the copies. He was glad she did not ask to go out. His watching had given him lately a powerful sense of possession. He did not want anyone else to see her—not now.

She slept naked, tumbling weightlessly in bed. She woke up quickly, at first light, and always seemed startled by her surroundings. Then she smiled, cursing softly in wonderment at the smoky dawn—and talked to herself, "Get smart, girlie," or something similar. She did stretching exercises very slowly, one limb at a time, and she growled in a way that always reminded Hooper of Fizzy's harsh catlike yawns.

Hooper had his favorite moments of watching her, but the best of the day was when she woke and winced at the light and remembered that she was in this pleasant tower. He hoped she was thinking of him at that moment, as she smiled and seemed to breathe *Alive!*

Her suite was full of mirrors, so that Hooper missed nothing. But neither did she miss anything of herself. She was obviously not used to mirrors, at least not ones this size. She found herself funny—teased herself and made faces. Sometimes her reflection seemed to arouse her sexually—she was less mature than her reflection—and that fleeting narcissism in her aroused Hooper more than he had ever known.

To start the morning she paced naked to the window and flung the blinds open and stretched some more—and more dance steps, pawing the floor and flexing her shoulders and scratching herself. She drank water thirstily in a neat licking way and then padded to the bathroom and stood in the tub and made a wishbone of her legs—arched her back and pushed and pissed hard into the drain. She washed in the tub after that, a shower, and then brushed her hair and dressed. By the time they met for breakfast she was a subdued and slightly different person from the swimmer who had surfaced on the bed.

That was what kept Hooper watching her this way: he loved the panting energy of the prowling youngster in the room, and he felt he knew her better than the shy and rather quiet and womanish girl who joined him for meals.

"I hardly see you," she said, biting an apple. "I don't know what I'm doing here!"

He felt he was taking a great risk saying. "Go if you want—"

"You're very kind to me," she said in a puzzled way.

His guilt stung him, and he hated his secrets. He wanted to tell her everything. That we are most ourselves when we are alone. That we are at our most natural when we are hidden, and that this is all a rehearsal. That for the pleasure of suspense he had been watching her closely on the monitor. That he loved her.

But just the word "love" frightened her—or else she raised her face at him and tried to repel the word with a laugh.

"I think you're rich," she said.

"Real apples. Real meat. Real vegetables. Potatoes with real dirt on them! Real firewood. Leather boots," he said. All his boasts had become jokes. "My own car!"

Yet she saw he was serious.

She said, "I never see anyone else at the swimming pool."

"I own that swimming pool," he said. "Here you can have anything you want."

"I can't swim," she said.

"I'll teach you," he said.

But another question forming in her eyes remained unasked.

She was still somewhat timid and obedient with him, and after the meal she quietly returned to her suite. She kicked off her slippers and became the prowling little girl again, and he became the hidden watcher.

He had only guessed from a few glimpses about her reaction to mirrors, but he soon realized that he had been right. Today, not long after she left him, she caught sight of herself in a full-length mirror, and lingered and teased herself. Then she went into a corner and lay on her side, facing the wall, with her legs drawn up and slowly scissoring. Her hands were clasped between her thighs, and she began chafing herself and uttering low sorrowing moans. Then she struggled with herself, and became frantic, as if she were being stabbed to death—each knife blow was distinct until they were too quick to see. And she died, too, but came alive some minutes later, looking shattered.

Hooper recorded this. He recorded her washing that afternoon, he recorded her trying on dresses, he recorded her painting her face. When she phoned him from her suite to ask whether he wanted to join her in the whirlpool bath he recorded in close-up the changing expression on her face. In the week after their return from Africa he had recorded a hundred hours of her on tape, and for about half that time he had been watching, directing the camera, changing angles.

He sensed that time was running out. They would find Fizzy—or more likely, Fizzy would find them—and Bligh's people would bargain for her back. But watching her, he had learned so much about her it was as though he had entered her life—known her for years. What husband knew as much about his wife as he did of Bligh? And it was an advantage that she was very young, because it seemed to Hooper characteristic of the young that their inner states were reflected in all their surfaces. He was seeing her naked, and while with some people nakedness was a special form of concealment, Bligh's nakedness said everything. She did not know he was watching.

It was always said that aliens were infectious—they were unhealthy, they were carriers of disease. It was the reason that they had no legal existence, that the cities had been sealed against them. It was not simply that they were regarded as career criminals, but that they were a danger to public health. Hooper had watched Bligh for symptoms of disease—sores, leaks, rashes, spasms. So far, he had seen nothing but her prowling and her dozing and her eager appetite: she lived like a cat, padding and stretching in her rooms. Yet even if she weren't carrying anything, she represented risks. But that was no discouragement to Hooper. He felt a kind of lust in being a lawbreaker; but he was justified, he felt, for if she were dangerous he was the only person who would suffer.

The possibility of danger—from the Feds, from Security, from Bligh herself—excited him and kept him watching her. He loved the hard muscles that moved under her curves, the colorless gaze of her large pale eyes, and her sunburned hair. Her buttocks were small and solid from her running, her legs slender, and her lips full on her wide mouth. She was lovely and so young; but her attraction was not only physical. Hooper loved her tomboy's daring, her curiosity, her darting glances, the way she paced at the windows. She had learned to use the binoculars and she remained fascinated by the city.

Without knowing it, she stirred his interest and took away all his loneliness. He had not even known he was lonely. She had shown him that, and he was anxious not to lose her, because he wanted to know more. Bligh was making him a better man. In spite of all the dangers associated with her being an alien, he felt very happy with her. And thinking about her, he dared to think about the future that had always seemed so familiar, and for that reason, so deceptive.

The image he always returned to was a simple one. It was not her youth, nor her nakedness, nor the fury of her eating, nor making love to herself, nor revealing herself to a mirror, nor energetically pissing. It was rather the sight of her standing at a large daylit window in a silk robe, with dawn showing through it and darkening the silhouette of her body, her small breasts and her boy's hips and bright hair, and looking like a princess in a castle tower.

Then he was burdened by the very beauty of it, and oppressed by everything he knew of her and all the hours he had spent watching her. He understood her well, and needed her, but without her realizing it she had become his secret life. He hated his sneaking and his excuses of work.

"What is it?" she asked. She had seen the strain on his face. They were in the whirlpool bath, bobbing in the warm currents, but at opposite sides of the tub. *I can see you better from here,* he had said, and meant it. She said, "Tell me."

He decided to approach the truth.

"I want you to let me watch you when you're alone," he said.

"How could you possibly do that?"

He explained how he would set up cameras and monitors and mirrors, and how they would work. He told her how he planned to watch her. He hoped she would not laugh.

"Is that all you want?" she asked in a wondering way. "To look at me like that?"

As soon as she said it in that certain way his desire for it died. He had never wanted her to know she was being watched. The pleasure lay in the secrecy. But her permission took all the blame away, and all the eroticism of watching her, and in that moment he wanted more.

Later, after their meal, when they lay on the cushions by the window—the yellow brightness of the early-evening sky-lights shining in on them from above the city—he touched her face. She was burning—he almost drew his hand away, he was so startled by the heat. But she was quicker, and snatched his hand, and took some of his fingers into her mouth. She moved nearer to him and rolled his fingers on her tongue until it seemed a bulb of heat traveled up his arm and burst, warming his whole body.

Hooper pulled the blinds, needing darkness, and tumbling into that darkness they struggled slowly with each other. It was as though they were inventing by trial and error an ancient ceremony, testing each separate move until it became part of the magic. It was a ritual he did not understand, but it changed him, and it could not be undone.

He woke, believing he had killed her by splitting her in half—he had a frenzied memory of lifting her by her ankles, one in each hand, and opening her wide to impale her and then devour her. But she had groaned with pleasure, and when he stopped she squawked for him to continue, and then she uttered little grunts until he was done. Now he was bumping against the ceiling, reawakened. He was horrified. He said, "You're wonderful."

The praise provoked her. She moved against him and dived deep, and then it seemed as though they were trying to drown each other, but were too buoyant to sink. The air was as thick as liquid around their bodies, and they held on as if performing a furious baptism in which two submerged lovers were purified to become one whole rising organism, flesh against flesh. Passion allowed this special creature to exist.

His heart was thumping in his ears. And then he woke again, but this time he was cold and solitary.

"I didn't think you were interested in that," she said, and drew him to her, warming him.

He did not speak. He was afraid again.

"I thought you might have some kind of infection," she said.

He was relieved to hear her say something he had himself feared. But he was still afraid.

"No," he said. "Do you?"

"I'm clean—cross my heart."

He knew it was the truth, and he caressed her, touching

her between the legs, wetting his fingers. It was as though he had put his hand on an open wound.

"You taste like smoked salmon," he whispered.

She smiled. She said, "I wish I knew who you were."

It amazed him to hear her say this, because he felt he knew her so well—every habit, every mumble and mood, every fleck on her body, her teeth, her toes.

"You'll have to stay with me to find out," he said, "because I want you for a friend."

He put up the blinds to see her face better. She seemed thinner, and rather small, but he had the sense that she was indestructible. He lay gently next to her, and the skylights gave them both a second skin. He became perfectly calm. He had not known such peace since early childhood.

He thought: I'm home.

His happiness with Bligh gave him a glimpse of Fizzy in O-Zone. In his vision the boy had grown older and had overcome his fears. He was stronger and more sensible, living among people much like Bligh—just as patient and watchful, just as gentle. The boy was happy at last.

Two days later (though it could easily have been more—after that night they abandoned their routine, and their exhausting nights turned the days inside-out; Hooper had stopped watching Bligh on the monitor, stopped recording her, and they went back and forth freely between her suite and his apartment, and bathed together, and shared one bed, and praised themselves—it could have been a week later) there was a message from Moura. She had arranged for it to appear as a priority printout, because he had gone off the air, he had closed his phone.

I must speak to you, the message said.

Hooper did not want her to visit him here. He took a different view of his apartment now that he shared it with Bligh, and he wanted to keep this second life, this real life, secret. He phoned her, and as soon as she identified herself he said, "I'll be right over."

On the way it struck him that she might have bad news of Fizzy. *We've just found his body.* Why hadn't he thought of that before? *Willis Murdick found teethmarks on the corpse.* No, not that. *We want you to be completely truthful and tell us everything you know about those aliens.* How could he begin to tell the strange story? He vowed to be cold and to let her do the talking. He was glad that the quarrel with Hardy was a thing of the past: it all seemed pointless nagging now. He wanted to see Hardy again and say, *No hard feelings!*

"Where's Hardy?" he said, stepping into the empty apartment.

"On a mission," Moura said very quickly, dismissing his question. "Will you help me?"

He was happy. He promised to do what she wanted—he felt he could do anything now—though what he longed for was very simple, to return to Bligh and take her downtown and urge her to choose something for him to buy.

"Let me talk," Moura said. She was edgy and trembling and her breathing was shallow. "If you're looking for someone who's lost, is there a central registry where they keep the names of people who pass through checkpoints? I'm not talking specifically about Owners. I mean anyone—can you locate them or pin them down to a particular area?"

"The Federal Census keeps track of everyone who passes through the Federal checkpoints. There's some sort of Health and Safety Department that stores the figures," Hooper said. "Some people slip under the wire, but not many."

"What if the person deregistered?"

"He'd still be in the computer," Hooper said. "Every time he's scanned his file's reactivated. We can't have unidentified people running wild in this country. Remember all those Mexicans during that border war?"

He saw the absurdity of it. Bligh had a false ID! There were probably millions of people like her—aliens living like Owners, and no one noticing.

"Where do I begin looking?" Moura said.

"This is the age of the ID," Hooper said. "In theory we know the identity of every single person in the United States. Everyone's got a number."

"What if he's an alien?"

"In theory, aliens don't exist—except for aliens wanted for crimes. But when they're caught, they stop existing." Hooper was disturbed by a sudden tension in her face. He said, "You don't have to worry. Fizzy's tough—he'll turn up."

"I'm not looking for Fizzy," Moura said.

Hooper laughed, feeling relieved.

"I'm looking for his father."

"I didn't think that was possible with frozen angels."

She made a face at the euphemism.

"Fizzy wasn't a test-tube baby," she said. "I went to a contact clinic. It was a man—a young man. I want to find him."

Hooper felt very close to her then and recognized the desperation in her voice: a panic of love.

"He shouldn't be hard to find. He had to have been an Owner or else fully registered, and even if he's cut himself loose, he can be chased. I'll help you." And then he felt it was safe to ask the question he had been pondering since he received her message. "What about Fizzy?"

"Hardy heard from him a few days ago."

"From O-Zone?" Hooper could not understand how the boy had managed it.

"No, but it wasn't far from there," Moura said.

"So you must know the coordinates," Hooper said.

Moura made a face and then said, "Hardy's gone looking for him."

"Alone?"

"With Murdick."

"In the Godseye gunship," Hooper said, seeing the big dark thing with the death's head on its nose and its Snake-Eaters insignia, streaking across the treetops, with its searchlights bleaching everything under it; and its urgent murmuring crew.

"I suppose so," she said. "What's wrong?"

Hooper saw the deadly thing against a clear sky at sundown, and the aliens below, with Fizzy.

"Give me the coordinates," Hooper said. "What did Fizzy's message say?"

"Hardy said he doesn't want you to interfere," Moura said. "He doesn't need your help—I do!"

Hooper said, "If you want me to help you find that donor, give me all the information you have on Fizzy. That's how we begin—we find him first. Then we find his father."

Moura began to cry, and it seemed odd to him that she knew so little about how terrible the situation had become and yet could still shed tears. She knew nothing of the aliens in O-Zone, nothing about Bligh, nothing much about the two abductions, and very little of the terror of Godseye. And she was not crying because her son was gone—she was crying for her lost love.

He saw the gunship again and the troopers peering out. It was a big wobbling wasp-shaped rotor, looking for someone to sting.

30

FROM WHERE HE STOOD, HARDY COULD SEE THIN HIGH veils of cloud ghosting in the blue sky of southern Indiana, and all around him the watery mirages and double images of the flat green fields—another hot day, another fuel depot. He had never known a rotor to use so much fuel. Even the depot engineer had remarked on it.

"Your ship's armor-plated!"

"We're security."

"What's it got—titanium shields? You carrying bulk weight? I guess it guzzles fuel!"

"That's all classified," Sluter said. Although he was outside the rotor, and just a cornfield nearby, he was wearing his mask.

"We don't have any trouble here," the engineer said. "Half the time the roadblocks are wide open—no guards or nothing."

The fuel was humming in the hose-pipe as they spoke.

"No roadblocks is just plain stupid," Meesle said through his propped-up faceplate. He had the thick upholstered look of an Astronaut. "You're going to pay the price for that. The price is aliens, robbery, rape, drugs, bad money, and disease."

"This ain't Florida or Texas," the engineer said. "This ain't Landslip."

He was smiling. He seemed friendly and unsuspicious in an old-fashioned way. And although this fuel depot was fortified, and most of it buried in the hillside, it seemed very peaceful: it was like the past. The engineer had planted gera-

398

niums in the dry soil, in flowerbeds around the rotor pad, and morning glories had leapt up the spiked fence.

Hardy had come to like these refueling stops and was glad the gunship was such a guzzler. He looked forward to seeing the star shape of the depot from the air, the glint of sun on the rotating radar dish, and then being on the ground—the easy conversation with the engineer, and a chance to hoist his helmet for ten minutes or to use a proper toilet—the Godseye troopers insisted that on-ground toilets were security risks; they used the inflatable shit-eater on the gunship.

The very desolation of these midwest depots was a relief after the confinement of the gunship. The big bug had seemed roomy and luxurious a week ago, but now Hardy regarded it as poky and rather noisy. He had been airsick on three occasions—clear-air turbulence. He found Sluter bossy and Murdick stupid and he had taken a particular dislike to Meesle, who had insisted on showing him videos.

"This one's kind of cute," Meesle always said of the cruelest ones, and of the most violent he said, "This one has an important message but it's in an easy-to-digest form."

Then Meesle usually smiled.

"It's full of geechees getting burned down."

He screened Intruder, Alienation, Time Travel, Godseye-Worldwide, and Reclaiming the States. Hardy watched them. How else to pass the time? But he hated them, and he hated Meesle for always sitting directly behind him, with his face against his neck.

Asians, Africans, Hispanics: they were shown committing dreadful crimes, and their faces were intercut with images of rats and roaches. Then they were chased and rounded up and killed in peculiarly horrible ways, often very slowly, in close-up.

"Omnifelons," Meesle said. "Lepers. Skells. Cokewhores."

Hardy sat stony-faced, with his helmet on and his faceplate locked into position, and his collar up, and even his gloves on. He went on watching because he wanted to go on hating these so-called troopers.

"You're as bad as your brother," they said.

At night, after scanning an area, they put the gunship down in darkness and kept a beam on for protection. They slept on board. Hardy was the first to begin wearing his mask every day and night, and he stopped taking his boots off. He used a breathing apparatus and assisted air.

"Worried about omnifelons?" Sluter said. "Meesle telling you about violent predators? That why you've got your armor on?"

"No, it's your feet," Hardy said. "And all the garbage we're carrying. This bug stinks."

Within a few days they were all wearing masks and air cylinders. But the Godseye troopers denied that they were doing it because of the smell in the gunship. It was preparation against aliens, they said. How did they know this kid Fizzy was alone? He might have fifty aliens guarding him. Some of them had technology! They might have rockets or land mines! They were desperate little geechees!

"This kid we're looking for," Murdick said one night. "He won't thank us. He won't like us. And we'll hate him."

The others looked to Hardy to refute this. But Hardy did not reply. He was ashamed of himself for having lived in New York his whole life and not known how vicious these people were. He had always assumed that Godseye was just another of the many security strike forces. But no—

"He's going to say, 'Make me captain or else I won't fly.'" Murdick had tried to imitate Fizzy's quacking voice, but he had overdone the wah-wah. It was a mistake. Now no one believed him.

"I don't understand how he got out of O-Zone," Sluter said. His incomprehension had made him grumpy. "You can't do that!"

"Not to mention the Red Zone Perimeter," Meesle said. "You can't get through the beam."

"He got through the beam," Hardy said. "He got out of O-Zone."

"You can't," Sluter said.

"He can," Hardy said. "Fizzy's area is particle physics."

The three men turned their masks on him. He could not see their faces, but he knew they were frowning at him.

"And fiber optics."

He felt pompous just saying the words—even the simplest description of Fizzy's research sounded boastful, and Hardy sensed the hostility coming at him through the painted faceplates. He had some sympathy for Fizzy then: the poor kid had to put up with this crap from everyone.

Sluter said, "Lots of people in this country know about

particle physics and fiber optics. But there's no record of them having busted through a Red Zone. And no one has ever entered or left O-Zone without written permission."

That objection made Hardy proud of Fizzy: it was like a testimony to the boy's uniqueness.

"He's a smart boy," Hardy said. His assertive tone said: Smarter than you.

"Years of research went into securing those zones," Sluter said, and pushed past Hardy on the way to the cockpit.

"He's barking mad," Murdick said. "Hates the idea of someone breaking through a zone."

"So do I," Hardy said. "Except this is my own kid."

"We always considered those places safe," Meesle said.

"No one ever considered them safe!" Hardy said.

"By safe I mean dangerous," Meesle said. He had unlocked his faceplate so that Sluter wouldn't hear him arguing on the phones. He was whispering under his uplifted mask. "Dangerous for aliens. When we had to dispose of them."

Hardy said, "So you're the ones who populated O-Zone with all those stinking aliens."

"It was before we switched to ocean drops. We booted them out of cargo planes. But we didn't always give them parachutes. Anyway, even if they survived the fall and managed to live with the radioactivity, they couldn't get out of the zone. If they didn't get cancer, they'd get nosebleeds. They'd start staggering. And they'd never get out of the zone. That's what I mean by safe—I mean very dangerous."

"Fizzy got out," Hardy said.

"Maybe."

"He was on the outside when he sent the message!"

"Then why wasn't he in Winslow like he said?"

The message was: *Have completed clandestine exfiltration O-Zone. The coordinates of my present position are 89°.58.027 and 37°.91.284, an unfortified farm near Winslow. Health okay except for feet. Very high exposure risk. Assistance required immediately, but do not alert Red Zone Rescue. Await instructions.*

It was unsigned but unmistakably Fizzy. A number of details interested Hardy. There was the astonishing news that the boy had escaped from O-Zone and broken through the Red Zone Perimeter—no one had ever managed that on the ground. There was *except for feet*, a very Fizzy touch. And there was the baffling *Await instructions:* this statement seemed more ambiguous as Hardy repeated it. Did it mean that Fizzy awaited instructions, or was it an order for Hardy to await instructions?

But unambiguous was Fizzy's order not to alert Red Zone Rescue, which would have been the normal procedure. It was the reason for their existing, to patrol the perimeter, and if Hardy had reported Fizzy's present position the boy would have been picked up within hours and spirited back to New York. But Hardy had a better reason than Fizzy's forbidding it. Alerting Red Zone Rescue to Fizzy's so-called clandestine exfiltration (no one was better at playing the trooper-hero than an irritating brat with no experience!) might also make the O-Zone project impossible. It would certainly endanger its secrecy.

So Hardy had accepted Murdick's offer of the Godseye gunship and crew, and now he was stuck with them. They had agreed to the mission in the hope of catching a band of aliens.

"We'll burn some cars. Shoot some dogs."

Hardy had expected that.

"Nuke some aliens," Meesle said.

"Wait a minute," Hardy said.

"Neutralize them," Murdick said. "Snatch the kid back."

But now, over a week later, they had found nothing—no one. It had made them bad-tempered and uneasy, and they were often frightened by the open spaces and the stands of trees. They imagined Diggers tunneling underground—thousands of them underneath the gunship as they flew low over southern Illinois. They saw what looked like bulges and breathing holes on the surface. They hovered and pumped gas inside and plugged the holes. They did not see Diggers. That scared them. It meant that the Diggers had outsmarted them: the beasts were clever.

They had flown toward Winslow on that first day worrying out loud. Hardy had imagined that they would be volatile and aggressive—their huge clacking gunship, with armor plate and mocking insignia; their arsenal of weapons; their helmets and wild-looking masks. Well, that was how they looked—like those space warriors that Pilgrims and Rocketmen fantasized about—but underneath it all they were worrying. Was the boy alone? Was he armed? Was he sane? Was he alive—or had he been killed and was the whole mission about to be lured into a trap? Was anything known about these aliens? Did they have technology—any irons, any fire-power?

Murdick had made matters worse by hinting that the boy might be unreliable, and not just ungrateful, but hostile.

The Godseye troopers were strangers here. They were New Yorkers, and like all the Godseye people they were part-timers, volunteer vigilantes. "I've got a couple of drug companies," Meesle had said, and Hardy knew that Murdick manufactured elevator equipment. This was a part of America they flew over at an altitude of forty thousand clicks. It was farmland, open fields, simple wooden houses, silos, and straight roads—some of it looked deserted, but most of it was in fairly good shape. Surprisingly, there were few check-points. Who lived here? Very few of the settlements looked fortified. It was fenced-in farming, but the land was poor or else underused. Perhaps it was too near O-Zone?

"Ground vehicle," Murdick said.

It was an old blue pickup truck, with six people sitting in the back and dust flying. The passengers were men and women, and the Godseye scanner did not find any weapons in the vehicle. But the troopers were not reassured. Those people in the truck were strangers; all strangers were dangerous.

"I'd like to nuke that vehicle," Meesle said. "Just take it out. I'd feel better."

But he did not shoot. They watched the vehicle head into Winslow.

"I don't like the looks of this," they kept saying, worrying themselves into a mood of aggression.

Winslow was a wide place in the road surrounded by watchtowers. There were farms and fenced-in fields nearby. Wind pumps had been stabbed into the landscape: they looked as simple and pointless as children's toys, their blades turning high above the still fields. Must be oil, Murdick said. Hardy did not bother to correct him—giving information to a stupid person only made the person stupider and more an-noying. They were pumping water, of course. This region had been drying out for years, but Hardy did not want to give them rain. He craved an empty place—one that would not be taken away from him after his rain began to fall.

"This area could be crawling with geechees," Murdick said. "There are whole towns out here that have been taken over by Trolls."

That was the talk: Hardy had heard it—everyone knew it. But it was city talk. There was very little hard evidence to suggest that anything had changed out here. In fact, just before he had left New York Hardy had watched a television program about how Easter was celebrated somewhere out here—Easter had just passed. But why tell the Godseye troopers that he had seen people, like those down below probably, eating ham, wearing new clothes and fancy hats, and going to church?

"Another ground vehicle," Meesle said.

"With a woman behind the wheel." Hardy had enlarged the image. She wore sunglasses and gloves. She steered around the holes in the road.

"Don't shoot yet," Meesle said. He rested his handgun on the dome of his belly.

"What do you mean yet?"

"I mean I don't like the looks of this."

They were flying high over the main street of Winslow, and what surprised them, when they enhanced the image on the ground-screen, was that none of the buildings was taller than five stories, and many stood alone, and some were unfenced. Their roofs were tarpaper and shingles and tin sheets—old stuff, with square patches showing. The watchtowers were empty.

"Look. Iron fire escapes. Haven't seen those for years."

"No security," Meesle said. "Must have a hell of a crime rate. Just kick your way into most of those buildings. Go through the roof."

"Maybe they don't need security," Hardy said. "Maybe it's peaceful."

Meesle found this very funny, and when his belly shook, so did his handgun, where it rested.

"Going closer," Sluter called from the cockpit.

He flew slowly and without banking, in order to keep the armor-plated underside of the gunship facing down. That was their protection. They dipped near a checkpoint at the edge of town, but there was no one near it—the gate was open, vehicles came and went. Meesle said he didn't like the look of that. There were stores on the main street, selling hardware and clothes and food and electrical equipment and farm implements. One of the largest buildings in town was a brick structure which bore the sign "Farmers' Market."

"After O-Zone was declared a Prohibited Area, these

nearby places just got sick," Murdick said. "The people are vegetables and simple-lifers. Scratching a living and saying prayers. Hell of a lot of Rocketmen in those towns." He smacked his lips and said, "It's all fucking terminal down there."

"Probably not an Owner or a taxpayer among them," Meesle said. "Probably all geechees, like Willis says."

"Why don't we go down and find out," Hardy said.

"I wouldn't go down there without a lot of firepower," Meesle said.

"We don't have to," Sluter called out. "The kid's coordinates are west of here."

Sluter had marked the spot on the ground-screen, but instead of flying directly to it he made a dogleg around a settlement on the outskirts of Winslow as a precaution.

"Missiles have come blasting out of pretty places like that!" Sluter said. He had shouted, Hardy thought, to cover his nervousness.

Some of these places looked idyllic to Hardy, with the sunshine on them and the roofs brown with rust and the pumps spinning and the wet ditches cut into the fields. It seemed amazing that these people had found a way to survive on the ground here, and in the twilight such places took on an almost nightmarish appearance. They were unknown, unseen; only talked about. They seemed to represent the confusion that Hardy always felt when he was away from New York: everywhere else was the past and paradoxical, the simple life that looked romantic one minute and savage the next.

"I'm not going down until we scan those buildings for lurkers," Sluter said. "And then we wait until dark."

"Just don't shoot," Hardy said. "I want that kid back alive."

Hovering over the cluster of dry wooden buildings, they were low enough to be drawing dust off the ground in their updraft.

From the cockpit Sluter called out that he was reading the scanner. He then said, "I'm not getting diddly."

No people—that frightened them. It made them imagine filthy creatures in underground burrows; dug in and swallowing and waiting. Sluter landed the gunship a hundred meters from the farm and kept the scanner on it. They expected to see heads rising from the ground—hairy faces, crazy eyes. But there was nothing. The scanner did not register either

movement or sound. Yet each of the troopers said he heard
human noises and could see shadows and licks of light—
antlers of flames striking through the darkness.

Dawn came and showed them nothing more. There was no
furniture in the main house, though there were some torn
curtains in the empty rooms. The ceilings had fallen, and the
floors were littered: animals had come and gone. Some
power lines still stood, and there was a dish in the yard.

"Probably got raided by Starkies or Trolls," Meesle said.

"Those people we saw in town looked pretty legal to me,"
Hardy said. "Just hard-pressed, as far as I could see."

Meesle paid no attention to Hardy. He was still looking at
the empty farmhouse. "Probably snuck in and burned the
people and butchered the animals."

"Maybe the people just picked up and went away," Hardy
said. "Maybe they went into Winslow."

He could see that these buildings were a skeleton of the
past: frail and hollow and dried-out, without any flesh, too
far from town. But its death and distance made it a safe place
to hide in.

Murdick said, "No sign of the kid."

"But this has got to be the place," Hardy said. "He could
have bounced his message off that dish in the yard."

They considered this, and Hardy knew that they hated the
possibility of the boy being able to manage that. They stood
in the farmyard in their helmets and flying suits—looking, as
always, like Astronauts. There was no sound now—not the
wind, nor the creak of the timbers, nor the complaint of
joists; the wooden buildings had stopped going *ouch-ouch*. It
was so still it seemed eerie and unnatural, as if some killer—
Meesle said—were holding his breath and hiding, and someone else lay dead nearby. It was that quiet.

"I don't like the looks of this," Murdick said.

"We should maybe search for a body," Meesle said.

"Sometimes they eat them," Murdick said.

They searched, they dug, they scanned, they used thermal
imaging and metal detectors. But there was no body. The
only bones they found were those of a cow, yellow and soft
with age. There was radiation still in them.

"Oh, sure, they took casualties," Meesle said. "O-Zone's
just across the river."

"Let's get off the ground!" Sluter called out. "I hate it
here!"

* * *

That failure their first day had made them impatient—and suspicious and sulky. They were not methodical or calculating men, Hardy decided—more reasons for him to miss Fizzy. Only since the boy had been absent had Hardy really begun to appreciate his uniqueness. And how often had he and Moura muttered about Fizzy being handicapped! But these Godseye vigilantes—these so-called troopers—were the opposite of Fizzy. They were frustrated, hurried and rather clumsy; they were quick to assign blame; and this fearful restlessness—their cowardice—had made them into killers.

Hardy was sorry he had asked Godseye to help him find the boy; and now there was no going back. They were always telling stories of how they joined the squad!

"I'm in Chicago on business," Meesle said. "This was years ago. They used to hijack cars and trucks in Chicago. You'd slow down on an exit ramp and they'd be on top of you. Anyway, I'm driving down a ramp and I see three Roaches squeezing through a fence. I gave them time to get near the road and then I pulled off and ran them over—bump, bump, bump. A week later I got the call. Someone had seen me and reported me. Do I want to join Godseye?"

"Mine was the same kind of impulse thing," Murdick said. "I had just bought a really neat iron and was taking a walk in Upper West, where we used to have a condo. I saw a Skell—incredibly old and ugly. I knew he was going to mug me, even though he was about a block away. I could feel it. And after he mugged me they'd put him away or burn him or whatever—but what good would that do me? I'd have scars for life! Maybe brain damage! Might lose an eye! So I lined him up and gave him a bead and stiffed him before he could lay a hand on me. He had money—he was a snatcher, no question of it. You've got to get the jump on them. Burn them before they commit crimes, because what good is it afterward? That's how I got the call. They liked my attitude."

"Memory lane," Hardy said, and turned his back on them to show that he had heard enough.

"You're as bad as your brother," Meesle said.

"I've burned so much trash I can't remember the first time," Sluter said.

They were still flying east of Winslow on the main line,

looking for the boy—or was it a kidnap gang, or half an army?

"Some of these aliens are so hungry," Murdick said. He spoke in fear and admiration.

The Godseye troopers were well-armed and yet they were reluctant to touch down, except at night to sleep. Hardy felt that they might have preferred flying blind in the darkness to risking the ground. It was almost as if they were afraid because they knew what fury they could unleash—afraid of their own firepower. They said they wanted to save time. They zigzagged and filmed; they radioed down to checkpoints, giving Fizzy's ID number.

They mocked the small towns, and yet they lingered over them, taking pictures. The places looked hard-up, with old cars and bad roads and acres of patched solar panels. Yet apparently they still worked. They had schools and stores and police, and most had checkpoints. They all flew the Stars and Stripes.

None of the people out here wore helmets and not many wore suits. It was rare to see a mask, and even then it was a nosebag, nothing fancy. Some of them had radios clamped to their heads. Their clothes were flapping and faded, the women wore trousers or skirts, and even though they might not be Owners they certainly were not aliens. They were working people and in some places there were fifty or more in a field, all together, hoeing weeds.

When Murdick said, "This reminds me of Africa," Hardy thought *Bullshit*, but he knew what Murdick meant. It was the contrast with New York—not nakedness and starvation, but another time zone. He was talking about the past.

"More irons," Meesle said again and again, in a kind of nagging notation. But it was true. Nearly all the adults out here, east of Winslow, wore weapons—real irons, pistols mostly, and the troopers were fascinated by them. These old irons were slow and inaccurate, they said, but it was touching and romantic nevertheless to see men and women carrying weapons in leather holsters strapped to their waists.

"Weapons with moving parts!" Sluter said, mocking and marveling.

"You couldn't carry them in New York," Murdick said.

"Why would you want to?"

"Allbright's probably one of these people that thinks the city's safe," Meesle said.

Hardy looked the fat man up and down, and sighed, audibly flunking him. This bug was too small for an argument, but Meesle got the message: Look at yourself.

"No city is safe," Meesle said, angered by Hardy's wordless scrutiny.

It is only a matter of time before he kills someone, Hardy thought. Of the three—Flatty had not been able to join the mission—Meesle was the most impatient to use his weapons, and it seemed as though his only motive was his impatience.

The days were full of silences, and the racket of the gunship was like another kind of smothering silence. They spent hours looking for fuel depots—like wanderers in a desert looking for oases. And because all the depots were fortified and some actually enclosed in garrisons, they lingered in these places, spending a whole morning or afternoon enjoying that safety at ground level. Then they ventured into what they thought of as the unknown: the pattern of towns in the midwest. They stayed away from the cities, believing that was what Fizzy would have done. Anyway, most of these cities were so hard to enter or leave. Cincinnati, for example: they were kept holding over the river for almost an hour.

"Checking credentials!" Sluter complained, and when the control tower asked for more information the others cried, "Snake-Eaters!" and "This mission is classified!" They flew off without entering the city.

Thereafter they kept to the small towns and the in-between stretches of farmland. When they took the trouble to look closely, they were impressed by the way some of the people in these towns lived so close to the ground—eating real food, drinking their own water, running factories and ingeniously irrigating their land. Many of them did not even bother to erect fences. From the air, their gardens looked like multi-colored rugs. There was large-scale farming, too—fields of winter wheat and newly sprouted corn.

Occasionally, from the air, they saw a white farmhouse and a barn and a paddock and a silo and a chicken coop and an old truck parked in front. And they knew there was a family in the house that had not been changed by either time or events. The family was at the table, eating supper in their overalls, their heads bowed toward the mashed potatoes and gravy and broccoli and the gleaming chicken—probably praying, and probably not even thinking of it as real food, but just food.

Yet some of those same families might be buying space in a rocket and paying a subscription to the Pilgrims and talking about leasing units and stations and orbits. They might be saying, "Let's sell up and get off the planet"—the poor deluded fools. Hardy felt they would be better off in Maine or Idaho. But they all worried; even those people praying over their mashed potatoes feared Diggers and Starkies and Roaches and all the aliens that sneaked into the States from the world, or were thrown out of the cities; and they braced themselves against the swarms that hit here and cleaned them out.

That was a fleeting thought over Indiana, but the rest of the time it seemed to Hardy that nothing had changed at all.

Toward the end of the week, Sluter said, "How do we know the kid got out of the Red Zone? We don't have any corroboration. That message doesn't prove anything—he could have sent it from O-Zone or anywhere, if he's such a brain. I think we're wasting our time. We should go to the Red Zone Perimeter and make inquiries."

"Fizzy specifically said not to alert Red Zone Rescue," Hardy said. "We should try Missouri State Security or the local police."

"The security people in the Red Zone will know if someone broke through," Sluter said. "We don't have to mention names."

"Do you have a right to go there?"

"Godseye! Snake-Eaters!"

They could seem clumsy and unsure of themselves, and rather dangerous because of that; but it was when they were arrogant and flashing their weapons that Hardy remembered just how dangerous they were, and that Godseye—in spite of all its pretensions about justice and brotherhood—was a death squad.

They lumbered around for most of the day in the gunship, looking for a fuel depot. By the time they found one and set off for the Red Zone it was growing dark. They put down and secured themselves for the night, and they grumbled: they were running low on air, food, and water, and so the next day they made that their excuse to stop where they did.

"You can keep Winslow and Booneville and Cincinnati," Sluter said, gloating at the ground-screen. "Just give me garrisons like this. The command post of the Red Zone Perimeter!"

"It used to be called Winterton," Meesle said. "Before the shit-storm."

It was a Federal flight garrison at the edge of the defoliated ribbon of land that ran around O-Zone. Hardy thought of it as a glorified sentry post, but the Godseye troopers were clearly impressed with the technology and the fortresslike aspect of the garrison that gave it a forbidding appearance. It was a control center and its purpose was to prevent anyone from crossing the red line and entering O-Zone. That anyone might want to leave O-Zone was unthinkable, since officially no one lived in O-Zone—too dangerous. That's what Hardy had thought until very recently. Now he knew that Fizzy had been kidnapped there by aliens who had probably been dumped into O-Zone by one of the Godseye squads.

"You're responsible for Fizzy's abduction," said Hardy. "Your people put those aliens in O-Zone."

"What was this kid doing in a Prohibited Area?" Meesle said, and laughter rang in his helmet as Hardy turned away.

They were making their final approach to the garrison.

"Just don't mention Fizzy by name," Hardy said.

It was always said that Godseye, and organizations like it—paramilitary groups, security patrols, task forces—were partly funded by the Federal government. That was what Hardy had heard. This landing was like proof of it: the control tower immediately granted permission for the gunship to land, and when they were on the ground they were given access to the provision warehouse. Two Red Zone commandos went aboard the gunship on the pretext of examining the flight recorder and logbook, but they hardly seemed to care about that. Their real interest was in the Godseye weapons and search system.

"You sure are ready for action!" one commando said, looking at the Godseye troopers.

The troopers wore helmets and masks and their sturdiest suits. They had tough ground boots over the liners they tramped around in on board. They wore their weapons, and communicated through headsets.

"Lovely boots, too!"

Hardy wondered whether any of the Godseye crew would give the real reason for wearing battle gear: the smell on board the gunship.

"We're on a mission," Sluter said.

Murdick described the features of his suit and the holding

and traction capabilities of his boots, and then he took out his weapons and showed them off. The commandos were so eager to see the particle beam in action they escorted their visitors to the garrison firing range to try it out. Even on a low charge it melted the steel target frame and turned a bag of sand into a pillow of solid glass.

"It shoots around corners," Murdick said eagerly.

"I wish we'd had this a week ago," one of the commandos said. "Hey, why do you private task forces have the best weapons!"

"What would you have done with that weapon a week ago?" Meesle asked.

"We had an incident."

Hardy said, "You mean someone penetrated the perimeter?"

"Suspected violation."

Sluter said, "Aliens?"

"Absolutely. But they had high tech." The commando was still holding Murdick's weapon. "This would have taken care of them."

Hardy said, "Was anyone killed?"

"That's classified."

"Have you issued a description of the violators?"

"You don't know what an alien looks like?"

"How can we help?" Sluter asked.

"Look for aliens," the commando said. "And shoot on sight."

It was remarkable how just that short conversation with the commandos at the Red Zone had bucked up the Godseye troopers. Hardy noticed a new resolve in the men and a determination and a sense of mission that had not existed even at the beginning. They started to call themselves by their nickname "Snake-Eaters" and they resumed their mutters of "I don't like the look of this."

But this new spirit in the mission worried Hardy. He saw them firing at anything that moved, shooting on sight, as the chummy vengeful commando had suggested. He feared that Godseye was a greater risk to Fizzy than the aliens, but how was it possible to neutralize them?

"I have an idea," Hardy said, after they were back in the air. "We head for Winslow. That's our best hope. We've got the exact coordinates."

"The kid wasn't there when we looked," Meesle said.

"We should stay there and await further orders," Hardy said, believing that they were likely to do less damage on the ground.

"Orders!" Sluter said. "From a kid!"

"Wait till you see this kid," Murdick said.

They all laughed, except Hardy. He had become convinced of Fizzy's versatility, and he was now ashamed of the many times in the past when he had complained about the boy. Fizzy was special—there was no doubt of that; and Hardy wanted him back.

"We'll look at Winslow," Sluter said. "It's not far."

But he took the gunship to a high altitude so that they could drop quickly into the farm complex without being seen or heard.

"There's lights," someone muttered. "There's a rotor down there!"

They were examining the ground-screen, the blip on the scanner—there was definitely a hot spot near those buildings.

Murdick said, "Where would he have picked up a rotor?"

"That wouldn't be too difficult for Fizzy," Hardy said. His mind was still on the boy's excellence.

"Except he can't fly."

Meesle was crowding the ground-screen and saying, "They're in the house. I'd like to drop a wipeout on them."

They cut the engines and drifted down silently, landing three clicks from the farm. Too far, Murdick said: they'd have to walk in the darkness, wearing their heavy battle gear—helmets, masks, armored suits, ribbed-sole boots, and two weapons apiece.

"This is ridiculous," Murdick said.

Their labored breathing came over the headphones, and soon they did not have the wind to complain. Hardy saw them in the starlight, and sometimes trudging against the sky. They were like big swollen dolls, with thick soft bodies and bulbous heads. They groaned and stumbled, cursing each other, blaming Fizzy, becoming grumpier. They were walking across the margin of a cornfield, past the papery flutter of the leaves. Hardy hoped they would not be seen by any of the local people—these leathery-faced farmers in dungarees would surely mistake them for the vanguard of an invasion from space, and they might be quicker with their old irons than Godseye with their beams.

Hardy was apprehensive, but all the more eager to rescue the boy, because of the gratitude he now felt: Fizzy had led him here, by a circuitous route, to the edge of the past. It was as if he had reached the shore of an island.

"I don't like the looks of this," Murdick said.

It was always the most worrying remark: the nervous cliché meant trouble. Hardy was afraid that Murdick was on the point of firing his weapon.

Meesle said, "Set up the scanner."

They did so, and found no wires or alarms. The rotor was parked on the far side of the barn—they took its profile, but could not read any of its markings.

They crept closer, moving clumsily in their suits and bumping each other, and swearing.

"Two of them," Sluter grunted, his faceplate against the scanner.

Hardy had crawled ahead, his hope making him bold. He had discovered his need for Fizzy and he knew he would defend him—he would certainly not hesitate to shoot anyone if it meant saving the boy.

"I'm almost on top of them," he said. The harsh breathing of the three Godseye troopers filled his headphones. He knew they were fearful: they had let him go forward. The death squad!

He halted and dropped to his knees.

"Hold your fire," he said. He seemed to be speaking to himself as much as to the others. He forced his weapon down. He had seen enough.

Yet it was the strangest sight. Standing framed in the old wooden windows of this farmhouse—just behind the cobwebs and the cracked panes of dirty glass—were two travelers in silver flying suits, with their helmets off: Hooper and that girl.

PART FIVE

GODSEYE

31

WHAT HAD AMAZED FISHER WAS SEEING MR. BLUE STAND
up and move away from the breakfast fire and in a voice of
quiet power say, "Shall we go then?" And the man set out
that instant for New York with the others behind him kicking
the dust—never mind it being fifteen hundred clicks and their
first time. It was a show of strength that matched the effort of
a great machine—everyone had obeyed and followed the
slender man to the edge of the cliff and down, walking in old-
style shoes.

Fisher had obeyed, following in his new boots: he was
impressed by the man who had made him do that. He wanted
to say: *I've never followed anyone before!* A month ago they
had put him in a bag and slung him from camp to camp and
pushed him and dragged him—even threatened him. Now he
was scuffing along with the rest of them. He was reminded of
the day he had left Coldharbor alone and walked around
New York. He had felt brave; it had been an unusual outing.
But this was extraordinary. They actually expected to make
it!

They took little except what they wore, the cast-off clothes
they had found in O-Zone, a little food, including some of
the sealed provisions, and some old weapons that doubled as
tools—axes, choppers, knives, billhooks. They rolled their
pots and cups into their blankets and twisted these rolls into
backpacks.

"You're a problem, Fish."

"What kind, Mr. B?"

They were descending the cliff wall, Fisher in his helmet

417

and torn suit, carrying his particle beam. His helmet contained him like a room.

"Your people are Owners. I mean, they're really powerful. Even I've heard of the Allbrights. If we stayed there they'd come and destroy us, for snatching you." He was talking quietly and choosing his steps with long loping strides.

The day was hot and bright and buzzing, what Fisher had come to see as a typical day in O-Zone. The sky was blue and high, not a cloud in it, no moisture, no wind. There was hardly any dew on the ground. There were scrub oaks and cedars here, and the flakes of sunlight beneath them were green and gold. At each clearing there was such stillness and such sky it was as though they were walking through a bubble.

"We'll find them before they find us."

"You had no right to take me."

"I suppose you think they had a right to steal Bligh."

He could have said, *But she's an alien*—and yet that didn't help. The word did not have quite the same meaning for Fisher now.

He said, "She wasn't legal."

"You ain't legal here, Fish," Gumbie said.

He was right—snuffling, frog-eyed DeWayne Gumbie was right. It was that sort of remark that made him qualify the word "alien," and they were aliens, no question about it. You only had to see them eating to know that.

Soon they were all perspiring and moving without speaking, Fisher at the rear, scowling, with his faceplate propped up, and the legs of his suit making a loud scraping as they rubbed together. He had begun to hate his noisy suit—it was a flying suit, totally wrong for the ground, and he swore at it—but he was afraid to take it off for any length of time.

He had never envied anyone before, and he told himself that he did not envy these aliens now. But he admired their guts and their dumb strength and their lack of ceremony. They didn't complain: that was very restful. You could probably teach these people enough math and physics to get them going. Their spelling and handwriting were better than Fisher's, but so what? Yet he liked the easy way they lived off the land—they simply stretched out and found something to eat, and left him the sealed provisions. They could smell water. He decided that they had to be very stupid to be so brave, and he somewhat despised them for their obedience. But how else was it possible to live here?

For Mr. Blue he felt not envy but regret that the alien had such inner strength. Although he was skinny and balding and had a bony face and was probably thirty, the man was very strong. Perhaps his strength came out of his silence and his narrow shadow. Fisher saw in Mr. Blue the qualities he knew he himself lacked. He needed that self-assurance, and there was something graceful about the man that made him feel ungainly.

"Never mind here in O-Zone," Fisher said, abruptly worried at what they were attempting and lapsing back into himself. "Never mind the low-level mutagens here. But what about the Red Zone Perimeter? There's a twenty-four-hour patrol! There's commandos! Checkpoints! Scanners! Spotter planes! Attack rotors!"

He hated his shrieking, but he wanted someone to reply, because he didn't have the answers himself. He struggled on the path, thinking: I'm on the ground! It wasn't even a real path—just the trampings of the feet up ahead.

"You'll figure something out," Echols said. "You're a smart kid."

Gumbie said, "And we'll give you some help, Fish."

They trusted him: they really believed he had the answers. He had overcome his fear of them, but this made him feel friendly toward them. They expected him to get them out of here. Was that possible? He realized the complication of having to save them in order to save himself. But walking to New York!

The name of the city made him think of his room, and Pap blinking at him; clean clothes, his bed, the bath, and a jelly sandwich and Guppy-Cola on a tray. He thought of his high cameras, and the view west that was always layered blue and purple over the dust-haze—the horizon that looked like sediment. He had been looking in this direction. He was now on the ground, part of the dust and residue he had always frowned at.

By noon they were trailing along the lower edge of the pan, where there was hickory shade. They kept to a steady pace until, near a rockslide, Mr. Blue led them to a pile of sprouting leaves and stalks that was tangled in a black patch of earth. It was a spring, rising out of the ground and seeping back.

"You smelled it," Fisher said, wondering how.

He picked some purplish leaves while the rest were drinking.

"What's the name of these?" he said. He had folded them, making a sandwich of them, and was about to stuff them into his mouth—he was certain he had eaten this cabbage before.

"We call that Sudden Death," Rooks said, and laughed as Fisher dropped the leaves and squawked.

But after that they showed him how to find potato beans and hawthorn buds and wild plums; and how to split roots and roast them and how to beat berries off the bushes. They tore up some weeds and said they were good for tea. They told him to crush the leaves and smell his fingers.

He put his fingers into the front of his mask and said, "Chewing gum. Toothpaste. Room freshener—the stuff you squirt in the bathroom. What is it?"

"Mint."

He did not hate them anymore. He pitied their foolishness and simplicity, and he wanted them to succeed, so that he would make it home. But they were aliens: savages didn't think ahead—illegals never made plans.

It was bright late afternoon when they stopped to make camp. They did not speak. Mr. Blue paused and they did the same, and when he began prowling they gathered grass for tufts to sit on, or looked for firewood, or sorted the food—wild food for them, provisions for Fisher.

They murmured as they went about their duties, not seeming to notice they were in a wasteland. It was wilderness! But they turned their backs on it and did their chores. Fisher wondered how long it would be before they died doing that.

"Do we have to sleep on the floor?"

"Not the floor, Fish. The ground. It's called the ground."

"And, Fish," Valda said. "It's bad manners to talk while you're yawning."

He laughed at this alien talking about manners—she had once tried to stuff her oinkers into his mouth!

It turned cool after dark, but the fire was doused nonetheless, so it wouldn't be seen. There were no planes today, they said, but there had been some recently. They said: Your people must be searching for you, Fish.

Fisher was glad they didn't ask him why. He knew that

none of the Allbrights liked him very much, and the Murdicks and the Eubanks and everyone actually disliked him. He thought: If you're indifferent to people they hate you. Now they wanted him back. He had been stolen by aliens—that was the reason. They didn't even know these aliens!

"You see something?" Fisher asked.

Valda was looking at the sky.

"Stars," she said. "Aren't they beautiful?"

"Arcturus in Boötes. The Galactic Equator. Hyades." He pointed. "And that thing that looks like Capella is a satellite. I've got an instrument in my emergency kit that will give me our position to five decimal places. Want the coordinates?" He was still looking at the starry sky. "Talking of pulsars, a few years ago I monitored energy emissions from pulsars in the Crab Nebula." Then, "Betelgeuse– "

He kept talking. At last he said, "Yeah, beautiful." And then they gave him a blanket and gathered themselves into a pig-pile under blankets to sleep.

Fisher crept away from them and lay in the darkness. It was always so noisy in the open air. Where were the solitude and silence people always talked about? The air crackled with the sound of beetles and locusts, and there was a continual rustle of insect wings.

Without asking whether it was all right they had placed their trust in him. *You'll figure something out.* He was grateful for their silent ways. What if they had asked him pointblank what his strategy would be? He would have had to admit that he didn't know how to get back to New York without a bird or a rotor; that he was afraid they would fail; that failure might mean dying. He had never walked anywhere. He might have said, "Let's stay right here in O-Zone and figure this thing out." But they had not asked.

It grew colder, and though they were sheltered by the sides of the pan, and there was no wind, Fisher shivered in his suit. The suit was in tatters—the elbows torn, tubes showing in the knees, the collar fastening gone. His helmet made his head hot, but when he took it off the cold penetrated to his skull.

From the pile of six aliens came the low rumble and flutterblast of snores. Fisher was wide-awake with discomfort, squatting in the dust and listening. He hesitated, and then he crawled forward and took his helmet off. An owl called out three clear hoots from a treetop. Fisher burrowed into the pig-pile between Mr. Blue and Valda, and sighed, and was soon asleep in that warm space.

This walk across O-Zone was not proving as bad as he had feared. Until now, he had kept himself apart from Mr. Blue, from everyone except Valda—that crazy spasm of hers; but she hadn't repeated it. Except for that, he had been alone, almost from the moment of his abduction.

Now solitude was not possible. The walking was hard, food and water were limited, and the nights were chilly. So he became one of them—walking in the column during the day, kneeling around the fire in the late afternoon, and part of the pig-pile at night. It vaguely disgusted him, but he had no choice. How else could he survive? He could not separate himself from them. Alone, he would die of exposure.

He came to see that these people survived because they had made themselves into an organism. It had been an accident, like the accumulation of a ball of fluff. They had been lucky in O-Zone; they had found everything they needed, they had lived by raiding the ghost towns, and they had stayed away from the areas of high radiation. The organism was a simple and fairly horrible thing: it was a blob, but it worked. It made headway through the wilderness, and when Fisher was part of it he felt anonymous.

They came to one of those towns—Talmadge, it was called, and on that same sign, *Visit the Distillery and the Old Undershot Mill.* But Rooks said he didn't see any Old Mill, and Gumbie said, "There's an ice-cream parlor." Talmadge had a town hall and a creek running through it—a trickle, but it had once been deep, from the look of the dam. The wrecked building on the dam must have been the mill. The town seemed full of bees, which gave it a hot, sleepy atmosphere. The lizards did not move from the sunlit shingles where they clung. The board fences had fallen.

"You're always talking about going to the bathroom, Fish," said Echols.

It was true: he used that expression whenever he unzipped his suit.

"Here's your chance," Echols said. He was pointing to a sign, *Rest Rooms.*

The main street was in good shape, but the gutters were weedy, and the trees had burst the sidewalks with their roots.

"I'd like to look in some of those houses," Fisher said.

"You wouldn't find much," Valda said. "We've looked in lots of places like this. Even lived in some."

"We don't need anything here," Mr. Blue said.

They walked through the town without entering a building, without disturbing anything, and it seemed to Fisher as though the town was not dead but asleep, and they had not woken it.

Afterward, he had a vivid memory of the town—its still-white houses, and the sturdy bridge over the creek, and the shady streets. It was a decent place. It hadn't been vandalized. No evidence of aliens having raided it. The people from Talmadge had moved out their belongings, and locked their houses, and driven off. It was in a curve of the road, its lilacs were huge and untrimmed, the houses had porches. You probably wouldn't even need a breathing mask here. Fisher hadn't been afraid: Talmadge was a pretty little place—he congratulated himself on thinking that was so— and it was still in his memory, sunny and buzzing.

But he admitted that there were times when he was afraid. It was intelligent fear, he told himself. These aliens hadn't thought ahead—they solved problems when they encountered them: they did not anticipate them. Mr. Blue was fine, but he was only a twig they clung to. It was so far an organism without a brain.

"You do everything the hard way," Fisher said.

"That's the best way, the hard way," Mr. Blue said.

He actually believed that! Fisher said, "Sure, if you're a per-vert."

Mr. Blue said softly, "We are what we are because of our difficulties. We faced them together. If it had been easy we would have come apart. Difficulties showed us how to live here—doing things the hard way. That's why this trip is probably a good idea."

If you're weak you need to stick together, Fisher thought. But he had only noticed this after he had joined them. He told himself he wasn't weak; he felt safer among them. But what next?

They covered the distance, one hundred and twenty-two clicks, in five days.

On that fifth day, Mr. Blue said, "That's the States."

"What the heck's this?" Fisher said, knowing the man could not say *This is our quarter*.

"This whole thing's the Territory."

"O-Zone, yeah," Fisher said. "And what's that again?"

"That's the United States."

"You are such an unbelievable tool," the boy said, feeling anxious and abusive.

They were at the edge of the last margin of woods, looking out across the long bald stretch of land that only Fisher called the Red Zone Perimeter.

"It's high security," he said. "It's deadly—there's commandos all over it."

Mr. Blue said, "Don't get upset, Fish. I always figured it was a good thing. It kept people out of the Territory, until recently."

The rest of them watched the flat land with interest, and Fisher gathered that Mr. Blue was probably the only one of them who had seen it before. And yet none of them seemed frightened—because they had no idea of the security here.

"Now what are you going to do?" Fisher asked.

Mr. Blue smiled at him and he wished he had not asked the question.

The man said, "Don't you want to go home, Fish?"

"This thing's lethal! There are aerial patrols with high-resolution cameras! They can shoot on sight!"

Fisher felt shabby and ill-prepared in his tattered suit and bruised helmet. He had not thought about Hooper for days, but he considered how his uncle had flown away without him, leaving him on the ground with these aliens, and all his bitterness and self-pity returned. That fuck-wit, that herbert, that willy. And he hadn't come back! In his anger was a measure of pride that he had done something that Hooper could never have managed: he had survived among these aliens, and more than that, he had walked across O-Zone. Hooper hadn't even been able to pilot his jet-rotor into the zone.

"The thing about those patrols," Echols was saying, "is they're just routine spotter flights. The high-resolution cameras mean that they're flying at tremendous altitudes. They've got so much technology they don't trust the naked eye."

"We're on the ground," Fisher cried.

"We're safer on the ground. If we were in a plane they'd take us out."

"If we walk across that perimeter we'll get burned. It's probably mined."

"No. It's a beam," Echols said. "Ask Mr. B"—and Mr.

Blue nodded—"It's the kind of chemical laser you're always boasting about. It's a red stripe running around the middle. You've just got to think of a way of interrupting it."

Fisher glanced around. Their mouths were open, which gave them, he thought, the look of hungry monkeys.

"You can't interrupt it, you dong!" Fisher said, and they shut their mouths. "It's a coherent flow of beta flakes! About ten kilojoules of energy per square centimeter! You don't just stick your hand up and block it!" Fisher turned to Mr. Blue. "This total dick wants to get us all killed!"

"That's why I'm putting you in charge," Mr. Blue said.

A scarcely human sound came out of Fisher's mask: it was a mutter of pleasure, but there was a small squawk of vengeance in it.

"Yeah," Fisher said.

Someone sneezed—the dust was terrible here because of the defoliated perimeter. And not only no trees, it had also been bulldozed flat, the whole boundary.

"Shut up—I'm thinking," Fisher said, and continued thinking aloud, saying, "Because if you could block it you'd be in trouble. They'd pinpoint your interruption and get at you from an attack rotor. No, the best way is to slip under it. We don't know the wavelength—okay, that doesn't matter. They're using about four megawatts. I've got six to ten in the short term. That chemical laser is practically on the ground—that's why this place has been leveled, to keep the beam low, to prevent any infiltration. Funnily enough, they never thought of clandestine exfiltration."

"What's that?" Gumbie asked.

"What we're doing."

"We'll never slip under something that's lying on the ground, unless we dig under it."

"There's no time for digging," Fisher said. "We bend it, instead. Boost it up a meter or so—give it an arch, using an alternative force field."

He saw that their mouths had dropped open again.

"With a counterbeam. It's fiber optics, fuck-wit. The beam bends." He was speaking into their mouths. "This weapon can do it. We just program it to fire a continuous exode full of Antigons."

"I've never heard of those," Echols said.

"Of course you haven't."

"I was a physicist, you dipshit!"

"I only discovered Antigons last year, wang-face!"

And then Echols smiled, and conceded the argument to Fisher and said he wanted to know more. But Fisher said it would take too long to explain, and even then they would probably not understand.

"An exode full of Antigons," Gumbie said. "That's powerful medicine!"

Mr. Blue said, "Give him room."

Fisher had never believed that he would be having this conversation early on a summer afternoon in this wild place of hot dust and still air, on the perimeter of the famous wilderness. He had always regarded himself as a theoretical physicist, dealing in the symbols at the margin of the keyboard and describing hypothetical forces. He had regarded numbers as primitive and misleading, like primary colors; but now he knew what "primitive" meant.

It meant this—these people in this place, sitting in the dust needing to be saved. And not just these aliens. "Primitive" meant everything outside his room at Coldharbor. Compared to the life he had led and the work he had done, all this was the past, and in some cases the distant past. He was with a tribe of savages, but even the commandos and technicians who secured the Red Zone were primitive—just a step up from the aliens. Their goonish delusion was their settled belief that they had the perfect security beam. But it could be bent!

"What if we get chased?"

"We'll unbend the beam and drop it on their heads!" He felt giddy, and then he went breathless again. "But they might try to jump us before we get set up."

"Then we'll burn them to a crisp," Mr. Blue said.

"Yeah."

The particle beam which Fisher had reprogrammed was mounted on a stone pedestal and secured with wire. Fisher gave the orders, panting and screeching as time passed. By late afternoon he was making his final adjustments. He had grown crankier as he worked—and more abusive. He had begun by shouting "Out of my way!" and "I'm in charge!" and at the end he was crying "Aliens! Aliens!" Then he went silent.

"The light's going."

"What's on the other side?"

"This dip better know what he's doing."

Fisher wasn't listening. He moved as though he was deaf, in a ponderous and mechanical way, and then he said softly, "We'll have to leave this beam to self-destruct, you know." There was steam on the inside of his faceplate, dust on the outside—smears of effort. "Then we won't have a weapon."

"We'll steal one. We'll snatch as many as you want."

"Yeah," Fisher said, and he brightened. "Hey, I keep forgetting you aliens are good at that!"

He did not notice the silence then.

"We've got about eight minutes to get across, and then it's out of power, the weapon self-destructs and the laser straightens—the kink goes out of it. We have to be on the other side by then."

He moved his thumbs on the weapon that aimed across the perimeter.

"It's working," he said. "My seven megawatts are boosting that beam. Hear it?"

There was a small continuous sound, like a bee in a jar.

"This is crazy. I don't see anything," Valda said.

"Believe me, I've made a space through there."

"Lead the way, Fish."

Fisher locked his faceplate and set off, holding his head down. The others followed in single file, keeping themselves at the same angle, as if ducking a low ceiling.

They were halfway across the gravelly perimeter when a spotter gunship appeared overhead and began maneuvering back and forth. As the gunship bounced, a ground patrol emerged in a dust cloud from the O-Zone side of the perimeter. It was a half-track, with a rack of missiles on its roof, and it was painted in both Federal and Red Zone stripes. It swerved and rattled at great speed toward the point in the perimeter where Fisher and the others had entered.

It had been Fisher's intention to make them believe that a break had occurred in the beam—after all, seven people were running across the perimeter. The driver of the half-track must have been fooled, because he raised his head above the hatch and steered forward, giving chase. Still speeding, he headed toward the ragged bent-over fugitives.

"Hurry up!" Fisher shrieked. He was sobbing with fear, and trapped in his helmet his voice deafened him for a while. He did not know that no one could hear him. "Clear the beam! It's going off! They're coming after us!"

His honking voice, crying *Hot pursuit,* rang inside his head.

But as he had promised, the beam wavered and went off. There was no question of that, and although they could not see it die or see the meltdown of its self-destruction, that puff of smoke, there was another piece of proof. At the moment the Red Zone beam dropped and reasserted itself against the perimeter, the half-track was passing through it, and the vehicle exploded with its commandos. Its four missiles were ineffectually launched into the air in a succession of gusts.

"No one's ever done that before," Fisher was saying.

He liked speaking with his helmet on and his faceplate propped up. He believed it gave a special and rather eerie quality to his voice.

"They've penetrated hyperspace, they're living in orbit, and there's a station on the moon. But no one's ever exfiltrated O-Zone!"

They were pig-piled under a bluff in a shallow cave of loose earth. Their instinct was to hide. On the way out they had crossed an old road and had seen some houses that may have been inhabited. Each of the houses had a sign on it saying *For Sale*. That was how you knew there had been a vast excursion of nuclear waste; half a state declared a Prohibited Area; America's first O-Zone; a monumental catastrophe: the bungalows just outside it had *For Sale* signs nailed to their walls. Fisher said wasn't that incredible!

The others were silent.

"They tried to nuke us. We destroyed those fuck-wits!"

Their breathing made the pile rise and fall. They had never even thought of breaking out before! This was as strange to them as O-Zone was to him. He had opened the door and let them out. And though he understood their fear, and had once shared it, he felt powerful here.

"Yeah. I like it on the ground."

Something happened to the sky the next day—it swelled, its dome grew and became cluttered with folding clouds, and even the horizon advanced to a greater distance and became as ambiguous as dust. But it was not the sky, it was the water beneath it, a slipping gray-green thing like another bald perimeter littered with branches and broken crates and odd bottles and logs, and the far bank trimmed so low that it seemed like more water.

"This here's the Mighty Miss," Gumbie said.

Hearing it said like that, Fisher wanted to cry, he was so pleased.

"I know," he said, but he hadn't taken it to be water. He had never imagined a river could look like this—he had only seen it from the tapes, when they had highballed overhead. But it was so different on the ground. It had a smell, it had a sound.

They lashed two logs together and made a long narrow raft that carried them up on a back-current and then downstream to the far shore. The river was so muddy it seemed to have no depth at all—they worried about going aground, though they bobbed like all the other pieces of spring flotsam.

"This suit has a buoyancy feature," Fisher said, and nearer the Illinois side he jumped in, shouting, "Wet exit!"

He was submerged in the river to his chin, and his helmet was all that showed. It was as though he were walking on the bottom. The raft made the shore, but the boy still paddled in his slow upright way. He was enjoying being a speck in this waterworld. His helmet bobbed across the water like a bucket in a flood.

"Fish," someone said.

They had seen Winslow some way off—the buildings, then the route signs, and at last the *For Sale* signs. Winslow's watchtowers seemed particularly ominous, and the land was flat enough for the checkpoints to be visible as gates on the highway. So they left the road and detoured around the town. High fences drove them farther away. They crossed farmland, some of it neglected and some of it still in use. The strips of trees that had been left as windbreaks had widened into shaggier patches of woods.

"There's plenty of water here," Mr. Blue said.

In O-Zone they had traveled only during the day; now, on the outside they traveled only at night. They marched quietly in the darkness. This terrain was different—wetter and unfamiliar. Unlike O-Zone it had a human smell—air soured by smoke, a whiff of decay, a sharpness in the light breeze that caught on their faces.

Keeping away from the lights of the town, they strayed into a cluster of darkened buildings, and they crouched near them until long after sunup, when it became clear that the place had been abandoned.

They sheltered in the farmhouse that day. They were disgusted by its dry rot and flimsy construction—the sagging roof, the shaky floor. The windows were dirty and useless, the barns still stank of sweating animals—of death and dirt. Rusty refrigerator, rusty kitchen machines, a sink full of spiders and mouse droppings, and strewn on the floor of another room old books that smelled like corpses.

"Is the United States all like this?"

Echols said no; Rooks said yes.

Fisher said, "I don't know!"

They moved into the overgrown garden, among fat flowering bushes and fir trees that had grown into steeples. Here they slept, beneath the sounds of insects and birds, while Fisher rummaged. His success had given him strength.

He found the car first—sunk in the driveway, buried to its fenders. Then he saw the dish and the cable, and he felt at last that he was in the same country as his mother and Hardy and that dimbo Hooper. He still had his helmet. He was glad that, even when it had seemed heavy, and he might have managed better without it, he had not chucked it. An alien would have shit-canned it! But the helmet had become a home to him, and he had stuck himself into it, and inhabited it, and had felt less lonely. He had not used the phone functions since his abduction—what was the point? It had a range of less than a hundred clicks. But using this dish to create a satellite link would extend its range, and he could transmit by relay.

He wished the aliens had been awake to see him tinkering with the dish and taking a reading of the sun. He took a malicious pleasure in mystifying them—there was power in mystery! He wanted to tease them, too. "What do you think I'm doing now?" he wanted to say. He could see them making monkey mouths. He wanted to quiz them and prove they were ignorant. "I live here," he could tell them. "This is my home!"

But he did not wake them. They knew now how smart he was. And why hurt them when he had gone to so much trouble to save them? The coordinates in his reading shocked him. He was still so far from New York! He put his helmet on to calm himself, and then he made a test transmission. He could not raise anyone at Coldharbor.

Then Hardy's voice, a recorded message: *The Allbrights are presently traveling in Africa and are unobtainable. Please store your name and number on the following—*

They had gone on vacation. They had known he had been abducted in O-Zone by aliens, and had packed their bags and gone tootling off to Africa, to sun themselves at some crummy garrison resort! The careless, lazy, irresponsible fuck-wits! Not only had they done nothing to help, they were not even in position when he needed them.

He began squawking. "Have completed clandestine exfiltration O-Zone. The coordinates of my present position are—"

He felt his strength return as he spoke, and he was powerful again, sitting under the trees among the wildly growing plants—the long-necked flowers and the shrubby garden— talking calmly on his satellite link to Coldharbor, using the dish in the yard and the booster in his helmet. He saw himself in the most dramatic way, like a man on a lonely mission to another planet.

When he had finished he stood up and faced Mr. Blue, who had been sneakily waiting for him to finish and perhaps incriminate himself.

"Who were you talking to?"

"Nobody."

That was not odd: he spent most days talking to himself, usually in two voices, young and old, a challenging one and a reasonable one, and when he went to the bathroom—as he put it—he talked the whole time, murmuring and reasoning with himself, though he was only dimly aware of it.

"I heard you, Fish."

"There was no one at the other end."

And why was this so? He had been away, kidnapped in a Prohibited Area for over two months. They knew he had been stolen—Hooper knew, and of course he had told them. They had not found him! They weren't home! The answering machine didn't even say where in Africa they were. They didn't care that he was being held captive by aliens!

Fisher was angry that he could not tell Mr. Blue how he had been abandoned by the Allbrights.

He said, "Why don't you let me go?"

Mr. Blue wore a smile of strain, his lips drawn down and his eyes hollow. His voice was a whisper in a monotone. Fisher knew the man was angry, but he felt stronger now—he had shown them he could work wonders.

"We'll leave you here, if you want," Mr. Blue said.

All at once it seemed a terrible place—dangerous, worse than O-Zone, probably full of crooked police.

Fisher said, "If I hadn't pushed that beam up you'd never have slipped out of O-Zone."

Mr. Blue said, "You'd have starved without us. You'd be dead by now. There's bears and bobcats in the Territory. You didn't even know that."

"Who stole me in the first place!"

But even Fisher saw the absurdity in arguing outdoors—yelling hoarsely under the sun that dazzled the whole sky.

"Your uncle snatched Bligh," Mr. Blue said. "And when we get her back we'll hand you over. Why else do you think we're going to New York?"

"We'll never get there," Fisher said, suddenly despairing and seeing this vast landscape of grass as an inescapable trap.

"Any other way is dangerous for us. We'd be ambushed. If we stay in control we'll make it. But if you contact your people you'll weaken our position, and then we'll all be in danger."

The phrase *your people* sounded so cold. It reminded him that he was a prisoner.

"You need my brains!" Fisher said.

"You need us, too," Mr. Blue said. In his quiet anger there was a kindliness, something reasonable and gentle. It was why they followed him.

A bird started squawking, and Fisher thought how stupid all animals sounded when they cried out.

"Remember we're in this together," Mr. Blue said, and he glanced back at the aliens slumbering under the trees. "Don't betray those people."

More birds came down like scraps of paper in the field.

"If you weaken us you'll be weak too," Mr. Blue said. "You can still die."

His parting words silenced Fisher. And now he was waking the others. They had planned to stay another day here, but Mr. Blue had probably not believed him when he said he was talking to himself—probably suspected the message, because he changed his plans. At nightfall they set off through the fields under a horn of moon.

Mr. Blue had alarmed him by reminding him how he depended on them. He wondered whether he should risk another message—or should he simply trudge with them until it was over?

He had also come to see this trekking as a pleasure. It had been very hard, but he had survived the hard part, and now his pride helped him on. They were not in O-Zone any longer. This was middle America under a huge sky—balmy late-spring days, thickened with heat. And when he wasn't worried he felt himself part of this band of people—and not an alien but their secret leader. *You need my brains.* Mr. B had not denied it!

They continued into the night, past the eastern side of Winslow. They heard a chugging, like a motorboat. Fisher said it was probably an old rotor. But the sound merged into a pair of yellow lights coming toward them on the ground, and they saw they were near a road.

Mr. Blue said, "It takes guts to drive out here."

"It looks pretty damn safe to me," Echols said.

"No, no," Mr. Blue said softly. He was smiling in the dark—Fisher could tell. The man knew something. "There's hijackers around."

"Where?" Fisher said.

Mr. Blue showed Fisher his moon-white face.

"Right here, boy."

He told them to pile straw and grass on the road, a bar of it, from one side to the other. He had wanted to use branches, but there were none around—no big trees. Fisher complained that they were so backward out here they cut down trees for fuel. The willies burned trees to keep themselves warm!

"That's the idea," Mr. Blue said.

When the next vehicle approached they lit the straw and fanned it with their shirts.

The truck did not stop, but it slowed down, and Mr. Blue, Rooks, and Echols leapt aboard, catching hold of the ropes on the load—no shouts, no orders, just grunts and the movements of three men who looked magnetized.

They were carried by the roaring truck into the darkness, leaving four people standing by the scattered fire.

"Now we're completely ballistic," Fisher said, and his voice broke. "Those fuck-wits left us! They're gone!"

He felt the night close over him like a rising tide.

Before he gathered his strength to cry out again, the ten-wheeler returned, Mr. Blue in the driver's seat.

"I'm navigator," Fisher said. "I'm riding up front."

32

"WE STILL GET MARRIED OUT HERE—'COURSE WE DO—
and we take our weddings kind of seriously in Guthrie," the
old man said slowly. He paused to let this sink in, so that
what he was about to say would sound like an outrage.

But he was too slow, and while he fuddled with his pipe a
red-faced woman behind him said, "They were animals. The
one wearing the helmet was the worst."

"He told us to call him Batfish," someone else said.

The old man resumed. "We had a preacher and a church
full of people. The whole entire town was there. And there
was food in the Grange Hall, three tables of it—a real
spread."

They were in the Guthrie courthouse. Hardy often heard
of such buildings, and had seen some, but he had never been
inside one. It was wood-paneled and smelled of dented var-
nish and leather cushions. It had an American flag, the state
flag, and three paintings in gold frames. The big lollipop-
shaped fan was dead. Hardy wondered whether they held
trials here, but he feared that if he asked they might take it as
a rude question—a suggestion that they were ridiculously
old-fashioned. But they probably did have trials here, and
church services down the street, and Future Farmers meetings in the Grange Hall. They had weddings!

Sluter was seated at the judge's high bench, Meesle and
Murdick on either side, all of them in their Godseye uniforms, with the Snake-Eaters insignia; high-tech helmets with
the faceplates down; and they spoke through the amplifiers in
the grillwork of the throatpiece—it made a piercing sound.

434

Their flying suits were black, with blacked-out masks, and their antenna-coils shining silver. They had put on this battle gear when the alarm came from the station at Guthrie.

Nothing had ever seemed so incongruous to Hardy as the sight of these three vigilantes—they were wearing gloves, too!—in the wood-paneled courtroom. The Guthrie people said they would agree to testify only if they could remain anonymous—no names, no IDs, no numbers. And no cameras or recording devices in the courtroom. They were anonymous—anonymity made them talkative. Hardy had already heard an hour of this.

"After the church service, some of us went next door to make sure everything was ready. And that's when we saw them. Must have been ten of them."

"They looked like wolves, with food in their hands and food all over their faces," a woman said. To justify her interruption she glanced around, showing an insulted expression, as though she had been wronged. "They just stood in the hall—didn't even run."

"They were all in old shoes, except for him."

Sluter said, "Why didn't you burn them down right there, knowing they were aliens?"

"They were armed," a young man complained. "They had our weapons! We weren't allowed to take our irons into the church for the wedding. We left them here with the food, assuming they'd be safe. That's the last time we make that mistake. They were the ugliest goddamn people I've ever seen."

"'Don't move,' they said—"

Witnesses were leaping to their feet all over the courtroom.

"'Don't do nothing. If you follow us, you burn.' The one with the helmet, he was the worst one. 'We'll nuke you. We'll lay the land open and drop you into the crack.' Stuffing sandwiches into his face mask the whole time."

"They would have killed someone, if we hadn't agreed."

Now Hardy spoke up for the first time. He was sitting under the American flag, on the steps of the aisle. He had taken his helmet off. He had become worried by the anger of the townspeople, and especially by the effect it was having on the Snake-Eaters.

"They didn't kill that truck driver," Hardy said. "They just threw him out of his cab."

"They hijacked the vehicle," Meesle said, leaning over to look at Hardy. "That's grounds for hot pursuit. The shoot-on-sight rule applies."

"No one was hurt here in Guthrie," Hardy said.

"They terrorized us," the old man said. "Anyone who doesn't call that a crime is as bad as they are."

Hardy knew he was losing. For the past two days the Gods-eye troopers had talked of nothing but killing the aliens. "Or else we don't have the right to call ourselves Snake-Eaters." It had been bad enough receiving explicit encouragement from the commandos at the Red Zone Perimeter; but the discovery of Hooper and that girl at the farm outside Winslow had maddened them much more.

"This mission is classified," Sluter had said to Hooper. "I could have killed you and your pup!"

Hooper had been shaken by the surprise visit from Gods-eye; and he had appealed to Hardy: "Let me help you look for the kid."

"We're looking for outlaws," Sluter said. "They out-smarted you—you lost the kid. You gave that kid away!"

"Please don't follow us," Hardy said, for what good had Hooper been so far? He had lied, he had stalled, he had been ineffectual, he seemed to care only for this young girl. "We can handle it. We'll find him."

And so Hooper Allbright had been left behind, but that conversation between him and the Snake-Eaters had seemed to whip up their blood. They were furious when they left him, and Hardy feared that in their anger they might kill Fizzy too. Now, in Guthrie, they seemed to make no distinction between Fizzy and the aliens—it was as though Fizzy had become an outlaw himself. And then he began to wonder whether the boy was still among them.

"Wasn't there a young boy there?" he asked in the Guthrie courtroom.

"They were all old and dirty," a man said.

"The one in the suit and helmet?"

"Old and dirty."

"I've never seen clothes like that," the red-faced woman said in a disgusted way. "Even Roaches and Trolls, the pictures I've seen of them, don't look that bad. We never had the real thing here. I guess we've been lucky—Guthrie's a quiet place. It's terrible to think there's creatures like that around."

"We'll find them," Meesle said. "We know what to do with them."

Hardy said, "I think they might have ditched Fizzy."

"He's with them. 'Batfish.' The one in the helmet. Snatching food. The worst one. That's got to be him."

"He's fifteen years old!"

"He seems to be able to look after himself," Meesle said.

Hardy hoped that was so—hoped Fizzy was alive and not in a ditch, where the aliens had thrown him after taking his suit and helmet. Hardy hated this talk of pursuit and pouncing, and though he was sorry he had started them on this chase, he was glad he was still with them: he still believed he might be able to restrain them. But Fizzy might not even be alive, and if he were, Hardy wondered whether he would be able to rescue the boy from their onslaught.

"I want to take down the testimony of everyone in this town who saw these aliens," Sluter said from the judge's bench. "I don't care about your names and addresses. But I need a complete list of missing articles and a description of the creatures."

Hardy listened very carefully to the statements. And he was impressed by the gentle, outdoor faces of the townspeople—their bewilderment seemed like kindliness. They were surprised and insulted that Guthrie had been invaded. They said they knew such things happened near Chicago and St. Louis, and all over the east—and no one was safe in Florida. But Guthrie was poor, remote, and self-sufficient. It was full of woodburners and simple-lifers. They had two gas stations. They made bread here, they raised chickens, they went to school, they got married. No one ever moved here and in the past few years they had hardly bothered to operate the checkpoints except when they received a raid alert, which was not even twice a year.

And that was why they had been so scared when they saw those aliens chewing their food and taking their weapons in the Grange Hall. This was the nightmare they had always been warned about by the Federal marshals. They saw how easily they had been invaded and now they would have to go back to the old time-wasting ID system, and all the checks: scanners, roadblocks, watchtowers, and aerial patrols.

"We can't afford that," they said.

"Want to know the price you pay for not securing your-

selves?" Sluter asked them. And then he told them the price,
in the Godseye formula: aliens, blacks, prostitutes, polygamists . . .

The aliens had come straight up the interstate, I-92, and
had turned off at Exit 29, the main road into Guthrie. They
had driven their ten-wheeler down Main Street without anyone stopping them. No one had even noticed that aliens had
come to town!

They had abandoned the truck on Curtis Street, behind the
bowling alley, and as it was a Saturday afternoon (this witness pronounced the word *Sarradee*)—and a wedding day—
all the stores were closed and no one was in the center of
town. That was a big mistake. The aliens had broken in
Warwick's and taken six pairs of trousers, a box of assorted
sweatshirts, five blankets, and some haversacks. They must
have stashed them, because they were not wearing any of
those clothes when they were next seen.

"Only six pairs of trousers," Hardy said, so that they would
remember.

But Sluter urged the witness to continue. "Where were
they seen?"

This was at Arthur's Rod and Gun on the Service Road
entrance. A woman passing on her way to the wedding had
seen some people fiddling with the steel shutters. She had
thought it was kids. There hadn't been aliens here for years—
high-school kids sometimes caused trouble, but aliens were
the last creatures she would have expected, though one alien
had apparently worked in the box factory for years without
anyone knowing.

"You mentioned kids," Hardy said. "So there might have
been a young boy among them?"

"Nope," the woman said, and Hardy hated her certainty.
She said she had *thought* they were kids, but later she realized they were adults behaving like kids, as aliens did.

A man stood up and said he was Arthur, the owner of the
shop, and that he could confirm that there had been damage
to the lock on the steel shutters. Nothing had been stolen
from him.

But Fizzy would have been able to burst a lock, Hardy
thought, and again began to doubt that the boy had been
among the aliens the woman had seen.

"It doesn't look too good for your kid," Meesle said, rubbing it in with a sort of cruel commiseration. "They might have chewed him up and spit out the pieces."

Hardy looked fiercely into the black faceplate: there was no face visible.

"But they're not going to chew us up," Meesle went on, defying Hardy.

It was now three in the afternoon. When the Godseye gunship landed just before noon it seemed that the only sighting had been at the Grange Hall—the aliens plundering the reception, stuffing their mouths with food, and warning the wedding guests to keep away. There was one story.

Murdick had said, "Let's go after the bastards!"

But Sluter said no. "Everyone's story is the same," he said. "That proves they're lying."

So he had held the hearing in the courthouse; and more sightings were remembered. *You don't forget a thing like that,* one man said, contradicting himself. The aliens had been seen behind the town hall, near Jack's Tractors and the Redemption Center and the firehouse; at the baseball field, near the War Memorial and on the way to the high school. Some people had seen two or three, others swore there were a dozen, and one man had seen twenty, marching four abreast like a color guard. They were bearded, they were black, they were dark, they were ragged, they were doglike; you couldn't see their eyes.

One man denied these various descriptions. "They blended in perfectly," he said. "They could have been citizens of Guthrie—let me finish!—on their way to the wedding. That's why I wasn't suspicious."

A woman said that she had seen some men, stark naked, at her bedroom windows. They had climbed up to the windows and stood with their feet against the sills, pressing their bodies against the glass and darkening the room. While she was speaking, the woman became short of breath and began to sob, and then she broke down completely, uttering a little threadlike wail that resembled a distant cry in a tunnel.

"This unfortunate woman is not responsible for what she is saying," another witness said.

Sluter said, "She's clinical."

"She was evacuated from O-Zone," the witness said.

"Some of those people settled here in Guthrie. Most of them died."

A tally was made of everything the aliens had stolen. It was a very long list, and it included food, weapons, clothes, and electronic equipment.

"And you say they left town on foot with all this stuff?" Hardy asked.

When they were challenged, several more of the townspeople contradicted what they had said, or withdrew their testimony.

"Why don't you just go after them, and leave us alone?" a man said, exasperated by the questioning.

"We want to know the size of the problem," Sluter said. "We need some more numbers."

Hardy guessed that, faced with these different versions of the alien invasion, the Snake-Eaters were becoming nervous and perhaps afraid—and he knew this was worse, because it would make them uncontrollable. He had long ago decided that it was ignorant cowardice that had turned them into killers. They were afraid of the aliens, and hated them, and because Fizzy was with them he seemed like just another fugitive.

Slipping out of the courthouse by a side door, Hardy stepped into the glare of afternoon sunlight. The air tasted of hot painted shingles and the sweet-sour tang of fresh grass clippings. He passed a telephone cubicle and dialed Moura in New York. His call was shunted to the answering machine.

"I'm standing on the main street of a town called Guthrie. We haven't found Fizzy yet, though there's apparently a band of aliens roaming around. They were here this morning. But I don't know whether he's among them. Call me on the Godseye number if you get another message from him."

He wanted to say more, and imagining the tape spools turning in the machine, he was reminded of his hesitation. He glanced up and down the street.

"They have fire hydrants and streetlights."

There were trees planted by the roadside, and neither the firehouse nor the police station was fenced in.

"Guthrie is indescribable, Moura."

Some children passed him and then turned and stared at him.

"They think we're aliens here."

After he hung up he looked more closely at the town. It wasn't indescribable—he hated the word anyway, as a result of Fizzy mocking it: *Nothing is indescribable!* But the town was not like any he had seen for years. He realized he had traveled too much in poor countries, his work had taken him too far afield, he had neglected the heart of America. They were still walking around in overalls here, digging potatoes, burning wood, driving cars. Guthrie resembled Winslow in its small size and its lack of security. In its way it seemed a fine old town, even if here and there it was a bit battered.

A great fear had come and gone, taking some people with it and leaving a few landmarks, like the watchtowers and the checkpoints. That was about fifteen years ago—the terrible alien scare that occurred at the same time as O-Zone was declared a Prohibited Area, the two events in Hardy's lifetime that had changed the country most. But that was the past: Guthrie was asleep again. It wasn't worth plundering, it wasn't touched by the world, and it had simply continued to exist without much crime or much technology. It was a town that stayed home—and that was so rare in the world. The townspeople were largely unguarded and respectable. Today was one of their terrible days: they were reminded of their old fear.

But they would brighten up. Many of them were old folks, who would have been shocked to see New Yorkers in masks, or painted, or stark naked in jewels, or wearing nothing but aprons. Even these Godseye helmets and faceplates seemed to startle them, and the gunship parked on the lawn in front of the town hall was still attracting attention hours after it had landed. No one seemed to mind that its presence had snarled traffic and that the Godseye troopers were a greater source of interest than the aliens had been.

The people in Guthrie seemed decent—and they were not very angry. They carried weapons, of course, but that was an old habit and a hard one to break.

A woman who had seen Hardy at the courthouse stopped him on the sidewalk and invited him to her house.

"Want a piece of pie?"

The sentence was so strange to him he found himself saying no and translating it to himself; and then he laughed at its beauty.

The afternoon sun shone on Guthrie without heating it much this fading day in late spring. A light flutter ran through the leaves in the trees above Hardy's head, and a ripple in the ivy on the brick wall of the library made it seem like a curtain swelling in the breeze. He heard the taunt of children's voices several streets away. He had the strong sense that the town was alive. It was not only the children and the lawns and the people gathered on the sidewalks chattering about the aliens and the troopers—but the very houses looked alive. There was something handmade and human about their chimneys and windows, their fences and gardens. You could smell cooking here. No rotors in the sky—he hated the thought of that racket in New York.

He was outdoors at last. It was not the New York sense of safety he had, that came from being imprisoned on the island-city; it was a looser, easier feeling of well-being—and it helped to be away from the troopers and their obsessions. He was glad in Guthrie that such places existed, where you could breathe without a mask.

He hoped that Fizzy had come here and had time to experience the same feeling.

All this while he had been walking along side streets, to test his impressions. Then he heard a harmless commotion, and following the sound to a sloping road, he came to a brick-and-glass building. Just behind it, enclosed by a high fence, a group of people on a set of bleachers cheered a baseball game. He had thought the whole town had turned up at the courthouse to describe the invasion of aliens, but here were fifty people who hardly seemed to care.

He took off his helmet and boots, unzipped his flying suit and stepped out of it. He made his equipment into a bundle, which he tucked under his arm, and in his street clothes he entered the ballpark.

He had never been interested in baseball, but this previous lack of interest made him especially attentive now. A man stepped to the plate and after several swings hit the ball into the outfield. Hardy was inspired to clap with the spectators. This happened again—another hit. Hardy stood up with the rest of the people. Then a young man hit the ball over the far fence and Hardy heard himself yelling with pleasure.

It seemed to him that these people in Guthrie knew a secret that he was still learning. He wondered how many other towns there were like this in America. Few of the people were Owners, probably, but that did not seem to matter here. Most of them were visibly hard-up, yet had their lives changed? It was not that the town was poor or bankrupt and that there was no one in the watchtowers; but rather that it went on surviving in a dignified and tidy way. They still cut the grass, and weeded the flowers, and put up the flag: that didn't cost anything. Guthrie was like a memory—not his own, but a recollection of stories he had been told. It tormented him to know that after seeing the white frame house surrounded by the green lawn and the clipped hedge, he would have to go away.

That was what "indescribable" meant: what he had not told Moura. The simple truth had not struck him then. He wanted to call her back and say *This is the past.*

And that was why the town had most likely suffered a greater violation from Godseye than from those aliens. He thought: They don't want us here, they don't need us here. The aliens had swept through, reminding them of the old world. But Godseye was still there, hovering and murmuring, like the intimation of a new kind of terror—frightening everyone with its masks, and demanding information, and filling the citizens with dread.

"Evidently one of them got into the high school," Murdick said. "We've got a witness."

Murdick had seen Hardy on the porch of the courthouse, leaning against a column, and while Hardy waited he went inside and found the witness, a boy of nine. He had a bristly head and a broken front tooth and he wore a T-shirt lettered *Obee's Apple Farm.* He seemed particularly afraid of Murdick, who was still in his Godseye battle gear—black flying suit, black helmet and opaque mask; and he was gesturing with his explosive baton.

"It was over there," Murdick said, pointing the weapon in the direction of the school. "In the basement or something. Speak up, sonny."

"The cafeteria," the boy said, clearing his throat.

Hardy said, "Can you describe him?"

"Kind of old. Kind of strange."

"So it couldn't have been your kid," Murdick said.

"We'll be right back, Willis," Hardy said, and walked over to the school with the boy. He easily gained entrance. He remarked that nothing seemed to be locked around here. He had simply strolled into the ballpark and now they were in the school. The boy did not seem to understand, which

Hardy took as a sign that he did not find it remarkable. It really was the past.

"He came out of that door," the boy said.

The cafeteria smelled of bread crusts and stale milk and fried food and ammonia.

"Where did he go?"

"He saw me in here, eating my lunch. It was just before the game. The rest of the players left. But all I do is help with the scoreboard, so I had some extra time."

"Did he say anything to you?"

"He made a funny noise. Then he picked up my sandwiches and smelled them."

The boy straightened his shoulders—he was afraid, remembering, and his fear stiffened his posture.

"He took one of the sandwiches. He ate the whole thing. I didn't care, as long as he didn't hurt me. He kept making these noises."

The boy took a deep breath, but did not exhale.

"It was my jelly sandwich. Then he called me Herbert. I was afraid to tell him my real name's Glenn. I didn't even know he was an alien. I thought he might have been one of the welders from the garage. Was he going to kill me, mister?"

"No," Hardy said, and was greatly relieved. "But what's in that room?"

"Computers?" Nervousness had turned his answer into a question.

At the farmhouse near Winslow, Hooper had first regretted that he was being forced to stay behind—and he hated the humiliation of being threatened. But then he realized that the Godseye troopers were lost and that Hardy was merely a passenger, so what did it matter if he spent the night there with Bligh? They slept in the rotor and when the sunrise warmed the windows they woke and made love, and slept some more.

"Such long grass," she said later, and left the rotor and ran into it.

Hooper, seeing her disappear ahead of him, felt he was in danger of losing her—the feeling was very distinct after they made love.

"I'll never be able to please you," Hooper said.

"I'm pleased here," she said.

She was very bright. She had the ability of the young to bounce back. Her memory seldom seemed to trouble her. She laughed easily, and became passionate quickly, and when it passed she was talking about the watchtowers and were there rats in that house?

Hooper had made love to her in an urgent and subduing way and yet afterward felt like a victim of it. She made an attempt to reassure him; but she did not understand. It was another paradox of her being fifteen that she was practically unconscious of her body, and yet he could hardly take his eyes off her. She was always half-smiling and saying, *What are you looking at?* She didn't know!

He wanted her to desire something that only he could provide. He needed her to tell him what she wanted. And his motive was not only to make her happy, but to make himself happy that way. But she was happy with nothing, so he was left out.

"I hated those men," she said. She was so young her teeth still seemed a bit oversize and her neck very thin. Her breasts were small, yet they were still growing! "I think they're dangerous. Not your brother, but the others."

"My brother's afraid—and he's given up on me."

And Hardy had not heard the worst of it. Sluter had hissed at Hooper, "If you follow us we'll shoot you down."

And they had flown the Godseye gunship into the darkness, their rotor blades whanging the low branches.

But, after all, staying behind had given Hooper and Bligh the advantage. On their return from the walk they had heard a signal from the rotor. The receiver was taking a directed message from a town three hundred clicks east of here—Guthrie. It was Fizzy, driving a transmitter in the high-school computer room—he had started calling himself "commander" again—and aiming at the dish in this ruined garden.

He had probably just walked into the room and walked out, for Hooper's message was returned to him with the code comment: *Not receiving.*

"At least we know where to find him," Hooper said.

Flying east with Bligh, Hooper had heard the general alarm—the Guthrie transmission: alien alert. He realized then that he was too late to find the boy. The aliens had fled and taken Fizzy with them, and the Godseye gunship—he could hear Sluter roaring on the alien-alert frequency—was on its way to Guthrie. So Hooper had done nothing more than circle the town.

"It looks like a nice place," he said. "They're wearing skirts. God, I love the word 'skirts.' Want one?"

Bligh laughed and put her knees together, and they had flown on, scanning the ground for the fugitives.

33

FISHER'S MEMORY WAS PERFECT. HE HAD TOLD MR. BLUE that, yes, unfortunately, he was afraid of the dark—Moura's fault for mashing the lights off once when he was three—but it didn't matter if he went blind, because he could remember clearly everything he had ever seen. What was the point in seeing it over and over again with his eyes when it was printed perfectly on his brain? Experience and memory made eyesight irrelevant, and Fisher had always been bored by repetition. He had never believed that the world outside his room mattered much.

He felt so foolish now. He wasn't afraid of the dark anymore—why had he blurted it out to this alien? And there was the other error—a great deal worse.

Months ago in Firehills, at the New Year's party, he had run the tape of the trip out. The party guests had watched it and they had congratulated themselves on having taken such a dangerous trip to O-Zone. And then Fisher had analyzed it. In his analysis, ruined towns and mobs and beaten people had appeared in the long desolate panning shot from New York to O-Zone. It had all looked like a route through the worst part of America, and shaken-down places like Guthrie and Winslow and Loogootee and Seymour (they had just left Seymour today) had seemed dreadful: hot dangerous horror towns in the dusty midwest.

No—leave it out! He had been wrong. But how could he have been so wrong? Anyway, he knew it now: he was on the ground. The camera had lied, overdramatized the action, darkened the shadows, exaggerated the poverty and ruin.

And the scanner had overreacted. I was frightened, he explained to himself, so it seemed dangerous. But where was the danger here? It was not only bearable, it could be downright pleasant. Those savage-looking towns were a pushover—practically harmless. The patched streets and stained roofs and empty watchtowers of these so-called outposts had misled him. They were simple little places! They had drugstores and bus stations and supermarkets and high schools. The stoplights worked. No one wore helmets, very few wore masks.

Fisher had said beforehand, "You're going to see some dongs and dimbos running around naked, pretending they're Starkies. Guys in horror-masks. Women in aprons, with their bums sticking out and their oinkers joggling. It's the fashion."

He had been thinking of New York. It was all he knew. But in Guthrie the people wore dungarees and overalls and sweaty hats, and some women wore skirts. The children ate ice cream. The wedding was well-attended. White dresses. Flowers. Church bells rang.

"Just because people are poor it doesn't mean they're dangerous," Fisher said soon after they arrived, when he knew he had been wrong. "It doesn't necessarily mean they're dimbos, either."

"What a wise child you are," Echols said.

"I wouldn't mind staying here awhile," Gumbie said. "Think my name's in their computer?"

"They'll kill us," Mr. Blue said.

"Not me, they won't," Fisher said. "I'm legal. I've got an ID. I'll say I'm Fisher Allbright, and they'll keel over!"

But then they had behaved like outlaws, taking the weapons and plundering the wedding reception and, as they moved through town, snatching what they needed. Fisher had felt brave and dangerous, and when the terrified woman in the Grange Hall had asked him who he was he had lifted his faceplate and yawned at her and said, "Batfish!"

They had lingered in Guthrie and put themselves into greater and greater danger, until at last they heard the approaching rotor and fled. After scattering, they evaporated, and regrouped in the dark. They seized a van from a pair of lovers, who were too surprised to do anything but surrender the keys when they saw the seven faces pressed against their windows.

"Aliens! Swarm crime!" Fisher cried, liking the game. And then he added, "Front-seat window for me! I'm navigator!"

They piled in and drove slowly all night on Route 50, stopping often—whenever they suspected they were being followed, and usually delaying themselves further by eating the food they had brought from Guthrie. They had sneaked into those other towns—Loogootee and Seymour: crawled down their streets in the van and read the signs, looked in the store windows. Shoe stores, banks, car dealers. Riteway Drugs. Alder's Griptite Tools. Ralph-O-Tronics. Pinsker's Pet Shop.

Fisher said, "It's the past."

"Looks like the future," Valda said.

"No," Fisher said. "The future's familiar. This is a mystery."

"Not to me."

Toward dawn they were rolling past damp fields, and way at the back of those fields the sun appeared in three wide layers of light in a dusty green sky. *Caution—Low-Flying Aircraft,* a sign said. Nearer the airfield, outside Marengo (another old-new town), they ditched the van and burrowed under the perimeter fence, using the tools they'd brought from O-Zone.

"These clunkers actually work," Fisher said, stabbing the sandy dirt with a shovel.

They positioned themselves in the bushes at the end of the runway, where the planes landed and turned before taxiing to the small terminal. "Looks like a shoebox! Traffic controller probably yells out the window!"

But no one was listening to Fisher. They were crouched in the morning heat, the fudgy-looking runway giving off a stink of oil.

"They'll just fly away when they see us waving guns at them," Rooks said.

"We'll command them to let us board," Fisher said, fussing with the radio in his helmet. "If they don't, we'll nuke them."

Just then a fat flapping plane submerged them in its roaring noise.

"Think you can yell loud enough, Fish?"

But Fisher's head was down. He had found the right frequency and was monitoring the approach of another aircraft.

They hid until a ten-seater radioed its landing and touched down, and when it swerved toward them on the runway

Fisher broke into the transmission and ordered the pilot to hold. The plane paused, and rocked. The control tower demanded to know who had overridden the instructions. Then seven people surrounded the plane, holding their weapons up.

"Swarm crime!" Fisher said, laughing because it was so easy.

The rest happened quickly: the steps were dropped and the passengers hurried onto the runway, and the seven armed people boarded.

"Aliens!" the pilot was hissing into his microphone as Fisher entered the cockpit and took the seat next to him. He pointed his weapon at the pilot's throat.

"I'm not an alien, you fucking herbert! Look at me!"

He was honking into his helmet.

"Your security here is terrible," Fisher said. "You people don't know the first thing about crime control. Haven't you heard of perimeter beams? You've got these stupid wacky fences that even a shit-wit could get through, if he wanted. I had a shovel—I dug my way in! You herberts deserve to get hijacked."

The pilot meanwhile was trying to answer him.

"Up!" Fisher said, outshouting the pilot. "Get us up! I'm driving the computer! I'm navigating!"

When they were in the air he turned and saw lowered heads. The hesitant plops of their puking disgusted him.

"Haven't you guys ever been in a plane before?" Then he remembered, and laughed in his strange groaning way, and tried to share the joke with the stone-faced pilot. "Hey, it's their first time up!"

The pilot's expression softened to pleading.

"Aliens!" Fisher said, intending to explain.

It was a short flight, less than an hour, but for nearly the whole of that time Fisher ridiculed the plane's instruments.

"These were obsolete twenty years ago! It's all needles! It's got bells and whistles!"

The pilot said they were low on fuel. Fisher saw it was true, and mocked him for not carrying a spare tank. Then he demanded to be taken down.

"Going down by hand! What a toilet! This is like driving an old car. You're actually using your feet, you willy!"

There was no airport nearby. They came down on a back road in Ohio, rolling past a sign that said "Bixby 4 km."

"Take anything you want—but please—" But the pilot said no more; he was too ashamed to say *Don't hurt me.*

"We don't collect antiques," Fisher said.

The others laughed, and over the next two days, hiking across fields by night, and sleeping by day, they repeated the sentence; and Fisher was proud of having pleased them—but what was the joke? All this time he was directing them, taking his bearings from the stars and monitoring police broadcasts. Roadblocks were common here on the interstates, but by following Fisher's directions they kept on back roads.

On several occasions, hearing low-flying aircraft or ground vehicles approach, they evaporated. Each time it happened quickly, without a word, and yet the method varied. The first time, they scattered and sank into the fields; the second time, they gathered, pressing themselves together, and moved in a mass and evaporated that way.

Fisher was impressed by these escapes—he called them monkey maneuvers. But he was prouder of the listening devices in his helmet, and his skill with radio navigation, and his reckonings by the stars.

"Think Bligh could do this?"

He meant: What good was she? He had always resented being swapped for an alien.

"Bligh wouldn't have to do that," Rooks said. "If Bligh was with us, we wouldn't be here."

"You'd be lost without me!"

Mr. Blue said, "If we didn't have you, we wouldn't need you. I told you, you're the problem."

"I'm the solution!"

But he was enjoying himself now. Being on the ground had corrected many of his misconceptions. He did not feel like a prisoner any longer.

"Next stop is Pittsburgh." He laughed, twisting his face into a frown, and the noise came out of his helmet. "It's a sealed city!"

"I'm going to miss that laugh of yours," Echols said.

Fisher explained that unlike Guthrie or Loogootee or Seymour or Marengo—those sleepy towns in the cornfields—Pittsburgh was very secure. It had rivers and bridges; all the access roads had checkpoints. Like New York, its physical features had helped make it secure. It was a natural fortress.

"You can't get in without an ID," Fisher said. "Without IDs you don't have a legal existence. They don't have any qualms about killing you, because you guys are already dead. But not me! I just flash my disc and they start saluting."

"Where are we?"

"Near Somethingopolis."

"We're skipping Pittsburgh," Mr. Blue said.

In their detour around the city that night they were slowed by fences, and rushing one in the darkness, Valda stepped on a rusty spike, injuring her foot. It was a deep cut, exposing the bone in one of her toes—raw meat and tattered skin.

"That's what you get for laughing at my boots," Fisher said. "You're not in O-Zone now, you know."

A new person had emerged in him over the past week or so—ever since crossing the Red Zone Perimeter. It had first seemed like a mood, and then a phantom, and now it had asserted itself and possessed him. It was older, bossy, mocking, confident: the "Batfish" from Guthrie, the copilot from Marengo. His voice was taunting and loud, his elbows stuck out, his helmet clattered on his head when he walked. I live here, he seemed to say. I know better. But he had also mastered many of the aliens' own skills. He could find food, he could sleep on the ground, he could evaporate when they did. He was stronger than the younger Fisher, but he was just as intelligent, and Fisher thought: When my brain turns to mush and I can't do any advanced math, I'll still be strong.

"If you don't get an antitetanus shot within forty-eight hours, you're risking lockjaw."

Valda worried and limped, keeping one shoulder high, and Fisher was so intrigued by her silent suffering he knocked his head against a low branch.

"Didn't hurt!" he cried, and it hadn't—he wanted them to think he was being brave. But he had cracked his radio, and thereafter its hum made it almost unintelligible.

"It hammered my accumulator!" he complained. He had been listening to Owners' and police broadcasts. Now, he said, he'd have to make a trip into Pittsburgh to find another accumulator.

"This is the best helmet you can get," he said. "It's better than most human heads!"

"Wait up," Mr. Blue said. He was looking at the lighted sky, a pile of yellow clouds: it was all they could see of Pittsburgh.

Fisher said, "We can't travel without a radio. And Valda's going to get muscle rigidity and tonic spasms. Lockjaw's a misnomer that some dimbo gave it. It's tetanus. The neurotoxic component's called tetanospasmin. It's one of the deadliest poisons known to man." Fisher grew excited as he spoke. "No one else can go with me! They'll get arrested! They'll get nuked!"

Echols was saying to Mr. Blue, "Is this a good idea?"

But Fisher gloated. "If Valda doesn't get a jab she'll be foaming at the mouth! And you'll need my radio to keep away from Feds and security people. I'm giving you raw data."

"He might not come back," Echols said. "What'll we do then?"

They had started talking to each other about him, as if he was deaf and didn't matter. Aliens!

"We'll put cowshit on the wound," Mr. Blue said. "Cowshit's great for tetanus."

"You horrible dim fucking willy," Fisher said—his wonderment gave a lilting tone to his abuse—"that's the sickest thing I've ever heard in my life."

"And yet it's true."

They were seated on the ground in the early-morning darkness with their backs against a grassy bank, preparing themselves for the dangers that daylight always presented. The aliens were silent, like small children or animals under a heavy falling sky of terrible blackness. They had never looked stranger or more savage.

When Fisher looked again they were gone: evaporated.

"Cowshit!"

He had thought of saying good-bye, or thanking them, because he had no intention of going back to them. It wasn't stealth that prevented him, and not the idea that they might conclude that he was running off, and seize him—no, he just didn't feel strongly enough about them to bother shifting his faceplate so they could hear him.

They had terrorized him, they had pushed him, they had forced him to walk and tried to wear him out, and then when they had needed him they had turned to him blankly and said, "Help." He had steered them out of trouble. And they had stolen him from Hooper's rotor! What was there to thank them for? He wondered whether they were really convinced of his intelligence. Possibly Mr. Blue and Echols realized that he had some power, but the others weren't bright enough to understand his special qualities. It took brains to appreciate brains.

That was why he had said, "I don't know what I'm going to do without you folks."

Because sarcasm was always best when it was used on people who didn't understand it.

Then he said sharply, "Don't even think of following me. If they catch you near that city, you'll get burned."

He could have disguised his feelings and said, "I won't be long." Instead he turned his back on them. He wanted them to suspect that he might not return; he wanted to put them in suspense. They deserved to worry for all the worry they had caused him. Would they, as aliens, be conscious of the fact that he had not said good-bye or thank you?

The full force of it had probably hit them now that he was gone and the darkness was piled on them. They knew that they were lost.

He found a main road.

"We've got a security check up ahead," the bus driver said in a cautioning voice, looking Fisher up and down as he boarded.

They had big wheezing rubber-wheeled buses here!

"I figured," Fisher said. "It'd be pretty pointless to seal the city if they didn't have tight security."

"They sometimes do spot scans," the driver said. "I'm telling you for your own good." He spoke in a voice of gentle warning. A stunner was strapped to his leg. He spoke from inside the driving capsule. "They can be very thorough."

"Good!" Fisher said. It was a torn-off squawk, as he pushed to the back of the bus, where he found a seat. It was the first bus ride of his life: But after what I have been through, why should I worry about taking a bus?

The stares of the other passengers annoyed him so much he clapped his faceplate down and raised his antennae. The passengers watched the slender probes grow out of the top of his helmet. Fisher folded his arms across his muddied suit. He had mended the rips on his knees and his sleeves with sticky tape from Guthrie. He had used adhesive filler on the gouges in his boots. His pale fingers showed through his split gloves.

He knew the bus passengers were interested in him—a bit too interested. They were commuters, probably not even Owners, just pass-holders and permit-people. They never went anywhere.

"Just back from a mission," he said.

The amplifier turned his voice into a series of wavering quacks and solemn chuckles. The defective accumulator had robbed his voice of authority.

"Cla-*heep*-ssified," he said, cursing the helmet and vowing to have it fixed.

At the security check—a gate, just before the bridge—a man in uniform boarded and looked down the crowded aisle. He examined the driver's ID, but did no more than that—no scan, no check of passengers' IDs, no photographs, no further questions.

"What a clam," Fisher said, as the big bus started across the bridge in the morning sunlight. "There could be a diseased alien riding on this vehicle! How do they know there isn't a weirdo illegal Roach on board just sitting here getting lockjaw and about to take a spasm?"

He enjoyed being watched like this: they were listening—you could tell.

"Maybe he's fungoid. Maybe he's got an iron. Maybe he's disguised as an Owner, wearing a lot of expensive gear, only underneath he's a stink-*heep*-ing wreck. Maybe he's got a forged ID. And he's going to be let loose in downtown Pittsburgh! What a great security check!"

Long before the bus pulled into the terminal, the passengers had begun drawing away from him and gathering at the doors. Fisher hated them for their rudeness. And they thought aliens were bad!

He attracted the same attention on the street. Was it this wonky helmet? It must have been—no one wore them here, no one wore masks. Yet he was happy. He liked these rising streets, and the bridges on three sides of the city, which bulked on the hilltop like a citadel, high above the empty steel mills.

Why had the bus been waved through the checkpoint? Mr.

Blue could have come with him. Any alien could penetrate this city!

"Excuse me, sir."

He heard that as the faintest whisper, and kept walking, until he was seized by the arms. His helmet was twisted off his head. He yawned at the two state security men—black uniforms, black helmets, funnel guns, stunners, shiny boots.

"It's about time," Fisher said, biting his yawn—tearing the sound with his teeth.

"Would you mind showing us your ID, sir?"

He had startled the men, he could tell. He yawned in their faces again, and handed over his ID. "Take a good look at the reference and the code number," he said. And he stood there gloating while the security men scanned him and phoned his ID through to the computer.

"You've got fabulous security here."

He snorted at them, seeing their bewildered reaction to his sarcasm. He wanted to go on ridiculing them with compliments, but they were not listening; they were looking closely at the taped patches on his suit.

"I'm afraid I can't tell you why this suit's in such tough shape," he said. "I've been on a mission."

The security men told him he could go: he was very pleased and felt powerful. This was more like it! Mr. Blue would have failed that security check. The alien would have been stuffed into a gunship and taken to a White Room for questioning. *Plug him in.*

"Correction!" Fisher said out loud. He had actually passed the security check! The computer had not caught his ID, even though he had been kidnapped in March. He was a hostage who had escaped and returned home to discover that he hadn't been missed. It was stupid, disgraceful, and inefficient. What if he had lost his memory and was stumbling around Pittsburgh this morning blinded with aphasia and loss of identity? The security goons would have let him go!

He found a telephone on a post and then saw it was outside a stand-up restaurant.

"Hardly worth using a credit card for that," the cashier said. She was black, her name badge was lettered *Herma,* and she was armed with a stunner. She frowned at the two jelly doughnuts and the vanilla milkshake on Fisher's tray.

"No cash," the boy said. "Too many weirdos around.

There are probably aliens right outside this city, sticking their noses through the fence and trying to break in."

"I don't know anything about it," the woman said quietly.

Fisher pushed the doughnuts into his mouth and took the milkshake to the telephone.

"Who is that?" Moura said, catching her breath.

"Batfish!"

"Fizzy, is that you? What's wrong—where are you?"

He had started to gag. "Milkshake," he said. "Can't get the stupid straw into my suckhole."

"Are you in New York?" Moura's voice was urgent.

"The herberts didn't even find me in the computer," Fisher said in his old snarling way. He hadn't spoken like this since the last time he spoke to Moura. He disliked becoming a child: it was the effect his mother's voice had on him. "Hey, that's what I call security! What if I'd blacked out?"

"Is Hardy with you?"

"I haven't seen the stiff," and then his anger overcame him. But there was pleasure in his anger, and strength, because he felt safe here. "Listen, did you report me missing?"

"Hooper didn't tell us you were missing until two weeks ago—"

"That willy!"

"Fizz, are you all right? Is someone listening to this? Because if they are, we'll pay them whatever they want."

She went on talking, sounding very worried. It calmed Fisher. His mother's nervousness gave him strength.

"Thanks!" he said. "You didn't report me missing!"

"Just tell me where you are—what's that noise?"

He was slurping the milkshake again through the suckhole in his helmet.

"On a mission," he said, and hung up.

He was still walking—it was so lovely on the sunny heights of this city. And he was less mocking about the security situation here, knowing that it had not been a computer error or a goofball or a police blip. They hadn't identified him, because he hadn't been reported missing. But why not? If Hooper hadn't told them, what had the fuck-wit been doing all this time?

He passed another telephone and punched Hooper's number and got his uncle's answering machine.

"You lost me and you didn't even say so! There's something seriously wrong with you, mister. You were responsible for my safety on that mission. I am very disappointed in you. This is Commander, Mission Westwind—"

He swung the phone from his ear, then thought again.

"Furthermore, you still haven't found me!"

He felt very happy after this. For once, he was not imploring these adults for help. He didn't need them. He had arrived here on his own—he had led the aliens here. He was not their prisoner but their leader. That knowledge, and the sunshine, and the sugary breakfast, gave him the lift he needed. It seemed official, it was confirmed. He thought: I'm a man.

It was a feeling of quiet power—something he had seen in Mr. Blue. It was not a show of strength: it was confidence. He had been tested. The test might have broken him—yet it had strengthened him. We are what we are because of our difficulties, he thought.

He needed a new flying suit and boots, but he decided not to buy them. He had begun to take pride in his ragged taped-up outfit. He liked the look. It showed what he had endured, and it was a kind of armor. He enjoyed being an Owner disguised as a trooper: a combination of cunning and technology, like an animal with indestructible circuits, an electronic wolf.

And of course people would know and be afraid. They would stare at him and say: *He's been on a mission. Must have been some mission!*

He frightened them, he knew, with his piercing look of having done something very dangerous. The man in Ray-Tech who sold him the accumulator seemed as fascinated by the scars on his helmet as by its many functions.

"A piece of equipment like this can be very important when you're in a Prohibited Area and you have to locate your ship," Fisher said. "And the place is crawling with aliens."

The salesman just stared, taking very small breaths, his tongue quivering behind his teeth.

"It can be the difference between life and death," the boy said. "Suppose you've been kidnapped, and there's contamination, and you have to locate the rest of your team?"

"You in the Pilgrims?" the man finally said.

"Shit-wit!" Fisher honked at him, suddenly angry. "Space

is nothing—the moon and these orbital stations are for tourists and fanatics. Any dimbo can go up in a space vehicle. Just remember not to puke. They're not heroes, they're not explorers! Fucking Christopher Columbus had a much harder time than any Astronaut—the dimbo didn't even know this continent existed, and you can see these space stations on a clear night. What's so hard about walking on the moon? Hey, I'm talking about the earth. Nothing is stranger than being on the ground!"

He loved saying that. He believed it, too. And he could tell the salesman was impressed.

But he was maddened again trying to buy the antitetanus serum—three drugstores said no. And, angered, he remembered his other grievances, the stupidity of Moura and Hooper, the incompetent secrecy of Hardy. And he felt more kindly toward the aliens, because they had helped make him tough; but he still had not decided whether to go back to them. For the moment, he was satisfied being alone.

The drugstores were so foolishly stocked! He wondered whether they were like this in New York. Toilet paper, pens, candy, radios, hair spray, tobacco, rubber hoses, electric fans, approved explosives, magazines and books, gardening equipment, potted plants, bicycles, wristwatches, children's toys.

"We've been carrying these items for years," the pharmacist said. "Where have you been?"

And he refused to sell Fisher the serum.

"I'm on a mission," the boy said. He was wearing his helmet, his faceplate was up. "It's classified. I need this serum for one of my people."

In his white smock, the pharmacist looked less like a medical man than a mental patient, and when he apologized it seemed like a crude form of gloating.

"I'm afraid I'll have to report you," Fisher said, and tugged at the cuffs of his greasy gloves. "You're highly unprofessional, and you're a complete and utter tool."

Was that man smiling into his hand?

Because he had been turned down, he was determined to procure the serum. It did not matter whether he needed it for Valda. He simply wanted it. All this time he was tramping. He followed a sign saying "University" to another rising road. He saw some boys, students probably, loitering near a building, and he butted his helmet at them.

"Where's the hospital?"

What were these dimbos looking at?

"Over there," one boy said, making a face at him.

Fisher walked through the entrance, pushed a door—no security—pushed another, found a corridor, and scuffed to the end of it. The legs of his suit still rubbed with a loud scratching sound. He pushed his faceplate up in order to read the small print on a sign, something about visiting hours, but hated the smell of the place. He kept walking—his boots going *Goom! Goom!* on the tile floor, and his legs going *Haust!* when they rubbed. Another sign, another door, a new smell: was that food or disease? This corridor was lined with doors.

He stopped, too furious to go farther, and rattled a doorknob. He pushed the stinking thing open. He squawked when he saw the woman in the chair—her white thighs.

She was young and she was just rising from the chair, her skirt rucked up—she hadn't expected anyone. Her face swelled with surprise, and then all the air went out of her cheeks.

"Who are you?"

Fisher was making noises inside his helmet.

"I can't understand a word you're saying." She seemed at once both frightened of him and eager to calm him, and so her voice was false and ineffectual.

"Antitetanus," Fisher was saying. He told the woman it was an emergency. What was wrong with these drugstores? He needed the serum for one of his people. He spoke of his mission, mentioning its secrecy. He spoke in his squeezed squawky voice through the trapdoor of his amplifier.

The woman smiled sternly in fear and urged him to sit down in her chair.

"They sell bicycles and candy bars and sex magazines," he said. "And they won't sell me the serum! But if I wanted a radio or some spermicide, oh sure! Want to see my ID? I'm an Owner."

But the woman had gone to the door.

She was frightened and preachy. She said, "Any injury involving a rusty nail must be taken very seriously, no matter who you are."

"And they said they were going to put cowshit on it!"

Fisher was pleased with himself when the woman left. She understood the urgent nature of the mission. He felt safe in disclosing it to her. He no longer feared the aliens, and since leaving O-Zone he had stopped seeing himself as their prisoner.

He now regretted that panicky message he had sent from the dish near Winslow, particularly *Very high exposure risk—send assistance immediately*. He was ashamed of the fear he had felt among the aliens, and even more ashamed of the fears he had felt in his room in Coldharbor. He had felt weak, and his weakness had shown him demons. It was all a memory of childhood.

"I don't need help from anyone," he said when the woman returned.

She held out a small pouch which contained a hypodermic syringe and a bottle of serum. Fisher snatched it and squeezed it in his dirty glove, and the woman looked frightened again.

"Don't be afraid," she said—her voice had gone hollow. "We get a lot of you people in here."

Fisher was having difficulty turning the doorknob—he couldn't grasp it in his oversize gloves, and the splits in the fingers loosened his grip.

"Wonky door doesn't even work!"

In the voice that seemed to come echoing out of her forehead with fear, the woman said, "Follow the exit signs and go straight out. But please be more careful in the future."

"It wasn't me! This complete tool stepped on the nail. I didn't tell her to! She probably wasn't even wearing any shoes!"

"I mean, telling people you're an Owner and your father's an Owner."

"I don't have a father!"

But the woman was still cautioning him in her fearful way.

"I knew as soon as you stepped in here that something was wrong. See, an Owner wouldn't have barged in like that. I could have set off my alarm—I'm glad I didn't, though. And an Owner would have said please and thank you. An Owner would have been wearing a clean suit—and that helmet is not convincing at all. These are all very simple things. But you should remember them. I'm not asking you who you are, or where you came from, or where you're going. It's none of my business to question anyone's legality—"

She had come quite near to him. She held her hand out in a peacemaking gesture.

"You porker!" Fisher said, and shoved the door aside. "You porker!"

Now he had what he wanted; but he wondered what to do with it. Yet he felt strong again, walking freely through the sealed city. And that porker had taken him for an alien! Each time he passed a public telephone he thought of Moura and Hooper and how they had let him down. They were too incompetent to find him. They hadn't even reported him missing. But their indifference had given him strength.

He thought of calling them and saying: *You are such total fuck-wits everything has to be proven to you!*

He laughed at this—his laughter was mirthless and energetic, like someone trying to blow out a small fire. But the effort of it gave him confidence.

The aliens were huddled under the evening sky. Thoroughly stupid people needed to be shown everything. He had shown the aliens he was strong by leaving them and penetrating this city on his own. There was a way he could show them he was even stronger: by returning. And they needed his medicine, they needed his helmet, they needed him.

"Excuse me, sir," the security guard said at the bus station as Fisher was boarding. "Step over here—we'll have to run your ID through the filter."

"Where the heck have you guys been!"

The guards did not laugh. The station was thronged with homeward-bound commuters. The guards stuck to the routine of their random check: filtering the disc, doing the numbers.

"You're a long way from home, Mr. Allbright."

"I've been traveling," he said. He decided not to arouse their curiosity with the word "mission." They were staring at his dented helmet and his patches of sticky tape. He said, "Wear and tear. Ha!"

"Notice any illegals in your travels?"

"Aliens—you mean real aliens?" he said, and swallowed and waited for their full attention.

"Any kind."

"No," he said.

Saying that, he transformed the people who were hiding and waiting for him. He made them better, he made them worthy of him; he appreciated them. And they needed him! He felt gladder—he had rescued them again. Now he was returning to them as a friend. Saying no to those cops proved it.

34

Tᴴᴇʏ ᴡᴇʀᴇ ᴍᴜᴄʜ ᴀɴɢʀɪᴇʀ ɴᴏᴡ—Sʟᴜᴛᴇʀ ᴀɴᴅ Mᴇᴇsʟᴇ especially; Murdick was nibbling in fury. And they flew the gunship recklessly, battering the turbulent air. They had received an all-points alert from Marengo—the airport had not been specified—and when they landed in the town center they were surrounded by armed men. One of the men said, "We don't care who you are or what you want—just get out of here, right now, and take that bug off the lawn."

Then a warning shot went twangling past the Godseye gunship.

"They think we're aliens!" Sluter cried as he spun the rotor into the air.

It was another bad day. The tension brought on by their frustrated pursuit worried Hardy. They had started out looking for Fizzy, talking of rescue; but now they talked about little except the criminality of aliens. Hardy was reluctant to give them any more information, and he didn't blame the vigilantes in Marengo for sending them away. He did not trust them anymore.

He radioed Moura from the gunship—the troopers would not allow him to use any telephones on the ground.

Seeing them adjusting the phones on their helmets, he said, "Don't eavesdrop."

Sluter said, "If we want to listen, we will. We've got her number, she's got ours. We don't need you, remember. But you need us. Why don't you jigs understand that?"

They heard everything of the conversation—that Moura had been phoned by Fizzy, that he seemed either very calm or very crazy, that she had traced the call to a public phone in Pittsburgh. "He said he was on some sort of mission."

"He could be wacko," Meesle said, without the slightest pretense of discretion. Hardy had just switched off.

He hated them, but without them what hope had he of finding Fizzy and freeing him from the aliens? Godseye was his punishment for the secrecy he had imposed on himself. Even Hooper had been excluded. Yet Godseye seemed a little too eager now.

Hardy said, "What are you going to do?"

"Find them!"

"I only want you to find Fizzy."

"If we can tell him apart."

"I don't care about the others. I'm not pressing charges."

They snickered at his innocence and headed for Pittsburgh. It was still only the middle of the afternoon, and there was plenty of daylight left.

Hardy was surprised, as he had been at the Red Zone Perimeter and elsewhere, by how easily these men picked up information. Over Pittsburgh, they radioed State Security and then the city police. As soon as they gave their code and identified themselves as Godseye troopers they were told everything. Hardy was appalled to think that an organization so vicious and bad-tempered had such good relations with legitimate police.

"Typical aliens," Sluter said. "They've left tracks all over the place. Three sightings in the city, a suspicious incident in the hospital, and detentions at two security checks. That proves it. Your alien sticks out like a real wolfman."

"What alien?" Hardy said. "He was describing Fizzy!"

Murdick said, "Maybe it's not him. Maybe it's an alien dressed in his clothes. Maybe they decided to eat him, and used his ID."

The furious smile on Hardy's face was intended to intimidate Murdick.

"'Eat' is just a figure of speech," Murdick said, backing away.

"Why don't you say what you mean, Willis?"

"Okay, maybe they killed him."

Meesle said, "Some of these kids that are kidnapped get twisted around. They begin to identify with their captors. Listen, we've got documentation—romances, marriages, slave relationships, puppet phenomena. Or they turn into animals. The average person can't take too much captivity."

"Fizzy isn't average," Hardy said.

"That's what we mean," Sluter said—and Hardy saw that Meesle and Sluter had doubled up on him. "It could be worse in his case."

They had hoisted their gunship over Pittsburgh. They collected the information about the sightings, and received a soundprint that was very blurred: it looked like a rotting Martian, or a collapsed Astronaut in secondhand space gear—the person's head deep inside the shadowy helmet.

Was that Fizzy after his ordeal?

"That's your career criminal," Meesle said. "That's your omnifelon. That's your animal. We're talking woof-woof here."

He stuck the smudged picture over the control console.

"Where are we going?" Hardy said, feeling the gunship gather speed as Sluter clutched at the controls.

"This is the bus route they mentioned."

The stripy road patterns moved across the ground-screen.

"A young, very dirty boy, wearing a helmet with a smeared faceplate." Meesle was quoting the security report and, Hardy felt, taking too much pleasure in it. "Extensive damage to new-model suit. Scarring on helmet. Boots plugged with filler. A loud voice. A noticeable laugh."

Murdick said, "Guess they didn't eat him."

At this high altitude, visibility through the windows and portholes was so poor they had to rely on the ground-screen and the infrared sensors and heat-seekers.

"There's no security out here. They could be anywhere. And we're going to run out of road in a minute." No sooner had he finished speaking than Meesle pushed up his mask and lowered his face to the screen. "Hold it. I've got a cluster."

"Count them."

"Seven. Isolated. Way off the road. Probably jigs, probably jabbering—they're always jabbering to themselves, never listening."

"We're going down."

"Be careful," Hardy said. "Fizzy's a very excitable kid."

"I'm getting a little tired of you," Sluter said, accelerating the dive, and his anger showed in the tilt of the gunship.

"Wait till you see this kid," Murdick said.

Meesle said, "If they put up any resistance, burn them all down."

"A shower of fléchettes!"

"No. You'll be putting Fizzy in danger."

"Get him out of here," Sluter said. "That's an order, Willis."

"Sorry, Allbright," Murdick said, and took hold of Hardy's arm. But Hardy immediately yanked himself out of the flimsy grasp and shoved Murdick aside. And when Meesle came toward him, Hardy dodged, let the fat man stumble, and went for Sluter. He intended only to jostle him—to arrest their nosedive—but Hardy realized too late that he had shoved Sluter very hard against the console of controls, causing the gunship to stall.

A sputtering and a hesitant chug of the rotor blades preceded a violent tilt of the ship, and it went lopsided, falling flat, with Sluter gasping obscenities and snatching at the console.

And then the engine started, the rotor began chopping, and the ship swung sideways in a pendulum arc. At its highest point it shuddered, spilling Hardy and the others onto the rubber deck. Then the gunship lifted itself farther with a roar, and it buzzed in flight.

"They're gone!" Meesle said, clawing at the ground-screen. "We lost them!"

Sluter said nothing. He steadied the ship and slowed the rotor, and using thrusters he brought them to where they could see individual leaves beating under them in the tree-tops.

Murdick said, "Are we going on the ground for them?"

He was always frightened by the prospect of ground searches, and had been terrified even in the harmless farming town of Guthrie. Hardy had long ago decided that all their fears of the ground—they were seldom on it: they made a fetish of flying—had given them dangerous fantasies.

"No. Your friend is."

Hardy had been bruised by the struggle, and by the stall and roll of the gunship. He had hit his elbow and thigh. His mask had been pushed hard against his face. He guessed his nose was leaking—he could taste the drab syrup of blood in the corners of his mouth.

With a springy stop they were on the ground and rocking gently, the rotor still spinning. The sun had just left the sky, and Hardy sensed darkness and a chill rising from the damp earth.

"We don't need you anymore," Sluter said. "Get out. We should have dumped you long ago."

Murdick and Meesle eagerly tipped Hardy through the hatch onto the ground.

They had seen the toppling gunship and heard its roaring straight overhead, and without thinking, Fisher clapped his hands over the earpieces of his helmet and began screaming at the noisy ship falling from the sky onto their heads.

He was rigid—stiffened by the unearthly noise and the sight of the black gunship plunging toward him. His throat ached as he tried to scream it away.

"Move!" Mr. Blue said, and hurried Fisher down the embankment.

The boy felt himself rising and being carried in the same toppling, lopsided way as the gunship was falling. And when he stopped screaming there was only a distant hum in the sky. He sensed that he had silenced the thing: he had repelled it.

"I did it," he said in an exhausted voice. The screams had taken all his strength. How had he gotten under this bridge?

Echols said, "Think we should dig in here?"

He was talking to Mr. Blue, who shook his head.

Rooks said, "That ship came straight down—I think someone jumped out."

"They're after us," Fisher said in a hoarse voice.

In the pause his words produced, the sky darkened and the great gusts of smokelike cloud that had been building up in the east began to crowd the whole sky with night.

"Let's stop a vehicle," Gumbie said.

"They won't stop for us," Fisher said, then showed his teeth and said, "I just said 'us' again." But it did not seem odd anymore. Returning to them, he had proved he was not their hostage.

"If we burn off a wheel it'll stop."

"How will we drive the wonky vehicle on three wheels?"

"Everyone carries spares, Batfish."

"Yeah."

They ambushed a small pickup truck just beyond the bridge, blowing out one of its tires with a silent rifle and an exploding shell. The burst tire caused the vehicle to swerve and stop, and they swarmed over it, hooting and showing their weapons, and terrifying the driver.

"He's an Astronaut," Fisher said, seeing the man's cap and insignia and finding it ridiculous on his faded farmer's clothes. "Hey, this dong's going into orbit!" He poked his old iron into the man's face and said, "Okay, Rocketman, change the tire!"

The man limped and set up his jack.

"He's probably in spinal shock," Fisher said.

After the man had finished, Gumbie said, "Can we drop you anywhere, mister?"

The man said no, and winced as they drove away.

"How did you know he was an Astronaut?" Valda said.

"I live here!" Fisher said, and liked hearing the confidence in his voice, for he had always thought that he lived in a room in Coldharbor. "I know these people!" But he was sorry he had frightened the man in order to prove it.

"What's this?" Gumbie said, and showed Fisher a plump copy of a paperback book, *The Tropes of Planet Alpha*.

"His bible," Fisher said, and threw it out of the window. "Nuke it!"

They drove on narrow back roads, heading east, until Fisher tuned into the frequency of a live roadblock near the settlement of Greensburg. It was shit-wits, he said, carrying out spot checks. He picked up the drone of their scanners and some of their talk.

"We'll walk it," Mr. Blue said, after they had abandoned the truck and eaten the Astronaut's sandwiches. "Let's go."

Fisher liked hearing this even more than before, in O-Zone, because now he shared the impulse. The simple statement of determination showed confidence and strength—like hatching and flying out of the shell—airborne as soon as the egg cracked open. *Let's go.* And look how far they had gone!

"Security's terrible out here," Fisher said. "It's really bad."

"That's what worries me," Echols said.

"Hey, stop worrying—it's lousy. Just dongs at roadblocks. They check vehicles, but if you walk through the woods no one bothers you. What kind of security is that?"

They were cutting across a field, but slowly, because there was no light. The moon and stars were hidden by the dense cloud. And Valda was limping, dragging her injured foot. The darkness made Fisher imagine he was in a forest, with masses of black boughs above his head.

"As if all aliens travel in vehicles—the dongs!"

They kept walking, and from the swallowed sound of their footsteps they sensed they were near another embankment.

"No one's safe here, except us!"

"Keep it down, Fish," Mr. Blue said, but he was laughing softly.

"I mean, that kind of security wouldn't make me feel safe if I lived here," Fisher said, and he felt even sorrier for the Astronaut in the pickup truck. No wonder they planned trips to the moon and read those stupid books and believed all that trash. "Hey, I'd get a dog!"

They sat on the embankment, listening to Fisher; then they slid down.

"I smell tadpoles," Gumbie said.

"And where's the security here?" Fisher said. "There's nothing in position. We just traveled halfway across America and no one killed us. And look at this—pathetic! An unguarded signal box! That doesn't inspire my confidence at all. Hey, you're better off being an alien!"

"It's a road," Rooks was saying.

"This tool thinks it's a road!"

Then they saw the dim light of the distant train.

Hooper had been certain of the spot. Fizzy's brief message had given him Pittsburgh, and Pittsburgh security had briefed him on the various sightings. "Missing person," Hooper had said, and he had found the people on the ground very helpful.

Following the bus route, he had picked up an emergency bleep which, strangely, had fallen silent moments after it had begun.

Bligh said, "What's wrong?"

"I think that distress call could have been the Godseye rotor. I know they're in front of us, and they've got a faster ship."

He could tell that Bligh was worried—she had been frightened at Winslow when Godseye surprised them, and was glad to leave Guthrie before they showed up. She seemed to recognize the troopers as her natural enemy. They represented everything that she feared and hated in New York; and yet the rest of the time she was happy, feeling freer in the jetrotor than she had in Coldharbor or the city.

Hooper loved her watchfulness, and the fact that she took

nothing for granted. At Coldharbor she was able to sleep for long periods, and there was a sensuality in her slumber—sleep heated her skin and made her damp—as if all her dreams were sexual. But here in the jet-rotor, Hooper's Flea, she was wakeful and always alert, and she vitalized Hooper with her energy.

But he was careful with her. He knew he had a rich man's presumption, and that his possessiveness spooked her. Whenever he reached out for her she drew away. She was like a cat: when he ignored her she crept into his lap, as if reassured by his inattention. This search for Fizzy had had the same effect: it was a distraction that brought them closer.

Each night in the parked jet-rotor they made love in a fierce way, losing themselves in it, and simulating rapturous murder—not only his old impaling, but all the interruptions of it, as she rode his face like a saddle and galloped him into ecstasy as he gasped between her thighs; but it was she who was winded and made the sounds of suffocation. And when she took him into her mouth and drank, it was he who howled as if he were dying. They lay head to toe, licking the dew from each other's bodies, and giving themselves life.

"What do you want?"

"You know what I want."

It was dark magic, and it worked. It confounded them, then helped them understand in a way that words would have failed to do. Sex took away their loneliness, then gave it back; and so desire returned.

Yet Hooper had noticed that at times his passion for her alarmed her. *I want to eat you*—and for a moment fear flickered on her face, as if he meant just that and would devour her with cannibal teeth. She laughed when he told her that she had the dark fishy taste of smoked salmon. He wanted more.

The sky was blue, but night was falling and the ground had gone gray.

"If that distress call was Godseye," Hooper said, "I don't understand why they went off the air."

Bligh was silent—the name Godseye reminded her of the story Hooper had told her of the hunt in New York. But he had not intended to frighten her. He had been trying to tell her that he loved her: he wasn't like the others, he was saying, and now he had stopped thinking of her as an alien.

"I wish we could see something," he said as the clouds

buffeted around them. "I was sure we were following that ship. Now we've lost them. No more landmarks."

"It's getting dark," Bligh said.

He had said: Only Fizzy knows how to fly one of these things in the dark.

"Are we going home tonight?"

Hooper stared at her.

"You said 'home.'"

The pinprick on the ground-screen was at just the point where the other ship had signaled, but now it was too dark to tell what the pinprick was. It seemed hotter than a human being, and not hot enough to be the burning wreck of a crashed gunship.

He flew closer and saw that it was a small fire—the sort of dinner fire that aliens might build to cook an evening meal: roast a dog, or soften potatoes, or stew the vegetables they were so fond of. Yet he could not pick up the heat of any humans. Perhaps they were sitting too close to the fire to be located?

He spun the rotor down with all his lights blazing and saw a figure separate itself from the fire. It was a person in a helmet, but with its arms up—welcoming, surrendering.

"It might be Fizzy," Hooper said, and hoped it was, so that he could bring him back to Coldharbor and vindicate himself for having lost him.

The boy wonder was capable of anything—even this, turning up beside a fire in a rural buffer zone in Pennsylvania.

"People always look so small on the ground," Bligh said. "So helpless and alone. I never knew that."

She's thinking of herself, Hooper thought. Flying with him had shown her the true size of things. She realized how precarious her life had been before they had met. She felt a sort of retrospective fear and was puzzled by the illogicality of her luck.

"And they always look desperate at night."

But even though she was reflecting in this way she still managed to work the spotlight expertly as they descended.

"It's my brother," Hooper said.

35

IT WAS RAINING—A SOFT RAT-TAT THAT BECAME A SIZZLING on the roof of the boxcar, and oddly quickened each time the train slowed down.

Through a crack in the door of the car they saw a spattery blaze of lights flash past. Fisher, speaking from within his helmet, told them about the people out here—commuters, simple-lifers, farmers, Astronauts.

"Some of them work in Philadelphia. Some of them want to go into orbit, though the program only takes one in two hundred thousand," the boy said. "Some of them don't even have telephones."

Explaining to them what they could not see strengthened his influence on them. He conveyed to them the sense of strange lives pulsing in the dark—it was the way he had told them about the stars, giving them names and shapes. He said there were people awake all night under those lights as the train slid past. He told them what he heard on his radio earphones, as he monitored local broadcasts: more mysteries.

"I've got a police patrol—a standoff with some aliens," he said. "I've got a roadblock incident—someone just flunked a security check. Dong! A suspected tax defaulter! And what's this? An unfortunate motorist, as this willy calls himself, is broadcasting from his broken-down car. It's a distress call. He thinks he's being watched by Roaches. What a dick! What if those Roaches have a radio? He thinks they're sort of subnormal peckerheads who've never heard of radios!"

The others listened attentively.

"Good thing we're in here," Fisher said. "There are a lot of patrols in this area. The private ones are the worst. I mean, who are they answerable to?"

Light from the door crack cut across their faces, and the boy saw their eyes flash at him.

"Don't be scared," he said.

"You're the one with gray hairs," Valda said.

The boxcar smelled of dusty vegetables. Foraging in the corners, they found onions, the remainder of a shipment—enough for three apiece. They peeled them, and chewed them, and wept.

"No one's going to want to kiss us," Fisher said.

He was still monitoring the passing transmissions.

"Altoona," he said at one point, and at another, "Harrisburg."

Place names meant nothing to these people, he could tell. They fell asleep, they stayed that way, and finally, banging across the trestles of an iron bridge, they were shaken by the clatter, and woke. The outside lights were dimmed by the oncoming dawn. Soon after, they looked out and saw horses, with smooth gleaming skin drawn tight over their muscles and their heads up at the approach of the train.

"Naked horses," Fisher said, and seeing a man on horseback, went on, "Some of the people here ride them. That's how they go to work." Yet he did not quite believe it, nor did he believe those men in black made a virtue of it.

The lock hasp swung and clanged at the boxcar door as the aliens gaped. Seeing their helpless curiosity, Fisher felt refreshed and strengthened.

"Bet you weren't expecting this, Elroy!"

Mr. Blue smiled.

"What are you thinking?"

"It's a long way back."

"There's a lot more ahead!"

"More of this?" Echols said.

Fisher snorted, because he didn't know and didn't want to admit it. But he knew that they saw the future outside and were alarmed by it. He saw the past and was consoled.

"You've been here before?"

"Oh, sure," Fisher said, exulting, because he meant the past. "But, hey, I always feel at home in my helmet."

He sensed that he had bewildered them by saying that. Good! Bewilderment would make them rely on him.

"I used to be afraid of places like this when I was a kid." He thought: I was a kid until I was kidnapped.

Valda was holding his free hand in her hot fingers. He was glad she hadn't given up on him. He had always regretted having said to her: *Shall I stick my finger into your bum?*

He said, "Know what? I've discovered I like weather. I never liked it before. You don't have to change it—you can change yourself. It can make you happy, too. It's better than music."

The morning was drizzly and still warm, and the foliage seemed swollen and sodden, like rags thickened by moisture. The trees were heavier in the mingled steam and smoke; the drooping branches hung almost to the ground. There was a blackness in the green that summer rain always brings to trees and grass—so the day seems gloomy. The pale sifting mist streaked past the door of the boxcar, and the warmth only made them more conscious of the humidity. The freight train moved along the tracks on screeching wheels.

"Philadelphia," Fisher said. As always his helmet distorted his voice and made him sound like a talking animal. "But this train's going straight through, so there won't be a scan. It's got checkpoint clearance."

He had just heard that phrase on his radio. He was monitoring the engine now.

"What happens in New York?" Echols said.

"We won't get that far. The city's sealed. Or do you have an ID and a work permit?"

"I didn't want to be here," Gumbie said.

"Then why did you come!"

He saw in their momentary puzzlement that they had forgotten why they had come, and when they remembered they blinked—did they regret it?

"Maybe your friend Bligh can take you back!"

He was hearty: this seemed to frighten them. He wanted to frighten them further. Fear made them so attentive! They had never listened to him this way before. He liked that. He knew it was not friendship, but there was something touching and equalizing in their dependency. It was not that Valda was holding his hand; he was holding hers too. He needed those people and he was glad they didn't know it.

"One of the biggest checkpoints in the world is near here," he said. "It's a high-tech filter. It can detect anything—drugs, weapons, diseases. Everyone is scanned—every vehicle, everything. Hey, don't even think of squeezing through!"

They were never more frightened than when they saw some people outside in flying suits and helmets and thick-soled boots. At first, Fisher did not understand their fear—the folks outside were lolloping in a park, faceplates down, probably children. Then it struck Fisher that they were dressed as he was, except in cleaner suits, and so he did not seem absurd anymore, but rather in his element. It was then that they realized that they were the aliens—strange, naked, and weak; and hunted.

"They call it the Wall, but it's not a wall," Fisher said. He was still talking about the checkpoint from New Jersey into New York. "And don't think we can sneak under it like we did in the Red Zone Perimeter. You want to drown?"

Talking in this way he had made them curious, but when they looked out of the moving train all they saw were huge rusty drums and girders, and flaring chimneys behind high fences, and tumbled stacks of broken bricks on the burned earth. Where it was not burned the ground looked soaked in black oil. This low scorched place, without a tree, without a person—and where was the checkpoint?—seemed to contradict everything Fisher had said about the high security and technology. For that reason, it was much more worrying.

"There's the river, too—they've got gunboats and missiles! They use them! And there's aerial patrols on twenty-four-hour watch, with high-resolution cameras. You'll hear them—aerial patrols make the most noise."

But it was quiet now, except for the rumble of the train. It looked as though a civilization had burned to the ground—not a great civilization, but a flimsy flammable one, with nothing under it but shallow cellars into which it had tumbled. And its embers lay in the streets—sprinkled with broken glass and looking greasy in the light rain. The civilization had been temporary but its ruins were permanent.

"You can't fly in, walk in, sail in, or drive in, unless you've got papers—an ID, a work permit, an entry pass or proof of residence. You need two stickers for a car. They detain people by the thousands every day, and if you look like a tool or a dimbo they'll jail you on suspicion. They're not supposed to, but they do."

"We never had anything like this in Chicago," Echols said.

"That where you're from?"

Echols said, "A long time ago," and left it at that.

Once Echols had said, *I abused my position*, and Fisher had hated him and imagined something very crooked. But now he felt sorry for the bearded, beaver-faced man, and the others, too, huddled in the boxcar. They had lain in the darkness ever since Pittsburgh, and even Mr. Blue seemed nervous. They had glanced through the crack in the door, but they no longer hung there gaping. It was as though they did not want to see too much, as though this was more reality than they could take. O-Zone aliens in New Jersey! He could tell they were shocked: they had not expected this.

He wanted to say, *You O-Zonians haven't seen anything!*

"What are we going to do when we get there?" Valda said.

"We're not going to get there."

"She means to the Wall," Mr. Blue said.

"I'll call my mother."

In a whimpering voice Rooks said, "He'll call his mother!"

Echols said, "You could call her now."

Rooks the toughie, and Echols the scientist, spazzing out at the sight of New Jersey!

"I don't have the range yet," Fisher said. It was a lie but it made them listen. When had they listened like this to him before? Yet, telling them not to worry and showing them this terrible place, he felt tender toward them.

Passing a settlement of old half-collapsed towers with lank gray laundry hanging straight down from clotheslines, they saw children playing among smashed cars in a sealed-off street. There were the inevitable fires: junk fires, children's fires, cooking fires, and smoldering dumps. The earth burned here—nothing in particular, just the oily ground. The drizzle made the fires smokier, and in their disfigurement was a look of utter futility. They had no fury. Their pallid flames and their gas were just another aspect of the ruin. And among all those fires a burning building—fifteen stories in flames—did not seem unusual. This one burned in silence. No fire engines, no hoses or alarms, no shouts: just a black tower going up.

"This is all Roaches. As soon as it gets dark they swarm outside," Fisher said. "There's a law against fires, but no one enforces it—too dangerous."

They did not talk much—the smell choked them. It was a dark brown stink of burned rubber and heavy gas, human waste, ditch water, and oil; it was scorched cloth and the reek of food being boiled in dented pots—bad meat and slop, that seemed the more disgusting when Fisher told them that someone out there intended to eat it.

"Retch-retch," he said, and clicking his faceplate into position, "Too bad you guys don't have masks."

They wrapped cloths around their faces and squatted like bandaged patients. They said nothing, and he admired them for their toughness. And he was grateful: they had made him tough. The very idea of this place used to paralyze him; so he did not blame them—they were aliens, after all, but not Roaches or Skells. And it was a terrible place.

"You get used to it," he said, exulting.

Once, long ago on that New Year's trip, someone had said that aliens had technology—it was Starkies with rockets. And Fisher had denied it—how could they? Naked people with matted hair and dirty feet and yellow teeth—who didn't even build houses! It was impossible to imagine them with missiles, or irons of any kind. They were fairly dangerous with their fires and their knives, but they had no technology—nor had Diggers, nor Skells, nor Trolls, nor Roaches, nor any aliens. If they had, they might have lived interesting lives; but, no, they survived by hiding. Mr. Blue and his people knew how to evaporate, but who except Hooper had ever bothered them in O-Zone?

Yet what this boxcar trip—and really, the journey from O-Zone—had shown Fisher was that aliens were tough. They were not the shaggy pathetic creatures they were always depicted as being—accident-prone and diseased. They were strong; they had to be strong to survive; and if they had technology they would have been superb. It was weapons that made Owners seem strong. Without them, they were naked. They weren't tough, they had no cunning, their senses were deficient. But an alien with technology hardly seemed like an alien at all.

Fisher said, "Don't be afraid. I'll take care of you," and saw himself in the boxcar as unique. He had the wealth of an Owner and the strength of an alien.

They were watching the smoke rise.

He said, "A little technology has taken us halfway across the country. You would never have made it without me."

And they were still relying on him, in a place he had always feared. Looking across at it from Coldharbor or from

Hooper's rotor, he had sensed a tightening in his throat, and he felt he would suffocate if he had to go on looking at it. He became a stupid animal and blamed Moura for choosing such an inadequate pedigree. My ears, my teeth, he thought. And he had been reminded of the size of the world, and how New York was surrounded by misery and danger.

"I like it on the ground!" he said.

Though it was awful here, and no one had succeeded in getting rid of these peripheral zones of gutted buildings. The attempts to burn them down had only made them more dangerous and uglier, and deepened the wasteland, and thickened the soupy air, like something out of the Jurassic Age—black rocks and big greasy birds. But he had conquered his fear and so he felt a wild affection for the place and a tenderness for these strangers who were still afraid.

"Bet you're glad you came!"

He had never imagined this: his standing in the boxcar, rattling through the smoke, frowning at the alienation out the door, and giving these O-Zonians encouragement. They had stolen him! They had not brought him here—he had brought them. And what had begun as his dependency had turned into his leadership. He wasn't leaning on them anymore, he was propping them up. He marveled at the change, and then thought: *I am Fisher Allbright!*

"I used to sit at Pap—remember I told you that's my computer?—and I was all hunched over. My membranes used to get all dried out because I never left the room. A flake of snot would drop out of my nose and hit the keys and I'd screech at it. My uncle saw me do it once. I didn't even care."

They were anxious and so they did not simply laugh but let go and screeched themselves hoarse, as if mimicking his terror.

"They thought I was a willy!"

They laughed again, the boxcar echoed with their shouts, and Fisher thought: They're mine. Their laughter proved that. But it also proved something else: they were good people.

He said, "If I ever took a spasm and decided to stay with you people, it wouldn't be because you're simple and primitive and wonderful, but because you're smart, and you learn fast, and you can use technology. And you know how to evaporate."

The laughter made them very quiet after that, and in the

silence of the boxcar they heard voices outside—the cruel-sounding whoops of wild children.

Gumbie whispered, "Get me out of here."

The door crack widened as the train lurched, and a chevron of daylight passed across the faces of the aliens. They were pale, exhausted from their cross-country push. Heaped there in the boxcar they looked brave and defeated.

"We'll have to get out of this freight car pretty soon. They scan these things at the checkpoint and then seal them. If they find us we'll get cooked."

He wanted them to react. No one spoke.

"You'll get cooked."

He wasn't needling them, he was warning them. But they were waiting for him to say more.

"There's no communications here—there's nothing. But I've got my helmet and I'm within range. I'll radio my mother pretty soon."

Rooks said in his whimpering voice, "He'll radio his mother!"

"How will she find Bligh?" Valda said.

"She'll call my uncle," Fisher said. "Hooper Allbright—remember?"

Kylie startled everyone by saying the jingle, "Allbright's for all bright things."

"Shut up," Rooks said.

They were quiet again, thinking: Then what?

"We'll get out of here," Echols said.

He was already thinking that far ahead. They hadn't arrived and he wanted to leave!

"Wherever we are," Gumbie said in a tone that meant *nowhere*.

Fisher said, "Don't you worry," and liked the way it made them purr.

"—the hell's that?" Valda asked suddenly, jerking herself around and then slowly backing away from the half-open door.

It was a tall shimmering vision, like a whole mirage, sky-high. Beyond the black earth and twisted wire and the fires and the junked cars of the foreground, which was both smoldering and wet—soot and steam mingled—was a towering island of bright metal and stone, across the water. Although it was about noon, the lights were on—windows and skylights; and the thin pale rain made it glitter in half a rainbow.

It rose, wreathed and sparkling in the haze like a city of crystal.

"New York," Fisher said, and he pushed up his scratched faceplate to see it better.

He had left it. He had been a child then, and had thought that New York was the center of everything. The rest of the country was primitive and insignificant, and the world was dark and dangerous. He smiled at the memory of his stupidity. It was not the world but New York that was dangerous. He was headed for that trap—these people intended to deliver him back into his old delusion. He would be shut up in it and kept ignorant. He would be a child in that room with Pap, and afraid again.

They were all staring at the city through the open door.

Fisher was behind them, zipping his suit, tightening his gloves, adjusting his helmet.

He turned to Mr. Blue, who had not spoken for hours—and his last words hadn't been much use. Silence always seemed to make him skinnier and more intense. He looked tough but unprepared.

"What I want to know is," Fisher said softly—and he loved the power in his whisper—"who's in charge of this mission now?"

36

FISHER, YELLING INTO THE BUBBLE ON HIS HEAD, WAS THE first to jump from the boxcar; and the others followed close behind. They took cover in a burned-out building away from the tracks. When they were inside, breathing hard from the effort, Echols remarked on how lucky they were that they had not been spotted by a security patrol.

"There are no patrols on the ground here," Fisher said. "It's all aliens."

They stared at him: they knew what the word meant now.

"I mean, real aliens," he said. "Dangerous ones. Skells. Roaches. Trolls."

They looked around as if expecting to see fangy faces with yellow eyes and spiky hair.

"Hey, the security patrols are dangerous too," he said.

He felt he was now between two worlds—the drooling aliens, the sky-diving Owners. He could think evenly in this in-between space—it was everything that he had seen since O-Zone, and it had seemed fabulous, like an undiscovered valley that had lain undisturbed and unchanged; like O-Zone itself. But he had explored the unknown and felt safe there, and already he longed to return to it.

"Take your time," Mr. Blue said.

Fisher had started to radio Moura. Until then, he had been monitoring the engine of the freight train, the aerial patrols, the transmissions from the towns they had passed.

"Got anything?"

He was fully in charge now. He held up his ragged glove to silence them. He was on the air. Then he heard Moura's voice, talking fast, like someone who has been waiting a long time to speak.

"I'm in the scab—New Jersey," he said, answering one of her many questions. "Let me give you my position. Ready for my coordinates?"

He paused before relaying the information. He liked seeing the patient trusting expressions of the aliens. They did not realize how tough they were. He clicked his faceplate up.

"She's calling Hardy now. He's out looking for us. A real yo-yo at search-and-scan. All technology—no muscle. We could have found him if we'd wanted. These people are such fuck-wits!"

"That's your father," Echols said, cautioning him.

"I don't have a father!" And he thought: That's part of my strength.

"There's no food here," Gumbie said. He was looking out of the cracked window. "That's why these people are crazy."

"They'll bring us food. We'll put it in the bargain!"

Mr. Blue said, "We'll need more than food. What about a truck or something?"

"He wants a vehicle," Fisher said, and made the request sound foolish as he repeated it to the others. "Hey, you won't get far in a vehicle."

Mr. Blue looked uncertain. He sniffed—the smell of this building, its crumbled plaster and burned floors, its lingering smoke-stink of shit, hung over them and made them itch. But their discomfort here added to Fisher's authority.

"You guys have to be prepared. Not a vehicle—a jet-rotor. Money. A program. I've got a great program—it would get you back there, no hands. You've got guts, but you need a little more technology. Hey, this is the world!"

"And Bligh. We want her," Mr. Blue said.

At her name they looked up at the city. It still gleamed through the mist, and the tops of its towers protruded into clear air and shone, silver and crystal, among the buzzing rotors.

The aliens were impressed by it—dazzled even—and Fisher was disappointed in them and wanted to tell them that this revealed the depth of their ignorance. The city seemed as magnificent to them as a castle, and even looked like one. But it was arid and haunted and sealed, hard to enter and after a time impossible to leave. They did not know that— but, really, how could he hold it against them? He had not known it until recently, and it was they who had shown him the true size of the world.

Fisher said, "We'll get everything we want."

They had taken up positions around the blackened building—it seemed more dangerous inside than out, and Fisher knew that if they wanted—if they had to—they could evaporate outside and wait that way: into the mud, behind the decayed houses, into the smoky air. But not yet. Their mission was so far uncompleted. One thing he had noticed, though. They had stopped using the phrase "hand you over."

There were aliens nearby—they could hear their whoops, their dogs, their tin-bashing. There was violence in their very mutters. Their stinking fires were suffocating. And because they could be heard and smelled, but not seen, they seemed turbulent and a greater threat. The rain came down and dribbled into the street and blackened further the poisonous-looking mud.

Fisher said he was trying to get a fix on the rotors. The dark hornets droned, and rose and fell, and some of them settled on the distant buildings. But most of the ones that landed did so on the rotor pads that were moored on the river.

"Not real rotor pads," Fisher explained. "They're just converted barges and lighters. Half of them aren't even safe. And after you put down you need to take a launch into the city."

Again he was describing something they could not see, so they listened very carefully.

"We've got our own pad on the roof of our tower."

"Wedgemere," Valda said, and smiled.

"No, Coldharbor Towers."

It was not a boast anymore. Saying it, he realized how paltry it was. It was a garrison in the Nineties, but so what? For him it had been no more than a safe room where he had spent his childhood with Pap. The journey from O-Zone had helped him discover the pleasure of space. That was his message to Captain Jennix: *There's plenty of space on the ground!*

The rotors flying very high over there made an odd overlapping sound, like a woolly roar. They nosed in and out of the clouds, and the roar suggested that there were many more up there than could be seen.

The clouds parted in places. They were discolored and ragged, and where they had separated were wisps, and in between a clutch of nose-heavy rotors, one with a curling scorpionlike tail, and another with twin rotors, and the shuttle sausage, and a black gunship with indistinguishable markings.

"I think I have contact."

The gunship detached itself from the passing swarm and dropped lower.

"That might be them."

It circled and came lower still, and then held its altitude and moved in a squarer way, tracing four corners in the air above them.

"They're doing short takes for their computer," Fisher said. "Just checking us out with scans, trying to get a soundbite. Hey, they're probably terrified."

He looked around and saw the others squinting over the cloth masks they had wrapped around their faces, against the smoke and the monotonous stinks.

"It's a big bug," Fisher said, and spoke into his mouthpiece: "Commander to Hardy Allbright. We are the mission from O-Zone. Do you read me? Over."

The rain obscured the gunship, and at times it was lost in a tuft of cloud. Fisher repeated his call. The gunship did not reply, yet seemed to drop lower.

"Give your position!"

The command thundered out of the crackle on his earphones. Fisher looked around him. The others had not heard it.

"This is the commander speaking—mission from O-Zone," Fisher said. "I gave explicit instructions for you to keep your distance. My people don't want—"

"We're talking to you, wolfman!"

"If that's not Hardy I'm not giving my position. Verify at once, or else that's negative, fuck-wit. Over."

Mr. Blue was next to him. He said, "What's wrong?"

Fisher did not want to say that he felt very vulnerable under the rolling gunship. But it was still high, and they were scattered beneath it.

"They could be security," Fisher said. "Maybe they haven't pinpointed us yet. I didn't give them our position."

There was an overtaking sound of human voices that made his skin prickle: some of the others had started to scream at the sight of the descending gunship. It disturbed him and made him want to scream himself.

"I'm going off the air. We've got to lose them."

The gunship was settling lower and turning toward them, whipping the rain.

"Get down!" Fisher said, and he stood up, holding one of the old long-barreled weapons they had brought from Guthrie. He hoped to fire into the throat of the jets and perhaps gag it. Now it had come close enough for its insignia to be clearly visible. He saw the skull and crossbones, the sunburst, the motto.

"Godseye!"

There was a mass of twisted snakes painted on the tail, and weapons protruding from under the black canopy, and howlers mounted on the midsection.

The gunship was shuddering, moving back and forth, beating the rain and spinning it in silver bursts from the rotor blades. The windows were blacked out. Fisher was trying to signal again. Hooper had told him of the Godseye hunt he had gone on, and how stupid and heavily armed the troopers were; how they burned aliens.

He could not warn the others. The howlers had started, deafening them, and the sound made them go small and look very compact. The howling was interspersed with blasts of simulated artillery, the terrible noise intended to paralyze them. But Fisher still wore his helmet, and when he switched it off and sealed it he heard nothing more than a distant whine and an odd popping.

Yet there was too much interference for him to go back on the air and tell them who he was. You're making a mistake, he wanted to say—and he kept thinking of the hideous irony in his having gotten so near to New York, and being burned here, in sight of Coldharbor, mistaken for an alien.

Mr. Blue lay on his side, and Echols near him, and Valda and the others crouched with small pinched faces under the ear-shattering noise. The howl alone seemed lethal, rendering muscles incapable of movement, and smothering the will in its rising pressure. But in his helmet Fisher was more indignant than frightened. He was outraged. How dare they! He had come too far and fought too hard to be wiped out by the dumb sadists in a death squad.

The rifle banged his faceplate as he tried to aim. He fired anyway, but made no impact—what good was this old iron? Yet their sensors must have picked up the slug, because the gunship immediatcly tilted in a lumbering way and presented the titanium plates of its armored hull.

And still howling, the gunship released a rocket. The slender thing flamed out of a side tube and tore off a corner of the building above them, spilling bricks on them. This was followed by a burst of fléchettes.

Fisher was swearing, but before he could fire again he saw the shadow of another rotor diving through the upper air. A missile twisted out of its nose and flashed into the gunship. In that same instant the gunship exploded. It blew sideways and dropped, burning fast. There was no thud—after the howling and the blasts there was only a loose sunflower of flame, coming apart as it fell. Then the great black gunship was simplified to a shower of sparks and bright petals, and fluttered noiselessly to the ground.

Bligh had begun to cry as soon as she had seen the aliens cowering near the building: they were magnified on the ground-screen. Even after the gunship disintegrated and vanished, they had not lifted their heads. She wept at the sight of them in that black ruin among the burned-out houses and the ditches and tracks. Steam rose around them, and bright pellets of rain flecked the smoke. Not even Mr. Blue was standing. She wondered whether they were dead.

Hooper had been shushing her, trying to calm her, for the entire trip, as he had radioed Moura and monitored Godseye. He had been tense for the past half-hour, knowing that Godseye had copied the message from Moura, and fearing that he might be too late. *Burn them all down* he had heard echoing from the gunship, and he'd flung himself at the missile release.

"Don't cry," he said.

She had sometimes become tearful when they made love. *I'm happy,* she said, blinking her smeared eyes and licking the tears from her lips. She said nothing now, she only sobbed.

He guessed that it was her shock at seeing the aliens in that terrible place, flattened on the ground, and Fizzy standing over them.

"He looks okay," Hardy said. "He's alive."

Hardy's words meant nothing, and he knew it. The boy was beyond description. It was as though a defiant and slightly taller stranger had slipped into his flying suit and was

shaking his iron at the heap of steaming ashes. Yet his faceplate was open; they recognized the boots, the gloves, the
helmet; and though the suit was tighter on his body, they
could see it was Fizzy. But that raised another question: Who
was Fizzy?

"They want to see Bligh!"

It didn't sound like Fizzy. The quack had gone out of his
voice. There was a growl in it now, his delivery was slower,
with a rumble behind it. His voice had broken: it had
dropped from his nose to his throat.

"Is Bligh in there with you?"

Bligh heard him and pushed her face to the window. She
looked out, trying to smile and keep her balance in the tipping rotor.

"They wonder if she's all right!"

Bligh heard this over the rotor's loudspeaker and waved.
Hooper flew lower, so that they could see.

"Don't come any closer," Fisher said. "You'll spook
them."

"Give us instructions for picking you up," Hardy said into
his mike.

Fisher stepped back. Who were these people? This was no
rescue. He had saved himself.

"They might have warped his judgment," Hardy was saying.

Fisher said, "We want to know who sent that Godseye
gunship here."

Hardy said, "Who's 'we'?"

"I'm putting this thing down, Fizz," Hooper said. "Get
clear of that building."

"They don't want me to. They don't trust you—especially
now, after those howlers and that rocket. They want to make
a deal."

Bligh was still crying softly at the sight of them crouching in
the mud; and circling in the rotor, she could see the city
behind them. It seemed to her now as though that was where
the world began.

"What do they want?" Hooper called out.

Fisher did not have to consult Mr. Blue, or any of the
others. He knew the terms, he had known them ever since
they set out.

"Hand Bligh over," he said. "And some hardware—a rotor, some weapons, some food, and cash. And get me a jelly sandwich."

Hearing this, Hooper brought the rotor to within a meter of the ground. He threw the side hatch open, so that Bligh could be seen. She hung on to the safety clamp and strap-loops, and stayed in the gaping hatchway. She lifted off her helmet and shook out her hair. She was not crying any longer, and yet she looked frightened as she glanced at Mr. Blue and Echols, who were kneeling in the mud in front of the others, as though they had been tossed there. They blinked back at her through the warm drizzle.

Bligh turned toward Hooper, as if imploring him for a verdict.

"It's your life," Hooper said, trying to find the right words, but expressing it better with a gesture—opening his hand and lifting it, as if releasing a bird. "You're free."

She smiled and held on. He had gambled on that. His decision to let her go—to leave the choice to her—was the proof of his love. In freeing her, he allowed her the decision. He now knew her well enough to realize that it was the only basis on which she would stay. She was so young, and he did not want her as his prisoner.

She had not moved; and it seemed certain from the way she was braced, with her legs apart, that she was not going to. The shadows had cleared from her face. She clung to the hatchway, but not in triumph. Her thin flying suit was blown against her body by the draft from the rotors—it was so tight its pressure outlined her nipples and her navel. Her expression showed relief, but her pale eyes showed sorrow and helplessness and eager hope: all the emotions of love—but it was part of her victory that she had never used that word.

"Look at him," Hardy said.

He had not taken his eyes from Fizzy. He was still trying to discern the nature of this beast. There was no doubt that the boy had become a man—he was bigger, hairier, and his voice had a growly authority. He wore his suit and his helmet. Their battered condition made him look wild. But he was calm, and there was something in that terrible patience that made him seem stronger and more dangerous. He was like one of those creatures that Hardy had heard of but never seen, aliens with technology, like the naked cast-out people who had rockets, and the Trolls who had gas, and the Roaches beams, and the Diggers who inhabited whole underground cities, in fabulous caverns—they were mythical almost, but Hardy believed he was looking at the real thing now.

They were asking for surrender, Fisher knew that. But he wanted more than New York—more than to be kept in a room, even one with Pap and his data base. He wanted to lay claim to his own life. So far, he had only had glimpses of what it might be like. He remembered it as triumphing on the ground—walking through O-Zone, blasting through the Red Zone Perimeter, entering the town of Guthrie.

"Batfish," he murmured, and saw himself opening another door and stepping through. "You porker."

He was smiling. He had not been rescued. He had made his own way back to New York. He had saved those aliens He had saved himself. He could do it again.

Beyond the black scab of this place, and the twittering rotor, the city mounted higher. The air was still gray here, but over there the sky had cleared. Rocket-shaped towers, and some like swords, struck through the parted clouds. Was that Coldharbor—was that the room where he had been a child?

He thought. What a world—and corrected himself. There were a million worlds; they contained all the past and all the future. Time was a matter of choice, if you were free. Every age was simultaneous upon the earth.

He wanted to choose. Mr. B had once said beautifully, "Shall we go?" The man had not needed to ask—that was why it mattered what he said. And Fisher, who had never believed in permission, and had seldom uttered a question, now had to ask one.

"Can I come with you?"

Their consent gave him power.

The uncertain weather and the way he stood in the rotor had masked Hardy by giving him a yellow mottled face, and he went very still and stupid, as if emptied of hope.

Hooper had never expected Fizzy to turn aside. He had agreed to all the terms, and had just begun to say, "You don't have to go all the way back."

But before he had got five words out—and as he was

speaking, which made it the worst interruption—the people shimmered into the drizzly heat. It made him feel temporary and unsteady, and he held on to Bligh, as the sun pierced the mist on this perimeter and broke through to reveal the people gone. They were all aliens again in the transfiguring light.

PART SIX

LANDSLIP

37

THE YEAR OF EVENTS WAS NOT OVER. FIZZY WAS GONE, and Moura noticed that everyone had returned to live quietly, at half-speed, renewing themselves on a routine. It was like load-shedding, a pause from the strain of having lived so fiercely for so long. But Moura was still alert—dissatisfied.

Then one day at the end of that same year Hooper called her to say that he had not forgotten the agreement he had made months before, and she had wondered *What agreement?* The earlier part of the year had been like another age, and most of it was buried and forgotten until certain words were mentioned, always the ambiguous ones that stirred her, like *alien* or *Owner* or *perimeter* or *clinic* or *O-Zone*. They had all acquired different meanings this year.

She was alone. Hardy was on an Asfalt project somewhere in Africa, but when had he ever mattered to her?

"We're back in business," Hooper said, explaining that he had just returned from California. He was flying everywhere these days, and not only to the south and west, where he had warehouses, but to Europe, and his factories in Mexico and India. He was energetic but still narrow and secretive—still in love, very frisky.

He had said to Moura, "Once you get used to having showers with someone else, it isn't the same when you've got to take one alone. It's like sleeping alone. It doesn't work."

It astonished Moura that he could say such a thing to her, but she knew that it was love that had made him insensitive. You could not be offended by his mushy logic.

He traveled for Bligh's sake, and they were always together. He was crowing *Look! See!* He took her by the hand and showed her the extent of what he owned—See how big! See how lovely! See how valuable! He showed her the world; and he had never been happier, for Hooper, who had never had a child because he had never had a wife he had trusted, now had both—and more. Bligh was a wife, a daughter, a companion, a friend.

Hooper had the boring habit of telling you how old she was—to Moura's annoyance there was never a polite reply to this old news. You just had to pretend that it was somehow a tremendous virtue to be fifteen years old; and really you wanted to laugh at the buffoon showing the space between his teeth and telling you how healthy this child was. Bligh, to her credit, found those moments awkward; and then Hooper seemed like the child, and she the adult. And Moura thought that in all such relationships that must be the case.

In other respects, Bligh must have satisfied a craving in Hooper for a child he could fondle and fuss over and blame—and rely on, too. "I've got to get back and give her a bath," he told Moura one evening, and she didn't know whether to regard that as very sweet or very perverted—but in any case she had always found Hooper both. And often it seemed that it was not even that one was an adult and the other a child, but rather that one was a child and the other a doll.

Yet it touched Moura to see this billionaire trying to impress the alien. It had a grotesque poignancy, like poor confused Fizzy long ago quacking, "Bremstrahlung!" to a room full of party guests. Hooper's love affair would work as long as he supervised everything and kept his own secrets. He was in charge, and so far Bligh was still a comparative stranger. While she remained a stranger she was dependent on him, and he was happy. Hooper's power lay in dazzling her.

Moura saw them fairly often, though she could never effectively separate them. It was always "we" now, and Moura was never able to have a private talk with the girl. It was as though Hooper wanted to prevent Moura from knowing too much, or saying too much—as if Hooper did not want Moura to influence her. But it was so silly of him. Moura knew nearly everything; and Bligh must have been very shrewd and hungry or else she would not have lasted this long with Hooper.

Everyone now knew that Bligh was an alien on a false ID.

Moura felt that it was what most men wanted: a simple soul to manipulate—a doll to play with. Owners captured them and screwed them and killed them. There was a story going around that Bligh was diseased. Moura knew it was not so. It was said because she was an alien. It wasn't true anymore to say that all aliens had diseases. Everyone had diseases. The difference was that Owners had doctors. As lovers and workers, aliens were in demand. Moura sometimes had the heretical thought that it was perhaps the aliens and not the Owners who would determine the fate of the world; but though the heresy gave her life—nothing lifted her spirits like the thought of rebellion these days—she also wondered: Am I thinking that because Fizzy is among them?

Some of them weren't so simple! And Hooper was also grateful to Bligh. She was his project—even he used that patronizing word—but she was also sensible and she was clearly able to make him happy. Moura guessed that underlying everything was a powerful sexual connection, as mysterious and unknowable as in any pair of people. It was a hot animating secret, and it energized them. In the sloppy and lavish ways that couples made themselves happy they were triumphant, and Moura admitted to herself that she envied them that happiness.

Hooper had such a large capacity for it. He was lordly with the girl, but he was also a boy, a husband, a father: Bligh brought out all these sides of him, and for whatever reason—her ingenuity, her peculiar beauty, her youth, the fact that she was illegal—there was no room, no time, for anyone else in Hooper's life. So they lived exclusively in each other's company. It might have destroyed another relationship. It strengthened theirs. Hooper was busy and interested, and who knew what this concentrated intimacy did for their sex life? Moura knew Hooper to be an avid photographer. His wife and girlfriends had always called him "the cameraman." You saw the gap between his front teeth and somehow you knew he was taking your picture. Moura did not want to know more than that. She had seen the strobe lights flashing at his windows in Coldharbor, and heard Hardy: "He's at it again."

There might have been another stimulus, every Owner's worry about his alien lover—that the alien was illegal and temporary and would never really belong to him, and it was because Hooper feared losing her that he behaved well toward her even though he monopolized her.

Nonetheless, Hooper was happy, and after this frightful year Moura wanted something for herself.

"I want happiness," she said.

"Why not ecstasy? It's the best drug." That was the new Hooper talking.

Now he was back from California, saying, "I'm a man of my word—I'm keeping my part of the bargain," and Moura had no idea what he meant.

She was smiling because he was—her smile an empty reflection of his huge illuminated grin.

"You've forgotten!" he yelled at her. All this energy in him made her tired. He was so pleased with himself. Did he still say that he had everything that he had ever wanted? That he was the luckiest man in the world?

Just his broad face was a boast, and the set of his teeth in his gaping mouth defeated her and made her feel weak. Hooper did not need to crow. He was somewhere and settled, that was obvious; she was nowhere, and for her it had been a year of losses and disappearances—Fizzy, Hardy, Hooper; and deaths too—stupid Willis Murdick up in smoke—and that had changed Holly.

Moura said, "Is it something about Fizzy?"

"No, the other man in your life."

She was not thinking: Hardy. Her mind was guiltily on Barry Eubank, who had stopped in to see Hardy; and she had detained him, simply asked for it by saying *God, I'm horny* or something equally awful. An hour of that, and now the word "man" confused her as much as any of the ambiguous code words. It was so easy to sleep with the husbands of her friends: her women friends always seemed to be pimping without being aware of it.

"Why are you blushing?"

She said, "Don't tease me, Hoop."

"That guy you were looking for in the New York area— remember 'Boy'?" Hooper said. "I think we found him."

At once she remembered more than she had ever dared, and he saw the eager questions in her eyes.

"In California. A week ago. Landslip. We had a network of warehouse facilities out there, before it cracked, and I'd been neglecting them—"

Get to the point, she thought. She was impatient now that

she knew the subject. He was talking about Allbright's warehouses, his work, his travel, where "we" had gone—he wanted to be given credit for taking trouble. He was making Moura pay for the information by making her listen to the details of how he had discovered it.

"—those warehouses are scattered all over southern California, in the most godawful places. You should see the zone."

He talked about the crack itself, how it opened, how you could see it from the air, the fault that had tipped the cities over and brought ruin and divided the state and given the name to the precarious new zone of Landslip.

She said, "Where is he?"

"I'm coming to that," he said. He looked pleased by her impatience, because it proved that she was really listening.

"I know about the crack," she said. "Everyone does."

"But do you know what it did to communications? They were without power for over a year—some areas still don't have juice. They've got dead lines, no phones except yelling out the window, not that they have windows. The computers went down, just died or strangled, and some dropped completely out of the system. I'm talking about security. Some are still out and are linking up slowly. The crack not only split up houses and roads, but also "

Lives, relationships, businesses, families—she knew what was coming, but Hooper went on at his own speed, keeping her swinging, making her work for what she wanted to find out.

"And security systems," he finally said. "They lost files! It was like being bombed! No records! No files, no wires, no information—the simplest data, like names and addresses. It's like O-Zone. It's unplugged."

All this while Moura thought how much easier Hooper had been when he was gloomy and womanless; and he had started to worry when he had stopped wanting anything—his imagination collapsed. It had been terrible for him. But he had been so simple then; so quiet. Now with this girl up in his tower he was so manic and spirited, ingenious and boring with his tiresome teasing. What an effort he was when things were going his way—so full of talk!

She could not separate his energetic good humor from his boasting. It seemed like the same thing.

She thought: I have no one.

He was still describing how parts of Landslip were not plugged in! She said, "But you plugged them in."

"Don't hurry me. I used my head. I know they're reconnecting the lines out there, so I kept hunting. I put out a query and let it float. Know what that means?"

"I can guess."

But he insisted on explaining.

She tuned out until he said, "I had this idea that if his name wasn't in any system, and the lines were down in Landslip, that's where he might be. His name just came up."

"He's in California?"

Hooper smiled, but it was not a smile—it was an expression she knew from the faces of all her wealthy friends, who hated to be hurried, or interrupted, or given advice. The rich went at their own speed and held to the view that they were always in charge.

"Landslip?" she said.

He shook his head to imply that she was being too impatient.

"Hooper, this is serious!"

He did not flinch at her cry. He stared at her and sized her up and made her feel weak again, and then he gave in.

"Just outside Landslip, apparently. A place called Forestdale."

"He's definitely there?"

"The fact sheet gave it as his last known address."

"He might have moved!"

"It was recent—he could be there," Hooper said, becoming stern under Moura's questioning. "He's not in regular touch."

"He's an Owner!"

Hooper relaxed, seeing that she was wrong. "That's the funny part," he said. "He's not down as an Owner. He's listed as unclassified."

"He must have lost his classification," Moura said, and remembered the ruined houses and towers around New York where she had searched for him. "I wonder how."

"There's only two ways: tax fraud, nonpayment, or criminality, and the Feds snatch it—or else you hand it over. He didn't have any convictions—a few noncriminal offenses, ID violations. I mean, he doesn't have a card."

"You're saying that he declassified himself! No one's that stupid!"

She knew at once she had said too much.

"It's been known to happen," Hooper said. His eyes were empty.

Like her, he must have been thinking of Fizzy. But she was grateful to him for not mentioning the boy's name. She did not want to be reminded of how completely he had gone. He had been untraceable from the day he had left, and she had thought: What freedom these aliens have! They could move, they could travel, they could adopt any identity they liked. But an Owner was fixed and measured—and an Owner was so easy to find. Yet the Owner was always safe, because he was always monitored. The alien was always in danger, because he had no legal existence. Fizzy had chosen that: he had vanished.

"Moura, I'm sure your man's there."

She remembered which man.

"A smile, at last," Hooper said.

This was the news she needed: that Fizzy's father had been found. It was not merely that he would help her understand Fizzy and give her access to his mind. She needed it more because over this past year she had accepted the passion she had felt when, in their masks, they had made love at the contact clinic. More than accepted it—valued it, counted on it, been vitalized by it, and wanted more. The mention of that name Boy aroused her as it had when Dr. Sanford had said it.

"You'll need this," Hooper said, and gave her a printout with the coded information. "Though there's not much here."

As if accounting for the few lines on the strip of paper, she said, "But he's still young."

"Forty-two!" Hooper said, still so frisky.

Could he be that old? The number startled her. She was on the verge of denying it and then realized that she would sound ridiculous. Yet she couldn't picture him at that age, or any age except twenty-six. Anyway, he was not like other men—not like any man she had known. Fizzy was the proof of his uniqueness.

She glanced at the paper printout: "WM UNC PAR 2 REF O CLASS SUBJ B NYC PED REF REAR ED REF PLUS"—indecipherable.

"Standard data code," Hooper said. "You won't have any trouble checking the references for detail, or finding prose equivalents. The important reference is circled."

The circle contained "CA-FO ZONE" and some numbers.

"Forestdale. Last sighting. And those are the coordinates."

Forestdale was one of those California names that described its opposite. There certainly wouldn't be any trees there.

"I appreciate this, Hoop."

He was looking into her face, beneath her expression, beneath skin and bones.

"It's usually a mistake to find what you're looking for," he said. "It's much better to find what you're not looking for."

In his voice was a kind of listening caution, as if he were testing this thought by saying it out loud. And she could tell from his tone that he wanted to get away now. He had delivered his message and lost some of his bounce. He didn't want her frustration to disturb him.

Hooper had become one of those happy people who went around repelling unhappiness like evil—not wanting to be tainted by anyone's bad luck. They frisked along, protecting themselves with self-congratulation, with boasts, with anything to repel low spirits. They could go very quiet and vanish, too, when they saw clouds blimping up—problems, whines, complaints, envious questions, urgencies. Happy people learned how to be great selfish preservers of their happiness, like strangers walking carefully in the dark—they feared holes and gouging corners and sudden shouts. Hooper wanted to be back with his snug leggy fifteen-year-old.

Moura considered what he had just said, and thought: What am I looking for?

Hooper was rising and bristling and beginning to flee.

"I'm glad you're happy," Moura said, putting it as unselfishly as she could and not asking why it was. His happiness was so unpredictable, so hard to comprehend or contain—and so full of secrets and evasions, like a child's hidden life, with its mingled pleasures and fears.

He said, "We're doing all right."

He's alive, she thought, and envied him. Why was she so jealous of this young girl? All their warmth made her feel very cold.

He said, "I was lucky."

He meant it as an attempt at humility, as if he wanted his ghosts to overhear that he was grateful; and yet even that sounded to her like a boast. Because he was so happy, everything he said sounded like a boast.

"I don't have a lot of time. I don't want to waste it."

I do nothing but waste it, Moura thought. She said, "This must seem so strange to her."

"No—this is very easy," he said. "She sits by the pool and paints her toenails and eats chocolates."

"And what do you do?"

"Buy the chocolates," he said. "She likes it here. New York is safe. But out there—that's hard. We're the ones on the fringe. We always thought O-Zone and those places were dead. But that's where most of the life is. It's a struggle!"

"Holly wants to talk to me about another party this year."

Hooper looked doubtful, and determined to go—more than that, looked as though he wanted to burst through the wall. The last party in O-Zone had been the start of everything for him. Trying to repeat it, he might lose his luck; he might lose everything. That fear was on his face.

"We'll see about that," he said, and made it sound like No.

After Hooper had gone, Moura grew excited. She had not wanted him to know how this man mattered to her. But from the moment she had heard the name she had begun to hope. She envisioned him and thought: I exist. And as she revived she realized how discouraged she had felt—how deep she had dropped. In all the losses, all the vanishing confusion in the inexplicable past, she saw a crumbling pattern in which one element was unchanging: this man, and her feeling for him—and it gave her hope for something more.

The alteration in her was sudden because her vision of him was so clear—not just his bold boyish figure as he approached and hovered over her; but the vivid sense—vibrant as a pulse—of his body humming in the darkness. And his special smell—not flowers, not perfume, but a ripe male smell that soaked him and reminded her of blood. And the smoothness of his skin, his feet, his hands—long gentle fingers, and his slender legs. The memory of particular postures, of his movement and his heat, excited her.

I never saw his face, she thought. But she remembered the beaky mask and she had always felt she knew the face behind it. She had decided on specific features—nose, ears, teeth, chin—and had seen her guesses confirmed as Fizzy had filled out and grown; as his face developed. Fizzy was special and terrible in his way, but he was handsome.

As for Fizzy's father—Boy—she had seen him so many times: glimpsed him in crowds, seen him on the street and in restaurants, and not only in New York but everywhere she went. Now she stopped seeing him; now she knew where he was.

The masks had made it perfect. Their meetings and their lovemaking in the clinic, and his whispers, had always inspired her the more because of their mystery—because of what she had not seen, never known, what she had guessed at and imagined. Over those two years of going to the clinic she had wanted him—woken up and desired him—and immediately afterward wanted him again.

It was so long ago, but the feeling was fresh in her. The loneliness, the longing: they were physical—she felt that longing in her belly, in her legs, on her face, in all her muscles. Desire was not a thought—it was a desperate thirsting of the flesh. It could hurt. She still wanted him, and now realized helplessly but with a surge of pride that she loved him.

38

AND I'M ALSO GOING SIMPLY TO VERIFY IT—TO SEE HIM and prove that he exists, and that it was not an illusion, Moura thought. That I lived once.

She was urged by her pride, and made excuses, but she knew that the risk was that if she were wrong she was left with nothing. Yet if she were right she had everything to gain. It was pathetic to say, "Even if I'm finished now, I had that—I had him," because she wasn't finished. But she was powerfully curious, and felt it in every muscle: it made her weak and eager like the worst hunger.

It was a way of reminiscing, too—going cross-country, getting out of Coldharbor, away from these New York towers.

After—waveringly—the decision was made, she felt courageous.

Until now she had avoided Holly, but with the prospect of finding her old lover she called her friend and they arranged to meet at Holly's new house.

"No one has a house in New York!"

"They're building them again—it's a town house, in Upper West, facing all that junk on the Jersey heights."

Moura kept herself from saying, *Near the clinic.*

"I've got a car, too—imagine! The permit cost a fortune, but I figured what the hell. Someday they won't even be selling permits for private cars. And it's nice to snuggle up with someone in the back seat."

Inevitably, Holly's talk turned to sex. But Moura shrugged. She could meet her without feeling like a failure or a sneak. It was not a question of telling Holly, but merely enjoying the thought that she had someone and that she had joined the two loose ends of her life with this one man.

But if she began to talk about it, she knew, it would seem a paltry story—mostly memory and not enough of it. She did not have the answers to her own crucial questions, so she knew she would not be able to answer Holly's sharper ones. Moura decided to say nothing about her lover, Fizzy's father. But it was not only caution: she was thrilled by her silence and that secret.

Holly sent the car for her. It was a kind of bragging and so Moura did not feel she had to be abjectly grateful. The house was less than a year old. A tower had been pulled down to make room for a development of tall narrow houses, like slender bottles in a row, their curved glass side facing west and the river.

Living so close to the ground was noisy—nothing like a tower and hardly anything like the cloudland of Coldharbor. But it was obviously such an expensive house, and Holly was so pleased, that Moura vowed to herself that she would not mention the noise—traffic, rotors, even voices and horns.

"We're at a very low altitude," Holly said, making a joke of her explanation, because she had had to stop talking when a rotor went overhead. "I used to hate looking at the ground."

She had been saying, "Who does your face?"

The admiration in her voice was undisguised, but Moura knew that Holly would never understand how her quiet life had kept her youthful.

"If you're taking something I'd like to know what it is," Holly said. "I need all the help I can get."

As if capsules explained everything. Moura exercised and ate well, and she felt rueful when she looked in the mirror and saw an attractive woman. She thought *What for?* and sensed her petals trembling and about to drop.

"You look great, Holly."

"I'm feeling piggy."

It was so exact Moura laughed out loud and saw a fat snout on Holly's face. The secret image a woman had of herself was often unexpectedly true—it came from studying the mirror and comparing other women and becoming obsessive about a single defect. Moura had sometimes thought: My ears—and had worried about making Fizzy bat-eared. "Pig" was perfect for Holly; not the huge oafish thing but a little selfish squealing creature with a piggy appetite.

Lust made people gleam like meat, and Holly had a lusty roasted look, which at its piggiest was like a kind of pork sausage. The year had left her fleshier and squinty, as if she'd had too much sun. Her lines marked expressions on her face—all her expressions, all at once—and it confused Moura to see amusement, pain, joy, and disgust scribbled one over the other in wrinkles, as though her face was a used bag of old emotions.

She looked lazier and smugger—probably the Godseye pension: somehow there was a Federal supplement in their insurance plan. Moura knew the government sweetened the so-called militias' funds—it certainly wasn't private money. And Moura had heard that Murdick Elevator Supplies had been sold.

"You could live here in the Colony and keep me company," Holly said. She wore a one-piece with windows and it crackled as she rolled over on the sofa and stuffed another cushion under her stomach.

"Is that what they call it, the Colony?"

"Yeah, that's why I sent the car. If you had come on your own they would have put you through the wringer. Live behind a high fence—that's what Willis always said."

Moura was thinking: *The Colony—*

"He believed in perimeters," Holly said.

She had never been faithful to Willis, but she had lost him in a good cause; and now that the nuisance had been murdered, and she was rid of him, she could safely think of him as a hero. She talked about him in a lying widowy way, as if she was proud of him. But Holly was also the sort of friend who could win back Moura's affection by saying something like: Of course, I'm not a hypocrite—the whole point of sentimentality is that it has to be insincere!

"And how's Hardy?" Holly said.

Moura was annoyed, because it sounded as if Holly wanted to compare husbands. Moura could not match that simple chummy tone. It was all right for Holly to ramble on about Willis—he was dead, after all, and safe. But Moura was uneasy saying anything about her husband. Apart from the fact that whatever she said would probably be wrong, it was also, she felt, a little dangerous. It was the live people who came back and haunted you, not the dead ones.

"Hardy's in Africa," Moura said. "He's got a big project there. Some sort of surfacing thing. Hooper told me about it—Hardy's so secretive. Apparently, it's to make up for that O-Zone fiasco."

"I love the islands in Africa," Holly said.

"There are no islands in Africa," Moura said. "You mean countries."

"No, islands. Like Earthworks. Those perimeter places with hotels. God, the guys out there were great stuff, weren't they?"

"I thought you had someone on board," Moura said.

"Can we talk about this next New Year's party?"

"That Woody-something you introduced me to."

They all had someone on board—Hooper, Rinka, Fizzy too probably, and Holly and her dumb muscleman. She imagined this man showing off in the pool of this housing complex in Upper West—the Colony pool, whatever it was called—in one of those little shiny bathing suits, strutting around showing his pouch, and Holly gleaming like a piglet. Undoubtedly Hardy had someone on board in Africa—the place was impossible without another friendly face. He was welcome to whoever—she could only do him good.

Holly said, "Woody's still around," and giggled and added, "I was going crazy, dating these guys. I think sex is part of my insecurity. I have to prove myself, like a kid. But it wasn't working. That's why I needed Woody."

"I'm glad things have worked out between you two."

"You don't understand. I needed him so that I could be unfaithful to him. Now I really am humping away. I've given up that stupid clinic."

"The routine," Moura said—lying, to keep her secret. She had not felt that way at all, but only a sadness when she became pregnant and could not justify going anymore. It had seemed worse than the end of a love affair. But at least I have his child, she had thought. Yet it had turned out to be Fizzy, and he had been like a death for her.

"No," Holly was saying. Her face had changed—more lines, conspiratorial, sharing a scandal; disgusted and glad. "A scare went around the place. Some fungus or another. Maybe a virus. At first I thought: This is supposed to be a clinic? Then I found out that this great so-called clinic lost its license a few years ago—"

"Holly, it wouldn't be the same party."

The suddenness of the interruption registered on Holly's face, and she blinked and squeezed her cheeks at Moura.

"Everything's different now," Moura said. Holly was pouting at her like a fat little baby. "Hardy's away. The Eubanks are in Florida. Fizzy's gone. Hooper's got that young girl—he'd never go. And Willis—"

"Is dead but that's not a problem," Holly said briskly. "You and I are here, and why shouldn't we do what we want?"

"We're a pretty small party, darling. And we'd never get there without Fizzy."

"I hate it when things change like this," Holly said, looking more brattish than ever. "It's awful when people tell you time's up, and you can't go back. I don't want it to stop!"

Moura made a sympathetic noise, but thought: I *am* going back, and not to the scene in O-Zone of that desperate party—it had been a failure as a party, it had overwhelmed them, it had changed everything. But no, she was returning to the deeper, the happier past and that lost love. The past wasn't a riddle: it was only illegible at this distance. Who had said that the past was a mystery, but the future was familiar?

"Fizzy's gone," Holly said, echoing what Moura had just said. "Don't you ever worry about him?"

Moura could not think of a way of telling Holly the truth—that she thought much more about Fizzy's father.

"He's so young to be with those aliens. What is he, fifteen?"

"Just turned sixteen," Moura said.

"You must wonder what he's doing."

No: her inability to imagine what the strange boy might be doing kept her from worrying. He was like a different species—like an alien himself.

She said, "I just hope he's happy."

"How could he be! Those people are animals! Look what they did to Willis!"

The official story was that the aliens had burned the Godseye gunship and that Hooper had been unable to rescue the crew. But Hooper had told Moura another story; and Hardy confirmed it—how they destroyed the attacking gunship and let the aliens vanish.

"Don't you want to save him?"

"If he wants to be found, he'll be found," Moura said. And she thought: We are the ones who are lost. "I'd only like to know what sort of person he is."

A loud pair of rotors went overhead, chugging and making the windows shake, and Holly's squint of incredulity—*what sort of person?*—was tightened by the squint the noise gave her.

Moura said, "I never really knew him. He lived his own life."

"But he's in O-Zone!"

"O-Zone might be the perfect place for him."

"O-Zone is nowhere."

"You want to have a party there," Moura said, but it was more a mocking reminder than a statement of defiance.

Holly made a mask of her face—she was thinking hard—and then she said, "Like a lot of really far-out places—like that Earthworks place in Africa, and some deserts and wildernesses and city-stains—the only thing it's good for is a party."

She smiled, thinking of the party in O-Zone.

"Willis would have wanted us to," she said.

She so enjoyed herself now. She had become an extravagant boasting widow. You couldn't dispute or deny anything she said or else she'd turn on you and cry, *My husband was killed!* And though it made no sense at all to Moura, Holly was happy, because as she said, she had Woody to be unfaithful to.

It seemed strange that this woman had once been her close friend. But now they had their own secrets, and Moura wanted to leave. And she had felt throughout the hopeless conversation that Holly wanted to be elsewhere—her blood was up, she knew she didn't have much time, she was dressed to meet a man. Moura lingered because she knew she would probably never see Holly again—a former friend could be so dangerous: there was no worse enemy. She never wanted to see her again, so she gave her another minute.

Why should I be sorry that Fizzy is gone? she thought. He had seldom been happy in Coldharbor, and never in New York. It was just possible that he was happy now, among aliens. And it was not that the year had taken so much away—those losses and disappearances—but rather that so much had become apparent. She had seen who these people were—who she was.

Holly seemed on the verge of speaking. She was holding her breath, wondering whether she should risk it. Moura stared at her and refused to be undermined by how obvious a sneak Holly was, how her trickery was always apparent on her face, and how her real emotions never were—only the creased surface of that bag in which they were jumbled.

"Say it." And Moura got up to leave this woman for good.

"You should really find someone for yourself," Holly said.

39

Moura wanted to rent a light plane and fly cross-country on her own, but at the last minute her impatience overtook her, the matter became urgent: she hopped by rotor from Coldharbor to the airport and went on the fastest flight she could find to Los Angeles, arriving at dawn, three hours before the time she had set out.

The speed frightened her, she imagined the crash, and her fear was so acute that she knew she would remember it as though the crash had happened, as though she had died. She had died that vivid death so many times before—suffocated in panic and noise.

In the sealed and windowless plane, flying at an altitude of thirty-two clicks, Moura could not see the country below. Yet strapped in and with her eyes shut, she had the impression that things had changed—the entire country, everything, everyone, all they overflew. But that was absurd: she knew it was her mood. She was ashamed that Holly had seen her loneliness. Sex was always possible, it was a fever that came and went; but how pathetic she felt, flying alone and blaming her odd solitary feeling on a world she had imagined was completely changed. She thought: the world is the same. The misery is mine. I need a friend.

But then on the low daybreak approach to Los Angeles the large ground-screen was switched on in front of her and she saw that the city had changed. It was almost unrecognizable. And it was not just the effect of the yellow smog, though she could see how much dustier it was. The smog lay thicker than any cloud, bulked between the mountains and the sea, and where there were holes in it Moura saw devastation, which was the severest difference.

To the southeast, bordering the area that everyone called Landslip, the fault line was distinct. It was a crack, a wrinkle, a seam—depending on the depth of the rupture. In places it looked as solid and upstanding as a curbstone. It had risen and cast a shadow against the powdery light. It was patchy and blistered, and in some places it was a physical feature, a rounded lump, like a bad vein bulging in an elderly leg; in other places it was a stain—the result of the way people had resettled an area, or stayed away. It gave the city a look of division.

The shadow at the southeast side of the seam was Landslip, distinct and depopulated, with the same kind of city-stains she had seen in O-Zone. There were some live or reactivated settlements here. It was not officially a designated zone of any kind, though everyone regarded it as a zone. The point was—and this was obvious—most people preferred not to live there.

That isolated area had dried out; the streets and freeways were broken, there were many shattered roofs, and everywhere the scars and sluicemarks from flash floods and burst pipes and mudslides. The memory of water was hacked into the land.

And even the rest—the whole of Los Angeles—looked so temporary to her; it was built so close to the ground. It was a large lopsided city, with a crack down one corner. Silvery and spiky with towers on its western side, it was mottled with bungalows and low houses everywhere else. The outer towns had shrunken and, ring within ring, had contracted to the small dark circle that had always been the crossroads or the central mall. But there were stranger settlements, too— Moura saw them in a glimpse as the plane sped by on its approach. They were the ragged huts and camps of desperate people, probably aliens, who had moved out of Landslip after the quake.

Los Angeles had always seemed to Moura a mixture of grandeur and ruin, with a look of seedy magnificence. Now it was divided, the crack of the fault line was like a wall, fifty clicks to the southeast, and on the far side a look that had become familiar to her. It was the look of O-Zone.

As soon as she was on the ground, Moura began looking for Boy, and seeing him—so often that she knew she had to be mistaken. But that illusion strengthened her and gave her hope. Frequently, in New York, she saw someone she thought she knew on the street, then realized she was wrong. But afterward and often on the next street she saw the very person she had imagined the moment before. There was a certain amount of clairvoyance in her imagination—probably in everyone's—and she began to understand what that person had meant a year ago by saying that the future is familiar.

"I want to rent a chopper."

She was inside the agency and yet still had to raise her voice, because the things were climbing and revolving around the building. All that yakking was like slow gunfire, and the drafts from the rotor blades made gusts of grit flicker at the windows.

"You licensed?"

Moura was insulted by the question, and when she gasped in impatience the agent looked rebuked.

"How many hours have you logged?" And now he began keying in the information.

"Four-K, plus."

"You must own one."

"We've got a Welly—the Thruster Three."

"A jet-rotor," he said. "People like you make me feel like a have-not."

"That's your problem, I think." She handed him her ID.

"Thank you."

Now, looking at her ID, the man was so attentive she could hear him breathe, and Moura pitied him for his sudden politeness. Then she was deafened again by a descending chopper.

"You flying alone today, Mrs. Allbright?"

She blinked, meaning yes and hurry up.

"We've got a lovely Hornet for you," the agent said, trying hard. "VFR today—great conditions—"

"Please make it snappy," she said, cutting him short. The fact that she was looking for one particular man made her intolerant of all other men.

The rebuke took away his false politeness and made him a robot. He stopped smiling his strained smile, and asked questions in a monotonous voice, and keyed in Moura's answers.

"Destination?" he began.

When he was done, and she had the keys and her clearance, the agent escorted her to the loading concourse and said, "Been there recently? The reason I ask is, you don't have to go to Pasadena Airport. There's a rotorport in Forestdale itself."

"Good. Tell them to be watching for me."

At the controls, Moura rose and tipped the Hornet and headed east, but stayed low for the pleasure of seeing the changes on the ground. Some hills had been wholly cleared—all the bungalows bulldozed and buried. In other places, the profusion of huts and faded houses lay in the flat geometry between the freeways, and some of the freeways had been closed off, or pinched, or barricaded.

It was the sight of the barriers on the coastal zone and the heavily policed access points that had determined her on renting a rotor. She would never travel on the ground—not here. She wondered who did. It was well-known that the main freeways stayed open, but beneath them and between them large areas were inhabited by people who had claimed the streets and sealed them. What the Owners had done in the coastal zone, in Santa Monica and Malibu, the permit-people and the poor had done downtown and in places like Anaheim. The fortified subcity called Mexico was famous, but there were other, odder settlements, and she imagined them populated by Koreans and Hindus and recent aliens who, in time, would be gathered up and flown offshore and dropped out of planes.

Moura had always felt free in a rotor. Never, even on the most secure road, had she felt safe in a car. Beneath her in the dense yellow air of the trafficky city the cars went grinding along the freeways, passing from checkpoint to checkpoint. She could see that the narrow roads were closed to traffic. It made the poorer neighborhoods on her flight path look like a parody of New York and all its walls.

Dropping to a lower altitude, into the murk, she used the ground-screen and looked for people. There were not many on the streets, but those who were out wore masks. Los Angeles was the place where the fashion had begun. It was a necessity in this sinister air (visibility was usually less than two clicks), and mask-wearing was a useful, practical fashion. Of course, the California models were better than the New York masks—they all had human faces and were beautifully molded, and she supposed they had better radios and transmitters.

She had never seen this many people in New York wearing masks—perhaps because it was so easy to duck indoors. It was healthy here to be masked, and while some people wore simple breathing masks and filters—pretty faces—others carried tanks and tubes, their own air supply.

What if he is wearing a mask? she thought.

If he had a mask and a suit, she might never recognize him; and so it would end dumbly, anonymously, with her stumbling, and him a mask among all the other masks.

But I have never seen his face, she thought. So his face is a mask. And all faces are masks.

She followed the flight path to Forestdale and put down in the rotorport, which was near his last known address—the coordinates Hooper had given her. It was a low-level tower; not old, but cracked, probably in the last quake. Landslip was not far.

A mask at his address—a guard? a landlord? a cop? it was impossible to tell these gun-freaks apart—spoke to her on a screen. Moura told him her name, and then the name and number of the man she was looking for.

"That a Federal rotor?" He raised his head. Moura guessed he was on the roof.

"No," she said. "It's rented. Don't worry. I'm not with the IRS, or the Feds, or any security. This guy's an old friend of mine."

The only friend, she thought.

"Too bad he slipped out then," the mask said.

The mask covered the man's face: it hooded his head and protected his neck with a bulletproof collar. But his body gave him away. Even on the small screen she could see that he wore a badly rubbed suit, with rips at the knees, and he was very skinny. The short, cracked tower had the same masked look—not very well-disguised poverty. It was dusty brick and faded paint on a street of dead still-standing palm trees—just bare poles.

Moura knew he was suspicious of her because she was expensively dressed and had her own rotor. He had probably seen her land: there was very little traffic here in Forestdale. Her goggles were stylish, but she was not wearing a mask. He asked her about that.

"I'm not going to be here long enough to need one," she said.

That stung the man, she could tell—not the words but her

tone of voice. Fear and uneasiness had forced her to sound tough.

"What does 'slip out' mean?"

"Sold his ID and flew. He's an Owner, you know—from back east. Supposed to be very smart. My wife liked him. He probably tipped one into her."

"Why are you telling me this?"

"Because I didn't like him," the masked man said. "He was arrogant. I'm glad he's gone. I got sick of hearing about him."

It was all abuse but it excited her because it made him seem real. If it had been praise it would have made Boy seem like an illusion.

"I hope they catch him," the man was saying. "I think it's sickening, misusing your citizenship like that. Ever hear of anyone deregistering before?"

Instead of answering his question, Moura said, "Where is he?"

"Where most of them are."

His anger made him seem bored, and he kept going out of focus on the screen. She had to prod him with questions.

"Landslip," he finally said.

"What doing?"

"They don't do much there. They live under bridges. They sneak over the perimeter and steal food and fuel. Half of them just wander around the zone in their bare feet."

"Where's the nearest rotorport?"

"La Plata's probably your best bet. It's not a big place. They might even know him."

"La Plata the resort?"

Now the mask moved forward into focus, and beyond, growing larger and fuzzier on the screen.

"That's a good one. La Plata the resort. That's very funny. I like that." The mask was twitching—the face beneath it was in motion. "La Plata the resort!"

40

Hᴉꜱ ᴘᴀʀᴛɪɴɢ ꜱʜᴏᴛ ʜᴀᴅ ʙᴇᴇɴ ꜱᴏᴍᴇᴛʜɪɴɢ ᴀʙᴏᴜᴛ ᴛʜᴇ mudslides, how they had buried some roads and severed others and covered up half the landmarks on her chart and made new canyons.

To shut him up Moura said she'd use her computer copilot, but once she was airborne and out of Forestdale she flew the rotor manually—slowly, marveling at the mudslides and the townships drowned in dust. The seam below her in the hills became a wrinkle, and beyond where it had risen was Landslip in clearer air.

The flood that had caused these recent mudslides had come and gone very quickly. There was no water gleaming anywhere, and instead of the familiar silver-blue peels were rough-textured scoops and snakes, which had once been lakes or watercourses. Great cataracts of dried mud had been left—and sliced-off hills, and screws and casts of bright dirt and sand.

The quake had brought the buildings down, and the floods had washed them away. But it was so dry here now! The broken bungalows had withered without decaying, simply become papery husks or splintered sections of prefab plastic. There was no smog—a few ringlets of smoke, no more; and a film of dust over everything, every roof, every road, even the leaves were coated gray. There were few clusters of green, almost nothing; but in that respect Landslip was like Los Angeles itself, famous for its water shortage.

Moura flew on, between more hills, into dry desert brightness. There were cars on some roads, but here it did not

515

mean traffic: nothing moved, the cars had no wheels—she guessed they were probably lived in by aliens. In another area she first took to be a vast parking lot, she saw that all the cars were definitely inhabited. Among the cars were cooking fires, and clotheslines, and canvas flaps outstretched for shade. The village of junked cars was especially odd, because farther on was a hillside of uninhabited houses—probably a quarantine order, or a subzone in the making. She flew over a wrecked trailer park, a small city-stain, and an elongated fire zone—a whole district burning and smoking, with a few fire trucks on the fringes spraying chemicals along a perimeter road to keep it open and to prevent the fire from leaving the zone.

That fire was just inside Landslip. Moura had been traveling parallel to the fault line, southeast. La Plata Valley led her deeper into Landslip and to La Plata itself.

She had remembered it as a resort town—Hardy had taken her, they had spent a week here, traveling in a ground vehicle in the shady valley between the high white hills. It had seemed to her a lovely place, small and sunny, with good water and secure hotels—green lawns, and tennis courts, and pools filled by waterfalls and elaborate fountains. The valley had been full of birds and wildflowers. Some people had complained: it seemed artificial, they said—the grass so green, the roses so red, the roads so tidy, and not a blemish anywhere. Something unreal about that, they said.

No more: now it had the same gray decomposing look of the dead half of Los Angeles, and it was not old enough or big enough to have become an interesting ruin. In any case, out here the ruins didn't last long. La Plata lay at the foot of a bright blistered hill forty clicks inside Landslip, and it seemed to Moura typical of what she had seen of that zone—rather tumbledown and unprotected, and close-up deranged. Probably it had lost most of its water—Moura was flying low now and looking for green lawns and swimming pools and trees. She saw a golf course gone to seed—but its sand traps were vivid scars; and broken roads, and abandoned houses, and people walking.

That seemed the chief characteristic of these ruined places—the people were more obvious; fewer vehicles. There were people on the streets, foraging, scavenging, peering up at her Hornet. People were always more visible in these dangerous outer districts. Trolls, Hooper called them,

Roaches, Diggers; and remembering this, Moura wondered what Bligh had been—what sort of alien.

After the mission to find Fizzy, Hardy had said, "Ohio, Illinois, Indiana—even Pennsylvania. There are towns in those states that haven't changed a bit."

He had described a wedding reception and a baseball game and the way they washed their cars and cut the grass. He was surprised and relieved—he urged her to believe him. He was round-eyed and pious, like a simple-lifer.

She said it didn't matter whether she believed it, but she had not known why until now.

This was where she wanted to be, and this had changed: time and shortages and a drought and an earthquake and aliens had altered it. Sixty clicks to the northwest people in Los Angeles hardly cared that this zone existed. They had received the same tremor but they had rebuilt and crept back from the brink. Here it had been almost a death blow. Like O-Zone it was an island; it had become like a foreign country, where aliens were the only real natives.

With her New Yorker's eyes, she had seen Los Angeles as a city of folly and free-for-all. It was another city on its back. It had seemed terrifying-looking but in some of its towns what Moura had taken to be rubble were houses, and within the county there were sealed settlements and secure zones that were elegant and had water somehow, maybe their own policed pipes and reservoirs. But of course they were surrounded by the scattered districts of handmade houses, where people lived in cars and under the freeways like wolves. It was not the nightmare that easterners claimed, but it was interminable, and that was nearly as bad: it was endless, and all of it lay on the ground, and it was impossible for anyone to leave, except by air; and only Owners had rotors.

The valley of La Plata had that same look: it had risen and fallen, and now it belonged to anyone who dared live there.

It was the look of O-Zone—bright and apparently abandoned, some of it fallen flat and other parts still standing and perhaps inhabited. That look provoked the suspicion that there were more people hiding there. The O-Zone look was the look of some of Los Angeles, and the whole of Landslip. To Moura it was the look of everything outside New York— the look of New Jersey and Florida, Mexico and Africa and poor overrun Europe. It was familiar.

The strangest thing about O-Zone was that it had not

seemed very strange. Moura had been fearful, but she had gotten over that. Her greater surprise was that it was not worse. Fifteen years ago the news had broken: "STORM SWEEPS THE MIDWEST"—and then "storm" was changed to "accident," and "accident" to "incident"; and finally it was impossible to know, except that the population of half a state was either dead or resettled. And that was where Moura and the others had spent New Year's this year. But where were the poisoned rivers and the fires? Where were the craters and the demons? Where were the monkeymen and the Shitters? It seemed much stranger to her that Hardy should return from his search mission and say, "They play baseball," "They have weddings," "They sell feed." That seemed much weirder and more exotic. They grew corn, they made quilts, some rode horses, and others drove nice old cars that they had learned to fix. That was very strange indeed and yet somehow very familiar.

Now here was La Plata. What was the difference? No water was an old complaint, and it was not odd to see houses down. It too resembled O-Zone. O-Zone was the look— more than a look, it was a certain sound, a kind of low wind-song, a high temperature, a smell of failure; but it was all too turbulent to be a bitter end.

She thought of Holly, planning another party, sitting with her googly tits pressed against the gaping windows of her dress, and saying confidently O-Zone is nowhere. Moura smiled: No. O-Zone was not a wilderness or a riddle—it was a condition and it was probably eternal, and it was everywhere. O-Zone was the world.

So when she received a stern set of warnings on asking for instructions to land, Moura did not hesitate and consider fleeing and spinning back to Los Angeles for a flight home; she maintained her descent and radioed back that she had noted and stored the warnings.

She liked the feeling that she had been here before, not only in the way that the New Year's party had prepared her for everything, but also in the sense that New York, too, was another part of O-Zone. But you had to have seen O-Zone to know that.

She came down among some hills that were textured like oatmeal. There were no live trees standing—it was like everywhere else on the fringes, the trees had been torn down and stolen for fuel. The government did nothing to stop tree theft, and some security agencies actively encouraged it, because with open fields and bald mountains and wide roads it was hard for aliens to hide. They exposed themselves by tearing down the trees.

"Got any weapons on board?"

The rotorport equipment handler was shoving on greasy gloves. *Bugbee* was stitched on a name badge over the breast pocket of his stained suit.

"No weapons," Moura said. "No offensive systems."

Bugbee dragged a heavy chain through the body grommet on the rotor's shaft.

"We've had thefts," he said, panting.

She wondered whether he was explaining the chain or the question about weapons.

"You must be on your way somewhere."

Moura did not say.

"Because no one comes here to stay," Bugbee said.

That made it sound perfect to her in her present frame of mind. She had started to walk toward the terminal building. It said "LA PLATA TERMINAL" but it was only the bones of one.

"Santa Barbara's real nice."

Now Moura turned and stared at this old man.

"What's wrong with staying here?"

Bugbee, to avoid her stare, was clamping a lock into the chain that held Moura's rented rotor.

"This has been a hole, ever since we lost our water," he said, keeping his head down. "We're just fighting for our lives here."

He was not challenging her—he was sad, he had dropped his voice. He was ashamed and bony, like the place. His chest was caved in and he labored for breath.

"You could go to Santa Barbara—someplace like that," he said. "This is trouble."

She didn't say anything. Bugbee glanced up with a twitch of hope on his face.

"You could go home," he said.

The hotel was bad, but they made no apologies and even implied that she should be grateful. She had a room at short notice, a view of the valley, her own bathroom. "We're the only ones here with real plumbing," the manager said.

Moura didn't argue. She did not say that the room was

dirty, that the view of the valley and its brown bushes and livid dust oppressed her. They probably wondered: What is this woman looking for? She hated the conspicuousness of being alone, and nothing seemed to her so melancholy as having to return each day to an empty hotel room—one with streaks on the wall and filthy windows. She didn't dare to sit out on the cracked balcony.

She began seeing him again—on the street, in the stores, even in the hotel. It was a glary haunted place—too bright, too empty, the floors stinging with the hot day, and water for specified hours. The men she saw all looked like Boy: that same eager taunting posture, the familiar aura. It did not matter to her that she had never seen his face. She thought: I would know him anywhere.

A second glance at these young men told her she was wrong, but she knew she had come very near, and each time she saw someone like him she felt she was getting closer. She had become a huntress, full of superstitions and hunches.

She spoke to one of these men on her third day. He was tall, rangy, the right build, with an intelligent face and pretty hands; and he had Fizzy's perforating gaze.

She said, "Do I know you?"

His smile told her she had the wrong person. Besides, he was not more than thirty.

"You're a stranger here," he said, and before she could explain he added, "You've got that look."

She faced him to make him doubt himself.

Without malice—with amusement even—he said, "Money."

Moura was the more embarrassed because he was not bitter. The man seemed to relax when he saw she was flustered and didn't have an answer—didn't even deny it.

"We're all burned here," he said.

It was true—literally so. He was darkly tanned, the backs of his hands were pinky brown and blotched, lines were cut into his face where he squinted, and there was a whitish scaliness on his arms, and a deep tan underneath. He had swollen peeling lips.

"Everyone wears uniforms around here," Moura said.

His was green—a shirt, a metal patch, a visored helmet, sturdy buckled boots, a weapon she had never seen before.

"Most of us are security, most of us are private. I'm a state trooper. We've got a post here."

She was staring at him, wondering whether she had chosen him for his resemblance to Fizzy.

He said, "We're holding them back."

"Aliens?"

"I don't use that word," he said. "They're illegals. I think of them as throwaways."

"Throwaway" described how she felt herself and she liked the man for giving her the word.

"How do you manage to hold them back?"

"You really are a stranger, if you don't know."

When Moura told him that she was an Owner, from New York, and showed him her ID, he said, "Allbright's—like the mail-order cable sales?" and invited her to his post. He was very proud of the fenced-in compound. He said, "They claim we don't do anything," and showed Moura his data base and his display units. He talked about his storage capacity and his data-gathering.

He did look like Fizzy, and he had Fizzy's enthusiasm for technology.

"We've got a satellite feed for an hour, twice a day," he said. "We go on rotor patrol every night and make tapes and analyze them on this machine"—he had seated himself at the console. "This is really elegant. This is so sophisticated we don't have to fight."

She could hear Fizzy saying that.

"We're not gunslingers like these other squads and militias. Ever hear of the Black Cars? It's a local squad that goes around blasting people. Sometimes they drop poison and wipe out whole settlements. They use screamers on anyone who looks suspicious."

"In New York there's a squad called Godseye."

"They love giving themselves names."

She thought: Having the right name is like wearing a mask. She said, "Don't you have a name?"

"Officer Pratchett. Unit Forty. State security." He was looking up at a monitor—two ragged women towing a tin sled heaped with wood. It was somewhere in the hills.

"If they want to live like prehistoric people, they're welcome to it. As long as they stay out of here, I leave them alone. I'm not like some cops. I don't go hunting."

Moura was looking at another monitor. A man had come into view.

"We know who's out there," Pratchett said. He was watching Moura now, the way she was held by the screen.

"Their movements?" she said tentatively.

"Mrs. Allbright," he said—Fizzy again, expansive among the complex monitoring equipment—"we know who they are and where they are and where they go. We know their ages, their sexes, their sizes, and what racial group they are. We know when they're born and when they die. There's no such thing as an unknown alien. We know the color of their eyes. We can hear them chew their food."

He was smiling at her as though he knew how keenly she was listening to what he said.

"In most cases, we know their names."

She said, "I have a name for you."

"Sure you do."

She said nothing.

"I knew you were looking over the wire," he said. "Into the Zone."

41

THAT MAN PRATCHETT WARNED HER, AND THE HOTEL manager warned her, and unchaining the rotor, Bugbee warned her too.

They were so often cowardly or fearful, the people who issued warnings and said Don't.

She told Bugbee, "I'm trying to find someone," and remembered Hooper's saying, *It's usually a mistake to find what you're looking for.*

"You'd find someone in Santa Barbara."

Moura was climbing into her rotor.

"Especially if you don't have a whole lot of time."

She could never tell when old men were mocking her.

"Where's your program?" He was fussing, he was afraid—fear made him bossy. "Don't tell me you're flying without one."

"It's VFR again today," Moura said. She had hoped to avoid another argument by not telling him that she was flying manually, but he knew and he hated knowing.

She had to wait for permission to take off—La Plata was a busy rotorport, probably because the roads here were so dangerous. Then she continued on her way southeast, using the coordinates Pratchett had given her.

He's living rough near a place called Ida, Pratchett had said, and didn't ask her to explain what she wanted; though she realized that out of gratitude she might have told him anything. She had needed help. It had never been a matter of following clues, but only of persisting and being lucky. There were no clues. There were only facts you had to be told. If

523

you didn't know the facts you were lost. She resented her life spent having to be shown the way. *He hasn't been there all that long.*

Did that matter?

The longer they stay, the worse they get.

Down below she saw brown bumpy hills and swatches of weed. There were town-stains and there were smears where smaller settlements had been. There were blobs where cars had sunk into the sand and showed their rusty roofs. She saw no people. Whoever lived here, lived hidden. It was another hot day. The stark sun had burned all the colors away. The rocks were split and white like broken skulls, and where it was thickest the weed was black. The old high-banked road into La Plata, the favorite of the weekend travelers before the quake, she mistook for an empty riverbed. It was strewn with stones.

Hardy would have laughed if he had known how much trouble she had taken to get here. But that was another reason she was here.

Gusts and downdrafts shouldered the rotor: it was the high temperatures in these valleys and the canyons farther on with their sheer walls. The rotor was punching along and she had begun to enjoy working it by hand. She was now used to the occasional hesitation in the wind, the tiltings and leaps.

She wondered: Was this lonely journey strengthening her, so that at the end of it she would not need the man she had searched for?

Her wondering stopped when, a moment later, switching fuel tanks, she saw the fuel indicator stutter back to zero and sensed the rotor losing power. It was first a rapping that was immeasurable, and then a stall for seconds that unconsciously she counted—*two, three, four*—and then a discharge and a hollering in the pipes as she restarted: cones of black exhaust fumes seemed to prop the rotor up. This happened three times. The bursts of energy seemed to weaken the engine, and she lost altitude each time the engine cut out. The fuel line was blocked or air-locked: the panel light flashed.

Then she was swaying like a basket on a line; and restarting aligned the rotor but did not keep it from dropping to the ground. The undercarriage tilted—probably broke—and a side piece shattered. Moura climbed out quickly, congratulating herself that she was alive. But her knees were tremulous and hardly supported her.

She decided not to use her radio, yet despised herself for testing it and for verifying that she had fuel and emergency rations—that ridiculous junk that Murdick had peddled. She turned her back on the leaning rotor.

This is where I wanted to be. I'll track him on foot—and laughed at the brave, wilderness word, because what did she know about tracking?

There was not much water, and she was wearing soft-soled flying boots.

I don't belong here. And then: *Does anyone?*

They attack you, they rape you, they take your machines, they kidnap your children, they steal your food, they rob you, they strip you, they bite you, they piss and shit on you, and at last when you're dead they insult your corpse by using your bones—that was what everyone said.

Besides the radio, Moura had a bleeper. If she called security they would come thundering down, the Black Cars streaking out of La Plata and plucking her back to Los Angeles, where she could sit by a swimming pool and drink mango juice, trying to forget the number of aliens they would shoot as a lesson. And if they didn't reprimand her, Pratchett would. They'd say: *You knew it was forbidden* and *What sort of a woman wants anything to do with people like that?*

She sat down to demonstrate to herself that she was going to wait calmly. She had not crashed, she hadn't even ditched, she hadn't been off course. She had stalled and somehow come to rest on her claws. There had been no explosion, no one had seen her. It was as good as a landing.

This could be a picnic! She had a radio, she had water and food—too bulky to carry but enough to last her for ten days.

She methodically made herself a picnic meal and ate it in the shade of the rotor; and afterward, drugged by the heat, she slept, perspiring, her hands clasped at her throat.

The shade slipped from her like a black sheet tugged away, and the sun blazed against her eyelids and gave her a painfully lighted dream. In this dream she met him in a pink room that had walls like flesh. She walked up to him. He smiled—that smile might mean anything, she thought: a smile could be so sinister and so hard to put into words. But he took her hand—his touch said something that reassured her. He was gentler, he took her deeper into this pink room, where she wanted to go, and thought: Imagination is clairvoyance. It was not a room; they were enclosed by the pink flesh of a mouth. He had Fizzy's face, and even in this dream she was conscious of the question, Am I looking for Fizzy?

"Who's there?"

She had woken knowing that someone was watching her. She stood up and listened. Excited by the early-afternoon heat, the insects made a ringing din like continuous sleighbells.

She saw just beyond the rotor a neat bundle of sticks tied with two fiber ropes—a small but obvious symmetry in all this natural disorder. She went over to the bundle and lifted it. It was hardwood—heavier than it looked.

"Please, officer," a small voice said.

A child—a boy of about ten—emerged from behind the rotor. He came out of the shade and she almost lost him, so well did he match the sun-bleached soil and burned rock. His hair was whitish and streaked with pale yellow, his skin tanned cinnamon, and his nose peeling pink and freckled. He wore faded denim shorts and rough sandals that were made of rope and rubber. What was it that Pratchett had said about these people being prehistoric? This boy had an overwashed look, as if he had been soaked and dried too many times—rained on and worn, like a small tired flag. But it was probably the sun.

Moura was cautious. These kids could be like little animals, some were dangerous: they were biters, and their instinct was to attack and run. They had weapons, they hunted in packs. There might be ten others hiding on their stomachs nearby waiting to leap up and jump her.

She had no choice but to stare him down and swallow her fear.

"Is this your wood?"

He nodded and she saw that he might be afraid.

She said, "I'm in trouble."

This bewildered him.

She said, "My rotor's broken."

He looked at the rotor: his lashes, his eyebrows, were bleached white and gave him a look of innocence she found alarming. But now she was sure he was alone.

"Who's going to fix it?"

The boy didn't hesitate.

"The biker," he said.

Moura said, "Where's the biker?"

The boy protected himself with his skinny hands, and she realized that she had come too close.

"If you find him I'll give you something to eat."

Keeping his hands up, the boy moved slightly, his body becoming tense. She wondered if in panic he might spring on her.

"Nice food—and a drink."

He said, "It might be poison."

Sometimes they drop poison and wipe out whole settlements.

"Won't you get the biker for me?"

"If you promise not to hurt me."

She did not hear him until the last moment. She had climbed up the hill to get a better look, but had not reached the top when she heard the clatter of his machine shaking on the stony ground. He was behind her, and when she turned back he was above her, staring down, with the sun crackling next to his head. She crouched below the brow of the hill, unprotected among the dead thorns and dusty cactus.

"That your rotor?"

At once she said to herself that it was not him, and felt fooled, so far away, clinging to this dusty hill in the heat.

He came toward her, kicking stones with his heavy boots, examined her with his face, and kept going past her, down to the rotor. She followed, because there was nothing else she could think of doing.

He was tall and slender, with hard stringy muscles and thinning hair. What distracted her was that so often in the past, and especially lately, she had seen a man and thought *It's him.* And now she was sure this man was not him— definitely not, and precisely because there was a slight whisper of similarity. She felt she was in danger of being misled by something very small—a hint of Fizzy in his posture, in his physique, in his attitude; but it was too elusive to pin down, and she had been wrong before.

Perhaps that was it, that he looked more like Fizzy than the man she had loved, and she was not looking for Fizzy anymore.

"It's rented," she said. "The rotor."

His eyes were perfect—a person's memory and intelligence and humor always showed in his eyes: all his life was there. His face was not battered but wounded, as if something within him had been hurt. Once he had been harmless and hopeful, and then disappointed or worse; and now he was beyond all that—yet his experience showed faintly on his face. She could see a very young boy in him, but not a young man. He had the sort of sensitive face that registers pain and holds it, so that in a certain light like the glare of this sun, his face was complicated by his history. And it was a memory within it, showing at his eyes; unlike Holly's—Holly was all surfaces.

Moura was disconcerted by this man, who was wrecked and interesting, because she suspected that she might like him more than the man she was looking for. But another of her new superstitions was that a sudden change of mind would be very unlucky for her.

The man said very little, and so she found it hard to study his face. His face took on a meaning only when he was speaking. It seemed to her that he could be wearing a mask—one which distorted his face but in which his face was still familiar. Was it his age—the sun, adversity, lost hope, searching? Anyhow, it was a traveler's face. She thought: Age is a mask.

"I had engine failure."

He said nothing.

"It's a new Hornet—do you know anything about them?"

It maddened her that he did not reply to her simple question.

"I need it fixed," she said, "so I can get to Ida."

"You don't need it fixed," he said.

He had no smile at all.

"Because this is Ida."

This hill? She did not want to see its rocks, its thorns, its hot sand. She thought: If I don't get help I could die.

"Then I need it fixed so I can get out of here."

"Right," he said, and it sounded like a farewell.

"I think it's the fuel line. When I switched tanks I stalled. The light came on, the readout clicked back to zero. Probably a valve, don't you think?"

He said, "I won't know until I look."

It was just what Fizzy would have said. She was reassured by it—by the man saying it, by the thought that Fizzy might learn to survive by being this strong and self-possessed. She felt a pang for the boy and saw his long white face surrounded by O-Zone. But she knew that the pang was also a sense of her own shame. What had she ever done except secretly sneer at Fizzy crowding his computer, and hope that someone stronger than she would get the better of him? But he was gone—for good, she felt now, and she was vaguely proud of him for going. She was awkward with the lame assertion *my son*, because he had dared to leave her.

"Probably a valve," the man said in her voice. He was mocking her with her own words. Then he turned—no smile—and took his slender hand out of the engine cavity and showed her his greasy fingers.

He said, "I bet you know a lot about pressure-alert multi-circuited linear hydrostatic valves."

Moura frowned and all her irritation with Fizzy came back. And who was this man who had ridden out of a gulch in the desolate zone of Landslip to mock her for something she didn't know?

He was tall like Fizzy, he had Fizzy's fleshy lips and narrow bones—and even this wilderness had not coarsened his hands. He was slim, he didn't smile, and like Fizzy—one of the oddest of Fizzy's features—he had patches and streaks of prematurely gray hair. It was whiter than the boy's but it was just as strange and stripy.

In contrast to his faded shirt and patched trousers and burst-and-sewn boots his dirt bike was beautiful, with chrome brush guards and highly polished paint—green lacquer—and bright shields protecting the heavy engine. The front fender was like an eyebrow raised high over the wheel. The wheels were its outstanding feature: silver spokes and hubs and rims fitted with bristling tires with treads like toes. The whole underside of the machine was lightly dusted the color of Landslip.

"They don't look after these rented rotors"—he had gone back to work, he was not talking to her, he was thinking out loud. "They just beat the hell out of them and buy new ones. They should be ashamed to use this for rental—it's full of loose connections. It's not even clean."

It seemed such a strange judgment for an alien to make. Talking about dirt and dents and loose connections on a hill of crumbled sand and rocks in Landslip.

But he was supremely confident. He looked out of place but contented here. It gave her hope. He was a severe man, but he was not a brute. It was hard here, she knew. But he was proud—like Fizzy. He had perhaps found greater courage in this wilderness. He would not give up. She suspected that without her ever guessing it, Fizzy had that obstinacy. Each insight into Fizzy taught her something that she needed herself.

"What does someone like you want in Ida?" the man said.

She objected to *someone like you,* but she was uncomfortably aware of the stylish way she was dressed—her perfect suit, her expensive goggles—and her food, her fuel, her rotor. He had nothing but his bike.

"Have you got something against Owners?" she said.

It made him pause and she was glad. She sensed his brain spinning behind his eyes. And still he had no reply.

"I'm just looking," she said, to fill the moment.

He recovered and said, "We eat people like you. Didn't they tell you that at the security check?"

"How do you know I'm not security?"

"Because you're on the ground."

"Couldn't help it," she said. "I stalled. Equipment failure."

"You would have signaled for help if you were in the squads. You would have bleeped your unit. You would have used the voice alarm." He was still standing under the engine, plucking parts from beneath the manifold. He turned and said, "I'm wondering why you didn't."

"I'm not afraid," she said.

"That's good."

She could see he meant it, and that instant she wanted him. She wondered whether she knew him. It amazed her to think that she might have had him—if so, she wanted him again.

She was sure that he regarded her as eccentric—a fool who had found her way over the wire because she had money or hunger.

She said, "Of course, I'll pay you."

He was attending to the engine. She had seen gynecologists put their fingers inside her like that—just as carefully, feeling and listening in just that way. He tricked a length of fuel line out.

"Don't talk to me," he said. It was not rude. It was Fizzy's voice of concentration.

She went silent and regarded him and saw Fizzy again: wonder boy, the genius in the wilderness, rebuilding civilization from its ruins. First the practical items—transport, the superior dirt bike, and then probably weapons and communi-

cations. Or did weapons come first? Anyway, later he would
be circumscribed by his own inventions—he would be safe.

She now knew that Fizzy would succeed—in O-Zone or
wherever he had led those people. Of course he had led
them. Wasn't this man a leader?

He had prodded and unscrewed—palpated an object like a
chromium acorn from one end of the fuel line.

"It's a valve," he said. "It's gummed up. But there's a
design fault in it, too. I'll give you a better one than that."

"You have spares—out here?" But somehow she suspected he had.

He said, "We have whole rotors. Better than this insect.
They fall out of the sky."

"Like me."

"No," he said. "Ever heard of the Black Cars? Hunters.
Searchers. Commandos."

Again he was looking at her in that suspicious and contemptuous way. But she stared back. She saw there was
something sexual in his look.

She knew when a man desired her; and there was a dreadful element in it, a kind of fascinated loathing, because the
man wanted her and didn't know her. Was it only surfaces
that men saw? She wanted just once to know what the attraction was, because she often felt barren and featureless—
often saw nothing in the mirror. But she knew when a man
was looking at her in that way. She was aware of sometimes
looking at a man that way, too, and she disliked the feeling in
herself.

Now she felt this might be worse—not that he desired her
and didn't know her, but that he desired her and did not
remember her.

"Would you like a drink of something?" she said. "And
I've also got some food."

"You'll have to do better than that," he said. "In terms of
payment."

His eyes were still on her. She felt naked, as if he could
pierce her.

"Fuel," he said. "I want the whole of your auxiliary tank."

But there was a stammer of interruption in his voice, as
though he wanted more than he said.

Or had he remembered?

"Otherwise I won't fix it."

"Take whatever you want."

She wanted to remember, she wanted him to remember. She had gone to the contact clinic because she had needed help, and she felt the same need standing near this elusive man.

Even if it was not this man, I might have married someone like him. She could almost picture it, and she mourned the life that she had missed in her imagination. She had lately come to despise herself for liking Hardy's wealth, the Allbright inheritance, and for not taking advantage of it. Her life was far from over, and yet—

The thing was to know how much time you had and not humiliate yourself by wanting more than you could manage. At thirty-seven she still sometimes saw that she had her looks—she was not always insulted by the mirror. She knew she was smarter than she had ever been. She had lasted better than this man, who was weather-beaten. And she had time, years more. She had stopped measuring her life by meaninglessly thinking: *I can still have another child.*

She remembered with the piercing clarity of this man's eyes everything that had happened at the clinic—every session, how he had looked, what he had whispered, how he had smelled, every detail of what she had seen, his mask. But if it was this man, time had wrecked him and caused him pain. Yet oddly it had also given him more life. He looked a little dangerous and if it were truly him he looked a lot freer and stronger.

The difficulty lay in being certain. She could not quite fit the lovemaking to this man; and yet she desired him.

You turn your back and you think people stop living and freeze just for you. But no, they go on, they live, they are wounded, they are altered by pain and bad news, and you turn again and it's all changed. Only happy people never change. She knew there was no certainty for her. The crushing thought was that she too might be ignorant of the past: *Because I have changed.*

He had scrambled inside with his tools and got the engine fluting. She could see he loved this, in spite of the fact that he didn't smile or show pleasure. It was how Fizzy would have behaved, probably what he was doing in O-Zone this minute—machine-mad, she thought, and felt tender toward them.

"I'm going to need this," he said, lowering himself to the ground and swinging a fuel tank out on a pulley. She knew it was full and heavy—and she had another tank. But how would he carry it?

He'll leave it, he'll come back for it, he has nothing else to do here but learn how to survive.

He stalked close to her and studied her with his bright eyes.

"It's a good thing I was here," he said.

She said nothing. She could stare back. What was that in his hand—another of those valves, maybe the old one, rolling in his blackened fingers.

"It looks like you may be able to use the full service."

She suspected that she knew what he meant. She wanted him to remember—anything. Whoever he was.

"I'm running all right," she said.

She desired him then most of all, as he was proposing and teasing her, and she was keeping him away. She searched his poor lined face for a flicker, but there was nothing. He still did not know her. Her desire for him was almost overpowering—she would do something ridiculous in a moment, she knew—snap at him, insult him, spurn him; because she felt on the verge of saying *Take me.*

Then she might know. That wild impulse might reveal everything, for sex was our deepest secret; the mask was tame and civilized, even the beakiest one, but the animal within it contained our identity. And shame was just another way of keeping the secret hidden. She almost reached out for him then.

His boots slipped and rolled on the stony ground as he stepped nearer to her into the sun, and the glare on him made him seem full of fresh wounds—his creased face, and the scratches on the backs of his hands, and the slashes in his shirt, and his boot heels worn flat.

He said, "Well, you know where to find me."

She hated his saying that. I'm wrong, it's a mistake, he's a stranger, he doesn't recognize me—because he is not who I think he is: her thoughts raced and jeered at her for coming all this way for nothing.

He cranked the ladder down, and helped her onto it, touching her for the first time. When he touched her he questioned her with the pressure of his fingers, and instead of being helped by them, the fingers made her hesitate.

She turned to face him, and he let go—embarrassed, a bit flustered, touched with innocence, as if he had given himself away. Was it to disguise it that he looked aside and opened his mouth and yawned? It was a hissing gasping yawn—he brushed it with the back of his hand, bumping it with the small bones of his knuckles.

His whole personality was in that yawn: it exposed and betrayed him. Was it this most human and unalterable gesture that he had passed on to Fizzy? She felt it was so, even more clearly than the way he had touched her, though that had said a great deal—the way his hand had lingered and the fingers had spoken, the abrupt and self-conscious way he had released her. His yawn had seemed to say the rest. It was loud and automatic, seeming to dismiss her, and his folded hand neither stifled it nor covered it. He had gargled air and snapped his teeth shut.

She felt strongly that Fizzy was safe.

"Yes," she said—and thought: I'm safe too; and paused on the ladder.

The December sun in late afternoon blazed without much heat, and already the land had begun to cool in the lengthened shadows. She saw that this broken-off part of America, Landslip, had a beauty she had never imagined. It was beauty regained after some centuries of civilization; and now it was redeemed by the wilderness that had taken over, empty flats and harsh hills. There was space here again. Why was it so precious? Because it had been wrecked and regained. It was beauty lost and found. That was the beauty of O-Zone, too. The beautiful sort of sexual cracks that splitting seeds make when they burst through fresh earth. And to live you had to match it, like this man and become wilder; as Fizzy had—and Hooper was trying.

"Because I was lost," she said, "looking for someone called Boy, or Boyd."

"You're not lost."

She was startled by the note of loneliness in his voice, and yet strengthened by it, because she was no longer lonely.

It had all been Fizzy's doing. His vanishing had left her free to get out of New York. *You should really find someone for yourself,* Holly had said. Was there anything more pathetic than searching for someone to save you? And yet her search for a man had shown her that she did not need a man.

Don't throw me a bone, she thought. She had found a father for Fizzy long ago. She did not want a husband—not a man or a motive. She wanted a lover now. Apart from him, she could look after herself. *I want more than a bone.*

Fizzy had led her here. She saw him in a landscape like this. He was the new breed, an O-Zonian, a sort of indestructible alien—stronger than any Owner. He had been a hostage in Coldharbor; he had freed himself. He wore a dusty helmet and a patched suit—still he never smiled. He led packs of hunched-over aliens through black pine woods. Sometimes at night he walked under the moon. She could see him distinctly, the dull, thick moonlight on his shoulders and on the dome of his helmet. He was big and because he was not naturally brave he was alert to all the risks.

The memory of his voice always brought her down to earth.

You are such a tool, he was telling someone, and he was probably right. He was standing triumphant, talking out loud, mocking the question, because he knew the answer. And if you demanded to know what he was doing he would say, *I'm on a mission.*

Moura reasoned that he was safe, because she was. And the point was not that she had come so far, but rather that, like her son, she could find her own way back. That was all that mattered. She had discovered what Fizzy had always known. He was not afraid. She was free—still finding out.

All this time the man had been watching her like Fizzy.

No wind, no odor, no sound: in the strangeness of this new valley of bones was a kind of safety—the best kind, for it had the appearance of danger. Yet it was a vast empty room, and they were both children alone in it. Outside it, she knew, the future changed every second.

He touched her again, and took hold, and his grip was single-minded with desire. She was still in suspense and yet joyous—tender sentences teemed in her memory. He brought her gently back to the ground, and she thought: In a moment I will know everything.

ABOUT THE AUTHOR

PAUL THEROUX is one of seven children, a member of the Peace Corps in the early sixties, author of five novels, including THE MOSQUITO COAST, four collections of short stories and several best selling travel books—THE GREAT RAILWAY BAZAAR, THE OLD PATAGONIAN EXPRESS, and THE KINGDOM BY THE SEA. He lives in London with his wife and two sons.